JUST KILLING TIME

It had been earlier in the evening that he had been struck by an urge, and he felt restless, leaving his residence for a brief interlude, just killing time by cruising the streets. These days he was in pain, not excruciating, but a dull and episodic throbbing that ran along his spine, giving him migraines, and he knew they would pass if he kept distracted.

When he opened the door to the passenger's side, the darkness remained, clinging to the alley like a sticky web, for the car's overhead lamp had been disconnected. And he stared woodenly at the young woman sprawled in the red leather seat. Her breathing was deep and laboured. He reached in, dragging her from the car, then dropping her along the curb like a sack of stones.

'We're out of time,' he said absently, studying the treeline for headlights, but the woman could not hear.

He closed his eyes tight, standing there in the dim light, the shadows failing into darkness, the darkness failing into death.

'Yes,' he breathed hard, and the moisture from his lungs held like a pale cloud.

'Yes, yes, yes . . .'

About the author

Derek Van Arman was born in Washington, DC, attended Cheshire Academy, Montgomery College, the University of Maryland, and served as editor of President Jimmy Carter's National Science Board for the White House. He currently resides with his wife in the Desert Southwest.

Derek Van Arman

Just Killing Time

CORONET BOOKS
Hodder and Stoughton

Printed and bound in Great Britain for Hodder and Stoughton Paperbacks, a division of Hodder and Stoughton Ltd, Mill Road, Dunton Green, Sevenoaks, Kent TN13 2YA. (Editorial Office: 47 Bedford Square, London WC1B 3DP) by Cox and Wyman Ltd, Reading, Berks. Photoset by Rowland Phototypesetting Ltd, Bury St Edmunds, Suffolk.

British Library CIP

Van Arman, Derek
  Just killing time.
  I. Title
  813[F]

ISBN 0-340-58091-7

For Susan

PROLOGUE

SECRET PLACES

The kid on the red Schwinn raced slightly ahead of the three-legged dog, down a dark and wooded hill, then back up into sunlight. Their competing shadows slid over the residential street like two eerie kites, moving slowly against the trees, moving faster against the sidewalk.

Just past Ridgefield Lane and River Road, a main intersection, Elmer Winfield Janson stood on his pedals, whistled sharply, then burst into a power drive, zapping over a sidewalk, a grassy strip, and crashing through a hedge. He emerged onto an empty parking lot and leaned his bike into full lazy circles, aiming his tyres at weeds, the small green aliens he imaged were sprouting a full-scale invasion from below.

The blacktop was fractured with weeds jutting through, easy targets for the deep rubber teeth of a dirt bike. And for the first time all day he felt free, swerving into expanding arcs until each tyre spun with earthen plugs which flew from the wheels as his speed increased. The circles tightening. Tyres and weeds, weeds and tyres, dog after boy, boy after dog, their pace quickening like a giant top; spinning and spinning, faster and faster until the universe whirled from focus and a drunken throbbing battered at Elmer's brain.

'Wow!' the boy breathed hard, hitting his brakes while climbing dizzily from his bike. 'There's nothing in the living world like mashing aliens!' And he gave a proud smile, standing on a flat of oozing green.

In the greying light Elmer's fine reddish hair took on the colour of smoked salmon, matching a mask of freckles that

3

seemed to tighten across the bridge of his nose. His eyes were a sparkling green, just darker than mint, and they always seemed fixed on some distant point within himself. Standing to his full height of four-foot-four he was able to stroke the Shepherd's thick mane without bending.

Now Elmer Janson was small for ten, he knew that, and the carrot-top and freckles made him look more like seven; but he was ten years and nine months old, and he kept track of details like that, just as he knew, or thought he knew, every inch of the parking lot to which he laid claim. A heavy mist fell through the air, the kind that leaves a waxy frost on everything when it freezes, and the boy could feel the wet chill on the dog's fluffy coat. 'Come on, Tripod,' he hushed, as in the dim afternoon sun he took a last furtive look over his shoulder and started towards the condemned structure at the end of the parking lot.

Damp and brooding, the building was old, and sad, and sick. A low slung fifties-style warehouse with plywood-boarded windows and crumbling concrete blocks that had been a twenty-six-lane bowling alley with a pool hall and gaming room. Front, facing the roadway and sandwiched between two pastel blue panels, there was a section of smooth pink aluminium big as a billboard that had once advertised Patriots Bowl in tall white letters. The colour scheme had been red, white and blue, suggesting a recreational duty to bowl; but the white characters had been torn off long ago leaving dark red splotches. The boy walked under the huge wall, crossing to the rear of the structure and hesitating only a moment near the back of the alley where the blacktop narrowed and there were signs.

Keep Out! No Trespassing!

He threaded his body first, then his bike, through a tight gap between a galvanised steel fence post and concrete corner, then walked his bike down under a dripping overhang that blocked the sun. Elmer paused, waiting for his eyes to adjust, testing the spongy pavement with his feet. Most of the black-top had broken free of the structure, eroding into a trench,

4

and he started along a length of dingy canyon, some four hundred feet of wet and troubled darkness. An occasional crack would nip a toe, a wad of concrete would belt an arch, boy and dog steadily working their way towards the small fenced area at the end of this tunnel.

To Elmer Janson this was a secret place, and from the halfway point he could just see a distant patch of sunlight reflecting against sloping blacktop. He knew this had once been a parking lot, and was now just a dump, but in his mind it looked more like the surface of a bright weird planet left to the ravages of time. More importantly, the dump was filled with curious things and was impossible for adults to reach without a twelve-foot climb over chain-link fence. As he walked he tried to imagine the scene in the alley's heyday, packed with '57 Chevys and Thunderbirds and huge Ford Galaxies. In his mind each car was red because he had such a picture in a calendar at home. And even though it was now late March, because of that one picture, Elmer's bedroom was stuck on July everlasting.

'Nothing better in the free world than July,' he said, smiling an easy summer vacation smile. School was almost over, that was the important thing, and he weaved his bike, dodging broken bottles and debris; a pile of wet boards with nails stabbing through, then car parts, including a broken battery and an oozing oil filter. He stopped and stared at a rainwater puddle, an oily brown skin floated on top, and his eye caught a thing. A dead thing. Bloated and half buried in the inky well.

'Tripod, sit!' he demanded to the curious straw-coloured dog. The boy leaned his bike against a wall, instantly searching out a length of spiked board. He started to rake.

The water rippled as the skin broke, releasing a smell like sweet rotting cheese as the freckles across his nose tightened. He snagged something. And although it was dark, Elmer could clearly discern the head, or what he thought was the head, badly swollen out of shape, more like a spongy fist of fur than a head; with eyes the colour of spit on asphalt. Elmer poked at it, studying each feature; a greasy snout, cuplike

5

ears, and toothy incisors like yellow needles. A tremble came over him like a chilled and unclean wind.

'Someone walked on my grave,' he whispered, pushing a beefy rat back into the water, as he felt an oily splash and a trickle run down his face.

It was cold, he noticed for the first time. The sun was dropping. It was getting colder.

At Patriots Bowl there were two spots behind the alley where the weeds sprouted taller than the others. One outcropping was a tangled swirl of growth which rose into an isolated fountain of grass. The other was a squat patch of plum-headed aliens that looked different from the rest, which were green or yellow. Elmer knew that ordinary plants came and went with the seasons, while these always stayed the same. They didn't bloom. They didn't die either.

They were living just past the *No Dumping* sign, next to a discarded V-8 engine block, and inside the fenced lot. As he pushed his bike out from the trench and up a slope, he could see Tripod's broom-like tail swinging full force, hind quarters extended, his entire body heaving as he dug with one front foot.

During the winter the team had made a dozen such trips, only to find the blacktop frozen. Elmer grinned, leaning his bike against the engine, then stretching catlike, watching with an intense concentration. The dog had broken through and down into the clay below.

'Today's the day!' Elmer beamed, crouching alongside Tripod, examining the torn pavement while breathing in the rich, earthy scent. Winter was behind them now, he reasoned, the ground would be forced to surrender. Pressing hard with both hands, straining against the asphalt until each finger went white, Elmer went on pushing until the soggy pavement moved. The dog was manic, clawing at the ground in a lathered frenzy as the boy removed a magazine from inside his sweatshirt.

'It is best to hunt while the ground is still wet, especially after a flood,' he read, his voice stirring. 'Look for any indentation where treasure may have settled. Study plant growth. Previous disturbances result in noticeable changes in vegetation. Adjust the metal detector to low yield.' A proud smile covered his face, for Elmer had accomplished that part months ago. Since it had rained for three full days, not a drizzle but dime-sized drops that had pounded at the cracks, the instructions had been followed to perfection. The blacktop was clearly sinking in sections, some small as a cup, some large as a tub, and he thought it no coincidence that the purple aliens grew where the pavement sagged most. Respectfully he rolled the magazine beneath the dry safety of his sweatshirt.

To Elmer Janson the written guide was a legacy of sorts, one of several that his father had left when he died, all neatly stored with a metal detector beneath the basement stairs. In them Elmer had found a world of excitement, in stories of treasure and exploration: caches looted by Confederate spies; Indian caves dripping with jewels; lost gold; ancient pottery; and all of it free for the taking. Until his discovery Elmer had only heard about history in school, but seeing the treasures and having a metal detector was real – like the difference between being told about germs and getting the flu.

And it didn't matter one bit that all of his previous efforts had produced only tin cans, car parts, rusted nails, and a trunk full of bottle tops. There was something spirited and curious and lonely trapped inside this one little boy that pushed at him, that pressed him onward when others would have quit.

Tripod barked. They began to dig.

An hour passed quickly and they were caked with mud, red like stewed tomatoes but thick as half-dried concrete. All the plum-coloured aliens were gone, ripped from the ground, and a small dark pit with a four-foot circumference surrounded them.

There was dirt, and digging, and more dirt, and more digging; with each stroke Tripod's rear quarters pressed high into the air, looking for all the world like a honey-coloured

7

bear fishing a water hole. The dog growled, low and hypnotically, his maniacal rocking unabated, deeper and deeper, down into the red crater, his broom-like tail smacking the tarry surface. Elmer felt a trickle of despair as the last vestiges of daylight began to close around them. Black clouds had formed. The smell of winter had returned to the air.

'Nothing ever goes off as you plan,' he spat, and a lonely tide washed through him. He had waited six months for the thaw, and he felt sad to the bone. He had wanted so badly to believe, to find something, anything, it didn't have to be a real treasure. And his lower lip started to quiver – when the world rushed into focus as something caught his eye.

A speck, a promise, a joy.

A fleck of metal sticking out from the earthen wall and trapping light, burning and burning like a diamond through the red beginnings of time.

Elmer's jaw dropped, the wind whooshing out of him. A nervous fluttering swirled from his stomach to chest, filling him with joy. This was no bottlecap. He dropped into the pit, scratching feverishly at the object with fingernails, grabbing it before it could disappear. It was cold and wet and slippery, a flat sliver poking up sideways through the dirt.

The boy tugged, the clay wall gave a rooted moan. Then holding tight with both thumbs and digging in with his heels, he pulled again. Small cracks snaked outward in the red dirt and his green eyes glistened with excitement. The shape was distinct. He could see it clearly now.

'A coin!' he exclaimed, and a sharp wind snapped the word away.

Elmer Janson knew without a second glance, he knew with an inner pulse – this thing was old. Ancient as a curse. Older than time.

He was working quickly now, wrapping a shirt-tail around each thumb, fastening a tight grip and pulling with all his might. The rain-packed clay fizzed and gave up its prize in one hot instant, like a stubborn tooth being pulled from tissue and bone, leaving the boy to tumble into a backward sprawl.

8

'Yeah,' Elmer whispered into a cold rush of air, his breath visible in small clouds.

An encrusted medallion gleamed in his outstretched hand, dangling from what appeared to be a length of wire; slimy, black and rotting. Nervously, he worked the coin's surface with his thumbs, rubbing off clay until words began to shine through. He squinted, holding the object to his nose.

'The Union . . . Must . . . and Shall Be Preserved,' he read slowly. 'Oh Yeah!'

The three-legged dog had never stopped digging.

In tandem they dug a trench sideways into the clay wall. Then working on all fours Elmer quickly nudged past and slipped his hand further into the wet darkness, down into the hollow. Just inside, just beyond grasp, he could feel a round thing – round like a ball. The cold slickness of its surface excited, the smooth hardness intoxicated his senses. He pushed further, the mask of freckles tightening with determination as he strained to work his face into the cramped opening.

'Tripod!' he screamed. 'We really have found treasure!' Elmer could just see the curving bottom of a container poking up like an inverted soup bowl, and he worked, widening the tunnel, pondering the delight and strangeness of it all. It looked like a bowl, but it had thin wooden legs poking out that made it resemble a small satellite with weird antennae. He dismissed that thought. 'It could have belonged to a slave, it could be African!' he puffed, having read historical accounts. 'Slaves couldn't have valuables, they buried them; maybe it belonged to a Confederate spy!' The possibilities blew quickly through his mind as Elmer grabbed the longest stick and pulled. The ground gave way and the object turned towards him, tilting. There was a muted thud as a wooden leg snapped loose and Elmer fell back into the dirt.

He held it in his hand. It was black. It looked like an old chopstick. The boy quickly folded this inside his shirt, reaching back, grabbing another. The object turned, then settled, the stick holding fast. He pressed his face to the wall. Now

9

he could see each of the feet clearly, jutting up from the red dirt like a giant pincushion, and his hand slipped back like a mole through darkness. Elmer caressed and stroked when he felt the jackpot. 'A handle!' he shouted. 'It's got a handle!'

White-faced with determination, the boy reached across the centuries, grabbing hold, his entire right arm plunged into the hollow. He pulled. Chunks of red clay spilled loose. Straining with his right shoulder and placing his full weight against the wall, he pulled again. Endless. Tiring. Resolute.

The earth groaned. Red clay poured from the hollow, flowed from the hollow over his belt and shoes; the wall beginning to crumble. The hollow became a cave as the wall fell, the object dragging closer toward his belly when his thumb punched a hole, a slick edge slicing one knuckle. It was thin, brittle, and sharp as porcelain, and although Elmer winced at the pain, he would not let go. It was coming free. The dirt fizzed.

With a deep sodden moan, the wall surrendered to the will that was Elmer Janson, and even as the image was slow to register on the boy's mind, his flesh began to ripple as his muscles went tight, loosened, and went tight again. Blood flowed from his fingertips and he shook the prize loose, letting it fall away from his body. Tripod barked, growling from a distance.

It was death.

The boy had found death and it had landed with a thud, pinning itself to the wet ground, grinning back at him with human teeth – grinning like so many thousand pictures of death.

Death as an entity. Pictorial death. A grin that could stop a clock but begged for something more, something living; and while Elmer told his feet to run, they would not obey.

'Tripod!' the boy tried to cry, but fear had snatched his breath, making Elmer pull back even as the dog leaned forward.

The skull was small and pink, stained from years at rest with the sap of red clay leaching through. Up from the pit, bony sockets glistened and stared, the nose forming a dark lopsided triangle. The teeth sparkled with Elmer's blood, the mouth hanging agape, torn open, leaving one good hinge.

'The bowl's handle,' his lips moved. But it was the grin that paralysed, sneering with ivory, offering silence as an explosion in his head. Laughing at him. Laughing.

Blood banged through the chambers of the boy's heart and he knew he should leave and take Tripod home. But Elmer Janson looked hard at the world, and once he did, he refused to look away.

ViCAT

The only thing necessary for the triumph of evil is
for good men to do nothing.

> Edmund Burke, 1751

They sleep not, except they have done mischief;
And their sleep is taken away, unless they cause some
to fall.
For they eat the bread of wickedness,
And drink the wine of violence.

> Proverbs 4:16–17

Talk of the devil and he will appear . . .

> Erasmus: *Adagia* XVII, 1500

ONE

The house was red brick. A colonial. A sedate residence located in an affluent suburb of Washington DC.

On the front lawn leaves were neatly raked, cherry trees were beginning to flower, hedges were squared and freshly groomed. From the back, similar dwellings ran in rows, nine deep, with sweeping lawns hidden by wooden fencing and ivy-covered walls.

Late on the evening of March 31st, the house was locked tight. In an upstairs bedroom Diana Clayton was sitting at her dressing table planning months in advance, turning pages in her desk calendar and preparing lists; groceries, school, work, meetings, vacation, and then sleep. At the age of thirty-nine, life had become a precious thing for Diana Clayton, a thing to be coveted and organised, a thing to be fought with and savoured.

Kim's 8th B-Day she wrote across the first page of June while glancing at the family portrait on her desk and into the face of her youngest child. Kimberly Ann Clayton was a deceptively fragile, almost perfect-looking little girl, and her impish smirk seemed to come alive in the silver frame as Diana positioned the picture closer to her calendar.

The resemblance between them was striking. Bright azure blue eyes and lightly freckled skin, with streaming blonde hair that looked equally good unkempt or combed. They shared a sly but natural turn to the mouth, a sensual turn that could have been a pout, but was not.

Behind Kimberly in the picture, and a full head taller, stood Leslie, three years older, more confident, less shy. She looked more like their father, Mark Clayton, and the woman gave a wistful smile, sitting motionless for a moment while studying the image. Leslie was only six when her father died, and since that time she had come to resemble him in manner as well as looks. She was a deep-feeling little girl, sensitive to a fault, and that single characteristic was even more like her husband than the child's brown hair, that was now beginning to darken into a fine chestnut glaze. And the penetrating hazel eyes. 'The best of him,' Diana whispered with a warm sigh.

She took a sip of hot herbal tea and returned to her note-book, her eyes flicking from month to month, week to week, then day to day. Hard enough to etch an impression through the following pages of July and August, she inscribed the words *Nag's Head* across the entire face of June. The decisive reference was to a North Carolina barrier island where the Claytons traditionally vacationed, and she was planning a special trip for Kimberly's birthday.

Diana smiled in contemplation, holding the pen against her cheek. As it had been with her late husband, the beach was the children's first love, she thought. First, that is, after Tofu, a large cream-coloured Angora rabbit with buttery ears that resembled huge velvet slippers. She shook her head absently. *Tofu to Vet* she dashed into the square for June 2nd, and then considered Leslie's pronouncements that Tofu would die of loneliness if left alone for a month. The children wanted to take their pet to the beach, a rabbit to the shore?

'Silly,' Diana whispered, tapping at the page with her pen, a ridge of concern forming across her brow. The children felt they would be abandoning Tofu, and that was not a matter to be taken lightly. *Absence makes hearts grow fonder!* This she entered cryptically at the top of the page, carefully reserving time on the morning of April 4th for a motherly chat, when it occurred to Diana that her daughters fussed over Tofu's every need like little mothers themselves. And that thought made her entire body sag with age.

Fatigue was returning now. There was a stinging to her eyes and a stiffness in her muscles that would not go away. With a sudden yawn she arched her back, glancing over to the brass clock on her bureau. 11:45 p.m. Her streaming blonde hair shimmered as it flowed over the blue silk of her nightgown, and she removed a dark comb from her head. She was closing her eyes when a strange chill suddenly swelled in her body. She curled one fist. Diana Clayton gave a quick shiver as it slipped through bone marrow.

'Funny,' she thought, sitting taller at her desk, letting her cup slide from her hands. 'Catching cold?'

She rubbed her forehead, feeling tiny hairs prickle as her heart fluttered with a strange sensation. It was as if a sour breath had entered her body and was gone in an instant, one heart beat off, and nothing more.

A shiver. A doubt. A mournful feeling.

In that same millisecond Diana Clayton inhaled, shaking her head, glancing down the hallway to where her children were sleeping. She listened for a moment while releasing her breath, but there was only the safe and familiar silence.

'Flu season,' she whispered, jotting a note to add vitamin C to the breakfast menu, and the natural curve to her mouth became a pout.

Kneeling in the master bathroom, she drew back a flowered curtain and adjusted the water to a tepid flow. A pool began to form, giving ghostly life to an inflatable pillow that had been lying limp in one corner of the bath. She removed a peach-coloured towel from beneath the sink, wrapping this around her head like a large bandana, tying a loose knot at the nape of her neck.

In the thickening steam, her pores were beginning to tingle and open, and she cracked the bathroom window, then dropped the silken robe off her shoulders, revealing a shapely form which she studied for a moment in the mirror. Although Diana Clayton was concerned with pending age, and saw an older image of herself in the reflection, in truth she was a handsome woman with a dancer's long legs and a body blessed with ample and sensuous curves.

She breathed deeply to clear her sinuses as she dimmed the harsh lights, then the water rippled as she climbed in, the warmth taking her like a glove; so relaxing, so quiet, she could hear cicadas outside her window. As she settled back, propping her head against the pillow, her thoughts returned to the shore.

She closed her eyes. She remembered the wild ponies as they ended their yearly migration, racing down the beach as the tide rolled in. And Mark, still half-asleep, chasing off in his pyjamas and carrying a child in each arm.

'I don't have time to be sick,' she whispered.

Diana Clayton dreamed of wild ponies.

Downstairs.

Moving soundless as thought while waiting for the bedroom lights to go out, a stranger strolled through the living room. A dark and seamless Dacron body sock covered him, rising into a hood that enveloped the head, the tight fabric masking throat, chin, and ears; leaving a pale and oval face seemingly floating in air.

The mouth protruded. Thin lips looked like sliced veal. And the nose, unusually faint, was cocked with self importance. Around each eye the skin was darkened with pitch and his expression seemed more lifeless than cruel.

He stopped, admiring this image in the mirror above Diana Clayton's babygrand, just killing time, playing with his reflection.

He lifted an upper lip, contorting his face with a grimace that was meant as a smile, and there was a flash from white even rows. The mask pulled tight across his cheeks, pinching his ears as he tugged it into place, enthralled with the feeling of being invisible, dressed for blending with shadow. With this disguise he knew he could have been anyone, man or woman, beast or angel; a school teacher, a salesman, a cop.

But he was not. And with a gloved hand he caressed the white notes, sweeping back and forth with fingertip strokes, entertaining himself with the image of smashing the keyboard. Sudden. Merciless. Terrible alternating blows, pounding and pounding, slow and methodical, building a tempo while calling for Diana; increasing the beat, then demanding each child by name.

The hardwood of the piano gleamed with lemon furniture polish, and his breathing went deep as he fingered the metronome next to the clock. It was 11:40. He knew the children were sleeping, and that delighted him.

And he knew about their empty little lives, boring as salt, regular as a plasma drip.

The heat snapped on.

A whirr of circulating air washed over him and he smelled apples, carried on the current. His eyes closed with a questioning wonderment, for there was a hidden scent, something deeper, more pungent than fruit or furniture wax. And his mind and his body wandered as he left the piano behind, moving leisurely through the house, stepping into the kitchen, following his nose.

A hard smell. Sharp as wetted wood yet bitter; and he stood at the floating island near a breakfast nook, sipping at the air. He opened blackened lids, closed them again, and rolled through his memory; every nerve coming alive in the puzzlement created by the odd smell when he heard a faint rapping.

Once, twice, again, coming from the far end of the kitchen.

'A fraying duct,' was his first thought. He moved closer. The heat died with a snap. Black canvas boots came moving across the linoleum shine, easing closer, stopping at the double sink where pans were carefully set on a dish towel for drying. He stood and listened. A brooding *drip, drip, drip,* from the sink. And he strained to place the unusual scent against a faint sound, his mind working fast and methodically.

Far away he could hear the distant bray of tyres on pavement. The wind licking a leafy branch. The mulling drone of a jet leaving Washington International Airport. And a rapping. Almost sickly. Like a whisper against glass, he thought, or severed fingers scratching inside an eggshell.

Thin lips curled with amusement; not a smile, but forming a slash across his face. And he moved forward, stopping to listen, then leaning over the end of the kitchen counter to peer down into darkness; down through the odorous bite of wet cedar chips.

'Well, well,' he whispered with excitement, as from between long buttery ears a small being awoke and blinked up at him, narcotic with sleep, the soft nose pulsating for a familiar scent.

'I should have known,' he said in a barely audible voice as he placed his tongue behind front teeth, producing a wet and pleasing noise. He squatted, pressing his face within inches of the cage.

Tofu, the Angora rabbit, could not sense danger. For she had never known anything in life but the gentle touch of a child's wet kiss; thousands upon thousands of warm wet kisses, and the animal gave a gentle hop forward, raising a velvet nose into the air.

Ever so slowly, dark and confident gloves lifted the small door while the rabbit's eyes blinked, soothed by human breath. Gently, he stroked the furry head with three fingers, the long ears bobbing, folding against cedar chips with each downward stroke.

'And who are you?' he intoned at the lop-eared fluff, placing his hands beneath each leg, lifting the creature smoothly.

Against the warmth of his body Tofu nuzzled a cheek, the sleepy eyes winking in metered time to each admiring stroke, the soft nose pulsing against Dacron.

Upstairs, Diana Clayton had felt a sudden chill that was gone in an instant. Instinctively, she had glanced down the hallway to where her children were sleeping, then stopped working for the night.

'Flu season,' she had whispered.

'I don't have time to be sick,' she had said.

He heard the tub filling.

He saw shadows against the stairway die as Diana dimmed the lights in her bathroom.

He felt the chambers of Tofu's heart pounding like a watch wound to destruction, nearly bursting with terror as he blew a foul stream across her face for a second time; the powerful rear legs kicking against his chest in a wild plea for survival.

Using the buttery fold of skin around Tofu's neck he fashioned a garrotte with surgical skill and began strangling the animal with its own flesh; watching the paws flip aimlessly, the torso writhing, dancing through air.

Relaxing his hold. Then pinching the skin taut, leading the animal across the countertop, down into the sink.

The once-trusting eyes teared, dilating into black pools as shock shut down the biological acceptance of pain. And Tofu gave an involuntary thrust, a spasm, her bladder releasing a short but steady stream.

Grabbing both front legs, he gave a sharp merciless pull, as for a second the body shook violently, followed by a predatory stillness that trapped time. Formless and pure. And a darkness that could almost be touched.

Intimate. Arousing.

There was a chill to the night air.

As he closed the front door behind him, he pulled his collar against the wind, and it was a quiet, sleeping suburb that greeted him.

And he felt curiously alive as his blood came pounding through the dark chambers of his heart, running down into every muscle and fibre and nerve, fuelling him with an almost unbearable delight.

No dogs came barking. No cars were turning. No signs of a suburb in terror.

Down and across the lawn he started, ever confident, ever at ease. He could see the mute sputterings from a television casting their glow, men like moths clinging to a bulb, he thought, empty lives flapping mindlessly.

And he knew all their names. Counting by house, row about row, he could recite their most personal concerns. One couple had a village idiot for a son. Another a spaniel with indigestion. One woman had been raped while young. Another was about to retire.

As he strolled, kicking through a small pile of leaves, he felt like a king, as if this were his village, as if these were his subjects.

He pulled back into shadow.

Headlights were approaching, filtering through a soft wooded lot, but they came and went like a hollow beam in a dreamscape. Against his cheeks he could taste the perfume of Diana Clayton's bath oil, this tickling his throat as he strolled out into the street.

He stopped briefly, glancing back over his shoulder. The house was now dark, save for a light burning in a bedroom window, and he saw her there, dressed and readied for school.

'Yes!' he exhaled forcefully, closing his eyes.

'Yes, yes, yes!'

Kimberly Clayton was staring down at him, watching his every move as he vanished into night.

TWO

A man in a battered grey raincoat strolled down the sidewalk, crossing the intersection at 37th and Park, having driven through a cold mist that had only threatened rain. As he walked he seemed to be talking to himself, quiet mutterings that no one else could hear or understand.

'Tofu,' he murmured, and he said this as if he were addressing an old friend.

His dove-grey eyes appeared red and swollen, while his hands ached with the slight tremor of arthritis as he removed his coat. He was walking quickly, making a casual effort of dusting lint and ash from a dark grey suit. As he joined a parade entering the lobby of the Sheraton hotel, he summoned his reserves as he checked his watch. He was late. It was 4:06 p.m., April 8, and at the age of fifty-six, he stood parked like a hydrant, a solidly built man of slightly less than average height who was wondering how many more hours his stamina would endure, how long until he could return to the quiet work which littered his desk.

His name was John F. Scott. And as he turned through the lobby for the hotel meeting rooms, he felt empty and unfit, as if he had abandoned the most desperate and forlorn of victims, and after willing them to life, was letting them die again and again. With each death, the grief was real. The grief his own.

From the corner of his eye he spotted a small sign that read *Welcome CAP Fellowship*, this in red on white, with a little arrow leading through a spotless corridor. Scott followed twists and turns until he stood before a set of towering double-doors. He ran his fingers through a mane of greying-blond hair that curled in every direction, buttoned his collar with one hand, then began pulling at the knot of a silk Dior tie. While inching the door open, he took a deep breath, walking out into a small sea of younger faces.

There were about a hundred men and women dressed in civilian clothes, and listening attentively to a woman of about fifty who was standing at the podium of a small stage.

'. . . so as our profile of this offender shows, Dennis Statler was in many ways like the series killer Theodore Bundy, with some rather subtle differences. In terms of their behaviour, they were the same type of individuals, but did they have the same motives for killing, and what were those?' she asked with a nod, watching as Scott approached.

He smiled in return, for Scott could hear the fatigue in her voice and knew she had been playing for time. The woman was a fellow instructor, from the federal behavioural research laboratory in Quantico, Virginia, and the hall was filled with police officers attending a special training course called CAP, the national Criminal Apprehension Program. The program was conducted once a year by the United States government for police forces nationwide, and included instruction by experts from some dozen federal agencies.

'Ladies and gentlemen,' she said with a bite, 'both men abducted and sexually molested their victims, both men preferred killing with a blunt instrument, and both discarded human remains in a shallow grave. Were their motives the same, in what other way were they alike?'

Scott raised his hand as he walked onto the stage. 'Bundy was a lawyer,' he said quietly, speaking directly to the men and women in the soft chairs. 'Statler was an accountant. Rather than motive, it is important to note that both were professional men who made their lives in quiet residential neighbourhoods. And while Bundy was engaged to be wed, Statler was already married and had two children.'

Scott was reaching into his coat pocket, producing a fist full of notes, and forcing his mind into paths of logic. 'Sorry I'm late, Dorothy,' he said quietly as the woman was collecting

24

her papers off the lectern. With a smile, Scott turned back to the students as the woman leaned up into the microphone.

'Our guest speaker has arrived,' she said, and a short burst of laughter filled the hall as Scott removed notecards from inside his jacket and placed them on the lectern.

'The important point about these two killers is not that they shared similar behaviours while stalking prey or even during the kill. No,' Scott said with a sharp conviction, holding up one hand while establishing eye contact with several students. He paused, scanning the crowd with precision. 'The important thing is their camouflage, the manner in which they were able to evade police investigators. During the next six weeks you will be learning from the leading experts on repeat violent crime and if you come away with nothing else, please learn this. Most serial killers have very little to do with the myths that are taking form around them. Most do not live in a kind of unemployed isolation, off in some distant wood or asylum. They are your neighbours. Just like Bundy, Statler, Gacey, Williams, Merrin, and a cast of hundreds, they are the people you meet at the PTA or little league, they ride the bus with you, your children play with their children, they may even break bread with you at family gatherings.'

A hushed murmur filled the hall, and Scott gave a knowing nod. 'First, as you may have guessed, I am Jack Scott, director of the federal law enforcement program known as ViCAT, the Violent Criminal Apprehension Team. Our job is in our title. I will be speaking with you from time to time throughout your course work, so if there is no disagreement, let's start with a few numbers that spell out the specific threat to the civilian population and domestic security of our country.'

He waited a moment, then read from a card. 'In 1985, there were 14,516 murders in America classified as without motive, that is homicide at the hands of a total stranger, someone who has nothing to gain but murder in and of itself. Now from this group of killings, only sixteen suspects have been captured. Nine have been convicted, and since I'm sure no one here tonight believes nine men could accomplish so much in so short a time, let's cut through the chase. Also, that number does not include an additional 5,000 bodies that simply turn up each year in the category of Unidentified, persons who only appear to be murder victims, so let the record show we're being conservative tonight.'

Scott watched the crowd of young police officers, they were silent and attentive, having been hand-selected by police chiefs to represent their home states. 'Now the question remains,' he continued, 'what type of human animal takes another life without motive, and why, and what does the incidence mean? First,' he said clearly, 'so-called motiveless murder is usually committed by a person from one of two classifications. The first has a major psychological abnormality, a type of mental illness. I'm sure everyone has seen the movie classic *Psycho*, this was based on a real case, so think of this as representative of the first group.

'The second, and by hundreds to one the larger population is classified as Recreational Killers, and they represent your Ted Bundys. Unlike the Psychos of America, they are considered to be quite sane and mentally fit. So who are they? Why do they kill?'

The crowd was silent, and Scott paused long enough to let the analytical framework sink in, combing through greying-blond hair with his fingers, brushing curls off his brow. 'Recreational Killers, also known as Rakes, are invariably male, while their victims are overwhelmingly women and children, and sometimes women and children together . . .' As he blinked, mental images tore at Scott, he fought back with a verbal detachment. 'Their killings are usually intraracial, that is white killing whites, black killing blacks, and so forth. As our population grows exponentially, so do the numbers of Recreational Killers, and just at a time when the judicial system is impotent to effectively deal with the mounting threat. We at ViCAT need your help, the help of an educated police force. But first we must have some basic understanding of why this killing population is so different from the rest of us, in addition to the scale of the problem.' Scott paused, scanning the crowd and maintaining eye contact for emphasis.

'By employing computerised Artificial Intelligence, we have

produced a statistic that sounds an alarm for every man, woman and child in America, and it translates in the following manner. If you are a middle or upper-middle class family of four, the chances are thirty-seven per cent that you will meet a serial killer in your lifetime, and the chances are one hundred to one it will be from our second group.' Scott gave a nod as a hand rose from the crowd.

'Why now?' asked a thin and neatly dressed man in his mid-thirties. 'That number seems quite high, why all of a sudden?'

Scott nodded thoughtfully. 'Well, it wasn't really sudden, although it might appear that way. The size of population has just grown until we have now reached a kind of critical threshold, in today's world we just have more of everything, serial killers are no exception. They have always been with us, and their numbers grow as the population blooms.' Scott paused again, recognising a large man in a brown vest who was standing at the back of the room.

'Sorry to interrupt, sir, I'm Sergeant Howard Means, California Highway Patrol. Is the critical difference between these two groups of killers a question of insanity?'

Scott smiled. 'Illness and insanity are legal terms, and while we would consider their actions to be quite sick by all human standards – Recreational Killers are *not* sick, according to current thought. Bundy wasn't sick, and I knew him well. He was, in lay terms, lacking or suffering a deficit.' Notepads were suddenly popping open and Scott held off for a moment.

'Most true serial killers,' he continued, 'are as sane as you or I, yet they treat other people without regard for human suffering, and they are in full control of their actions. They know what they are doing when they kill, indeed many are cunning predators. The critical difference between them and seemingly normal people is that these killers are born without the ability to feel emotion.'

A hand rose in the front row. 'Sir, Kevin Mullin, Boston PD. Isn't it true that all humans have feeling, just to varying degrees, and that many of these killers could have been victims of severe child abuse that numbed them somehow?'

27

Scott returned a sly but understanding smile. 'Officer Mullin, you said?'

'Yes sir.'

'Thank you for hitting the target on the first shot, I'm drafting you for an experiment.'

'Sorry?'

Scott carefully summed up the young man with his eyes, making sure the audience knew he was doing just that. 'Officer, would you humour an old man and cover your eyes for just one moment, we will be giving you a quick test.'

Kevin Mullin quickly glanced about the room, preparing himself in case his powers of observation were called into question, and then covered his eyes.

'Thank you,' Scott offered. 'Now, today I am wearing a grey suit, I want you to describe this for me, not the suit, but the colour.'

'Well,' Mullin sighed and hesitated, 'that's a tough one. Grey would be like a blue but not as bright, it's really not much of a colour. Damn,' he shook his head. 'Sorry, I don't know how to describe grey except by comparing it to other things of a similar colour.'

'Fair enough,' Scott offered, 'you must compare the colour of my suit to other things that you have experienced, so this little experiment is over. Now what is colour to a blind man, a person who has never seen?'

The officer looked pensive as a hush started to swell in the room.

'Anyone can step in at any time and field this question for Officer Mullin,' Scott offered, concerned he was embarrassing the man. But there was only silence as Scott's eyes fell back to the policeman before him. 'Want to take a shot?' he asked quietly.

'Well,' he offered, 'to a person who was born blind, they would never really be able to fully understand colour, it would always be just a concept. You would have to have lost sight to understand it.'

'This is quite true. Now let's take it one step further. Ladies and gentlemen, would someone please explain to me the feelings of the following sensations,' and with that Scott held up one hand, slowly counting on his fingers. 'Joy, sorrow, anger, fear, or hate. There are six basic emotions, I have intentionally omitted love from our list so that we can avoid a battle between the sexes.'

A small wave of laughter bloomed and died.

'These, then, are the six basic emotions, all the rest are subsets or variations of these. Now I have named them, but I don't know how any of them feel,' Scott said with intensity in his voice. 'I was born emotionally blind. So please, isn't there anyone who can help me?'

A noisy wave rolled through the hall as a smaller man stood excitedly, waving his arms. 'Detective D'Angelo, sir, NYPD. In order to explain either colour or emotions, you would first have to experience them.'

Scott nodded. 'That is very true, and what, detective, do emotions do for us, how do they serve us?'

'Well,' he chuckled, rolling his eyes, 'emotions give men and women something to share.'

Scott interrupted a humorous chatter with a forceful and dismissive wave of his hand. 'He's right, let's give him a chance, please. What else, Officer D'Angelo, what other part do emotions play in our lives?'

'Everything, I think, emotions are the reason we enjoy things, and they also keep us in line. I mean emotions serve as a system of checks and balances on our behaviour.'

'This is true, and without them what would we have, certainly no highs and lows in our lives, no joy or sorrow or love. Without them, every stimulus on planet earth plays to the intellect alone, and while I can't ask you to fully comprehend this just yet, I would ask you to grasp this concept.' Scott paused and began to pace, his hands clasped behind his back.

'Without feelings, everything becomes meaningless except on a purely intellectual basis. Issues and events and characters, life's comedy and drama, are all meaningless. Without emotions, nothing matters, anything becomes possible. Recreational killers are born without emotion – we label them Devoids, in fact – and if you would like to explain feelings to

29

them, I would suggest you practise by describing colour to the blind.'

Instantly, the hall broke into a noisy chatter, as whispers were gaining tone, and Scott paced to the edge of the stage. 'Our studies now indicate that people like these, devoid of emotion, comprise the largest and most dangerous population threatening civilian life. As is the case with Ted Bundy, most have had above average child-rearing, but as adults they kill women and children with the mercy you might afford a cockroach.'

Scott glanced at his watch. 'As individuals these killers tend to be quiet socially, their physical appearance is usually neat, and they may be pillars of the community. They function well within society, and can share experiences with others with a rather critical exception. Since they are born nearly devoid of emotion, they must constantly measure their behaviour by studying others. For instance if they see us laugh or cry in a theatre, they know they must follow suit, or over time they will face detection. They parrot our emotional displays, and here lies a key for spotting them, which we will delve into at our next meeting. As food for thought, I will tell you that they do recognise this inability to feel, which potentially sets them apart from others.' He began collecting his notes as an excited debate began filling the hall.

'It has been a pleasure to meet you, and I wish you well throughout the course. Get your pens at the ready, and write down the following research question, I would like an explanation next time we meet.'

The audience went silent.

'Auschwitz,' Scott stated coldly. 'No place in history ever attracted so many Devoids in a single wrinkle of time.'

'But that's not a question,' a young woman offered in confusion.

'Yes it is,' Scott nodded bleakly as he left the room. 'And Dachau. Treblinka. Bergin-Belsen. Buchenwald . . .'

Scott walked through a downpour, climbing into his car at Park and 37th, where his engine caught on the first hit. He pulled into the street, heading south towards the World Trade Center, the mulling of tyres on wet pavement producing a monotonous and hypnotic effect, Scott letting his thoughts drift with traffic, his mind unable to concentrate further.

He knew the neighbourhood well. Almost operating on automatic, he slowed at the awning of Enrico's Fine Italian, the windshield wipers slapping at sheets of rain. Once, long ago, little David had worked there as a waiter, he remembered, and Jack Scott smiled darkly.

'I knew you were the one, I knew you could talk to Sam,' he blurted, before he started to cry.

David Berkowitz believed what he told Scott, that he was a 'Divine Messenger'. And Scott had taken all the pieces of his sorry life and put them together. That he was the killer of at least thirteen young women was not a question, what remained a mystery was why. Little David would not tell.

One August evening in 1977, after hours of mindless discussion, Scott faced the one-way mirror of the interrogation room, about to signal release, when he winced at the reflection. It was there, in the mirror.

'D-O-G?'

Scott choked on his drink, turning on the demented young man, having solved his motivational riddle, an anagram that sent him off into the night to kill. In frustration, Scott had scribbled case elements in large block letters on a legal pad, while for days Berkowitz had babbled about the beagle in the backyard that barked, keeping him awake – the nights he took human life.

'The dog told you, didn't he, David?' Scott had asked with mercy in his voice. 'The dog told you!'

'Yes, oh yes.' Berkowitz was excited and relieved. 'I knew you would understand . . . I knew you were the one . . . I knew . . .' And he broke into a fit of tears, reaching to hold the agent, love the agent who would now take over for him. The messenger who would carry his burden.

Sick, tormented bastard. In his lonely, twisted world, David killed because the dog told him, woke him at night and told him. The beagle named Sam asked David to kill and he obeyed. For David was his son. David needed love. Because D-O-G spelled backward is G-O-D.

The Son of Sam could not tell right from wrong, and barely left from right. Mentally ill, a true psycho untouched by reality, incapable of understanding the world into which he was born. Compared to what ViCAT faced daily, David was almost shy, an excitable boy who lacked direction.

He was not the devil incarnate, cult leader, conspirator and death master portrayed by tabloid hucksters.

David Berkowitz was a sick, sick man.

But he was *not* a Recreational Killer.

THREE

With a sharp snap, a flood of light covered a desktop littered with photographs, while a hand was adjusting a beam of glare. It was a tired hand with the small liver spots of encroaching age.

'The moment of death is not as arousing, not as important to you as just being in control – that's what you're after,' Scott said aloud, and he moved his pen, entering a notation in a yellow legal pad. He shook a head of greying hair, propping his elbows against the desk, his body sagged slightly forward.

'The ability to decide life or death, the process,' he repeated, rubbing his palm against his forehead. 'The whole time you were after the goddamn process?'

Scott felt as if he had been looking through a kaleidoscope, turning it aimlessly for hours, staring at fragments and meaningless patterns, then had by accident turned it just right and had the bright bits form a realistic image. He made another notation, lifting a photograph from a seemingly endless series.

Beneath the focused beam he studied this image for a moment, then flipped through a sequence of close-ups, every detail magnified and preserved.

There was a bowl of apples, and again he recalled the smell of fresh fruit. His own daughter had once kept a rabbit, and he stared at the horrible form of Tofu, bound in a blue ski parka, lying dead on the kitchen table.

33

Scott swallowed hard. Suddenly he felt uncomfortable in his clothes and tugged at the collar of his white shirt, then removed a cufflink from each sleeve, dropping these into a shirt pocket. Fatigue was returning, and he drained the last from a cold cup of coffee, standing behind his desk, then cracking the blinds of his fifteenth-floor window and hoping for a ray of sunshine. He looked out onto the Manhattan skyline, but the world to John F. Scott had gone dark.

That morning, in a Washington suburb some six hundred miles to the south, Diana Clayton had been buried. She had been dead for nine days, except in his mind. The mind of Scott, Commander of the elite and little known investigative division of the United States National Security Agency, ViCAT. And he wondered how many more hours his stamina would endure as he returned to his chair.

'I am the killer,' he closed his eyes to say. 'His skin is my body.'

Impossibly soft.

He imagined laying Tofu's body out across the kitchen floor by pulling and caressing each ear, tucking her inside of Kimberly Clayton's jacket. He was examining that photo now, tacking it gently against a wall of decorative cork using a clear plastic stick pin.

Drawing upon emotion, creativity and training, he imagined positioning the bunny's face up through the hooded parka and slowly zipping the jacket closed. 'What moved inside of you?' he whispered in a flat voice, working his hands as if tying long ears into a hideous knot. 'Like wrapping gifts, but a package for whom, for what purpose, for what occasion?' Again Scott evoked the sweet smell of apples from his memory, lazy and tranquil, like a crisp morning far away in time, far away from his office, as he began leisurely stuffing the hard fruit into each sleeve, in his mind, arranging them just so and adding a fullness and bulk to the carcass.

The parka had hung in the kitchen closet near the back door, and he checked the distance to the cage against a blueprint. Nine feet. Estimating twelve feet from the window, with at best, street lights to work by. 'Now,' he said, checking a computer-generated time series chart against a stopwatch, 'the bath water being turned off now.'

He tried to evoke that sensory experience, the absence of sound, as a safe little house returned to sleepy stillness. Soundless as thought he began moving quietly for the staircase, the waiting over, towards Diana and her children; moving room by room through a photographic sequence. He followed champagne carpeting, starting with a wide-angle view of the stairs, a hallway landing, and a dimly lit bedroom entrance. The door opened wide. He pinned this photograph at the centre, and then like building spokes on a wheel, placed two more pictures on either side, each detailing the hallway's interior.

Although critical detail had been lost to the camera, he could tell the family portrait was the type taken with studio lighting in the better department stores. He made a notation to have the picture removed from the house and copied for the files, while applying pressure to the small of his back with one hand, emitting a heavy sigh.

The master bedroom came next, and he gently affixed a photo, centre, above the rest. Her bedroom looked untouched, unmolested. Dark grey business suit still on a hanger just outside the closet door, pressed and cleaned. An ecru coloured blouse, ruffled at the collar, folded and placed on a chair. Shoes beneath. Light brown pocketbook resting on the carpet next to a maroon briefcase, both closed, the briefcase leaning against her dresser. The room was tidy in a feminine sort of way, there was no doubt that Diana Clayton had planned on living.

He examined an enlarged snapshot taken from the family room. She was standing at the water's edge in a red and silver one-piece bathing suit. Nag's Head, perhaps, and Scott's eyes worked quickly, soaking up the image like a sponge; well muscled legs, flat stomach, ample cleavage, short brown hair with blonde highlights. He checked his notes.

Married in 1972 at age twenty-five, her first child was born 1974. The years had been kind, he thought, either maturity

35

or motherhood brought out a refined woman who had been more girlish before. A good-looking woman, not a beauty, but unusual.

His fingers flicked from file to file.

A third photo, Diana Clayton's nude body, eyes open, staring up from her bathtub. Her right hand extending, palm down, towards the sink. A northward direction. Towards her children. Her chest thrust up, her spine arched, not even relaxed in death. Scott cleared phlegm from his throat and swallowed. Four scratch marks. Blonde hair caked in the darkness of congealed blood which had spread into a horrible pool. This picture he studied a moment longer, then placed it on top of the centre column, which was now four frames high. He made a notation, fumbling for a cigarette in his top desk drawer. 'Keep it clinical,' a voice inside him warned. 'Slow it down.'

Stink of sulphur, a few puffs, smoke filled his lungs. The harsh burning threw off other, more choking sensations and he pressed the recording button. 'Although victim was found in tub, victim's body cleared water by two to three feet for several seconds resulting in blood stains on carpet.' She had been held down for a brief duration. 'Scratches and bruise on left quadrant, upper-chest and neck, suggests assailant is left-handed or ambidextrous,' he continued. 'Extension of right arm, fingers spread, evidence of reflexive shock.' He rechecked the autopsy report.

'Cause of death: cardio-pulmonary arrest from cranial bullet trauma.' This confirming a single lethal blow from a .22 calibre truncated hollow point bullet, which entered her mouth through the upper lip, splitting teeth, then exited the rear lateral cranial posterior, or the back of her head. Scott closed his eyes and swallowed hard, having dealt, like most policemen, with debunking the media myth that a bullet to the head is always fatal and instantaneous.

'What went through her mind, what did she perceive was happening?' he wondered aloud. 'She couldn't even move.' Scott was breathing heavily now, pulse quickened, his thoughts beginning to blur. The coroner estimated that although she was paralysed at the instant of bullet's entry, it had taken her between three and five minutes to die. And the killer had waited. The killer did not want to use a second shot.

'The process,' he swallowed, a quiet rage stirring Commander Scott to his feet, the black bile rising in his throat. Suddenly his right foot tore into the side of a grey metal trash can, the object hurtling across the office, clattering as it spun.

'What did you do to her those last few minutes, you evil bastard!'

He stood fixed, blood throbbing at his temples, his grey eyes burning sharp and without mercy.

He closed his eyes.

In the bedroom, standing, I am the killer.

She relaxes in a warm bath, so she does not see my approach up the stairs and into her bedroom.

Soundlessly, I push the bathroom door wide on its hinges, and Diana's horror begins with a cool, sudden draught.

'Who's there?' she asks, peering through the doorway into the bedroom, feeling the unexplained chill on her wet skin.

I do not answer, Scott reasons, I wait so the victim does not scream. By now she is thinking the foundations have settled, popping the hinges, or the heat has come on, pushing against the door. She is seeking a justification in her mind while I know her disorientation will last just long enough.

I walk in, talking. 'Let us be calm about this,' I say very coolly. 'I'm lost, is this the Smith household? Do I have the right address?'

She wakes into a nightmare bursting, exploding in her head, the blood pounding so hard, so fast, she cannot hear, she cannot think; operating on instinct, starting to rise while trying to focus – when a forceful hand strikes her neck and chest.

Godless reality.

She is trying to comprehend, to see, but the room moves frame by frame in anguished slow motion.

'Oh God!' she prays instantly. 'Who are you?' Trying to find logic while trying to stand, the hand strikes, knocking her downward, grabbing her by the hair and preventing her fall.

'Does he know about the children? Kimberly, Leslie?' Thought number one.

'Is he lost? Does he want money? My children! God no!'

With all her worth Diana fights to stand, the slick surface of the tub working against her feet. Scott turns to the wall, thinking, 'I am between her, the door, her babies.' Pushing her back, beating her down with both fists.

'I only want you,' I comfort. *The process.* I understand what she is protecting; I know the hope she is clinging to.

She nods her head without making a sound, as Scott returns to his chair.

Behind my back I steady the gun in my fist, coming out now, quickly with a dull pop; a silenced gunshot splits through her teeth. Her body jerks back in a cough of blood, her hands fight as her body freezes.

I remove my gloves, five minutes pass.

She dies there.

Footsteps.

Mercifully, Scott thought, he heard footsteps approaching. A door opened and there was a familiar voice saying, 'Talk to me, Jack, do you need anything?'

And he tried to break loose from the death that was Diana Clayton, his thoughts failing as thoughts, that were now failing as words. The voice became a hand, and then a mug, that became the smells of freshly brewed coffee lying beneath the Commander's nose, tugging away at his senses with a warming reality as he leaned forward, his hand groping like a small animal, feeling its way across the desk. He was lifting a cup that seemed made of lead.

The hot liquid splashed back through his throat, mixing with bile, and he swallowed hard. His eyes looked red and swollen as he glanced up quickly at the figure who stood beside him, then quickly away, fumbling through his drawers.

'In the ashtray,' the voice corrected, and Scott saw a crooked white spire already rising from his desk.

'Sorry,' he exhaled, then pulled a long draw of hot gases,

filling his lungs. He sat back in his chair. 'What was the question?' he asked distantly.

'Nothing pressing.' Matthew W. Brennon was smiling at him.

Special Agent Brennon was a tall man, in his late thirties, and dressed in a dark blue suit with red tie. He was now examining the photographic matrix on the wall as Scott pumped down more coffee, finishing off a stale Marlboro.

'With what we're facing, I don't know why the death of a rabbit gets to me so badly, but it does,' Brennon confessed, looking away from that series of photos, then peering at Diana Clayton's body. No answer came back, so he turned, establishing direct eye contact with Scott.

'Tofu,' the Commander said quietly by way of agreement, releasing a frustrated sigh, removing his glasses and rubbing fists into each eye. 'I really appreciate the coffee,' he took another sip. 'You have no idea.'

Brennon turned his back to the matrix and leaned forward, both hands on Scott's desk. 'You've been at it for three hours, want to toss it around?'

Scott shrugged. 'Tofu was a member of the family, otherwise the bastard wouldn't have cared enough to give the bunny a slap. Killing as an end in itself doesn't do it for him, what he craves is domination, absolute control, that's key.' Scott stood, stretching his back, and with a neatly manicured thumb smudged away the term *Lepus Angorus* from the white margin of an 8 x 10 glossy. He then inserted the rabbit's proper name with a black grease pen and sat down again.

'Did you come to rescue me or did I miss an appointment?'

Matthew Brennon handed him a fist of pink message slips. 'Captain Drury has been calling constantly, he attended the Clayton funeral and wants to talk with you. He said he's willing to put the entire Maryland State police on this case if you so order, so I told him you'd be in touch.'

'Thanks,' Scott sighed. 'Anything else?'

'A woman called from the National Neighborhood Watch crime prevention program, she's writing a nasty letter to the

Department of Justice. I told her that was the wrong branch of government, her comments are on the note.'

Scott shook his head.

'And that covers immediate demands.' Brennon picked a file off the desk and placed it beneath his arm.

'Matt, have you worked through the path reports on the Clayton case?' he asked, pushing the spring-loaded beam of his desk lamp higher against the wall matrix while opening Diana Clayton's appointment calendar.

'Twice, the second time was to review your notations.'

Scott nodded. 'Do you recall if they found any traces of infection, bacterial or viral?'

'Negative, they were all in super health, why?'

'Playing a hunch, but it could change the course of the investigation, which I had planned on reviewing only for procedural advice as a favour, then kicking back to the Maryland State Police.'

'Here we go,' Brennon smiled, 'give it to me, Jack, make it a good one.' As senior field agent, Brennon knew that in order for a homicide to become a ViCAT investigative, the crime either had to classify as serial, or be an atrocity committed by a total stranger, what was referred to as motiveless homicide. These were two types of assault local enforcement had little chance of solving without help.

'Until now we've been operating on the assumption that Diana knew her killer and that the attack was motivated by anger or revenge of some type,' Scott stated in a flat voice, 'and that, of course, would have kept this one out of our formal purview.'

Brennon leaned against the desk. 'It's a nasty event, Jack, but I haven't seen any evidence to the contrary.'

'Take a look,' he said, ignoring the comment, pointing to the notation *Vit. C* on Diana Clayton's calendar. Each page was carefully sealed with a pliable acrylic for protection, and Scott had circled the marking with a red grease pen. Brennon did not respond, but stood fast, a pensive look framed by neatly trimmed black hair, his hazel eyes reflecting confusion.

'Damn it!' Scott spat impatiently. 'She felt him coming and

mistook that for the flu . . .' his voice sagged abruptly.

'Woman's intuition,' Brennon sighed. 'We've seen it before, but I don't know, Jack, what you're suggesting is that this notation reflects an instinctual error and that somehow, and God knows you'll come up with it, this will change the scope of our involvement?'

Scott tapped at the appointment pad with his pen, pushing out from his desk, then started to pace. 'I don't recall her stomach contents or blood chemistry, except that she was clean, but we were looking for pollutants, drugs or poison, not vitamins.'

Not prepared to argue, Matt Brennon leaned over, placing an index finger on the notation. 'You're right, Jack, if she had been taking vitamins it would have shown in the path report and I'd remember.'

'And if she knew this man, if this killer was known to her, do you think she would have reacted to his presence so viscerally? No, she thought she was catching the flu, and I also believe she was taking a hot bath to cure the chills. Diana Clayton felt him with her maternal gut, just like hearing a time bomb tick, only she miscued. Why else would her last request be a reminder to take vitamins, unless she erred on instinct, unless her body warned her, unless she knew but could not interpret her feelings, unless . . .' his voice trailed off sharply, his nostrils flared with disgust.

Brennon stood fast. It was starting to make sense. From a micro-analysis of her handwriting, such elements as decreasing downward pressure, the loosening of curves and swirls, the amount of perspiration on a page, the incomplete closure of circles and loops; ViCAT technicians had scored each of Diana Clayton's notations in a time series based on the combined effects of fatigue on penmanship. *Vit. C* was her last entry in life.

'She did *not* know him,' Scott concluded as he paced, his hands behind his back. 'The killer was a total stranger, unfamiliar to the family, and for that reason alone, she felt him.' He crossed the room, grabbed the grey metal trash can and set it back on end.

'This killer wants us to believe he knew her, but he did not. The Claytons were selected and stalked. And, I might add, that process does not appear to have been random.'

Brennon's brow pinched. He knew that less than one per cent of all motiveless homicides were ever solved, and Scott was moving towards having the Clayton case reclassified. More to the point, under Executive Order 14595, signed into law by President Jimmy Carter, under the National Security Act, ViCAT could take authority over the investigation.

Scott sat back down. 'Let's key on a criminal profile where single mothers have been attacked by strangers.' He tried to make the request sound like an offering instead of a direct order. 'Forget other similarities, wounds, weapons, body positions, sexual contact and the like. Start from scratch, maybe the computer will give something back this time.'

Brennon was jotting into a black notebook.

'There's something familiar here, Matt, I can taste it. Right now I'm betting this man will match against one of our known offenders who has just graduated into the big time. The computer robbed us last time, let's hit a home run.'

Brennon shook his head against a mounting case load. 'What priority?' he asked with a sense of dread.

'According to the forensic pattern left at the scene, our offender even doubled back to rough up the pile on the carpet where he had stepped, erasing footprints. He has a working knowledge of police science and that, my friend, bothers me a great deal. Let's go First Priority.'

Brennon released a troubled sigh. 'Okay, Jack. Kick the grey intercom if you need me,' he offered, as Scott began to focus the beam on his desk, lifting a silver frame into the light. It was wrapped in clear plastic and sealed with tape.

'Don't forget your dinner party tonight, I promised to push you out of here about now,' Brennon cautioned on his way through the door. 'And get some sleep, you look like a parlour corpse.'

Scott ignored the comment. Once again Kimberly Clayton's impish grin was melting his heart, and even as he heard the footsteps vanish and the door close quietly, Scott felt his mind beginning to crawl.

'An almost perfect-looking little girl,' he said, plunging back into a dark well of cruelty. He hesitated only a moment, taking a deep breath from his own childhood, and then a long step forward in time.

According to Captain Maxwell Drury of the Maryland State Police, it had been a neighbour who first stumbled onto the crime scene. Her name was Martha Cory. According to the report, she had been walking her dog by the house when she saw Kimberly and her sister staring out from a bedroom window.

Martha had waved, the children did not move.

Martha had rung the doorbell, there was no answer.

She had been staring into the lifeless eyes of the Clayton girls, each dressed and positioned like store mannequins in the bedroom where they had been sleeping.

FOUR

Down the hall in the fifteenth floor of the World Trade Center, Matthew Brennon returned to the Mix Master, a main frame computer capable of grinding through a population of close to three million known offenders and prior cases, keying in on related information, then spitting back data in micro-bursts.

Is weapon correct as listed? a message popped onto a green video display terminal as Brennon returned to instructing a recent graduate from the Federal Law Enforcement Training Academy by the name of Daniel Flores.

Flores was twenty-six and had been first in his graduating class, specifically requesting assignment to ViCAT in New York. It was his career ambition to work alongside Commander Scott, training on state-of-the-art equipment and studying with America's elite manhunters. Files in hand, Brennon stooped over the keypad as Flores sat in mute attention, staring at the sign over the door through which Brennon had just appeared.

> *We are the last defence.*
> *We are the last detail.*
> *Sentries at the door of hell,*
> *Who can't afford to fail.*

> N. Dobbs

It was heady stuff to the recent graduate, and Brennon waited patiently before clearing his throat.

'Who is Dobbs?' Flores asked.

44

'Who *was* Dobbs,' Brennon corrected. 'The first ViCAT commander, he's been dead a long while.' Agent Flores smiled up at the lean agent, who stood about six-foot-two, his dark black hair contrasting against a face grown pale from working too many nights. Matt Brennon was a soft-spoken thirty-nine year old, trim with an intention to stay that way.

'Now look at the prompt on the screen, the program is challenging you. It is questioning if you entered the data on the murder weapon correctly. Why would it do that?'

Flores looked blank.

'Artificial intelligence does not give leeway for user error, it works on strict probability, and the weapon in this case, a firearm, doesn't make sense with what the system already knows about home intruders, specifically home intruders who kill,' Brennon explained. 'These types of killings typically are beatings, strangulations, stabbings; anything rather than shootings. The computer thinks a gun is too impersonal a choice for this type of killer.'

'So it was expecting a device that required touching, physical contact?'

'Exactly. Now look at the second question, the computer is asking if the weapon was found at the site, so it's trying to classify the man's personality.'

'As a potential repeat offender?'

'Not yet, but it will lead to that. If the killer used whatever weapon was available, a kitchen knife or a lamp cord, that points to a more disorganised personality. If the killer brought his own weapon, which is the case here, it points to a stalker, someone who is cunning. If the stalker brought a gun,' he shrugged, 'who knows what it will come back with. Enter .22 calibre pistol,' he said, 'brought to scene by the killer.'

'Do we have evidence for that?' Flores asked correctly.

Brennon reached into the file and handed him a black-and-white enlargement produced by an HVEM, high voltage electron microscope. The photo looked like the surface of a weird planet exploding. 'All of the bullets were .22 calibre, something called a hornet, mass produced, easy to purchase. Muzzle velocity estimated at 1,600 feet per second. No shell

45

casings, and they only recovered bullet fragments like this one, from Diana Clayton's tongue, and she did not own a gun.'

Agent Flores' hands trembled slightly as he typed the salient data into a form on the screen. He pressed the enter button. The screen went blank and delivered another prompt.

Entry Forced/ /Type of Entry? the computer asked.

'The program is comparing the degree of sophistication of implements and tools used by the killer, looking for burglar equipment. This is the same logic we applied, but in a pure mathematical form. The program assigns skill levels based on the coding of different tools. Unfortunately we have nothing to feed it, so type in *unknown*,' he said, pulling a sheet from the file. 'No sign of forced entry, in fact, no sign of entry at all. You should also note that the locks in the house are registered and were installed by a bonded company, who claims no other keys were issued except those found with the bodies.'

It took a few moments, but Flores typed, beginning to understand the sophistication of the case and the computer. The screen swallowed data, went blank, and another prompt appeared.

Other Material Evidence Outstanding? the computer asked.

Brennon was at the ready. 'Two strands of Dacron taken from between rear feet of family pet,' he paused. 'Make that Tofu,' he said. 'Identify the pet as Tofu.'

Flores stared up at him. 'Sick bastard,' he spat. 'The rabbit was kicking its heart out and . . .'

'. . . she caught the killer's clothing with her rear claws giving us better data.' Brennon completed the statement in a positive way, placing another HVEM photo on the desk. The Dacron fibres were rendered porous as Swiss cheese and shaped like alien wasps. Agent Flores typed the data in slowly.

'There were also a dozen strands of nylon rope taken from the children's room, checked under HVEM. There are about twenty-five possible U.S. manufacturers, more abroad. You can buy it anywhere, boat supply, hardware stores, sporting goods.' The graduate punched it in, the screen swallowed.

Offender's Blood Type/ /DNA Code? came a prompt.

Brennon released a sigh, pulling a series of stills and reports from the file. 'Body evidence negligible,' he said. 'Saliva shows AB positive, but the FBI techies don't have enough for DNA decoding. Not even one eyebrow hair, he must have used tape for those or was completely shaven, although Jack thinks he was covered by a Dacron hood.'

Agent Flores' chin was against his chest. 'Then she was raped,' he concluded.

'No,' Brennon answered, his face worked into a cold mask. 'Enter that we have no fingerprints, no footprints, no latents.'

And Flores stood, his face and neck flushed with blood. He was a human fireplug, five-foot-seven, with wild hazel eyes and thick lips that looked parched.

'Matt, are we going to get this guy?' he asked with a sudden sadness.

Brennon stretched like a cat and then pointed at the sign over the exit door. 'Like the man said,' he smiled, 'take a break and I'll get us some coffee.'

Daniel Flores had already spent the better part of a week reviewing the top ViCAT cases, every type of violent crime the human mind could fathom and in horridly graphic detail; investigations ranging from multiple rape and child molesting to mass murder and serial killings. Through the use of the Mix Master computer he had already met more human monsters than most cops meet in a lifetime, and he continued to enter data, or what the program saw as a lack of data, the screen swallowing information as fast as it was entered.

The computer prompt returned, and Flores' eyes flared with horror.

1. Evidence negligible for severity of crime, the computer spat back.

2. Expert pre-forensic evaluation by suspect.

3. Police or law enforcement officer probable suspect.

Daniel Flores pushed away from his seat in a horrified dash to find his training officer.

47

FIVE

He was a dog of unknown years, for he had been found fully
grown along River Road in Bethesda, Maryland, near the
posh and aristocratic neighbourhood of Kenwood Forest.

It was Elmer Janson who discovered him, having heard a
whine come from a ravine while riding his bike home from
school. The boy had pulled the wounded animal to safety,
then using his jacket as a litter, dragged the dog several miles
to the Glen Echo Fire Station. A paramedic applied a tourni-
quet to a badly mangled left front leg, stabilised the dog's vital
signs, and sent for a vet. That was two years ago, according
to a newspaper article, and rush hour commuters never
noticed the child fighting his way along the road, pulling with
all his might to save a dying dog.

'Give me a break,' spat the hard looking man in a tan
Crown Victoria, and a gob of shine flew from the window,
landing on the 7–11 parking lot. 'A little kid dragging a fully
grown Shepherd down the road and no one noticed?'

He stuffed the newspaper clipping back into the forward
pocket of his sweatshirt while speaking to a dirty windshield
and sipping at a styrofoam cup. A flush of cars already blocked
River Road with gridlock and he figured that the more likely
scenario was that hundreds of motorists had seen the child's
act of mercy but that no one cared. That would be more
typical of Bethesda, he thought, drivers who routinely cursed
like cheated whores, making obscene gestures at the slightest

48

provocation. And he remembered a lawyer who had slammed into the side of a school bus while leaking verbiage over his car phone, then later filed suit against the school district citing the colour yellow as a non-reflective road hazard. That was the suburban city he knew. He eyed a pair of women in a red BMW who had pulled into the parking lot and were now swishing towards the door.

The larger of the two seemed to have a post-nasal drip, and was pulling at her front lip while tickling her gums with an index finger; symptoms classic of cocaine abuse. Dirty blonde, dark blue designer threads, about five-foot-eight, 155 pounds, slight scar on chin, Rolex-type watch, red fingernails. He let them pass, studying his reflection in the rearview mirror and grabbing a beaten pack of Marlboros from the dash.

His name was Frank Rivers. At the age of thirty-eight his once all-American boy appearance was fading fast into the worn flesh of middle age, producing a severe-looking man. His sculpted chin appeared hard and chiselled, the pleasing boyish eyes now seemed menacing, a piercing blue, almost deadly. His hair was thick, the heavy yellow of ripened corn with a thinning patch at the crown of his head that revealed a troubling scar that snaked outward like a pale worm. He licked a palm and batted the hair backward with both hands.

'Dispatch, this is One-Echo-Twenty,' he stated quietly, holding a radio mike in his palm, thumbing the indent button impatiently.

'Go ahead, Echo-Twenty . . .'

'Wants and warrants,' he glanced at the plates. 'Victor-Alpha-King 5-2-5, Maryland,' he instructed, 'BMW convertible 1987.'

'Roger, Echo-Twenty.' The radio went silent as Rivers returned to studying a folder marked Jane Doe, the case of an unidentified female, human remains found at County Plat 178, better known as River Bowl. He counted backwards.

The remains had been exhumed last Tuesday. The case was closed on Thursday. In two days the County Medical

Examiner had identified the bones that Elmer Janson had unearthed as belonging to a girl who had died of unknown causes somewhere before the turn of the century, and that was all that was known. As of today, Friday, 8 April. Rivers knew that the County authority would be filing the bones away in some drawer, to be forgotten until another generation was cleaning through the ME's warehouse, and so he returned to studying the news clipping, a story on Elmer's adventurous activities and those of his family. The article had appeared in the *Tempo* section of the Washington paper the day after the boy's discovery, and Rivers gave it a good scan.

Elmer Janson's father was described as a jet-setter who preferred travelling through Europe over raising a child, and *Tempo* staffers pulled the stops to back that theory. 'A real gambler,' stated one source, 'very hard core.' In addition, the boy's mother was an extra special juicy item.

'She's a party girl, she doesn't care about that child,' stated a neighbour who asked not to be identified. 'It's all a charade, a marriage of convenience. It's no wonder that boy is digging up graves, he should be placed in a home . . .' Rivers stopped to spit out the window, dropping *Tempo* onto the seat while picking up an official-looking report, then checking the news feature against the facts.

Elmer's mother had seen the grave and then called the Montgomery County Police, who had notified the state, who had referred it back to the ME, who in turn had declared it all a worthless issue. Routinely, the case was being dismissed, and while Rivers had objected to his captain, he had been ordered to stay clear, being told that further investigation was burning precious man hours.

Rivers shook his head. If the body was interred one hundred years ago, how come Elmer Janson suddenly connected, finding the site, then digging it up? He checked for some type of dating on the bones, radiocarbon, isotopic tracing, and there was only a work order, the tests had not been completed. Since the County had failed to bring in a forensics crew to excavate in the first place, how were they to know this boy didn't find the body somewhere else and was just now disposing of it? And more importantly, why no one seemed to care about this dead child, no matter when she died, was even more of a mystery, a mystery that disturbed him; and while questions raced through his mind, Rivers started to anger at the insufferably weak detective work. Incompetence leaped from official-looking pages.

'Dispatch to Echo-Twenty,' a girlish voice came over the speaker, breaking his concentration just as the two women were leaving the store, heading for their car.

'One-Echo-Twenty, go ahead.' Rivers spat, and his shiny gob sparkled from the pavement.

'Registration, BMW, Dr Alan R. Munstein, no wants, no warrants,' the dispatcher replied. Rivers' shoulders sagged as he watched the upper class users pulling away. His jaw ticked. He felt like kicking them into the next world.

'Requests, Echo-Twenty?' the female voice asked.

Rivers hesitated. 'Negative,' he stated. 'One-Echo-Twenty clear.' And he studied their faces as they glided past, edging toward a Montgomery County police patrol car, then stopping to flirt with that driver for a moment. They were higher than kites, giggling at each other like two schoolgirls.

The uniformed car pulled through the 7–11 lot, parking, and a large officer with a belted gut waved as he walked by, a kind of jaunty salute. Halfheartedly, Rivers returned the gesture, noticing with some disgust that the patrolman's ample midsection was stained with tomato sauce.

'Get them carbos, Lardass,' he grinned under his breath, waiting for the officer to pass. And he started his engine, edging out from the parking lot, placing a fireball on his dash and pulling into traffic.

He checked his watch. 4:50 p.m. School had been out for an hour and he powered up his window, leaning into his siren as civilians cursed his approach.

Frank Rivers circled the block before making a final turn into the shopping centre across the street from the abandoned bowling alley. He parked his cruiser facing the intersection of River Road.

As he stepped into the chill of late afternoon shadows, he tightened the laces on each running shoe and discreetly studied the angle of the sun. It was a savoury time for boys after school, he remembered, too early to think past dinner into homework, yet late enough to kill the pressures of new math, or whatever they called it these days. And if anyone understood little boys like Elmer Janson, that man would be Frank Rivers, he thought proudly to himself. No boy with any spirit in him would be shut in on an early spring day like this.

He quickly studied the layout of the building before deciding on his approach, around the back of a Mobil gas station. From the rise in the pavement he could look down into a caged clearing beyond a No Dumping sign and into a trashed lot with fountains of weeds. He could just discern the figure of a young boy with light reddish hair sitting on a junked engine block and scratching the ground in lazy circles with a stick while stroking a large blond dog.

Rivers gave a low whistle, then waited for the wind to carry it along. He nodded, for the dog raised a massive head.

The man came directly towards the building in a half-jog, not slow, not fast, just sure and steady. And from a distance, the boy watched, pondering the ease of his movements over busted concrete, glass and litter; a catlike certainty, a quiet power, almost deadly in purpose.

As he came closer, Elmer saw the sharp blue eyes under a brow that was fixed in alertness, and he felt his heart beginning to race. The stranger was moving swiftly upon them, the eyes endlessly searching from side to side and forward, taking it all in, missing nothing.

The policeman jogged through a short ravine, skipping puddles of oil and battery acid, moving quick and silent in lengthening strides. The boy stood suddenly, his heart racing, staring at the dark and forbidding figure that glided towards them. There was a laziness to his movement that suggested danger, an easiness of stride that suggested tension.

It was the tension of a pending trap, and even as the boy turned and started to run with fright, the man scaled the fenced compound with one powerful leap, landing lightly on his toes and blocking his escape.

Elmer Janson caught his own footing and tumbled backward as his dog growled through a quivering muzzle.

Rivers was standing to his full height inside the dump, instinctively keeping his hands where the Shepherd could see them, palms outward, steady by his side. He leaned back against the fence and smiled, showing white even teeth.

'That sure is a fine looking animal,' he said quietly, and his voice caused the fur on the dog's back to stiffen and ridge. Rivers watched intently as the boy applied a soothing stroke against the dog's fur, righting himself against the engine block at his back, then dusting himself off.

'I once had a Bay Retriever, but I don't think as smart as this one,' Rivers continued, taking a step closer. 'I'll bet he let you know I was coming even before I made up my mind.'

The dog moved forward a foot, in perfect balance, 100 pounds with menacing, exposed fangs. 'Easy, boy,' the child whispered, stroking the dog's back while staring up at the stranger. 'Sit,' he said, and the dog obeyed.

Rivers waited. He had intentionally rushed the child and the boy's heart was clearly thumping, his breath falling in short bursts. 'Who are you?' the boy asked suddenly with a sense of dread and excitement.

The stranger nodded thoughtfully at the question. 'Well,' he said slowly, 'who do you think I am, Elmer, friend or foe?'

The mint green eyes grew wide with the sound of his own name, the boy backing up onto the engine block.

Rivers smiled. 'What are you thinking?' he asked quietly, taking on a relaxed posture and pulling a smoke from inside his sweatshirt. He lit up with a flick of his thumb.

'I sure hope you're a cop!' the boy rattled out, and his voice broke.

Frank Rivers felt a tickle. He smiled warmly. 'You knocked it down on the first try, Rooster, I am a cop,' he confirmed. And the boy quickly slipped his rump off the engine and stood, looking up at the tall policeman.

Rivers pushed his posture straight for effect. Although he stood six-foot-one in socks, he regarded this as only slightly better than average.

'You don't look like a cop,' the boy said cautiously. 'The others I talked to were wearing suits and ties,' he glanced down at soiled cross-trainers with double knots in the laces, 'and dress shoes . . .' He then pointed at the red globe and anchor on Rivers' grey, hooded sweatsuit. 'You're a Marine,' he concluded with a worried tone.

Rivers studied the boy's eyes, they burned with the fires of intelligence. The child looked at him cautiously and then pulled himself back up onto the rusting block with the big dog standing between them.

'I was a Marine, Elmer,' he said through a puff of smoke. 'I'm a Maryland State police detective and I want to talk.'

'And how do I know that?' he asked nervously. 'You didn't make an appointment . . .'

Rivers exhaled a puff of smoke. 'I'll show you my badge,' he offered, 'and my ID.'

'Do you carry a gun?' the kid cut right to it. He was now eyeballing the man's hip, looking for a metal bulge as the dog crept forward by inches.

Of course, Rivers thought, by this time he's seen so many badges he couldn't care less. 'Gun, badge, handcuffs, the complete kit,' Rivers offered. 'When I turn around you can take a look, but don't get grabby. You move on me and that dog of yours will eat my stones, do we have a deal?'

'Deal.' The boy smiled for the first time.

Rivers turned, exposing his right side and lifting his sweatshirt to reveal a large automatic with ivory grips in a tan high-ride holster. It was no small pedestrian police shooter. Alongside, two stuffed clip carriers were loaded with .45 hollow-points, dark and deadly, and a set of Smith & Wesson cuffs in a leather pouch. When he turned back the freckled face was smiling at him, even the three-legged dog was thumping its tail. Rivers grinned, 'Boys and dogs, weapons and secrets,' he thought to himself. 'At least some things in this neurosis factory haven't changed.'

'Can I see your badge?' Elmer asked shyly. He knew a good thing when he controlled it.

'No way, deal's over,' Rivers said. 'You've been staring at County tin, that should be good enough.'

'They're a bunch of twinkies, I wanna see *your* badge.'

'Twinkies?' Rivers asked.

'Sugar and air,' the boy smiled.

The detective chuckled, this child was old beyond his years. 'You said you didn't care if you saw my badge, your only interest is in fireworks.'

'That was then.'

'And this is now?' And he laughed the laugh of time, remembering those days when minutes crawled like snails. 'No deal, Mr Janson, I've got work to do,' he chuckled, then he started to walk. Without losing a beat the boy came following after, catching his stride as the dog ran ahead.

'Hey there, please wait a minute, I got another deal for you . . .' he said, and his voice dripped with a certain loneliness. Rivers stopped, abruptly meeting green eyes in a head on blaze.

'You let me look at your badge and I let you pet Tripod. He's smart, I've trained him to do tricks . . .'

Rivers stifled a laugh. 'Is that his name, Tripod? That's a terrific name, why, he looks like a Belgian Shepherd.'

'He's part wolf.' The kid upped the stakes.

'No shit?'

'No shit.'

Then Rivers said, 'Okay, you introduce me to Tripod and I'll let you have this for a while, but don't take off on me.' He pulled a black leather case from inside the hand warmer on his sweatshirt and flipped it open, a seven-pointed star produced a brilliant yellow flash. 'Deal?' he asked, offering the case.

'Wow,' the boy said with excitement, grabbing the badge, then pulling the dog by the mane. 'Tripod, this is . . .' he looked at the ID, 'Detective Sergeant Francis Dale Rivers, Maryland State Police, Bureau of Violent Crime . . .' and his voice went shaky, trailing off, and he swallowed hard.

55

'Frank to my friends,' the cop said quietly.

The boy exhaled, staring at the gleaming star. 'Right,' he swallowed. 'I'm Elmer Janson,' he extended his hand, which Rivers shook with firm precision, '. . . and this,' the boy tugged on the collar, pushing with one hip. 'This is Tripod.'

The Shepherd sat up on hind quarters, exposing a white stomach. 'He wants to shake hands,' the boy suggested.

The jogging policeman held his hand, palm down, under the dog's muzzle, then bending at the knees, shook a furry right paw. 'Well, you're a good old boy,' he said, 'did you meet Rooster in that ravine I read about?' His fingers were scratching through the thick fur, and Rivers could tell that this dog was groomed often. Tripod was swinging his tail, kicking up a small dust devil.

The boy gave the badge a long admiring inspection, then dropped it into a deep pocket.

Elmer Janson, dog at his side, turned down the sidewalk and over a small grassy common with the detective following after, heading up a concrete walk toward the front stoop of the Jansons' compact townhouse. It was an expensive unit, free-standing with its own small yard and iron gate, and Rivers watched carefully as the boy removed a pocket knife from his trouser pocket, then held up a key which dangled from a single ring; Tripod's tail slapping against his jeans as they hurriedly mounted the steps.

'Frank?' Elmer asked shyly, inserting the key into the door. While he had been insistent that Detective Rivers meet his mother, he now seemed uncomfortable with his own request.

'What's the trouble?' he asked thoughtfully, standing next to the steps where he could look directly into the boy's eyes. Elmer was nervously working his hands into fists.

'I just remembered I forgot my bike.'

Rivers nodded. 'After we speak with your mother, I'll walk back with you.'

The child turned to the door, reaching tentatively, when he stopped again. 'Frank,' he suddenly sighed, 'my mom asks a lot of questions . . .'

'I understand,' Rivers said thoughtfully, considering his dilemma. 'And she will ask you where you left your bike, and the bowling alley is off-limits?'

The boy nodded.

'Elmer,' Rivers sighed, taking a step forward. 'That's none of my business, but just this once, if she asks, I will refer the question back to you.'

'Thanks,' he said sincerely, turning back to grab his key, which suddenly veered away from his reach as the door swung wide and a woman appeared.

The dog stood in greeting, wagging his heavy tail with intensity. 'Hi Mom!' Elmer blushed quickly, dropping his hand as she swiftly glanced down at the stranger.

'Hello,' she offered without expression, moving forward, then reaching down for her child. She placed a gentle hand on his shoulder as Rivers' pulse immediately began to thicken.

Wrapped in a pink apron, covered with flour and crumbs, a truly beautiful woman stood before him; slim and curvy, her shiny blonde hair tied on top of her head in a strange little ponytail. Rivers was sure his breath made an annoying sound as it left his body, and he swallowed against the fluttering he felt inside.

'Hello Mrs Janson,' he said, unable to divert his eyes, remembering his mission, then quickly patting through his pockets for a lump of identification. Elmer was already handing this to his mother.

'Mom,' he announced proudly, 'this is Frank, he's a state trooper.'

She smiled only slightly, holding the badge in her right hand, scanning the particulars, then comparing the photo to the stranger before them. Her green eyes were like large sparkling pools dancing over Rivers, with a voice that was equally fluid.

'Has Elmer been playing at the bowling alley?' she asked with annoyance. Rivers chuckled quietly to himself, watching as she leaned down, handing back his credentials as his hands were just ending their search.

'Pleased to meet you, Mrs Janson,' he said, extending a

57

hand in greeting, which she shook lightly, and he felt her cautious smile like a small tickle against his ribs.

'Jessica,' she nodded at him.

'Mom,' Elmer interjected, 'can Frank stay for dinner?'

Rivers grinned. 'I just stopped by to ask a few questions,' he explained. 'I thought we'd better check with you first.'

At this Elmer cocked his head.

'You do know,' she sighed, 'that we've already spoken to the county detectives at some length?'

'I understand, Mrs Janson, and I won't push. I used to live nearby, so I was just curious.' He glanced down, the boy could barely hold still, his feet nearly vibrating as he tried to maintain his position. 'He's quite a handful, it's good that he has a dog like Tripod.'

Jessica was stroking the boy's fine hair, her green eyes filled with pride as she looked directly at the tall policeman. 'Do you have any children?' she asked quietly.

Rivers shook his head. 'No Ma'am, I'm not married.'

'For the past several months Elmer's been an explorer, and before that it was stuntman,' she explained. 'He doesn't mean any harm.'

'Oh I know that, Mrs Janson,' Rivers smiled warmly. 'I feel honoured just to have met him.'

She nodded.

'If it's all right I'll walk with Elmer while he retrieves his bike, ask a few questions, and then I'll be on my way. I apologise for any intrusion.' And Rivers felt her eyes covering him, seeing him clearly for the first time, summing him up. And he wondered what she saw, suddenly wishing that he had dressed better, when he realised he had been holding his breath. The pent up air seeped from his lungs.

'You're welcome to stay,' she offered, taking Elmer's hand as his excited voice filled in from behind.

'Thanks Mom!' he grinned, snapping into motion, heading across the small porch for Rivers. 'Hey Frank,' he offered with excitement, 'we're having homemade pie for dessert . . .'

* * *

It was almost seven o'clock by the time he walked Elmer home, the boy pressing him again to stay for dinner. The detective could see the disappointment in his eyes when he declined the invitation.

'Some other time,' he had said, and he wondered what had changed so badly in a society so affluent, that a boy's best friend was a thrown-away mutt and the loneliness of an abandoned building. Frank Rivers didn't know, but whatever it was, it made him feel empty inside and he blamed Bethesda.

It was a strange and alienating place, an ostentatious bedroom community of Washington DC, where adults were rarely held accountable for offensive behaviour, while those with diplomatic immunity never were. Once it had been a sleepy little Southern village, then in a brief twenty years, the town boomed with concentrated sprawl until it split at concrete seams forming instant megaburb, when in the strictest sense Bethesda was just another city. But without that title. Bethesda was a city without a soul.

Maybe that was it, he thought to himself, little Elmer Janson and his three-legged dog were the soul of an otherwise ruthless and uncaring city. The plain truth of the matter was that Elmer's act of mercy restored some of Frank's faith in the town where he was raised. And not faith in humanity. Rivers had lost that long ago.

'They used to park right here, Frank!' Elmer said with excitement, leading him by the hand, showing him the remains of a burned out '64 GTO that had gone to rust while discussing the old alley in its heyday when people drove muscle cars. 'And they'd bowl until the lanes closed and drag race all night.'

The detective smiled through his years and received the full tour, inspecting the pit where the bones were found, stomping on weeds that had sprouted through broken asphalt, examining every inch of the boy's hideaway. On the way home, Elmer, dog at his side, asked if he could keep the gold star.

'But don't they give you extras?' he asked.

'No, a detective only has one badge and it's real gold, very valuable.'

'Can we trade?'

'No deals on this subject.'

But the kid came up with his best offer. 'I have a coin that's real, real old,' he said proudly. 'This coin goes back to the Civil War, only one of its kind. I worked real hard for it.'

'Then you should keep it, save it for a rainy day when you need to trade for something better.'

Without warning, the boy stopped, and turned to the buff coloured canine. 'Tripod, sit!' he demanded. The dog obeyed, and Elmer unbuckled his leather collar and removed it, then turned to the detective. 'Look here, Frank.' He held the collar by one dog tag. 'See this coin, I gave it to Tripod, says right on it *The Union Must & Shall Be Preserved!*'

Rivers was fascinated. The coin was the size of a quarter. On one side there was a small house, entwined by a serpent, with the word *Beware* at the bottom. It specified no denomination. He wondered where it had come from, what it was doing on the dog's collar. It really must have value. Did his parents know about it? Something smelled.

'It belonged to a slave,' the small historian stated, 'it's worth a fortune, let's trade!'

'I'm sure it is,' Rivers smiled thoughtfully. 'Where did it come from?'

'Between us?'

'Sure.'

'And no one else?'

The detective sensed something amiss, the child was avoiding eye contact. He had been too eager, now reluctant. 'Elmer, tell me where the coin came from, if there's a problem I'll be able to help.'

The evaluation of trust was not a slight matter, so as they walked the block towards the townhomes known as Ridgewell Hamlet, Elmer thought about the tall policeman in jogging clothes, and the stories he had told him about Bethesda when he was a kid, and about the bank robber whose car broke down and hitched a ride from him, and about River Road before the offices and shopping centres. This stranger had spent time with them, had trusted him with his only badge,

60

and it wasn't a silver crest like the others. Frank Rivers was a real cop. And Tripod liked him. After all, he was the best judge.

'Promise you won't tell?' Elmer finally asked.

'I promise that if you ever need a partner, you can count on me.'

The boy was anxious, feet dragging, then he stopped and blurted, 'I lied to those County cops.' Just coming straight at you, a matter of fact. 'And they asked for it,' he added shyly.

'You did,' Rivers agreed, crouching down, placing elbows against his knees and looking the child straight in the eyes. 'You lied about what, Elmer? Did you find the coin in the grave?'

He nodded. 'They asked my mother if I found anything else and then she asked me, and that's . . . second hand . . . like a rumour or something, like I wasn't even there. And I was told not to take part in rumours . . . and so I said no. And that's it.'

Rivers observed that there was an odd truth to his logic. 'All right,' he probed, 'that's what, exactly?'

'The coin!' Elmer stressed, a worried look crossing his face. Rivers noticed his green eyes had gone to glass, there were tears just under the surface. 'That's what I lied about,' he said solemnly. 'The coin was chained to the body, only I didn't know that at the time. I really didn't. I told them Tripod found the bones, I have a metal detector, and . . .'

'You're not in any trouble, Elmer, no one's going to blame you for anything,' Rivers cautioned. 'I think I understand, you were working with your metal detector and this coin set it off?'

'Yes, sir,' said Elmer, 'and then I dug and it was right there, only it was attached to a chain so I pulled it loose. Then while I was cleaning it off,' his voice trembled, 'Tripod started barking and that's when I found . . .'

'The bones?'

The boy nodded.

'And don't you think you should tell me what else you found?'

The boy shook his head. 'Some weird sticks is all, they were right on top, poking up next to the coin. I think slaves used them for trading.'

Rivers was concentrating through a puzzle that was getting deeper and deeper, the boy was guilty of something, but what? 'Elmer,' he said, 'why are you so sure these sticks, and the coin, belonged to slaves?'

The child squirmed. Then he took a deep breath and rubbed the back of his neck. He pinched at one ear. Then he said, 'The date on the coin is 1863 and this used to be the South, only Rebels around here, and slaves. The Rebs buried a slave there. I was grave robbing.'

Grave robbing at a bowling alley? Rivers shook his head. The poor kid actually believed he was committing some crime. 'Elmer,' he said, 'it's impossible to guess where that body came from, but you weren't grave robbing, you were exploring, there's no law against that. Tell me about the sticks, how many are there?' he probed, finding a Marlboro, lighting it with a battered Zippo.

'Ten, but two are busted up,' Elmer explained. 'Some were stuck real hard down in the dirt, and I had to get pliers to pull them out.'

And Rivers reflected back on the County report, a passing reference to postmortem boring of the skull that was unexplained. 'Sure would like to borrow your collection, if that's okay with you?'

'Are me and Tripod going to get into trouble?'

'No trouble at all, in fact, I'll be back to see you in a few days.'

'Great,' a smile returned to his face. 'Why do you want them?' he asked with an uncertain voice.

The tall policeman smiled. 'Just fishing for a bigger catch, ever been fishing?'

The boy shook his head.

Rivers tousled his red hair while leaning over to scratch Tripod's chest. 'Then ask your parents if I can take you on a fishing trip.'

Elmer's face beamed as he ran up the street to his house,

the three-legged dog shadowing his every move, and Rivers watched them vanish up the sidewalk.

The thought of a dead child overlooked these many years and discarded beneath the once busy parking lot didn't make sense. Over the last thirty years, every square inch of Bethesda had been dug up at least once in the process of laying foundations for urban sprawl, and as far as he remembered, the bowling alley was no exception. No matter how he ran the equation – an archaeological site that had been missed by earth-movers, a Civil War child buried in the mists, a quickly fashioned grave for an ancient murder victim – the concept left an overtly foul taste like a sip of dirty cat litter. And as Elmer had shown him, the site was shallow, nowhere near the six-foot depth required for health reasons during the nineteenth century.

The team was back before Rivers had finished his cigarette, and Elmer Janson was handing over a brown paper bag flecked with dried clay. 'This is all I got,' the boy puffed, catching his wind. 'My mother says I have to come in . . . she has to talk to you again before we go fishing . . . can you stay for dinner? Please? Can you stay for dinner, Frank?'

'Some other time,' he said; and Rivers heard the breath leave the boy's body as his lower lip began to quiver.

'What's wrong?' Rivers asked quietly, as Elmer turned to walk away.

'You believe all those lies about us,' he stated sadly, and Rivers overtook his retreat with a single giant stride.

'Are you talking about that *Tempo* story?'

The boy gave a silent nod.

'That's just Washington talking to itself, don't take it seriously,' Rivers offered, but still the boy's eyes were moist and questioning.

'Then why do they say things to hurt people, why do they print rumours?'

It was not the question that made Rivers pause, it was the child's innocent voice poking at his heart, and he was thinking, 'Because they need fuel to burn, Elmer, food for their dirty engine. You don't want to understand their itch, how they chuckle through the breakfast obituaries, how their thirst for human suffering is never quenched.' He looked down at the child and stroked his hair.

'They hurt because they don't know any better,' Frank Rivers said quickly, and he was gone, just a shadow among shadows in the day that was dying around them.

SIX

If it was noticed at all, then the Maryland State Police sub-station on Rockville Pike was once considered by civilians to be a desolate outpost at the edge of the world. The low-slung brick building was located on a tiny hill in the rolling country-side, far from the famed Washington Beltway with its growing suburban blight.

It had been a quiet little place until 1976 when vandals carted away the station's only coke machine. In retrospect that act was a harbinger, sounding a big city death knell for the highway patrol ambience of the place. By 1980 the population had exploded, bringing the Maryland/District line over thirty miles to the substation's front door, and things changed, seemingly overnight.

Walls were torn down, additions were made, parking lots were paved, ceilings were raised, and decorators were hired to finish off the station's interior. Because of the strategic location near the sprawling cities of Bethesda, Rockville, Gaithersburg and Wheaton, Substation-4 became headquarters for the Maryland State Police, a regular police department no different from any other citified nerve centre for trouble. Frank Rivers braced himself as he pushed through modern glass doors to face an insulting throng of humanity.

It was a plush and neatly appointed lobby for a police station, with wall to wall carpet, sofas and coffee tables, and idyllic landscapes of the countryside that had been ploughed under. He entered to the competing sounds of dime bag pushers; prostitutes clutching their credit card presses; illegal aliens; thieves and pickpockets; speeders and drunks; every type of Mook imaginable after a routine day in the 'burbs. With bickering voices they were demanding their rights to a speedy process, demanding action from a detached bureaucracy incapable of quick solutions. Above the din was the familiar bark of uniformed Sergeant Sven Tompkins, a burly desk officer who had the courage to handle complaints according to number.

'Wait your turn!' Tompkins pointed a fat finger as a middle aged man in a tailored suit approached. Rivers recognised him as an uninsured motorist.

In places like Sub-4, Bethesda's true personality popped to the surface very quickly, and it was mostly unpleasant.

'Number thirty-one.' Tompkins waved a ticket at the air and a family rushed forward, emptying two couches. Mother and father with five juveniles, all neatly dressed, batting their way towards the desk, parting around Frank Rivers like noisy ants around a tree. It had taken him the better part of an hour to drive twelve miles from Elmer Janson's house, being curbed one more time didn't phase him. With a long reach he grabbed a fist of messages from the desk, raising his eyebrows at the weary sergeant.

'Check the can,' the burly officer whispered, and Rivers moved forward with a nod, dodging civilians, stepping around toys and tots, through a double door and into a hallway, moving towards the back of the building. He stopped at the men's room to relieve himself, and was standing at a urinal, giving a shake to help the water flow, when he heard a strange moan drift up from the stalls. He recognised the sound, which resembled a small animal's dying gasp.

'You okay, buddy?' Rivers asked with a smile.

'Goddamned gut,' came a voice from a far booth as Rivers heard the telltale sound of a Maalox bottle being popped, the pillow-sized pills being crunched by greedy molars.

'How ya feeling, Captain?' he asked calmly, giving a flush. 'It's Frank Rivers.'

66

'Oh, hello Frank, how'd the interviews go, anything solid we can hook into?' Captain Maxwell Drury, head of the Maryland State Police, had a voice that sounded like gravel being churned by a blender.

'You there, Frank?' he growled.

'Max, I've been looking into your Jane Doe and you've got real problems,' Rivers stated cautiously. 'It's possible we've hit on a . . .'

'Oh God, Frank!' he groaned, thumping the stall with a flat palm. 'Is that what you've been doing?' Drury exclaimed. 'Jane Doe isn't a case, it's an archaeological site, you've been away from your unit since two o'clock, and I told you to recheck sources on the Claytons. You were supposed to be in coat and tie talking to their neighbours, why,' he moaned from the can, 'oh why can't you follow instructions?'

Rivers leaned against the sinks, lighting a cigarette while waiting for the old man to finish. He shrugged in the awkward silence. 'Listen, Max, the kid who found the bones was holding out, I need the complete path report, it's not in the files.'

'No! We've got real problems,' Drury cut him off. 'Frank, forget that shit, please, I'm begging you . . . I'm dying in here. Why do you torment me? The Clayton killing is heating up in the press and I've been dodging calls all day. God save us, wait till you see the news tonight, the maggots are having a field day with this, the funeral was a media circus . . .' The Captain popped another tablet and bit down.

'Max, I think this little Jane was tortured, I recovered implements,' Rivers stated flatly.

'What?' Drury sucked air while chewing. 'All right, Frank, what's this about?'

'The ME had a passing reference to cranial punctures in the report, only he said it was caused by worms or some sort like that, postmortem, long after death. I need to examine the skull.'

'Oh no you don't, Frank!' his voice boomed and echoed. 'That bag of bones is small enough to fit in one hand, forget it, she's been dead a hundred years, can you hear me? We don't have time. It's all very unpleasant but it would prove nothing.'

Rivers heard the toilet flush and turned towards the mirrors, checking his smile. Captain Maxwell Drury appeared, his face ashen and drawn. He was a small but neatly dressed man, balding on top with a crewcut fringe that was going grey. His marine green uniform was expensively hand tailored and heavily gilded with stars on the epaulettes. He shot Rivers a hot glance in the mirror as he stooped, adjusting the flow of water into a sink.

'You've got two detectives on the Claytons, Max, what's a few moments of my time? Besides, a carbon test was ordered on this, and hasn't come back.'

Drury shook a balding head in despair. 'Let's say she was murdered, that means the killer lived a full life and died in his sleep – fifty years ago, Frank!' Drury reestablished eye contact with Rivers, who was fidgeting with a paper bag. 'If I didn't know better, I'd say you're trying to throw the investigation off, this is very counterproductive.'

The detective pulled a handful of towels from a white dispenser and handed them to Drury. The Captain soaked one and then patted his face, neck, and the top of his head; while Rivers quickly removed one of Elmer Janson's dowels from a bag, examining it for a second time.

There were ten of them, all identical, like chopsticks. They were four-sided and thick at one end, then tapering down into tips sharp as icepicks, even after being buried in wet clay for so many years. He balanced it across his finger, and gravity pulled it downward at the point, or what he guessed was the point.

'They look like small spikes, Captain,' he said slowly, trying to gain Drury's attention. 'We saw something similar in '68, used in conjunction with wet rope it's real effective for obtaining information. I remember a guy we found from the Third Platoon, he was still talking when . . .'

The Captain's harsh brown eyes held him off. 'Korea was nasty too, Frank,' he said, his voice gravelly. 'I'm putting you on narcotics first thing tomorrow, I'm really quite angry about this.'

'Max,' Rivers said cautiously, 'who's your agency pal who's reviewing the Claytons?'

'Frank, why are you pushing me?' He turned to the detective. 'I've got serious problems.'

'Just kick it into the system and let's see what falls out.'

Drury cringed sharply, staring at him, then rubbed an aching belly with one hand.

'Have you seen these bones?' Rivers asked, shadowing him out the door, just one step behind, down the hall, and into his private office. Drury sighed, shaking his head, returning to his swivel chair just as a secretary came forward, handing him a form. He quickly scanned a narcotics search warrant while reflecting on Frank Rivers. Drury knew his subordinate's game: attrition. The bastard enjoyed wearing other people out.

'Yes I have, Frank,' he said calmly, 'I've seen the bones and there's nothing there, you're pissing into my ear.' At which point he signed his name across the wrong line. 'Damn it!' he spat, staring at the form, then handing it to a tall female officer in State greens.

'I'm sorry,' he said, 'can you white it out?' The woman smiled weakly, carrying the warrant out through the doors as Drury stared at Rivers' sheepish grin.

'That's it, Frank, one more chance, you canvass the Clayton neighbourhood first thing tomorrow.'

'Tell him, please.'

'Tell who?'

'Tell your friend, I heard from dispatch that ViCAT's involved, it's no big secret. Didn't you train with these greybeards?'

'One greybeard, Frank, may you live so long.'

'Tell him, Captain, I've got a bad feeling about this . . .'

'Sweet Jesus, tell him what, Frank?' Drury jumped to his feet and started pacing angrily behind his desk. 'Tell him that I can't control my troops? I've got a bad feeling too, right here,' he slapped his belly, 'a feeling that this sickoid will kill again, and if not here, then somewhere else. So what do you want me to tell him, that I'm really quite upset with you?'

Rivers looked Drury hard in the eye. 'Max, I don't know what I've got, but I sure as hell got something,' he said in a pleading tone. 'Tell him that the generations may ring true, like father like son like grandson like great-grandson . . . Hell, Captain, I don't know what to say, or I'd say it. Just tell him us Smokeys don't believe in coincidence – that we got one very bizarre murder on our hands less than a mile from where the Claytons were killed.'

'Yes Frank,' he lied with dripping sarcasm, turning back to his desk, sifting through the pink message slips that had mounted there, dealing some into the trashcan.

'Can you afford not to?'

Drury ignored him.

'And what if you're wrong, Max,' he pushed, his voice filled with a quiet but troubled rejection.

Captain Maxwell Drury thought it over, for about as long as it took Frank Rivers to leave the room.

SEVEN

'What a bitch,' hissed Gregory Corless, a soft, round looking man of about fifty, as he walked from Bakker's Diner on Interstate 41. It was still a balmy seventy-two degrees, about average for early April. The index finger of his right hand kept disappearing into cheeks that were naturally puffy and red as he picked Irish stew from between his front teeth. 'Did you hear what she said when I asked for a toothpick?'

'No, Greg, I didn't,' answered Seymor Blatt, a thorn of a man with a thin neck and large larynx that resembled a rock stuck in a rubber pipe.

'Buy a toothbrush,' Corless cursed, 'the bitch told me to buy a fucking toothbrush.'

'I stiffed her,' Blatt returned proudly as they crossed the parking lot.

'You can't get stiff,' Corless sneered, as Blatt instantly blushed at the insult.

'I tipped her five per cent, she's a one dollar whore.'

'Well, what she needs,' Corless paused, 'is a good beating and a hard fuck.' The duo stopped alongside a white Dodge van as Corless fumbled in pastel blue pants that were too tight for his heavy build, producing keys, then sliding the bay loading door open. He retrieved a dark blue sports jacket with shiny gold buttons that was hanging on a hook.

'Should I drive?' Blatt asked.

71

'You read the map,' Corless hissed, putting on his jacket. 'Let's get clean.'

And together, like a drill team, they swept through the cab, tossing out wrappers and empty cups and old newspapers, which they had gathered along their journey. Seymor Blatt was checking under the driver's seat when his hand touched one of Greg's trophies, and he remembered the taunting voice which Corless had used on him all day.

'Better rip this up before we throw it out,' he smiled, the lump in his throat bobbing as he talked. Gregory Corless glanced up from the carpet at the picture of a girl, naked except for a collar and leash. His fat face froze into a mask of hate.

'I'll kill you,' Corless said in a quiet, relaxed voice. 'I'll kill you until you beg me to die!'

Without a word, Seymor Blatt placed the picture back where he had found it, under Greg's custom seat, and not in the box with the others in the back of the van. He was too scared of Greg Corless to question anything he said. With a gun or knife or a club in his hand, fat Corless was the most frightening man he had ever seen, a natural Santa Claus with a passion for hate and violence. If there was one thing he knew about his partner, it was that Gregory Corless never threatened something he was not prepared to deliver.

'Just kidding,' Blatt sniffed.

'Check on her,' Corless ordered as he moved behind the wheel and fastened his seatbelt.

Seymor Blatt pulled back the curtain between the seats and slapped the form that was wrapped in an old blanket behind where his partner sat. There was a whimpering movement.

'She's okay,' Blatt offered, turning back, then opened the Rand McNally. The fat man was staring at him in contempt.

'Last chance,' he stated without tone.

But Seymor Blatt did not respond, he just stared out the window at the people eating in the wayside diner. He did a lot of that on his expeditions with Fat Corless, stare at other people. And he wanted to say it right now, right to his face for all the abuse he had taken that day.

72

'You aren't what I look at Corless, you're just an obese and ugly fat man.' But instead he remembered Greg's courage to make real what to others remained fantasy. His strongest suit.

'I spoke with Maxine before we left,' Blatt's smile showed frail greyish teeth that looked small for his mouth. 'She said Donald has been accepted at Yale . . .'

'Ah, sweet Maxine, my wife, my dream,' Corless interrupted with a song as he started the engine and pulled away. 'All she cares about is having one of our children graduate from Yale. She never even considers the cost, twenty thousand a year, did you know that? And this time next year I'll have all three kids in college at the same time. Where does it go?'

'Money?'

'The time, you idiot.' He shook a round head covered with a cheap black wig.

'Goes fast, Greg, they're still babies in my mind.'

'And I was going to buy a Beechcraft jet when I retired, just think of the possibilities . . .' his voice trailed off. 'I don't see that coming for a long, long time now.'

'You'll do it,' Blatt assured him in a perky voice. 'You're the envy of the flight club.'

'You're right,' he quickly agreed, 'but it's just not the same as owning your own plane, a nice one, that is.'

'You'll find a way.'

And the three riders moved forward in silence, up a ramp and back onto the interstate, heading south towards the Florida Keys.

During dinner they had avoided rush hour.

They were making good time.

73

EIGHT

9:05 P.M.
LONG ISLAND, NEW YORK

Scott coasted slowly through the neighbourhood of Greenlawn, letting his headlights soak a few lawns as he looked for signs of spring, for signs of renewal. Things were going green in the yard across the street. Flowers blooming next door. But Jack Scott's perennials merely pitted flowers against squirrels, resulting in a mangled multicoloured row which led to his front door.

The rain had ended. He parked his blue Chrysler in the driveway, removed a heavy black briefcase from the trunk and walked, tamping with an angry right toe while moving slowly up the path, cursing at each half-eaten crocus bulb. 'Nasty little bastards,' he sneered, kicking wet earth into a hole.

The house was the oldest in the area, a two storey Victorian, and it had been home to the Scotts for three decades. Linda, his wife of thirty-six years, had left the portico light on for him, and he opened the door to an emptiness that seemed to buzz from hidden recesses. Years past, Scott would arrive to a mad concert of televisions blasting at record players competing with telephones, and the pounding of feet against stairs, rolling after him with the turmoil of adolescence; anxious questions and despairing tears, every triumph and failure, the fabric of a family. Their lives were melded with the old house, and to Jack Scott, the silence was deafening.

With his right hand he entered a sequenced code against

74

a soft button pad, disarming the alarm system which emitted two beeps, and he thumbed through the mail on an antique library table. A few bills specifically for him. And a postcard. He studied this for a moment staring at a moonscape with mountains and cacti, then a signature. 'Jody's in the desert,' he said sarcastically, dropping the card back into a decorative silver bowl. 'Who the hell is Jody?'

He popped the briefcase open, tucked a file beneath his arm, and headed towards the kitchen, where he dropped his wet shoes by the rear door. A note was posted on the almond-coloured refrigerator with a shell magnet, the cooler served as both feeding station and information centre.

'Dinner,' it said. 'Heat chops for three mins. on medium, apple sauce in white bowl, make some rice.' He grabbed the message and continued to read while digging through an assortment of bottles and containers.

'You forgot Bill and Judy's party,' it continued, and Scott winced, lifting a plate covered with plastic wrap, two thick lamb chops cooked many hours before. He searched deeper for mint jelly.

'Matt Brennon has called you twice, eat first.' Scott didn't bother to heat the food, but laid it out cold on the table, removing his jacket with one hand, then peeling off a shoulder holster, slinging the blue steel and leather across the back of his chair. He spooned apple sauce into his mouth, filling both cheeks, letting the coolness slide down his throat.

'And Jody,' the note explained, 'is the Secret Service agent you consulted with on the Meade case two years ago, he's semi-retired to Arizona. He's fifteen years younger than you are, John.'

'Oh,' Scott shook his head. Linda knew him better than he knew himself, and he began spooning green jelly over the chops, slicing the cold meat into sweet slivers that tasted like a world of wonderment; that in his mind simply tasted like home. He was slicing more, slurping sauces, fuelling a worn and tired body that had all but forgotten about food, when the phone rang. He picked it up on the fourth ring.

'Commander Scott,' he stated firmly, walking the phone from countertop to table.

'Have you eaten, Jack?' asked Agent Brennon.

'What's up?'

'A couple of wrinkles you should know about. We've rerun the Clayton crime scene data through the Mix Master . . .' he paused, wondering if the news could wait until morning.

'Yes,' Scott interrupted, lifting a spoon of applesauce. 'And it said to start looking for a police officer, we're looking for a cop.'

'You knew that?' Brennon was startled.

'No,' Scott answered flatly. 'One never really does know, it's just logical, the killer has made a study of police science. What better way to enjoy the pleasures of slaughter than learning to work with a skilled impunity? Did you push the program?'

'Until I thought it would implode, Jack. The computer comes back negative every time. This jerk doesn't even hint at any of our known offenders, so I think you should help me with postmortem behaviour, what he did after the killings, so I can build a profile. Tomorrow, I mean, maybe we'll get a hit against some other behaviour.' Brennon was standing in Scott's office.

'It's a waste of time,' Scott assured him. 'I already ran the positions in which the bodies were found looking for similar criminal behaviours in the existing population, and it came back empty, and that's all we have left to run. Every move this bastard takes is aimed at erasing evidence, he kills the way an artist paints; conception, imagination, technique, method, organisation. I've broken down each step, every move, and behaviourally, we've got a cop.'

'Bastard,' Brennon mumbled.

'I'll give you an example of what's left, that is if you're looking at the reconstruction,' Scott offered.

'Sure,' Brennon responded, sitting up at Scott's desk, staring at the display, the horrid photographs mounting up and across on each other.

Scott breathed deeply. 'Take it from the beginning, which

is crime scene forensics, furthest left. It only gets worse from there.'

Brennon agreed, looking at a picture of the living room, champagne-coloured carpeting, a babygrand piano, plush sofas.

'You knew our offender doubled back to rough up the carpet where he had stepped, erasing footprints, compromising any accurate estimation of body weight and height determination. Who but a professional would have that kind of critical knowledge of our best technology?'

'I programmed all of that in.'

'Yes, Matt, I'm sure that you did, but I intentionally withheld how he accomplished this task, hoping we'd get a match from a more general approach, and I tried not to bias your interpretation. Count nine photos from the left, moving through the kitchen towards the back door, what do you see? There's an enlargement.'

Brennon's eyes flicked from room to room, Tofu's body lying on the table, an empty cage, a kitchen door where Kimberly's parka had hung, and something blurred, something fuzzy. His eyes hit the last shot. It was an enlargement of a vacuum cleaner on the back of the kitchen door, strung on a hook next to Leslie Clayton's green ski jacket.

'Jesus,' Brennon exclaimed. 'That fucker knew how to . . .'

'He really took his time, Matt. That's Diana Clayton's Hoover Upright, which she kept in a broom closet on the other side of the room. He kept track of the areas where he had walked and on his way back out used the vacuum. He took the dirty bag with him. That's rather telling, in two ways. Not only does he know about micro-forensics, he knew enough about Diana to trust her vacuum cleaner, which was in perfect working order, otherwise he'd have brought his own.'

'God save us, Jack.' Brennon swallowed. 'Is there anything we could have missed, an additional motive, perhaps?'

'He left two twenties and a five in the master bedroom, along with a one-carat flawless diamond ring, he couldn't care less. Did you read the field interviews from Captain Drury?'

'Sure did,' he sighed. 'They're detailed, Drury's got some good people. There were no other keys to the house outstanding, including neighbours. The locks are first rate, registered, installed by a bonded company and the serial numbers checked against a technician, who happened to be a female locksmith, married, four children. The Claytons had no known male companions. And no one saw or heard anything. A quiet neighbourhood.'

'It's grim,' said Scott, 'a hand dealt by the devil. It reminds me of one of my first cases when police science was still in its infancy, a serial sex killer who subscribed to the *FBI Law Enforcement Journal* through a public library. This is not a good feeling for me . . .' his voice started to drift.

'I don't remember hearing about that . . . Holy Jesus!' Brennon spat suddenly, having wandered some distance from the wall, taking in the whole photographic collage for the first time. 'You've formed a cross, Jack.'

'What?'

'You've laid out a cross on the wall, a crucifix.'

Scott pulled back from his subconscious, finding a smile in his voice. 'That's because I haven't finished yet, smart guy,' he said. 'I have two more sequences left.'

But Scott didn't really, he was finished. On the wall he had left empty patches reserved for Kimberly and Leslie Clayton, he couldn't force himself to post those graven images. If their short lives had meant anything it was that other children and other families would be safe from this obscene destruction.

'How long have you known Captain Drury?' Brennon asked.

'Why?'

'He's called several times, but keeps saying not to disturb you, and that smacks of a long-term relationship. Just keeping my wits sharp.'

'Very good, Matthew,' Scott responded. 'Maxwell Drury and I went through the Federal Law Enforcement Training Academy together about thirty-six years ago, I better call him, poor sorry bastard. Running a police agency in the Washington area is akin to managing an insane asylum under a full moon. His whole jurisdiction swarms with the most important people on earth, just ask them.'

'He's grasping for straws.'

'So are we.'

'But his last call was about an archaeological find, the guy is desperate. They're pushing at the envelope, he admitted as much.'

'I'll call him, what about archaeology?'

'He said a site was uncovered beneath a parking lot that's near the Claytons' house. Civil War, it looks like, he said you should know.'

'I should, I told Drury I wanted information on anything that seemed out of the ordinary, especially in the immediate area. What else do we have?'

'He said the bones date back to the mid-1860s.'

'What bones?' Scott barked. 'You didn't say anything about bones.'

'That's what an archaeological site is, Jack. Relax, it doesn't relate.'

'And how do we know that, an important person tell us?'

Matthew Brennon gave a sigh, reaching into his hip pocket to produce a black-cased notebook. He started flipping pages. 'Skeletal remains of a child were discovered by a boy sweeping with a metal detector behind a condemned structure. The boy thought he was digging for treasure when he hooked a jawbone. His mother called the County, who called the local police, who called . . .'

'Metal detectors don't register bone, Matt. What exactly did this kid find?'

'Hell, I don't know, Jack. This all took place last month. The kid found the site, his mother called the County, and a set of human remains were picked up by the medical examiner's office. One of Drury's detectives also found a Civil War coin.'

Scott had lost interest in the story, except for the sloppy field procedure, which was unlike Drury. He was by-the-book, a real detail man. 'Why wasn't the coin recovered with the remains?'

'Sorry Jack, I don't know.' He glanced back at his notes. 'On the day the bones were reported, March 25th, the County Medical Examiner performed the usual routine. A small female, one century worth of dead.'

'You're not answering my question, Matthew.'

'Right,' he sighed. 'I'm not sure I can, the coin was just recovered today, looks like pure enterprise work. After the case was closed, a State detective read the field report and went to see the boy. Drury didn't know what he was up to, so technically this detective wasn't assigned. I guess the guy was just curious, I understand he grew up in the area.'

'Go on,' Scott said, holding the phone to his ear, searching through the refrigerator for dessert.

'Here it is, Jack, *Archaeology*, I just found the definition under garbage from the past, relics, forgotten monuments – the study of ancient life and boring cultures, lost civilisations,' and his voice was flush with cheer. 'Ah yes, come away with Indiana Scott to those golden years of yesterday,' he was puffing into the phone. 'Send now to ViCAT Old World Video and you will also receive . . .'

'You're a very funny guy, Matt,' Scott found what looked like a slice of leftover cheesecake, which he placed on the table.

'So how was your meeting?' Brennon asked, changing the subject. 'That fulfils our service requirements for the quarter.'

'They were very attentive,' Scott smiled, digging into strawberry cheesecake, flushing down a bite with a glass of milk. 'Tell me about the coin, Matthew.'

Brennon looked at his notes. 'Not much to tell,' he said 'According to Drury it was made during the Civil War, there wasn't any other metal found, no belt buckles or buttons, just a few inches' worth of silver from a necklace.'

'And the boy's discovery of this coin resulted in recovery of the bones?'

'Right.'

'Where are they on the autopsy, how far along?' Scott was focusing on the last sweet mouthful.

'Jack,' Brennon laughed, 'they don't do autopsies on fossils, neither do we, so I thanked Drury for the information and got off the line. They also uncovered some utensils made from a black wood . . .'

And Scott froze as an image suddenly tore through his mind, a horrid and painful image vanquished for years, stirring, then stabbing faintly inside, coming into a soft focus. He felt his body go stiff.

'. . . and that's it, Jack. But I think you should talk to Drury.'

Scott closed his eyes and swallowed at the pounding behind his temples.

'Jack?' Brennon asked.

'Was it sharp?' he asked flatly. 'This utensil, was it sharp?'

Brennon sensed alarm. 'I can't say,' he said in a confused voice. 'What gives?'

'What do they look like?' Scott's tone and blood pressure climbed, his knuckles were turning white against the phone and he changed hands.

'What are you asking me, Jack?'

'The wooden utensils, what do they look like?'

'There's just one, a shaft or fork or something, I don't know. I think Drury said it looked like a stick, a chopstick, a black chopstick.'

Scott winced, then cleared his throat. 'Chopsticks,' he stated flatly.

'Right, that's all he said.'

'It couldn't be . . .' Scott's breath fell loose as he pressed his ear into the phone. 'Were they fire-hardened? Blackened from fire?' his voice rose sharply.

Matt Brennon took a step backwards.

'Talk to me,' Scott pressed with an angry tone. 'The stick, there was only one? Are you sure? Was this crime analysis team comprehensive? They didn't cover everything, they didn't take this seriously, did they?' His voice was racing, his face flushed with blood, an angry force pulsing through arms, legs, torso.

Brennon swallowed hard. 'They didn't send in a team, Jack. Like I told you, first a few guys from the ME's office, that

81

was last month, and today some detective followed through. What is this? Do you want me to get further information on the stick?'

'No,' Scott said, voice suddenly quiet and resolute. 'Who was this detective, the one you said freelanced in the field?'

'I don't know.'

'Track him down, I want his complete State and Federal records on my desk in an hour, have them faxed from Washington and don't trip his wire. I want to know this man, where he lives, how he lives, his home phone, everything. Don't forget tax data, school records and military service. And call Drury immediately, talk only to him. I want stats of this stick, we'll handle the interpretation. Get copies of the coin too, and this is very important,' he said slowly, 'I don't want those human remains touched any further, understand? If they have a photographic sequence of the unearthing, let's get that.'

'Yes, sir,' Brennon snapped. 'Is this in some way related to Diana Clayton and her children? Is this detective a suspect?'

But Scott didn't hear the questions. 'I'll be there as soon as I can,' he said, blind to the outside world, operating on instinct as he hung up the phone. In his mind he was seeing faces, once forgotten, and their words were soft and kind.

'She's not coming back,' the voice repeated.

Scott ignored the comment, lighting another cigarette. 'Nothing to do for her now, nothing left to do for her family,' was his thought. 'No words of comfort, no assurance of police protection, no psychological counselling. Nothing.' And he was filled with despair, just another fool strapped in a watch and counting the minutes, waiting for her to die.

Mary Beth Dodson was sixteen years old. A machine was breathing for her now, and once again, Scott could hear the pistons of the artificial lung plunging, driving air into her broken ribcage. He stood at his kitchen window and remembered with a terrible clarity the girl's pale and beaten face, the movement of the hands batting at the air as if chasing away deadly insects; just as he knew he would remember during every weak and insufferable turn of his life. Remember. How Mary Beth's eyes had stayed open, stretched with terror but unable to see. From the waiting room outside came the sobbing from parents and siblings.

Scott turned away from the bed to the hospital window as they began strapping her down, and he watched a mad parade filing past; doctors, nurses, technicians and visitors. Some were smiling, greeting each other, walking arm in arm unaware of the horror he was living with. As he walked from the room his eyes briefly met those of Mary Beth's father, his steeled silence sharper than any words of blame. Scott hesitated a moment, then pushed himself towards the end of the hospital corridor. Dr Chet Sanders, director of internal medicine, found him a moment later.

'Jack,' he called softly, a towering man with tan and wrinkled skin. Sanders stood attentively in a blue surgical gown, patting blood from his shirt sleeves, removing a mask of white gauze.

'There's still hope,' Scott answered, refusing eye contact. Mary Beth Dodson was the only victim to have survived an attack by a sadistic killer who had stalked the suburbs of New England for several years.

'She's too badly beaten, Jack. The meninges,' he explained, 'the protective membranes enveloping the brain and spinal cord have been punctured, and she was shaken so hard that her brain literally bounced within the skull case. It's swelling too rapidly, the next stage will be multiple organ failure.'

Scott's grey eyes flashed with violence. 'There's still hope,' he stated again through clenched teeth.

Dr Sanders laid a gentle hand on his shoulder. 'If we could control the swelling she'd have a chance, but I'm afraid that's beyond control. For all practical purposes she was dead when you came through the door. I'm sorry.'

The young woman had been missing for ten days when Commander Nicholas Dobbs and Special Agent Scott had narrowed their search to within a single neighbourhood. She was found in the closet of an abandoned building.

'You look tired, Jack, you've lost weight, there's nothing you can do here . . .' Sanders was saying. 'If she did survive, she would have severe brain damage. That's not a life. You've done all you can. It's better this way . . .'

'Yes, better,' Scott interrupted, his voice mechanical, lighting a cigarette end-to-end from one that was still burning. He rubbed his eyes with fingertips yellowed from nicotine.

'Jack, I've been treating patients for thirty years, some that have ripped apart, take some advice . . .'

Scott breathed deeply.

'Heal thyself,' said the doctor.

Scott turned, his eyes burning. 'What are you saying to me?'

'How old are you, Jack?' the words bubbled back from beyond time.

'Twenty-four.'

The aged medical practitioner bent his tall frame from the waist, until Scott felt his breath against his face. 'Take some advice from an old man,' he whispered. 'You must learn to detach yourself clinically or you will not survive your work.'

Scott looked up into eyes that were pools of pained wisdom. 'Inside,' Dr Sanders thumped Scott's chest, 'you must learn to walk away or you will lose your humanity; all that protects us is our training, our jobs, and we must remember our professional parts at every instant without exception.'

Scott rubbed the back of his neck, for suddenly he felt very cold.

'The moment you stop thinking like a cop,' Sanders continued, 'or I stop thinking like a doctor, we lose the ability to practise effectively. And that is the worst failing of all, I believe. If we faced this brutality like normal men, we would lose ourselves to our own caring, to our own pain.'

Scott studied the horror behind Dr Sanders' quiet demeanour, it was etched in lines on his face.

'But I did fail, and now this bastard will be going after a seventeen-year-old, any seventeen-year-old, what are my chances now?'

Chet Sanders pulled the cigarette from between Scott's fingers and snuffed it into a standing ashtray. 'Jack,' he began, 'you will get him, and you'll do so with a system that's designed to fail . . .' when Scott's words suddenly caught the doctor by the throat.

'Why seventeen?' he asked incredulously.

Scott paced, hate erasing the humanity from his face. It was a younger man with bright blue eyes and thick blond hair who was talking now, the older man at his kitchen window could see himself clearly.

'He's playing a sadistic game, and I think he's playing it for me,' Scott said quietly. 'Mary Beth Dodson was the last victim, she's sixteen,' Scott explained. 'Genie Katz was fifteen. Lora Baker, fourteen. We haven't found the others. Our man is working his way up the chronological scale of birth, claiming a victim for every year, like a trophy. Seventeen would be next.'

Dr Chet Sanders rubbed both hands into his eyes, letting air seep slowly from his lips as Scott smiled weakly. 'Chet, what else do we have?' he asked nervously, lighting another cigarette.

Dr Sanders reached into his coat pocket. 'The patient has a punctured lung, low,' he pointed to his own sixth rib, 'and that tear seems to extend down to the third lobe of the liver, which is very deep. We removed this during surgery,' he said, holding up a wooden dowel sealed in plastic, handing this to Scott.

'What is it?'

'A clue, Jack, I really have no idea.'

'And this was stuck in her lung?'

'Lung and liver, it took a great deal of force to drive it there.'

Scott winced. 'Then the trauma was caused by stabbing?'

'Possible, but I don't think so, at least not with a hand motion, the wound was too clean and without surface bruising.'

Scott slipped it into a pocket as Sanders pointed at his cigarette. 'I just received a paper from Sweden that suggests a relationship between that and cancer,' he said. And Scott remembered as the harsh smoke drilled his lungs, throwing off other, more burning sensations.

85

Mary Beth Dodson died that evening, March 31st, 1957.

Dr Chet Sanders was felled by a heart attack in 1963 at the age of sixty-two.

And Jack Scott felt the haunting of time in the arthritic ache across his knuckles. He left the house an old man with his familiar ghosts, driving into a night in which he could not have been more alone.

NINE

Under Matthew Brennon's watchful eye, Agent Flores moved from his usual place at the rim and into his first watch. The physical position was in the cut-out centre of an enormous circular desk that shined with a fresh coat of battleship grey. The surface had been recently padded, though the desk itself was a relic, pirated away from an old evening daily.

This position was known as the slot. It was the hot seat, the heart of ViCAT, and Daniel Richard Flores had been months in the standby, working the outer rim with his training officer and waiting.

Eventually every ViCAT agent served here, a swarm of green computer screens around him. There were eight of these, representing each region of the country, divided by two. Just above the slot, nearing eye level and suspended from the ceiling, there was imaging equipment, fax machines, and an array of recording equipment. In many ways taking up the position was like sitting at the control board of a missile silo, and emotionally it was a lot more dangerous for the attendant. An hour never passed without a direct challenge with potentially horrid consequences.

'If you can't answer a question or if you don't know the correct response from computer templates, just have them stand by,' Brennon instructed. 'It's always better to wait than to give a wrong response. If it's an emergency request, if the information is critical, one of us will always be here. Always check the Duty Sheet when you come in so you'll know who's available.'

'How about Commander Scott?' Flores asked. 'When is it proper to call on him?'

Brennon raised an eyebrow and smiled. 'Believe me,' he said, 'you'll know because your guts will tell you. His home is line one on the re-dial.' He pointed to a keypad, then continued to collect forms and dossiers that were pouring in from a dozen different agencies that were answering a blanket ViCAT request. The outer rim was starting to take on the appearance of an embassy shredding room during enemy assault; there were papers everywhere, which Flores was methodically checking off from a shopping list of demands.

'Five years' worth of tax returns from '82 through '87,' Brennon said, shuffling a stack. 'And four motions to postpone payment.' He held up one sheet and chuckled. 'Where does Jack find them?' he laughed. 'Look at this.' He pushed the paper across the rim to the slot. 'This guy declared a failing season for the Washington Redskins as grounds for a tax hardship and ended up paying a six-hundred-dollar fine.'

'That's an expensive sense of humour,' Flores agreed.

The pieces of Frank Rivers' life were being assembled into a composite that started with his first public record, an application for a Social Security number, lacking a date, bearing his father's signature. From the Defense Intelligence Agency came a demanding form requiring an official justification for his records; bureaucrats buggering bureaucrats, Brennon thought, and he put that aside in a special pile. Surprisingly, the CIA admitted having a file, and fired off a quick fax of Rivers' Marine Corps discharge, which Brennon thought a bit odd for there was no record of direct employment. JRS, a cheque assurance company, complied with a complete financial history, most of it average for a cop, but claiming bad paper for a fifty-dollar Chinese dinner. A bell chimed a gentle alert through the chamber, not unlike a doorbell, and Brennon walked around the rim as Flores put his headset with microphone on.

'It's Duncan Powell in Florida,' Brennon explained, recognising a series of alpha numbers which were walking across screen number two, the United States Southern Region. All that was required for accessing ViCAT was an ongoing case with a previously assigned code, and the recruit punched his authorisation onto the pad. A hard disk whirred as green characters began filling the video void. Brennon pressed an intercom button.

'Duncan,' he said without tone, 'we are receiving your file now.'

'Reporting Case 217,' a deep voice responded. 'We believe we have a sixth victim.'

Brennon pointed a finger at the younger agent, who was waiting at the keyboard, tape had begun rolling the instant the phone line was opened. For the past month Daniel Flores had studied the coordination of Multi Agency Investigative Teams, or MAITs, as they were known, using hightech equipment and analysis that was made available nonstop to agents in the field. Calls were constantly being received, updating or requesting information, seeking emergency advice on the behaviour patterns of violent repeat offenders. As was the case with Duncan Powell, the state contact was usually the local chief of police, although that varied depending on jurisdiction.

'I'd like to introduce Daniel Flores who is handling the slot tonight,' Brennon offered. 'This is Captain Duncan Powell of the Florida State Police . . .'

And the two men quickly exchanged greetings as Matthew Brennon walked back to the rim and began assembling stacks of paper. Flores spun in the slot just in time to see Brennon leave the chamber, and the detached voice of a stranger boomed through his ears.

'Victim discovered April eighth, twenty-hundred hours, description as follows,' he said, the deep voice conveying critical information as a photographic transmission hovered overhead like a black wing, sharpening into a focused image. The young girl Flores was now staring at had been beaten into disfigurement.

'We believe her attacker is repeat offender Case 217. Our postmortem investigation has just begun, but the victim has the same unusual odour emanating from the oral cavity. We would like assessment for your possible interdiction into this case.'

Powell described the victim as four-foot-two with short brown hair, hazel eyes and a light complexion, although Flores knew they would never have been able to tell from the body. He guessed they were operating from a missing persons list and had obtained a potential match from more obvious physical characteristics, as Duncan Powell's deep monotone continued to fill his ears.

'Probable name, Lisa Darlynne Caymann, DOB 7-1-81. Reported missing 3-27-89, Clearwater, Florida. Parents' address, 1606 McDowell, subdivision Silver Shores. Salient detail as follows . . .'

Agent Flores had retrieved a computerised registration of missing persons that had been compiled for the five-county Florida area, and had found the name. He punched in a code and read quickly. Lisa Caymann had been abducted in the daytime from her backyard, where she had been using a swing. Parents and relatives were cleared as potential suspects. Her mother, Denise, had gone into the house to answer the phone. When she returned, her child was gone. Flores bit a lower lip and waited for a hard copy of Lisa Caymann's portrait to materialise.

'Location and general position of victim as found?' Flores asked, and his voice trembled.

'Spread eagle,' Captain Powell responded without tone. 'Face down in an open ravine off a back road near Route 41.'

Flores had one thirty-six-inch computer screen filled with a detailed chart of the Florida Gulf coast. 'Yes sir,' he said, 'help me find it.'

'Hit Sarasota and move south until you see the off ramp marked Hillside Cemetery. If you reach the town of Saint Luke's, you've gone too far.'

Flores moved a green cursor across the map, then back up, highlighting the general area off the Florida Interstate, just as Jack Scott appeared at his back. Scott's necktie was missing but he was still dressed in a white shirt with a grey sports jacket. His face looked distressed, his eyes red and tired. Above the slot, a photo prompt emitted three short beeps, and Flores pulled a photograph from the image pan. Scott watched the agent compare the third-grade picture of Lisa Caymann with the battered image at the rim. He stood silently, looking every bit like the stalwart federal Commander, skimming details that were pouring from a laser printer.

'Agent Flores?' Captain Powell asked suddenly, and Scott saw a physical jolt hit the new troop as the voice filled his ears. The photographs, once compared, were truly sickening.

'Yes sir,' Flores stammered.

Scott quietly reached into the slot and switched the call back to *audio intercom*, placing a warm hand on Flores' back while pulling a chair against the outside metal rim. 'How are you, Duncan? Jack Scott here,' he said. 'Can you tell us about the position of the body please?'

'Spread, face down, no clothing or personal material items recovered. One blanket, the site is a gravel . . .'

'One step at a time, Duncan.' He nodded at Agent Flores who seemed intense but relieved. 'You found no clothing, so you're saying the body was completely exposed to the elements?'

'She was partially covered with a blanket, Jack. We're sending that for lab . . .'

'Give us a photograph of the body as found, please, with the covering. While you're doing that, tell me about the disposal site.'

'Very close to a paved access road off 41, complete gravel, no hope for shoeprints. The road shows no recent treadmarks.'

'Easily seen from where?'

'From nowhere at night, not much traffic and too far from the interstate. The body was spotted by a young woman who swerved to avoid a jacklighted deer. Do you want . . .'

'Duncan, did the body look articulated, as if it had been

carefully positioned? Were the arms and legs fully extended?'

'No, it was sort of haphazard.'

'And the blanket looked like what, tossed on, or carefully draped?'

'I'm not sure, Jack, a bit ruffled maybe. We're transmitting the film now, you'll have it any second.'

Scott looked at Flores, whose face could not mask the rage that was burning inside him. 'Duncan,' Scott said, 'I missed the beginning, was her mouth cleaned of any fouling?'

'It looks so, Jack, I explained that to Agent Flores, we think it's the same medicinal odour. Her teeth were without the expected tartar, which is also in keeping with . . .'

'Cause of death strangulation?'

'Affirmative.'

'It's him,' Scott sighed. Agent Flores lifted a wire photo from the pan above his head and quickly handed it across the rim. Scott studied this for a moment, looking beyond the readily apparent for small details, micro-behaviours, seemingly insignificant clues that the ordinary policeman could easily miss.

'Duncan,' he said, 'stand by one.' And Scott turned his attention back to the man at the slot.

'Agent Flores,' he cautioned in a direct tone. 'Right now minutes don't count for anything, this child is already dead, so take your time. Develop some feeling for this tragedy, tell me what you see.' He placed the photograph in front of Flores' chest. 'Start with the history.'

Flores nodded and cleared his thoughts. 'Yes sir,' he said, 'Case 217 involves a series killing through the Gulf States, two victims in Mobile, three in Florida, Lisa Caymann would be victim number six. Although there's some evidence of oral rape, no traces of semen have been found. Teeth have been excised from some victims. Cause of death is the same in each case, strangulation from behind with slight variations.' Scott nodded approval as Flores turned his attention to the print, studying it closely. Against the grey peppered landscape of a gravel pit there was a form covered with a dark green blanket. A pale arm protruded. One leg was exposed.

'What can you tell me?' Scott pressed. 'And take your time, that's all we've got right now.'

Flores knew that the chances were excellent he was looking at the work of a Recreational Killer, savage and emotionless. But he knew something was amiss as he recalled Scott's profiling seminars. His mind engaged. A man who clothes or covers a victim usually has a small degree of guilt or shame for his act; and covering the body is his way of saying *I feel bad*. Also, if the body were placed where it could easily be found, that would point to a killer of some feeling who wants his victim to have a decent burial and not be left exposed. If there's any remorse, however slight, micro-behaviours hint at the story. And as Flores was taught, a killer with a hint of emotion is a killer who can be caught.

'Captain Powell,' Flores asked directly, 'would you consider the spot where the body was found as a hiding place?'

'It's a remote location,' the deep voice answered, 'and the body was lying at the bottom of a wide ditch, so some effort was made to conceal, though not well. Does that help?'

'Yes sir, stand by one, please.'

Flores turned to Scott. 'It doesn't compute. If the disposal site was remote, then that suggests hiding the victim, and that behaviour points to a ruthless man without emotion. Yet the use of a blanket to cover her suggests our killer does feel some guilt. We have two conflicting behaviours.'

Scott smiled. 'Why the blanket?' he asked. 'If this man feels shame, why doesn't he simply allow the victim to get dressed?'

Flores thought for a moment, but drew a blank.

Scott rephrased the question. 'Why leave a perfectly good blanket behind, covering a body that, as you pointed out, was already hidden in the ravine?'

Flores shook his head. 'He feels guilt?'

'Yes he does,' Scott agreed, 'but then why didn't he place the body where it would be an easy find? If he uses the blanket to protect her from the elements, wouldn't he also want her to have a quick and decent burial?'

'I don't know,' Flores sighed.

Scott gave him a knowing look. 'We are dealing with two people,' he concluded.

· Flores' eyes went wide.

'Understand this, Daniel,' it was the first time he had ever used his first name, 'you are dealing in a brutally violent world where coincidence doesn't count, there's no such thing, so get coincidence out of your mind.'

Flores nodded.

'Coincidence is a luxury used by civilians to explain things away, we do just the opposite.'

'Yes sir,' Flores agreed.

'Now you were right about the conflicting behaviours of hiding the body without remorse, and then covering the body with a sense of shame, but you didn't allow for the phone call.'

Flores smacked a palm against his brow.

'If memory serves, Lisa was playing in the backyard when her mother went for the phone?'

'Two people,' Flores said foolishly, and a telltale anger flamed in his soft hazel lenses. 'They were stalking this one particular child.'

Scott hit the speaker switch. 'Sorry for the delay, Duncan. Have you contacted the parents yet?'

'Negative, we're waiting on dentals, also a news reporter picked up our radio call, so I'll have to go soon.'

'Mrs Caymann was in her backyard when the phone rang, and she left the child for only a few moments. Talk to her again, find out everything you can about the voice before they're informed further. We believe the person who called is the one who covered the body with the blanket, was that a man or woman?'

'It was a man's voice. Do you really think it's connected?'

'Yes,' Scott assured him. 'They just slipped up. We have conflicting behaviours which indicate we should be concentrating on a team, at least two men. In their early fifties, maybe late forties.' There was a pause on the line.

'We didn't find footprints . . .' Powell was questioning.

'The other victims were alive for three days at best, and their bodies were hard to find, if I recall?'

'Affirmative,' Powell said.

'Duncan, for whatever reason they held this child longer. They knew her. And although the actual killer would have still been content to just toss her in a ditch, as an afterthought, somebody else covered her up. It's that second man that feels something, ashamed, maybe a sense of loss, it's hard to say. His partner is the more dominant personality. The second man is the type who gets annoyed if he sees a wrinkled shirt.'

'You're an amazing man, Jack, how did we reach that conclusion?'

Scott looked at Agent Flores, whose eyes reflected admiration. 'Strangulation smacks of a disorganised personality,' he stated, 'not the type of individual who has tidy personal habits, and that's bothered me. Each victim had their mouths washed, depriving us of any hope of retrieving fluids for DNA decoding. A very organised person. I'm betting the man who made the telephone call to set up the mother, and who later draped the body, is also in charge of this oral hygiene. He is doing the bidding of the dominant male who understands how good our technology is.'

'Are they faggots?' Powell asked.

'Whoever knows, Duncan, sex isn't what this is about. Sex is a secondary act to the excitement of abducting, then killing. One is a Recreational Killer, and his boyfriend is probably a psychopathic voyeur who enjoys watching other people being dominated, which takes the place of sexual activity.'

'I've got to put them away, Jack, I need assistance,' Powell's deep voice demanded.

'I understand, Duncan, but this is the first break we've gotten. I've got nine agents in the field and I can't afford more at the moment. I'm putting Agent Flores in charge of this case, and as usual, I'll be available at all times.'

Flores' face flushed and seemed to go blank.

'Duncan,' Scott said, 'in the meantime you should be concentrating on a late model stationwagon or van. One suspect should be relatively thin and neat, the other overweight, possibly obese, that's just a guess.'

'Based on what?'

'Opposites attract, the emotional partner has a health and cleanliness fetish, I'm sure he watches every calorie. And you might suggest to your detectives that they keep a close watch for signs that would be emotionally disarming.'

'I don't follow.'

'These characters are cunning, mocking of authority, treating parents with an unusual degree of contempt. They'd get a real charge from throwing suspicion off, so look for anything that would retard normal doubt if they were spotted with a child, a bumper sticker like *Have you hugged your kid today?* you know the type.'

'I know the type,' Powell said grimly.

Jack Scott turned the slot back over to Daniel Flores, who managed alone well into the night with Commander Scott's instructions echoing in his mind. 'This is your case. You will assign the file name. You are now the desk officer in charge.'

Scott left the rim for his office where he monitored the twenty-three other on-going cases that came through the slot before midnight.

Scott aimed a cone of light at his desk, staring down at the photographic image of human bones nestled into a shallow grave. Without looking away he padded through the inside pockets of his coat, removing a crumpled pack of cigarettes, and quickly lit up.

There was no doubt that the remains were that of a child. The skull was small and the hands were underdeveloped, coming apart at the cartilaginous digits. The ribcage was brittle and broken in several places. The teeth had begun falling from the jaw, some lay in the dirt surrounded by rotted cloth. He was looking at the products of decay and time.

According to Captain Maxwell Drury, the site was found by a boy named Elmer Janson, who roamed the neighbourhood with a three-legged dog. They had snagged a human jaw while digging for treasure, and if all of that wasn't strange enough, no one seemed to care. Not Captain Drury, not the Medical Examiner, not the County Homicide Bureau. Some cop by the name of Frank Rivers had mysteriously tracked the kid down; a cop who knew how to press Maxwell Drury's buttons.

But why? And with the scant evidence facing him, Scott contemplated the coincidence, feeling as if he were drowning inside, slowly coming apart into tired pieces.

The bones looked a century old. The image of the coin bore the date 1863. Rather than concentrating, though, he found himself listening to the constant hum of imaging equipment, drilling away at life from the ViCAT slot and producing victims by the score. Scott had decades of experience with the kind of horrid detail that buzzing sound produced, day and night, without stop, a manic buzzing that reminded him of the electric chair. And his mind skipped off track as he found himself visualising the way the buzzing volts had hit Theodore Bundy; his brain pan smoking while his body curled into a human snail. And the eyes. Even at their last they burned with that cold strange light that no man of conscience could hope to comprehend. Then Scott remembered all of the killers with that icy inhuman stare; of charges dismissed for lack of evidence, of courtroom theatrics with high-priced lawyers, of lame judges and politicians handing pardons to men who slaughtered women and children for recreation.

He walked across his office, shutting his door to distractions, then lifted the two enlargements from his desk. An ancient coin. *The Union Must & Shall Be Preserved.* His mind fogged.

If given time, he knew they would eventually be able to track the artifact with precision, back to its very maker. Civil War relics were a well documented element of Americana, and he made a note to have a filing removed for radiocarbon testing to determine age. But if he was right, time was a luxury he lost long ago.

Antique coin or not, this grave had been dug by a predatory animal who stalked his victims in a pitiless game, man against child, killer against mother. He felt blood pulsing behind each

97

ear. A sourness rose in his throat and he flushed it down with freshly brewed coffee, setting out to tackle the abandoned site, prepared to manipulate facts if necessary in order to build a case for official involvement. A justification. He hated the word, though he placed the photos of the coin under the heading *Case Similarities* and began working on a yellow pad.

The Clayton girls had been found adorned with jewellery, Latin style gold crosses; the killer had not been interested. He theorised that this coin was also a child's keepsake worn around the neck, a charm of some type, for it had been drilled to accommodate a chain, three inches of the rotted silver were recovered. On either side of the hole there were block letters in near perfect condition. On one side *JO*, and on the other, *IN. JOIN.* But join what? Did the keepsake even belong to a child of this century?

'Jane Doe,' he sighed, picking up the photograph of frail bones. 'You deserve better.' And he dug into a mountain of paper, retrieving a colour glossy of Elmer Janson's stick. Though he thought about it, Scott did not want to look at this picture, and as he held it in his hand, his mind and his body and his soul warned him off.

'Jennifer?' he asked quietly, returning to the first image, and his voice sounded like a man who had lost his way. 'That's always been a favourite of mine.' He retrieved the Medical Examiner's report and reviewed the laboratory examination. 'Small female, height and weight impossible to determine. Skull plates and dental evolution provide age distribution estimate, ten to fifteen years of maturation. Date, time, cause of death unknown.' From the photograph Scott knew it would be a difficult, almost impossible job to determine much more, though he pulled the phone closer on his desk, fumbling through a grey rolodex wheel for a number. He dialled. Only then did he think to look at his watch.

It was 11:33 p.m., Friday, April 8th. A brief twelve hours had passed since he had received the Clayton files. By morning it had seemed a week. By nightfall, a lifetime. The phone was answered on the fourth ring.

'. . . I need someone I trust to tell me about this child,

about her life,' Scott said with urgency, bypassing hellos and shared experiences.

The voice laughed, the amusement deep and resonant. Scott had reached Dr Charles McQuade at home, the first time they had spoken in almost a year, and their conversation, as usual, started somewhere in the middle.

'Of course you do, Scotty,' the deep voice said calmly. 'If this wasn't a problem you wouldn't call, so why don't I take a look?'

And that's all there was to it. For all of his authority and skill, McQuade, a hulking bear in a white gown, was a frightening man who clipped small talk and enormous tasks like so many blades of grass. And Scott knew what *taking a look* meant to the specialist.

Dr Charles Rand McQuade was the unsung champion of the laboratory war against missing persons, his formal title was Chief Medical Examiner for the Armed Forces Institute of Pathology in Washington DC. He first became prominent in the late sixties for identifying plane crash victims burned beyond recognition, and then for producing faces based on just bone fragments.

'They tell me she could be from the Civil War period, but I don't think so . . .' Scott continued, about to go further, when the bone doctor interrupted.

'Do you have a case, Jack, under what authority is the work assigned?'

Scott released a troubled sigh. There was no case. There was no authority. The job he was requesting could cost an easy sixty thousand federal tax dollars, and for those law enforcement agencies not in the mainstream budgets were so tight, audits of every department now fell on the quarter. Scott was asking a giant favour.

'There, there, Scotty!' McQuade's voice boomed in his ears. 'I'm always prepared to move on your verbal authorisation, so let's get started.'

'I don't have a shred of evidence,' he cautioned weakly, 'if you want to postpone.'

'Hell, trust your instincts, Jack, that's what you always say.

Have them send the child along, we'll see what we can do. You sound tired, go home, get some sleep. I'll call the moment I have word.'

McQuade hung up the phone leaving Scott flushed with guilt, feeling manipulative, like he was taking advantage of an old friendship. But with McQuade's assistance, he felt suddenly satisfied that the world would again know this destroyed child. Within hours, the director would be applying calipers, rulers, X-rays, magnifying glasses, sketch-pads and clay to bring her face back from the grave; and Scott had marvelled many times at the man's hulking artistry.

Long tedious hours without food or sleep came first, with McQuade endlessly stooped over a chrome operating table. He would start with a determination of the victim's age and sex. Then, combined with thickness of bone, he would calculate depth of muscle and facial tissue. Any missing fragments would be cast from plaster and added, filling in voids. From that, he would judge and reproduce the victim's facial planes, building and moulding realism with artist's clay. Few details would escape him.

Though soft tissue like ear shape and eyelids cannot be inferred from skull configuration, McQuade had calculated rules of flesh based on anatomical averages. The mouth, as wide as the front eight teeth. If the teeth are missing, aligned with the centres of the eye sockets and widest points of the chin. The nose, roughly two times the length of the nasal spine; the ears, about as long as the nose. As a final touch, glass eyes of a neutral colour would be positioned.

It made no difference what condition the remains were in, or how many there were. Computers and mathematical models would be employed if necessary.

McQuade, the pacifist and former war protester, had produced entire faces from skull fragments, identifying remains returned in cardboard boxes from Hanoi. And even while he had begun to work, trusting Scott's instincts absolutely, for Jack Scott, doubt festered like an open sore.

TEN

As far as Matthew Brennon was concerned, there was only one reason to live in New York. Availability. Night or day you could find anything you wanted in Manhattan, it was the city that never closed. He had doubleparked in front of the Central Records building, a massive marble expanse with skylights, and once inside he felt like a weak duckling trapped in a stone shell. From the main rotunda with sixteen pillars supporting a giant dome, there were twice as many hallways with doors peeling off to unknown places. At 11:12 p.m., all rooms were locked shut, except for the stone bell-jar where he stood, waiting in line to view a display.

On two sides of the echo chamber, uniformed guards watched each time a visitor came in, studied a moment, then went back to scanning the crowd. Brennon guessed both were former NYPD, in their late fifties or early sixties, carefully avoiding eye contact with each other. A two-man ring of protection. A large black officer with peppery white hair had nodded when he came through, and every few minutes he would turn, alert to potential trouble.

Brennon knew that locked behind each door there were chambers for every pursuit, from the map centre which preserved original charts of New York City and almost every other major Eastern municipality, to specific reading rooms for specialised subjects, Art through Zoology. Each was connected to the central library and rotunda by a labyrinthine maze, and while Brennon was pondering this, he took a place in line, studying the firm calves of a woman's legs. She could be a dancer, he thought, standing just to the rear, the muscles were long and tight and well toned. There were better things to do late on a Friday night, he thought, than visiting a collection called *Prizes of the Civil War*. He smiled absently, though he said not a word, as the line edged forward.

Within half an hour he was standing before the first display case, a nine-foot glass enclosure crammed with Civil War canteens, belt buckles, daggers, hats and accoutrements from Dixie, none of which he found interesting. He hopped in line to the next, a glass-encased flag with bullet holes, the Stars and Bars of the Confederacy. Oh for joy, he thought, a worm-eaten battle flag, where's the good stuff?

He glanced around for an authority figure, the stooge responsible for a lifeless, non-interpretive display of relics which no one could touch.

Near the far end of the exhibit he found his mark, a dumpling of an old dandy, white fringe of hair, blue blazer with patch. Under the sentinel's watchful eyes, Brennon edged forward, and the dandy seemed ruffled by his approach.

Brennon stood over six feet tall and was lean, while the dandy stood about five-foot-two, and plump as a neutered house cat. 'Hello, are you Dr Robert Perry?' he asked.

'Yes I am,' said the dandy, gazing upward, twisting the right end of a handlebar moustache. 'And who are you, may I inquire?'

'Special Agent Matthew Brennon, sir, I spoke with you on the phone about an hour ago.' He produced a badge, then shoved it back into his coat pocket.

'Yes, Mr Brennon, as I told you, I don't like phones – no use for them whatsoever.'

'Yes sir, that's why I'm here.' He produced two eight-by-ten photographs from inside his jacket and stripped the rubber band from the roll. 'I was wondering what you could tell us about this coin,' he said, handing over the package.

Dr Robert Perry tied his face in a knot. 'I thought you were going to bring the coin with you, can't tell much from a picture,' he puffed.

'Yes sir, we don't have the coin in our possession at this

time, so I'm afraid the photo will have to do. Would you try please?'

'Oh, all right, young man, but I would rather have the actual coin.' His thin voice seemed annoyed as he balanced a set of Civil War period spectacles, the wire kind, across a button nose.

Brennon thought himself mad, for he could have waited until Monday and pushed the lab in Washington, but it all seemed urgent the way Scott was behaving.

'Well, sir, what do you think?' he asked, but only after Dr Perry had had a sufficiently long time to appraise the grainy photos.

'Very interesting, would you like to donate it?'

'I'm sorry, no, we just want to know what it is, the coin doesn't seem to have any denominational markings. Is it real?'

'Oh it's very real, and fairly rare. But it's not a coin.' He took another look, studying the enlargements closely.

'Then what is it?' Brennon felt like he was pulling teeth.

'Hold your britches!' the dandy snapped back, pushing the photos out across a glass case. 'We'll start with the obverse, which is the order in which you handed me the documents.' Dr Perry pulled a chrome telescopic pointer from inside his club jacket, extended the device into a long rod, then reappraising his stature in relation to the table, adjusted it back to two feet.

Brennon stifled a laugh at the pudgy curator who stood one foot away and waist high at the glass counter. All of this to look at some pictures?

'The bust of the bearded gentleman,' Dr Perry continued with authority, pointing with the red-tipped silver rod, 'is Major General Andrew Jackson.'

Brennon doubted this was important, but he produced a pad and jotted notes, a psychological signal that said the listener was intensely interested; the opinion valued enough for the record. Dr Perry noticed this behaviour and paused so that Brennon could catch up, the downside risk of the technique.

'And this phrase here, *The Union Must & Shall Be Preserved*, is a modified quote from Jackson's famous speech on states' rights and constitutional theory, which he gave, let me think . . . in 1830, which of course was several years yet before the war. You can quote me.'

Brennon was looking at his reflection in the glass case, he didn't think he had such a dumb face.

'The stars at the bottom represent the Union States, of course.'

'Of course.'

Dr Perry turned to the other photo and laid it over the first. 'This,' he said with a pause, 'is the reverse.'

Right, thought Brennon, heads and tails. He was staring down at a little house, a shack, entwined by a snake.

'The key here is the serpent, which is symbolic of a Confederate or Southern sympathiser, hence the warning BEWARE in capitals underneath.' The red tip flicked from top to bottom.

'I don't follow you, sir.' Brennon paused in an effort to dig some details.

'Look at the token, Son! Look at the token!'

The red tip was suddenly rapping the counter as Brennon stared down in disbelief. 'Sir,' he said cautiously, 'why do you call it a token?'

Perry sighed with displeasure. 'Because that's what it is,' he said incredulously. 'It is *not* a coin, or any type of currency, but a patriotic token made of copper. These enlargements ruin the aesthetics of the work, the actual token is slightly smaller than a quarter, but much, much thinner.'

Brennon took a note. 'And what were these tokens used for, how many were there?'

At this question, Perry's eyes flared. 'You did come to waste precious time, didn't you!' And his face twitched like a squirrel with a nut. Brennon stepped back, thinking quickly.

'Oh no, sir, everyone said you were the best man to seek advice from, so I came directly to you, I don't wish to waste your time.'

Perry breathed deeply. 'Then why didn't you bother to look at our display of tokens, we worked very hard to collect them – they are quite precious.'

'Yes sir, the display. I was just saving it, hoping you would show me personally. It would mean a great deal to me, er, us.' Brennon was lying, he dared not search the room now, as the aged agent of history suddenly waved him aside, lifting the photographs from the case. Beneath a waxy glass glare, was a bronze plaque: *PATRIOTIC TOKENS & MEDALS FROM THE SOUTH.*

Three tokens like the one in the photographs shone in the light, and Brennon felt dumb as the day he was born. 'Aren't they handsome,' he exclaimed, when at his back he heard the laugh of a rent-a-cop.

'Well then,' said the curator, sounding relieved by this display of enthusiasm. 'You understand that before and during the war, many states in the South were divided, some leaned towards the Union, others not.'

'Oh, yes,' said Brennon, really starting to get interested, shooting the guard a nasty stare.

'All the way from Kentucky and Tennessee, up through North Carolina, Virginia, West Virginia and Maryland, there operated what we call the Underground Railroad, an elaborate network for rescuing and freeing slaves.'

'Yes sir,' now he was interested.

'It was a frightfully dangerous business, a man couldn't trust his neighbour and sometimes even his own brother. During the effort to bring the slaves north to freedom, where they could fight for the Federal forces, the single largest threat to the operation were Confederate spies. They were everywhere. Confederates, you know, had an elaborate network of spies?'

'Oh, yes sir, that much I knew, but the way you tell it one feels transported back.' As Brennon said this, he really felt like he was stroking a house cat.

'Yes, of course one does. Now,' Perry was rapping at the glass, 'with the exception of clandestine meetings, the workers of the Underground Railroad communicated mostly during

normal social activities, such as shopping, banking trans-
actions, dances, fund raisers, and the like.'

'Now, since merchants and shoppers couldn't openly discuss their feelings or activities for fear of retribution, these
little tokens were a way of communicating. Do you
understand?'

'I think I do, go on.'

'Now let's go back a moment. I shall become the proprietor
of a cotton or tobacco auction house, and you are not only a
grower but we are both operators of the Underground
Railroad.'

Brennon nodded. He noticed that the black guard had
taken several steps closer and was also listening.

'Now, let's suppose I have reason to believe that a merchant
who has come to town is really a Rebel spy. How can I warn
you without exposing both of us to arrest or kidnapping or
execution?' The little man's eyes danced in the light as he
looked up through wire spectacles at the tall investigator.
'Humm? What shall we do? What shall we do?' he urged,
rapping the counter with his red-tipped wand.

'Well, secret meetings are hard to arrange and wouldn't be
practical . . .'

'Correct!' snapped the clandestine curator, whipping his
pointer through the air.

'So I would stop by to see you, say, in the middle of town
surrounded by people and you would pass me a token?'

'Not quite,' he shook a fringe of white hair, 'that could kill
us both. But if you came and sold me some cotton or tobacco,
or asked for a small advance, I would have to hand you change
and I would drop this token in among the coinage – and
nobody's the wiser!' He lifted the reverse photo to the centre
of the counter.

With his pointer again, 'It means just what it says, Beware,
there's a Rebel spy, a Confederate snake nearby, do not work
the railroad. Pass the word – we are in danger!'

'That's amazing, that's what it is?'

'Yes, son, that's what it is. A patriotic signal token used to
secure the Underground Railroad, a way of talking without

being heard. And you, of course, would pass the token to someone else.'

Brennon had been writing furiously, thinking about the relationship of the token to the human remains found by an abandoned building in the middle of a modern city. 'And what about the house being entangled by the serpent?'

'Well,' Perry explained, 'that's symbolic of what they called a safe house, a hiding spot for slaves and Federal troops escaped from prisoner of war camps.'

Brennon chuckled, truly amazed, 'I wonder if that's where the CIA came up with that term?'

'That, I assure you, I wouldn't know,' Perry huffed. 'I have no interest in modern politics, none whatsoever.'

'Then it's no house in particular?'

'No, I don't think so, but it's possible, depending upon where it was minted. Tokens were produced at the California mint, a few were made at Harper's Ferry in West Virginia. Let's take another look.' The bespectacled man was bent over the glass comparing the photograph to tokens in the collection.

'Look here at this one.' He tapped the glass with the red tip. 'Notice at the top it says White's Ferry? That's the name of a town, and a token was specially made to alert the community there. So that coin, which is cruder in detail than specimens made in California, was produced at Harper's Ferry. The ones from the West Coast are without names, except for the tiny S trademark of the San Francisco mint, which can only be seen with a jeweller's loupe.'

'Dr Perry, in the photograph there is a name at the top with a chain hole through it. The word looks like *JOIN*, what do you think?'

'I noticed that, a tragic defiling of a historical record. No, it does not say *JOIN*.' He studied the photograph. 'It must be the name of a town once held in high esteem by the Federal forces at Harper's Ferry. A great tragedy. The token was most likely hand-drilled, separating the letters *JO* from *IN*. Several other letters, and hence the meaning, were punched out by the drill. A tragic loss, but I would be willing to acquire the token. This one I would let the public hold, provide a chance to touch the past. The others, of course, can only be handled with gloves and rarely then.'

'Of course,' Brennon smiled. 'I'm afraid the token belongs to another party. Do you know of any town on the railroad with a name that comes close to the word *JOIN* in configuration?'

'No, sorry I don't. But in addition to our collection of tokens, we do have many of the original maps and heirlooms from the Underground Railroad system. Let's take a look.'

The stubby curator walked around the display case, passing the Confederate flag and protected gun racks, then stood facing a series of hand-drawn charts encased behind heavy glass. 'These are Confederate,' he said, and the red probe crossed and ticked against the glass faces, again and again, stopping, ticking, moving onward, then stopping.

Finally he turned and said, 'I'm sorry, but there is no logical choice. There is one town, Cabin John, but that doesn't seem close.' For the first time, the curator noticed that only he, Matt Brennon and two guards were left. 'Young man, may I suggest we continue tomorrow, as arranged by the building engineer we should be closing. You do realise our extended hours only last one more night, after which *Treasures* will be moving to New Haven for three months, and then Philadelphia?'

'No sir, I didn't realise,' Brennon said. 'You've been very kind. One more question?'

'Yes, one only.' He twitched.

'Where can I obtain copies of these charts of the Freedom Railway, I would like to . . .'

'You cannot,' Dr Perry said indignantly, 'there are none, which is why we have a priceless exhibit. I would be pleased to provide you with a list of illustrated books on the subject, and while they're inaccurate in many ways, scale and detail, they should do for amateur purposes.'

'Could I have a technician come and take a photograph of the maps?' Brennon suggested.

'My Lord, no!' Perry's faced steamed with red. 'That's out of the question! These are fragile, light-sensitive parchments, they will never be attacked by flash or daylight. And, I might add, many have tried to produce renderings, which is why the history books are rife with inaccuracy. You are welcome to visit the collection any time you like.' He was now leading Brennon by the arm, walking past the guard, into the rotunda.

'Of course,' Brennon smiled as he shook hands and headed out into darkness.

The crushing sound of a heavy iron door being bolted rang out behind him as he took one step, a century forward.

ELEVEN

SUBDIVISION TARA, POTOMAC, MARYLAND

'Full name?'

'Debra Ralson Patterson.'

'Her nickname is Dee?'

'Dee.'

'And you said she was going to the store for a few items?'

'Milk,' Jonathan Patterson said, shaking his head with anger and a quiet resentment. He was Debra's father. Debra was missing. She had driven to the store and not returned. Not even her car had been found. That was twenty-six hours ago.

'Goddamn you!' he said suddenly, his voice rising. 'We've been over and over this . . .' Jon Patterson was a meek looking five-foot-six with a gaunt face and pale expression. He was usually very reserved and friendly, and he felt himself coming out of character. He hadn't cursed with anger since his college days. He was forty-eight years old.

'For the report, sir, we are filing a formal missing persons report, we need accurate data and documentation that's verified.'

'What is it with you people?' Patterson was on his feet. 'You *must* have her driving permit, and she's been gone since eight o'clock last night. You have pictures of her. She's never run away before, damn it! She's never even been late . . .'

'I understand that, Mr Patterson,' stated Sergeant Tyler Conroy of the Montgomery County Police, looking for all the world like a coiffed and manicured diplomat in a starched tan uniform. His hair was a healthy jet black without a parting and combed thickly back over his head. He carried an expensive leather briefcase instead of the standard clipboard or duty book. 'It's a difficult situation, a painful process to go through, and we're doing all we can. The County Code states we have to wait a minimum of seventy-two hours, so we are pushing the rules a bit.'

'Pushing the rules, pushing the rules?' Patterson mocked coldly. 'We're talking about my daughter's life, I'm not interested in your lousy bureaucracy!' And he sat back down on his living room sofa, nervously scratching a buff-coloured cocker spaniel.

'Yes sir,' Conroy said, 'and her birth date is July 3rd, 1972?'

'Yes.' He shook his head with an irritated gesture.

'And what was she wearing when she left the house?'

'I don't remember, like I told you before, I didn't see her. I was in the den working on taxes and she called out she was going to the store for some milk. Would her birth certificate help?'

'And what did she say?'

'She said . . .' and he was standing again, his face twisting with a slow anger that was unlike Jon Patterson. 'She said she was going to the goddamned store!' he spat.

'Please don't make this any harder, Mr Patterson, did she say which one?'

'No. No she didn't.'

'And you said Mrs Patterson is currently in Stratford, Connecticut, is she the natural mother?'

'Visiting her parents, I told you that . . . of course she's the mother, I've only been married once and I only have one child. Let me get Dee's birth certificate.'

'Do you know of any reason that Dee might have been upset, was there anything going on in her life that may have . . .'

'What are you getting at?' Patterson asked coldly.

'Any problems we should know about?'

'What?' Patterson barked. 'What kind of problems? She's

a perfectly happy, well adjusted child – even her grades are good!'

The sergeant cleared his throat. 'Mr Patterson,' he said slowly, 'why is your wife in Connecticut with her parents?'

'That's none of your fucking business,' he said, rising from his seat, staring the uniformed officer directly in the eye. 'Now you listen to me,' he said, 'your job is to find my little girl, you have a photograph of her car, you have three current pictures of her, you know all that I do, and now you have even met her dog!' The spaniel was upset and climbing at Patterson's trousers. 'Now why are you wasting time talking to me?' He moved the well groomed policeman towards the front door.

Sergeant Conroy read back through his list, closing his briefcase. 'Is there some reason for your wife being out of town that might have upset Dee?' he asked again, just as the telephone rang. Jonathan Patterson shook his head.

'Just one moment,' he said, picking up an extension in the foyer. He had a brief conversation with his back to Conroy, who was waiting at the front door.

'That was Beth Meyers,' he told the sergeant.

Conroy's face was a perfect blank.

'My daughter's best friend, you know, Beth Meyers, the other little girl from Montessori School with straight As and a bright beautiful future.' His tone dripped acid.

The sergeant did not respond directly. 'Mr Patterson,' he said slowly, 'are you and your wife . . .'

'And Beth Meyers says,' he interrupted, 'that she hasn't heard from the police, that no one has even checked with her! And further, she says, that this isn't like Dee. No, Sergeant Conroy,' he hissed, 'not at all like our girl unless someone has detained her while I worked on my taxes to pay your damned salary!'

'Are you and Mrs Patterson . . .'

'The only reason I'll tell you is because this County police force is my only hope, and I don't want you wasting any more time.'

Sergeant Conroy backed out the front door.

'You see, Sergeant, my wife's mother is having a hysterectomy, nothing immediately life-threatening unless you're a woman. In the meantime my little girl is out there,' he pointed with a shaky hand, 'and she *did not* run away from home!'

'Yes sir,' Conroy said, 'and if we want to verify this with the mother?'

'Then you find her maiden name and use the phone book like anyone else. In fact, I think I'll let my fingers do the walking right now and find the best way to sue this miserable county into a subterranean existence. Now stop wasting time and find Debra. Please. I beg you . . .'

From habit, Jonathan Patterson closed the door softly. In his mind he slammed it shut, but fear had stolen his anger. And he sat, sobbing in the darkness, wondering who he could call for help, who he could turn to, who did other men turn to?

Jon Patterson could not answer, so he cursed at his career, twenty years of being a tax consultant had not prepared him professionally for the events that were transpiring on the nights of April 7th and 8th. He called the FBI, who referred him back to the county police, back into the hands of Sergeant Tyler Conroy. And time was wasting. Without a ransom note, there would be no FBI involvement. Precious time. Wasting away. Minutes becoming hours becoming days.

His child was missing. That's all that mattered. And even a mild man, a very cordial man like Jonathan knew in his gut the cruel and bestial things that other men were capable of; sick men with nothing in life worth losing. The thought made him shake physically.

In his heart he considered violence, but there was no one to fight, so he thought about his age and experience. At forty-eight, Jonathan Patterson had never even fired a gun, much less owned one, so he considered lawyers, which brought him back to the beginning. A lawyer required an opponent. There was no one to fight. Then the family doctor popped into his mind, but there wasn't an illness and he wasn't thinking clearly now.

He decided to call a private detective and ripped open the

yellow pages, staring down at the book, wondering how to make such a critical decision; by the size of the ad? Despair was setting in, hopeless despair, and he picked up the phone and dialled, mustering all of his courage while his spine was going limp beneath him.

It was answered before the first ring had ended.

Alice Patterson, his wife of thirty-two years, had been waiting with the phone clutched in a shaking hand.

TWELVE

VICAT

Chasing shadows.

Scott's dream was vague, as he was following the sounds of running water down through a dimly lit hallway. There were human cries. There was an empty house where he was arriving too late, again and again, the sounds vanishing, only to be replaced by the bray of pistons sucking air through an artificial lung.

Dr Chet Sanders was there. And Commander Nicholas Dobbs. And the clutching hands and anguished words of Elizabeth Dodson, Mary Beth's mother. 'Catch him ... please get him ... Get him for me ...'

Just as he was about to respond, the man behind his desk heard a distant chiming in his memory, thin as a dreamscape, like a doorbell, or a faraway church, or the hazed recollection of a clock ringing. It came again and again, and he drifted up to his desk, lifting his head, staring at the phone and connecting his thoughts with the outside world. Before he could identify himself, Scott recognised Maxwell Drury's voice.

'Sorry Jack,' the Captain offered, 'I asked to be put through.'

'Yes,' he stammered, 'yes Max.'

'Jack, will you tell me yes what the devil is going on, I've had tag teams filling your demands all night, and then a courier from the Armed Forces Institute showed up to transfer bones from an archaeological site, and under your authority. Do we have . . .'

'Max,' Scott cut him off, his eyes glassy. 'It's good to hear your voice, but I'm afraid I have nothing for you, I'm just playing a hunch.' He poured cold water from a thermos bottle into a glass and swallowed. 'Unless you have something better,' he added, wetting his fingers and rubbing the cool water into the corners of each eye.

'No, heavens no, Jack. It's just that Matt Brennon made it sound urgent. What's going on up there, is there anything I can do?'

Scott turned in his chair, lifting a file, forcing his mind into logical paths. 'Let's start with Francis Dale Rivers,' he said, his right hand searching out a cigarette. 'Tell me about him, is he trustworthy?'

There was a heavy sigh, followed by a pause on the line. 'Personally I like Frank,' Drury finally offered, 'but he's a misanthrope, he really hates people. A very antisocial type of guy.'

'Be specific, Max, back up your claim.'

'Rivers has gone through more partners than anyone I've ever known, he's a one-man team, a walking attitude, let me put one of my other detectives on this for you.'

'Not what I'm after, where'd he come from?'

'Residence or career?'

'Both.'

'Well, he was born and raised in Maryland, has a few political connections too,' Drury said thoughtfully. 'Served in the Marines, plus I think a freelance stint with Langley or one of your agencies. I heard he turned down an offer as a career spook, and that sure wouldn't have been with the diplomatic corps.'

'Who recruited him?'

'One of my team, Roland Russell, cancer hit him five years back.'

Scott turned to a list of commendations attached to Rivers' State folder. 'According to your personnel file, he's received two awards by the Council of Governments as Outstanding

116

Detective of the Year, two years in a row,' Scott read on. 'He's made more arrests resulting in conviction than any other cop in the tri-state area.'

'All true,' Drury confirmed, 'best detective of the year and then Rivers fails to show up at a black-tie reception to collect his award. The following Monday he told me the blue fish were running that weekend.'

'Were they?'

'Oh shit, Jack!' Drury cried. 'You should have seen me sitting with the Governor, acting like I knew what the hell was coming down, and with the local press waiting outside to take photos. "Oh, it's an emergency, your Honour, hush-hush police business . . ."'

'Did he buy it?'

'No, the Governor demanded I write a memo detailing Rivers' activities, why he didn't show, and when I asked Frank to play along, like a sudden break in a case – he looked me right in the eye and said, "I'm a cop, not a politician. Tell them anything you want to, Captain." I'll never forget that, Jack. The Governor of the State, tell him anything?'

'So what did you say?'

'That Rivers was deep cover. Every time I eat seafood I think of him and the Governor. "The fish are jumping?" It was not pleasant, Jack, the man has a real problem with authority figures. Fortunately the Governor has the attention span of a poodle, and this year they're giving the award to a young officer who will show up for the ceremony.'

'Then it worked out fine.' Scott was reading the personnel file, which had its weaknesses. 'When were the awards, Max, it doesn't say?'

'First week in May, same time every year, why?'

'Curious.'

'It doesn't matter, like I told you, Jack, he doesn't have an attitude problem, Frank has an attitude that produces problems. He's made Lieutenant three times.'

Scott noticed, a professional Sergeant, first in the Marines, then in the State Police. His DD214 listed three tours in Southeast Asia; a Silver Star, Bronze Star, Presidential Unit

Citation, and two Purple Hearts. Activities between 1969 and 1972 were still marked *Restricted*, which meant he had the misfortune of working with Military Intelligence, a true oxymoron if there ever was one. Scott made a note to sequester government files coded for his civilian activities prior to becoming a policeman.

'Max, Detective Rivers worked patrol his first three years, how did he make out in uniform?'

'Make out?' Drury cried. 'The last incident before I put him in plain clothes he was clocked at 130 by a Delaware unit fouling up the State lines chasing after two fugitives. Frank kept running jurisdictions on me. I got a call in the middle of the night, he wasn't even on duty. If the driver hadn't been kind enough to eat a bridge abutment, Rivers would have chased them all the way to Canada. Shit, I took a lot of heat for that one too, Jack, what are you asking me?'

'That's not in the file, those suspects were wanted for what?'

'Hell, I don't remember, we let Delaware take the collar. Armed robbery and I think a rape or murder was involved somewhere, sorry, I can't recall details, just the political fireball that hit when our State had to file the chase report and make the identification for two bodies stuck in Delaware. Rivers had been investigating the case without authority, breaking every written procedure. It was a mess.'

'Sounds like it,' Scott soothed, 'so why did you keep him?'

'Like I said, I really do like Frank, he's a big dog that's not housebroken. I keep hoping he'll change, but I have serious doubts. The chopper pilot who picked up those materials at his house tonight reported that Rivers was all teeth, like a Cheshire cat.'

'Sounds like he has some growing up to do.'

'My point exactly. Why him, Jack? What does he have that you want so badly?'

'Just playing a hunch.'

'It's your call,' Drury agreed, 'but I've got a couple of real up and coming young detectives, detail men, team workers.'

Think about it. And just in case you need anything, let me give you my beeper number.'

'I have it, good talking to you, Max,' Scott said as he terminated the call with a thumb. And he stood, cranking the window open to let the cool air flow through.

Outside, sounds churned in the humid air, voices and boom boxes and car horns echoing skyward from the street. And he recalled Mary Beth Dodson in her hospital bed, weak as a kitten, her hands and arms flailing at the air to fight off unseen blows. He returned to the Clayton family and Jennifer Doe.

All that connected them was physical proximity on a map, and the personnel files of a recalcitrant State Police officer who disliked authority, and Scott stared down at the folders on his desk, then set out to organise documents into units marked *Physical Evidence, Personal Histories*, and *Case Similarities*. He knew it would take the better part of three hours to collect his thoughts and impose order, and he sat, stretching backward in his chair until his spine cracked.

'So what pushes you, Mr Rivers?' he asked flatly, draining the water from his glass. 'What devil do you fight alone this evening?'

The errant fisherman held a secret only Scott knew existed.

Through the shallows of night slid the coldest animal of all.

THIRTEEN

11:25 P.M.
SENECA, MARYLAND

The cramped forty-foot space was not just a room but a small block house with a red shingle roof. It smelled damp as a root cellar, even though the floor was a carpeted slab of concrete. There was only one door. There was only one window.

Once it had been meant to be a three-car garage for a mansion, but that was never built, and the little white house sat turning grey like a bad tooth lost in a sweeping field of weeds and eroding red clay.

The cramped interior was decorated in early American honky-tonk. There was an ageing couch, badly in need of repair, and over this hung a nude on black velvet with breasts like purple footballs, blowing a kiss from a face which resembled a football player in drag. The picture was covered with personal autographs. On top of a small beaten curio cabinet stood a haphazard row of award trophies, the gold and silver chipped and covered with dust. There were baseball batters, and little dog handlers, flycasters, sailboats, and marksmen, the latter pointing bent rifles aimlessly under aged icons like James Dean, Marlon Brando, Clint Eastwood.

In the centre of the room there was a movie poster of a surfer from *Endless Summer*, and a dartboard with open wooden doors. On the opposite wall, surrounding the door, hung a series of flags, a rising sun from Japan, a Viet Cong battle star, a battalion group insignia with a Pink Panther clutching the numeral one and dancing merrily through a field of red.

The television was on, a thirty-six-inch colour hightech wonder that filled the space with light, belting out a quiz show in stereo, competing against the sound of a ham radio hooked to cheap bass-heavy speakers. The local police channel was being monitored, and a human form was rolling over on a twin mattress in the far corner.

'M-P-R 280,' the speaker popped loudly. 'Name, Debra Ralson Patterson, age sixteen, missing four-seven . . .'

It was getting hot. The man on the bed felt that it was getting hot. And suddenly he leaped into the air with a heavy thrust of his legs, just as a piece of cigar ash burned down through his white T-shirt.

'Goddamn!' he cried, smacking at his stomach with both hands as the timer on the microwave oven screamed. He dabbed at his stomach with a wet napkin while grabbing a fifties-style microphone from the shelf next to the bed.

'Repeat your date and data, Missing Persons Report,' he hissed. There was a pause.

'This is County-One, M-P-R number 280, state your authorisation . . .' a woman's voice demanded back.

'Ahhh,' he sighed, feeling the hot sting subside, checking the bedspread for smouldering ash. He had fallen asleep in the middle of his favourite game show.

'Rivers,' he said flatly, 'State Sergeant Detective 140, radio car One-Echo-Twenty.' He pulled off his shirt, dropped it onto the floor, then went for the scalded milk in the micro-wave. He grabbed a bag of chocolate chip cookies and returned to the bed, waiting for a response, increasing the volume of his TV show with a remote.

'. . . and in the sports category, for an additional 500 points. In 1916 Washington State University played Brown University in what famous event?'

Rivers shook his head at the idiotic music, breaking a hand-ful of cookies into his mug. 'The Rose Bowl, you bimbos, Washington fourteen to zipper.'

'I'm sorry, contestants, that would be the first Rose Bowl.

Washington won that game, fourteen to zero. Grant, it's your turn at the board . . .'

Rivers was still half asleep, his eyes were slits, his blond hair a matted mess. 'Let's try technology, Mike,' the contestant cheered, 'we're a technology minded family . . .'

'Look out Japan,' said Rivers.

'For one hundred points, in 1915 this man developed the farm tractor. Who was . . .'

'Henry Ford,' said Frank.

'Gee, that's more of an agriculture question, Mike. I'd like to trade in my option before the clock.' He moved towards the board.

'In two for one, and Grant is betting his option which might take him out of the game . . .'

'I'm going to take the hill, Mike, let's stay with technology!'

'Yeah,' said Rivers, 'his strong suit.'

'In 1915 Dr Thomas A. Watson received a telephone call from this famous man of the time . . .'

'Al Bell,' said Rivers, 'everybody knows that.'

The crowd was on its feet. '*Zapp-pp!* I'm sorry, Grant, would you like to take a shot?'

'Ah, 1915, that would be President Wilson who called?'

'Dipshit.'

'That was Alexander Graham Bell calling from New York, the first transcontinental telephone call. Tough break.'

'Yeah, tough break,' Rivers chuckled as the radio sputtered and came alive.

'County to Echo-Twenty.' The cheap speakers buzzed with a woman's voice, and Rivers turned down the set with his remote.

'This is One-Echo-Twenty, go ahead,' he said, draining the last from his cup, then grabbing his duty book. He pressed the button on a blue Papermate and scribbled a star to get some ink flowing.

'M-P-R 280,' she said without tone. 'Caucasian, brown hair, green eyes, five-foot-six, Weight 110, DOB 3-7-67. Name, Patterson, Debra Ralson. Last seen intersection River Road and Falls, green 1988 Mustang convertible. Maryland tags Victor-Echo-Zulu 9–1–8. Registration Jonathan T. Patterson. Relationship, father.'

Rivers waited. 'That's it?' he asked.

'Echo-Twenty, please follow police radio procedure,' the woman ordered.

'One-Echo-Twenty-County-One,' Frank swallowed his spit, sneering into the microphone. 'Why wasn't State Police notified?'

'Echo-Twenty,' the woman intoned, 'procedural guidelines permit notification of State authority on 9–4–89, within forty-eight hours, contact case officer Sergeant Tyler Conroy.'

Rivers smiled. 'Not in your lifetime,' he said as he switched off the radio, placing the microphone back on the shelf. From a pile on the floor he lifted the Maryland telephone book and flipped through P, finding the address with an index finger. He considered the hour and calculated the basics.

Rivers had been off duty for six hours. He was fed. He was rested. He was bored. He dialled the phone while toying with one of Elmer Janson's wooden sticks, glancing at a passage from an old red-back encyclopedia opened to the naval history section.

Marlin-spike. It was illustrated. *n. a pointed iron instrument for separating the strands of a rope during splicing or marling.*

'Hello . . . hello . . .' the man had a quiet, distressed, but somehow pleasing voice.

'Is this Jonathan T. Patterson?'

'Oh my God, no!' a terrified voice cried with confusion.

'Relax,' Rivers said calmly, 'if this is Mr Patterson, then I'm a friend.'

There was a lengthy pause. 'Yes. Yes it is . . .' the voice said shakily.

Phone in hand, Frank Rivers began to pace in tight circles, giving Patterson time to gain his senses. 'I'm a cop, Mr Patterson,' he said slowly, 'I'd be glad to give you my badge number.'

'No, no, that won't be necessary, do you know about Debra, have you heard anything about my little girl?'

Rivers felt a pang in his chest, and he breathed hard. 'I'm

really not related to the case, sir, my name is Frank Rivers, I'm a State Police detective and I just heard the Missing Persons Report come over the radio. I'd just thought I'd call, I grew up a few miles from your place.'

'I've heard from no one, God, this is awful, can you help us?' Patterson blurted with desperation. 'We don't know what else to do, Debra's a good child, a responsible girl . . .'

'I'm sure she is, Mr Patterson, really.'

'This is not like her, Debra wasn't raised like this . . .'

Rivers' brow knotted with concern. 'Why are you so defensive, sir, I haven't said anything negative. Is there a reason I wouldn't think she's a good kid?'

'You said you're a State Trooper?'

'Sure,' Rivers smiled, 'a real trooper. Mr Patterson, can you answer that question? Why are you defending her character, is there something I should know?'

There was a silence on the phone, and Rivers thought he heard the man sob. 'They think she ran away from us . . . They think she left home because of us, my wife and me.'

Rivers looked at his watch. 'Did she, Mr Patterson?' he asked coldly.

'No!' he fired in an instant. 'No, I swear, something is seriously wrong,' he cried without hesitation. 'Help us, please, Debra would have called if she could . . .'

Rivers sat on the edge of the bed and re-lit his cigar. 'Have you spoken with her friends, is Debra an only child?'

'Yes,' said Patterson, 'yes to both questions. Her friends have not seen her, can you help us?'

Rivers clipped a gun and holster into his pants, stuffing his wallet, badge, cigarettes, knife and watch into a slate-grey windbreaker. He laid this across the bed, strapping a small automatic pistol to his inside left calf, putting down the phone to unfold a clean sweatshirt from a footlocker, which he then pulled on. He propped the phone back under his chin and was tying his running shoes when he heard Jon Patterson cry out.

'Mr Reever? Mr Reever?' his shaky voice asked.

'Yes sir, I'm right here. It's Frank Rivers, and no need to

apologise for the name. Look, Mr Patterson,' he paused. 'I'll be there as soon as I can, but it's an informal visit, if that's okay?'

'Anything,' the distressed father sighed.

'Good, that's real good, Mr Patterson, because if you want to find your daughter you've got to understand what you're up against. You are dealing with bureaucrats and politicians, that's what police agencies are all about, and this County is particularly bad. I'm a State man, so I've really got to watch myself.'

'I understand,' he said weakly, his voice becoming more sober. 'Anything you want . . .'

But what Frank Rivers really wanted was to live in a world where life wasn't considered so cheap, there for the taking. Druggies killed innocent people in cross-fire, then referred to them laughingly as mushrooms, as in, 'I made a mushroom today, think I'll buy me a Porsche.' In open court, group rapists called their victims strays. Pornographers called smut literature. Hitmen referred to their prey as leftovers. And sexual killers called stalking their victims wilding or trolling. Life was as cheap in America as it had ever been in Vietnam, and any fool who told you different never saw the Nam; or never saw American justice defending the little people.

On the Maryland side of the river, the three most prestigious neighbourhoods had always been Chevy Chase, Kenwood and Potomac Village, slices of real estate that started at more than a half-million dollars a throw. While a teenager, Frank Rivers had dated girls from all of these areas, the daughters of lawyers and government executives, retailers and corporate men. He came flying down River Road in his tan Crown Victoria, slowing only a moment to study the lights that were burning in Karn Foster's window; a second-floor room in a massive stone mansion with marble pillars and rolling acres.

His head turned slowly as he remembered a pink canopy bed with the image of a fragrant girl drifting through his mind, every soft, sensual curve and caress that was Karn. And he wanted to relive the sins of that room as they were then;

carefree, young and reckless. Rivers winced at how things had soured since then. The house had exchanged hands three times that he knew of, Karn had an unhappy marriage of nearly twenty years and lived in California with her four children. The Crown Vicky rolled silently through the intersection of River and Falls Road to Tara, where he turned right, studying the sweeping front lawns and arched entry ways. Only one house on the small cul-de-sac had lights still burning, and he swung into the tiled circular driveway, checking the address, then looking at his reflection in the rearview.

As the sound of the engine died, he rubbed his front teeth with an index finger, then dug at the corner of each eye. He licked one palm, patting yellow curls back over the crown of his head, then grabbed his clipboard as a man appeared at the front door.

On any good night, the drive to Jonathan Patterson's house in Potomac was forty-five minutes. With siren and fireball, Rivers had arrived in twenty, and he studied Patterson's approach. He was small and frail, balding on top, and dressed in rumpled but expensive grey slacks. He wore a thick white braided sweater, and suspenders hung down from his waist to his knees, swinging as he trotted forward. Before Rivers had closed his car door, the man was on him.

'Thank God! Thank you ... thank you for coming,' he gushed, extending a shaky hand through the grey light.

'Pleased to meet you, Mr Patterson, I was ...'

'We've got to get started, where do we begin?' he sputtered frantically, and Rivers could hear dogs barking a block away.

'Well, can we start by taking it inside?' he suggested calmly.

'Yes, I'm sorry, oh yes, oh yes,' he repeated to himself, biting his lower lip, then scurrying up the pathway. He swung the already open door wide, and they walked in.

From the hallway, Rivers could see into the family room. There was a phone surrounded by the symptoms of waiting: dirty glasses, plates of half-eaten food, notepads, personal telephone book, and clothes that had been discarded by the wearer where he camped. Jonathan Patterson led him into the livingroom, it was as plush a domestic dream as any man could envision, a room larger than Frank Rivers' entire house. The detective stood, waiting for instructions, facing a marble coffee table.

The sofas and chairs were arranged in a semicircle, an expensive green velvet on thick beige carpeting with an oriental rug positioned in the room's centre. Above a jet black Baldwin babygrand hung an oil of a gorgeous brunette in a lacy low-cut gown. Patterson caught the policeman's stare.

'My wife Alice,' he sighed. 'She's in Connecticut with her parents, her mother's quite ill, she'll be flying home first thing tomorrow,' he said apologetically.

'A beautiful woman,' Rivers said in a genuine tone, looking around the room. He spotted a picture of a girl in a crystal frame on an end table. 'May I?' he said, reaching.

'Please,' Patterson nodded. 'Can I get you a brandy or . . .' he was trying to sum up the hard-looking stranger in a hooded black sweatshirt, 'maybe a beer?' he asked nervously.

'No thanks, Mr Patterson.'

'Jon, please call me Jon,' he pleaded, and Rivers saw pain edging out across the little man's face.

'This is Debra?' he asked, looking Patterson in the eyes.

'At her confirmation several years back,' he said. 'She turned sixteen last July.'

'Does she have any lovers?'

Instantly, Patterson's face flooded with hurt. 'She's only sixteen.' He swallowed and an insulted look began to spread across his face.

'Jon.' Rivers rose and put his hand gently on the man's shoulder. 'Maybe I will have that drink, do you have any coke or coffee? Anything will do.'

Jonathan Patterson smiled dutifully, running on automatic, his mind flipping into the role of host as he started for the kitchen. Rivers held him by the arm, detaining his escape.

'Listen to me, Mr Patterson,' he said slowly, 'if we are going to find your daughter, you had better start getting real. She may be your baby, and I understand all of that, but Debra's a sweet looking kid and they grow up faster these days. If you don't know her boyfriend, you're off to a tougher start.' Rivers tried a smile. 'I'll bet half the boys in her class are chasing her.'

Patterson gave a troubled sigh. 'Well,' he cleared his throat, 'her phone does ring quite a lot.'

Rivers nodded as he released his grip. 'Think it over, I'm going to poke around.'

Patterson wandered off in a trance while Frank Rivers examined the room. There were three telephone lines coming into the home, he jotted them off. He heard a scratching behind a door at the end of the living-room and walked over. There was a bark as he released a cocker spaniel. Patterson returned with a tray.

'You locked the little guy up,' Rivers stated.

'Some people don't like animals, you just never know.'

Rivers was kneeling by the marble table, scratching the little dog on the head. He then sat Indian style on the rug as Patterson placed drinks in front of them.

'Do you want me to run through what I've told the other officer?' Patterson asked plaintively, sitting down into green velvet.

Rivers grabbed a cold glass of coke and took several swallows. 'No, I'm sure it was pretty routine. Just tell me the last time you saw her, how she was dressed, and where you think she was when she disappeared.'

And Patterson complied. They talked for a good thirty minutes, then Rivers finally said, 'You really don't know her very well, Mr Patterson, you've chosen to only know the little girl when the rest of the world is interested in a woman. Does she keep a diary?'

'I don't know,' he answered thoughtfully.

'Does she always go by the name Debra?'

'That or Dee, I think so . . .'

'And her best friend, Beth Meyers, you can talk to her?'

'Yes, yes I can.'

'And how are you fixed for bucks?' Rivers asked.

'Anything you want!' Patterson responded quickly. 'I'm not rich but we're very comfortable, if you need money . . .'

'Hold it, sir, that's not what I mean.' Rivers stood, corrected him firmly. 'You're a taxpayer, I already work for you.'

Patterson sighed, his shoulders falling forward. 'I'm sorry,' he said. 'I've never been through anything like this before.'

'Most folks haven't, there's not much in life that prepares you either.' Rivers looked him hard in the eye. 'Here's the thing, Mr Patterson,' he said cautiously, sitting back down, then leaning forward on the carpet so his chin hung over the coffee table.

'The County Government is in charge and they're following the seventy-two-hour rule, that is, until your daughter is missing for that long they won't put their full weight behind the wheel. And right now the wheel is turning slowly.'

Patterson's head swung on a weakened stalk. 'Who can I call?' he asked. 'How can you get them moving?'

'Well, I can't,' Rivers stated honestly, 'I'm just another cop, but you sure as hell can, and you can't afford to wait.'

'Tell me,' Patterson cried out. 'Debra could have been abducted, she could have amnesia . . .'

And Frank Rivers thought about the myriad times he had heard that amnesia fantasy, in many cases parents held onto the belief decades after the fact.

'Mr Patterson, the radio report said Debra's car is still missing, you have to start there and be prepared to really turn up the heat.'

'I don't follow you,' he said, leaning forward in his chair and reaching for a pad of paper.

'Right, I'm not making myself clear,' Rivers reconsidered. 'You need three things, Mr Patterson. A loud voice, a few extra bucks, and as many air taxis as possible, ah, helicopters that is.'

'Of course,' he smiled, 'to find her car! How can I get them moving?'

'The County has two choppers, the State has four, and there are an additional ten or so in private hands. Use the phone book.'

Jon Patterson was on his feet and starting to move.

'You'll have to wait, sir,' Rivers stopped him, 'I'm precluded from participating because of departmental rules.'

'Oh?' Patterson sucked air. 'You can't use a phone book?' he asked incredulously.

Rivers smiled broadly. 'That's not quite it, but close, I can't participate in an investigation conducted by a citizen in my presence.'

Patterson nodded, he was beginning to get the picture.

'Look up WMAL radio in the book, they have a contract pilot, Dan the Airman, he reports on gridlock, I don't know his real name.'

'Yes, I've heard him.'

'Start there, tell him your story, flip him a couple bucks. And wake him up tonight, don't wait until morning. If you can't track him down, find someone else, there are dozens of traffic reporters. Just call the stations, you'll find that night workers are universally easier to get information from than the morning crowd. A lot quieter at night, people are more friendly.'

He nodded agreement.

'Then look through the book and find a private pilot, ask for someone experienced in search pattern navigation, it's a speciality, a former cop or combat pilot is always best. And get some bids. After that, pick your best shot, your gut will tell you. And listen carefully, I'd bet on the guy who's more interested in your story than how much you're gonna pay.'

'I appreciate that,' he nodded.

'In the morning, call each of the local television stations, they all have pilots. Ask for the metro desk and sweet talk someone. Let them know how you feel about your kid, and that you've got a local radioman and private jockey in the sky. They're going to ask where the cops are, tell them they're too damn busy. Say that and they'll go nuts, Mr Patterson,' Rivers was smiling, 'everyone's going to go nuts!

'The TV and radio folks will fear if they don't roll on this, then they're going to be losing a hellava good story. And the County cops . . .' Rivers chuckled, 'instead of breaking their seventy-two-hour rule of non-involvement they'll write a new rule for action and name it after Debra.'

Patterson smiled for the first time. 'I'm following every bit of this,' he said, his hand moving furiously across a legal pad.

'Just remember that you're not looking to place a news story, though, you're looking for Debra's car. Don't lose the focus. That's first, Mr Patterson, you've got to find Debra's car, and right away . . .' his voice sagged.

'I understand,' he said.

'When the County Executive hears what you've done he'll call the police brass, and next thing you know, a case will be opened and then I'll ask for State Police involvement and the assignment.'

'But I thought there was a case, there isn't a case?' Patterson asked with alarm, his tired eyes blown wide open.

Rivers slowed his speech, combing his fingers through curly yellow hair. 'No sir,' he said, 'I know this doesn't make sense, but like I told you on the phone, we're dealing with bureaucrats. All we've got right now is a Missing Persons Report, which means uniformed units will keep an alert eye for a person matching Debra's description. You won't get a case unless it gets worse, evidence of foul play, that kind of stuff . . .' he saw the horror register on the man's face and backed off quickly.

Jonathan Patterson was living the worst of all dreams, the kind of event that transpired in other people's lives. They had a good life, a good and wholesome family. They were not heavy drinkers, they did not live near transients, they were a loving couple with one child. The Pattersons never even raised their voices at each other, no matter how angry or upset. Rivers saw the man drift off in thought.

'Listen, Mr Patterson, if you raise enough hell you could get a case officer by this time tomorrow.'

The man's face was twisted with pain and Rivers didn't know if he had done a good job of explaining himself, or if this father had the courage to follow through. Then Patterson lifted his weary head, locking eyes with the tall policeman, and extended his hand. 'Thank you,' he said, and that took a great deal of physical strength, he looked like he hadn't slept in two days. 'Thank you so very much.'

'Sure,' said Rivers, 'that should get you started. Do you or Mrs Patterson have any relatives nearby, any male relatives?'

'No, there's just my older brother, he's retired in Florida. Alice's parents are it from her side of the family.'

Rivers studied this answer closely. 'Any men come to the house for work, yard help, plumbers, pest control?'

'Joseph Mallery does all of our yard work, but he's an older man, a nice man.'

'Could I have his number and schedule anyway?' he asked coyly.

Patterson nodded, leaving the room for the kitchen, and returned with a slip of paper. He found Frank Rivers standing in the hallway by the front door.

'Are you leaving?' he asked, handing him the paper.

'We've both got work to do,' he stated, examining the particulars on the sheet. 'When's the last time another workman came to your house?' Rivers pushed.

'I don't know,' Patterson sighed, 'I'd have to ask my wife, she manages that kind of thing.'

'Do that,' Rivers suggested, 'and another thing, Mr Patterson. Do yourself a favour and toss Debra's room.'

'Toss?' he asked.

'Search it, maybe she has a diary or something else. If we can't find her in a few days we'll be here to do just that, so give a good look. It will be easier while her mother's away.'

Patterson's swollen eyes blinked, brimming with a film of water. The detective was right, Alice Patterson would regard that as a violation of Debra's privacy. 'I'll toss it,' he said solemnly.

Rivers smiled, walking out the front door into the cool night air. It was overcast. A slight breeze was blowing in from the Potomac, he could feel the moisture on his face.

'Detective Rivers,' Patterson said, following after him and, again, extending his hand. 'I really don't know how to thank you,' he said in a sincere voice.

'No sweat, Mr Patterson,' Rivers gave him a firm shake, 'but you could do me a small favour in return?'

'Anything, just name it,' he offered, 'anything at all.'

'We never talked, not that I care, I'm just not in the mood to play politics, it slows me down.'

'I understand.' He smiled gravely. 'I have some idea of what we're up against.'

Rivers raised an eyebrow. 'Good luck, sir,' he said, 'I'll see you again when the system catches up.' And he strolled over the tiled drive, making a mental note to check on the family in the morning.

From inside his jacket pocket he removed the colour print that Patterson had given to him, and he sat in his radio car with the light on, attaching it to the top of his clipboard.

Debra looked like the portrait of her mother, he thought, her hair was shiny and soft to look at, her figure was subtle and genuine, and it made Frank Rivers all the more disheartened.

He gunned his engine down River Road and into the familiar darkness.

He felt truly sorry for Debra Patterson.

She was a pretty little thing.

FOURTEEN

Daniel Richard Flores had gained a feeling for the ViCAT Slot. He felt as if he were trying to build a fence around a sandstorm.

He filed a report off screen number three, watching bright columns vanish and the blinking cursor reappear. Phones and computers and imaging equipment hadn't stopped buzzing all night, with a new report about every twenty minutes, the emergency requests flowing from every American region; as far away as Honolulu, as close to home as the Bronx. The police officers reporting had a variety of voices, young and old, male and female, some blistering with hate, others choked with intense sorrow.

Captain Duncan Powell had wired a positive dental match from a missing persons sheet, a victim had been identified by medical examiners, and he was now requesting that Scott come to Florida. Flores promised to speak with his Commander, and he tried to read Powell's state of mind, but Flores could not read Powell, his voice was deep and hard with a commanding bite.

As he concentrated, the young agent tried to imagine their features, all of these pleading and detached and demanding voices, and in his mind he would assemble composites from faces he remembered, people who had drifted in and out of his life. That effort made him feel sadly alone, and lonely, Flores knew, could be a danger. The slot was a difficult job, worse at night, and his goal was to survive until morning. In retrospect, Daniel Flores thought it unprofessional when his emotions slipped to the surface as he was talking to the Sheriff of Tucson, Arizona, who had invited him for a holiday weekend.

He had been sharing the man's frustration, assisting with behavioural keys in a search for a twenty-three-year-old woman abducted from a convenience store. He had been on the phone for exactly 16 minutes 22:03 seconds, and their relationship had gotten that close, that fast. A total stranger. Flores couldn't explain it.

A call from Santa Cruz, California, followed, where a boy had been thrown from a speeding car along a dark interstate, the Highway Patrol remained at the scene.

In Jacksonville, Florida, a young woman had vanished from a department store parking lot while waiting for her husband, and the Dade County Police were reporting their case as a series. Dade had four similar incidents with no survivors.

At 9:10 p.m. in Christy, Texas, witnesses reported seeing two children being forced into a car by men they could not describe, and the offender's vehicle was found abandoned.

At 9:45 p.m. in Fort Wayne, Indiana, a serial rapist announced his retreat from the home of Joyce and Suzanne Williams by throwing a woman's shoe through a neighbour's window. Joyce, seventeen, had survived, and Flores had pushed detectives to make a last ditch effort to obtain a dying declaration from her that might provide leads.

At 10:12 p.m. in Jackson Creek, Wyoming, eighteen-year-old Bonnie Caputo was found dead, stabbed a total of eighty-one times and dumped in a graveyard; the Jackknife Ghoul had struck again. And Jack Scott stood at the rim in the ViCAT situation room, his grey eyes knowingly tired, his face drawn into intense focus. He listened to Daniel Flores, watching patiently as he completed the Jackson Creek call, and he felt lucky for his young understudy. It was a slow Friday night for a warming April, only six previously registered ViCAT cases had gone active.

Scott checked the computer printout. There were killings and rapes and abductions, and Flores even handled one arson, a series crime terrorising residents of a small Pennsylvania township. Scott handed him a fresh cup of black coffee as

Flores dropped his headset onto the battered grey desktop, breathing a sigh of relief. His eyes were clear and bright and Scott admired the young man's stamina.

'I've been listening,' he said, 'you're doing very well, Daniel.'

Flores spun his chair in a semicircle like he was born to the slot. 'Thanks,' he responded, taking the cup in his hands, sipping at the hot liquid. Scott noticed he did so rather gingerly.

'How do you take your coffee?'

'This is fine, thank you sir, I'm not much of a coffee drinker, but I guess I'm going to start.'

'Any questions so far?' he asked, looking over the edge of his cup.

And Flores propped his elbows against the desk while stifling a yawn. 'Nothing that's case-specific, but I am worried about Captain Powell, he . . .'

'Don't,' Scott smiled, holding up a hand. 'Duncan Powell is acclimatising to his own skin, it's part of the hunt, and his behaviour gets rather testy at times. Florida is a tough state; in addition to drugs, there's more series crime than they can deal with. Ever heard about the sticky wheel?'

Flores smiled.

'That's Duncan,' he said, 'and we will become the grease. Believe me, this is a man who will not take no for an answer. Does anything else come to mind?'

'I do have a question that's not in the literature.' Flores sipped his coffee. 'I've read the incidence reports, but what do you really think?'

Scott gave a knowing smile. 'Well, at any given time, between one and about two hundred active serial killers work the land, maybe more, maybe less, it's very hard to say. There aren't any reliable statistics, but I have always believed that we touch the bare tip of the iceberg. Does that help?'

The young man went silent, considering the number, which seemed quite high to him. 'Where the hell do they all come from?' he asked gravely, and there was a fire to his hazel lenses. 'I mean, why now, this wasn't happening when I was growing up.'

Scott forced a stiff grin onto his face. 'I'm afraid it was, Daniel, it's a question of scale. Serial killers have always been a threat to society, our planet is just more crowded now, so we have more of everything. But those responsible for telling the tale, government officials and writers, have managed to mask the threat in various ways. That's always been the case, though it's getting more difficult for them now.'

Flores shook his head with confusion.

'I'll give you an example,' Scott offered. 'Have you ever heard of Vlad the Impaler?'

'Did I miss a ViCAT case study?' he piped with concern.

'No, that I would doubt very much,' Scott smiled. 'Vlad was in his prime around 1465, his real name was Vladimir Basarab, a sadistic serial killer very much like the suspects we track today. He was emotionally devoid and his recreational thrill came from abducting innocent people off the streets of his hometown, then putting them to a painful death. The circumstances surrounding his place in history are rather telling, in terms of human behaviour.'

'Then I should know of him,' Flores agreed.

Scott leaned against the grey rim and took a sip of coffee. 'Over many years he was given a dozen names, at one time they called him General Basarab because he controlled the military. The town's population lived in terror, unable to cope with the fact that Vlad could come marching into their homes at any moment, kidnap them at will, and then impale them on a sharpened pole. He liked to watch his victims suffer.'

'It does sound familiar,' Flores said, searching his memory. 'Did they stop him?'

'No,' Scott sighed. 'They explained him away. And they explained him away in much the same way society is explaining away the growing population of killers you've asked about. Then, as now, people had great difficulty accepting the concept of a *sane* human predator who kills for pleasure.'

Flores gave Scott a questioning look and raised one eyebrow. 'I don't really follow you, sir.'

'Well, instead of facing the harsh reality, they began justifying their inability to stop him, imbuing Basarab with a divine will, attributing superhuman powers for what he did.'

Flores connected with a chill. 'Count Dracula?' he murmured, leaning back against his chair.

Scott smiled. 'The very same, and he did exist, as real as you or I, only there was nothing occult about him. In fact, Basarab had no interest in cannibalism or drinking human blood, that was a writer's invention. Today the same man would be given a sugar coating of mental illness, instead of giving him divine powers they would make him into a psycho. Such tales make the whole damn thing easier to swallow. But either way it's mythology, nothing more, nothing less.'

Flores looked pensive, remembering the Count's movie exploits. 'But why didn't they tell the real story?' he asked with excitement.

Scott's grin was genuine as he placed a hand on the young man's shoulder. 'You tell me, Daniel, why doesn't our government tell the real story about all the little Draculas we monitor on a daily basis, that's a better question, I think.'

And a chiming overhead filled the chamber signalling a case alert as green alpha letters began marching across screen seven, the Northwest Region. Flores quickly put on his headset, then waited, checking the transmitted code against a clipboard, his index finger moving down the pad. 'The Home Intruder,' he said flatly.

The case was named for a countryside killer who took residence in the houses of his victims until all their food was eaten or their bodies had started to decompose. He punched in an authorisation.

'Sir, do you want me to handle this?' he asked, working the keypad, his eyes intent on the copy that was starting to fill the screen.

There was no answer, so Daniel Flores spun quickly in his seat to repeat the question, prepared to open a phone-line with his left hand.

The Commander had already gone.

*　　*　　*

For a long time Scott sat in silence at his desk, one fist curled under his chin, listening to an inner complaint. He fumbled through a drawer for a fresh pack of cigarettes and struck a match, the tiny blue flame coming to life, reflecting in his soft grey eyes like a hellish ember.

And Jack Scott felt equally possessed.

Matthew Brennon had returned with a report of his findings; Elmer Janson's coin was a metal token, one century old. The expert's name was Dr Robert Perry with credentials that were beyond reproach, and Scott dropped the file back onto his desk. His mind began to wander.

Flores had dubbed the Florida case the Devoid Callers, and Scott thought it fitting for emotionless animals who used a telephone as a distraction to snatch children in one deadly moment. The Cub Scout Killer had left another victim along a California roadside, he had last been active in New Mexico months before, and from the sounds coming in, the Home Intruder had found another meal. And there was more. Every hour of every day. By midnight of Friday, April 8th, 1989, Jack Scott felt the oppressive weight of a lifetime pushing him down, and his cigarette burned to his fingertips, jolting him back to attention. He snuffed it out.

With meticulous effort he started clearing his mind the way he was clearing his desk; reflecting on files only he understood, then walking through memory rooms, closing doors while opening others, lifting, sorting, disposing, and examining motive. It was raining outside his window, thick heavy droplets, and he could hear them falling. It was a quiet rain. And Scott craved quiet the way most men crave a vacation. He pulled it over him like a favoured old coat and flopped back in his chair.

He lifted a file and unfolded it across his desk, adjusting the light, just so, to reduce shadow. There was an area map of Bethesda, Maryland, he had scanned it once, now he studied it with care. The modern suburb sat broad with printed legends advertising Subway Station and Public Parking and Future Skating Ring and Historic District and even New Sculpture; making promises in every direction like a fat concrete politician. To the north there was endless urban sprawl sprouting titles like Potomac, Cabin John, Rockville and Wheaton. To the south there was Chevy Chase, an older village well known on the East Coast for affluence. Following that, there was the Nation's Capital.

Scott turned a page, and was now examining a statistical breakdown of the Bethesda population that had arrived from the Department of Justice Research, interpreting as he read, looking for figures on Ridgewell Hamlet, the Claytons' neighbourhood. According to the report, they had lived in a rather small neighbourhood for the area, occupying one of sixty-seven homes with a population of 268 people. The hamlet, in turn, sat in an urban ring of sixty square miles with a population nearing two million people; which was about as far as Scott went. All elements were there. Three critical factors associated with a high incidence of serial killings, abductions, and similar types of violent crime: a large population, rapid growth, a high number of transients. Diana Clayton was raising her family in a modern killing zone. His anger sparked, Scott lifted a bound report from the local Chamber of Commerce which promoted Bethesda as an urban township within easy commuting distance to a city, then flipped the advertisement into the grey can.

That Bethesda was a quiet residential community away from the multitudes was the illusion that allowed the killer to mask himself, the more quiet the neighbourhood the better, the more detached each neighbour, the more effective the camouflage. With her surrounding communities, when it came to population, Bethesda was twice as large as Buffalo, three times the size of New Haven, as large as the city of Cambridge, almost identical to San Diego. Yet who had ever heard of this strange bedroom city?

Scott shook his head, turning his attention to the skeleton found due east of Diana Clayton's home, checking the address of the condemned building, then finding Elmer Janson's house on the map.

With a red grease pen, he circled Ridgewell Hamlet, darkened River Road, then drew a square around Elmer's house.

Changing to a blue pen, he coloured in the neighbourhood where the grave had been found, and using calipers, estimated the distances at one point three miles along the same highway. He made a note. The map made the locations impossibly close, a sharp lopsided triangle covering a specific plot of territory. Even in timely context with the Civil War, it was just too pat for coincidence, and he thought back to his history, when five hundred years ago Vlad the Impaler proved the importance of territorial claim. In behavioural context, feeling at home, knowing the population well, and being comfortable in the workplace was of primary concern to a devoid killer. Selection, stalking, and an adequate study of prey could not be accomplished as quickly in a strange environment. He folded the map, then placed it into a file marked *Case Similarities*.

Scott was standing now, facing his wall with the two-storey brick house tacked beneath the detailed shot of Diana Clayton's master bedroom. Breathing deeply, he removed a folder from his briefcase, producing a picture marked *Kimberly's Room*. With a clear stickpin, he tacked this enlargement in place, left, next to a wide-angle perspective showing the upstairs hallway.

Kimberly's door was open. The tiny doorway disappeared into the grain of darkness and he shook another photograph loose. Kimberly's room was pinkish or peach in colour with posters of rock stars on her walls.

A close-cropped shot of the bureau came next, the mirror above it shattered in the centre, cracks snaking outward and meeting the frame. He checked the analysis report on his desk, no pieces missing or fallen out, and he hit the button on his tape recorder. 'Notation,' he said thoughtfully, 'mirror struck by a blunt object, swift, precise blow. Suggests extreme control, perhaps familiarity with tensile resistance of glass, sample required for test and type manufacture.' He checked the files, searching for a report of other broken glass or mirrors in the house. Nothing.

Another photo showed a close-up of the bedding area, a night stand with picture and lamp still in place, pink slippers next to the bed; wall-to-wall carpeting was freshly vacuumed. He checked the report, three-quarter inch nylon pile. Between the night stand and bed frame, just next to the slippers, a small splash of blood. He pulled another enlargement and turned a page in the crime scene analysis. Kimberly's Type, B-Positive, with slight evidence of drainage from sinus mucosa. He had either struck the child here or she had been startled and hit her nose.

Where was Kimberly when the intruder entered, he questioned. Although the County report concluded that the 'attacker had found both girls together, asleep in Leslie's bedroom', Scott did not believe it now. He hit the recorder: 'Notation, killer did not bring Kimberly back into room, as suggested. Rather, killer woke child in bed, struck child in facial area with small blunt object used on mirror.'

He pressed both hands into the small of his back and stretched, then checked the crime scene report. 'What did you take?' he muttered, scanning the pages. 'If it wasn't a sliver of glass, then what souvenir gave your shallow little heart a knock?'

As was the case with most Recreational Killers, Scott knew the chances were excellent that this stalker had removed some item from the Claytons' house, a trophy which he could later fondle to increase the intensity of his fantasies. He quickly scanned each photograph, trying to gain a sense of what was missing, as opposed to what could be easily seen. Besides a cruel death, what men like these were after was the production of memories; something to feed on long after the event was over.

Something tangible.

As he searched, his mind skipped through an inventory, the macabre and twisted collections they had recovered through the years; toys and clothes, photographs and films, ears and teeth, toes and fingers, scalplochs and bone. Sometimes even the flesh was removed, sexual organs carefully dried with salts for tanning. If nothing else, he thought, the Claytons had escaped that atrocity, and his mind suddenly turned to Captain Duncan Powell. If he had been right, a killer was collecting the teeth of each victim, sparing Lisa Caymann for reasons that were not known, and Scott swallowed hard, glancing at his watch.

He knew the detail his old friend was facing.

Captain Duncan M. Powell of the Florida State Police stood at a door, a towering man who seemed larger than life. His troops liked to point out that he looked a lot like John Wayne as a senior, kindly yet strong, with a presence that could fill a house.

He had known John F. Scott since the early years, when he and Captain Maxwell Drury had all graduated, together, from the enforcement academy at Glenco. Along with Joe Taylor, Alan Grafton and Leslie Vance Doyle; they had been known as the infamous Team Tiger. The manhunters. Their skills placed them top of the class of 1954, and they were among the few original greybeards who still ran the enforcement establishment and refused retirement.

More than most men, Duncan Powell was a natural and gifted leader who would send no other to do what he alone felt was responsible, what was right. And so it was that he found himself at 1606 McDowell Drive, removing a gold braided hat, standing with military precision in a dimly lit porch in the subdivision known as Silver Shores.

Powell had come in full uniform. He had stopped at the rectory of Our Lady of Mercy and asked for the assistance of Father Thomas O'Brian, a small man who was clutching the good book beneath his left arm, standing in the shadow just off to his right.

Since their daughter had been abducted twelve days before, Duncan Powell had come to know Mr and Mrs Phillip Caymann as good and downright decent people, and of all the details in the world, the Captain now faced what he knew as the hardest. He had started to ring the bell as the door was cracked, revealing a pathetic figure of a man, his head bowed with a deeply troubled resignation. Duncan could hear a woman sob convulsively from another part of the house.

'I am truly sorry,' Captain Powell said, extending a massive right hand. Phillip Caymann took it limply.

'We saw you pulling into the driveway,' he cried at the policeman. 'You have news about Lisa?' he asked, fighting to maintain his composure, then his eyes flared, focusing downward on the little pastor.

'May we come in?' Powell asked kindly.

'I'm sorry, but I don't want her mother to hear, tell me first, please, Duncan, I beg you, I'm begging you. Is it Lisa? Did you find Lisa? Is she dead?'

Captain Powell stood silent at the doorway watching the terror contort and stretch across the man's face. Powell released a heavy sigh, giving the man time to prepare himself, to steel himself, if that were possible.

'Earlier this evening,' he said slowly, 'a patrol car found the body of a young girl near the highway . . .'

And Phillip Caymann took a sharp step backward, hitting the door with his back. 'Please!' he interrupted with a cry, feeling his knees grow weak, holding up one hand to silence the senior officer.

'Please, her mother will hear . . .'

And then the man began to tremble violently as the reality took hold with the logic of a scene reeling like a tape in slow motion. The police would not have come without calling first, unless they were sure, the red lights pulsed from the driveway. There was no siren, no rush suggesting that life was hanging in the balance. Instead the police had brought the church . . .

And the primaeval role of father quickly superseded the braver role of man and protector, as his knees folded beneath him, and Phillip Caymann double-stepped, tripping forward against the Captain's barrel chest.

'What kind of animal would do this?' he cried helplessly. 'What kind of monster would kill my baby . . .'

The Captain propped him up as Caymann released a horrible scream into the night air, a painful, deafening and terrifying roar that sounded like a lion whose heart was impaled.

And at that tragic moment, as the pastor prayed, Duncan

Powell turned his face into the cold night, holding the shattered man together with all his humanity. Only one thought came to mind.

Find Jack Scott.

There were no others.

FIFTEEN

Scott's desktop was nearly empty.

There was an ashtray and coffee mug, which he now moved aside, and with a tired hand he reached for his bottom drawer, a large wooden file box that had served as his catchall since 1956, the year he had purchased the executive-style tank.

He felt haunted, as if while surveying the contents he were surrounded by ghosts, moving backward in time, moving back through the darkest corners of his life. He aimed the hinged cone of light, clearing shadows, then looked down with intensity. The pack-rat things of his life stared back up.

On top there was an assortment of newspapers, haphazardly thrown in, each covering various ViCAT cases, and he lifted them out in a pile, dropping them into the trash. A special edition of *Look* magazine surfaced. Scott paused, trying to remember when he had aspired to the theme issue of country living. The date on the cover was 1968. He quickly dropped it into the can. Next came a worn World Almanac for the year 1964, which in turn rested on top of a hand calculator that was about the same thickness and weight. He discarded them both. Underneath there was a large manila envelope containing an original poster of 'Speech', one of the Four Freedoms painted by Norman Rockwell, and he set this aside, recalling how he had meant to frame it for the country house.

There was a box of white linen handkerchiefs, which he

146

had forgotten, yellowed from smoke and age, and as he lifted this, a gold-plated lighter fell to the carpet. He smiled. This he did remember, it had been given and broken nineteen years ago, and he held it in his palm. *Congratulations Dr Scott.* It had been inscribed for his graduation. He turned it over. *Love, Linda.* He could not throw it away.

Out went a tie clip, a badge, assorted buttons, then a variety of relics stuffed into a cracked and swollen Belvedere cigar box. He was about to toss the box when he stopped.

'Bless this day with a healthy child,' the voice of Nicholas Dobbs bloomed from memory and filled his ears. Scott had purchased the cigars in 1959 when his first child was born, and had opened the box for his Commander. The old Irishman was so touched that he raced for the door, returning with peppermint candy for Scott to keep under his bed.

Beneath the box sat an outdated doubled-edged safety razor, blades long spent before a youthful mirror. Next came a small brown cardboard box marked *Colt*, containing a pocket pistol. And finally he reached bottom.

And it was there.

In a mass of lint and litter, flecked with grey ash and covered with dust, a thick pile of bound reports and case summaries about the size of the Manhattan Yellow Pages. Most had been kept, not as trophies, he reasoned, but as important precedent-setting documents advancing techniques of criminal investigation. Others had simply been closed by command when leads ran out and budgets went dry. His heart raced as he reached deeper into shadow, his mouth went dry and he could not swallow.

And it was there. In the darkness. Waiting for him like an ancient and evil debt.

Scott hesitated, a pack-rat staring down, a yellowed folder staring back up. He shuddered, awash in adrenaline, his sphincter pulling unpleasantly tight as he recognised his own youthful scrawl on the outside tab. No secretary or assistant back then, and he felt an ache, a curse of time racing across the ridge of his knuckles.

With a deep breath he reached, pulling it free, preventing

the contents from spilling with his left hand. With a faint tremble he laid it down across his desk. Scott was breathing deeply now. He swallowed.

ZACHARIAH'S ONE-MAN CIRCUS!
Magic*Clowns*Fortunes*Puppets*
For Children Of All Ages!
--Zak the Master--

Scott was reading the advertisement in his mind even before he had opened the file, and his throat burned uncomfortably as he removed the printed flyer. He took a sip of cold coffee.

Time had not changed a thing, he thought, adjusting it into the beam. There had been a hundred similar flyers left in boxes on the day they arrested Zak, and Scott leaned back against the night, staring into space, remembering a more civilised, less complicated age.

American values were more pure then. Or perhaps better defined. Maybe his youth was a factor and he was now shaping and distorting the past with the resentment of age. And he fixed on the memory of seeing Zachariah's collection, coming up from the bathroom floor. In 1989 it would appear fairly tame, he thought, but in 1960 all such legal products limited their displays to bikini-clad pinups, and Scott, like most law enforcement professionals, knew that there was a direct link between porn and violent behaviour.

The search of Zachariah's apartment produced a depraved assortment of pictures and film, including graphic photographs of women and children being sexually debased. Even more damning, the seizure included stacks of police procedural manuals, some with detailed instructions on current investigative techniques. And Scott spoke suddenly to himself.

'Sonofabitch!' he hissed. 'Sonofabitch, Nick, over here!' Scott remembered with an uneasy clarity how he had cursed while pulling up a bathroom tile with a pocketknife. In an instant Nicholas Dobbs was standing over him, his command-

148

ing voice providing an edge of caution while six other agents were hacking into the floor and walls.

'By the book, fellas,' Dobbs would say. 'Scotty, mind your procedure . . .' Scott waited for his commander, then removed four tiles with gloved hands while keeping a tight rein on adrenalin. He placed each element of the collection into an individual evidence bag, while Dobbs recorded the event with a box camera.

Scott was looking at that picture now, a record of Zak's shower coming apart in the hands of a younger Jack Scott. Under the harsh white beam he could see a blur where his young hands would have been, shaking then as they were now, disappearing into a carefully constructed hollow beneath the drain.

One by one, elements of the collection came free, manual after manual, book after book, primer after primer, diagrams and photographs and films. Scott leaned back on his haunches, handing a book to Commander Dobbs; he was looking at that photographic sequence now, of a man Daniel Flores' age handing a book to an old and trusted friend.

'Expert Restraint, How to Work Livestock with Rope,' Dobbs read aloud.

'I'm going to skin him,' Scott spat, remembering what he had said while reading marginal notations in the killer's workbook. 'I'm going to cut his goddamned liver out!'

Immediately Dobbs stepped into the shower, leaning over so that only Scott would hear. 'Attend to me,' he whispered, biting off each word. 'We are going to prosecute this man and he is going to the gas chamber, so as of now we start tempering every comment as if a judge were listening.'

'But how can you be sure, Nick?'

Scott listened intently, then as he was doing now, but it was an older man, less brave and more alone, who waited for his commander in the patter of rain drifting against the tall windows.

The sound of the rain. Hardly a sound at all.

*　　*　　*

149

The One-Man Circus.

His full name was Zachariah Leslie Dorani, and between 1955 and 1960 he had advertised to parents throughout New England. During that period, four bodies had been recovered, women and children mostly, and though more were reported missing, they were never found. Zak Dorani was a Recreational Killer, a self-taught master of cruelty, illusion and deceit.

After that brief conversation with Dobbs, Scott returned to digging through the apartment, removing a plethora of the macabre including a definitive medical reference on poisons, Arsenic to Zyklon-B; along with a collection of Second World War manuals on silent weaponry. These lay next to classic texts on the mortuary arts, with sections dedicated to embalming and cremation. At the end of a series of pornographic materials, Scott found several self-help books for women, long before the pop publishing craze, and these had been stored alongside *The Complete Encyclopedia of Child Psychology*.

There had never been a doubt that they had arrested the right man, for the abductions had stopped immediately, September 5th, 1960. Mary Beth Dodson was Zak's last victim. Scott had watched her die. She might have been the only person on earth whose words could have put Zak on death row, and without her the case shattered like a glass house.

Since the forensic sciences were still in their infancy, case elements had to be inferred without the luxury of today's comprehensive crime analysis, and the evidence against Zachariah was, at best, circumstantial. From bruises and rope fibres found on each victim, it was clear that they had been bound with strips of cord in a skilled manner remarkably similar to those found in the manuals. And death always came from critical punctures of the brain.

Pathologists never could determine what caused the destructive cranial holes, what kind of offending instrument was used in killing, for Zak would remove the lethal evidence precisely at death's onset. As Dr Chet Sanders testified, the reaction of the brain to grievous insult is to swell until the organ bursts, turning to jelly within the tight skull case, destroying wound channels while also killing the victim. Whatever it was, the technique rendered the help of medical professionals worthless, they were never able to make a precise reconstruction of events based on the equivalent of shattered bowls filled with a gelatinous soup.

Using time series analysis, Dobbs and Scott had attempted proof of Zak's heinous crimes through a reconstruction of events. All of the dead women and children shared one thing in common; they had been entertained by the One-Man Circus. Two children testified that Zak had offered them free magic in a special place where their futures could be seen, an invitation they wisely declined, and in spite of the fact that he was a known friend who had been the featured attraction at their birthday parties.

The defence made it sound very innocent, portraying the killer as the victim, a tragic figure missing the companionship of his own family. In 1953 Zak had lost his wife and two children to a freak traffic accident, and with the help of his attorney, Meyer Coleman, Zachariah explained away every claim, skilfully painting the image of a grieved and model husband. In his last year as Assistant U.S. Attorney, David Satter headed the prosecution.

'Your honour, the State would like to point out that the accident left the defendant sole beneficiary of a substantial insurance policy, paid for by the defendant . . .'

'Objection.' Meyer Coleman rose sharply out of his chair, pleading to the jury. 'Mr Dorani is not on trial for a great personal loss, your honour.'

'Sustained,' ordered Judge Owen Lymann without hesitation. And so it was that Zak was able to relay an incredible yet convincing tale of coincidence and association, explaining away the materials found in his shower.

'They are all very innocent!' Zak cried, sobbing expressly for the three women of the jury. 'They belonged to my wife, she was studying sexual response in hopes of earning a college degree and becoming a counsellor in sexual dysfunction.' He wiped his eyes and paused for effect. 'She only wanted to help others . . .'

Coleman introduced the dead woman's college transcripts, she had taken two lower level courses in human sexuality, and Scott remembered how Zak played the crowd, with daring and skill, an accomplished actor giving the performance of his life, for his life.

The jury was his stage, and he cried over everything, right up to the point where the state introduced the illustrated guides on livestock. At this his eyes flamed with indignant rage.

'I have never seen them before!' he huffed, crossing arms against his chest, his face flushed with the hurtful suggestion. 'I have told you quite honestly, my wife and I did own the literature, they were scientific research, and we hid them so the children would not be exposed. Maybe they belonged to a previous tenant, why would I lie about books on farming . . .' And so it went.

After a protracted trial which lasted nine months, for lack of conclusive evidence, Zak Dorani was found not guilty on nine related counts of abduction and murder; but guilty as to felony possession of pornographic materials in the third degree, by reason of insanity. Today, Scott reflected, such possession is not even considered worthy of court, but in 1960 it was simply unexplainable and revolting, the kind of cruel trash that crawled from human sewers.

On that much the jury agreed, recommending the maximum sentence, and Zak was given eight years in the Adjunct Psychiatric Facility at Woodside Prison in New York, after which Scott fell into a deep depression. He took leave, returning to complete his degree at Yale University, Dobbs attending his graduation, then assigning the young agent to the new concept of criminal behavioural profiling. They never spoke of Zak the Needle again.

'When we lost this case, why did you promote me?' Scott asked, holding his failings with both hands, the brown coffee ring on the file placed there nearly thirty years ago when fatigue and morning glare could be shaved away, washed off and left in a sink. Scott always regretted not asking for an explanation, and Dobbs had taken the answer to his grave over a decade earlier.

Like so many others, Commander Nicholas Alan Dobbs had fallen to the agent's curse, the policeman's disease. After retirement, when the painful roar of silent images accumulated over a lifetime had filled his ears one too many times, refusing to let him go, he placed his gun into his mouth and pulled the trigger. In the end, it was a symbol of his failing, of his humanity, of his caring too much to fail.

For some professionals, teachers, editors, accountants, merchants, even doctors, failure was a part of the job. It made you a member of a humble species. An error apologised for, then forgiven, often adjusted. When Nick Dobbs or Jack Scott failed, innocent mothers died with their children. Bombs were set. Infants and small animals were torn apart. Acid was thrown on unsuspecting tourists. Grandparents mourned before closed caskets. And there was no one to apologise to, not even each other. Commander Dobbs had succumbed to a personal demon that held him, seduced him, that finally took him once and for all.

From inside a glassine evidence bag, Scott removed a honed, tapering spike given to him by Dr Chet Sanders, excised from the left lung of Mary Beth Dodson. He held it under the light. It was black, hardened over fire, sharp as a needle. He held it tightly in his hand, comparing it with the photograph of Elmer Janson's souvenir.

Rough estimates showed six inches of wood, but from a facsimile, critical detail was hard to discern. The boy's stick was worn, eaten away by years underground. Physically they were not exact analogues, but in his mind it was all the same.

'You will pay,' Zak Dorani had admonished Scott as he left the courthouse for the last time, fists manacled to his belt, his legs bound by chain.

Scott closed his lids, straining to recall the killer's voice, but the memory evaded him as he remembered the eyes, burning like cold empty lanterns, and just as a warmth licked against his wrist, jarring him from thought.

Blood was flowing, but Scott didn't feel pain.

He had worked the spike up into his palm.

SIXTEEN

After hours on a weekend, Georgetown was a scant thirty
minutes from Bethesda, Maryland, a straight shot down
Wisconsin Avenue through the upper northwest part of the
city.

It had been earlier in the evening that he had been struck
by an urge, and he felt restless, leaving his residence for a
brief interlude, just killing time by cruising the streets. These
days he was in pain, not excruciating, but a dull and episodic
throbbing that ran along his spine, giving him migraines, and
he knew they would pass if he kept distracted. He pulled
his car through the alley behind Zephyr's Bar and Grill on
Wisconsin Avenue, a shabby little dive five minutes from
Georgetown University.

The bar was a local landmark of sorts, and he knew it well,
having been a regular since the late 1960s. It was centrally
located in the city and well known for serving drinks to
minors. As he stepped from his car, he placed one hand
against the small of his back, then stretched while releasing
a satisfied yawn. The only light in the alley came from a naked
bulb which hung over the Zephyr's rear door, the feeble glow
too weak to illuminate much detail.

Standing in this ordinary light he was a plain and little man
who could have been anyone; an insurance salesman, a car
dealer, a clerk. His features were bland. He had an oval face
with a high forehead and receding hairline. What was left of

his fine brown hair he parted on the left, combed like an altar boy awaiting inspection.

Earlier in the evening he had been restless. Now the lateness of the hour took him by surprise and he felt tired to the bone, and released another deep yawn. When he opened the door to the passenger's side, the darkness remained, clinging to the alley like a sticky web, for the car's overhead lamp had been disconnected. And he stared woodenly at the young woman sprawled in the red leather seat. Her breathing was deep and laboured.

A silver Mercedes turned from a back street and moved slowly past the alley's entrance. Two older women in fur coats glanced his way, then averted their eyes as the man smiled. 'My kind of town,' he said with a nod, and he knew it well, all the paradoxes and refined illusion that fuelled this particular city. To him it was simply a place where it was easy to procure human flesh, night or day, that made no difference. You could romance it, pay for it, or take it by force. These were strictly personal choices that depended more on whim than on wisdom, for there were few rules in the nation's capital beyond *don't get caught*. By day, a land of monuments. By night, a city that swallowed life.

He reached in, dragging her from the car, then dropping her along the curb like a sack of stones. She moaned up at her assailant through a trance, her blue eyes rolling, her lids streaked with mascara, blinking shut with a heavy narcotic slumber. He pushed her closer against the curb, then kneeling down, manipulated her legs to remove her shoes.

'We're out of time,' he said absently, studying the treeline for headlights, but the woman could not hear. She had not known the cocktail she was drinking had been laced with succinylcholine, a powerful but tasteless muscle relaxant with hypnotic consequences.

It was a quick twenty paces from the alley to the sidewalk above, and in between there was a covered storm drain on a grassy knoll. He pulled the woman onto the grass, then bending over at the waist, removed the iron lid with a simple T-bar he carried in his belt. Placing a penlight between his teeth, he stuck his head through the opening to inspect the pit.

The beam struck concrete walls, failing to reach the bottom, and the corrosive smells of wet iron and stone filled his sinuses. The little man huffed, turning to examine her sprawling body, the dishevelled slacks and blouse, the torn stockings over bare feet. Without ceremony, he grabbed her beneath the arms, flipping her over, then dragging her, toes up.

He was supporting her weight, and her stocking feet left no visible mark in the coarse brown grass, and he dropped her again, fumbling at the small of his back with one hand.

With skilled precision he leaned her shoulders and head backward over the gaping darkness, exposing pale breasts and admiring the flow of her brown hair. Parting lids over helpless eyes flashed in his mind like a glassy blue stain.

'It's been fun,' he said, rubbing her neck where it strained, then grabbing a fist of hair he suddenly pulled her face towards his, and in one smooth motion, fired a single shot from a silenced pistol.

There was a dull clank as the bullet hit the concrete below. *Clank, clank.*

And her body followed through the darkness, falling freely through the air as the world went silent and still around him, the sounds of traffic failing, sirens dying, jets finding a void of quiet above his head, her body landing with a harsh thud.

He closed his eyes tight, standing there in the dim light, the shadows failing into darkness, the darkness failing into death.

'Yes,' he breathed hard, and the moisture from his lungs held like a pale cloud.

'Yes, yes, yes . . .'

And he flipped her shoes into the seamless dark, covering the drain again. The second and third shots had removed her dental forensics, and he knew time and sewer rodents would accomplish the rest.

He was happy now. He returned to his car.

With one hand on the wheel he coasted through the alley, attentive to rules of the road, slowing carefully for a blinking red light at the intersection of Wisconsin Avenue and Foxhall Road. A war-battered District of Columbia police car appeared, moving in his direction, and he gave a weary nod at a tired blue uniform.

Not that it mattered, but he drove a black BMW with red leather seats, and he snapped a cassette into the tape player while settling back for his midnight drive, finding the road for home. He fancied himself a cultured man, so he listened to things like Chopin's Nocturnes, which he had discovered resting on a babygrand next to a porcelain ballerina.

'Would you mind if I borrow one of your tapes?' he had asked of Diana Clayton on the night of March 31st, as he tested her bath water with an index finger, toying with her mind, her body and heart.

'No,' he quickly agreed, 'ask me nicely and I'll think it over.'

SEVENTEEN

Well after midnight a telephone was ringing.

A hand hovered in front of a television, moving over a footlocker that served as a coffee table, then lifting Mickey Mouse onto the bed. Francis Dale Rivers was watching what is known to cops throughout the Washington area as Midnight Mass, a local news show second to none in doom and shabby production. A commercial was coming up, so he let the phone ring while waiting to see if they previewed his announcement concerning the disappearance of Debra Patterson.

There had been five drug-related slayings, a report on a serial rape in Bethesda, a hit and run, two suicides, one bombing, three reported burglaries, and a replay of Bush's latest law and order speech. An average six-hour run. Rivers guessed a story about the Patterson kid had been bumped, even though he had stopped by the station to ask for their assistance.

'Yeah,' he answered, crunching an aspirin into Mickey's ear.

'Sergeant, my name is Scott,' said the voice. 'Commander Jack Scott, I'm with ViCAT in New York.'

'So that's your name.' Rivers smiled.

As Scott had requested, Captain Maxwell Drury had dispatched a helicopter to Rivers' house earlier in the evening in order to recover Elmer Janson's evidence. Scott carefully considered the nature of that intrusion, rubbing one hand through his hair, choosing his words thoughtfully.

'I'd like to thank you for the materials which you sent to my attention,' he said. 'I'm sorry for the delay, I'm looking forward to your cooperation.'

Rivers was immediately fascinated with the voice, it was mellow and urbane with a cultured enunciation, yet there was a hint of anger, like a steel hand in a velvet glove. 'My cooperation, Mr Scott?' he questioned sarcastically. 'I was cut out, I didn't know who I was dealing with or if I was even dealing. I kicked that stuff into the system to see what would fall out, and I guess that's you. Drury sent a chopper to my house and that's about all I know, what's your badge number?'

Scott considered the suspicious tone. 'One,' he said.

'Just routine,' Rivers offered, 'always like to know who I'm talking with. That would be Badge No. One, NSA ViCAT, USA,' he repeated.

'That's correct, do you require verification?'

'Negative,' Rivers spat quickly. 'So what winds your clock, Mr Scott, what can I do for you?'

Scott paused. 'Perhaps a great deal, or perhaps nothing at all, but I like your style, Frank. Could I ask a few questions?'

'Sure,' he baited, leaning back across his bed. 'Fire away, but you don't have to stroke me first.'

'Am I interrupting anything?'

'No dates, no ball game, a rather slow Friday night. I was just doing a little research and writing up an APB for one Debra Patterson, a local kid about sixteen years old.'

'What?' Scott hissed. 'A missing child, why wasn't I informed . . .'

Rivers listened intently to his tone, he could sense the glove coming off.

'. . . I asked to be kept posted on any wrinkle.'

'Well, I'm sure I wouldn't know, Mr Scott, might be you're asking the wrong bureaucrat. But if you want my opinion, this is a real sweet-looking kid, and some Mook could be dressing her down right now. It won't be on the wire for another twenty-four hours. Rules, paperwork, the usual crap, you know the drill.'

'I know the drill,' Scott lamented.

'Her parents are going nuts, I don't blame them. Why don't you lend a hand, I mean, Badge One and all, it's very impressive.'

'All right, Frank,' Scott chipped at the sarcasm. 'I'll see what I can do. So what's your story, what winds your recalcitrant ticker?'

'Mine?' Rivers chuckled. 'Chevrolet and applepie, sounds like you've been reading my sheets.'

'Every word, an interesting profile,' he stated flatly.

'Well, nothing special in there, but I really hate being treated like a weak-kneed sister to some old billiard, so why don't you tell me what you need, maybe we can work something out . . .'

'Jack.'

Rivers did not respond.

'Is Captain Drury the old billiard?' Scott smiled.

No response.

'Frank, we've got a serious police apprehension problem and I need your help, I apologise if we stepped on any toes.'

Rivers pulled himself forward on his elbows. 'Well, I appreciate that, Scott, cause you're Bigfoot. Listen, sure as hell burns I'd like to help with the Claytons, but do you have assignment authority?'

'At the highest level,' he said, 'in the interest of national security.'

'Yeah, yeah, that's not what I mean, Jack. When you duck, who gets hit by the shit?'

Scott pushed off his desk and settled back in his chair. There was something brutally honest, almost severe, about Frank Rivers. 'My people come before my career, I've told that to three presidents.'

'Interesting,' Rivers responded absently. 'Tell me something, are you a shrink, that's been the talk for years, you know, that NSA Enforcement is run by a bunch of shrinks.'

'I have a degree in psychology. A shrink has an MD and hands out pills, I'm a cop.'

'I like that,' he chuckled, 'how can I help?'

'Let's start with the Claytons, what else do you know about the killings?'

'Just what I hear, plus I conducted a few field interviews, I'll bet they're on your desk right now. I was one of the first

161

at the scene, just about the cruellest case ever. I heard you guys were called when the investigation stalled out, the County was handling it, that was a big mistake.'

'Why?'

'They're like McGruff the crime dog, all warm and fuzzy at home, but in the field, forget it. The severity of this case was too important. Did you know Drury only took over as an advisor at the request of the Governor and then got stuck with the investigation?'

'I figured as much. Tell me about Elmer Janson, how did you know to track him down?'

'Just curiosity, I read about his finding bones in the local paper, got a copy of the postmortem, and went to see for myself. I also read a report on the territorial imperative of the series killer a few years back, and based on that, Elmer's little discovery bothered me. It's within a mile of the Clayton place, but I guess you knew.'

'Yes I did. And Elmer gave you the evidence?'

'That's affirmative. He's quite a kid. So what do you make of it?'

Scott paused. 'What's your theory?' he asked.

'Hell, I don't know, but we got something. Based on the territorial imperative I was thinking we might have a family of wackos handing down their expertise from generation to generation, maybe the guy who buried that child is the great-grandfather of the Claytons' killer. How's that for a start?'

'Well, it's definitely murder-one,' Scott said provocatively.

'I thought so too, Jack, that child had been tortured, I've seen sticks like that in Southeast Asia. You know it's interesting, during the Civil War this town was swarming with troops while some sickoid was getting his rocks off hurting little kids. Humanity sucks, I've always believed that.'

Scott let the man talk, agreeing when he could, building a foundation for trust and common ground. Rivers was a serious man, that much was clear. He also cloaked himself in the demeanour of the common man to shield his insight, and there was no doubt in Scott's mind that the classic dagger was close behind. That unassuming diamond in the rough bit had CIA training stamped all over it.

'Frank,' Scott interrupted him, mustering a voice of reserved authority.

'Yeah?'

'The grave Elmer found is modern, post Civil War, your Medical Examiner is sleep walking.'

'What?' his voice fell short of a cry. 'You better beam up, Scotty, you need mission control.'

Scott heard him chuckle.

'The body found by Elmer Janson and the Clayton killings are the work of the same man,' Scott stated in a more formal tone.

'Nope,' Rivers spat with contempt, 'that's crazy talk.'

'Is it?' Scott asked quietly.

Rivers carefully considered the claim, the grave found by Elmer Janson was close to becoming a bag of dust. 'Dr Talbard who worked the bones is a good ME, Jack, I've seen better but I doubt he'd miss something like that.'

'He missed.'

'Give me some evidence,' he demanded.

'Fair enough,' Scott offered calmly. 'Answer me one question, and if I'm wrong I'll buy you tickets to a ball game.'

'That's a deal.' Rivers smiled, lying back down across his bed. 'How about the World Seriousness?'

'Frank, you turned in a piece of wood to Max Drury, looked akin to a black chopstick?'

'That's right.'

'And you spent some time with this boy who found the grave?'

'I'm a pretty fair detective.'

'I have no doubt, so be straight with me, Frank. A great deal depends on this.' He was staring at his wall, into Diana Clayton's lifeless eyes, trying to fend off guilt with his intellect.

'I'll be straight,' he promised.

Scott took a breath. 'There are at least nine more of these sticks, but maybe twelve,' Scott stated coldly. And the resulting silence was chilling.

Bile quickly filled Scott's throat, he mixed it with a splash of cold coffee and swallowed hard. 'Isn't that correct, Frank?' he asked, clearing phlegm from his throat.

'Holy Christ!' he cried with a painful excitement, hopping from his bed, lifting Elmer's paper bag then shaking the contents. Scott waited for the excitement to pass, and Rivers sat nervously on the edge of his bed. 'There's no way you could have known that, I've withheld the evidence . . .' he started to say, catching his words, then closing his eyes.

'Yes you did, Rivers,' Scott said coldly, 'and you made yourself suspect in the process, so why did you do it?'

Rivers paused, knowing if Scott wanted to file papers, then his State career was over, and he had just started to figure it was time for a change anyway, that the job was growing stale, when Scott spoke up.

'I don't care, Frank, but it's not a good practice.So why did you do it?'

'Just a precaution,' he answered slowly. 'I don't like having my cases jumped, and down here it's routine, politics all the damn time. But how the hell did you know?'

'I think I've arrested the same killer before, but I'm still waiting on evidence. Between you and me I'm running on empty except for the help you've supplied.'

'But how could that be?' Rivers charged. 'This is getting weird, that body was almost dust, ancient, and the coin . . .'

'I do have my doubts,' Scott confessed, cutting him off. 'I'm guessing it's the same man.'

'And he killed the Claytons?'

'Possible.'

'God, how long has this guy been killing, what's his name?' His voice was starting to race and Rivers felt his body charge with adrenaline. 'Hey, what did he do to those little girls, Jack?'

'Frank,' Scott said cautiously, 'would you like to work with me on this case?'

'Sure,' Rivers stated. 'What are these sticks about, what a slimy bastard, I'm going to break him apart . . .'

'No you are not, Sergeant,' Scott spoke quickly. 'If you want in, then we have some ground rules.'

'Anything,' he promised vaguely.

'First, you answer only to me,' Scott said, biting off each word with precision. 'Second, you do not discuss this case without my authorisation. Third, if you cause a problem, it's over – no second chances.'

'If that's it, you've got yourself a deal, Commander, let's get started,' he spat out casually.

Scott contemplated his situation. 'I'm going to start processing papers to assign you to us on an interagency request, what we call a Multi Agency Investigative Team, you'll still carry your State badge with our ID. Now, this is important . . .'

'I'm listening,' Rivers was taking notes.

'Call Captain Drury at home, wake him up if necessary, tell him I told you to. Don't discuss the case, just tell him to dispatch two officers to the home of Elmer Janson for surveillance. Men you trust, you pick the officers and tell Drury.'

'Oh God, are they in danger?' Rivers exclaimed, images of a beautiful young mother and a lonely little boy tore through his mind.

There was a blistered silence.

'You answer me, Scott!'

'No, Frank,' he corrected quietly, 'you answer to me.'

Rivers dropped his head into his hand. 'Right,' he sighed, staring indignantly at Mickey's puss.

'Is Mrs Janson still married?' Scott asked. 'Is her husband at home?'

Frank bit his lip, 'Shit, I don't know, now that you mention it, the local paper said he was in Europe, they invited me to stay for dinner. Jack . . .'

'This is just a precaution, I don't think our man will hit a family again this soon, he'll go after single targets, what we call a quick fix.'

'Christ!' Rivers spat. 'Then what about Elmer Janson, the kid's a real player, he . . .'

'He'd require too much planing for the killer, at least for the time being, but they *would* be a likely target.'

'But how would our man know?' Rivers pondered.

'You said you read Elmer's story in the newspaper, and you're not the only subscriber, Frank. There are other case elements as well, so just pick two good men, have Drury assign them. Now according to your jacket you've lived near the area most of your life, how long?'

'I'm thirty-eight, my folks moved here when I was in eighth grade, so twenty-four years on and off, why?'

'Does anyone know the local history better than you?'

'Only one person I know of, but there's a local historical society . . .'

'No!' Scott blurted. 'Stay away from them, that's important, and stay clear of preservationists.'

'Why, what's this about?'

'We'll get to that in the morning, I just don't want second-hand history from an egghead dropping nose hairs in books. How long has your friend lived there?'

'Forever, he was born here, Jack. Personally we're very close and he's also my landlord, a fourth-generation Mary-lander. He lives in Cabin John, that's a town real close by.'

Scott opened a file and circled the name on the Bethesda map. 'We're going to need his help, give him a call.' Scott knew the man was trustworthy, anyone who could get close to Frank Rivers would have to be, by definition, quiet as a lump.

'Anything,' he said.

'Good, I appreciate that, Frank. Now tell me about Debra Patterson, you said you needed an assist.'

Rivers gave Scott the details, as much as he knew. 'Last seen in her car headed for the store, I need an air search and I don't have the clout.'

'But I'll bet you know a decent pilot?'

'Affirmative, damn good, three tours in air cavalry, name's Steve Adare, he's a State boy, why, he could find a tick in a . . .'

'Ask Drury to get that man airborne, my orders.'

'You're kidding?' Rivers laughed. 'Easy as that, order Mad Max to . . .'

'Be nice about it, Frank, that old billiard is a dear friend of mine.'

'Affirmative,' he said quietly.

'And Frank,' Scott warned, 'at all times try to remember that the man we're hunting knows exactly what he's doing, for all practical purposes he's as sane as you or I, and he's real clever.'

'Who is he, Jack, what's the fucker's name?'

'Doesn't matter, like I said, he's smart, changes identities like you or I change socks. But if you can follow orders, we'll get him, are we on the same wavelength?'

'Yes sir, but I don't get it,' Rivers questioned. 'Why didn't someone keep an eye on this bastard, how the hell did he get away?'

Scott closed pale lids over eyes that had grown dark and bloodshot, the eyes of an older man who had brooded long after normal people were asleep.

Frank Rivers understood the silence. 'So you pooched the tiger, Jack, everybody does at some time, forget I asked.'

Scott wanted to comply, he wanted to forget, he wanted to go back in time so forgetting wasn't necessary.

'I thought he was dead, Frank, and that's just what he wanted me to think. I'm staring at his obituary right now, Zachariah Leslie Dorani, dead at the age of thirty-three, and that was back in 1966. I should have examined the body before the cremation.'

As the call was terminated, Scott placed the obit under *Case Similarities* and reached back into the file marked *Children's Room*.

He felt a shiver. He felt cold to the marrow.

Leslie's bedroom overlooked the front lawn and street, two windows large enough to allow a full blast of morning sun. Scott checked the analysis report. The room and front of the house faced due east.

In another shot Leslie Clayton sat in a white wicker chair,

167

dressed in a pastel flowered blouse with charcoal grey slacks, ready for school. A blue denim totebag rested against the chair. He cross-checked the forensics report.

Although only fibres remained, she had been left tied in the chair for hours after death, until rigor mortis had begun to set in, accounting for her rigid posture. The rope was gone, but from lacerations and bruises it was certain the killer had left the moribund child bound from the neck, arms and back for over two hours. Her eyelids had been held open until her body stiffened, and Scott felt his eyes tear, he was thankful death had been instantaneous.

He recorded a notation: 'Had the killer left the house and returned? When did he place the dead child in front of the window?'

The cause of death was nearly identical to that of Diana Clayton, a single shot, with the exception of the wound channel. Scanning the report, he saw the bullet had punctured the hard palate inside the oral cavity, exiting at the top of the child's cranium. Only trace elements of the slug had been recovered. Notation: 'How did killer trap and capture the bullet?'

He placed the photo alongside the last, building out from the left. The third was a wide-angle of the room showing the lifeless bodies of both children, sitting in separate chairs, Leslie at the window; Kimberly positioned just behind at her sister's dressing table, seeming to look out towards the street. She was partially dressed and appeared to be untying her hair, her arms suspended in death.

Cross-referencing, she had been bound in a similar manner until her body stiffened, and knowing that he would live with this image for how long he didn't know, Scott could not bring himself to study the picture too closely. Words on a page, safer, antiseptic.

Kimberly had not been shot. Cause of death was listed as 'sequential multiple organ failure', compound trauma resulting from rapid 'acceleration-deceleration movement of the head'. When death is not instantaneous, Scott knew, the body reacts to acute shock by shutting down organ functions.

The most common cause is a swelling of the brain against the tight skull case, the type of trauma most often seen in automobile accident victims. The child's brain had literally bounced within the cranium case, causing massive swelling, haemorrhaging and death. The image did not reflect the face of a little girl.

Gently, Scott tacked each exposure into a godless matrix, and closed his eyes, no longer able to concentrate, so he did not notice Daniel Flores standing silently in the doorway. The horror of the wall had reached out and touched the young agent. Flores cleared his throat.

'I'm sorry to disturb you, sir,' he said, shifting his gaze towards the tops of his wingtips. Scott didn't respond, but fumbled through his drawers, lighting a match. Harsh smoke, old and stale, burned in his lungs as he leaned back in his chair, back into the night.

'What is it, Daniel?' he asked, sightless, rubbing fingers into tired eyes. He glanced at his watch, it was 1:46 a.m., the night had ascended into Saturday morning.

'Dr Charles McQuade wired into system one, the computer automatically authorised his entry, so I thought it might be important. I tried to keep him on line, but he ended transmission.'

The young agent stepped forward, handing Scott a sheet from the laser printer along with a file, which the Commander then laid across his desk, seeing nothing but a wasteland of white, characters of ink marching in tight little lines.

'That's the report on Mrs Janson you requested, is there anything else I can do?' Flores asked with concern.

'No, no thank you, Daniel, what time does your shift end?'

'In an hour, but I'll still be fresh if you need me.'

'Has Brennon returned?' Scott asked without looking up.

'No, sir, he just radioed to say he's on his way.'

'I want to see him the moment he's back, tell him it's urgent.'

'Yes sir,' Flores said as he closed the door softly behind him.

* * *

Tricks of time did not evade Dr Charles McQuade.

'So what's worse,' Scott asked aloud, hesitating at the report. 'A child afraid of the dark or a cop afraid of the light?' With a hand that ached with age, he lifted the printout from his desk.

Black female. Time of death: spring/summer 1958. Age: twelve years. Cause of death: small, critical punctures of cranium. Material Evidence: Rope fibres. Materials Postmortem: traces CaO, calcium oxide, commonly known as lime. Traces of mercuric acid.

Scott nodded thoughtfully. He knew first hand the caustic effects lime could have, and working in combination, acid would have speeded the decomposition process until the ground was smoking, bubbling in a corrosive brine that would rend flesh from bone, that in turn would dissolve bone back into its organic elements. With anger, he lifted the file marked *Jennifer Doe* and removed a photograph of the burial site during excavation, examining this closely, then checking against a report from the U.S. Soil and Conservation Service.

'Maryland substrate,' he was reading aloud, 'a fine-grained earth . . . composed chiefly of hydrous aluminium silicate materials.' They had been produced through the millennia by the breaking down of rocks, mineral and stone. The soil of the Potomac River Valley was a fine reddish clay, a hard combination of sandstone and granite, so pliable and dense it held rainwater like a tub. And the photograph showed a pit, a hollow beneath the blacktop that held a good six inches of rain and was unable to drain. Scott immediately concluded a refined knowledge was involved in disposal, the killer had intentionally dug an earthen pool so that the victim's body would be submerged, soaking for years in a bath of vitriol. He now understood why the remains appeared to have been interred over a century ago, they were lucky anything was left.

With a stirring rage, he grabbed the file marked *Zak* off his desk, slapping the summaries inside, and Scott thought about the region, if it was possible that this killer had been operating that far south, and that somehow, they had never known. Even after three decades he could recite the case from memory, Dobbs had officially ended the pursuit, his initials were in the upper corner of the file, a faded signatory attesting to failure: *Case Closed, September 14th 1960.*

And Scott considered the possibility that he was chasing old ghosts on a futile and endless run backward through his own worst imaginings; that the Claytons were merely a coincidence, that their deaths were not his fault. This he wanted to believe, that he was simply falling apart with the agent's disease and that such delusions were merely a symptom.

But his gut told him differently, registering cold spasms, his heart pounding the human spirit from his body. He leaned forward in his chair, pushing the cone of light against the background on Elmer Janson, and the data forced sweat to pop into beads on his forehead.

The boy's father was dead, his mother had never remarried, and that alone made them the most enticing of prey to Zachariah. His speciality was single mothers, the sex of a child made no difference. Scott's mind drifted absently as he leaned forward, grabbing the file forcefully.

On the outside of the old jacket he punched downward with a rubber stamp, slick with red ink, then routinely initialled the upper right corner:

CASE ACTIVE.

EIGHTEEN

BETHESDA, MARYLAND

'What that woman *really* needs,' the manicurist had said under her breath, 'is a plastic surgeon.' And although it wasn't completely untrue, Irma Kiernan, who knew the remark was directed at her, thought it unfair. Or at least uncalled for. But that was early on in the day. Throughout the afternoon and well into the night, she had considered this haunting insult and was starting to agree.

It was now after midnight. Now Irma sat at her first floor bedroom window, combing short-cropped hair, feeling like some old and rejected Cinderella. She studied herself in a hand-held mirror, trying to imagine a young and shapely woman, but with a doctor's effort. A pinch here, a tuck there, a bit of liposuction, maybe an implant. What Irma Kiernan desired was beauty, to be in demand by the best of gentlemen. But plastic surgeon or not, at age fifty-four, she knew that no coachman would be bringing a prince to her door.

All through the day, what she had on her mind was seduction, pure and simple, not an exacting plan, but more of an intensified and concentrated effort. She had spent the entire morning at Jean Claude's Beauty Salon in Bethesda, Maryland, where she had ordered the works. Hair, nails, facial and wax. Back to the mirror.

The grey was now gone, replaced by a muted brown with a style that was meant to lend a modern pageboy look, more youthful in appearance, almost perky. Yet the hair kept curling up at the ends and taking on a life of its own, while the bangs had begun to frizz. Irma tried parting it in the middle, but it looked like a sick animal was sleeping on her head. She tried curling the ends back under, they popped like rows of corn. No matter how she tried, the image in her hand did not even loosely resemble the slim woman of regal bearing and proud bone structure which had been her mother, though Irma had once been sure that the girl in her would grow into such a handsome woman. Her mother's hair had been a sweet golden brown, soft and silky, framing eyes that were a robin's egg blue, and this was the truth the woman in the mirror faced daily.

'I'm not like her,' she said aloud. And she was correct. Irma Kiernan was just short and plain, bones bland, with a figure befitting a baker's wife. Daily she fought weight and lost, and she peered deeply into the glass, applying a gentle dusting to the lines across her brow. Her skin looked tired, even after a facial, and she imagined the wrinkles that time would soon deliver. That was it, *time*, she thought. Time was running out. Her hands began to tremble as she quickly shoved the glass into a bureau drawer, shutting out the image that mocked at her.

Growing old was Irma's worst fear. But growing old, alone, was an absolute terror.

Deep into the night, she applied two drops of Heavenly Lace behind each ear, and then directly on to her pillow, a sweet lilac perfume which she had purchased at Jean Claudes that morning. A man would soon be coming for her, and she had prepared well, every detail down to the choice of sheets, which were a pale rose-coloured satin. Her mission in life was to retain a vestige of her youth while proving herself fit for marriage.

Her body trembled.

Irma Kiernan saw headlights approaching. He was coming home. The wait was finally over.

His name was Jeffery L. Dorn.

And the fact that he sometimes stayed out until the early morning hours while Irma waited, and the fact that they

173

maintained separate lives, plus the fact that he would rather sleep alone than with a woman; all of these things didn't bother Kiernan so much as the reasons.

Which were not his fault.

Jeff Dorn was in great physical pain, as well as suffering from emotional scars, which Irma knew was not uncommon for a decorated hero of such tremendous substance. In 1951, as a young man serving in the Korean War, he had received a blow to the back that had all but disabled him, and although it was true that there were no outward physical signs, at the age of fifty-five, the old and lasting injuries prevented Jeff from living any kind of normal existence. Because of severe and chronic pain, he was unable to work. He could not concentrate more than a few hours at a spell without suffering excruciating muscle spasms along his spine; spasms severe enough to steal his breath.

While Irma never really did understand what triggered these awful spikes of pain, this price for his heroic service was something which, over the years, they both had come to accept and share. And that price was quite high.

As Irma understood the event, Jeff had charged directly into an enemy bunker in order to save the lives of his men, who were pinned down in a fire-fight and running out of ammunition with no hopes of reinforcement. In one decisive moment, carrying a grenade in each hand, Dorn flung himself into the concrete shell. Although he was able to climb back out before the explosion, avoiding the deadly metal shrapnel, the resulting blasts were so powerful they caught him with a violent force while he was running for his life; blowing him head over heels, breaking his back in several places and crushing his spine in one. Although he was later credited with saving the lives of many American boys, and was later honoured with an officer's rank, it was now clear to the woman that only part of him had ever come home. Only part of him survived.

The lack of intimacy between them was the least of it, she thought. At times Dorn's pain was so excruciating that he couldn't eat or even walk. And this was just physical. The woman could only imagine what the psychic trauma was like.

It was the rarest of nights when Jeff was able to sleep without an episode waking him, sending him off into an agonised world of quiet despair. There were nights when he woke in such terror that from another room she would hear the screams produced by the terrible images that came to him in dreams. Then he would describe these in detail so that Irma might understand, as for days after he would be a changed man.

Cold. Detached. Quiet.

Irma Kiernan feared the nightmares worse than he did.

Since Dorn's injuries prevented him from being the family breadwinner, a role which Irma knew he craved, she wilfully chose to earn the household income; though at times she feared this was depriving him of his self-esteem, a silly sense of manliness which she didn't quite understand.

'Life has cheated us for my bravery,' Dorn was fond of telling her, while Irma considered quite the opposite to be true. Though not perfect, their lives were rich for having found each other, and they had also been blessed by Irma's abilities, which neither took for granted in a suburb of Washington renowned for its expensive lifestyle.

Irma Kiernan was a nutritionist by profession and worked for the Montgomery County School System, earning a wage of better than fifty thousand a year, nearly twice the national average for such employment. So her income allowed them a few little extra pleasures which they would have ordinarily been denied. Like visits to Jean Claudes. Irma thought back as she watched his headlights flooding into the driveway.

Though the night had been riddled with problems, the day had begun with great promise.

Irma Kiernan's office was located in the administrative wing of the Westwood Elementary School, and although there were no classes or meals to supervise in the county on Friday, April 8th, she had stopped by on the way home from Jean Claudes to collect a score of dietary plans, as well as to collect her thoughts. As she strolled the halls she had received several compliments from her fellow workers over her new and youthful appearance.

Irma was grateful for the admiration and tickled that she had been so daring, placing her sinfully out of character with herself. It had been other women who had egged her on, and she had spent the entire day pursuing her expectations. By the time she left school, she felt beautiful and sexy, longing for the man who shared her life and loved her, and her alone. As a woman, Irma Kiernan wanted so much to give, but more than that, she wanted to be taken.

It was a short walk home from her office and she could feel her pageboy haircut tickling the back of her neck as she put a youthful bounce into her step, turning onto the flagstone walkway down into Wooded Acres. It was warm for April, much warmer than she remembered from previous years, and she gingerly patted the makeup on her brow with a tissue to keep fresh. Around her, cherry blossoms and dogwood trees were beginning to bloom, and the air carried a sweet and fragrant almost magical scent.

The Kiernan house was a two-storey colonial, and as she approached she noticed that the white exterior was in need of some paint, as were the red shutters on the upstairs dormer windows. These, more than others, were badly peeling, and in her mind she was considering the family budget as she paused at the mailbox out front, seeing that the contents had not been collected. With nimble experience she thumbed through a fist of envelopes, noticing mostly bills, and decided that the front door could also use a fresh coat. She stopped, studying neighbouring homes. In comparison, their house was beginning to look like an eyesore, so she forced her mind from unpleasant thoughts and back to the mail, heading again for the front stoop.

There was a card in a plain envelope addressed to Jeff, lacking a return address, and she puzzled at this, then placed it on top. There was an overdue notice from EuroCoupe on his automotive service contract, she placed this on the bottom.

She was just fumbling in her purse for her house key as the front door swung wide.

'Hi, Sweetheart,' she smiled, straightening her posture and pushing her shoulders back to give her chest a little extra. But there was no answer.

Without a word Jeff Dorn had opened the door, then walked back to his easy chair in the living room and sat down. His eyes were fixed and unfocused, his face seemed flushed and waxen.

'Oh, Honey,' she cried, dropping her briefcase and purse, propping the mail between them, then running through the hallway to stand by his side. 'It's your back, isn't it? Oh, let me help.' Gently, Irma leaned him forward, propping a pillow low, just above his belt-line.

Still no response.

She was now reaching to touch his forehead, to check his temperature, when the little man suddenly grabbed her arm forcefully with a twist. 'How many times,' he mouthed, closing his eyes, 'how many times have we decided to leave the air-conditioning set at no more than seventy-five degrees?'

To Irma, the man's teeth seemed clenched with pain.

'Oh, Sweetheart,' she sighed, 'I'm so sorry. I thought you were going to be out all day, and the electric bills are just killing us. I forgot, I'm sorry . . .'

Dorn looked on vacantly as her voice trailed off, he was pausing for effect. 'Irma,' he whispered, and his voice became soft like a prayer. His head was stationary, his dull brown eyes glaring in the half-light of closed draperies.

'Yes, Hun, I'm here,' she comforted, stroking his head as if he were disoriented.

'Irma,' he said, 'you must remember, it's the pain, I can't stand the heat for very long . . .' and his voice tapered off as he twisted in his seat, seemingly fighting a spasm in his back. The woman looked on in helpless desperation and was about to speak when Dorn held a finger up for silence.

'Have you changed your mind about us?' he asked quietly. 'I'll understand, but you should be truthful with me, Irma, be truthful.'

177

And for the first time, Dorn's eyes suddenly locked onto her, Irma Kiernan, the woman who dreamed of fairytale knights and princes who rescued their maidens. She knew better than to ask why he had not simply adjusted the thermostat to a cooler setting, a man like Jeffery Dorn was simply too proud to surrender to his own pain.

'He must have thought I had purposely wanted the house to get hot, that I was trying to drive him away,' she thought sadly, unable to look into his eyes. 'It's so hard for him to admit I'm the breadwinner, he doesn't feel in control.' Guilt instantly consumed her and her eyes began to well and tear.

'Oh, Honey, I do love you!' she cried suddenly. 'Nothing will change that!' She started to weep, wrapping her arms around his neck.

He did not respond.

'This flare-up is my fault,' she admitted with a shaky voice, and through all of her efforts the little retired army colonel just looked up at her from his chair and blinked feebly.

'Oh, Sweetheart, do you want me to get your medication?' she asked nervously, and it was thirty seconds before Dorn broke the silence of suffering.

'No, no.' He exhaled. 'It's passing.' Then he stroked her lightly on the thin flesh inside her left arm and said, 'I just wasn't sure you wanted me any more.'

The worn and worried dietitian walked over to adjust the thermostat in the hallway, promising herself, punishing herself, that she would never be careless again, when she remembered the compliments at school; when she remembered her womanly role as seductress and lover. A rather shy mistress, Irma Kiernan summoned her courage and slowly, suggestively, unbuttoned her blouse. She removed her bra, quickly returning to his side, and nearly stumbling as she walked.

Dorn appeared unable to see as she gently pulled his tortured face between naked breasts, giving a squeeze, then releasing him.

'Do you notice anything different?' she said perkily, using her most girlish voice and teasing her hair with one hand.

'Different,' echoed Colonel Jeffery Dorn. 'Very nice, you've had your hair done. It's . . . becoming!'

Irma smiled warmly, walking her fingers across his shoulders as he clutched his hands around her waist, delivering a limp embrace. It was a non-response. Kiernan's jaw tightened until her whole face and neck trembled with fear of rejection.

This was a very minor behaviour, what Dorn called *A Tell*. He had planned for it, had waited for it, just hours before when he had set the thermostat in anticipation of her arrival. As he felt her body quiver, he wondered if she had bothered to plan anything for dinner, a trip to the beauty parlour could mean she was expecting an evening out.

'I missed you, Honey,' Dorn said, pulling her closer, tightening his grip, and she sighed with relief, feeling at ease for the first time all day. 'It was all I could do to just go downtown and get my uniform from the cleaners.'

But the woman heard only a meaningless patter as she revelled in his voice, for it was gentle and loving and kind. Through his touch Irma Kiernan had entered the sanctuary of her secret world where she was beautiful, and filled with life, and married.

'Well, Irma, tell me about school,' he demanded for the second time.

And she obeyed.

Earlier in the night, Irma was thinking a romantic evening on the town would have been in order. Now she was just thankful to be home with him.

It was clear from his attentiveness that the painful spasms were subsiding, and he had taken his pain medication before dinner, ten milligrams of the synthetic morphine Percodan. As Irma scrubbed at the kitchen sink, her mind wandered, and she thought about how his day must have been. Difficult, she decided. Jeff had picked up his uniform from the cleaners, a uniform which he only wore on special functions, and she knew that he missed the routine of being on active duty. For a passing moment she wondered why the Veterans Administration could not do more to help him.

'God knows,' she said aloud, 'it's all I can do to pay the medical bills and coax him into swallowing his medication.'

There was a problem there. According to Dorn, the pills made him feel drowsy, and he did not like the light-headedness that they produced, affecting his ability to concentrate. Irma, who was practical when pushed, knew there was no other choice, and her efforts to force him into swallowing usually prevailed. After seven years she'd lost count of the number of specialists he had been to, and each said nothing else could be done. 'The bravest man I'll ever know.' She smiled warmly, remembering how she had once demanded to speak directly to his doctors. But Colonel Jeffery Dorn wouldn't condone interference.

'Irma,' he had said, and she could still hear his words, 'a soldier's pain is a personal cross, to be borne alone and with pride.' While she admitted she understood very little about men like him, warriors and heroes, it just didn't seem fair. And she stood at the sink, hesitating, wondering if she should scrap an entire portion of meatloaf, when she remembered an earlier spat.

Meatloaf dried out quickly, then tasted like sawdust, she recalled, and she scraped the serving plate clean, poking the leftovers into the grinder, then hitting the switch.

'It's the Percodan,' she spat angrily, 'it just wrecks his appetite!' While Dorn had never admitted this, the woman knew it was true, for all through dinner he had just played with his food to keep her company. And it hurt to see him pushing potatoes and meat and carrots around his plate, while fighting to keep a straight posture.

'*Pain management*, that's what the doctors had said,' she muttered to herself while her man dozed in the living-room. She could hear the canned laughter of a sitcom on TV, but knew he wasn't watching. When Jeff hurt this bad the set was just a distracting flicker.

Irma's mission in life was to help him find comfort, and

she truly accepted him for who he was, a badly injured hero whose life was lived mostly in the past.

By eight o'clock she had finished the dishes. By nine she had reviewed the County grocery bill and prepared most of the week's menus. She didn't need her watch, she could tell time by the theme from MASH, which Jeff always let play at high volume.

Even after seasons of reruns it was the one show he would not miss, and Irma knew that making comic theatre from a tragic period in his life helped to soothe painful memories. She rose from her place at the dining room table, turned off the overhead light and walked towards his chair.

'Can I get you something cold to drink, Sweetheart?' she asked from behind, holding the corners of the large buff recliner, peering down to see if he was awake.

The little man, his body stationary, reached with his left hand up over his shoulder to pat her wrist. 'No thank you, Honey,' he said absently, his eyes intent on the screen. 'Grab a seat.'

Irma returned to the dining room, fetched a hard wooden chair with a straight back, and dutifully placed it at the Colonel's right. As she sat, waiting until a commercial to ask if the medication was working, she studied him.

'Jeff Dorn,' she thought, 'with the dark and radiant eyes, the strong chin and proud posture, you are my champion. You are not just any man, you are mine, like it nor not, for better or for worse . . .' And she began to giggle like a schoolgirl.

'Stop!' Dorn said tonelessly, lifting his right arm. Irma quickly covered her mouth, feeling the laughter bubble through her fingers, as the cool air circulated, while the slapstick surgeons of the Korean War produced comic theatre.

That was the best part of the night.

Every few minutes Jeff's eyes would sparkle and he would point with an index finger at the screen. And she thought about asking, again, if they could sleep in the same bed, just for a night, playing with that thought until the show was over.

She decided not.

The answer was always the same.

Her turning in bed would cause spasms, robbing him of sleep on those rare nights when he fell naturally into a slumber. Most of the time, when he could not sleep, Jeff feared that she would be the one deprived. He was always thinking of her. Jeffery Dorn had spent his entire life thinking of others first, and as far as Irma knew, in 1951, it had nearly killed him.

She went to bed early, somnolent and tossing, chasing frantic dreams of old age through the night. She had wanted to make love, to be touched, fondled, caressed, and held; for them to mingle and sweat in each other's arms until their bodies and breath and smell were one. Yet she understood the painful limitations which bound him.

In a fit of desire Irma Kiernan woke sometime during the night, part of a sordid parade marching in step to the national anthem, a brassy chorus rising from the television downstairs. The late-late show had ended, and already Jeff wandered through the house alone, staying awake to prevent his nightmares.

She heard the garage door open and his car pull away.

Irma Kiernan feared the dreams more than he did.

At 1:12 a.m., some forty miles to the north, Detective Sergeant Rivers was also considering the unusual heat wave while thinking about sex. He couldn't even remember the last time he had been seriously attracted to a woman, beyond some transient physical need.

But Jessica Janson, he thought, she was a much different item. Her figure was as genuine as her manner, which was warm and maternal in a way he had seldom seen. The job, he reasoned; most of the women he met in the line of duty were hard-bitten characters, even nasty, their demeanour like a cold shower.

For Rivers, matters of the heart produced memories instead of dates, and the warm, humid night quickly brought to mind the lovely vision of a fragrant young woman by the name of

Tammy McCain, a highly educated and sensuous research scientist whom he had known since her days as a tomboy. He smiled. She looked very much like Jessica Janson, he thought with intimate knowledge; her hair was a shiny dark blonde, her eyes a knowing and deadly green, while her figure curved and cushioned in all the right places.

As he remembered, the warming weather had started it all, for the shoes had come off first, after which he removed his shirt. And while he had been thinking of how to delicately romance her, Tammy suddenly appeared with a mischievous giggle in her voice, dragging his twin mattress out into the moonlight.

Once, Frank Rivers thought they would marry, but their careers had interfered and they drifted apart. With a smile on his lips he was sitting outside in the darkness. A small grey tabby strutted and rubbed against his back, and Rivers fluttered his fingers over the soft fur.

One short month ago there had been but two of these little monsters, now he counted seven, all lapping away at the little round cans which he had opened. They were feral, ever vigilant and ever hungry.

His favourite was an old bruiser of an orange tabby who had a notch missing from his right ear, a big old tom of a cat with a heavyweight's constitution. This animal had finished off his last few bites, and the detective sat on his front stoop almost eyeball to eyeball with the distrustful stranger. The cat was watching him lick a cigar, rolling it against his tongue, then take a clean bite off the end.

'It's like this,' he spat, 'one more can and you'll own me.' He dropped the cigar into his mouth and lit up with a smooth stroke, while the orange tabby sat parked like a battered hydrant, staring up at him with owlish eyes. The grey female had curled against his leg.

Without street lights and with an overcast sky, the little house sat on a gentle rise in a pitch-black open field. After speaking with Jack Scott, Rivers had turned off the lights and taken up a position outside. He liked it dark, darkness helped him think, and except for the contented purring of his grey companion, it was quiet as death. He could feel his eyeballs swelling to absorb what little line and form were visible in the glow of his cigar.

There wasn't any doubt in his mind that this guy Scott had the real juice, of the political kind. One word to Captain Maxwell Drury and the State Police had put their best pilot into the air in the search for Debra Patterson. That would help a great deal, he thought, and Rivers knew that she would eventually be found, for those were the odds. At the same time, that's what worried him.

As he stroked the grey feline, an old image flashed through the smoke of his cigar. An image of limbo, the nether world produced by sadism and sexual attack. It was different for male survivors, but for women victims of atrocity there was an inbetween.

And that was not alive. And that was not dead either. Like zombies. Their bodies still breathing, still walking, but their minds reduced to lather. In Phu Bai Province the first platoon had found a whole village of them, walking aimlessly, bumping into each other, then shrieking, then walking; while their husbands and fathers lay half-buried, rotting away in monsoon-swept rice fields.

He shivered, forcing the image from his mind, placing an aspirin against his rear molars, crushing the pill down into paste. Rivers liked the acid bite. It dulled the throb that emanated from the right hinge of his jaw, and as he was chewing, the bass-heavy speakers suddenly boomed through the little doorway, scoring a direct hit against the orange tabby, who vanished into the night.

'This is Eagle One!' the impatient voice repeated.

Rivers leaped inside the house, crossing the room, moving by feel. He grabbed the microphone. 'This is Echo-Twenty,' he returned flatly, dropping his cigar into an ashtray. The sound of chopper blades tore from speakers, vibrating against the artwork on his wall.

'We've got a Boggie,' the voice said sharply. 'Mustang, top-down convertible.'

'Is it green, is it a new one?' he asked calmly.

'Hard to tell, Franko, late model, over.'

'Abandoned?'

'Hard to say. Possible. Do you want units, over . . .'

Steve Adare, the pilot of the Hughs-500 Loach, a jet-powered chopper, was asking if the assignment officer, in this case Frank Rivers, wanted a police car dispatched to the scene.

'Immediately,' Rivers spat. 'Can you put down?'

'Sorry, Frank, I'm regulation poor and running on empty,' the voice lamented as Rivers heard the blades begin a hard accelerated whirr, and Steve Adare peeled Eagle One into the sky.

At exactly 1:48 a.m., Frank Rivers headed out to the location, one click north of the intersect, Foxhall and Wisconsin Avenues, directly across the street from a local dive known as Zephyr's Bar & Grill. As he drove he forgot about Jessica Janson, and his cats, and Jack Scott, and the animal they were chasing.

All he had on his mind was a girl he had never met, and a village in Vietnam, and the man with torture spread across his face.

Jon Patterson.

Jon Patterson loved his daughter more than life.

With her hands trembling ever so slightly, Irma Kiernan closed her mirror into a bureau drawer. Headlights were coming. Jeff was returning home to her.

The wait finally over, she quickly composed herself, strolling seductively down the stairs, then taking a position near the door, and waiting, as Jeff was lingering in the garage.

He reconnected a fuse beneath the dash of his BMW, and now, with the car door open, the overhead domelight functioned normally. In the white glow which had been absent before, he quickly scanned the expensive red leather upholstery. There were no stains. There were no signs of another occupant, save the lingering of a woman's perfume. Casually he removed a small can of AirWick from the glove compartment, giving a quick spray, then leaving the windows open.

He came through the back door and braced himself, knowing that Irma would be waiting for him. From the street he had seen her bedroom light go off, and he could imagine her high-pitched whine even before she spoke. He shuddered in anticipation, placing his car keys on the kitchen counter.

'Is that you, Sweetheart?' Irma asked, and Dorn winced visibly.

'No,' he hissed quietly, 'the tidy bowl man has come to clean up your shit.'

She was gliding through the hallway, around the corner and towards him. 'What dear?' she crooned. 'I was upstairs, I didn't hear you.'

'It's been a hard night, Irma,' he said flatly, 'I said I'm tired, very tired, I think I should sleep.' The man quickly hobbled, as was his way at times, into the family room where he set himself down in his easy chair. It was not the events of the evening that ran through his mind, it was simply the thought of dealing with Irma again, his lifetime with her seemed like a suffering eternity.

'Oh, Honey.' Irma crossed after him through the small hallway, into the living-room, standing by his side. 'The nightmares woke you, I heard you leaving. Let me get your medication.'

Dorn agreed in an instant, to him Percodan was better than earmuffs or a double whisky, it helped to make the grating sound of her voice almost tolerable. Like clockwork Irma reappeared with a glass of water and a pill, which Dorn pumped down without delay. 'Thank you,' he said. 'Irma, why don't you go along and get some sleep, I'll be up shortly to say goodnight.'

'Oh, Sweetheart, I'll stay with you,' she contested, 'does it hurt that badly? It's been a rough night, hasn't it?' And Kiernan sat beside him in silence as the little man blinked, his dark eyes like wet stains against his face.

'Come up to bed, Jeff, let me rub your back for you,' she

pressed, leaning over into his space, and he could feel her hot breath and smell the heavy scent of lilacs, and it was hard just to stay in the same room. He couldn't even imagine pinning her to a mattress, and in his mind he had never even touched Irma Kiernan, it took all of his courage just to look at her.

As the drug began to work its effects, fuelling his body with a light-headed tingle, his thoughts went adrift, and again he was unwrapping the girl in the bright green convertible. She had cried for her mother, and that had amused him. He had made the woman a statistic in the American war against the sexes, and the numbers didn't lie. In the sports category, he thought, rape, murder, abduction and mutilation were on the increase anyway, the bitch was at risk the moment she was born.

So in his mind, Dorn reasoned, she could have been anyone's kid, and if her family merely applied a little logic and a few numbers, the loss would not seem so great. 'Irma,' he spoke quietly, 'I'm bone tired, run along and get some sleep.' His face was a perfect blank. The girl's compact body had been much more generous than he had suspected, and drugged with fifty milligrams of Pow, she had performed like a trained seal, depleting him until nothing was left.

Clank, clank. He could still hear that sound.

'Honey,' Irma whispered seductively, 'let me make you feel better.' She was pressing her body into his, moving to touch his thigh with a nervous hand. But the man she knew as Colonel Jeffery Dorn suddenly grabbed her wrist, forcefully pulling her face into his.

'Leave me!' was his toneless demand.

And she did.

At 2:08 a.m., Frank Rivers arrived at the scene on Wisconsin Avenue and spotted a green convertible parked directly under a street light. He checked his duty sheet.

That it belonged to Jonathan Patterson was without doubt, the tags were correct, and the parking sticker on the rear bumper was from Debra's high school. Walking from his radio car, he searched the interior with a halogen beam, looking for smears of blood or body fluid, but there were no signs of a struggle, only the usual fouling on the front carpets. There was no evidence to the naked eye that would leave even the slightest clue, save the faint smell of perfume or after-shave.

He opened the passenger's door and checked under the seats. They were clean. In the corner of the dash was a lipstick. On the rear seat a Raggedy Ann doll looked up at him with shiny button eyes. He was about to move the front seat when he spotted the keys dangling from the ignition.

He stopped, the chambers of his heart crashing, then beginning to pound. He swallowed hard.

Soundlessly, in one giant stride, he reached his car, grabbing the microphone through the window. 'This is Sergeant Rivers,' he sneered, leaning halfway into the cruiser.

'Go ahead Echo-Twenty,' came the refrain.

'I ordered a backup unit thirty minutes ago, and I'm telling you now they'd better be humping or I'm going to kill something . . .'

There was no response. He took a breath. He drove images from his mind. 'Scratch that,' he stammered, his voice regaining a calm, deep edge. 'Dispatch a crime analysis team, stat, and I mean now,' he said. 'Notify Captain Drury if necessary, and get those bums out of the sack.' Before the confirmation arrived, Rivers tossed the mike onto the seat and began to cross the street.

A DC cab hurtled in his direction, horn blaring. Rivers gave him his best gob of spit, then waited for a confrontation. A middle finger appeared but the cab continued, as he walked to the front door, checking through the windows for signs of life. It was empty. Chairs were parked on tabletops.

'The infamous Zephyr,' he said to himself, and he stood at the door wondering if Debra Patterson had been inside, and why? He looked around. He checked up and down the street in both directions, there was nothing else open after 11:00, and he reached up, grabbing the lamp that was mounted next to the front door.

It was warm. It had been off only recently, and the bulb was just going wet with condensation.

As he waited, instead of thinking of Debra, he saw only Jon Patterson's spent face in his mind. And then the zombies, walking through the killing fields of his youth.

NINETEEN

2:33 A.M.
NEW YORK CITY

John F. Scott emerged from the Central Records building facing Lexington Avenue, smelling of mildew, the time-worn scent covering his clothes as he stood between marble pillars.

He was a *thief*.

In his mind there was no other word for it.

The black briefcase resting at his side bulged with valuables for which there simply was no higher price, he had paid with his principles. The coin Jennifer Doe had been wearing was a clue without perspective, that's what he was stealing, he told himself, perspective. But there was no excuse. As Matthew Brennon had explained, the exhibit was Dr Robert Perry's mission in life, his reason for living. Scott was stealing a man's life.

His strides lengthened down ten long flights of circular steps. Fleeing beneath two massive stone griffins, he glanced up and the menacing symbols became fixed in his memory. The thief paused. A slight rain. His senses were waking.

Across Lexington and down 43rd Street into the dark, he walked, looking at his watch. The night was beginning to clear. Thick blankets of steam dissipated into patches that scurried like phantom crabs over pavement. Except for an occasional jogger, a couple strolling, a passing delivery truck, the street seemed quiet. On any other night he would be going home, leaving the city by way of the Long Island Expressway.

Scott left 43rd Street, darting left onto the sidewalk, bathed in the halogen glow of low cost anti-crime lights. There was something wrong, he reasoned, with lights that cast no shadow, and in the wash of manufactured daylight he felt detached, a strange isolation.

Between blocks he ducked into an alley. Empty. A wet chill climbed the back of his neck as the smells of human waste took him by the throat. Two boys, unaware of his presence, peered with a penlight into the dark blue Chrysler parked at the curb. An AM radio, a tattered blanket, good tyres with deep treads, but too much work. They wandered on, howling obscenities at the approach of an ageing prostitute. Acne scarred, eyes yellow, she gave a futile kick in their general direction while a middle-aged man tightened his dog's leash, threading the small animal through human barriers.

'Keep moving,' the thief whispered.

Headlights approached over wet pavement as a child scampered from a doorway, hurling a brick at a passing car. The projectile shattered on the street, multiplying into smaller weapons as other moppets joined chase. The car rounded the corner and vanished. This was not his business, not his place. The city was closing in on him.

He walked for the car, unloading stolen treasures, placing them securely into the trunk and positioning ancient charts beneath a blanket. A Cadillac filled with middle-aged men roared by toward Times Square, he recognised them as Chicken Hawks cruising for boys before Brother Dow opened again, and without thinking he soon followed their headlights through the city's poisoned arteries.

Traffic slowed to a crawl as he turned onto the Deuce in the Square, the city pulsed and rocked to its own twisted, paralysing rhythm. Sex parlours shimmered in neon. Doormen promised to deliver. In the window of a fast food store, a large black woman craftily slipped heroin up into a vein. Children peddled drugs. Adults supervised. By day, withdrawal sucked life from the newborn. A city gone mad. His type of guilt had no place here.

Despair for his fellow man gripped him, and he pushed the

Chrysler hard down the ramp and into the Lincoln Tunnel, away from Manhattan. He tried the radio, music held no meaning.

He took a ramp, veering left towards the turnpike, heading steadily south into New Jersey, chasing high beams. Billboards, motels and parking lots bloomed from darkness, then were gone in a blaze. Images fast appearing, then fading, 60–70–80; the window open, the wind burning at one ear. And he stretched, pushing down hard against his seat with the events of the past twenty-four hours reeling through his mind.

'Something familiar here,' he had told Brennon about the Clayton case. 'I can taste it.' And it seemed like the years were running them all down.

Nicholas Dobbs, Dr Chet Sanders, and the voice of a young mother who had died of old age, 'Just get him, get him for me, get him . . .' Scott's mind skipped, and for a passing moment he regarded the noisy images as ghosts, stages of the agent's disease on an endless mental run backward through his own worst nightmare.

The Claytons were merely a coincidence, he told himself. Jennifer Doe was a Civil War child. And for seamless miles he held tight to that belief, simply because he needed to. Zak was dead. But Scott knew better.

Old enemy. Old friend.

How long had it been? 80–85–90, the speedometer soared, the Chrysler lurched on open road towards Washington and his enemy.

For more than three decades, helpless mothers and their children had been set upon by the same human predator, an animal without a soul. And at the age of fifty-six, time was running backwards for Scott and everything he believed in – dignity, hope, humanity – raced beyond him through the night.

DAY TWO: THE DEVOID

I cut her throat so she could not scream. . . . this
went on for a while, but she kept passing out.

> Theodore Bundy, Jr.

Ted, our hearts are with you!

> Protest sign at the Execution Vigil of
> Theodore Bundy Jr.

TWENTY

The Carefree Diner on Wisconsin Avenue was a landmark of sorts. Once it had been a truck stop, now it more resembled an upscale imitation of itself with chrome that was too clean and brightly polished, a menu that was too elaborate and pricy, and coffee that had gone from freshly brewed to electric drip.

When Scott and Rivers arrived it was quiet inside, and mostly empty, but with the sunrise locals began lining up at the door, reading their newspapers and being admitted by name. Rivers watched this with some contempt. There was something wrong, he reasoned, with a diner that accepted reservations and prepared Eggs Benedict, which was what Jack Scott was eating long after Rivers had polished off two stacks of flapjacks with Polish sausages and eggs over-easy.

'So what do you think of the odds?' Rivers asked, having explained the discovery of Debra Patterson's car.

'The odds that she's still alive, or that she was abducted by Zak Dorani?'

'Both.'

'On her life I'd guess fifty-fifty, based on personal experience, but on Zak's involvement, I'd rather doubt that. We're only guessing that he's alive and this is a large metropolitan

195

area. Would you like me to come along when you tell Debra's parents?'

He took a sip of coffee and shrugged. 'It's not necessary, Captain Drury volunteered and he's been through that drill before. But what about you, Jack, where will you start?' Rivers had opened a ViCAT folder and was studying the contents, it captured another era back when individual police files were comprehensive, stuffed with mugshots, measurements, fingerprint records and lab work showing detailed analysis. A black and white photo of the man had faded down into shades of grey, and the detective could tell that it was taken when law enforcement did not include pampering. 'He was cuffed in the nude?' Rivers smiled.

'Strip searched, a violation of his civil liberties,' Scott stated coldly. 'We found a woman's engagement ring taped behind his scrotum.'

The smile went sour.

'Zak had reasons for everything he did,' Scott continued, dipping a piece of muffin into congealed yoke. 'My guess, he was about to force some woman to search for it, but we never did find the ring's legal owner.' He returned to his eggs, while Rivers concentrated on the photos.

According to measurements against a prison wall, Zak Dorani stood exactly five-feet-five inches, with a natural posture that curved slightly to the left, and Rivers searched for a physical imbalance. The legs were well formed, with the knees at a correct angle, not overtly bowed or knocked. The stomach was tight, and the torso was well proportioned to the body. 'He's athletic but has a crook in his spine, that would get worse with age.'

'There's a doctor's report, Zak was under treatment for scoliosis in 1959, physical therapy for a rather common condition for lateral curvature. Nothing too serious, about one out of every hundred are born with it, but it can be painful.'

Rivers nodded. Because of the smooth complexion, oval face and brown hair, he thought Zak so plain as to be of almost any descent. The eyes were deeply set like the Dutch, small black mirrors, and the chin was sharp and flat. The nose seemed bobbed, almost too small for his face, and his lips were thin, like slivers of veal. 'Will you know him on sight?'

Scott took a sip of coffee, pushing his plate off to one side. 'Perhaps, those shots were taken over thirty years ago, there wouldn't be anything that he hasn't changed through cosmetic surgery, hair transplants, face-lifts, you name it. We're dealing with someone who is more vain than the most narcissistic female you've ever met, and he's an expert at preventing detection, a real actor.

'Physically, he's small, tough to hide that, and his eyes used to be so brown they appeared black in a poorly lit room. But maybe that's changed as well.' Scott shrugged. 'Surgery or coloured contact lenses, who can say.'

Rivers fumbled in his sweatshirt pocket, found a roll of small cigars and continued searching until his hand produced a crumpled pack of Marlboro, which he offered across the table. Scott pulled loose a bent smoke and then lifted Rivers' lighter, expertly thumbing the wheel, then examining the battered relic with some interest. On one side was a Pink Panther, on the other a grinning death's-head, images that seemed in sharp conflict with one another.

'A lucky piece?'

'A gift,' Rivers responded, remembering back to when the Zippo was America's weapon of choice. He extended his hand across the table, palm up, and Scott placed it back into the man's hand. A waitress appeared with a tray, re-filling their mugs, then began clearing the table as Scott produced two black-and-white wire photos and laid them down.

'I think this was a lucky piece, or maybe a gift of some type,' he suggested. 'Have you ever seen one of these before?' They both looked down at copies of the Civil War era signal token.

'Negative,' Rivers said, lighting his smoke, 'first and only time I ever saw one was when Elmer Janson gave me this.' He reached into his pants' pocket and retrieved a glassine evidence pouch containing the small medallion, dropping the coin on the table.

'Anything else today, Frank?' the waitress interrupted, placing a check and pot of coffee between them.

'No thanks, Kathy.'

She replaced two spoons and moved on as Scott carefully studied the coin, flipping the pouch over from front to back. 'Can I keep this?'

'It's on loan.'

'And you're sure the boy found this where he said?'

'Absolutely, he's a good little kid.'

'What do you make of it, Frank?'

'Hell, I don't know, Commander, it's an old coin. Do you have an artist's rendering of what our Mook would look like today?'

Scott smiled. 'Mook?'

'Pervert.'

'Let's talk about him later,' Scott suggested, turning the conversation back to the coin. 'Notice at the top that a drill has punched through a word, or possibly a series of words.' He pointed, looking up into tired eyes.

'Yeah,' Rivers squirmed, 'I saw that.'

'Well, we've established that the coin was made in 1863 at Harper's Ferry, West Virginia.'

Rivers leaned back into the bench seat. 'So what's that have to do with Zak?'

'Evidence, Frank, and directional forensics.'

'What?' he shook his head and then leaned over the table at the older man. 'Look, Jack,' he said in a biting tone, 'if it's the same guy what do we need this for? If you can spot him, it's over, the guy's a grease stain, let's start from there.' And Rivers coughed, waiting for an angry response. But Scott just smiled, leaning back into the soft leather banquette.

'Humour me?' he asked, holding palms up in supplication.

'Sure,' Rivers agreed. But he didn't really. He was thinking that if the killer was territorial like Scott had said, then they already knew he frequented the River Road area, which meant they could flush him out in a sting using a decoy and stakeout.

He knew the perfect chick for the job. Scott cleared his throat.

'Age before beauty, detective?'

Rivers chuckled at the old corn. 'Haven't heard that since I was a kid.' Scott produced a cardboard tube from beneath the bench and started unscrewing the aluminium cap on one end.

'What's in that anyway, you've been guarding that real close?'

Scott didn't answer but reached inside, producing a scroll of heavy paper, then wiped down the surface of the table with a linen handkerchief. What unfolded was a detailed pen-and-ink chart of the Potomac River Valley. The map was painted, Rivers guessed watercolours, and it looked ancient.

'Damn me for a mutt, where in hell's creation did you get that?' he asked, leaning across the table with excitement.

'It's on loan,' Scott lied. 'It's from a series produced by the Confederates before shots were fired at Fort Sumter, this is how the Rebs saw this part of Maryland in 1860.'

Frank studied the antique closely, the strange odour of parchment mixing with the aroma of coffee and sausages. He could see the Potomac River and the Chesapeake and Ohio Canal very clearly, these were a tropical blue. But the city of Bethesda was not on the map. 'This is great, Jack,' he said earnestly.

'Take your time, a quiz will follow.'

'Right,' and the State Trooper moved closer, inhaling through his nose like a bloodhound on the scent.

He loved the names, they were rich and amusing. The river fell from the map, emptying into Old Georgetown in Washington at a place called Frogland. 'Some of the most overpriced property in the nation, Froggie-Vill? Jack, this is . . . fantastic!' he exclaimed, moving closer still, invading Scott's air space. Near Frogland, a tract of property was labelled Conjurers Disappointment.

'Look at this,' he laughed, 'they probably ate at one of the French restaurants in Georgetown!' And he followed the blue-wash of paint as the river curved back up into Maryland.

Two landmarks were clearly marked, an aqueduct known

as Widewater and the Great Falls of the Potomac, but the famous nearby townships of Cabin John and White's Ferry were strangely omitted. They were gone, or they didn't exist at the time. The detective shook his head. He found River Road, and a little too far north there were two small intersections along the river, called John's Revenge and White's Crossing, which he had never heard of.

'The devil be damned, but I can't find Bethesda, Cabin John, White's Ferry, and there was no town of Potomac?'

Scott was watching intently.

'Darnestown is here, and so's Rockville,' he said, following an index finger, 'but they got the river areas all screwed-up, Jack. Where's Cabin John? My family used to have a house right here.' He pointed to a bluff overlooking the canal.

'You tell me, Frank, I know Bethesda wasn't named yet, but Cabin John and White's Ferry definitely existed as far back as 1839.'

'Look,' he said with excitement, 'they left everything out, they'd be right here,' and he jammed a thumb on the chart. Scott cringed.

'Sorry.'

'Now let's take a closer look,' Scott offered, placing photos of the coin back across the map. And Rivers pushed his fingers over the word *JOIN* which stood out in capital letters.

'What does it mean?' he asked, picking up the real coin and squinting at the little house entwined by a serpent.

'Do you know of any neighbourhood with a name that comes close to the word *JOIN* in configuration, a name having the letters J-O-I-N, in that sequence?'

Rivers applied pen to pad, scrawled a moment and pulled away. 'Nothing,' he said, 'the word is *JOIN*, I think that's what it means, how about you?'

'Look again,' said Scott, pointing to the letters. 'The only logical choice is *Cabin John*, and we know these coins were made bearing the name of other towns. The coin is a patriotic signal token minted by the Union. On the map, *White's Ferry* is labelled *White's Crossing*, but there's a similar token that claims another name, which one of my agents tracked down. That coin says *White's Ferry* just like it is on the Rand-McNally today. I think the charts, and hence the modern maps, are in error.'

'No shit?'

'It's a theory.'

'Was it intentional?'

'My guess is that the map-makers didn't know any better, these towns were just small communities during the Civil War and hostile to any outsiders. A Rebel spy might have been ignorant enough to ask for help with this chart, and was misled, anything's possible. Remember, in the 1860s they didn't plant signs on the road when it came to smaller Southern communities, and Maryland was a state divided.'

'But how do you get the words Cabin John out of all this, when the coin was minted?'

'Okay, let's take another look,' Scott said, 'but remember, this is just speculation.'

'Right.'

He sketched on a napkin. 'Take I-N from the word *Cabin*. And the J-O from the name *John*. Now that won't work in sequence, but it works. And it works in only one way, unless we're dealing with a code, and I doubt that.

'J-O-I-N is a combination of the first two and last two letters of the name John and the word Cabin, in that order. So if you drilled out the centre to make a hole for a chain, what would remain is J-O followed by I-N.' *JOOIN* he drew on a pad. 'John Cabin. And over the years it was forgotten. What do you think?'

'Are you saying that based on some old coin that all along the name of the town was John Cabin?' Rivers asked sarcastically. 'I grew up in Cabin John, Maryland, I would have known about something like this.'

'It's just an educated guess,' Scott concluded. 'Take a look at the house on the coin, looks like a cabin?'

'Right.'

'In New York, Agent Brennon interviewed an expert on the Freedom Railroad, and these tokens were used as a way of warning underground operators that they were being watched, explaining the word *Beware!* stamped over the cabin.' He pointed. 'My guess is the town now called Cabin John was an important link for slaves fleeing oppression, and today these coins are very rare.'

Rivers was excited but confused. He slid back in his seat, wondering. 'The killer left the coin on this girl's body some thirty years ago, he must have seen it. No way he didn't.'

'He didn't care, Frank.'

'Do you think he knew what it meant?'

'That doesn't matter either. Do you think the little girl who was wearing it knew what it meant? She was a black child, where did she get the token?'

'It must have been a gift, a black couldn't have afforded it back in 1958, so it must have been a family heirloom. If what you're thinking is right, I'll bet she was a local kid, but I checked the records and no black child, boy or girl, was reported missing in this County until 1971. That's a long time, Jack.'

'Yes it is. When did the County start hiring blacks?'

'Oh, hell, when was the Equal Opportunity Act?'

'That would be sixty-nine.'

'Well, it wasn't until then for sure, they wouldn't have integrated unless forced to.'

'I believe the life of a local child fell through the cracks, unless a black family would have gone to the white police?'

'Not hardly, I see where you're going.'

'When we find out more about the coin's history, we'll start to gain hard insight into who this child really was, when the killer first arrived here, maybe what his disguise was at the time, and maybe still is. The list could prove endless, it's the best lead we've got. Eventually we'll have photographs of this girl, making it easier to track relatives, and there's a few other tricks we can pull, but that's down the road.'

'All right,' Rivers conceded, 'but what about the killer, you mentioned the Janson family, are they safe?'

'You checked on them?'

'Right until the sun came up, radio reports all clear.' He

smacked his forehead. 'Christ, I feel like I'm talking about a vampire.'

'Worse than that, vampires can't work by day.'

'And you think this coin is our best lead?'

'Except for the little girl's body, it's about our only lead. Certainly have damn little from the Clayton murders.'

Scott drained his coffee cup, and Rivers saw the blood pumping into his neck and face, the guy looked like a candidate for a stroke. 'What is it, Jack, are you all right?'

Scott cleared his throat. 'Sure, getting too old for my job. What I would like to do, Frank, is set up a command post, and I'd like you to be the officer in charge.'

'Depends on what value you're willing to assign the Debra Patterson case, they're counting on me.'

'Priority One.'

Scott watched as Rivers examined the breakfast tab then dropped a twenty dollar bill on top.

'Then the meal will be on me,' Scott offered as Rivers suddenly leaned across the table.

'What did Zak do to those children?' he asked coldly.

'Killed them very methodically.'

'I read the report at least a dozen times, I couldn't make sense out of it. Did he rape those little girls, Jack?' Rivers' blue eyes glinted with a murderous fury, a vein stood out on his neck.

'No, Frank, he didn't rape them, he did not force them to engage in sexual activities, at least the way you and I think of it.'

'Are you being straight with me?'

Scott was watching the man's jaw ticking. 'Yes, as honest as I can be. The killer is not capable of having sex so he finds other means, but we can get into that later. We have got to bring ourselves up to speed and you, my friend, have some catching up to do.'

Rivers' eyes narrowed, the vein in his neck pulsed. 'I'd like to gut this bastard like a toad,' he spat, as they both stood, Scott picking up his things.

They went silent as they approached a line of patrons on

the way through the door. Rivers fought with himself to keep calm, while the cooling air and the coffee had helped Scott. He could feel his senses waking, every nerve suspicious of the new city surrounding him. From the front of the diner he could see traffic starting to swell with a morning rush, backing up at a light on Wisconsin Avenue one block up. Rivers slowed his gait, noticing that the older man had to make an extra effort to keep astride.

'I've read your sheets, Frank, your complete file. I still don't know much about you,' Scott offered, his eyes straight ahead as they walked.

Rivers pondered this a moment. 'Not much to know,' he answered quietly.

'Everyone has a history.' Scott paused, making eye contact. 'I'm the oldest from a large Catholic family, my father was uniformed NYPD. I had eight brothers and two sisters. One brother was killed in Korea, my twin sister was snatched from a school playground in 1938. A few years later we buried an empty box.' He blinked.

The pent-up breath left Rivers' body in a small moan. 'I'm sorry,' he swallowed, 'I suspected something like that, it explains a great deal.'

They stopped at a crosswalk, waiting for a light to change, the sign went to blinking green. 'I believe good cops are made, not born, tempered from desire and fashioned from circumstance. So what about you, Frank, why are you a cop?'

Rivers shrugged, looking off into space. 'Hell, I'm really not that deep, I'm not even sure I know.'

They crossed again at the intersection of Cordell and Wisconsin Avenues and into the public parking garage. The blue Chrysler and Crown Victoria were parked side by side in one corner, and Scott stopped between them. 'Frank,' he asked cautiously, 'was your father's last name Rivers? The Social Security number under that name wasn't active until after the fall of Saigon.'

The State Trooper raised an eyebrow, then gave a knowing nod as he unlocked his car. With his eyes on Scott he reached inside, turning on the radio and grabbing the mic. 'I'm on your side,' he stated without tone, hitting the indent button with his thumb. 'Dispatch, this is One-Echo-Twenty,' he piped routinely as the Commander checked his watch.

Rivers noticed his behaviour and quickly sought to change the subject. 'This job gets old,' he offered. And Scott smiled, nodding his agreement.

Old as a lifetime, dark as a childhood scar.

TWENTY-ONE

The house was red brick, three storeys of townhouse with sidewalks instead of a lawn. Treeless and indifferent, it loosely followed the colonial style, any character derived from paste blue shutters. Looking south from the front stoop, a supermarket sat at the end of a patch of green. Across a cramped and busy intersection, the east side faced a retirement home. One short block down Ridgefield Drive was the four-lane highway River Road, where the condemned bowling alley waited.

Scott stood in the harsh sunlight shielding his brow, staring up at the skinny house. 'This is to be used as the command post?' he asked.

'Captain Drury's instructions.'

'Was he supposed to meet us here?'

Rivers tossed his dutybook back into the car and removed a black gearbag from the trunk. 'Last I heard,' he said, heading for the front door. Scott tried the latch while Rivers circled the house, checking windows and screens, and a moment later he was back on the front stoop, watching Scott select a pick from inside a black zipper pouch.

'I can radio for dispatch?' he offered. But Scott was already at work, carefully inserting the pick into the lock. It looked ridiculous. Rivers knew a specialist who could zap a deadbolt in less than a minute, but Scott was far from that practised truth. He was pushing his entire head up to the keyhole, his face was knotted with intense concentration. The doorknob poked him in the nose.

Then there was the sound of shattering glass, and Scott

was rising, one hand against his back, as the front door opened and Frank Rivers walked out. His right fist was wrapped in his T-shirt.

'That's Hollywood shit anyway,' he said, and Scott nodded gratefully as he wiped his brow with a clean handkerchief.

The ceilings were vaulted with recessed lights and the decor was a rather nondescript abstract modern. There was blue carpeting throughout, and bright metal sculptures that resembled large paperclips. The furniture itself was leather, a sandy colour with over-stuffed pillows in shades of neon. All the tables were glass and chrome, lending to the detached and antiseptic feeling of the place. There was no personal warmth, no hominess, no give, and Scott stood in amazement, then chuckled to himself as he watched Rivers carrying sculptures to the hall closet.

'I really can't live with this one,' he said, lugging away what looked like a twisted brass pelvis.

'Don't break anything,' Scott suddenly cautioned. 'What do we know about this place?'

'Drury said it belonged to the State Department.'

'I was afraid you'd say something like that, our tax dollars at work.' Scott stepped carefully from the foyer, around an enormous brass swan, then down into a sunken room. There was a gilded fireplace that was decorated with pine cones and plastic logs, and Scott knew it had never been used. Up through an arched hallway he found a massive kitchen with floating island and tiled counters, and he strolled to the sinks which overlooked a rear deck and patio.

To the right, a carpeted stairway led down to the garage or up to six bedrooms on two additional floors. It was the type of town-house that offered sunken tubs on a postage stamp lot with a view of your neighbour's bathroom.

'Bet some junior ambassador hired his main squeeze to decorate,' Rivers offered from the kitchen, checking the contents of the refrigerator. The unit was built into the wall, something called a Sub-Zero, and it was empty. 'If your average wage earner saw this he'd march on Washington.'

'Not a chance,' Scott corrected, 'we're a nation of sheep with an electronic shepherd.'

'Then let's unplug them.'

Scott shrugged as he walked for the stairs. 'It's a nice thought, but let's just settle for showers and a change of clothes.' And he took the entire third floor which offered a better view of River Road, while Rivers selected the gaming room on the basement level, which offered a Brunswick Slate-top, the kind of expensive pool table that he had always dreamed of owning.

While Scott was changed in scant minutes, Rivers took thirty, steaming himself in a sunken tub that was larger than his living-room, twisting a gold-plated gargoyle's head with a ruby eye for hot, and an emerald eye for cold.

Though he was slight of build, Captain Maxwell Drury was a formidable man who wore a full uniform, a stern countenance, and jet black boots. His olive jacket was accented with gold braid, his white shirt looked starched to excess. From his left shoulder a chestnut bandoleer crossed his chest, attached to an old fashioned Sam Browne belt at his waistline. In his right hand he carried an officer's campaign hat and a two-way radio, in his left a smallish bundle of cloth sealed in plastic.

He was thin, too thin, worn from worry and aged with dread. As Scott closed the door behind them, he could tell from Drury's expression that his old friend was cooking inside with political fallout. 'Max,' he said warmly, embracing him.

'Sorry I'm late. You're looking well, Jack. Like old times, just like old times.' He tried to put a smile in his voice, but it sounded like stones rolling down a sheet of tin. 'I stopped off to see the Pattersons, Frank filled you in?'

'Come in and sit down, Max.' Scott led him by the arm.

'They're taking the news about their daughter's car being abandoned very hard, very hard indeed. If we find a body I'm not sure they'll be able to live with it. Mr Patterson told me he'd rather die than entertain the possibility that some bastard has destroyed his daughter. I feel for him, the mind can endure only so much pain . . .'

'Max,' Scott tried to interrupt.

'She's their only child, maybe some of your psychology would help.'

'Anything I can do, you know that, but let's not bury her yet, Frank said the car was clean of assault forensics.' Scott led him into a grey kitchen chair, which he pulled from the table. 'I'll get something to drink.'

From the bottom of the stairs, Rivers watched with an uncertain curiosity as the two men talked; he had never seen Drury emotional, it was unlike him, or so he had thought. He pulled a T-shirt over his head, saddled his gun in a high-ride holster at his back, and listened as he combed through a tangle of wet hair.

'Debra Patterson, at least in her pictures, reminds me of my Martha. Maybe it's the hair, I don't know, there's a certain innocence. She's seventeen now, you haven't seen her for ten years, she's a beautiful young woman, John, you won't even know her.' Drury set his hat, parcel and radio on the table, and took a glass of water from Scott.

'Was the information on careers in the social sciences of any help, has she made a decision about college?' he asked.

'Nothing yet, but I thank you for your trouble. Martha's been chasing some sports car enthusiast around, the man will amount to nothing.'

Scott smiled. 'As I recall you were a car enthusiast.'

'Humph. So tell me, Jack, what first? How many men for this detail?' he rattled.

'First would be Patriots Bowl, we excavate the building from the inside, the entire alley if necessary, and then . . .'

'It will take time for search warrants, and we don't have much of a case, but I have a few favours I can call due.'

'If we have to deal with some slack-face judge over probable cause, we're dead.'

'Hail Mary!' Drury breathed hard.

'Max?' Scott nudged.

The man's voice went to glass. 'Don't ask me to condone this, no petition before a judge, no justified cause, it's a gross violation of procedure.'

'Max?'

'Oh God, Jack,' he cried, 'that same little bit in sixty-eight set my career back ten years.'

Scott nodded. 'I remember, you said it was worth a hundred suspensions.'

And Scott waited as the Captain considered the stakes and odds. One thing was certain, it was nonfeasance, and inexcusable, and unforgivable. If caught he would be facing a quiet, political type retirement, but there would still be a partial pension, he thought, he'd check the book, he was almost certain they couldn't take that away.

'You've got twenty years in, Max, they can't take your pension unless it's a Class-B Felony, and even then I'm not sure it's indictable.'

'You know what you're asking,' he said tonelessly, 'sweeping uniformed regulations into the can? This may look like Maryland but it's Washington, Jack, the political theme park, make no mistakes about that.'

'I understand.'

'And my men? Even if I did commit, I can't expose my men to charges.'

'Then offer me something else.'

Drury began to ponder, taking a deep breath and a sip of water just as a shadow moved over him. Rivers stepped forward into the kitchen.

'Oh, hello, Frank,' Drury said, his brown eyes moving under heavy brows.

'Have a seat,' Scott offered, pulling out a chair.

Rivers shook his head. 'I'm going to pick up some supplies and fuel the tank. Is that my package?' he asked, lifting the plastic covered bundle from the table. He examined the contents from the outside, pressing hard with his fingers. There was a gymshirt, socks and some panties, these were an acid green with large black dots.

'Mr Patterson was very uncomfortable with the request,

most of Debra's clothes were freshly cleaned, so I urged him to search the laundry facilities. We found the undergarment in the hamper.'

'Thanks, Captain,' he said, 'is her mother home?'

'Debra's mother?'

Rivers nodded.

'Yes, she's distraught, the family doctor is treating her.'

Rivers popped an aspirin into his mouth, opened the back door, and was gone.

'Frank's in some type of physical pain?' Scott questioned, but Drury's attention was elsewhere.

'I have it!' the gravel voice took on an excited tone. 'Let's set up an ambush and drown the bastards in paperwork, they'll never know what hit them. I'll contact the property owner and smack him on the forehead with a citation, then we'll go directly for the keys and demand their full cooperation!'

Scott was listening intently. 'I don't follow.'

'I saw the alley on the way in, technically we're dealing with a condemned structure, so I can employ the guise of inspecting a health hazard. It's not my department, such a case would belong to Health and Welfare, but that should take at least a week for a good attorney to figure out. By then we'll give the place a clean ticket, return the keys and blueprints, and keep sets of our own.'

Scott smiled. 'An excellent plan,' he raised his glass of water in salute, 'you still have the touch.'

'A bit of bureaucratic buggering.'

'It should work, but if you can't locate the proprietor or if they are noncooperative, drop the matter and get back to me. I do not want the County notified, and under no circumstances apply for a Court Order.'

'Out of the question, but I'm far more comfortable with this approach. I'll find someone to lodge a complaint this afternoon. Now tell me about manpower, that could present a problem.'

'Frank and I will work the field from this command post, one of my agents should be arriving sometime tomorrow. I have most of the communications gear I need, but in the meantime you can provide two guards for inside the alley, round-the-clock surveillance.'

Captain Drury made a notation. 'Morning and evening shifts split at 5:00 p.m., their movements will be lost in peak activity.'

'Old clothes, no police cars. Have them park elsewhere and approach on foot.'

'I can't afford senior detectives, Jack, the Governor attended the White House conference, we've had our priorities shuffled to narcotics and . . .'

'I understand.' Scott raised a hand. 'If you can't find a budget I'll sell some fruit.' He pointed to a bowl of sterling silver apples that sat between them. 'Just have the officers dress for the weekend, drive their own cars, and report to Frank. They'll get the short course. Frank has also requested a sound truck in case we need a more sophisticated surveillance, and I agree. I'd like a laser parabolic plus two additional men for that unit, I don't see any other way.'

'A laser?' Drury laughed. 'Jack, my department can't afford something like that, we still use hard wire for taps. The Secret Service may have one, you'll have to use your own juice.'

'You do have a surveillance truck?'

'Yes,' he growled defensively, 'and it's complete, a very fine rig. At the moment it's in use, how about late this afternoon or tonight?'

'That would be great. Rivers handpicked several men, what do you think? I can't leave the Janson family unguarded, no second place winner in this game.'

'Human pitbulls, Frank's type of cop, they work on our Violent Offenders' Unit.'

'Availability?'

'I'll see to it, but we've known each other too long, Jack.' His voice raised a pitch.

'How's that?'

'ViCAT's always been poor on manpower, so why didn't you just say you needed three men for your MAIT team?'

'Because you would have baulked and I need seven.'

'Wait just a minute.' Stress brought the gravel back to his voice. 'I'm giving you four men plus Rivers.'

'I understand that,' said Scott, 'I'm including Frank, plus my guy makes five.'

'And another?'

'To stake out the Claytons', I need a senior man.'

'Come off it, Jack, do you really think this killer will return?' Drury asked sarcastically.

'Can we afford to ignore that possibility? We just had a case in Atlanta where . . .'

Drury nodded. 'I know just the man, but I can't get him until tomorrow.'

'And the others?'

'Right now they're on other details, but it will be done.'

'Thanks, Max, I know you'll be pitching a lot of excuses on other fronts, you'll keep me appraised of political blowback?'

'If it threatens to affect your operation.'

'And as policy, all communications will run directly from this command post, without crosstown traffic?'

Drury forced a smile. 'We'll do our best.'

'Good,' said Scott. 'What else do we have?'

Drury reached into his coat pocket and handed Scott an envelope. 'Keys to the CP, the Riser slug is for the Claytons', works both front and back. Now what about our suspect, Frank mentioned you have some history with him?'

'That's what worries me, if it's the same man his behaviour has become unpredictable, he's not following the rules, anything goes. As of the Clayton killing there is no predictive model for him.'

'You're holding something back, John, what is it?'

'I'm not holding back.' He ran both hands through his hair. 'I just don't have a clear picture, a comprehension of what we're up against. For reasons I can't figure, this killer has become brazen, overt, and defiant, which makes no sense with who he is. At one time he used to make a concentrated effort to hide human remains, and by now he'd be an expert at disposal.'

'So why the Claytons, the ghoulish stage setting?'

'In times past that family would have just failed to return home one night, and in time the case would have been dropped, which as you know is not uncommon.'

'I see what you mean,' Drury said, 'it's the timing that's bothering you, why now?'

'That's it, something is pushing on him. I don't have a clue. If I could figure that out I might be able to anticipate his moves a little better.' Scott's voice was tense with frustration. 'He's capable of anything, he can't be predicted.'

Drury thought for a moment. 'Perhaps he's just lost his rational abilities, years of killing caught up with him, he's gone insane? Or he's seeking some kind of credit, wanting to punish society with his cruelty?'

Scott shook his head. 'No, the detail, planning and skill with which the Claytons were slaughtered could not have been done by a mental case.'

Drury sighed. 'Then maybe he's just dying, terminal man getting in his last licks?'

Scott winced, and this was followed by a brooding silence.

Finally, Drury said, 'I'm sorry, but that makes a lot of sense to me, Jack, try this scenario. The physician has just given you six months, once you're over the shock what do you do?'

Scott leaned forward in his chair, tapping on the table with a pen. 'There would be a lot of loose ends, I'd have to get my sordid little world into order, check with the insurance companies, execute a list of legal forms, and of course I'd say a few goodbyes . . .'

'Yes?' Drury pushed. 'You thought he was dead, and if he's not, and he is dying, how many other cops has he become acquainted with over the years? How many good men have spent part of their lives trying to stop him?'

Scott's eyes flared with a strange light as he slowly pushed back his chair. 'The big goodbye, the bastard's got nothing to lose this time!'

'It's possible,' Maxwell Drury offered grimly. 'Here's hoping I'm wrong.'

TWENTY-TWO

With disgust he jabbed a fork into the hard yellow eye that had been staring at him, the silly bitch couldn't get anything right.

Eggs over easy not poached, toast buttered lightly not greased, juice instead of frozen concentrate – Jeff Dorn couldn't understand it.

Was this a difficult order to fill?

And the phone was ringing. The house phone. Not his private line, and he threw his napkin on the kitchen table with contempt, pushing the plate away from him. 'What are you doing that's so damn important you can't get that?' he wanted to scream, but instead he said this under his breath while staring up at the ceiling. It was the fifth ring.

'Sweetheart, would you get the phone?' Irma Kiernan asked from above.

'God,' he exclaimed, 'how I hate that sound!' Her voice echoed through the ductwork and Dorn knew she was in the bathroom again. Then the seventh ring as a flush of water moaned through the pipes, coming towards him, rumbling by into the basement. Eight rings. He could barely stand her miserable incompetence, and it finally stopped.

'Honey?' Irma cried from upstairs. 'Sweetheart, are you there?'

The party dosage of Percodan he had taken the night before had given him a hangover, a slight headache and sour stomach, and Dorn did not feel much like conversation.

'It's for you, Sweetheart, do you want me to take a

message?' she cried, and he mustered his patience to deal with the inane demands that were crowding his morning.

'No, no, no, thank you, my love, I'll get it,' he sang, reaching from his chair and lifting the receiver from the wall. He then listened carefully, not for a greeting, but for background noise that would give the caller away. He groaned. Typewriters and bickering voices, and he knew immediately that it was Marcy Newman, director of preservation for Partners of Living History, the PLH.

'Colonel Dorn,' he barked, sounding very much like the professional military man. But what he heard in reply was the reverberation of office clatter from a sparse little hovel where everything echoed.

In the PLH brochures, and in the brochures only, the nonprofit foundation was housed in a massive federal office building and maintained a staff of hundreds. In reality, PLH had but two employees, Marcy Newman and a secretary, and as far as Dorn was concerned, the difference between the two was that the secretary got paid for her time.

PLH was a tax exempt organisation that, as Jeff was fond of saying, provided for the future by preserving the past. 'Colonel Dorn, will you please hold the phone for Marcy . . .'

'No, goddamn you, I pay your salary!' he snapped.

'J-J-Just a moment, please,' a confused young woman put the call on hold while Dorn double-checked the contents of his briefcase. He lifted a leather zipper pouch containing a small pistol, and immediately wanted to fire it into Marcy Newman's substantial gut. But he knew he could not. He needed her, though he loathed that thought.

When Jeff had first met the woman she was a Senate staffer on an environmental subcommittee, a brassy power-hungry bitch who, over the years, had made him bleed for every little political favour. Now her tenure was over, a failed election took her PooBah's seat, and she hit the streets peddling her knowledge, which was meagre; her contacts, which were questionable; and her looks, which as far as Jeff was concerned could be deployed for the national defence.

The phone was still on hold in a nasty little power game,

and he was revelling in how Marcy always underestimated people, she was freelancing the weekend away, using PLH resources to turn a buck. She would be making sure he wasn't coming to the office and crowding her paying clients.

'Hi, Jeff, what a glorious morning, it reminds me of Paris when . . .'

'Others may fall for that crap, but I happen to know you've never been there. What do you want, Marcy?' Dorn hacked away at the political gadfly.

'You should be nice to me, Jeff,' she said.

'Why, because I'm right about Paris?' he laughed. 'Now that I know the truth I'm going to tell everyone.'

'Oh Jeff,' she lamented, 'I've been on the phone for an hour with Mrs Warren, she's pledged four thousand dollars for the bridge project, it's wonderful!' and she bubbled with a practised enthusiasm, usually reserved for those in her Washington appointment book who really mattered; since Dorn had hired her at no cost he knew, by definition, that he did not.

'Wonderful,' Jeff repeated, 'just send her a brochure on Great Falls Park and write a letter for my signature.'

'Jeff, are you coming in today?'

'No, I have meetings, and now you have made me late,' he said, pausing for effect. 'But if I miss my appointment, I could come in . . .' Dorn's voice sang suggestively.

'I didn't mean to delay you, I was on another line. There's really nothing you can do here, I've got it well under control!'

He hated the exclamatory suggestion. 'Well, thanks to you I don't have time to write a proper note to Irma explaining that I'll be detained until late after dinner.' To Marcy Newman, this was a familiar drill, and after working on the Hill, she played like a pro.

'Let me call her for you later, what time would be good, what time is she expected home?'

Dorn dropped his edge. 'She'll be back around five, could you do that?'

'Oh, I'd love to!' exclaimed the contrite voice, which Dorn quickly cut off with a blind thumb just as Irma Kiernan came strolling down the stairs and stepped into the kitchen, whirling like a dervish in her new sun dress and carrying a picnic basket in her hand.

She placed this on the counter, smiling coyly in a manner suggestive of wine, shady trees and soft blankets. Dorn winced visibly.

'Who was that, Sweetheart?' she said brightly, walking to his side.

'That was Marcy, I'm needed on an emergency, something about a permitting process. They need my testimony ASAP, and I haven't finished writing it yet.'

'Oh dear,' Irma said, 'I'd thought we'd visit the park together, it's a beautiful day.' She saw the breakfast plate he had pushed aside. 'Are you in pain, Honey?'

'No, I'm feeling quite well, and I was looking forward to spending time with you, but . . .'

'I know, Sweetheart,' she soothed, 'duty calls. Can I help with the report?'

'No, it's a one-man job, unfortunately, there's nothing you can do.'

'Will you miss me?' she sighed, draping her arms over his shoulders.

'More than you'll ever know,' he said flatly, stroking the back of her hand as he returned to reading the morning paper.

When he had to, Jeff Dorn could be very agreeable.

Downstairs at the Kiernan home in the Wooded Acres subdivision, was the pride of Jeffery Dorn's existence. A windowless, seamless place in the basement, just below the family room and kitchen. The room was fifteen feet by twenty, but it looked deceptively large, the walls finished with soundproof panels, which were painted an eggshell white, while the floor was covered in outdoor carpeting, a dark leafy green.

In the ceiling, recessed cylinders could be dimmed from a switch at the bottom of the wooden staircase, and he made this adjustment in light levels until a soft romantic glow was achieved. It was clean, spotless, and private. The room had only one door, also painted white, which Jeff kept open most of the time so as not to arouse Irma's suspicions. He had recently read in a woman's magazine how the weaker sex did not understand a man's need for personal space, though he thought that odd for the manner in which silly bitches crowded their kitchens. There had been three in the Clayton house, each one had marked personal space with clothing, notepads, and utensils. It was laughable.

He closed the door, turning to examine himself in the Irma Solution, a full-length wall mirror that looked a tad off centre, for it had to be hung low enough to accommodate her stubby body. This security device was silver-edged, tasteful, and it hung just opposite the door where Irma would immediately enter to meet her own reflection. Dorn knew she would be unable to stay more than a brief moment with her own face, and he was rather proud of that, the simplicity of it all.

In the room's centre, there was a glass desk with a type-writer, an organiser, and a tape recorder. He strolled across the carpet enjoying the feel of cloth tiles beneath bare feet, and pressed the Play button on the recorder. The basement office snapped to life, filling with the sounds of a writer at work; keys clattering, papers turning, punctuated pauses at just the correct intervals. He listened to the floorboards creak above his head as Irma settled into her routine and trotted up the stairs to her bedroom. Quietly, he locked the door and removed the key, surrounded by white. Cold, disorienting, disarming. Looking out from the centre of the room, the door had vanished into the seamless walls, the human eye was lost for a focus.

Canisters on the ceiling repeated themselves in the mirror, reflecting on the glass table. One spin in place, and direction became skewed. East became west. Time became trapped. The tape provided a typewriter's march under dim lights, the little room was glowing and he loved it so; his entrance to a world that nurtured him, seduced him, that gave life meaning.

There was but one picture on the walls, on the far side of the room, nearest the mirror. Just a few moments bathed in white, and the colours nearly screamed from the walls, vibrating, demanding to be recognised. It was an eerie Pop Art collage of a sidewalk bistro, part painting, the awnings, people and tables; part photo, the diner glowing under the black flower of a mushroom cloud; part food, rice raining from the sky; and part ink, the faces of patrons sketched with gas-masks and helmets. They ate merrily under flame-like letters that said *Welcome to the Atomic Cafe*, and he lifted the heavy frame, setting it on the green tiles.

Under the metal lip of a forty-five pound test hook was a hole that on first inspection appeared to be a black smudge. Upon a second look it seemed a shoddy attempt at picture hanging with an oversized nail. From his briefcase he fetched a child's hooded skating key, the antique type once used to adjust vice-like binders against leather shoes, and with nimble experience he inserted it, then spun the key while pressing against the wall until a machine bolt spun free, hanging loose from its anchor.

With a two-handed push along the panel's invisible seam, a spring-loaded panel swung loose on hinges, opening slowly like the door to a bank vault, and there was darkness, formless and pure. Jeff Dorn stooped over at the waist, walking crab-like, then vanished into the black maw, closing the panel behind him.

The room outside was seamless white, with the sound of a report being hammered into life.

The hallway was a concrete tube, about ten feet long and rounded at the top, some three feet wide and four feet high. It resembled a miniature train tunnel, the darkness leading to a second door where an egg-like chamber sat at a depth of twenty feet under Irma Kiernan's backyard.

That this structure had once been intended to protect a family from something as remote as a nuclear attack always amused Dorn, who considered it without the perspective of the period in which it was built. Washington in 1962 was a world that had seen the sole of Khrushchev's shoe as Jack Kennedy ordered the blockade of Cuba, and America waited for a communist promise. In Washington, news pounded at the population, neighbours donned helmets, theatres filled for the movie *Fail-Safe*, and even at public schools children were trained to keep their mouths open to prevent blast damage to eardrums. Wooded Acres, among the better planned communities, gave home buyers their choice of luxuries, a swimming pool or a bomb shelter. And so it was that Dorn stood in the coolness of a bunker twelve foot by twelve, among the smells of liquid Teflon and Hoppes nitrogen solvent. It filled the dead air space, and he threw a light switch, setting the ventilator on low, bringing life into the stuffy relic.

From the backyard, a quarter-acre lot, the only visible sign was a breathing snorkel, which resembled a stovepipe and was about the size of a skinny fire hydrant. This poked up through the ground but had been carefully disguised as a Japanese lantern so that it was functional as well as pleasing. Dorn had constructed the housing device as a filtration system, building elements into the window-like lantern on three of six sides, then presented this as a gift to Irma, who unknowingly completed the camouflage, planting an elaborate flower garden around the oriental hydrant; mostly coloured perennials in honour of Jeff's comrades who had died on foreign soil.

And if you asked Irma Kiernan, she would say that the shelter was gone, ripped out and filled in, and that her Jeff had managed all of this for a tremendous saving, and thereby proving that the world is filled with crooks. Most of her neighbours had paid a group rate of upwards of five thousand dollars each to have their backyards dismantled, and Irma didn't seem to mind that it took Jeff nearly a year to complete the work, even though a strange and unpleasant thing happened.

During demolition, Irma was forced by events to take up residence in a cheap motel, for during the peak of Dorn's efforts, rodents started invading her home. For a short time she had tolerated the field mice.

Soon after she found two dead rats in her kitchen sink.

It took almost a year for the Atomic Cafe to take form.

Once clean air was circulating through filters, Dorn began patching the concrete, sealing and painting, building shelves, carpeting the pad on which it was built, then adding two chairs and a loveseat. Like the den that preceded it, the walls were painted white, but this carpet was red. The work was completed in 1981, and since that time he had added little finishing touches; a dehumidifier, a space heater, a magnetic fan in the floor, whatever the family budget would allow.

The ceiling was a small concrete dome with a white pebbled surface, and the door was double reinforced steel, lockable from the inside only with a bolt and crossbar. These two features were original, the door forged from high-test steel, then packed with molten lead for weight and protection against nuclear fallout. Over the decades, even the hinges held true, and he guessed that the Atomic salesmen had used these in showrooms as a selling tool because the integrity was beyond question. On the turn-bolt crossbar, the same type used on hatches for large ships, was stamped *W. Charles & Co.*, and he pulled on this, stepping down five wooden steps and into the sunken confine.

From the outside, the door appeared to swing shut without a sound. But from within there was a deafening thud and a shock of air as the faint hum of the snorkel's magnetic fan began to whirl. He stopped to admire the steps, the original white spruce which he had painstakingly sanded and refinished to their natural complexion.

Just inside the chamber, to the right, was a wall plate with a series of black toggle switches and a captain's chair. To the left of the door, between a taupe-coloured loveseat and recliner was a large wooden armoire which was painted a flat black. He opened the door to rows of clothes, freshly cleaned, some still hanging in their plastic bags, and counting seven across, he removed a uniform. It was a pale blue jumpsuit with more tool holders than a watchman has keys, and across the breast pocket was the name *Ben Johnson, Supervisor.* On the back it said *C&P Telephone Company*, and on each shoulder was an embroidered logo of a bright blue liberty bell. He laid this across the loveseat, then stripped down to his underwear.

For an hour Dorn sat on the small sofa while running

through a checklist of equipment, then pulled a filebox towards him, the ball-casters sliding easily over the outdoor carpeting. He opened a drawer and retrieved a file, removing a news clipping from a New York newspaper. It was a photo-less story, less than two column inches long and lacking a byline. Dorn wished the editors of the community page had included more detail.

LOCAL MAN HONOURED BY BROTHERS

John F. Scott of Greenlawn was honoured today with a Lifetime of Service award from Big Brothers of America for his work with children who are lacking male role models.

Scott, a government analyst, is due to retire from federal service later this year.

He read it again. It had not been the first time. And he knew the Clayton package would be sitting on his desk, and that stirred an excitement in Jeffery Dorn.

To this he clipped the small white envelope which Irma had retrieved the night before, and his hand shook uncharacteristically as he held the paper to the light. Earlier in the month he had specifically requested that all such communications be sent without a return address from his doctor on Foxhall Road. It was a dying man's wish. As a patient he could not be denied.

During a routine checkup, Dorn's quarterly trip for pills of various kinds, a blood test had revealed a white cell count over 1,500, indicative of advanced cancer. The shock had crippled him for days as he quickly investigated the possibilities of therapy; chemical, radiation, even transfusion.

Having studied the effects of healing, in many cases worse than simply dying, Dorn held further treatment in abeyance until the specific type and location of the disease could be found. He was scheduled for an extensive battery of tests at the end of the month, and did not want to read more about his fate. When faced with his own mortality, Dorn simply wished to fill his last days with as much living as possible, which meant keeping the secret from Irma, who would fawn over him in such a way that death would be preferable.

Dr Thomas Landry, who Dorn considered a basic pill doctor, was lost for words in the first place. That the patient would die was without doubt, the cells and platelet count proved that, however sloppy he considered Landry to be. This was the fourth message from him in a month, the last described what to expect, how his body would grow weak, how his strength would ebb. Dorn was tired of dealing with it. Whatever the outcome he planned on living to the last, pushing his entire life into a remainder of months.

Six of those, or maybe a year, no one knew.

And while Dorn started to consider this, anger stirred him to his feet and he slapped the envelope inside the file. Life was cheating him. He was still young. His prime was not yet over. And if he had believed in God, which he did not, then he would have considered this a message.

But Jeff Dorn knew better.

On planet earth there was only mortal man, that was the being that left messages of reason. No wild dog could ever do the same, no Christ-like figure, no apparitions born of insanity from the foolish sands of mankind's collective past. He hated mythology. From the Greeks to the Bible to the Gods of Mormon hope, to the babbling fools in their sanctimonious stained glass towers; they spent their lives interpreting messages, reading tea leaves, searching for reason.

Men like Dorn created the messages, lasting messages, and he had left one for Scott, a masterpiece of play, a little retirement package; and their name was Clayton. He knew the case would be sitting on Scott's desk, it filled a dying man with a wicked delight and special sense of purpose.

That Scott was Catholic only made it better, guilt ran his soft and shallow life from the confessional to the squad car to the streets; he couldn't act on a whim without permission from the saints. And he imagined that his enemy had grown quite complacent over the years, his futile little job failing to provide meaning where the church had promised, but could not deliver.

'Elmer Janson,' Dorn spoke aloud, selecting another newspaper and scanning the page. The reporter from *Tempo* was a soulmate to Dorn, though he did not know him, they both were itching for details on this slut of a mother.

It delighted him.

A hundred times he had read this thing, he would read it a hundred more.

And in three steps he crossed the bunker to a supply closet which sat against the furthest wall. It was large, metal, with double doors. He opened them, then leaned forward examining rows of sophisticated weaponry, carbines and assault rifles and machine guns. There was a speciality shelf for knives. On each side of the vault, pistols hung suspended from trigger-guards lying three rows across, ten deep; a total of thirty semi-automatic handguns.

Below, in an enclosed locker, a padlock promised accessories; picks, blades, suppressors, clips and ammunition, pipes, holsters, and cord. He surveyed the inner walls, and from among many gleaming possibilities he selected a .22-calibre Rohm automatic, which he lifted from its hook. For the better part of an hour he stripped, cleaned, assembled and polished the little weapon, loading the clip with hollow-tipped bullets. Dorn held it to the soft overhead light, releasing the slide, and it snapped shut with a deadly clap, feeding a cartridge. Safety activated, he inserted the clip.

Oiled with a liquid Teflon, the flyweight alloy gun, silencer attached, was swift and soundless as a sewing machine. He removed a tool bag from behind the loveseat and began to dress.

Within fifteen minutes, Ben Johnson was emerging from the shelter, a field supervisor from the local telephone company being dispatched on an emergency assignment; a role Dorn favoured almost as much as Veteran. And he played for the most personal and ultimate stakes. Deception to Jeffrey Dorn was a deeply personal and satisfying amusement, a hobby, a challenge, and a way of life. The role he was now wearing would not fade in the wash of humanity, for he knew it, tried and true, an experienced lineman with the credentials to prove it.

On his way to work he paused, lifting a small but exquisite leather case with a reddish hue which sat by a shelf near the shelter's door. As far as he was concerned there was nothing finer to be had anywhere in America, at least not as a symbol, and he took it from its case.

The Legion of Merit sprayed a sparkling glint of yellow as he held it in his hand, the light streaming in tiny lines across the shelter, dancing on concrete walls, reflecting on the pebbled ceiling. A blue ribbon lay carefully folded into rows, from which was suspended the heroic shield, and as he touched, caressed, and held it Dorn felt an excitement that had not waned, not even after millions of inspections. There was an enchantment that he could not shake, though he had worn it for years around the collar of his dress uniform, and his breath fogged the shiny medallion, one of America's highest rewards for sacrifice and gallantry.

Before leaving he wrote a note to have Irma apply polish and elbow grease. *White hot*, he penned, that's the way he liked all of his medals, and he left this upstairs on the kitchen table.

Now it was true that, under another name, he had served in the Army as a private during the Korean War. But he had been court-martialled for sexual assault and held a Dishonourable Discharge to prove it.

During his four-month tour of duty, he had never left the United States.

TWENTY-THREE

In the northwest section of the Potomac River Valley, a gentleman's country estate sat on a piece of land just skirting the edge of Great Falls National Historic Park.

The vast private property was so close to the highway that during the summer months, tourists often mistook the little farm house by the road as a Department of Interior food concession, and would knock on the front door of the residence expecting menus. The man who answered was James Lee Cooley.

Once, not so far back in time, the Cooley family had maintained a working farm in Cabin John. But with the massive housing development that came to the area during the early seventies, property taxes increased to the point where the only solution to a pending government foreclosure was to sell a tract of land once used for shedding tobacco. And it was thus that the man who was now standing before John Scott and Frank Rivers had become an overnight millionaire.

'Hey, Jim,' Rivers said cheerily as Cooley stepped out onto the front porch. The country gentleman had heard the siren approaching, then the car pulling over gravel and into the long circular driveway.

'Hey back at you, Frank,' he smiled. 'Would you like a menu, special of the day is lemonade, or beer, if your friend wants one.' He extended his hand to Scott who was standing a little off to one side. Greetings were quickly exchanged, and they found themselves following the lean farmer through the hall, living room, kitchen, and out to an open-air patio.

Frank Rivers had known the entire Cooley clan, so

watching Jimmy was like casting eyes upon the stern countenance of a ghost from early childhood. He knew Jim as a
compact version of his father, with looks and a manner that
were deceiving. Though he was thirty-eight, he could easily pass
for fifteen years younger, making him easy to spot by former
acquaintances. He was quiet, almost pensive, and his once
wild head of reddish hair was a thinning chestnut brown.

'I'll get us some drinks,' he said quietly, glancing at Rivers,
then to Scott, as the two men settled into lawn chairs, and
there was an awkward silence.

'That sounds grand,' Scott smiled.

'Anything's good for me,' Rivers returned, and Jim Cooley
crossed the grey slate patio, vanishing through the rear door
as the two men sat in quiet admiration. Looking out onto
Jim's world from the rear patio, there were meadows and
rolling green hills as far as the eye could see, an enormous
island of calm in the middle of a ruthless city. And Scott
found himself imagining what the Cooley farm must have
once looked like, corn rows reaching, golden fields, earthen
patches ploughed into neat columns. Far off near the roadway,
before a stately oak, he spotted a tractor's rusting hulk, the
front blades still attached, locked and frozen above the
ground. The open fields, the bright sun and smells of damp
humus stroked the senses, deepening a foreboding silence.

On second look, it was a mournful sight, and Scott's brow
was heavy with concentration. Clouds moved through sunlight
casting shadows at their feet.

'What happened to him, Frank?' Scott said quietly, pulling
his chair closer to the detective.

'In what sense, Jack? Jimmy's good people.'

'His parents, you knew them?'

'Died within a year of each other, his mother had a stroke,
Big Jim died from a coronary, they found him sitting at the
wheel of his Cat.' Rivers pointed to the tractor. 'It's a hellava
machine, straight eight, don't see many of those any more.'

The Commander prodded gently: 'In the hallway I saw a
picture of you and Jim with another boy on what looked like
a camping trip. Who is he?'

Rivers' eyes shifted to Scott, then back out to the fields. 'You don't miss much, do you Jack? That was his older brother Michael. We were three buttons off the same shirt, couldn't keep us apart. He got wasted, spring of '68.'

Scott could see the man's jaw tighten, a cool breeze soaked the landscape. 'The first week in May?' he asked softly, and Rivers stood, fumbling through his pockets for a smoke, then popping an aspirin instead.

'Outstanding detective of the year, the awards ceremony is about the same time, being with Jim is more important to you, does he know?'

Rivers' eyes turned to ice. 'No, and you aren't going to tell him, and I mean that.'

Scott had no doubt that he was digging into a wound, so he quickly dropped the matter as Cooley appeared, tray in hand. He poured three glasses and settled into his seat, watching Scott with a subtle interest, but annoyed by the occasional rumble of cars leaving the National Park across the way. Scott took a long hard swallow from his glass.

'Thank you,' he said, waiting for his host to speak, but Cooley said not a word as he quickly stood to freshen his drink. A calico cat appeared, rubbing against Scott's leg, then plopped down at his feet. He leaned over and stroked the small animal.

'What's his name?' he inquired.

'Buttercup,' said Cooley. 'He's a she.'

At the sound of voices a basset hound slowly sauntered over, licked the cat and lay down alongside, vying for attention. 'Buttercup's friend?' Scott asked.

'Downboy, only dog you'll meet scared of his own bark,' Cooley offered, just as a large black feline leaped up and crawled over his back, draping himself across both shoulders. 'Hunley,' he smiled as the cat purred loudly, amber eyes glowing in the Commander's direction.

'Good name for a cat,' Scott offered. 'Wasn't Horace Hunley the inventor of the first American submarine?'

Cooley nodded. 'Yes sir, a Confederate captain, 1864 was the date. The sub went down in battle with all hands.'

Rivers was dunking cubes in his glass with a straw.

'So what can we do for you?' Cooley asked, placing the cat in his lap. 'Frank made it sound pretty urgent, but he always sounds like that.'

'Thanks Jim,' Rivers replied.

Scott put down his glass and removed a notepad from his blazer, which was draped across the chair. 'We're trying to understand a relationship between . . .'

'You have three dead children and one woman, Frank explained all that,' Cooley cut him off. 'How can I help?'

'The black child,' he said gratefully, 'I have someone working on an identification but I need to know, if she still had family or friends, where would they be now?'

'If she was a city kid, Washington, it's a black city, and I don't mean that in an uncharitable way.'

'And if she lived around here?' Scott asked.

Cooley looked at Rivers. 'She was a local child?' he asked, and his voice seemed trembly.

Scott nodded. 'We're not certain, but let's presume that she was.'

'And she died when?'

'She was killed in 1958.'

Cooley stared into the distance and took a sip from his glass. 'Then Tobytown would be my guess.' He pointed. 'About ten miles north as you head out to Frederick.'

Scott opened his black briefcase, removed an area map, and then handed it to Cooley. 'Will you show me?'

'Sure,' he said, leaning forward, and the cat jumped from his lap. 'Here's River Road,' he pointed. 'A few years ago I sold a tract of bottom land a few miles up, we used it to shed tobacco, that would be a good landmark for you.'

Scott circled the spot on the exploded view.

'Look for a housing development right there with a gold sign that says Tara, you'll find Tobytown eight miles up.'

Scott chuckled, 'From *Gone with the Wind* Tara? That's the best they could do?'

Cooley shrugged, remembering the honey smells of barn-curing tobacco and thinking about the mansions with their purple doors that developers had just seemed to drop there. 'Instant identity for thieves,' he said, reaching to the lawn, and with the practice of a field hand he pulled a blade of dry grass and dropped it into his mouth.

Scott caught the man's grimace.

'Tobytown,' Cooley volunteered, 'used to be near where you and Frank are staying, back when I was a kid. It could be she lived there once.' He shrugged. 'But her family would have been forced to move north.'

A puzzled expression spread across Scott's face. The command post was at least ten miles south, going in the opposite direction, and the only town there was the city of Bethesda. 'Jim, do you mean another town used to be near the bowling alley?'

Cooley nodded. 'Tobytown,' he said again.

'Tell me about that,' Scott dug, 'government records don't reflect what you're saying.'

'Jack,' Rivers put in defensively while reaching for the pitcher, 'if anyone would know, Jimmy would.'

'I'm quite sure, thank you Frank.' He turned back to face the lean farmer. 'What the devil happened, Jim?'

'Well,' he drawled with a slight Southern accent, 'Tobytown was a mixed village, black and white, poor but proud. My grandfather lived there for a short time when he was down on his luck, so Tobytown was established long before this farm. During the States' War, as people would flee from the deep South, they followed the river. Once they got to Cabin John they took River Road towards Washington and just settled there, up by the railroad tracks where the high-rise buildings are. That's the short version, there was an entire town that spread down to Kenwood Forest past the bowling alley.'

Drury's office had supplied detailed land records of the area, there had been no mention. 'I'm sorry, but I'm confused,' Scott said, 'you're saying Tobytown is now in the other direction?'

Cooley nodded. 'North,' he said, 'look for the sign that says Tara and just keep going, you'll find it.'

'And this town, this Tobytown, used to be near the bowling alley?'

'All true,' said Cooley.

'Then why did they relocate?'

'Why?' Cooley repeated the question with a forced laugh, staring at Scott. 'Poor people don't have lawyers is why,' and there was anger in his voice. 'Didn't matter that nobody owned that land, it was sold out from underneath them. Did you notice the small Baptist church between the bank and the gas station?'

'I did see that, yes,' Scott answered.

'That's all that's left, the one thing Tobytown residents refused to give up, now it sits in a concrete wasteland. Next to the church there was an adjoining cemetery, they built right over it. When Frank called I thought for sure somebody hit on an old Tobytown grave, but he didn't agree.'

Scott winced. What better place to hide murdered women and children, the killer had planned for the future, and he recalled Elmer Janson's remark about slave burials, perhaps a loose rumour based on historical fact. And the lime to quickly dissolve bone, forcing early decomposition, masking victims among graves of the disenfranchised. Who would have searched there, and if anything was found, who would have cared?

'And the church is all that's left,' Scott's voice sagged. 'Do you know what took place there?'

'This isn't ancient history, Jack,' he said sarcastically, 'I know what happened to Tobytown because the goddamned sky turned red, lighting up the horizon for miles. She burned for three days. Somebody torched them and the town went to ashes, it was the week of my eighth birthday, I was born July 21st.'

Scott sat back in his chair, it sounded like behaviour from the turn of the century. 'Then that would be around 1957?'

'No, Frank's got a year on me, that was 1958. From my bedroom I could see the flames from Tobytown, and the local men all gathered outside, right here, talking and drinking, but there wasn't anything they could do. Just working men, they didn't want trouble not of their making.'

Rivers gulped his drink, nervously stabbing ice cubes with a straw for more liquid. Cooley reached over and refilled his glass. 'I don't mind,' he said to him, though looking in Scott's direction. 'So anyway, they were moved way out, we can take you there. You'll see a large sign that says *Tobytown, Established 1865*, and behind that you'll find some cheap apartments built by the County Government. Around here, signs help some people sleep at night, the River Road properties had become too valuable to let the poor keep them.'

'There are laws,' Scott commented absently.

'No,' Cooley frowned, 'this is Washington, land of lawyers. Around here the thieves make it up as they go, some work for the feds, some for the County, some for private companies, but it's all the same, glove in hand corruption. Very safe, and very lucrative. Way out here they forced me to sell a field, got better than two million for it, and that's nothing compared to what Tobytown was and where it was located. Difference is, I'm a white boy, they had to pay me.'

Scott's lips pinched tight, he was beginning to understand. 'Frank tells me that there's a lot of history around here and that you used to find Civil War artifacts on your farm?'

Cooley glanced at Rivers and smiled. 'Frank told you that?'

Scott glanced at him. 'Was he wrong?'

'No,' Cooley laughed, 'but to Frank, history was last night's dinner.'

'Dogs and beans with slaw,' Rivers added.

'Well, I researched Cabin John,' Scott pressed on, 'and there's very little mentioned, no battles, anyway.'

'There wouldn't be,' Cooley explained. 'River Road was an immediate route to and from the major fighting at Antietam, Manassas, Gettysburg and other battlefields. Federal and Confederate boys would actually pass each other in broad daylight and not fire, a lot of 'em were neighbours.'

'Then there was no fighting,' Scott concluded.

Cooley leaned forward, straightened the map, and pointed. 'You're here directly across from Great Falls National Park, one-quarter of a mile off the main roadway. Anything on either side, including this farm, was free-for-all. Do you remember seeing the punch-press housing developments on the way in?'

Scott nodded.

'Once they were fields and farms, in those areas, especially down here by the canal or river, it was a No-Man's-Land, hundreds of men in blue and grey fought viciously as they were returning from major campaigns, and fighting so close to home, this area saw some of the most desperate hand-to-hand combat of the war, but no historic engagements. Some guy was dying right there one hundred and twenty-five years ago.' Cooley pointed to the large oak near the roadway.

'Fascinating,' Scott said. 'Were you hunting for artifacts?'

'No, I don't believe in that,' he replied, taking a long sip of lemonade, then locking eyes with Scott. 'When I was ten we were tilling near that tree after a storm and the plough blade bit cloth just under the soil, we uncovered a Confederate boy still clutching his cap, so we fetched the pastor and interred him, he's still there. A few weeks later we snagged bone near the park, found a Yankee, and buried him alongside. The Yank faces north, the Reb faces south, that was my father's idea. Our guess is that they were on their way home after Antietam in 1862 and killed each other, but who knows? They were young, no wedding bands or filled teeth, but if anyone found out today,' the man blinked, 'they'd be sold at a flea-market.'

Scott emitted a sigh and faced Jim Cooley directly. 'So we're dealing with a relocated village, a church cemetery and public records that were destroyed?'

'That would be my guess.'

Scott smiled thoughtfully. 'That explains a great deal, I've dealt with this type of greed before. You have a beautiful home, Jim, and I thank you for sharing it with us.' He started to rise from his seat when the man suddenly barked at him.

'How did it happen?' Cooley blurted, and Frank Rivers stood quickly, watching anger take hold of his friend.

'What's that?' Scott responded, looking to Rivers for direction.

Jim Cooley seemed confused, his fists were clenched. 'One day,' his voice quivered, 'this was a real nice town, I mean, all places on God's earth have their problems, but it was a real place. Next thing you know we're overflowing with crooks, everything's bulldozed flat, and it happened so fast no one saw it coming, like we were sleep walking . . .' his voice trailed into sorrow.

Scott studied the two young men. 'I'm not sure exactly what you're asking, but most places with a cultural legacy would never have allowed this much development this fast. A construction avalanche usually starts when history is forgotten or rewritten, that's obviously what went on here,' he said, watching their expressions. His words were having an effect.

'Oh come on, Jack,' Rivers suddenly blurted. 'What great fucking history were we known for?'

Scott waved him off with one hand, offering silence.

'Freedom,' Cooley stated at Rivers, finding his voice. 'Freedom, not the concept but the courage to find it, the strength to allow it. The very name Bethesda means House of Mercy, from the Old Testament.'

'But the Urban District, the people who put out that dining guide said Bethesda took its name from a pool in Israel,' Rivers fired. 'They even imported a rock from there, it was in all the papers.'

Cooley sat back in his chair shaking his head. 'And where do you think they came from, Frank? You should know better!' He turned to Scott. 'My father was a boy when Bethesda was named, the town was titled for the courage of a Freeman, a former slave.'

'John?' Scott asked.

Cooley nodded. 'The city was named to honour him, in the bible it says, "Go without fear with him whose name is John, for upon his promise thee will find Bethesda, house of mercy, of freedom, and of God." That's where the name came from, Frank, I really can't believe you!'

And Scott knew. He knew in his instinctual gut the way

Diana Clayton had felt Zak Dorani enter her house, a shiver, a chill, a heartbeat. He leaned over and handed Jim Cooley a glassine evidence pouch, and the farmer's eyes instantly burned with anguish.

'Was this found in the grave?' he asked solemnly.

Scott nodded.

'And Frank told me that this man's been killing for thirty years?'

'Closer to thirty-five,' Scott answered. 'What is this?'

Cooley's eyes did not need to focus, he closed fingers around the medallion. 'It's a John's Warning.'

'The same man Bethesda was named for?'

'John-the-Free. These coins would be put into circulation as a warning that Confederate spies were infiltrating the river area. The only other type was a Scarborough warning.'

'I don't follow,' Scott said.

'Southern Lynch Law, if they caught someone helping slaves or Federal prisoners they'd kill you on the spot, you'd be found swinging from a rope. Only two types of warnings back then, a John's Warning like this coin, or a Scarborough Warning, which means hang them first and they'll get the message.'

'First a blow, warning after, the spies were ruthless terrorists which is why the tokens were so important. Faced with such brutality, no one could be trusted.'

Cooley nodded.

'And the house on the coin?'

He shook his head, 'It's a symbol of many cabins that were built near here to hide refugees, it would take a long time to explain.'

'Maybe not. What type of child would be wearing this?' Scott asked.

'A child who was well loved,' he said, staring at the coin. 'A good token is worth several thousand dollars to a collector. My grandfather gave me one so I'd remember what this town is about, I still have it.'

'And Frank told me you were born on this property,' he

paused. 'Your birth record doesn't say Cabin John, does it, Jim?'

The intense green eyes sparkled with recognition. Rivers sat mute, since childhood Jim Cooley had been his closest friend, they had no secrets, or so he had thought.

Cooley carried his cat into the little house which drifted in acres of rolling green, and returned with a bound leather album, handing it to the stranger.

'I was born in a place that no longer exists,' he stated, his face a mask of hatred. 'A town where it never mattered to anyone what colour you were, or religion, or how much you made, or what land you owned. We were hard-working Americans, that used to count for something.'

Scott began to examine the first document, his fingers lightly stroking the words on a Certificate of Live Birth as Cooley handed him a gold wooden frame. It was a country landscape with a village green, a town, a white church steeple, a waterfall, and inset at the bottom was a token in mint condition.

'John's Cabin, Maryland,' Scott said with a tone of defiance. 'I was right, the birth certificate and the coin are the same!'

'Once the greatest town in the Free State,' Cooley responded proudly. 'The name was changed the year Toby-town burned.'

TWENTY-FOUR

He had started to sweat in the hot morning sun, and although he had dressed using the finest of talc, his blue uniform was already clinging. It sagged at the hips, weighted down with tools and equipment, the most awkward of which was a telephone lineman's test set. This was a self-contained telephone with push-buttons and a rotary dial built into the handle, and as he climbed the rungs on a pole on Westbard Avenue, it swung from a cord at his waist, slapping against his thigh.

His technique was only fair, not good, and a passing uniformed patrolman knew immediately that Jeff Dorn, an older man who looked out of practice, was a C&P Telephone Company field supervisor who had been short changed over the weekend.

Other tools sprouted from chest, belly and thighs, and he climbed higher as the police car sped by. He was resting at the twelve-foot station where the metal struts began, providing a ladder for authorised workers. He attached a leather safety strap and, holding on tight to the pole, wrapped it around the sticky pylon, clipping the left end first, then the right, to the steel turnbuckle at his waist. Leaning back gently, he felt the support across the small of his back and climbed slowly as he caught his breath.

Now it was true that on some rare occasions Jeffery Dorn had some back pain, he had inherited a curved spine that could cause muscle spasms when the weather was inclement. And it was also true that the local telephone company issued a quality suit with more holders than a watchman has keys, but the material was still inferior to what he was accustomed

238

to. Cotton would have breathed better and would have been the more logical choice, Dorn thought as he started to sweat. Then again, he only became a lineman in the best of seasons.

He was moving quickly now in an upward crawl, using the metal rungs, passing the twenty-five foot mark, then the fifty, and resting again. Soon he reached the top of the pylon, eyeing a large grey terminal box that connected with power-lines and rows of industrial cable.

To repairmen across the land, this type of unit was referred to as a junction box or terminus, but to Dorn it was the Hydra, a slang used in the parlance of clandestine surveillance, which he had picked up from detailed manuals he had discovered years earlier at the annual State Department book sale. Such proceeds always went to charity, which Dorn found ironic, and with a single controlled stroke he slit the back of a cable housing with a straight razor. He then reached inside the hose with a small chrome hook, pulling free a nerve bundle of multicoloured wires in every hue of the rainbow.

Methodically he laid these across his palm, searching for one with small white bands, and then denuding a sheath using a special tool, and attaching an alligator clip to the raw copper wire. He leaned back against the belt and studied the massive grey Hydra, the black cords playing out to countless rows of houses, and leading to a second box a few hundred yards down River Road.

Throughout his life, Jeffery Dorn had always depended on the predictability and general competence of other people, and he knew if the telephone maintenance crew for this block was any good he could save hours, working by colour code and geographic distance. It was a simple thing. The closer the house, the closer the Hydra, and inside there were sequentially coded wire leads from near to far. He could count the houses visually against each coloured lead, but if the maintenance crew was sloppy, it could take all day.

Dorn clutched the tarred and sticky pylon looking down from the metal struts beneath his boots to the street. The bastards were oblivious, their puny lives looked as dwarfed as their cars two hundred feet below, and he began to work, counting against a notepad. Life itself, he reflected, was an orderly process of elimination, just like working the wires, old against young, sick against strong, mind against will, man over beast, a progression of time and endurance; and he counted seven strands, yanking a red wire free, reaching to a breast pocket for another tool and stripping that line down to metal. He then searched for yellow, and one green, fourteen wires in, snapping these to bare copper and attaching clips to each. He held the test set to his ear and listened for a dial tone.

Nothing.

Checking for an unstable ground connection he freed the white ribbed wire, licked the teeth on the clip, and replaced the contact. The headset snapped to life, the connection was true, steady. He dialled, watching his meter, and a phone rang twice.

'Westwood Elementary,' a woman's voice filled his ear.

'This is telephone repair,' he said in a dry but commanding tone. 'We are checking a faulty line, is this Westwood school?' he asked.

'Yes it is . . .' sang a Valium voice.

The woman had to be sixty. 'Can you hear me clearly Miss?'

'Yes I can, I can hear you . . .' she sung for a stranger on a pole.

He glanced at a gauge, the voice registered .9 Biddles indicating weak resistance on the line for a half-mile span, and knowing that this could be improved, he prepared to terminate the call.

'Thank you, I believe we have the trouble corrected.' His words were firm but routine. 'If you have any complaints, please contact your local C&P telephone repair, it's been a pleasure to serve you.'

'Oh, thank you . . .' she fluted, as he pulled the plug, made a notation and secured the book to a belt clip. He replaced the hold on three clips, checking for dust or any fouling, and swabbing these with a pre-moistened chemical pad. The lines had not been disturbed, number fourteen yellow-and-green was the switchboard at Irma's school, he had established a baseline he could easily follow. Without further delay he tore into number seven red with tiny metal jaws.

'I don't care, Donna, my father hates him,' the voice of a young woman filled his ears. 'Did you hear that?'

'What?'

'That click on the line, it sounds like someone is on the phone.'

Dorn was cleaning his teeth with a thumbnail.

'I didn't hear a thing, Donna, it's not over here, are you sure you're going through with this, I'm late for school . . .'

He wanted to listen, but didn't have time, and hit blue. '. . . we've got to unload,' harped a man's voice, slightly effete. 'We've been sitting on it too long, we're not collecting interest on our investment – did you hear that?'

Static boomed, then died.

'What the fuck?' a second man responded.

There was an extended silence, Dorn shrugged, making sure his fingers were far from the transmitting bar and checked a ground lead.

'I don't know what, but I heard it!' whined the effeminate male. 'Do you think our phones are tapped? God, maybe it's the DEA, we've got to unload!'

'Shut up, you fucking idiot!' came a sharp retort. 'Not on the phone, I'll meet you.'

'Where?'

'In the lobby of the Air Right's building by the photo counter, ten o'clock?'

Dorn pulled the plug and remembered to laugh. He was fascinated by suburban life, the closed doors and private conversations, residents ran in circles like mice on a wheel, chasing each other, then dropping with exhaustion into twisted nests. The nice young men down the street were really idiot faggots selling dope. Donna worried about father who was probably doing Donna anyway, who was he to intrude? He wormed through the coil for a silver line and attached.

'Oh, it's so hard, Beth,' she pleaded, 'ever since the children left for college he's been difficult, we just don't talk any more. Mop the floors, clean the toilets, feed the dog, starch the shirts, do I have ambitions? No, I couldn't have.'

The lineman could also hear a television soap in the background.

'When's the last time he told you he loved you, appreciated you, took you to dinner?' asked a sedate woman.

She sighed, 'I can't even remember, it's been that long.'

Dorn had been on an open line, and since the static interference was weak, the signal clear and steady, he knew he was in close proximity to his target. Since they hadn't commented on the intrusion, he decided to perform a trial run to determine where he was in the neighbourhood telephone loop. He smacked the transmitting button on the test set twice, his eyes dropping down a list in his notepad.

'Telephone repair, sorry to bother you ladies, there seems to be some trouble on the line. Is this 1107 Kenwood Forest Drive?' he asked with authority, charming them with his rounded tones.

'No,' said the distressed woman, 'this is 1103, you must have the wrong number. Beth, do you have any phone problems?'

'No, Maggie, you know Mark does all of our installation, and we never had a problem. Not one . . .'

'Sorry about the intrusion, ladies, we've crossed a wire,' he comforted, writing in his book. Number 1103 was Maggie Lubbo, at least he was close.

'. . . you just don't know how lucky you are, Beth,' the conversation resumed before the lineman had disconnected. 'He's such a talented and considerate man . . .'

Was it green-on-green or white-on-green? He selected the first.

'. . . but we don't know that much about him, Honey. I'm sure he's a fine man, a perfect gentleman, but think now. How many times have you met him?' she prodded gently, a creature with an elegant voice. The lineman was enthralled.

'Twice, Mom, two times, why can't I go, you met him?'

'Only for a second, just long enough to say goodbye, and that's not good enough.'

'But Mom, please?'

'Well, I'd like to talk to him again before I allow you to go traipsing off into the woods to some fishing hole. Did he leave a number?' she asked gently.

'A con artist fleecing a house of suckers, snatch the kid for a snuff flick,' he said aloud. 'It's a dealer's market.'

'We can talk about him later, Hun, are you working on your homework, you have two tests on Monday.' Her voice was firm but soothing, and Jeff Dorn remembered the first time he saw *Bambi*, how the little creature loved and obeyed his mother. And he imagined that feeling. It was a good but bitter memory, he could whistle the music to the death scene, the doe had gone down hard.

'Yes, Mother,' he sighed. 'When are you coming home?'

'Elmer, I've got a meeting in a few minutes, and I'll be home right after. Then we'll go out for some treats, would you like to see a movie tonight?'

'Yes,' his voice sounded perkier, *'Indiana Jones!'*

'You've seen that twice, pick something else after you've completed your studies, and we'll talk when I get home. And no TV or running around until you've finished everything, or there'll be no movie, understand?'

'Yes,' said the voice huffily.

'I love you, Baby.'

'Tripod says hello.'

'Hello Tripod, now please get some work done, and if you have any questions call me?'

'Yes Mom,' he said grudgingly.

'And no more sweets until after lunch, it's in the re-fridge.'

'I know.'

'Call me?' she tested.

'Yes, Mom.'

'I love you.'

'Love you too, Mom.'

And Dorn mocked their conversation, imitating their voices, listening carefully as Jessica Janson hesitated, just a fraction of a second, raising a brow before hanging up the phone as Jeffery Dorn worked his face into a cruel knot.

If anyone knew about maternal instinct, it was the lineman.

TWENTY-FIVE

The detail moved forward like the hands of a clock with the two men arriving back at the command post on Ridgefield Drive at 3:10 p.m.

To Frank Rivers it felt early, his spirit was depressed by his lack of knowledge about the town where he was raised, while to Jack Scott time had been forced into a precise stillness. He was wandering the dark corners of his life, counting faces in a morgue, those bearing the marks of Recreational Killers. His mind flipped back over thirty-five years at a speed that stood the world in slow motion as the horrid truth became inescapable.

In that period, Zak Dorani could have easily claimed hundreds of lives, but by the time the Crown Victoria edged into the driveway, Scott was contemplating the gender ratios of girls to boys to young mothers, considering their fate as his personal failing just as a giant of a man emerged near the garden gate.

He stepped from the shadows near the garage, black and looming, in his early forties, and wearing a light blue beret with a purple T-shirt.

Quickly the man made his presence known, and quickly he took a step backward into shadow. He was a severe-looking sort with a face that seemed chiselled from a block of wood.

'I do hope he's friendly,' Scott said as the engine died.

'I should have known about John's Cabin,' Rivers said absently.

'By the time you were old enough to care, the name was

long gone, changed when you were a baby living in California, so don't get down on yourself.'

Rivers chewed on a bit of flesh inside one cheek as he opened the door and stepped out, waiting for Scott, who drew up alongside.

'How do you want to handle tactics?' Rivers asked.

'You have my every faith, you know what we need to cover our position, and I will leave that in your capable hands.' They were heading towards the side lot.

'And if you don't like my techniques?'

'Every faith, Frank, you know your capabilities, men and resources. If I'm free to concentrate on the hunt while you're minding the store, we'll make better progress. If you hit a wall, let me know, but I'm placing you in charge and I speak for Captain Drury.'

Rivers nodded as they approached. Travis Bernard Saul, or Toy as he was known, greeted them both, then slapped Rivers' palms hard enough to sting. He led them between houses and through the garden gate, where three other men in old clothes waited on the patio.

It took five minutes to get acquainted and unload equipment into the house; radios, field parabolic, spotting scopes, cameras, and several banker's boxes filled with files and forms. As Scott looked on, the State Policemen hashed over the interior decorations before settling down into the garish leather chairs and sofa.

'Where are you parking?' asked Rivers.

'In the NIH lot on Westbard, two blocks up,' Dennis Murphy responded, a large officer with red hair, his fair skin covering a massive skull and bone structure. He was known to Frank Rivers as Mule Murphy, not for his size, but for his tenacity. They had known each other since the Christmas truce of 1968, Da Nang Airbase.

'Any problem with the keys to the bowling alley?' Rivers asked a pair of younger men in street clothes.

'No, the captain gave us an extra set,' answered Marcus Koczka, the shorter of the two, mirror sunglasses slung over thinning hair. He handed the copies to Rivers.

'The lock's cheap, no alarms or loose windows,' said Rudolph Marchette, a slight man with a thick black moustache.

'Ditch the lip, Rudy,' Rivers demanded, turning to unroll the blueprints.

'What, Sarge?' the rookie responded assertively.

'The fake brush.' He reached over and ripped it loose. 'Stick it on your tool, you can play Dick when you get home.'

Toy laughed, slapping him on the back, almost sending the light man into a tumble.

'Listen up,' Rivers demanded. 'We're going through this once, no screw-ups. Marchette,' he bore down, 'do you know about the fool who went to the Red Cross and gave all his blood?'

'Ah, no sir,' said Rudy the Lip.

'You screwup, you'll wish that was you, now listen up!'

Faces registered a serious focus as all eyes shifted to the floor where the blueprint lay weighted down in each corner by Frank's running shoes, gun and handcuffs. He studied the chart on one knee for a moment, pushing over blue paper like a bloodhound chasing crickets. He stopped, straightening his back, deadening eye contact with all four men in a semi-circle.

'The detail is physical security and surveillance. There are two teams. There are two targets.' He studied expressions, they were on cue.

'Target one is the home of Mrs Jessica Janson, their town-house borders the parameter here.' He darkened the north side of the bowling alley parking lot with a felt-tipped pen.

'There are two entrances, front door easily seen from the street, back door opens into a small yard connecting to the rear of the alley parking lot. Mule and Toy,' he motioned to the white and black pair, 'were working the house last night. They know the property.'

'There's a wood basket-weave fence between Janson's and the parking lot,' Toy offered.

Rivers drew in a dark slash, then reaching into his top pocket to produce a picture. He passed the images around.

'A boy and his dog,' Rivers stated. 'Child is Elmer Janson, the canine is Tripod.'

Toy, who had sides of beef for arms, started to laugh, elbowing his partner with the heavy bones.

'Did I say something funny?' Rivers barked.

'No, Frank, but the dog is missing a . . .'

'How many legs you got?'

'Three,' he smiled, 'brothers all got three.'

'Dog has four, one up on you.' Rivers' eyes were like frozen flames. 'Anything happens to that boy, you'll be walking with two of something and I get to pick.'

Toy pulled back instantly. 'Hey, Franko, lighten up, I was kidding,' he smiled, instinctively leaning over to protect his crotch as Rivers continued.

'That's the first set, boy, woman, dog – no other players on stage. Understood?'

Four men nodded. 'Do we have a picture of Mrs Janson?' asked Rudy.

'By this time tomorrow. She's a real fox, trust me on that. She's slim and has blonde hair, which she parks on top her head in a weird ponytail when she's at home.' He made a cone with both hands. 'Looks like a straw fountain. Mule and Toy will take the front, do we have the surveillance van?'

'Affirmative,' Mule Murphy responded, 'the panel truck, do you want a sign?'

'We've got Pest Management,' Toy added.

'Your cover is congestion monitoring for neighbourhood traffic, there's a roll of cable in the rear, just lay it across the street like you're setting up a metered system and park close enough for a clear view of the house. Remember the dog's sound range. Mule, what's the name of that football team you were on?'

'Huskies,' he said proudly.

'First team is Huskies,' Rivers announced, 'responsible for observation of all activities on the street and surrounding the house up to and including the backyard. Rudy,' he looked at the Lip. 'Your wife gave you a puppy last Christmas, what's its name?'

Bewilderment spread across Rudy Marchette's thin face. 'How did you know about that?'

'I'm looking to eliminate provocative words, there's a chance someone could be using a radio scanner. Give me your dog,' he demanded.

'Uh, Pogo, Sarge, her name is Pogo.'

'Second team is Pogo,' he stated, 'have you been inside the alley?'

'Side door by the gas station,' answered Marcus Koczka, 'just to look inside.'

'Use the rear entrance away from the road, there's a stairwell. Be cautious of observers filling their tanks at the pumps, it's a direct line of sight to an all-night gas station. If you find you are being watched by some pain in the ass civilian, just act like you belong there. Cough, yawn, stretch your legs, if they don't look elsewhere, grab your balls and scratch. Which one of you is working nights?'

'I am, for three running,' said Rudy.

'You're first man in, take the equipment and leave it by the large window in the northeast corner overlooking the Janson's backyard, that's your position.' He darkened a line with felt-tip on the rendering.

'Rudy, you've been out of the academy for two years?' he asked.

'No Frank, just one, starting my second.'

Rivers turned to Marcus Koczka, 'Have you ever worked old clothes before?'

His face begged forgiveness. 'No Sarge, this is my first assignment off patrol.'

'You'll do just fine, now listen up, I want you two to appreciate distance.' He pointed at Rudy and Marcus, then from side-to-side on the drawing. 'I eyeball about ninety, maybe even one-hundred feet from each wall, and even deeper heading down the lanes,' he stated.

They leaned forward on the couch and nodded.

'Now no one can sneak up on you at that kind of distance, do you understand me?'

They looked at each other.

249

'Sometimes it gets pretty spooky in a large building at night, you hear things that aren't real, a backfire becomes a gun blast; a falling branch, Ninja assassins; bottles tossed in the parking lot, Molotov cocktails – all you need is a little imagination and you'll think you're under siege, understand?'

'Sure,' said Marcus. Rudy nodded.

'You both trained on a twelve-gauge pump, I want you to take my riot gun. Keep the chamber empty, and if you are certain someone has entered – and only if you're certain – pump a round into the breech. Nobody in their right mind would challenge the sound of a riot gun feeding, nobody.

'Commander Scott and myself might be checking on you, we will identify ourselves very clearly. Now you two like your old sergeant, don't you?' He pulled back and presented a friendly face.

Team Pogo smiled.

'Well so help me,' he pointed at them, 'if you blow me away I'm going to be disappointed, and then I'm going to re-group in hell with some of my old pals, and then I'm coming back to fuck you over with a fork, do you understand what I'm saying?'

Team Pogo fought confusion, the Huskies wore masks of stone.

'Any questions?' Rivers offered.

'What are we looking for?' Mule asked.

'A killer. Like I said last night, I can't give you details, all we know is he works solo, no team or anything like that, and he's Mr Slick.'

'Is this related to the Clayton homicides?' asked Rudy.

'We're not sure,' Rivers responded. 'Set your radios to Channel Fourteen, high frequency.'

Both teams adjusted their sets and checked batteries.

'Okay guys, now if you see anything, a car pull into the lot, a flasher in the brush, a dog taking a shit – I want a picture and I want a radio check. Pogo,' he looked into young faces, 'there's nothing to be ashamed of if you pull a chill, talk to us. There'll be someone on every minute, and you can count on Huskies. Either way, we hear from you on the half-hour.'

Their faces registered a touch of relief.

'Now I want you to look at the drawing.' Rivers pointed down. 'The Janson backyard is blind-side to Huskies. You will be covering their backs, they are covering the family. The world depends on Pogo, you are no longer rookies.'

Mule Murphy swung a grinning, massive head, and Rudy-the-Lip noticed that Mule had no neck. In the meantime Marcus Koczka eyed the giant black man they called Toy. Even at roll call they used his nickname. Marcus suddenly noticed a pink tattoo, a panther on his right forearm – and the rookie jumped, his pants literally clearing the couch.

Toy was deadlocked on his curious eyes, staring right down into him while digging between his molars with a sharpened icepick.

'Settle down, Marcus,' Rivers demanded. 'Toy will be there if you need him.'

Mule slapped Toy on the back and grinned. 'Give us five minutes, then a radio check,' he offered to Rivers, rising from his seat.

At 3:45 p.m. teams Pogo and Huskies were deployed.

TWENTY-SIX

She was there. She was beautiful. She was waiting.

Brought back from the grave, a bust of clay and plaster that stopped just short of breathing, golden eyes that followed Scott's every move around the dimly-lit study. He eased closer, placing a hand against her cheek, it was smooth as thought, slightly warm, and he emitted a frustrated sigh.

'It's the light, Jack,' comforted a hulking bear of a man in a white gown, stripping off his lab jacket. His powerful hands gently adjusted the desk lamp beam a fraction.

'The eyes are actually a prosthesis used for cosmetic purposes on living patients, they trap low level ultraviolet emissions, makes her seem alive. I think I'll have a cognac, are you sure all you want is coffee?'

Scott nodded. And Dr Charles Rand McQuade left him alone with his thoughts, watching as he leaned over the desk, peering intensely at the haunting child.

Her face was soft and angelic, the front teeth sparkled between cupid lips. A sweet, sculpted chin with high, subtle cheeks. There was a special innocence that glowed, radiated and filled the room; it was not the sunlight dying through the windows. 'How could it be?' Scott thought, and he stroked the black hair, silken to the touch, as he remembered the grave she had been found in, and his shoulders fell slack. For more than three decades she had lain in desolate abandon, a

252

destroyed child, her nameless face a prize from some killer's private burial pit.

Scott grabbed the edge of the mahogany desk, shaking a mane of greying curls, slowly swinging his head back and forth over the edge, his mind leaping, whirring into a smear of thoughts. Good cops are cut from circumstance and experience, he reminded himself, artists like McQuade are born. Because of his skilled hands the child before them was wearing a face of love; artistic licence, or it could have really been her face. Scott didn't know and he had begun to ask just that, holding a finger into the air, then stopped himself. He didn't want to know. It was late, he told himself, he didn't have time to inquire. A coward's invention, time always the excuse, fools strapped in watches and waiting in crooked lines. Failure was a part of it. The job, he told himself, breathing deeply, what in all of his years had he not seen.

McQuade rested his glass on the desk, handing Scott a cup of stiff caffeine. 'Better than three thousand unidentified youngsters are turned into our office each year and the numbers are growing. You can't save them all, my friend. The cause is noble, you are but one man.'

The bile had returned to Scott's throat, he took a sip of coffee and swallowed hard.

'The hair is real.' McQuade's voice was deep with resolve, echoing into itself like a tunnel through madness. 'I selected a wig with very fine husking, not coarse, in keeping with her bone density and structure. A rather attractive little girl.'

There was silence. From the window Scott could see the last cars leaving the Armed Forces Institute of Pathology for the day. Two young boys in shorts began tossing a baseball over the grassy quad, a beagle barking for attention and racing between them. At the far end of the military complex, a uniformed sentry closed a security gate and returned to his booth just as the ball landed beneath their window. A dizzying race between boys and dog ensued as a towheaded girl in blue jeans appeared to tussle for the sphere, the contest taking on a life of its own, carrying them back to the mall.

'She came from attractive parentage, notice the high

253

forehead, the splendid shaping across the nasal bridge to the eyes, the slight and angular brows.' Dr McQuade was admiring his craftsmanship. Scott turned and wondered.

'Yes,' he said, studying the child's features, 'she is beautiful.' A pause. 'How did she die?' He picked up his cup and sipped bleakly.

'Not sure, there wasn't much left to work with, mostly bone scatter of a sort, lime mixed with acids, it did the job. The head was easier to reconstruct than the face, but I did find ten complete cranial punctures, one partial, each about twenty-five millimeters in circumference. Any one of them could have been fatal. You knew about them?'

He nodded, his eyes focused downward on the child.

'I excised each area,' McQuade pointed at the head ten times, 'building duplicate plates, then sent the originals to Mike O'Hare at the FBI, he was waiting on them. He had been alerted by your New York office.'

Scott turned away from the child and began to pace. 'Tell me about her, Charlie, what do we know?'

'If you don't hold me to it.'

'Speculate, I'll wait for absolutes another time.'

'Agreed,' said the laboratory director. 'I believe the blow that killed her was a puncture low on the crown, about halfway to where the spine joins the skull.' He gently rotated the bust and pointed. 'It was not a gunshot, the wound channel reveals some shatter, very slight, my guess is the splintering was caused by the surface tension of an object moving with rapidity through bone. O'Hare said he is running a battery on wooden shafts, it's possible they are arrows, but not likely. Too much penetration in curved density, but definitely not a hand-held striking implement. She was hit with something from a distance, perhaps four to six feet, the FBI will be able to tell us more.'

'Surface tensions, you mean the shaft of the instrument rubbed against the bone hard enough to cause the fracture?'

'Yes, that's close enough, Jack. A smooth object that is moving fast during penetration, let's say a bullet, simply bursts

254

through bone, punching a hole. The heavier the object, at higher velocities, the cleaner the wound. Although a wooden stake may look smooth to the naked eye, friction is created between striking surfaces, in this case bone and wood. A fracture results. I can't tell you much more than that.'

Scott's face tightened and he fought to relax, reaching into his coat for a cigarette, McQuade spotting this behaviour and lifting the window open. Boyish voices filled the room, a girl's giggle floated through like a thought balloon, failing in a puff of swirling smoke. He winced.

'Did she suffer?' Scott heard himself asking.

'Impossible to tell, Jack, let's believe she did not.'

Scott understood and turned back to the childish form. 'She was twelve,' he confirmed.

'A positive identification, skull plates and dental evolution matched against carbon dating, buried in 1958. Porous fibres, strands from her clothing, held residue from a yellow weed, almost like a mustard stain. We're waiting on verification from Mike, but our analysis, both chemical and electron microscope, suggests a wild flower is the culprit, a member of the Primrose family.'

'What's your source?'

'We ran the molecular structure through the Armed Forces Institute of Pathology's Cellular Registry, they maintain a computer log of all known plant and animal cells. Sometime before she died, she had come in contact with a flower, leaving us with a reliable indicator for the time of year she was killed.' The gentle Goliath strolled over to the liquor cabinet and returned with a bottle and file folders in his hand. Scott smiled, Dr McQuade had been using personal time if research materials were stored there.

'Notice the tiny flecks of red inside the leaves at the stalk.' He motioned with a massive finger.

'Very unusual,' said Scott, 'a bundle of yellow flowers with red flaring along the petals.'

'Hard to miss in laboratory work, you're looking at Yellow Loosestrife, the species is one of several local to this area, this is the rarest of the lot. There's a number on the back, a graduate student at the Smithsonian who is writing his thesis . . .'

'Thanks Charlie,' he interrupted, tossing the picture on the desk. 'I have a local man consulting who will know, but how the hell do you derive any accurate time of year from these?'

'It's only an approximation, we'll keep working, but you said you were rushed?'

Scott baulked. 'I'm sorry, I did sound ungrateful.'

The laugh was resonant. 'Heavens, Scotty, you an ingrate? I know better. When you catch this man, you'll sleep, until then grateful is in your manner, not in your heart.'

Scott smiled weakly.

'The flower is a stalk which stands about three feet tall, this child stood six inches higher. The stain was on fabric stuck to her fourth rib, I am presuming her clothes crumbled inward during decomposition. If so, that means she was bending over and examining flowers during the day, or she was buried with one, and I doubt that.'

'So she had a soiled blouse?'

'No, she had a specific stain from a rather peculiar species which blooms only in late March and early April, maintaining ribbons of red for just a few weeks. Then the yellow takes over completely. The composite residue was biased with reds. Early April, that's when she died, before the Swamp Candle loses its fire, about the fifteenth of the month. You might have Mike double-check, but from sample analysis with the scope, I'm certain enough. The stain had never been cleaned, and . . .'

'What did you say, a Swamp Candle?'

McQuade nodded, the failing sunlight playing in soft brown eyes which followed Scott in circles around the room. 'All in here, Jack.' He handed him a folder. 'That's the common name, we also included colour shots of the child from every angle, and black-and-white in case you need to distribute.'

Scott glanced at the girl, the behaviour fitted her image. 'She was picking flowers,' he stated without reservation.

'I didn't say that,' the scientist countermanded, 'I said I

256

thought she came into contact with one, you're reaching back over three decades with your assumptions.'

'You said you trust my instincts?'

'Absolutely, but as a scientist I don't want to force you into conclusions.'

'Charlie, a Swamp Candle, it must grow near water?' he asked, looking around the room for direction. 'It's only the ninth, they should be in full bloom about now, yellow and red, easy to spot.'

Dr McQuade smiled. 'Going to pick flowers, I like that about you, Jack. No chore too great, no challenge too small. Let me freshen your coffee?'

'No thanks,' he said reflexively. 'An isolated, quiet community, and the residents bound by a Southern tradition of avoiding strangers, minding their own affairs . . .'

'You're running ahead of me, friend.'

'Sorry, thinking out loud. In 1958, Good Friday and Easter fell in the first two weeks of April, she could have been preparing a centrepiece for the family table, little girls are brought up to think that way, poor children improvise. As the city of Bethesda started to grow, there were two small towns, Tobytown was for predominantly black families near where she was buried. The other town was four miles away down by the river. The Swamp Candle grows near water, so she was down where the flower grows.'

'That's the ticket, swampy places, grassy shores, a very hardy little weed. If you're right, she would have headed for water.'

'John's Cabin.'

'If you say so, Jack.'

'So let's presume she goes to the river, on foot we're looking at a rough eight-mile round-trip, but children were more industrious then. Someone must have seen her, but adults in that area were leery of strangers, afraid of getting involved. They would have never challenged a uniform or official looking car, unless she was in obvious danger, it all makes sense.'

'He uses a uniform?'

'Once he did, and very effectively, the world was less

complex, less populated. It's possible he stalked her, maybe even her mother or another child, and while they were picking flowers he appeared in uniform, demanding to take them home. He drove in the right direction, from John's Cabin towards Tobytown.'

'And they never made it.' McQuade took a shot of cognac. 'As good a theory as any, how can I help?'

'Well, as a start, I need to find where the flowers grew back then, and I need to find her mother. I was hoping you'd ask.'

McQuade smiled. 'Would it have made a difference?'

'No.' Scott pursed his lips, there was misery in the confession, and he stood at the window staring out. 'This will help,' he said, turning to face the scientist directly. 'And I have one other minor problem, rather pressing, I'm afraid.'

'I'm not avoiding you, Jack.'

'The burial site could have been a full blown cemetery that was never completely exhumed, and I've got to dig there.'

The doctor shrugged. 'Of course you do,' he responded, reaching for the rack that held his sports jacket, 'and you need on-site interpretation in your search, and I'll also bet you don't have a search warrant, or even a budget.'

'You understand everything.'

'Not hardly.' McQuade swallowed the last of his drink. 'How much trouble do we risk?'

Scott sighed gently. 'Well, even though it's been gutted, we still have a Fourth Amendment, plus the privacy act, in addition to trespass law. Since the site is privately owned, I'd say if we get pinched the fallout will be substantial.'

McQuade nodded. 'Then you better have a decent cover, Jack, it's not worth either one of us going to jail. As for funding, I'll cover my equipment, lab costs and time under another case, but we'd better hit pay dirt or they'll be digging up my bones.' He turned to his desk, removing another folder which he handed over. Scott gave a grateful smile.

'What's this?' he asked, turning the cover.

'That's the jacket you requested on Vietnam, Operation Phoenix, to be specific, we pinched a copy from the clubhouse at Langley under the auspices of identifying skulls from Hanoi, we really do have two boxes sitting in the lab.'

'Boys from Vietnam?'

'In this case Cambodia, but we'll never be able to give them names, that much I'm fairly sure of.'

Scott began to flip through the lengthy treatise.

'It makes for interesting reading, I've seen similar files before, there are dozens of Phoenix Operatives still unaccounted for, MIAs, so our office has been involved in identification for quite a while. I might be able to help if you tell me what you're looking for.'

Scott sighed, pushing through the pages. 'A young man I happen to be working with who has some rather unusual qualities. His last name is Rivers, but I think he had it changed, or someone changed it for him. That smacks of either criminal or governmental behaviour, and since he was a marine, I think I'm heading in the right direction.'

McQuade raised an eyebrow.

'Explain it to me, Charlie, Operation Phoenix was what exactly?'

'Well, for public consumption it was something called a Pacification Program, but behind all the cloak and dagger stuff it was terrorism of the worst kind, state sponsored, in this case Uncle Sam. Brought to you by the very incredible CIA, take a look,' he said, reaching over to help turn a page in the report and revealing a summary statement.

'The Phoenix mission,' Scott read aloud, 'to infiltrate and destroy the Vietcong infrastructure by whatever means possible, specialised units to include assassination, terrorism, and forced interrogation.'

'A nice word for torture,' said McQuade. 'It started around 1967 and in my opinion the entire operation was a crime against humanity, a very dark period in American history.' He watched as Scott searched with an index finger. 'Looking for something specific?'

'A name,' Scott replied bleakly.

'That's what I've been trying to say, Jack, you won't find any, so imagine trying to identify human remains when you only have numbers and codes to work with. That report's no different than others, no photographs, no medical sheets, no physical descriptions, no personal histories, and no names.'

'Then how do you get an identification?'

'We don't,' McQuade shook his head, 'because the record isn't made available, and that's how we know when we're dealing with Phoenix. When Hanoi coughs up a set of bones, and once we have exhausted the standing MIA list, I have to send a complete description of my findings through the State Department, they take it to CIA for possible identification of a Phoenix agent. The process always ends there, I'm still waiting for word on four skulls from the '76 exchange.'

'I don't understand,' Scott said, 'these agents were military men, why the tight lid after twenty-some years?'

McQuade shrugged with heavy eyebrows. 'It's politics, Jack, what is it always? For the most part they were military men, but once recruited the rules were changed on them. The CIA claims that it is protecting those Phoenix agents who survived, but I rather believe they're just covering their own silly butts.'

'Who's to care, Charlie, that's ridiculous.'

'Is it?' McQuade responded. 'You do know that America is now seeking diplomatic ties with Hanoi and that the United Nations is involved?'

Scott nodded.

'Well, the boys from Phoenix are wanted men, war criminals, and so branded by the government of Hanoi, and more recently the Soviets and East Germans. Behind all of the nice political table talk between these countries, these poor sorry bastards have had the rug pulled out from under them again. You know about the numerous sightings of MIAs, verbal reports, sometimes even photographs?'

Scott nodded, his face intense.

'Well, while they feed the public on a steady diet of "ain't it awful but it's just not true", our government has really had the shit laid on their table. Hanoi wants a simple trade, the boys from Phoenix and then a public admission of our actions, and in return we get everything on the MIAs, names, places, real accountability; and it goes even deeper than that . . .'

Scott held up a hand. 'I don't even want to hear it, Charlie. You're saying our potential allies consider them international outlaws?'

'That's correct, Jack, right or wrong all that matters in Washington is that these boys are an issue, a diplomatic sticking point. Hanoi wants them for public trial, and we've been saying they don't exist, but more importantly, that they never did.'

'That's nuts,' Scott spat.

'Perhaps, but atrocities did occur, documentable crimes, and in some cases there have been international rewards posted for those who were involved. It doesn't matter if you agree or not, for some the war goes on, and the U.S. is taking extreme measures to hide any official government involvement.'

Scott nodded thoughtfully. 'So these Phoenix agents, their identities are classified, and those among the living have been changed?'

'Yes,' said McQuade, 'only numbers and general codes, the heat is on and the lid is tight. Do you have anything else that might help, a unit number, perhaps a mascot? They all had those.'

Scott remembered the Zippo. 'How about a cartoon character, a Pink Panther?'

McQuade frowned. 'Nasty group, that would be Marine Phoenix, the Pink Panthers. There were two platoons and four squads. Group One specialised in field terrorism and kidnapping, Two was an ambush team, Three was explosive ordnance, Fourth Squad was a sniper unit. Only a handful survived and it's little wonder, they did three, sometimes four tours apiece.'

'What can you tell me about them?' Scott asked, reading between the deletions made by a heavy handed censor.

'Panthers were run directly by CIA through a field psychologist by the name of Dunn, Major Bradford E. Dunn, who was killed in action, may the bastard roast in hell. His unit was one of the deadliest legends to come out of the program.'

'Dunn was a CIA psychologist?'

'Trained in techniques of terror,' McQuade stated coldly, 'and he enjoyed his work, hand selected his men too, except most of them were really boys. My understanding is that he preferred to work with teenagers who had been victims of child abuse, if you get the picture. Rather cunning CIA tradecraft, I really do loathe those maggots.'

'And Dunn searched out men according to the depth of their emotional scarring, using his background and access?'

'That was only true of Panthers,' McQuade corrected, 'the other outfits had their own variations and peculiarities, there were four programs under Phoenix, Panthers belonged to Red Rover, kidnapping and terror. Major Dunn gave the orders directly from Washington, playing a childhood game.'

Scott held his hands to the air. And McQuade chanted, 'Red Rover, Red Rover, the lawn's gone to clover. Red Rover, Red Rover, send Jackie over.'

Scott winced.

'That's the way Dunn declared a state of emergency, then ordered abductions behind enemy lines. If you were Jackie, Panthers would track you down no matter how many they had to kill or torture to find you.'

'And the pink mascot?'

'Most of these men were so young when they arrived in Vietnam that their folk heroes were still from cartoons, Pink Panther, Bugs Bunny, Felix Cat, Tweetie Bird, that kind of thing. I suppose it was part of the killing game, children are more willing to play.'

'Not always,' Scott corrected. 'Is this first hand, were you stationed overseas?'

'Me?' McQuade smiled. 'I was protesting the war on the Berkeley campus, or any other place where there was serious intent. About a decade ago I used my clearances to assuage a guilty conscience. If your request is official I can give you a name at Langley who will talk off the record.'

'No.' Scott shook his head while holding up the report. 'Burn it for me, Charlie, war's over, these boys have a right to privacy.'

262

And McQuade closed the file into a grey safe behind his desk and spun the combination. 'I'll give you a lift, Jack, you'll never get a cab at this hour.'

Scott stood and worked his features into a smile.

From Georgia Avenue in Washington to Ridgefield Drive in Bethesda, more than an hour of debate fell by the road, and they covered nearly every subject on which they could disagree. They continued with Vietnam, then world population, moving into abortion versus right to life, then hitting on the cultural effects of rap music. By the time the death penalty popped up, McQuade knew that words would not bridge the chasm between them.

'Have you ever considered gardening, Jack? I find it very rewarding,' he said.

Scott lifted an eyebrow, he was thinking about the old fashioned gallows. With help from a sympathetic hangman, prisoners would last a good minute after their spines splintered into jelly, a technique that allowed a cop to get a word in edgewise. He was staring at his watch and carefully counting sixty-seconds' worth of words.

'We'll be there soon,' McQuade said, mistaking this behaviour, waiting for a light to change on Wisconsin Avenue. And he turned the subject back to star-like yellow flowers.

'Many of the wild loosestrife do well in cultivation,' McQuade offered.

The windshield fogged from within.

The street was slick with rain.

TWENTY-SEVEN

6:20 P.M.
UPPER NEW YORK STATE

In police lore they used to say that Old Woodie will swallow no more, by which it was simply meant that the State Cemetery at Woodlawn, New York, was full, or had been buried out, depending on your point of view.

It had first opened its gates in 1902, so the only bury room left was in a used grave, on top of someone else's casket, and this was an insignificant thing, or so Matthew Brennon had always thought. But standing in the dying light at a place called Rabbit Run, a hilly drive that was more of a dirt path than a road, the reality was overwhelming.

He had parked his car at the end of the road and stood near the rear of the cemetery where the older graves were, staring out at thousands of headstones. These had been smashed and twisted by vandals, overgrown by weeds and strewn with litter. As he walked they seemed to be mourning for his attention, a country mile of greying slabs, and with a sudden gust, yellowed newspapers flitted over them, shifting with the wind, dancing like a parade of lost souls.

Brennon walked casually, briefcase in hand, following an overgrown fence while looking down onto a swell of green. The hills seemed to be rising, then falling, rolling with endless rows of white crosses. These, he knew, were the New York doughboys that the caretaker had mentioned, ploughed under in their youth, now standing in waves as far as the eyes could

264

see. Down the path, it was a full five minutes before he had left them behind, then he approached a valley of travertine crypts and mausoleums which resembled huge marble tanks tilting towards him in reckless abandon.

For eighty years the dead had been coming to rest at Wood-lawn, and Brennon was just beginning to fathom the magnitude of lives past as he approached an elaborate and ancient gateway that seemed dark and forbidding. He stopped. It was a huge iron arch which had been cast onto circular sandstone pillars, and in the lattice-work above him, a pair of iron cherubs wept rust on their journey to heaven.

The gate itself was thick wrought iron, sealed by an old chain and padlock, strangled by ivy and crawling brambles. Beyond this a dirt path vanished down into dark, rolling hills, after which he could see nothing. He removed a notepad from inside his windbreaker, checked his notes, and glanced at his watch. Then cupping his hands to his face, with a deep breath, he forced all of the air from his lungs.

'Hello,' he yelled, and his voice went rolling down the hills, reflecting through the crypts like a desecrating scream, then filling other tombs in the distance. The silence quickly returned to his ears, not even a bird came to life.

It was gate No. 11, Woodlawn's northern arch, and at this spot he knew the graves continued for ten square miles into Poughkeepsie, tens of thousands of souls harvested over time and then put to rest by the State. Yet for all the memories among the living, Brennon could not see even a withered flower down the path, the graves crowded in death as they were in life, close enough to hear your neighbour drip. He cupped his hands to his face.

'Hello,' he tried again, and his voice blew through the tombs, echoing back at him like a lost twin.

'Hold your water!' a harsh voice suddenly roared.

From behind the gate's thick ivy mane he heard a man cursing. 'Goddamned pile of rust,' followed by heavy breathing.

'Hello?' Brennon asked.

'Relax, young fella, you're among the living.' And with that the brambles parted and Brennon was staring directly at gloved hands that were holding back the vines. A face protruded from shadow.

'Are you Mr Dudley Hall?' Brennon asked.

'That I am,' he chirped, the brambles closed, and he returned to working the thicket, removing a badly overgrown chain, then pumping hinges with an oil can. The man was completely hidden by the dense foliage.

'I'm Matthew Brennon.'

'Justa moment,' he chirped, 'was doin' just fine a moment ago.' The voice sounded like he had swallowed a bird whistle, Brennon guessed the man was missing some teeth.

'I could just climb over?' he offered.

But there was no response. In short moments Brennon saw the gloves thrashing away at the vines, ripping at the brambles, and a beefy plaid shoulder pushed against the iron door, forcing the gate into a painful groan as daylight burst through and onto the path. What emerged from all of this looked like a human fireplug, short with massive shoulders and legs, plus a barrel chest covered by a worn checkered jacket.

'Call me Duddy,' the man whistled, removing a glove and extending his hand, and they were standing face to face as the man released a red stream of tobacco juice from the side of his mouth.

'Yes sir,' Brennon said, 'I'm Matt, pleased to meet you.' He could see from the smile that Hall's lower front row was missing as the man gave him a powerful shake. His whiskers had gone to grey, not a beard, just a face badly in need of a shave, and it was a worn face, beaten into a patchwork of leathery lines and crevices. Brennon guessed he was in his late sixties, although in excellent shape.

'We talked on the phone, didja bring da papers?' Hall asked. 'Sure hope ya got copies, I called that judge of yours, gotta have copies.'

Brennon sensed the uneasiness. 'I understand, sir, I brought you a set, all signed and sealed, all you have to do is fill in the details.' He popped open the briefcase, reached inside, and handed over a series of official looking documents.

The caretaker began to read, taking his time, and Brennon was concerned that they would soon be working into the darkness. He needed to be back at the ViCAT slot by midnight.

'Ain't seen wonna these for a time,' Hall finally said, examining a Writ of Exhumation. 'Why you folks so anxious to have him back?'

'I wish I knew, I just follow instructions,' Brennon lied, and he did this well, sounding more like a pleb than a senior federal agent backed by the State's highest court.

The man humphed, then whistled. 'Jest like me,' he said, 'wassa time a body only got three things at old Woodie, a plot, a stone, and me. Real personal. Now I'm retired, and dem still ordering me around like a damn night porter.'

'Well, I appreciate all your help, I'm really being hammered.' He smiled. Brennon's call had woken Dudley Hall the night before, it had taken twenty-four hours for a judge to sign for exhumation.

'Old Duddy understands, son, higher ups is always pickin' and pantin', don't matter none if you're dead.' He spat again. 'Sorry to lead ya here but you'll save an hour gettin' to it.'

'How can I help?'

'Just follow me,' said Dudley Hall, picking up a wood-handled spade with one hand and an apple-picking basket with the other. 'What dis man do, anyway?'

'A bad guy,' Brennon answered, following him down the path, down the hill and towards the crypts. As they walked, Brennon thought Duddy's arms looked comic, like small suspended hams, and his thumbs nearly touched his knees.

They had strolled in silence for about ten minutes when Hall spoke out. 'So what do you think of 'er, Matt?' he asked in quick doublestep, not turning his head as he talked, marching along like a one-man army.

'Woodlawn?'

'Yep,' he whistled, waving the spade with his right arm at the rolling hills. 'I settled 'ere in '43, was nothing but a big pretty forest with lotsa meadows, it's all been buried out, tain't no more room.'

And Matt Brennon remembered the stories of Old Woodie.

There was a time when he had thought it was poker piss, just greybeards filling your ears, then telling you that it's raining. 'Have you been the caretaker since then?' he asked, for Dudley Hall walked with unseeing eyes, as if strolling through his own living room.

'Caretaker, hell you say, never heard that doggone word until '64, that's the year we got the backhoe. You musta found my name in the State book, only place I know they call me that.'

'Yes I did,' he confirmed.

'I'm the Diggerman, best thar is, bury 'em by hand,' he chirped as he moved effortlessly beyond the greying stones to those of a more modern design, some of them sculpted, praying hands, doves, symbols of eternity.

'Until '58 I'd dig and bury on a first come basis, those days was good, the way it outta be. I'd take my time, dressin' a grave up real nice, then stay for the funeral, I'm proud of that. You remember Boltin' Joe Sharkey, the prizefighter?'

'Well, that was . . .'

'Right dere.' He swung at a headstone that stood higher along the path than the others. 'Dug 'em myself, that grave's a seven-footer, most sevens are for man and wife, used to be we'd place 'em side-by-side, but we ran out of room. Buried dem on toppa each other, real symbolic like, Joe wouldda liked that.'

'Very interesting,' Brennon sighed, keeping the pace, watching the stones as they came and went. 'Do you have the plot number that we're . . .'

Duddy Hall spun in his place, walking backwards, eyeballing the young agent. 'Hell you say, this is my yard, son, got all the numbers.' He put a finger to the side of his temple. 'And I got all the plots.' He waved the shovel.

Brennon smiled.

'These aren't just sections and graves to me,' said the Diggerman.

And Brennon was worried, hoping the batty old man was up for the task.

'See that large marker over dere?' Hall pointed to a large

sculpted angel with outstretched wings, never once slowing his pace.

'Yes.'

'That's Pancake Louie, just buried his wife this past year. Louie's family had spent too much on his stone, then put him in a cheap box, the weight of the dirt just crushed it, made an awful damn sound and all at once, *KaaBoom!*' he yelled, slapping the ground with the shovel's flat side.

Brennon started. 'What did they do?'

'They watched the dust jest belly up from the pit, I hate for a family to see that, weren't the first time neither. Old Louie's widow never said a word, but we buried her in a Burns casket with a copper lining in it, that's a whole lot of money to be putting into a hole. She's riding on top of old Pancake Louie in a real money box, wonder if their marriage was like that?' And he spat, the red stream as true as his step.

As he talked, Duddy Hall the Diggerman never dropped a stride. Soon Pancake Louie was far behind and they were approaching a row of markers that looked like graves in miniature.

'Duddy, what about the State prison system, how do they bury?'

'If dere's family left?'

'Just the State.'

'Cremation and a cardboard box, then I'd stuff 'em into a hole any time I'd git to it. You asking 'bout this Zachariah fella?'

'Yes, I guess . . .'

'Ashes in a box, Rigby'd kept the teeth if dere was any gold.'

'Who's Rigby?'

'Runs the crematorium in town.'

'Works for the State?'

'He's a cooker, burns by the job, he don't care who pays.' And Dudley Hall stopped at a small iron fence that stood about a foot high, surrounding a grassy mound.

'Here she'll be,' he spat, pacing into the field, counting

rows, measuring by the place markers. The light was starting to grey.

'Three deep, four across,' he said, 'and three foot deep, don't take much for a burnt man.'

'And you're sure . . .'

The basket fell and the shovel blade sliced neatly into the dirt, the damp earth giving way as Duddy Hall applied his full weight over the hilt. With his bright chestnut eyes locked onto Matthew Brennon's, he began effortlessly rocking the handle back and forth, back and forth, very slow, boring down on the agent.

'So what'd ya say this fella do?' he demanded.

Brennon could feel the Diggerman's penetrating stare, and the eerie quiet of the yard, and the oppressive weight of the stones surrounding him.

'He killed women and children,' he said, and Dudley Hall nodded thoughtfully, continuing to rock the wooden handle.

'Ya know, Matt, in my day I could dig a five- or six-footer in eight, maybe ten minutes.'

'Very impressive,' Brennon said sincerely, watching the ground quake with each shift on the shovel's handle. They were surrounded by dozens of little white markers, most of them crosses, but two of them oval stones.

'Urns jest don't take no time at all,' said the Diggerman.

'Why is there a difference in these markers?' Brennon asked, as Duddy Hall pulled a flashlight from his belt, turned on the beam, then laid it on the ground.

'Just like plunking olives from a jar,' the man stated, giving the shovel a final push, and a bright gold lid slipped to the surface, shining at their feet. They were looking down at an urn, and as Hall twisted the wooden handle it popped free of the earth in a wad of dirt and turf.

'That really is impressive,' Brennon said, bending over, inspecting the burial can.

Hall quickly eased forward onto his knees, brushing at the urn with a gloved hand. 'No,' he said, shaking his head, 'something's not right 'ere.'

'Wrong grave?'

'Nope, checked the records after you called, this is it, but it's not prison cardboard.' Carefully, the Diggerman lifted the urn, cradling it in both hands. It was about eight inches high, a blue enamel with gold inlay.

'Are you sure this is right?' Brennon asked.

'No, but it's him inside dere,' he stated, 'look at the collar.' He spat a red stream and the lid dripped. He waited a moment, then brushed it off with his fingers.

And Brennon read, '*Zachariah Leslie Dorani, Born 11/18/ 33, Died 2/21/66.* That's him all right, where's the problem?'

'For one thing it was a prison funeral service, and this is a state plot, so all we should have is a pile of ashes. That's why I bit so far down with the blade and brought the basket, so as to fetch a complete pile, the cardboard pancakes and seepage turns a burnt man to concrete.'

'Then how did he get an urn like this?'

'Don't know, but it's a money box, that's real gold. And here's another thing, your papers list him as an atheist, that's why the stone marker instead of a cross like them others.'

Brennon's eyes grew wide as they studied the container, on two sides, and on the top, there were gold crosses. 'Could it have been a mix-up, could the prison authority have made a mistake?'

'Naw, not like that,' he said emphatically, 'them's Latin style crosses, Roman Catholic. Someone bought this urn, paid top dollar too, then had him poured inside.'

Brennon leaned over and stroked the thing. 'But you're sure he's in there?'

'Oh, he's in dere,' Duddy said, shaking the can with both hands, then checking the lead seal at the top. He pointed with a finger, 'This ain't been broke neither.'

'Would there be any records, how can I find out where the urn came from?'

'Well, not 'ere there wouldn't be, we just put 'em to rest, wouldn't know who the burnman was neither, but there's a way to tell.' His chirp raised a pitch.

'Anything,' Brennon said, 'it's important.'

'It's against the law.' He chirped again.

'What is?'

'Gotta check the ashes, I can tell lots from the ashes, but breakin' that seal's against the law.'

'Then I'll do it,' Brennon offered, but by the time he had reached for the urn, Duddy Hall was sitting in the dirt, prying at the top with a penknife. There was a scraping sound as his large hands began screwing the top, back and forth, back and forth, then a thump as the cap came free.

He looked in with his flashlight, then wetted a finger and dipped it inside. 'Got some baby killer on me,' he spat, rubbing his forefinger and thumb together.

'Then it's full, the urn, I mean?'

'Oh yeah, and it was a slow burn,' he said, pouring a stream of ash directly onto the lawn until he had a pile the size of a tablespoon. 'See here how it's grey and peppered, should all be a bright white powder. What you gonna do with 'em?'

'Lab tests for blood type and anything else we can get.'

'Then you got plenty,' and he continued to pour, the pile growing like the bottom of an hourglass, when there was a clink as a piece of bone fell free.

'What the hell?' asked Brennon, staring at what looked like a chip of charred wood. 'Don't they pulverise the remains?'

'Leon Rigby don't,' Hall responded, 'man's got no pride of work, never did, slob of a burnman. Don't bother to do the ashes with a rolling pin neither, good houses mash 'em flat, cook 'em twice, nothin' left but powder. He's been cheatin' the State for forty-some years, don't even wait for his fires to go blue.'

'Would he know about the urn?'

'No way he'd fill some other burnman's bottle, so it musta been his. You may need that chippy,' he offered, picking up the bone and handing it to Brennon.

In the dim light he held it with an uneasy grip, then wrapped it into a clean white handkerchief. 'Where would I find Rigby?' he asked.

Hall stood, stretching his back and arms. 'In his house or the creamer, I'll take you, you'd never find it.'

272

'I appreciate that,' he cautioned, 'but I can't ask, your orders end when you give me the remains.'

The gravedigger did not answer, instead handed Brennon the elaborate urn, turned his back, then leaned against his shovel. And in the darkness that had closed around them, a hollow sound erupted, a soft sound that trilled like the gentle roll of a drum pattering against the turf.

'Baby killer,' Brennon heard the Diggerman say under his breath.

Dudley Hall was urinating into the pile of ash.

TWENTY-EIGHT

BETHESDA, MARYLAND

By seven o'clock, Rivers had answered Pogo's radio check, returned from Foong Lin's carry-out, and was awash in Szechuan dreams of dim sum, spicy san shien Wor-bar, oysters in black bean sauce, hacked Chinese cabbage, and hot Singapore rice. He had also ordered chilled crabmeat and asparagus soup. He hadn't eaten since dawn, and had doubled orders of everything. Scott found him on the rear deck, hovering over little white boxes, the aroma that gave life meaning.

'What am I eating?' Scott asked, pulling up a seat and grabbing a plate.

'You'll like it, try the soup, it's terrific,' Rivers slurred, pushing a container across the table. Scott poured this into a white plastic bowl, studying the greenish broth as he laid a handkerchief across his lap.

'Is this vegetable soup?' he asked, dipping in a disposable spoon. He swallowed and looked up, his eyes instantly welling with tears.

'Hot stuff, Jack, be careful,' Rivers said, and Scott could feel the cold brine pumping down hot, the back of his throat tingled and he took a quick sip of water.

'Very good,' he said, digging for more.

'It's got everything, white fish, crab, asparagus, seaweed, bean curd, egg white, mushrooms, peas and rice.' He gave a dumpling an expert chew and swallowed, lifting another with chopsticks and dropping it into a plate of hot sauce.

'You know that old chart I let Jim Cooley borrow?' Scott asked, giving up on his chopsticks, reaching for the dim sum with a fork.

'Yeah, he was real excited,' Rivers said, gathering containers around him and filling his plate. 'Try the oysters with black bean sauce, they're terrific.' He leaned his head back, dropping a fleshy plum into his mouth, then draining the shell as Scott placed four large molluscs into his dish.

'It's stolen property, felony material.'

Rivers looked puzzled, popping another fishy blob into his mouth, moving clockwise around the table and filling his plate. 'How so?'

'I stole it, breaking and entering, premeditated, first-degree. If it went to trial I'd lose my badge.'

Rivers was stunned. He stopped eating and studied him carefully. 'You're not kidding, are you, Jack?'

'Not about something like this, no.'

And the detective grinned, shaking a mane of blond hair, searching through shells for a plump morsel.

'That chart is from a series of three, its insured value is seventy-five thousand,' Scott offered, dropping a shell back on his plate. It tasted bitter, and he moved on to hot Wor-bar.

'Seventy-five large?'

Scott nodded, puzzling over the sticky food smothered in black bean sauce.

'Bad oyster?' Frank asked.

'Tart, puckers your lips.'

Rivers handed him a cup. 'Sweet Hunan fish sauce, try dunking it in this first.' Scott followed instructions, and the meaty blob mixed in his mouth and slid by his palate.

'Very nice,' he said, reaching for another. 'Very nice indeed.'

And the men chewed and passed containers, fuelling bodies that had all but forgotten about food.

'Frank,' he asked, prying another from its shell, 'if we wanted to construct a silencer from parts where would we go?'

Rivers smiled. 'Depends on the calibre, any good junkyard

would have most of the stuff, are we making a Death Whisper or a Hush Puppy?' he slurped.

'You tell me, smart guy, what's the difference?'

'Quality is what. If you're disposing of the weapon we'd just screw an oil filter onto the end, that's good for a few dozen rounds or so. If you want real control, it takes more work. We had a saying, *one shot one kill, no sound not found*. Anyway, it always comes down to quality.'

Scott's teeth dug into a lip. 'Let's go first class.' He grimaced.

'How versed are you?'

'Just the basics, you're obviously the expert, Marine Phoenix, wasn't it?'

Rivers shook his head and laughed under his breath. 'You obviously know it was, Jack, you must really be tired. I've watched a lot of your starring roles, dumb's not part of your Thespian forte, pal.'

'Very good, Frank.' Scott raised an eyebrow. The man seemed to be letting a little of himself slip through.

'Used 'em and built 'em,' Rivers offered. 'Our first requirement would be a light metal tube for the suppressor, then a good drill press. We'd also need threading equipment, unless you want to clamp the extension on the gun barrel, that is.'

'Go with the best.' Scott drained his water glass.

'We start with the tube and drill holes, which would bleed the gases off slowly and deaden the vacuum.'

'Vacuum?' Scott inquired.

'Sure,' the tall policeman leaned forward. 'Most of the noise doesn't come from the charge going off, that's a misconception. When the bullet leaves the muzzle a tremendous vacuum is created within, gases are driven out and air rushing back into the barrel makes a loud retort which is confused with an explosion. Once holes are drilled in the extension tube, bleeding the air back in, you've solved sixty per cent of the problem. The rest is just padding, what they call buffers, usually a combination of fibreglass with metal retainers.'

'And you think that's what our killer used on the Claytons?'

Rivers nodded thoughtfully. 'The better suppressors actually catch the gases going out and coming in, dispersing them internally.' He poured more food on his plate. 'But I think he used a combination of techniques.'

'And how quiet could you make a .22?'

'What type? You're talking about the most underrated and least appreciated calibre.'

Scott leaned back in his chair. 'Is this from CIA training?'

'What?' Rivers asked incredulously, letting a laugh slip free. 'Silent attack is an art form, Jack, they're just bureaucrats who invent names for what real people do. Are you going to eat that last oyster?' Scott shook his head and Rivers' chopsticks reached, plucked, and dropped it home. He then rose, crossed the redwood deck and quickly returned with a 7–11 bag from the kitchen.

'Coffee?' he bowed stiff and Manchurian.

'Why yes, Chinese coffee, very thoughtful.' Rivers laid large cups on the table, popped plastic lids and watched the steam rise.

'You were saying silence is art,' Scott pressed.

'Absolutely, I know a man who could land from a swinging rope onto rice paper without tearing it, zap you with a Hush Puppy, catch the shell in his right hand and vanish before anyone noticed.'

'A cop?'

'Hardly, he's a thief, and rather proud of that, a real professional. One of America's best, highly decorated, carried four wounded men out of a hot LZ when their chopper flamed. The CIA wanted to keep him, but he'd rather rob from the rich and give to the poor, being himself, an orphanage and the Catholic church. He's really a pacifist.'

'Sounds like it.' Scott shook his head at an entire generation of lost boys. 'Pick the most high-powered .22 you can think of.'

'For range or destruction?'

'Destruction.'

'If we want to stay with commercially available ammunition, I'd say hyper-velocity truncated hollow points, travel better than sixteen-hundred-feet-per-second at the muzzle.'

If there had ever been any doubt in Scott's mind about wanting to work with Frank Rivers, it had just been vanquished. 'Tell me about impact power, what's their capability?'

'Varies with the target, pick a target.'

'Human skull, the cranium.'

Rivers thought for a moment. 'Hard but thin bone, all mush inside. From a few feet away the bullet is at maximum speed, the soft hollow nose penetrates and expands, then begins to tumble, cutting a path.' He picked a small bit of oyster off a shell with his fingers and chewed. 'The shock wave surrounding the projectile burns a channel of its own, rather devastating, burns the brain to jelly, leaving only a small puncture. It's the bullet of choice for professional assassins, you knew that?'

Scott nodded.

'Because skull plates are tough, curved, and the slug is travelling roughly one and one-half times the speed of sound, a glancing blow could actually ricochet. It takes a well placed, direct hit. Is this helping, sir?'

'Yes,' Scott answered. 'One shot, one kill. Where would you aim?'

Rivers patted the crown of his head. 'Shooting from the front or rear, that's the target,' he said. 'We were taught that anywhere above the spinal cord, in that general area, death is instant or as close as possible. Passing from side to side,' he placed a finger on his right temple, 'could leave an enemy disabled.'

Scott swallowed as Rivers grabbed a leftover piece of hacked cabbage and crunched.

'That helps, I want to think like this killer, the fascination with an object like that is foreign to me. So how silent can you make this weapon?'

Rivers thought a moment. 'From how far away would you be hearing the sound?'

'Like we are now, about six feet.'

'Okay, Jack, listen up,' he said, wiping his mouth with the back of his hand.

'I didn't hear anything, what are you doing?'

'Sorry,' Rivers stared, his penetrating blue eyes sparkling with mischief. 'Let's try again, but you have to listen very carefully.' He stirred his coffee while lighting a cigarette with his Zippo.

'Okay, smart guy, what's up?'

'You missed the point, Jack.' He smiled, and recognition spread across Scott's face.

'That's it?'

'Yep, and I used a staggered clip, ten shots through the mouth, you're rather dead, nothing left but pulp.' Rivers flushed down a piece of cabbage with black coffee.

'And how did you catch the brass shells, with a canister made specially for this particular firearm?'

'No,' Rivers stated flatly, 'a hanging canister's just one more part to foul up, plus adding bulk and weight. Wasn't there a trace of plastic found on a bullet fragment, the one taken from Diana Clayton's brain?'

'FBI suggested it came from a factory bullet coating.'

Rivers shrugged, grabbed a white carry-out bag off the table and stuck his fist inside, aiming a finger at Scott. 'Thump, thump,' he spat. 'Tell your beloved Bureau to check their evidence against Gladbags, keeps your kitchen clean without odours.'

Scott's eyes narrowed. 'You're suggesting he used a trash bag?' he asked incredulously.

Rivers nodded. 'Yes I am, the technique's called Bagging, and for stealth, practicality, and maximum control of the weapon it can't be beat by modern technology either. Hell,' he crumpled the paper in his hand, 'if you really bag a gun properly and use light loads that don't produce a sonic boom, you don't even need a silencer.' He smacked his hands together. 'Sounds like hands clapping, and not only will you catch the shells, any fouling remains trapped and you're ready for storage, no fuss, no muss.'

Scott suddenly looked pensive. 'The hot gases would fill it like a balloon, not to mention it would hide muzzle flash, it's so . . . simple!'

Rivers smiled, 'Gladbags, Jack, aren't you glad?'

'Very funny, Frank, how does it work?'

'Nothing to it, just stick the gun inside the bag, put rubber bands around your wrist for a seal, make it really tight, and then pull the trigger.'

Scott leaned back in his seat. 'It's a good thing that's not widely known, we're a real gun crazy society.'

Rivers shrugged, breaking open the lid on a second cup of coffee. And for a few moments the men were silent as their food settled, producing a calming fatigue after so many hours without sustenance. After a time Scott yawned deeply as Rivers leaned forward, propping his elbows against the table.

'I've read everything that's out there on serial killers, fact and fiction, and I still don't get it,' he stated.

'Get what?' Scott responded absently.

'Exactly why do they kill? If they're not sick and it's not a crime of passion, then what's the motive? All the stuff just dances around the issue, there's got to be something I'm missing.'

Scott nodded thoughtfully, reaching across the table for a cigarette. He flicked the tired old Zippo, breathing deeply, and the harsh and familiar smoke drilled his lungs. 'It doesn't take a degree in science to comprehend what they are. Shall we take Zak as an example?'

Rivers nodded.

'Zak Dorani is what we call a Rake or Recreational Killer. On the outside he appears to be perfectly normal, he's unusually bright, educated and polished. And yet he doesn't feel – there's not a glimmer of emotion left in his soul, if he even has one.' Scott thumped his chest while Rivers raised his eyebrows.

'You're suggesting that he has no feelings?' he asked in a startled voice.

'He's what we call Devoid, no emotions of any kind, and that's the only thing that makes him different from you or me. Do you understand the principle?'

Rivers thought it over. 'Sure, I understand what you're

saying but somehow I can't grasp it. No emotion, so do these Rakes know what is missing, I mean, instead of feelings what do they have?'

Scott smiled, his voice steady as stone. 'What is colour to a blind man, Frank, to a person who cannot see?'

'Either a memory or a concept.'

'Exactly,' Scott blinked, 'and emotionally Zak is blind.'

Rivers cocked his head. 'They never felt emotions? That's really weird, if he can't feel then he's more like an android than a human being.'

'Bingo, emotions *are* what makes us human. Now take the case of innate intelligence, IQ if you will.'

Rivers nodded.

'We are all gifted, or cheated, in that department as well. Take Albert Einstein, then compare him with all the poor creatures who are born so deficient in intellect that thinking itself is damn near impossible. In this same manner, some are born with such a puny emotional base that they are blunted, barely human, as you say.'

Rivers sipped at his cup. 'So if one of these blunted people had some kind of trauma, like abuse at an early age, they'd have nothing left, it would finish them off?'

'That's it, Frank, technically we are all born with emotions, but some are born with barely a glimmer. Drive that out, and you produce a Devoid. Without emotions there is no regard for the suffering of other living creatures, anything becomes possible.'

As Scott waited, Rivers nibbled a fleshy corner of his mouth, playing with the concept in his mind. 'A blank slate, an emotional void, so then why do they kill? Without emotions they wouldn't feel anything in return?'

Scott leaned forward. 'Let's go back to our example. If you were blind, what would you give to experience colour and the wonders of sight?'

'Anything, I would imagine.'

'And if you were emotionally blind, what would you give to experience a bit of that?'

Rivers breathed deeply, the roots of the idea taking hold. 'I think I'm getting the picture, you're saying that killing enables them to feel?'

Scott shook his head. 'Get the concept first, it's not that simple. If you didn't have emotions what would your world be like?'

'Well,' Rivers thought aloud, 'I'm sure there wouldn't be much excitement, a very boring existence, I'd guess. Could I make love to a woman?'

'Physically you'd be able, but I'm afraid sex won't do much more than raise your blood-pressure and respiration rate, so why not swim, it's better for you?'

'Then I guess I'd read a lot, and watch sports and movies, but without emotions, would I care?'

Scott smiled. 'You're starting to understand them now; without a vested interest on an emotional level things would no longer matter. Without feelings,' he rubbed his heart, 'issues and events and characters, life's comedy and drama, are all meaningless except on a purely intellectual basis. Without emotions, nothing matters, like being stranded for a lifetime in the middle of a big grey desert, no highs or lows, no peaks or valleys, just a torturous monotony.'

'So you'd resort to mental pursuit, challenge yourself, break the boredom that way?'

'True enough, the raw intellect takes over without any emotional checks or balances. As they go through life they are truly unable to comprehend what causes others to smile, laugh, frown, or even cry, and no one could explain that to them, just like describing colour to the blind.'

Rivers' eyes went wide with excitement. 'But they must show something, otherwise they'd stand out like store mannequins, they'd be easy to spot.'

'Correct again, Frank. As children they recognise this glaring deficit which potentially sets them apart, so they learn emotional displays, reproducing what feelings should look like.' Scott parted his lips in a strange grimace. 'What's this?' he asked, pointing up at his own face.

'Hell if I know,' Rivers chuckled, 'you're showing me your teeth?'

'Sure, showing teeth, isn't that what a smile is? Remember you can't feel it inside, you don't understand joy. When normal people feel emotion, we respond physically, laughter for joy, tears for sadness, violence for hate, that kind of thing, but the important point is that we usually don't notice until we begin to display one of these. It's all second nature, thought simply does not go into it.'

Rivers' jaw popped open. 'Holy shit, Jack, you're saying they're human parrots?'

'More like accomplished actors, and their performance is very realistic. They teach themselves how to turn their displays on or off like a switch, but surrounded by others for too long a period it becomes obvious from their miscues that they're acting. They smile at the wrong moment, or even worse, become confused with their displays.'

Rivers leaned back, a pensive expression on his face. 'I think I understand, but they do feel the killing response?'

'Precisely, the tiny spark of emotion left in them only ignites when they experience the most extreme of human behaviours, such as killing, which carries with it some rather unique physical responses as well. Anyone who has ever killed another person knows this, a change occurs in the body, and it doesn't matter what level of emotions you have. Most combat veterans have felt this sensation, however primitive it might be.'

'I remember,' Rivers said quietly, 'your body and your mind go berserk all at once, and everything becomes crystal clear in the chaos, you feel like a bottle being filled. God save us, that's what they crave?'

'The killing response and the emotional response are very similar, like identical twins. When our emotions excite us in the extreme, our bodies undergo drastic changes, blood pressure, alterations in blood chemistry, respiration, gastrointestinal activity, erection of hair, pupil size, sweat, almost anything you can name – and that all comes from feeling. Here's an obvious example I use with students, the so-called butterflies in the stomach, you've felt them?'

'Absolutely.'

'That comes from emotion, and we take the butterflies

for granted unless they become an ulcer. But if you were functionally devoid, you could not experience any such sensations without the administration of drugs . . .'

'Or killing,' Rivers replied bleakly. 'You feel very, very different, the body and the senses go wild.'

Scott took a deep breath. 'Rakes become hooked on this high, these sensations which mime emotional response in the body, and that's as close as they ever come to feeling, to having emotions, to breaking the dull sameness in their sorry lives. Killing is the only thing that excites them, and even then, it's brief.'

'Holy Christ,' Rivers exhaled, 'this Zak really is a cold-blooded monster.'

'They don't come any colder, no hesitating on the kill, no repulsion at pain or gore, no remorse. Cold and calculating. When you strip emotion from a human being all you have left is intellect, the ability to reason without the checks and balances of a conscience. Anything becomes possible, and he feels he is a superior being, we're just fish in his tank.'

Rivers was stunned.

'So what do you think?' Scott asked, reaching across the table and grabbing Frank's cup of coffee, then taking a sip. 'My office is currently tasked with twelve on-going series, and of these, eight involve men like Zak.' He paused and studied Rivers, the man's eyes were slits of concentration.

'So he feels a glimmer of emotion, plus the physical high, which is sharper than anything else in his existence, like a blind man seeing a flash of colour and then darkness again,' Rivers concluded.

'Correct, between episodes they live on fantasy, imagining in their minds what they have done or what they would like to do. Fantasy sustains them, at the same time driving them.'

'Do they always rape before killing?'

Scott nodded. 'To men like these, people are things to be possessed and then destroyed, sex is the ultimate control next to execution, otherwise they wouldn't care, it's just another physical act. They crave power over their victims, to them sex is power, and they confuse that with the feelings we would normally associate with intercourse. Also, their desire to control extends to us, the authorities, it's an element of their possession, another type of rape, if you will.'

'I don't follow,' Rivers cautioned.

'Domination of the worst kind, did you notice when the Claytons were discovered, the children slain but dressed for school?'

'Last day in March.'

Scott nodded. 'In this case a Rake crawled out of his stink and challenged me, a feeble cretin who he wants to dominate and break. This is all an April Fool's joke to him,' Scott stated with a sorrowful resignation, 'it's no deeper than that . . .'

As his voice trailed off, Rivers felt the butterflies. Whatever emotion may have caused them, they were twisting his gut into a tight and sorry knot, as Scott was staring absently into space.

'I once knew a guy who couldn't show any emotions,' Rivers offered, 'maybe he didn't have any. When he smiled, it was unreal, like his face was a rubber mask you could just yank off. The bastard loved war, he used to slice men's hearts out and feed them to his dogs.'

Scott nodded, 'I suspected that. Major Bradford Dunn?'

Rivers immediately tensed at the name, his jaw stiffening as his stare became ice. Scott reached gently across the table, placing a hand on his arm.

'I'm not prying, Frank, just concerned. You don't open up to anyone, you're very quiet, sometimes that's not healthy. It goes no further than us,' he offered gently, 'maybe talking would help some.' And Rivers leaned back in his chair, studying the older man who sat before him.

'Well,' he released a troubled sigh, 'I'm not sure what it will help with, Jack, that was a long time ago. I was just a kid, real young and real, real stupid.'

Scott smiled, 'Young is stupid, Frank, we've all been there.'

Rivers nodded. 'For years I thought the major was my best friend, but he wasn't any friend of mine . . .' and his voice trailed off suddenly. 'I'll tell you what, Dunn liked to say that Vietnam was what we were having in place of a happy childhood, that says something.'

Scott nodded, 'Yes,' he said grimly, 'and how did Major Dunn find you?'

At this Rivers smiled, leaning back into his chair. 'He was a psychologist, an expert in the polite wars, so it wasn't very hard.'

Scott shook his head as Rivers stood, pushing away from his chair, then slowly bowing at the waist as he parted his hair. At the crown of his head there was a large and noticeable tear of flesh where the hair would no longer grow, the scar itself looked like a large pale worm. Rivers forced a smile as he sat back down.

'Then that didn't come from Vietnam?'

'Nope, that little tattoo came from my senior prom, Jack. I was dating one of the prettiest girls in school. Anyway, we were all set for that big date, I had rented a suit and was about to pick her up for the reception, when a strange thing happened . . .' Rivers paused and looked skyward, Scott could tell the man was struggling.

'Who hurt you, Frank?' he asked quietly.

'Well,' he breathed hard, 'I had asked my dad for the keys to his car, and earlier he had agreed, but when I started out the door that night,' Rivers shrugged. 'My father busted an entire fifth of whisky over my skull . . .'

Scott cringed.

'The polite wars, Jack, they're the ones you can't win. All very secret, and it's shame and disgrace that makes them so hard to fight in the first place. Like I said, it was a long time ago.' With that he took a swallow of coffee and lit a cigarette.

'Then what happened to you?'

'In Vietnam?'

Scott shook his head. 'That night, what happened to you and your family?'

'Hell, I don't know, it was business as usual, or at least there was nothing my mother could do. I spent prom night with Jimmy Cooley down by the canal where no one could find us. He put seven safety pins through my scalp so that I'd clot by morning . . .'

'Sweet Mother of God,' Scott breathed hard, 'why didn't you go to a hospital?'

Rivers smiled, genuinely tickled at this. 'You still don't understand the town you're in, Jack. You read that *Tempo* article about Elmer, what was their crime, but you saw how they slammed his mother?'

'Yes.' Scott's voice was puzzled.

'If there had been a police report the same little bottom feeders would have destroyed my family in public, only they're much worse now, a new and improved generation. All you need to become a worthy target is a little social prominence, and my father was well known, he owned a huge plumbing company. If people knew how he beat his family, we'd have gone broke, then everyone would have starved. So what's the point?

'Anyway, a neighbour who heard what happened had the kind sense to call the Cooleys instead of the police.'

'So Major Dunn spotted your scar?' Scott pressed, but it was clear that Rivers would not go much further.

'Sure, Jack, he knew what to look for. You know it's funny what you remember, but to this day I imagine old man Cooley watching *McHale's Navy* as the call came in. Jimmy was only fifteen, but his dad let him drive the truck rather than miss that show. We still laugh about it, that was a fairly corny show.'

'I remember,' Scott forced a smile. 'And soon after meeting Dunn, you found yourself in a program with others who came from troubled homes?'

Rivers chuckled. 'Nothing wrong with the homes, Jack, it was the kids who were abused. Anyway, I can live with it.'

Scott nodded, sipping bleakly at a cup of cold coffee.

'No, Jack,' he shook his head, 'what I can't live with is what I read, that victims of abuse lose their emotions over time, or worse yet, revisit the sins onto others. You've probably guessed that I'm not all that great at forming certain relationships?'

'Well, I don't know if that's true, Frank. You may have a hard edge, but you obviously feel things quite deeply. Is that why you're not married?'

Rivers nodded. 'She wanted children, I was afraid of myself, what I might do . . .'

Scott released a stream of smoke. 'Sorry,' he smiled, 'but you have nothing to worry about, unless you've ever raised your hand to . . .'

'God no!' Rivers cut him off, with a nasty stare. 'That's a hell of a thing to say.'

Scott gave a good natured smile. 'You obviously ask it of yourself, so what are you worried about? Trust your feelings and the rest will follow. Frank,' he looked at him with dismay, 'can't you see how foolish your doubts are when you bond so quickly with a little boy like Elmer?'

'Well,' Rivers sighed, 'he's a special little kid.'

'Sure.' Scott dismissed this with a wave of his hand. 'I don't think it would matter to you what child was in danger, it cuts deeper than that. You're a good man, Rivers, take it from there and just get on with your life. If you can't trust yourself, then trust me.'

'And you're a good judge of character?' Rivers smiled.

'The very best,' Scott returned.

And they talked well into the night, fighting to understand what each of them had become in life, and why.

It was a waiting game.

They were killing time by opening wounds.

TWENTY-NINE

Slung low on the horizon an angry sun blazed for the last time before falling off the edge of the world. The Gulf of Mexico was unusually calm, so the flames dropped through a placid green mirror, then burst with an eerie afterglow.

Overhead, scattered clouds pulsed with incandescent light, casting shadows, and as the light died, the colours changed. As the clouds moved, the dunes were rocked with shadow. Far off to the right, an inlet had become a mystical river of fire that resembled fingers of smoking white lava.

'The beach looks alive,' Carol Barth exclaimed, releasing a pleased sigh and pointing towards the coast. To her friend, Lacy Wilcott, the entire scene was like a huge red planet exploding, for she had been born and raised in a place called Moxie Pond, just a bump of an agricultural town in Western Maine. She had never travelled this far south.

'We're in another world,' she answered, her voice filled with a soft wonder. 'How close are we to the equator?'

'Close enough so that even the palm trees look different,' said Carol.

They were first-year students at Loyola University in New Orleans, taking a short vacation before returning home for the summer. Carol was from Newport News, Virginia. They had been on the road for two days, having spent that afternoon touring the Selby Botanical Gardens in Longboat Key.

Lacy Wilcott was a shy and well developed young woman of nineteen with a light complexion and sandy blonde hair, casually dressed in a pink V-neck sweater and white shorts. Carol Barth was the same age, only taller and slim to a fault, with dark hair and violet eyes accentuated by a powder blue tank-top and matching shorts. These pinched at her waistline, flattering her long legs. Together they leaned against a white Pontiac Firebird, the only car parked at the Coral Cove scenic overlook along the old Coastal Highway. A cooling salt breeze washed over them.

'Whadda ya say?' Carol asked as the day burned into terminal orange. She was bent at the waist and slipped off her blue canvas boatshoes, which she tossed through a window and onto the back seat.

'My tummy's growling,' Lacy agreed, 'I think we can make Fort Myers by midnight.'

'Let's just grab some food on the way, how hungry are you?'

'Snacks will do, the first clean store we see. I also need a bathroom.'

'I'm for that,' Carol urged sharply as they climbed into the Firebird and closed the doors. It was Lacy Wilcott's turn to drive, so she moved the seat forward and buckled her seatbelt while her friend switched on the radio, searching for a weather report.

'It's got to be ninety-five degrees,' Carol said. 'I'm still sweating.'

'That's humidity,' Lacy suggested. 'We'll be wearing our jackets in another few hours.'

And in local news, the search for seven-year-old Lisa Caymann ended in tragedy late last night when her body was discovered along Route 41 in St Petersburg. In a press conference this morning, State Police Chief Captain Duncan Powell discussed what he called a mindless atrocity . . .'

An official sounding voice filled the speakers and Carol Barth pushed a tape into the slot with a troubled sigh. 'Who'd do a sick thing like that?'

'Animals,' Lacy answered, and she adjusted the volume as the white Firebird pulled out into the traffic.

The sea was unusually calm that night as they drove towards Venice, discussing their futures in the manner of the young, as if time were a lasting friend which you courted and fashioned from leisurely pursuit. And they returned to discussing the College of Arts and Sciences while listening to rock and roll, cruising towards a destiny that their young minds could not possibly have fathomed.

Gregory Corless was seething with anger, and Seymor Blatt looked startled as the waitress brought a tray and began clearing the table. It was just after sunset and the pair had said only a few words to each other since breakfast.

'Anything else?' The waitress held a check at the ready.

'No, nothing,' Blatt responded flatly. As the woman disappeared, Corless pushed his rotund face across a spot of heavy syrup that short moments ago had been a large stack of waffles. His face was red, flushed with hostility, and his voice was choking with rage.

'How the hell did he know that?' he cursed quietly, his eyes burning with contempt. 'This cop, how did he know there were two of us?'

Following a commercial-free half-hour of easy listening music, the evening news had been piped directly into overhead speakers, and the partners had heard the announcement of Lisa Caymann's death, which registered visibly on other faces throughout the Wayside Pancake House.

Upon hearing the news, a husky truck driver at the counter had thrown his napkin onto the floor, stomping it, while another spun on his bar stool, slapping a fist into his palm. Far off near the cash register, an older woman began to weep as a younger teller spelled her, and she walked past the two men and towards the kitchen.

In the report, a police captain cautioned motorists to be alert for two men, one heavy, one thin, both late middle-age, and travelling together.

'I dunno, Greg,' Blatt chirped nervously. 'I dunno where he got that, but I'm scared.' He scratched at the gold vinyl tablecloth with his fingernails, watching the faces of patrons who were coming in his direction, towards the men's room in the hallway, each stranger making him feel threatened.

'Did you catch his name, did you hear this cop's name?' Corless was whispering, shielding his face with one hand.

'Ah, no, no I didn't.'

'You fucking asshole,' Corless growled, settling back in his seat and scanning the small dining room. They were silent for a moment, Corless sipping his coffee, the other finishing his milk.

Then Blatt said, 'I think we better leave one at a time, Greg.' The fat man's face instantly turned into a mask of red fury.

'We leave together, this cop knows nothing, absolutely nothing,' he hissed, trying to pin Blatt into silence with his eyes.

'Well, I don't like this,' Blatt whispered anxiously, 'how could he have known?'

'Shut up,' Corless sneered, again shielding his mouth. And at this Blatt's eyes narrowed with hurt, he was incensed by Gregory's disrespectful treatment of him, and they had been quarrelling all day.

Just as Jack Scott had suspected in his review of the case from the ViCAT slot, there was a thread of guilt running through the partnership, in the person of Seymor Blatt, who had not wanted Lisa Caymann dead, indeed, had even argued for her life, only to later cover her naked body with a blanket.

As far as Blatt was concerned, Lisa was an angelic specimen with a serious occlusive overbite, a medical condition, and with treatment he knew she could have grown into a beautiful and pleasing woman. He felt as if his partner had betrayed him. Blatt leaned over the table.

'Lessa,' he fired tonelessly, watching Corless squirm in his seat, uneasy with the nonsense word, then turning to face the wall. Blatt waited.

'Lessa,' he fired again, and Corless looked away.

Throughout the day Seymor Blatt had used a hundred such words, meaningless to anyone else, and he used them as clubs with which to beat the fat man, pressing his buttons at every turn in the road.

'Can't you just let it go?' Corless had begged as they left Sarasota. 'You know the rules, and there'll be others that you'll like.'

But on April 10th, 1989, Blatt didn't think so, Lisa Caymann was simply his girl, the child of his dreams, and now he was breaking the rules at each and every turn. Years before they had taken a solemn vow that once a game had ended, when it was done, it would not be discussed again.

'Rules of the road.' He remembered how Corless had explained, and once Blatt had agreed, but right now he no longer cared.

'Why did you do that to her?' he had asked Corless over eggs and coffee, but the fat man did not answer. 'Why did you want to hurt Lisa so bad?'

'I didn't,' he stated calmly, almost absently.

'But there wasn't anything left of her,' Blatt cried.

Fat Corless hissed. 'I didn't want to hurt her,' he explained, speaking very slow while dunking his Danish. 'I wanted to destroy her, there's a difference.' Blatt could still hear those words, and it was then, in that mental fog, that he felt his anger starting all over again as he leaned across the table.

'Lessa,' he hissed suddenly into Corless's ear. 'Lessa, Lessa, Lessa!'

Corless recoiled from the sound, forgetting for a moment that no one else in the diner could possibly understand the imitative voice Blatt was using.

Lisa Caymann's deformed bite had produced a lisp.

Lessa was the way the child had said her name.

By eight o'clock, the students in the white Firebird and the partners in the Dodge van were both weaving through traffic. This time Blatt was driving, so he refused to allow Corless use of the overheads to look at his scrapbook; Blatt even objected when he wanted the domelight in the van's cargo bay turned on.

At this time, Lacy Wilcott was fighting monotony as well

as a bit of depression. 'I'll be working all summer, but I'd rather be in school,' she said, and her voice sounded troubled. 'My father wants me to take my degree in agricultural science and then manage the farm. I think landscape design is a coming thing, so we fight . . .'

'Is it bad?' Carol asked with concern.

'No,' Lacy shook her head, 'we just argue, and I hate that. When my brother declared a major in law, Dad threatened to disown him, but now he calls him every week to see how his studies are coming, there's lots of stress running a farm, I understand all that.'

'He wouldn't take you out of school, would he?' Carol asked.

Lacy smiled. 'No, once he gets over the shock that his kids have their own plans, he's supportive enough.'

'Well, at least you had a brother to pave the way, I'm the oldest and my folks think I'm going into nursing, they're in for a big surprise.'

'Then you're going to tell them?'

'What's wrong with teaching, I'd rather treat the ignorant than the sick. Try this,' Carol offered, drilling her lungs with smoke, then holding her breath. She had fired up a joint she had saved through the semester, and handed it to Lacy.

'What would they be doing in Hog Howler right now?' Carol asked.

'In Moxie Pond?' Lacy smiled. 'By ten the town would be gathered at the Stock and Feed, drinking beer and waiting for something to buzz. They slap flies with a wet mop. "That thar one was a blue-face,"' she said in her most manly voice as she slapped the dash. Carol shrieked with delight.

'You're kidding?'

'Oh, maybe a little,' said Lacy. 'What about the shipyard, do they have Saturday night rust patrol?'

'No, they stay up and worry about the Navy, budget cuts, that kind of thing. To hear them tell it the government never buys enough ships, and when that argument grows old they'll talk about the ironworkers at Groton where they build inferior boats.'

294

They had been on the road for an hour when they whisked past a sign that said *Restroom/Groceries/Gas.*

'Let's give that a try,' Carol suggested, 'somewhere in the next mile, I think it said.' Lacy began looking for an exit, steering the car loosely with her left hand.

Soon they were coasting down a wooded ramp towards a smallish street that reminded them both of backroads in the towns where they were raised.

At the intersection a stop sign was peppered with buckshot, leaning up from weeds on a greenway.

'Welcome to Butcher Howler,' Lacy smiled, slowing a bit, then heading towards a two-pump store with a billboard for a sign, spotted by canisters of light.

'Grafton's General,' Carol said, 'I can almost smell the blue pills in the toilet bowl, bet it hasn't been cleaned in this decade.'

'We can wait?' Lacy offered as she braked, inspecting the parking lot and store. It was well lit and looked clean enough from the outside. Carol was dabbing her lips with a stick of gloss.

'What the hell,' she shrugged as Lacy swung the wheel, creeping towards the top of the small parking lot, towards the bright lamp that reduced shadow.

There were two other cars parked side by side, an old Volkswagen Bug and a new Buick Skylark with New Jersey plates. Next to these were a delivery truck and a battered van, each parked tail first against the curb. They were clearly for daytime use.

'So what makes him the World's Greatest Grandfather?' Carol asked as they pulled alongside.

'Don't grow old,' Lacy Wilcott suggested.

The cargo bay was a steamy parlour of sorts, and with the heat from the engine compartment stirring up humidity, water was leaching down the walls in small rivulets. Gregory Corless was on his rump, changing his shirt and sweating like a sow, which Seymor Blatt thought he surely did resemble.

The partners were both tired with each other, sitting in the cargo bay arguing. When they talked, their words seemed disconnected, going past each other as if the two had nothing in common. They sensed the partnership crumbling. Each resented that fact, and Blatt was worried by the frequent radio reports.

The van's rear doors were open, facing a thick wall of hedges and allowing privacy, while the cool night air blew through the foul interior.

'I think we should just go home,' Blatt whined, and his apple bobbed in his skinny throat. He had removed an extensive dental splint made of gold-filled porcelain which left his own frail teeth planted in his gums like sharpened grey posts. Without the false choppers, Corless thought he looked like a refugee from a gulag.

'This cop, Duncan Powell, is chasing his own ass,' Corless offered. The discovery of Lisa Caymann's body was being repeated on the hour, and that was about their only concern. 'There are hundreds of men on the road who travel in pairs,' he continued, 'truckers, tourists, campers, even bikers, he doesn't have a clue, though I'd like to know how he figured out you're a scrawny little wimp.'

'What else does he know about us, Greg?'

'Nothing, if they had a description they would have broadcast it, no way we were seen. Besides, we've used the backyard snatch before, we're experts, way too good for them.'

'I don't know,' Blatt was whining, 'we shouldn't just sit here, what if a cop pulls in?' The light streaming through a side window made his teeth look like little grey nails, and Corless was about to suggest he rinse his mouth and plug the damn bridge back in, when they heard a car approaching from the roadway.

Corless quickly snapped off the overhead light, Blatt started to fidget, fetching his teeth from a gearbag.

The car moved closer over gravel, crunching, slowing down to inspect the lot. At this, Blatt was having dark visions, running for his life through the woods, dogs rending his flesh, a hick of a sheriff watching him bleed to death. 'Greg?' he cried.

Corless lifted a lip, he was fantasising about a girl he had never seen before, ripping off her clothes, making cruel demands on her. An engine died on their left and they felt rock music thump against the van's interior wall. The brassy chorus was quickly followed by silence. And then voices. At least two, maybe more.

'Get the rear door,' Corless said quietly, buttoning his shirt, putting his book into a banker's box and closing the lid. 'And don't make any noise, we'll leave after they do.'

Blatt ignored him, rising to his knees, then parting the curtains an inch and peering out the window just to make sure they weren't cops. By now he didn't even trust his own senses, and he could just see the driver from the lips down, while the girl in the suicide seat was no more than a torso, one hand pulling a tape from the stereo, the other holding up a marijuana cigarette that was burning to a stub. Blatt breathed a sigh of relief, his thin neck twisting as he spoke.

'There's two of them,' he whispered, 'and I think they're getting high.'

Corless barked something under his breath, moving slowly on his knees, the van rocking with his bulk as he closed the doors, slowly, carefully, quietly as possible, and with a great deal of resentment in his body language. Feeling safe from police dogs, Blatt was enjoying the view, peering down into the white Firebird.

'I like her very much,' he said, and on his return trip, Greg Corless smacked him on top of the head.

'You said there's two of them, don't waste your time,' he responded. And Blatt smiled, thinking about Lisa, thinking about ways to make the fat man pay. These were attractive girls, and if Corless would only look, he knew that alone would drive him insane.

In combination with the Rule of One, Blatt knew the slob would hyperventilate, maybe even go into cardiac arrest. *Pick more than one and they'll end your fun*, Corless was fond of saying, the premise being that abducting one person was easy, with two or more the risk of something going wrong out-weighed the benefit. Blatt smiled, this time Gregory Corless would face fruit he couldn't pick, and Blatt swam in that joy, digging at him with a vengeance. He studied Lacy Wilcott's mouth as she talked, her lips were full and wet, her teeth were bright and evenly spaced.

'She's still in her teens,' Blatt offered from a short dental review.

Corless hissed, preparing to leave as Blatt made a haunting moan deep in his throat.

'So, what's she look like?' Corless barked, the curiosity starting to gnaw at him as his partner giggled.

'I can see the driver pretty good, you'd like this, she has really big tits,' he announced with a teasing whisper.

'Well, don't get used to it, too risky, can you see the other one?'

'Not really.'

'And they're smoking pot?'

'Not any more, they're just talking and . . . Look at that!' Blatt breathed hard. 'She's getting out, arranging her shirt, what a show, her sweater's stretching tight, no bra, her shorts are pulling up . . .' Blatt started heavy breathing just to piss the fat man off, and Corless could stand it no more. He pushed hard on his hands and knees, forcing his considerable mass into the small space, bumping into the thin wall, then straining to catch his breath.

Together they filled the cramped area beneath the window like two evil Kilroys, staring over the edge as Lacy Wilcott and Carol Barth stretched in shadow, oblivious to the menace above.

'A beautiful night,' Carol said with a yawn, looking up at clouds covering a pale moon.

Lacy shivered, crossing her arms against her chest. 'Sandwiches and a pit stop, then let's get back on the road, I don't like it here.'

'The pot makes you paranoid,' Carol offered.

Lacy frowned.

'You mean *women*,' Blatt stabbed sarcastically. Corless was going crazy, he really had said *mature girls*.

'No, women are a pain in the ass, I mean girls whose changes are complete, a woman's body with the mind of a child. Girls. The English language is inexact.' Blatt could see Corless was breathing hard over a game that could not be played because of the Rule of One, it was driving him over the edge.

Blatt was rejoicing, watching the girls enter the store, using his voice to drive Corless into a lathered fit. 'Big bouncing tits, the girl in pink just loves you, the one in blue has legs so long she'd make like a river pump and drain your life away!'

Corless huffed quietly.

Blatt was about to continue when he saw the fat man tremble, unable to sit, trying to maintain his balance, and then losing it. His rear slammed onto the deck like two giant hams. 'I've got it!' he stated before the floor had stopped shaking.

But Blatt knew he had nothing, except for maybe the cold sweat that was dripping down his fat neck. Gregory Corless was trapped in his own rules like a pig cooking in his own hellish juices.

'Did you hear what I said?' Corless barked.

'Got what, Greg?' Blatt asked aimlessly.

'I've got both of them,' he said, grabbing Blatt by the arm. And he had said this with a resolve that frightened Seymor, with a voice he immediately recognised from other games, and he found himself speechless.

He tried thinking of something to say, of something with which to appease the fat man, of something that would put them back on the road.

'The two-minute drill,' Corless ordered, grabbing him by the throat.

By then Blatt was moving too fast to think.

They worked quickly, and with a nimble experience.

'The puppy won't work,' Blatt cried, 'they're going to scream, we're going to get caught!'

'Get the cage,' Corless ordered, 'and I'm also using the cast.'

They thrashed about the steamy cab, pulling the pieces

299

together, setting them down in the middle of the cargo bay. Corless was stripping off his pants and then shirt.

'But Greg,' Blatt cried weakly, 'the rules, what if one of them gets away?'

Corless shot him an acid stare. 'That's your job! Do your job, there's nothing to worry about.'

Blatt worked quickly through the van on his hands and knees, bumping into fat Corless who was digging through a box. Within less than a minute they had assembled an odd assortment of trash in the centre and were looking at coils of rope, rolls of silver duct tape, handcuffs, an icepick, a black leather sap, an expensive shirt with a torn sleeve, a pair of navy blue slacks, a dog's dish, a bag of feed, a can of food, and a small portable kennel with the word *Happy* hanging over the cage door.

'Get it in place,' Corless commanded, struggling to pull the designer T-shirt over his head as Blatt arranged the cage just opposite the double loading doors, covering this with a towel, just so, then placing the dog's dish close to the metal seam which connected to the van's outer stairs. Then using a can opener and spoon he quickly filled the dish with a smelly pile of Kal Kan puppy chow, sprinkling a handful of dry crunchies across the top.

'I don't like this,' he whined, grabbing a roll of tape and a pair of scissors. 'You're going back on your word, you're breaking the . . .'

'You fag,' Corless cut in, 'you said *you* wanted these two, and we will, clear down to Highland Point. Now get with it!'

'I never, never said that,' Blatt sniffed.

Corless ignored him, unwrapping a large plaster cast that had been covered in bubblewrap and safely tucked into a soft brown leather suitcase he called The Bag. He sat in the centre of the van, extending his right arm out towards Blatt like a rotund knight awaiting his armour. 'Make sure you only use a small bit at the wrist this time, I need the hand free, and I don't mean for peeling off your screwups.'

Blatt covered the arm with a plaster cast that was craftily slit open at the back. With some help, the medical device encased the man's arm and shoulder like a shell, covering the entire appendage, including the wrist, thumb and fingers. It closed tight and seamless, fitting like a glove.

Corless proudly held his arm from above as Blatt worked, placing a large strip of white tape under the armpit, and a tiny one under the elbow and wrist.

'And what if they scream?' Blatt asked again.

'Add a little more under the elbow, I don't want this falling off in the parking lot.' Dutifully, Blatt thumped the area with his knuckles, and then complied.

'Greg,' he tried again, 'you just can't walk up to their car! This is a death state! In Florida they have a death penalty and they actually use it!'

Corless smiled where he sat, rotating his entire body, for the cast was now in place and his right side was completely rigid, stiff as a block of wood. His arm was cocked at a forty-five degree angle from the elbow. In turn, his forearm was positioned high in front, almost touching his double chin.

'Apply the brace,' he ordered, and Blatt worked quickly to position a chrome support bar, placing this into a special slot at the elbow, then applying more tape to seal it in. He quickly attached the pillar to the man's belt, and when this was done, he searched through The Bag for a suitable knight's crown. Blatt held a neck brace towards him, a stationary medical support collar made of white plastic.

'Not too tight,' Corless cautioned.

'Sit up a little,' Blatt returned, and he closed the velcro snap, adjusting it, just so, in order to allow for expansion.

Suddenly, Corless was struggling to his feet. 'We're out of time,' he said coldly, having monitored the two-minute drill. And what stood was a pathetic figure of a broken man that would easily spark pity in any caring human being.

His entire right side looked fractured, possibly crushed, and his neck brace tilted his head back, pushing under the chin so that he had to swing his entire body in order to see. His shirt was torn to accommodate the cast in two places, the shoulder and then the waist, where the metal strut attached to a metal cleat that doubled as a gun hook. His shirt remained open at this spot.

'Quickly,' he ordered, and with a shaky fist Blatt handed him his gun, frightened of dropping the heavy steel thing. Corless held the large black revolver high into the air, up to the light where he could see it.

It was no ordinary gun. This .357 Colt Magnum was a weapon designed for psychological intimidation, and had once been commissioned by the U.S. Border Patrol. The short heavy barrel was not tapered like most, but cast into a straight black tube like a stovepipe, as round at the muzzle as it was at the breech.

'Just aim it,' Corless hissed, 'they just curl up and die, you don't even need a trigger.' Without ceremony, he pushed this into his pants, pulling the shirt down, turning to his partner.

'The girl that you'll meet is the only one who can scream, see that she doesn't.'

Without another word, he opened the door and was gone.

Lacy Wilcott waited at a glass sandwich bar, comparing the tuna with ham while Carol finished in the bathroom. An older couple were at the cash register now, getting directions from a clerk, and she could tell by the nasal accents that they were the ones from New Jersey.

Next to the sandwiches she found a row of drinks. She was opening the glass door and selecting a carton of chocolate milk as Carol appeared. Lacy could see her smiling as she came skipping down the isle towards the back of the store.

'Did you see the blue pills in the bowl?' she asked.

'Imported from Newport News, what'd ya get?'

'Ham and cheese with chocolate milk, the tuna looks bad.'

Carol examined the shelves. 'All they have is white bread?'

'The egg salad is on rye.' She motioned to the top row.

'I'll try that.'

Corless came through the door, turning sideways with his

chin braced back and clutching a piece of paper in his left hand. He was careful not to look directly at the girls, but he saw the blonde's head turn his way. They were aware of his presence. He walked on.

Gregory Corless strolled leisurely down the aisle for Canned Goods while holding the list to his nose. About halfway, just after the tuna and soup, but before the canned peaches and pears, he stopped and listened. The girls were now one aisle over.

'Donuts or chocolate chip?'

'You're having that awful milk, sure you want more chocolate?'

'My middle name.'

'I was hoping you'd say something like that.'

With his left hand and arm he collected six cans of Puppy Chow to his chest, then brought them to the counter, only to return for three more. Behind the register sat a kid, about sixteen, Corless guessed, sitting on a stool and entrenched in a comic book.

Corless swung his massive frame, looking for other employees milling about, satisfied that they were alone. He could just see a pink sweater and a blue top reflected in an oval shoplifting mirror above the door.

'How much?' Corless asked the boy, using his most mild voice as he pulled a wad of bills from his pocket. The clerk got up from his chair.

'Dog hungry?'

'Yes.'

The kid grabbed a can, turning it upside down, then ringing the same number nine times on the register instead of multiplying in his head. Corless sized him up as someone who didn't have the mental capacity to store a man's description longer than a few seconds, and he tried to keep his behaviour invisible.

'That'll be five dollars and eight cents, please.'

Then the clerk fumbled in the drawer to make change from a ten.

'Thank you,' Corless said. 'Would you have a box? An open beverage tray would do nicely.'

The clerk glanced at the extensive cast which was supported by a polished chrome beam. 'Wanna bag?'

'I'd prefer a box.'

He ducked under the counter and produced an open Dr Pepper box, then stacked the cans into place. 'Thanks,' Corless said in a genuine tone, sliding the crate across the counter to his waist, then lifting with his one good arm.

'Wanna hand?' the clerk offered.

'Ah, no,' Corless said quietly, 'I have to get used to this thing, seven more months to go.'

The kid shrugged and went back to his comics, and on the way out Corless glanced up at the oval mirror above the door. Two girls were headed towards the checkout, and he stared at their curves, undressing them with his eyes. He felt a fire growing inside him.

He felt the thrill of the hunt.

They paid and left.

The cool night air greeted Lacy Wilcott and Carol Barth as they walked out into the parking lot. The high clouds had been driven away by the wind revealing a sliver of a moon, faint, almost a scratch on the night sky. Carol stopped to look up.

'The pollution's gotten so bad in Newport I almost forgot how beautiful the stars can be,' she said.

'In Moxie we write songs about them,' Lacy smiled. They strolled away from Grafton's General Store, sipping their drinks on the outskirts of Route 41 near the town of Laural.

'Did you see that schoolboy looking at you?' Lacy quizzed.

'Very funny, he's younger than my brother.'

'He's in love.'

'With a comic book.'

They were about halfway across the lot to the white Firebird when a can rattled by in their direction, across the parking lot, and they watched it roll as if this were an alien thing, not a can of dog chow, but a foreign object they had never seen before. When they looked up, an invalid of a rotund man was bobbling a box of cans, two more of them slapping the ground with a knock, the man locked helplessly into a huge cast and straining to balance the load.

'Oh my!' Carol exhaled as she watched another roll in her direction, down the blacktop, nearly bumping into her toes. She bent over and picked it up. 'The poor guy,' she said, starting towards him.

'Carol?' Lacy cautioned.

She kept walking, but turned her head back towards her friend. 'He's in a cast, silly, he can't hurt anyone.' Just then the cripple at the edge of the parking lot lost his balance completely and the box fell with a crash, cans spinning, Gregory Corless sweeping the air with his stiff appendage.

He smiled good-naturedly as Carol approached, and instead of shaking his head, he shrugged with his entire body. She stood four feet away, looking up into his face, examining his eyes, while Lacy followed after, swinging their dinner in a brown bag and clutching a can of dog food.

'Let me help,' Carol offered, picking up two of the cans just as Lacy arrived alongside and tugged on her arm.

'I'm sorry,' Corless said, releasing a dejected sigh.

'Don't be silly,' Carol responded, her pretty violet eyes darting nervously, reflecting the light. She looked up and saw a wedding band on his good hand and figured it was quite safe.

'Is that your van?' Lacy suddenly asked, and her voice was ripe with concern, even a bit displeasing.

'Lacy?' Carol queried disapprovingly as she placed all of the cans into the fallen box, then took another from her friend. She stood and started to hand these back to the owner, and an awkward shuffle ensued, reminding Carol of crowded encounters, nearly bumping into someone, and then waltzing in place.

Corless laughed gently, it seemed like an embarrassment. The man only had one hand, and it was obvious to Carol that he couldn't carry the whole box, for that's what had gotten him into trouble in the first place.

'He's been parked there a long time,' Lacy cautioned.

'Yes I have, and I appreciate your help, but I can take it from here,' he offered.

'Good luck,' said Lacy, and she started to walk.

Carol was still holding the box and looking at the labels for the first time. 'Do you have a puppy?' she asked, and Lacy stopped, emitting a frustrated sigh.

Corless turned, his right arm stuck in the air like a frozen crane. 'My wife and I are heading south to see my oldest daughter, and we were bringing my grandson a puppy. When we stopped here for a snack late this afternoon, he jumped out of the van. My wife's still looking, we're taking turns.'

'Oh, that's terrible,' Carol responded.

'Then why all the dog food?' Lacy asked.

'I couldn't think of anything else to do, so I thought I'd buy some extra cans, open them up, then place them around the area in case the little guy gets hungry.' He tried to shake his head but the brace wouldn't budge, so he rubbed the back of his neck with his left hand.

Carol was staring angrily at Lacy.

'I know it's dumb,' Corless said, noticing that the brunette was now starting for the van, carrying the box, and walking slowly.

'You the Greatest Grandfather?' Lacy asked as they approached the bumper.

'Not any more, I'm afraid, not with a missing puppy anyway. We had one for each grandchild, looks like we'll arrive with only one dog.' And he stopped at the cargo doors, his face sad and strained.

'You have another puppy?' Carol asked, standing by the van. Lacy Wilcott stood just behind her friend, feeling a bit uncomfortable.

'Yes,' Corless smiled, 'a baby cocker spaniel, cutest thing in the world. They're brother and sister. Well, thank you very much, girls, you've been so very kind.' He reached forward with his left hand, awkwardly trying to open the door while his right arm swung, arcing through the air. The door would not budge.

'I'm still not used to this cast,' Corless sighed, about to try again.

'Let me,' Carol offered, handing the box to her friend.

Lacy Wilcott took a step back, Corless was standing to her immediate right, and slightly behind, and the girls took no notice as his arm eased through the splayed bottom of the cast and hung limp at his side while the medical prop stayed in place.

'How do you open this?' Carol asked, having turned the latch.

'Oh, I'm sorry,' he said, 'it slides, you have to pull.'

Carol Barth pulled back the door, and there was darkness.

Lacy Wilcott stood her ground just as Carol stepped forward, first smelling, and then seeing a bowl of puppy food inside the steps.

It was reassuring.

Just behind this she saw the little cage draped for the night, and over this, the name Happy.

'Is that her name?' Carol asked sweetly, turning to collect the box from Lacy.

'Yes,' Corless cooed proudly. 'I cover her at night when she's sleeping, but you can talk to her if you like, she's very loving. I don't know how she's reacting to the loss of her litter mate.' His voice sagged. 'Maybe she doesn't notice, seems all puppies do is eat, play, and sleep.'

Corless was taking another small and unnoticeable step backward as Carol smiled. 'Oh Happy knows,' she confirmed, moving forward and peering into the van, placing the box of cans on the floor. Then she stepped up, leaning over the cage, and bent down. She approached with a soothing voice.

'Hi Baby,' she cooed, 'hi Baby,' and she started to lift Happy's curtain.

There was horror. Not at once but building slowly, mixing with confusion as she strained to focus her eyes on what was before her.

It came into focus as the world around her whirred into a smear of horrid and confusing images. At the bottom of an empty cage was a photograph of a nude woman being bound into a chair – terror hit Carol Barth like a bullet in the chest.

Time stopped.

Fear stretched across her face, contorting her features, and she tried to scream and stand at the same time.

'Run!' she had started to cry, but the word just fell from her mouth as she fell, a black leather sap coming out of the air, silencing her with a crippling blow.

Blatt had delivered a dull punch to the back of her head; just as two massive arms swung around Lacy Wilcott's throat, grabbing her from behind, then lifting her by the chin into the air.

Her feet dangled and she kicked frantically with overpowering fear, struggling for breath and fighting to scream. But her throat was pinched shut and her lungs burned for air as she felt faintness crippling her.

'Go ahead and fight,' Corless hissed into her ear.

Seconds crawled by. She felt her strength draining away as Corless slapped the deadly stovepipe revolver across the bridge of her nose, being careful not to draw blood, then jammed the gun up under her chin.

'Make one sound and you're dead!' he sneered under his breath, and his lips touched her ear.

Still, Lacy Wilcott gave a futile last kick as she felt her body being crushed and overpowered, then going limp beneath the attacker's violent hold. There were two of them now. She felt two of them.

Blatt and Corless were dancing together, pressing the girl between them, using their bodies as a human vice with which to force her movements. With expert skill, Seymor Blatt slapped Lacy's wrists with handcuffs even as Corless was rolling her onto the floor of the van.

'Tape her,' he ordered, lying on top, then smacking her hard across the face, drawing blood at the corners of her mouth. He held her jaw shut with two massive hands as the cargo door slid shut.

Darkness.

It only took seconds, then Lacy was taped and bound, and

then Carol, who lay unconscious near Happy's cage. The men were congratulating each other in the darkness, united again, catching their breath.

'Get the blonde naked, I don't want anything else in my rearview for the next few hours,' Corless ordered without tone while climbing into his seat, adjusting his mirror.

This done, they headed south.

They were happy now. They were just killing time.

THIRTY

Dudley Hall, the Diggerman, wound his Chevy four-by-four up into second gear, churning dirt with his tyres, roaring down the curving hills on Rabbit Run. As he talked he swerved occasionally to avoid door-sized potholes which were puddled with leaves and rain water.

To Matthew Brennon, it looked like a miss would spell certain death, and he grappled for his seatbelt, snapping it tightly into place, Hall observing this.

'Ain't been a road crew by for a good while.' He spat out the window. 'Prison shut down the chain gangs, was violatin' their *serval* rights.'

Brennon knew what he meant as he sat clutching the urn with both hands, hoping that the man they called Leon Rigby would be home, and that luckier still, he would have some recollection of the burial jar which held the remains marked Zachariah Dorani.

'Shouldn't we have called?' he yelled back, glancing discreetly at his watch so as not to offend.

'Nope,' the Diggerman hollered, 'where dere's smoke dere's fire,' and he swerved off onto a circular clearing by the side of the road and stopped, dust funnelling over the cab. Dudley Hall waited for it to clear.

From this elevation on Woodside Mountain they were looking down a country mile onto the small town, a patchwork village of houses, farms, and manufacturing buildings all saddled into a tight valley. Abandoned railroad tracks skirted the edge of the development closest to them, and Brennon noticed a boarded up train depot and switching yard. There were no cars on the roadways below, and he quickly concluded that Woodside New York had been dead for some time, decay had taken over completely.

'What are we looking at?' he asked, setting the urn on the bench seat between his legs.

Hall pointed through a hazed windshield. 'See the blinking lights over dere?' In the distance Brennon could just discern a series of small red beacons flashing from the other side of the depot, and knew he was seeing aviation strobes attached to an aerial obstruction. Something was jutting up into the sky.

'Radio station?' he asked, unable to discern the object's form.

'Chimmy,' said Hall, by which he meant chimney. 'That's Rigby's creamer, gettin' it fired up too, can just make out the heat plume.'

Brennon could just see a ridge of white clouds slung low on the horizon, they were being sliced in half right over the obstruction. 'Would anyone else be operating it?'

'Justta old fool hisself,' answered Dudley Hall, pressing the pedal to the floor, and the Chevy truck bolted over dirt and gravel, belting Brennon back into his seat. The truck rumbled along, carrying the men towards a destination Brennon could only imagine, so he tried concentrating on other things. The cool air at his sleeve carried a clean wet smell that reminded him of Vermont where he had spent part of his childhood, but for reasons he didn't understand, the smell made him think of dust, human dust, and how a real wet season could leach and jell a man down into a concrete shovelful; then a thousand years' worth of people all slipping around under the earth, while others blew on the wind, flitting up some cooker's chimmy. And at that moment life seemed a strange and futile thing for Matthew Brennon, his mortal place merely a troubled speck as he clutched the urn and the truck hurtled through time.

Hall had started fishing under his seat with his right hand, producing a pint bottle of sloe gin, then unscrewing the top with his thumb. He offered this to Brennon.

'I appreciate it, but no,' he said, as they rounded the bottom of the hill and hit pavement, the truck's tyres biting with an angry chirp. Hall placed the bottle between his lips and gave a long pull, taking a right onto a side street. Soon they were speeding through the village, houses came and went as the four-by-four clattered along railroad tracks and towards the red beacon.

'Did ya see all the vandalism at Old Woodie?' Hall asked, taking a small sip. Brennon remembered hundreds of over-turned stones, it was a dreadful sight.

'When I was a kid we wouldn't dare even raise our voices in a cemetery, it makes you wonder.'

'Ain't no kids,' he huffed, 'an unemployed welder, lives right dere.' He slowed in front of a small grey house set back from the street. The glow of a television flickered through the window. 'Sheriff knows it too, can't prove a thing, a whole family of shit people live in dat house.' He took a long pull of the bottle, then rolling down the window, slung it at the litter-strewn yard. It landed with a crash as a pungent odour filled the cab, hitting Brennon like an acid kiss. He covered his face and coughed.

'What's that smell?' he sputtered.

'That,' the Diggerman smiled, 'is the creamer.'

The truck turned onto a lash of a gravel, through a picket fence, rolling towards a large Victorian house with a blaze of red strobes pulsing from a dark round funnel that towered like a scar against the night sky.

Rigby's crematorium was a concrete room that had been con-structed at the back of his residence. Inside, the walls were painted white, the floor was a slab of finished grey with a fresh coat of shiny sealer. As they walked through the door, a tall figure in blue surgical scrubs turned their way, made eye contact, then went back about his business.

Dudley Hall led them to a spot across the lab near the only window, and Brennon did a quick inventory as they passed. There were wooden cupboards, a glass laboratory case, and large stainless steel sinks at the end of the room near the oven. In the centre of the cubicle was an examination table, the older type once used in city morgues with chrome drip gutters and drain holes at head and feet. Mercifully, he thought, this was vacant.

From the far end, a noise blew through the space, first starting as a whisper, then sounding more like a jet engine firing up. It emanated from a vast chrome tube that resembled a huge septic tank, half buried in the furthest concrete wall. As Hall moved about, making himself at home, the sound was increasing, nearly roaring, then blasting at them with a penetrating whine. They watched as the man Brennon surmised was Leon Rigby peered through a heavy glass porthole at the end of this massive steel chamber, turning a little wheel that sprouted copper tubing from two sides.

Above his head ran a series of analogue gauges with pie zones in the colours yellow, red and blue. He made an adjustment and the room screamed, while Rigby began turning another knob, this one producing a deep sound like the roar of a boiling ocean. Brennon glanced out the window and could just see a spire of black smoke. He realised he had been holding his breath.

The smell was suffocatingly sweet, like bacon being torched on a bed of apples, and it filled his lungs as he watched a stream of fat flowing down a stainless gutter.

'Why don't you jest let the damn flame go blue?' Hall was shouting above the din, criticising the red glow that was reflecting against the walls. Leon Rigby waved him off like shooing a fly, his wet cough sputtering through his surgical mask. He removed the asbestos gloves that had been shielding him up to the elbows, then untied the blue gown. He was tall, thin and gangly, with a voice that slurped like a bad drain.

'What?' he wheezed, and Brennon guessed the man suffered from advanced emphysema, his husky wet cough shook his entire body as he moved back to the chrome counters, making adjustments, putting away tools.

'Eight and eight,' Rigby yelled, and the two men strolled to the chamber, glancing up at a series of glass encased gauges on top of the pot. One read eight-hundred degrees, and

Brennon cringed, thinking the body inside might cook for eight hours. He watched as Rigby spun a little wheel, and the roar suddenly went deafening, like standing at the end of a jet runway on takeoff.

The blue man hit the light switch, transforming the space into a white hot glow that screamed through the porthole's glass face, washing the cell with fire, making Brennon conjure images of earth's end. Casually, Leon Rigby walked by and through a skinny door.

Inside, the Rigby residence was a stuffy little hole with wooden flooring, a couch covered with an old Afghan, a matching plaid easy chair torn at the seams, and a coffee table that was a slab of raw oak, round with concentric rings. Opposite this, the television set was vintage black and white, and somehow Brennon found himself pleased that creaming bodies wasn't that lucrative. He guessed that Leon Rigby was not a man who parted with money easily. The three were standing.

'This is Special Agent Matthew Brennon, he's on official gov'ment business,' Dudley Hall said, using his most authoritative tone. And Leon Rigby seemed to be studying the lean agent, sizing him up, gauging the importance of the visit. He fought a cough as he extended his hand, which Brennon saw as a thin and fragile cage of bone.

'Glad to have the company,' Rigby said.

Brennon greeted him warmly.

'Let me wash up, like a beer?' he wheezed, pulling off his gown and laying it over a wooden chair.

'That would be fine, thank you.' Rigby disappeared across his living room, leaving them in the dingy light cast from an ancient floor lamp with tassels on a yellowed shade. Beneath this Brennon spotted a green oxygen bottle with an inhaler attached. The house reeked of smoke, dampness clung on everything.

Gently, the Diggerman placed the urn on the coffee table, then sat on the couch while lifting a pillow. 'Make sure he don't charge for the beer,' he said mockingly.

'How's that?'

'Rigby's so tight he squeaks, can't close his eyes, they'd stick shut.' Brennon smiled as the Burnman returned, carrying a wooden tray, then laying it down alongside the urn.

'So what's this?' he directed to Brennon, handing him a cold bottle of generic suds. He then gave Dudley Hall a double shotglass filled with bourbon, and sat down on the couch next to him. The two men had said nothing to each other.

'That was exhumed with a court order, and we were hoping you could tell us something about it,' Brennon offered, lowering himself into the tired easy chair. He could feel a spring poking one cheek.

'Cigar?' asked Rigby, lifting a box from an end table and waving this at Brennon.

'No thanks,' he said, then watched as Hall took the box, placing one cigar in his mouth, then dropping another into his top pocket. Rigby was twisting the urn 360-degrees.

'Oh, for Christ's sake, talk to the man!' Hall suddenly cried through an angry face. Rigby ignored him.

'Son, do you have a budget?' he asked, lifting his shotglass and taking a generous sip.

Dudley Hall splashed liquid back against his throat. 'Damn it, Leon, that's a baby killer that's bottled up dere, you white trash rummy nigger!'

Rigby coughed, his lungs going into a spasm. 'Well,' he stammered, rattling like a jump-started car, then clearing his throat. 'Well, how could I know?' His thin face was flushed with red, and he stood, walking from the couch, then returning with a bottle of Old Crow. He refilled his glass as Hall held his over the urn.

'Seal's been torn,' Rigby stated, examining the bottled man.

'We broke the goddamn seal,' said Hall.

'Did you sell this urn?' asked Brennon.

'What are you going do with him?' Rigby wondered.

'We're sending the remains to the FBI forensics lab in Washington,' he explained, 'then try for a blood type.'

'Don't know his blood type?' asked Rigby.

'That's his business,' Hall snapped.

'We just want verification,' Brennon offered kindly, 'but I'm more interested in the bottle right now.'

'Won't get no identification from those ashes,' said Rigby, moving the Old Crow to his side of the table as Hall just slugged down his drink.

'Why not?'

'Fires burning at over 2,000 degrees, nothing left, no cells anyhow. Carbon, that's all you'll get, unless he was burned slow, but in that,' he swung his glass at the expensive blue container, 'he would have gotten the best, blue flames, there's nothing in there but dust.'

'Show 'em the chippy,' Hall suggested, puffing his cigar and standing to reach for the whisky.

Brennon handed Rigby a white handkerchief, which he carefully unfolded into his lap. The Burnman was holding a piece of porous grey bone between his thin fingers and squinting. 'Calcaneum, tip of the human heel,' he said. 'That came from the urn?'

Brennon nodded as Hall humphed.

'Let's take a look,' Rigby offered, handing Brennon the whisky bottle, then clearing off the table. He popped the urn's cap, and with both hands began pouring a stream, watching the speed with which the flakes were falling. A pensive expression moved across his face as Brennon watched carefully.

'Ah, you did that, you old cheap screw,' Hall cursed over his drink as Leon Rigby ran his finger through the pile. Rigby frowned, then shook his head at the urn.

'Are you from the prison authority?' the thin man asked nervously.

'No,' Brennon shook his head, 'we're only interested in learning about the deceased, we don't care about anything else.'

Rigby rubbed his fingertips together, dipping back into the pile. 'That's a discounted job,' he said, 'a burnt up yardbird. To torch a body right it takes nearly fifty cubes of natural gas, top Fahrenheit costs plenty, the State has always paid about half the going rate.'

'He burns 'em real slow, uses charcoal at the bottom,' Hall explained.

'The less gas, the cheaper your cost, and the charcoal continues to burn after the gas is shut off?' Brennon concluded.

'Or I'd never show a profit from the State, but I only do that to penitentiary men, or derelicts. Who was this?'

'Career felon, died in prison,' said Brennon.

'I think not,' Rigby corrected, 'at least not in this jug.' He lifted the urn. 'It's top of the line, and spare no expense. If I burned this man it would have been fast, all carbonated powder, not grey with chippies. If someone was around to buy a pricy bottle like this, the State wouldn't have carried the cost of cremation.'

'You're sure?'

Rigby nodded. 'Either the prison pays or the family has to carry all costs, can't have it both ways.'

'What he's saying,' the Diggerman added, 'is that a slow burn is easy to spot, and this ash should have been dumped into a cardboard bury box.'

Brennon nodded, writing into a black notebook. 'What can you tell me about it?' he urged.

'Well, it's definitely my work and my can,' Rigby confirmed. 'Back when we were fed by the trains I did a big city business, and I'd sell bottles to funeral homes and private customers.' He read the date on the gold ribbon. 'By 1964 I had sold most of these because the style was going out, but this,' he paused, 'doesn't make sense.'

'Could bodies have gotten mixed up somehow?' Brennon asked.

Dudley Hall laughed as he spoke. 'Never,' he said. 'Leon keeps better track of a corpse than you keep on your dick, a body means money.' And Brennon knew there was some truth to this because the Burnman had gone stone silent and was shifting uncomfortably on the sofa.

'Sir, is there any way to tell who bought the urn?'

Rigby shot Diggerman Hall a crooked glance as he stood

and left the room. Hall quickly grabbed the Old Crow off the table. 'He's gone for his records,' he said, 'hassa mountain of boxes and crates filled with useless shit, maybe something will happen this time.'

'This time?' Brennon repeated. Hall had spoken as if they were watching a routine, then suddenly the Diggerman leaned over and slapped Brennon hard on the knee.

'Lotta old family ties 'ere at Woodie,' he said through a cheery alcoholic glow. 'In my time I've known most all serious manhunters, least in these parts, same's true with old Leon.'

Brennon smiled weakly and took a sip of beer, that bit of bragging was old as the academy, everybody knew everybody, only they didn't really.

'It's true nuff,' said the old man, 'some came lookin' for the Diggerman hisself, others just led by the fate of two million dead, that's a lotta bodies to be telling stories.'

'Yes it is,' Brennon agreed, 'lots of stories,' and his voice sounded worn, even a touch sarcastic.

'Name of Nicholas Dobbs mean anything to a man your age?' Dudley Hall asked suddenly, and Matthew Brennon nearly inhaled his beer.

'And Tombstone Taylor, Popeye Doyle, the Real McCoy, big Duke Duncan, Mad Max Drury, and that Scotty Dog of yours? Saw him water a few graves in my time.'

'Jack Scott?' Brennon sucked air as his jaw sprung open.

But the Diggerman fell into a silent and toothless grin as Leon Rigby walked between them with three fileboxes in his hands.

The thin man was rather proud of his organisational skills, particularly the multicoloured rows of plastic file tabs, which arranged hundreds of white, lined, three-by-five cards.

On the outside of the first box it said Supplies Wholesale, and he gave a wet cough as he pulled the floor lamp closer. 'You'll have to bear with me,' he said as his bony fingers began scratching through the cards. 'These are categorised by dates, but that urn could have been a personal sale, wholesale exchange, or even a barter, it could take some time.'

'No problem,' Brennon said. 'Is this cataloguing required by code?'

'Hell,' the Diggerman grinned, 'that's jest in case the IRS wants a nickel, he's been preparing for years, ain't that right, Rigby?' The thin man worked unimpaired by the distraction as the Diggerman settled back in his seat.

'Is the gold inlay real?' Brennon asked, leaning over to finger the urn.

'Eighteen carat, six millimeters deep, roughly 1.2 troy ounces.' He pulled a card from the box. 'In 1960 that metal cost eight dollars wholesale, real money.'

'May I see that?' Brennon asked, retrieving the card, then reading meticulous handwritten notes. 'The urn was hand-crafted in 1964 at Peterson's Mortuary Services, St Paul, Minnesota?' he asked.

'A very fine house, they went belly up that same year, always keep your overhead down and the profit up, they did neither. The inside is glassblown, the outside is leaded copper, and the finish is blue cloisonné enamel with gold inset.' He went back to the box.

'Then these bottles would be filled by you and delivered back to a funeral home?'

Rigby shook his head. 'If the beloved were to be buried at Woodlawn, and the church services were elsewhere, the undertaker would just use a duplicate empty bottle, a dummy, I'd keep the real one here.'

'And then these ghouls would charge the family for a phoney transport, priest would be blessin' an empty can,' Hall sneered.

Rigby shrugged. 'By 1964 I had sold seven as dummy bottles to various homes, here's the list,' he offered, and Brennon examined the card.

'Then these homes could have been involved in some type of mix up?'

'No,' Hall corrected, 'after they milked the bereaved family for a worthless transport, the funeral home would send the empty can back to Leon as trade for the real one he filled.'

'Or they always had the option of keeping the can and splitting all bogus fees,' Rigby corrected, 'but this particular urn wasn't involved in any type of wholesale exchange, or it would be in here.' He scratched at the index cards with yellowed fingernails.

'Then it was retail,' Brennon pressed.

'It's possible, but I thought I'd remember that, those purchases were always bereaved walk-ins. Apparently I had four in stock, I thought it was three.' His hand flicked from red to blue tabs, searching out the correct year.

'What was the month he died?' Rigby asked, holding a spot in 1966.

'February,' Hall said.

Rigby fished for a card, reading as he went, his eyes darting across the lines. Then he pulled one loose and nodded his head. 'Here's the answer,' he sighed, 'imagine that, it was a telephone order, fairly rare, I should have remembered.' He read aloud, interpreting the note.

'Someone who couldn't attend the services paid for the jar, and he just made it under the wire too. According to this, when the order was placed I had already performed cremation and was about to stick the deceased into a prison box, that's why the slow burn job.'

'May I?' asked Brennon, and his eyebrows were knotted with anticipation.

'February 24th, 1966,' he read, 'Peterson's Eternal Promise ordered by phone for Dorani, Zachariah. Cost of purchase, $1,200?'

'It was my last one,' Rigby shrugged.

'Under method of payment it says PPO, what's that?'

'Personal Purchase Order, shorthand of mine, it's the method of payment, which would be cash or certified cheque before services.'

Brennon nodded. 'Then under that it says Paid in Full, which means you received the money?'

'Believe it,' Hall stated.

'And what's Dryer's mean, for twenty-six dollars?'

Dudley Hall spoke first, putting down an empty glass. 'That

would be Al Dryer, the engraver who did the gold, he's been dead a while.'

'That's all included in the ticket price,' Rigby clarified, 'just a personal record if Dryer ever said I didn't pay, which he sometimes did.'

'No claim there,' Brennon offered, 'says Paid in Full on the 25th. Then under that, the name of the company that bought the urn, DIDS Ltd of Dallas, Texas, and an old address.'

'I wouldn't have settled for that!' Rigby looked insulted, reaching for the card, turning it over, then holding it under the yellowed lamp. He then leaned towards Matt Brennon, his thin face worked into a broad smile.

'See here,' he said proudly, 'just ran out of room, I even copied the telephone number. DIDS stands for Dallas Instrument & Dental Supply, and the man I dealt with, Mr Aaron, was the owner. That's him right there,' Rigby pointed, sniffing the air for Hall's benefit, and Brennon quickly scanned the data.

That Zak Dorani was a devout atheist was well established, yet the President of DIDS had requested very clearly, and in some detail, that the deceased be buried in a religious bottle, specifically a Christian urn with five gold crosses. 'Is there any way Mr Aaron would *not* have known about Dorani's religious concerns?' Brennon asked.

'Naw,' Hall waved him off, 'the prison would've kept it on file, and Aaron would've been told the moment he offered to pay for services.'

'And if they didn't, then I certainly would have,' Rigby added.

'Then why did you comply with the request?' Brennon asked. 'It could have been meant in some mean spirited way, intentionally failing to honour Dorani's last request to be buried in an unmarked urn, he didn't have any family left?'

'Can't make much sellin' a pickle jar,' said Hall.

'Oh, what's the harm?' Rigby asked defensively, his wet cough making his body shudder.

'Well, puttin' a man in a jar he don't want is like pissing

on a grave, only worse, denying a request that lasts an eternity. You should be ashamed,' Hall admonished. And Brennon watched as Rigby reached for the oxygen bottle, pulling the mask to his face and turning on the gas.

Brennon thought back. If what Dudley Hall said was true, then purchase of the Christian urn could have been meant as an act of retribution, an insult of some type, albeit an expensive one. And Brennon wondered about Mr Aaron's relationship to Zak Dorani, if that's who was even stuck in the jar. It was with this puzzle on his mind that he felt strangely on edge, his instincts warning him into action, and he used Rigby's phone to call the ViCAT slot and order a nationwide computer search on DIDS Ltd.

A half-hour later, 9:45 p.m., Saturday, April 9th, Special Agent Daniel Flores called back, and Brennon answered on the first ring as Leon Rigby and the Diggerman looked on.

'I've found the urn's buyer listed as the CEO of a major dental supply corporation,' Flores announced. 'According to Trans-Union's credit sheet DIDS was a one-man outfit until the seventies, now they have offices in twenty-three states.'

'Big and prosperous,' Brennon responded. 'So Aaron's still alive?'

'Very much alive, and I just spoke with Commander Scott, he said to tell you this is urgent, so we're pushing the search first priority. He also said to draft Dudley Hall into service, we need his help.'

'I beg your pardon?'

'Jack said ask Mr Hall to come to Washington, for old times' sake. You are to buy his ticket.'

Brennon's head fell on a weakened stalk. 'Anything else?' he asked quietly.

'No, but you have a minor slip in your data, a simple inversion, I had to run combinations with Aaron before I got a hit.'

'On the name?'

'Yes sir,' Flores stated. 'The man's first name is Aaron, you have it reversed.'

Brennon scribbled a correction into his notebook. 'So I should read *Aaron Seymor Blatt*?'

'Yes sir,' said Flores, 'fifty-one years old, single, and no police record.'

THIRTY-ONE

The phone at the command post had been ringing through the early hours of evening, and Jack Scott terminated a call, his face tired but knowing. It did not matter that he had never heard of Aaron Seymor Blatt, he immediately ordered that all ViCAT stops be pulled out at once, that his New York office concentrate their energies on him, that his history be uncovered and his life laid bare.

Frank Rivers had been testing electronic tracking equipment in the parking lot across the street, and he returned through the rear door to find Scott working on a collage of Diana Clayton's house, scanning her personal appointment calendar as he placed a photo on the table. 'Is that necessary?' Rivers commented as he strolled into the kitchen, peering over Scott's shoulder and down into a silver-framed portrait of Kimberly Clayton.

Simply put, the image was haunting, and without a clear purpose which furthered the investigation, it seemed a bit macabre. Scott inhaled a puff of smoke, then lifted the glossy of Jennifer Doe, the lifelike clay image staring up with penetratingly human eyes.

'Something precipitated the attacks,' Scott offered quietly, 'I'd like to know what that was, and the answer lies in who they were.'

Rivers frowned. 'So you're getting to know them?'

'I am, but a bit more. These two families shared something, possibly an activity, I don't know.'

'Jack,' he said sceptically, 'if that child had lived,' he picked up the portrait of Jennifer Doe, 'she'd be older than me.'

'That's quite true, and the Clayton girls could have been my granddaughters, but age has nothing to do with it. I consider them each as individuals, their behaviours transcend time.'

'Then what do you see?'

Scott smiled. 'Nothing so far,' he changed subjects, 'how about the field equipment, is it functional?'

'Sure, but it's primitive stuff, the locator will put us within a mile, not much more.' He had planned on dropping a small transmitter behind Jessica Janson's car bumper, but was now wondering if it was really worth the effort. He picked his gearbag off the floor.

'Did Captain Drury call about the Patterson kid?'

'Max said the dogs did find Debra's scent in the women's room, but nothing else, she was there, and that's all they got.'

Rivers remembered the acid green underwear that Mr Patterson had found in her hamper, they looked ripe for a successful K-9 attempt, their best team had been assigned to search the Zephyr Bar and Grill earlier in the day. 'And the witnesses?'

Scott shook his head. 'According to the field interviews, there are none, and the owners were very uncooperative, they immediately threatened with legal action for unlawful harassment and we have no grounds for a search warrant. I'm afraid it's a wash unless we petition a court on Monday, but I think probable cause is going to be a real problem here.' He handed over a note. 'Those are the owners.'

'What the hell,' Rivers growled, 'it's been going on eight hours since her car was found.' He shoved the slip into his pocket just as Mule Murphy's voice cracked through the kitchen radio, reaching their ears like gunshot.

'Base, this is Huskies . . .'

Rivers reached across the table, lifting the microphone, turning the volume down on the receiver. 'Go ahead.'

'A car's pulling in, white Oldsmobile Cutlass, woman driving, do you want plates?'

'Negative Huskies, is it mother?'

'Must be, the boy ran out the front door to meet her. He's

hugging her back, so yeah, but this lady's nothing like your description, we are exposing film now.'

Toy Saul was using a telescopic lens through the van's rear windows, taking pictures on a high-speed emulsion.

'Roger that, Huskies, are they parked in the garage?'

'No, in the driveway, they're walking for the front door.'

Rivers nodded. 'Base to Pogo.' He was checking the stakeout position at the bowling alley. 'Do you copy?'

'Ah, yes sir,' Rudy Marchette's thin voice chirped with excitement, and Rivers quickly made a notation of the time in his duty book. Jessica Collier Janson had arrived home at 6:08 p.m., Saturday, April 9th. 'Keep us posted,' he demanded, then released the toggle with his thumb and began searching through his gearbag.

First he removed a soft leather Galco shoulder rig, slinging this over his left arm, then pushing an automatic into place, adjusting the holster's tension spring with a small screwdriver which he kept on his key case. It was an unusual-looking gun for a State man to carry, the metal was a bright shiny blue and the grips were an inlaid ivory instead of rubber, like most serious combat pistols. Both the front and rear sights had been removed, and Scott recognised the piece as an old Combat Commander. He watched for a few moments as Rivers fidgeted until he was confident with the ease of the gun's release.

'Going hunting?' Scott asked, as Rivers grabbed a light grey windbreaker, then placed a small radio receiver on the table.

'Promises to keep,' he answered tonelessly, and there was a curious tension in the room that made instant strangers of the two men.

Elmer and Jessica Janson strolled hand in hand up the front walk, the three-legged dog vying for their attention as they climbed flagstone steps, the boy talking excitedly as they disappeared through the front door.

They walked through the hallway and into the kitchen.

The truth was that Jessica was an attractive blonde, and Elmer was rather proud of that fact, although today his mother was dressed for work in a navy wool gabardine suit that suggested only sexless and cool decisions. Her matching slacks had creases that could slice, and she removed her jacket, folding this carefully across her briefcase, dropping them both on the tiled counter. As she unbuttoned the choke collar on a white blouse, she dabbed her neck with a wet paper towel. Elmer dutifully poured from a pitcher of ice tea in the refrigerator, then handed her a cold wet glass.

'You're an angel,' she sighed, sipping gingerly while removing tight two-toned business pumps with open heels. She bent at the waist, placing these on a sheet of newspaper near the door.

They were both standing, Elmer fidgeting at her side, Jessica massaging her feet with one hand as the dog nearly rammed her in the thigh, his ears pulled tight across his head. 'Hello, Tripod, have we been ignoring you?' She smiled sympathetically, crouching to stroke the large Shepherd, who immediately sat up on his haunches, batting his good foot at the air. She gave him a handshake, then sat Indian style on the white linoleum floor, the dog immediately pushing his muzzle down into her lap. Elmer drew up alongside, staring at his mother.

She was tired, that much was easy to see, her eyes were red and bleary, and her voice was worn. Elmer knew from experience that she was catching her second wind, so he gave her time to relax.

'Mom,' he said quietly, working his hands into nervous fists behind his knees, rocking on the floor. Jessica glanced at her boy, and as often happened, saw the haunting reflection of his father, the mint green eyes that were a Janson family trait. She felt a hollow thump inside.

'Yes?' she responded, rubbing Tripod's ear.

The boy hesitated, leaning forward, nibbling his upper lip. 'Mom,' he said slowly, 'do you think I'm a good person?'

'Why do you ask?'

'Dad said the most important thing was that I grow up to be a good person,' he explained, and the innocence on the boy's face radiated uncertainty. For whatever misguided reason, he was unsure of himself, and Jessica Janson felt a mournful ache in her heart as her mind drifted, his voice becoming a whisper in the background.

Elmer was remembering words that he couldn't have possibly understood when he had first heard them, he was too young when his father died, yet now he was playing them back and trying to grasp their meaning. She swallowed hard.

'. . . and Dad said that it's not as important what you are, as who you are inside.'

'Come here, Red,' she whispered, and she pulled him close, nuzzling her face into his neck, then holding the boy at arm's length.

'Daddy would be very proud of you,' she said, looking him straight in the eye. Elmer hugged his mother, holding her around the neck, and although they stayed that way for only a few quick minutes, to Elmer it seemed forever until she found her reserves, and her lips produced the magic words used in the Janson household every Saturday night since he could remember.

They were joyful words that spelled the end of a working week, that told of only good things to come.

'Pepperoni? Rigatoni! Who's your friend?'

'Mom!'

'At least you're not too old to play.' She kissed him lightly on the forehead, then she attacked his ribs until Elmer was covering up, no longer able to control the giggles, the dog barking furiously until their ears hurt.

'Wash up, silly, we'll go to Tony's.'

And on his way up the stairs, Elmer suddenly stopped in his tracks. 'Are you working tomorrow?' he asked.

With the plaintive sound of her son's voice, Jessica immediately felt the latchkey guilt of a single parent. 'No, Elmer, Sunday is our day.' She walked to him, working her features into a smile.

'Can we go to Great Falls Park?'

'Oh Red, what about tonight, you wanted to see a movie?'

'*Platoon*'s at the Circle Uptown!' he beamed.

'No,' she said quickly, 'you know the rules.'

'*Untouchables* is PG-13?'

'And you finished your studies?'

'Not the math.'

She nodded thoughtfully. '*The Untouchables* then, and I'll call Gram while you take a bath, now don't forget to wash up top.'

She ran her fingers through his hair.

'That's what bothers me,' Jessica Janson said from her bedroom, changing ears, trapping the blue Princess phone beneath her chin. She removed an earring from her left lobe and slipped this into a lacquered tray on her nightstand, shaking her head, strawberry blonde hair falling forward across her brow.

'What does, dear?'

'Oh Mother!' she fumed. 'You don't listen!' She plopped on the edge of her bed, unbuttoning her blouse with her right hand, then wriggled away from its cling. 'He's lonely.'

'Nonsense, Jessie,' Mrs Martha Collier corrected her daughter. Although she lived in Long Beach, California, like clockwork the two spoke every Saturday evening.

'He has you and his school mates and Tripod, now stop worrying about his every little mood.'

'I'm concerned,' she sighed, 'I think he'd rather be by himself than with other children, I just don't understand.'

'Now Jessica, just allow him to be a little boy and he'll find himself.'

'Well, that's not what he finds, Mother!' her voice rose sharply with frustration. 'Remember his last little stunt?'

'He's adventurous, just be glad he's not a video game addict, turns their little minds to mush, other parents would be extremely jealous.'

'Mom, we're talking past each other. I didn't have a clue as to what he was doing at that bowling alley. When I'd ask, he'd just say he was *mashing aliens*, which means running over weeds with his dirt bike. Next thing I know he's dug up a human skull, the police are asking questions, and when I asked Elmer he said he was just *roaching* around. God, it just gives me the creeps.'

'You forget too easily, dear, you were quite a handful. Remember that time you and Lynne Meade had those little mice?'

'You're a great help, Mother, I call for advice and you're still grinding your axe, that was an accident!'

'But you did let them escape into the doctor's office, as I recall Dr Meade had patients passing out from fright months after you said they were all captured, weren't you about Elmer's age?'

'Oh God, Mother, you are such a bitch!'

'Of course I am, dear, it takes years of practice. Just don't be too protective. How's the studies?'

'Fine, his lowest grade this week was a B in math.'

'You're the envy of the Long Beach School District.'

She sighed. 'Mother, maybe I should reconsider work, not ending my career but cutting back, maybe I should spend more time with him?'

'Nonsense, Jessie, you're doing a perfectly capable job.'

Janson removed her bra and slipped a pink long-sleeved T-shirt over her head and wriggled through.

'Are you there, Jess?'

'Yes, last night, and again this afternoon, Elmer mentioned his father.' She said this with a questioning sigh, then switched ears and pulled a pair of light grey slacks over her knees.

'All perfectly normal, a death that early in a child's life is very difficult.'

'Mo-ther!' she bit the word in two. 'It's the way he asks. "Mom, do you remember Dad's face, do I look like him?"' she said wistfully. 'How can I answer something like that?'

'With honesty. Tell Elmer I'll be visiting in July and bringing something very special for his birthday.'

'You're hopeless.'

'And you're in fits over nothing. Is the job going well?'

'Yes, just fine. I'm taking Elmer to Tony's for pizza, then we're going to the nine o'clock show at the cinema, he wants to see *The Untouchables*, I don't think . . .'

'Jessie, I've got to go,' Martha Collier interrupted, 'someone's at the door. I love you, baby, don't worry so much?'

'Love you,' Jessica sighed, hesitating only a moment as she hung up the phone.

And in the gathering darkness of a night sky, Jeffery Dorn felt his blood crawl.

His heart was beating behind each temple as he clutched a steel pylon, staring down from a telephone pole onto the little people who strolled the sidewalk below. He closed his eyes to this inner pulse, having nearly forgotten just how good it felt, eavesdropping on the strange emotional voices, being back in action, being back in the hunt.

As he removed his metal clips from the Hydra, he felt a thunderous pulse, his stomach stirring, his brain going light. And the more he thought about Elmer and Jessica Janson, the faster the blood went pounding through the shallow chambers of his heart, racing through his body, reaching down into every muscle and fibre and nerve, fuelling him with an uncontrollable pleasure.

As he started a downward climb, he felt struck by an urge to laugh, and so he opened and snapped his jaws, wagging his tongue, twisting his face into a hellish obscenity. He was remembering a page from his own childhood, how he had been forced by his mother to stand for so many hours at her bedroom mirror, and how she had coached his efforts to produce what feelings should look like.

'Not like that, baby,' she would say. 'Now laugh for Mommy! A big laugh for Mommy!'

And if he teased her too often, making these hellish little expressions, refusing to perform, a brutal slap would sting his face.

Looking back, Jeffery Dorn could honestly say that he had grown attached to his mother, a middle class housewife who knew from the very beginnings that something was terribly wrong with her child.

'Zachariah, smile!' she would demand.

And with each stinging backhanded kiss, the boy produced until perfection was achieved.

can be described as a page number distracts our eye to describe this area. Other shadows were so dark it was nearly possible to see or to keep or know we are below the shade.

Turning the story creates a writer that can to very fifty hazardous...

... But it was the other face than to say and that any of it in the more work. But here some shapes it was also and generally interesting life in which most...

THIRTY-TWO

Like most of Washington DC, the Zephyr Bar and Grill had two distinct faces, depending upon which personality a customer sought.

One was pleasant enough, of a neighbourhood gathering place in the upper northwest part of the city where the younger crowd could meet on College Night, which always fell on a Friday, and was so marked in a front window.

But it was the Zephyr's other face that troubled Frank Rivers; a face of unparalleled depravity for other patrons who knew what specific Saturday nights were reserved for them, and he reasoned it was by the drawn shades, or perhaps the light that was left burning in the rear alley.

He had been watching from a grassy hill overlooking the back of the building, and now he broke into a run, moving with powerful leonine strides down the gentle slope, the long muscles of his legs stretching tight, the sculpted arms at his side slick like pistons, hammering him forward through a light mist. Behind this dampness he could feel the building threat of monsoon rains, the sky turning black, swallowing shadows.

His effortless glide brought him down onto broken cobblestone, down into the alley behind the Zephyr Bar and Grill, then he moved through this darkness, swiftly approaching the young woman who was hobbling across the rough patchwork. She turned her head, glancing back, picking up her pace.

She was tall and fashionably dressed in a tight blue knit suit with a split seam revealing long legs, and glitter stockings with stiletto heels that made her wobble just enough to be sensuous. Rivers had been watching her seductive approach with a smile, thinking that with her tight long waist and swirl-ing hips she resembled an expensive fishing lure, but by this time he was already moving to overtake her.

He checked his watch, it was 8:17.

Before she arrived, he had had the entire block staked out, watching customers drift through his field of vision and enter the bar from the rear. All of these were men, in their forties and early fifties, were well dressed, carrying briefcases or clutching leather folders, some arriving on foot, others park-ing on the street with a freehanded ease, then entering and exiting like hungry ants in a food line.

Rivers carried a thick canvas leash in his left hand, complete with a chain choke collar, and since he had dressed casually in jeans and a light grey windbreaker, it looked like a natural thing for him to be roaching about, searching for his dog in back alleys.

He slowed his pace, coming up behind the woman just as she turned, her eyes meeting his, her hand snapping open the brass catch on her purse, which she clutched to one breast. Her red hair was below the collar, flowing in streams as she moved, too perfect to be real.

'Hi,' Rivers offered, closing the gap with one long stride. And he couldn't help but stare, from this angle the woman was all cleavage and legs, her perfume enveloping him like a cloud. He took a position just alongside and was trotting in place.

'Get lost, creep,' she puffed, rattled but confidently picking up her pace, the pavement dangerously broken and her heels moving delicately. She stepped lightly, wiggling as she went.

'Looks like rain,' he offered.

'My hand is on my gun, my finger's on the trigger,' she said coolly, not looking up, her face a pretty slab of stone.

Rivers gave his best smile, raising his hands to the top of his head, then trotting backward with his elbows poking the air.

'Where are we going?'

'We?' she mocked with an icy voice. 'We are not going anywhere!'

333

With this she stopped, a small chrome pistol flashing in the dim light while her heavily painted eyes covered his form, summing him up, seeing him for the first time.

They stood about a hundred feet from the Zephyr's rear door.

'I've already surrendered,' he smiled weakly, then quickly shuffled back a few feet as the woman tensed.

'Look, creep,' she sneered, and her face became quite unpleasant, 'I can't run in these shoes, so either I pull this trigger or you leave me alone!'

Rivers shook his entire torso, then closed his eyes. 'Sorry, you'll have to do it.'

'What?' At this her shoulders sagged, and the little gun bobbed nervously.

'I'm really sorry to be a bother, my name's Frank Rivers, it's always good to know the name of a hostage.' He pointed down at the gun with a finger and smiled.

'You're crazy!' she fumed, starting to walk again.

'I'm hoping you'll feel you've made a good choice, I'm a very low maintenance Frank. I only need one walk a day and come with my own leash?' He waved the canvas trotter with his left hand, keeping his arms high while walking backwards.

The woman was grasping the absurdity of it all, pinching her face at him, then offering a slight smile. Very slight, but a smile all the same.

Unexpectedly and with a tilt of the head, she slid the small weapon back into the purse, stopped, then removed her wallet.

'I need help,' his voice was sincere, even a bit nervous. 'I'm not used to asking . . .'

'No,' she said, raising her eyebrows, 'I can see that.' And she removed a crisp five-dollar bill, offering this to him, and it was offered so genuinely that he wanted to accept it, but shook his head.

'No?' Again she reached for her gun, her hand plunging back into the purse. 'What do you want?' she demanded coldly.

'It's about a missing kid,' Rivers said slowly, 'her car was found out front last night.' He nodded at the Zephyr.

334

'And you're a cop,' she nodded unpleasantly, 'now it all makes sense, you lousy bastard!' Her body slumped, the last bit of defensive posturing vanishing as her purse closed tight.

'If I had started with a badge you wouldn't have talked to me.'

'You're right, I would have called my lawyer, which is just what I'm going to do, what's your badge number?'

'Look, lady,' he lowered his hands, 'I'm a human being, and while I'll admit that's hard to believe, at the moment what I do doesn't matter so much as the why of it.'

She gave a tight frown, raising one eyebrow.

'Give me a chance, please?'

She watched him closely as he pulled a photo of Debra Patterson from his jacket and held it out. The girl in the picture was standing with both parents, her expression sweet and proud, bedecked in her white confirmation gown. The woman looked closer, studying the face.

'She's very young, are you related?'

'No, no I'm not. This was taken two years ago, but you're right. This missing kid could have been anyone, my niece, your sister, the girl next door, all I know is that she's some-one's baby, and that should count for something in this world of hurt . . . she should count for something.'

The woman studied this man's eyes, they radiated a kind of deadly blue concern, yet underneath, there was pain. She took a step forward and gave a small nod.

'Okay, low maintenance Frank, I'm a player, you have ten minutes from the time you show me a badge, and I can spot a fake.'

Rivers flashed his shield, hiding it in his palm as another man walked into the alley clutching a briefcase. There was no doubt that the badge was genuine.

'The only bust on record for these guys is for serving drinks to minors.' He nodded at the Mook who was now unlocking his car, and they both watched. 'There's one hell of a lot of activity in there, I need to know what it is, gambling, designer drugs, girls, that's all there is to it.'

'And why can't you go?'

'My guess is they know all their customers, so they'd make me, plus we had a K-9 team in there this morning.'

'But they'd never suspect a call girl?'

'No,' Rivers smiled warmly, 'they'd never suspect a lady.'

Instead of ten minutes it took nearly a half-hour. Rivers spotted her immediately as she came through the rear door, her face and posture stern, her eyes cold and sad.

He quickly strolled down the grassy hill overlooking the alley as she glanced back over her shoulder, quickening her pace. In doublestep, Rivers drew up alongside.

'Come with me,' she ordered, taking up his hand, leading him back to the hill. They quickly walked the distance together, then settled down at a kerb. Marcy was tugging at her skirt and staring off into space, her eyes glassy.

'I feel dirty,' she said quietly, and with that her body shuddered. Again she tugged at her skirt, sitting tentatively against the gutter staring up at the sky, but clouds had now blocked the stars. 'Do you smoke?' she asked, rattled.

Rivers started to rise, the lean muscles along his jaw pulling tight, when her hand reached up, grabbing his arm. 'Squares, dummy, cigarettes. I don't do drugs, although you should try a Valium.'

'Sorry,' he rolled his eyes, then reached for a smoke, lighting this for her and handing it over. They made eye contact. Rivers noticed that her eyes were a pretty hazel, almost green, and he guessed her real hair was a soft and shiny brown.

'I'm thirty-four, and I've seen some bad shit,' she offered, inhaling deeply, 'but that's a real nasty freak show you've got in there.'

Rivers nodded. 'How so?'

'The place is full of Little Men, and they're buying Pop, and there's even two teenagers minding their beer, they have no idea what's going on!'

'Neither do I, Marcy, what are Little Men?'

She looked at him with wide eyes. 'Child pornographers, Frank, freaks, perverts, sadists, call them what you like . . .'

336

'And what's Pop?'

'You're a detective?' she shook her head. 'Pop, Candy, Lickers, that's kiddy porn and real deviant shit. I told them I had a client with special interests and they showed me some really rotten things; men, women, bestiality, bondage, children, real kinky . . .' She made a funny clicking sound with her teeth.

Rivers touched her lightly on the knee.

'This is some very sick shit,' she cried, 'and they enjoyed showing it to me!'

Rivers nodded sympathetically. 'What did they have?'

'Books, films, magazines, tapes, everything, they were very proud of themselves.' She looked at him. 'They said they fill orders you can't get elsewhere, they should be shot, I could do it, too . . .'

Rivers swallowed hard. 'And they keep this stuff where exactly?'

'I'm not sure, they were real crafty about that, in the kitchen, I think, but they had photographs under the bar. They had one shot of a little boy and girl . . .' her voice trailed off and Rivers could see she was fighting back tears. 'It was inhuman.'

'How old?'

'Eight, maybe, ten, I don't know. And they have film of teenagers, they couldn't be of age.'

Rivers placed a hand on her shoulder, handing over a slip of paper. 'Take this,' he said, and she glanced at it with questioning eyes, there was only a number.

'Call me if you ever just need a friend.'

'And what about you?' she sighed.

Rivers stood and watched a middle aged man stroll out the Zephyr's door, the bag in his hand had taken on a special new meaning. 'What about me?'

'What are you going to do?'

Rivers nodded at the bar. 'I have to know if they've seen my girl.' And he started to walk as Marcy jumped to her feet, cutting him off as Rivers had done with her, holding her hands in the air.

'I'll call for you and get some backup, these are very cruel men,' she cautioned.

He shook his head, staring past her into an outer darkness, then moving there; so quiet, so easy, it was hard to appreciate that he had even gone.

They were twins.

Kenneth and Bart Dix, two late middle-aged men with sagging guts, both hard-looking characters working side by side, tending bar, filling and washing glasses.

As Marcy had suggested, they were ugly Little Men, each slightly better than six feet tall with pan-flat faces and unruly brown hair. On both heads, this was thinning above dull looking eyes that resembled dirty marbles, bulging fishlike from thick skulls. The eyes followed Rivers as he quietly came through the front door facing Wisconsin Avenue.

The twin on the right spoke to the other, removing a white apron, then tossing this onto the bar. As he walked by, selecting a corner table, Rivers heard the word *Cop*, though he didn't respond as he counted heads.

There were four men seated at the bar, in addition to the twins, two larger men playing cards at a rear table, and only six drinking customers, mostly girls, one looked underage. He considered his options. A nickel bust for serving a juvenile wouldn't slow them down for an hour, the twins would be out before the paperwork was cut, and he pulled out a wooden chair and settled in with his back to a corner.

Over the bar he could just see a blur of faces reflected by a mirror which advertised Bud Light in gold metallic letters, as a burly twin approached, leaning over the table and slapping once with a wet dish towel, his shoulders looking as wide as the table.

'What's your drink?'

'Slice.'

The twin shook his head. 'We've got beer, wine or whisky, no mixed drinks, there's a cafe down the street, try there.'

Rivers was flaming a cigarette with his Zippo, looking over this and studying the dull eyes, the turn of his mouth, and

338

the double-chin. He released a stream of smoke in the man's direction. 'Which twin are you?'

'They call me Snake, what's it gonna be?'

'And him?' He pointed to the bar with his cigarette.

'That's Younger, he came out second, what's this about?'

Rivers shrugged. 'I've got some special interests, thought you might be able to help.'

The human Snake turned, Younger snapping into eye contact with his brother, a kind of an invisible form of communication dating back to the womb. The man came forward from behind the bar.

'Didn't catch your name?' Snake hissed from a massive face.

'Francis.'

'Well, Sweetheart,' he mouthed, 'let's see the colour of your money, then I'll see what we can do for a cop's pay.'

Rivers nodded, digging for his wallet, laying some green on the table as the other twin approached, standing a few feet back, watching with intent.

'That's twelve bucks,' Rivers offered as Younger hopped forward, his face a hard and heavy mask. A scar ran along his chin.

'What's that for?' he asked in a menacing voice.

Rivers was silent.

The twins looked at each other. 'Don't even play with him,' Younger suggested. 'Do you have a warrant?'

Snake placed his hands on the table and leaned into Rivers. 'Let's play trick or treat,' he hissed.

Younger grabbed his brother's arm. 'I'm calling my attorney, she's gonna bust your silly ass down to humping meters, so I suggest you leave.'

Rivers nodded thoughtfully.

Just then another customer strolled through, Snake spotting him, returning quickly to the bar. Rivers watched carefully, the man was well dressed, short, in his early forties. He handed a satchel across the counter, and Snake's whole head vanished from sight.

If he was counting cash, Rivers figured it could be a few

thousand dollars' worth of purchase if the bills were small, and what then emerged reflected off the bar's countertop, staining it with bright fleshy tones, filling empty beer mugs with pink.

He stood, travelling swiftly past Younger, and in three long strides was at the bar. As Rivers approached he could just discern a colour glossy, not the magazine type, but an expensive colour print which Snake skilfully hid beneath the counter, flashing his empty palms.

'Lose something?' he grinned.

Rivers quietly took a stool as the front door opened, and another man walked in. Mid-to-late forties, six-two and thin, black hair, pale complexion, five o'clock shadow, scar mid-forehead. Rivers observed his grey Italian suit was in need of pressing; scuffed black shoes, wedding band, expensive watch. The man nodded as Younger returned behind the bar and poured a draught, pushing the mug directly in front of the customer as he was settling into a chair.

'I just heard you've got fresh Poppers,' the man smiled, and Younger moved forward, leaning down with a whisper and nodding at the detective.

Rivers reached into his jacket, then held the photograph of Debra Patterson out in front of him, slowly turning in a circle on the bar stool, watching faces, then dropping this directly between the older twin and his customer. Snake's eyes darted nervously in their sockets as Younger rushed forward.

'So what's it gonna be, pal, isn't it past your bedtime?' he asked, and his voice lost its edge.

Rivers' eyes were like hot pokers. 'I'm not your pal,' he returned flatly.

Without concern, Younger shrugged with massive shoulders, picking up the phone beneath the counter, then walking over to a row of bottles in the corner where he soon stood in conversation with his back turned. The men seated at the bar were avoiding eye contact, so Rivers tapped the taller one on the shoulder, leaning over, pointing at the man's gold wedding band.

'Does she wipe your pictures when you're through?'

340

The thin man twisted uncomfortably on his stool, then stood, quickly walking to the back of the room, passing another customer who saw an altercation brewing and scurried back out. Younger was holding the phone against his chest, staring at Rivers.

'Hey, buddy,' he said in a loud voice, 'legal counsel says if you don't leave we are well within our rights to protect our customers, and to use bodily force if necessary.'

'That a fact,' Rivers returned without tone.

Suddenly Snake was leaning up into his face, poking him once on the left shoulder with a fat thumb. 'You should find another line of work, you're not very good at this one.'

Rivers glared, 'That's *my* finger.'

'What the fuck?' Snake hissed. 'I'm going to break your head!' And he turned, lifting a heavy black sap from behind the bar, slapping his left palm.

Rivers ignored him.

The bartender hung up the phone as two shadows approached from the rear, then Younger stepped out from behind the bar with an insolent grin, a towel draped over his right hand. He stopped within feet, studying him closely, then adjusting that view. Rivers kept his eyes to the mirror, rolling the picture up, placing it inside his jacket as Younger sniffed, mocking at his airspace.

Customers scurried off to the corners as two large men in soiled T-shirts flanked Rivers on either side. The smaller of the two had the battered face of a former boxer, which resembled a block of clay awaiting features.

'Does your dog bite?' Rivers asked without looking up.

'That's it, you crazy scrot, you know we can't swing first, so why don't you stop running your fucking mouth and do something!' Younger charged.

Rivers propped his elbows on the counter, watching the three men reflected in the mirror. They were the types that would sport with a cripple, and Younger dropped the towel without further ceremony, resting a broad-bladed meat cleaver against his shoulder just as Snake leaned forward across the bar.

'You're gonna hurt bad,' he whispered with delight, 'my brother will split your fucking skull, you weird asshole!'

'Oh, you silly queen,' Rivers smiled.

Without warning, Younger suddenly bolted forward to protect his brother's honour, the two men grabbing him, then restraining him as he struggled for freedom, Rivers turning casually and standing directly up into the threat.

'You got something to say to me?' Younger screamed with an indignant rage. 'You want to threaten me?'

Frank Rivers turned away slowly, easily, effortlessly.

Without another word, he was gone.

THIRTY-THREE

'Wow!' Elmer Janson exclaimed, and the mask of freckles across his face drew tight. He placed an empty box of popcorn on the seat and turned to his mother.

'That *was* a good show,' Jessica said, 'please throw that away.'

'It was wicked!' Elmer sighed. 'The way Eliot Ness saved that baby from falling down the stairs!'

'Good old Eliot,' she smiled, rubbing the boy's hair. And they strolled after the crowd, up through the theatre doors, and out into the lobby. Elmer put his litter into the can and followed her to the windows.

Outside the tall glass entrance of Bethesda Square Mall was a solid sheet of rain which drove patrons back inside in a mad dash for cover as the wind howled through doors, the water spraying in machine gun bursts, flowing through the underground parking garage. There were about a hundred people milling into a crowd, more coming in, and the giant slabs of glass started to fog from so much breathing. Elmer rubbed a circle with the flat of his hand, watching a river flow down and over a concrete gutter as Jessica turned to face the shopping mall.

In the background there was the eerie calliope sound of a carousel firing up, the music starting as a brassy moan, then grinding into a loud symphony. Elmer's attention was focused on the stream of children headed in that direction as his mother stared back out onto the streets, knotting her brow. 'We shouldn't drive in this,' she said as the wind rattled against the panes.

343

'Svensk's Icecream is open,' Elmer offered, 'it's just past the merry-go-round?'

She shook her head, 'I know where it is, silly, you've already had pizza, popcorn and soda, you'll get sick.'

'No I won't,' he rolled his eyes as she stepped back, out of the traffic pattern, the crowd starting to mill about anxiously as more patrons came rushing through the door for the next showing. She checked her watch, it was 10:33.

'Come on, Red,' she smiled, 'are you too old to ride the carousel?'

Elmer's green eyes sparkled, 'How 'bout you, Mom?'

She grabbed him by the hand and followed the music.

It was a winding concrete path with high railings, solid pastel walls in a rainbow of colours, and store windows boarded shut with plywood. They moved hand in hand, following a crush of patrons, slowly being swept up by the flow as they approached the lobby, the music wailing, growing louder, deafening.

The hallway teemed with people, filling from the rear of the cramped corridor like a bottle, loud voices trying to reach above the din as wet blasts of cold air created a wind tunnel effect. The doors at either end had been opening, closing, and Jessica held tightly to her son's hand, looking down into his eyes, moving in small steps, unable to see over the crush of humanity.

Without warning, the marching line came to a halt.

'Now what?' she asked, and there was shouting from the rear which carried on another cold blast of air.

'What?' Elmer cried, and she shrugged, shaking her head.

Jessica felt her legs starting to cramp at the knees, it seemed as if they had been standing forever, the tunnel teeming with faces, throngs of people; the combined body heat, smell and voices creating an overwhelming sensory explosion that was battering to the brain. Suddenly, they felt a tremor in the human wall, and then the sounds of shattering glass as the wave surged with an angry power and two hands pushed Jessica violently in the small of her back, whipping her spine.

344

She had just started to turn in confrontational fury as a heavy-set man stumbled backward, crushing her left toe, and the crowd pushed forward as her hand slipped free.

'Elmer!' she cried, seeing him vanish into the crush of adults. Jessica watched his face, only for a moment, growing smaller and smaller, carried down the corridor, away in the writhing madness and he looked for all the world like a drowning child waving a small arm in the air.

'This is nuts!' she cried, the stale air snapping at her brain. Her body was pushed again, and she followed helplessly, her feet working into small steps as she tried not to trip. She mustered her reserves, pressing defiantly, then taking another hard punch from behind, surfacing near the front of the room like a battered diver with worn and aching lungs, fighting for breath as a distressed man shook a finger into her face.

She ignored him, grabbing the wooden railing as the carousel spun at her feet.

She gulped air, searching the crowds.

It was short minutes later when Elmer saw his mother appear, and he came unseen from behind, unthinkingly slipping his hand inside hers.

Jessica jumped, crossing a hand over her heart.

'Mom, are you okay? I saved us a place.'

She reached out, holding the boy's head tightly to her waist. 'What happened?' she breathed.

'Someone made a mistake, all the theatres let out at the same time, and the storm brought more than they expected.'

'Oh,' she nodded, 'it's hard to manage schedules for six whole theatres, very complicated.' She was about to suggest finding somewhere else to wait, realising there was none, and trying to find tranquillity under the ocean blue carousel tent that was spinning into a patterned swirl; fiery painted constellations that seemed to flame like shooting stars as lightning cracked outside, pulsing through the tall windows.

At this time, a strange thing happened to Jessica Janson.

Elmer, in an attempt to protect his mother from the crowds,

345

pulled her gently forward against the carousel railing, but when she looked up, she did not see a childlike playfulness in the wooden menagerie; but rather a menacing parade of trapped animals that filled her with horror. The lightning fired like strobes, with every burst creatures were frozen into silent agony, their painted eyes stretched with terror, muzzles carved into a white lather, their witless strides futile, their spines impaled on shiny brass poles.

She shuddered as they twisted without mercy at her feet, the tearing, painted eyes begging her for help.

'Fatigue,' she thought to herself, 'a touch of claustrophobia?' She touched her brow lightly for the fever she suspected, but found none.

'Good lion,' Elmer smiled.

The machinery rattled and slowed, the race grinding to a tilted rumble, the calliope releasing a mournful, sleepy sound as a man in a red barker's suit quickly moved the line forward, holding back the over-eager, placing his arm at chest level, counting saddles, lifting his arm again.

Elmer scrambled, watching his mother stroll to a giant rabbit and grab him by the ears, swinging herself into position. The uniformed man circled the platform, threw a lever, and the music wailed, growing louder; the animals lurching, spinning, until they seemed to be galloping with fright against the lightning bursts.

Once, twice, again, the carousel spun, gaining speed, Jessica whirling with painted constellations, feeling her world spinning through time until the faces around her became a blur and the frozen kingdom snapped into a sharp focus.

And she felt a thousand adult eyes.

With everything that was woman, Jessica Janson sensed these eyes undressing her, they went slithering across her flesh, dancing over her form, dropping into her shell. She felt naked and cold to the bone, leaning forward onto the cottontail's ears to partially conceal her splendid shape.

'What's wrong with me?' she thought, as the giant rabbits went leaping, as the wolves snapped their pursuit, as the sound of a child crying in the distance tugged at her heart, then turned into a vicious snarl that chilled her blood to ice.

'I'm cracking up . . .'

'Boy, that woman over there is a fox!'

'Ooo, would I love to make it with her!'

There were two young men following the rabbit with admiring eyes, then remembering their roles, keeping a sharp watch for their wives while holding their children in line. Their exchange was easily overheard by an older woman who stood rooted behind, her presence noticed by none. She was alone, but more than that, she was lonely.

She pushed back into the thinning crowd, unwittingly shielding her face with one hand as if the sun were bright and her skin flawed. And having studied Jessica Janson's graceful and ample form, her long legs straddling the bobbing creature, chest thrust forward to taunt, blonde hair falling downward like a shiny cascade she had become self-conscious beyond fault.

The woman was seething with envy, nearly nauseous with self-pity, and was wandering aimlessly through the mall when she was grabbed forcefully by the arm.

'Oh my!' she said.

'Oh my yourself, Irma, let's go.'

'Jeff, do you think she's pretty?' she tried to whisper, following his anxious pace, her face tied into a knot.

Dorn's voice held an edge that could cut. 'That will make *your* job a whole lot easier,' he said. 'I saw the way you pushed her, Irma, hitting her like that in the spine.'

He imitated her aggressive display, ramming the glass doors with the heel of his palm; they shook violently as the couple walked out into the underground parking garage.

Dorn shook his head. 'That all looked very personal to me,' he criticised.

'Oh, Sweetheart,' she smiled, wrapping an arm around his waist, 'you said you like it when I'm spunky!'

THIRTY-FOUR

Three hours earlier Jeffery Dorn had arrived home, having spent his day on the line. He loved the intimate voices, the emotional twitterings, the graphic displays of human behaviour in all of its forms; and he almost hated to leave the unanswered riddles behind. The sorry truth was that he had to, forcing himself, for the conversation between Jessica and Elmer Janson disturbed him, the way they toyed and teased each other, flooding him with memories, filling him with regret.

He knew that his own childhood had deadened his core to wood, Zak Dorani was not a stupid man. Once he had known human warmth, and it frustrated him if he tried to remember that.

'Laugh for Mommy?' he huffed aimlessly, sitting in his car inside the garage. Never, he recalled, could he feel that natural joy swelling inside him, as it once had, he was sure it was so.

It was time that beat him. Time. Beating him down into a mannequin man; his face moving with conscious efforts only, muscles tugging into an alien mask.

I cannot feel, you cannot feel . . .

Large woman, tall woman, hands like a club.

Blood mouthfuls.

Red teeth in a shattered mirror.

You will laugh for Mommy now that Daddy is gone.

'Jeff, Sweetheart, is that you?'

Dorn winced at the sound as images collided, back to the

348

business at hand. The blonde was a slut, the boy was a mutt, that dog must be killed.

Crying is a waste of water.

And he made a mental note to look up Tony's Pizza in the Yellow Pages, not that it mattered, but it would be nice knowing where the Jansons ate regularly, and from the tone of conversation, he knew it was a routine.

Jeffery Dorn thrived on routine. It was the stuff of life. He preyed on predictability.

Jessica Janson spoke with her mother each and every Saturday night, just like clockwork, and Dorn had been enjoying that, he was planning on using little snippets of their most personal conversations on her, but that would come later in the evening. As he strolled across the bare concrete floor towards the kitchen, he stopped to eye a thin metal rod that was leaning in the corner, and which he used for various purposes, like killing spiders on the ceiling.

It was then that he heard her coming with a more serious intent, and he lifted the metal shaft, fingering it thoughtfully, examining its hard straight edge, wanting to bring it inside and beat her without mercy until nothing was left. A fleshy, broken sack. Just a stain on the carpet, but a silent stain . . .

'Oh, Honey.' Irma opened the door, and Dorn winced visibly at the sound.

'Is that you?' he mocked to her face. Who else would come for her? Not even a travelling freak show.

'Hi, Sweetheart,' she mewed, and he dropped the shaft and his equipment bag, which landed with a sharp knock. Dorn was stone to the form that had appeared, mousy hair combed back and tied with red silk, grey eyes thick with makeup, rouge slapped across thin cheeks. A walking corpse. She hovered in a transparent negligee, moving closer as he came into the kitchen, the folds from her midsection crazed for a belt to lean against.

He swallowed hard. 'Leave me alone, Irma.' He turned to the sink and began washing his hands. And he wanted to turn off the lights, the woman's ageing body spawned an illness in him.

349

'Oh, Sweetheart.' She pressed closer, the harsh light revealing a flat plate of skin where cleavage should be. Dorn quickly glanced into the sink as Irma embraced him from behind with pale arms and the heavy smell of lilac perfume.

'Your office called, Marcy Newman has explained everything. I'm so sorry, Jeff, it's been a bad day, hasn't it?'

Dorn quickly tried to figure what lies the little lobbyist bitch had contrived, overstepping her bounds, what could Irma possibly be sorry about, perish the thought.

'Come, come sit down,' she sighed, taking him by the arm and leading him into the living room where he plopped into his chair, unable to talk, unable to think, still clutching a dish towel and drying his face. The woman was about to flap at him again when Dorn could stand it no longer. He felt time slipping away, he glanced at his watch.

Jessica had told her mother it was to be the nine o'clock showing, and Dorn reached up, grabbing Irma by the arm and twisting.

'Water!' he cried, pulling her face to his, then pushing her away forcefully. He wasn't sure why, he needed time to think, and water was the first thing that came to mind. With a nervous blink, Irma raced for the kitchen, feeling alive, excited by the manly order which Dorn had just issued, excited further by her own desires and the demands she knew he was capable of making.

Masculine demands. Ordering a woman to use her charms for a purely selfish and uncontrollable end, and as she poured a cold glass, she steadied herself, preparing to do her duty. But when she returned, he was staring off into space, his teeth set with pain, his eyes unfocused.

She lifted his right hand by the wrist and delivered the glass, watching his fingers close around it. 'Oh, Honey,' she cooed, 'it really has been a bad one, hasn't it? Does your back hurt?'

She was breathing hard, pressing her stubby body closer against the padded arm. 'I've held your dinner, ground veal just the way you like it, let me heat it for you?' Dorn could only imagine the slop, like a road kill thrashed in a blender, the woman's cooking was like her appearance, heavy, comic, and tasteless. He was about to politely decline the invitation when he felt fingers walking across his neck.

'Let me rub your back for you?'

Instantly, Dorn heard his own voice blow through the room as if another had spoken. 'Why don't you just die, you miserable cunt!'

The words hit Irma like a club.

'Oh my!' she exclaimed pensively. 'That's not good, is it?'

'What?' Dorn's head twisted on its stalk, the dark eyes glinted slyly.

'Jeff, why are you upset with me?'

The pupils glared with a cruel intelligence shining in the half-light. 'Will you be a good wife to me, Irma?' he said, carefully snipping off each word with his teeth as he watched the woman's knees tremble into a kind of putty.

She couldn't believe her ears, was he proposing?

'Oh Jeff!' she swooned, the breath driven from her body. And she locked her arms around his head, pulling his face to her chest.

'Answer the question!' he demanded, pushing her back, then reaching out with both hands and pinching the nipples on each small breast with his thumbs. The woman's body quivered.

'Oh yes, yes, yes,' she mewed. 'I will, Jeff, I promise, I will be the best wife . . .'

He pinched harder. 'Did you get my note?' he hissed.

She nodded, a nervous smile twitching at the corners of her mouth.

'Well?'

Irma Kiernan all but flew to her bedroom, thumping back down the stairs again, rushing to his side, offering up a small red velvet pillow with both hands.

Dorn refused to look.

'Put it on!' he demanded. And with reverence, Irma Kiernan lifted the multi-coloured ribbon, tossing the pillow aside, then carefully draped it around his neck as Dorn tilted his head back proudly.

Just below his throat, the Legion of Merit shone in glory, polished white, gleaming with distinction. The woman stood back, anxiously awaiting his approval.

'It's a beautiful job,' he said finally, fingering the medallion while forcing a smile. He opened his arms, offering an embrace, and she rushed forward, burying her face in his chest, feeling the coolness of the metal against her cheek.

'Irma,' he said quietly, closing his eyes, hugging her. 'There's something you must do for me.'

He made his demands, holding back nothing, just shading the truth the way he liked it.

To Jeffery Dorn, truth was a simple thing. There was reality, of course, but above all, there was what he wanted to believe, what he wanted to make true.

'And you must help me attend to her,' he dictated quietly, then pulled Irma away, holding the woman at arm's length, feeling her body shake, watching her grey eyes glaze over.

She was breathing hard, struggling with his hold.

'But Jeff,' she cried, 'the last time they were all found dead!' And she began to sob.

'That was not my fault!' he screamed with indignant rage.

Irma Kiernan dropped to her knees in tears, crying quietly. Dorn recalled the expression on Diana Clayton's face as her bathroom door swung open. What was it, a startled, waking expression? Certainly not surprise, more like shock, and her face changed again and again, recognition, or realisation, and at the end . . . He shrugged, he couldn't be sure, really.

'Jeff,' Irma sighed, 'you're sure someone killed them after you left?'

Dorn grabbed two fists of hair and pulled. 'What? I told you! Clayton killed her own children, then shot herself while relaxing in her tub. You don't listen to me, Irma. I've changed my mind about us!'

With that he stood, storming away down the stairs, leaving behind a pathetic puddle of humanity which sobbed into the empty chair. 'But what about being married?' she cried after him.

Dorn gave her time.

Right to the minute, time was something that he knew how to give.

By 7:29 p.m., April 9th, 1989, there were no more tears left in the Kiernan household. Jeffery Dorn would not speak with Irma, other to say that he was packing. In truth he was preparing to receive guests. And planning. And reflecting.

This widowed blonde was trash, he could see that, even her voice was cold and harsh. Since her telephone calls were an open book, he knew this to be true, and he found everything about her too assertive, too demanding.

If there was one thing he couldn't tolerate about career women it was their sense of self-importance, their egocentric appraisal of self-worth. Marcy Newman came quickly to mind, she was classic, overstepping at any little opportunity, a simple call to appease Irma became complicated. And Dorn wanted all of the working bitches to be where they belonged, serving a daddy or walking the goddamned streets looking for one.

'Jeff, Sweetheart, are you there?' a voice floated down the stairs, and Dorn casually sealed the shelter, checking his watch, laying out a change of clothes which he planned on returning for. A heavy rain was predicted, so he made a note to place his umbrella in the car.

'Honey,' she cried. 'Oh, Sweetheart, please answer me . . .'

With his head hung low, working his features into what he knew as sadness, Dorn walked slowly up the stairs, embracing the woman, then caressing her gently.

She started to speak, but Dorn held a finger across her lips, then worked her back with both hands; her neck and breasts, then beginning on the inside of her thighs until her body shuddered and her legs seemed no longer able to support her weight.

'You're beautiful,' he smiled.

'Can we sit?' she mewed.

With a clinical eye, Dorn watched her pass into another world with her excitement, walking her back to the chair, sitting first, then grabbing Irma around the waist, pulling her to him. She was so willing her entire face seemed to be coming unstuck, and he looked away.

'You will please me, Irma,' he said in a husky and demanding voice. 'You will be a good wife!'

She nodded bashfully as Dorn dropped the garment from her torso, the woman quickly stepping out and kicking it aside as he brought her to her knees, directly between his legs. 'Pull your hair back,' he demanded, and she did just that, holding it with her left hand as Dorn opened his trousers.

'Listen to me,' he said quietly, and he could hear her heavy, laboured breathing.

'Today I was on a mission of mercy, you saw my telephone gear in the kitchen, yet you said nothing.'

'Yes,' she breathed, 'yes I did.'

'Well,' he cleared his throat, 'the woman I'm speaking of is evil, I've heard her telephone calls, she is selling her child for immoral purposes. I am the only one who knows this, hence the only one who can save them. Would you have me just turn my back? Is that the kind of husband you want?'

Champion was the word on her lips, yet before she could answer, Dorn grabbed hold and was pulling her forward, as Irma was losing control. It was only then that he began to really work on her, caressing her, manipulating every inch of her frame, leaning over, then finally placing his hands beneath her bare buttocks. He helped to lift her as she gave a breathless hop, her fingers reaching down, guiding him into herself as Dorn gave a wild thrust.

Irma Kiernan felt fire pass between her thighs. She gasped. She shut her eyes and whined gently, closing arms and legs around him, lost in rapture, every thrust bringing with it an unbelievable pleasure until she fairly screamed and collapsed forward into his arms.

It was over that quickly, so he did it again, wondering why people didn't jog and produce an honest sweat. He felt sticky and didn't care for it.

'You will be a good and lasting wife,' he commanded as

354

the woman caught her breath, gasping for air, coming to her senses as he lit a cigarette. 'Gain their trust. Once this is done, you are free to leave, it shouldn't take long . . .'

And although the words were clear enough, there was no verbal response, and if Dorn had not made a study of this particular woman, he would have sworn that Irma Kiernan was stone deaf.

'Just love me,' she breathed, sweat dripping from her chin. 'I couldn't bear to lose you . . .' She started to sob again as Dorn lifted her face with two fingers.

'Tears of joy, I hope?'

'Oh Jeff,' she swooned, 'I do love you!'

Before going off to take a shower, preparing for the show, Jeffery Dorn drew more promises than he needed, giving Irma several good rides on his chair.

He used mirrors to finally ejaculate.

He made passionate love to his own image.

By 10:48, as was the plan, they were working on the ground level of the mall's covered parking garage, in a premier spot near the stairs. Irma's job was to wave off trouble-making motorists who mistook their very presence as potentially available parking space which they could take.

'Irma Dorn,' she cooed, 'it has a nice ring.'

But the words did not break Jeff's concentration as he opened the passenger door of what he called the Irma mobile a 1978 Ford Maverick that was simply the zenith of automotive ugly. The colour was a nondescript pale green, a hatchback with black vinyl interior, two doors, and plain bench seats. The heavy body was badly chipped and bruised, with dark horizontal streaks where the side-moulding had been torn away.

Dorn also liked to say that it was a previously owned vehicle, having bought the car at government auction, but the truth was that neither one of them liked to park it in their driveway for very long. It was an eyesore. Irma had been saving her kitchen money to have it painted, but Dorn insisted it wasn't worth the effort.

'After this can we trade it in?' she asked, now standing in the open door.

'Beauty's in the eye of the beholder,' he said, trying to be somewhat amiable, and lifting a one-inch box socket wrench from his tool box. This in hand, he swung his small body into the passenger seat, pulling at the seatbelt's anchoring plate, which was mounted against the transmission hump.

'Well I know that, Honey, but it's an embarrassment for me to drive to work, I'll buy us a car as a wedding gift.'

Dorn ignored the comment as a middle-aged couple wandered out from the mall and into the garage, glancing at their position near the stairwell, summing them up. The structure was a covered five storeys, two down, three up, and by early evening it was already full. The man seemed to be having some difficulty remembering the colour code for his garage level, and was now moving away, following his wife in the other direction.

It took Dorn but a minute, the ratchet spinning at the single bolt-head, and the entire seatbelt assembly came free in his hand. He removed a replacement from a cardboard packing box, then tightened this down into place.

'We can't afford it,' he said tonelessly, rising to his feet, pulling the passenger seat forward. With his left hand he was feeling along the back, along the outside seam, examining a chrome release plate and latch whose only purpose was to allow the seat to come forward, enabling riders to duck into the rear.

'I've saved some money, Jeff.'

It was attached by two machine screws, and without ceremony, he quickly removed this, leaving an empty hole in the black vinyl. That's all there was to it. With a few turns of a wrench, the Maverick was transformed into a rolling house of horrors for anyone who stepped inside the pale green trap.

Anyone, that is, except Jeff Dorn or Irma Kiernan.

'Oh, Honey,' she asked nervously, standing over him. 'Are you sure this will work, it just seems so easy.'

Dorn was lifting his tools from the pavement and carrying them to the trunk. 'Always keep it simple,' he mumbled, 'life's complicated enough.' He lifted a roll of silver duct tape, snipping off a large piece, then making a sticky loop.

'It's just that . . .'

'Irma!'

'But last time they were teenagers, this one thinks she's awful damn smart.' She was about to speak again when Dorn's punishing stare held her off.

With practised skill he slithered onto the rear seat, grabbing this at the bottom, then slapping once with his palm. He lifted it off its mount, and the trunk immediately filled with a wash of bright fluorescent light from overhead; the cardboard partition between the trunk and cabin had been sliced in half and discarded, leaving a hole about the size of a window.

Dorn poked his head up through the trunk and watched as a family of four trotted from the sidewalk into the underground parking area, their clothes soaked and their faces dripping; mother, father, and two adolescent boys. They passed the Maverick without notice, moving on towards the theatre entrance.

'The goddamn tape?'

Irma spotted the loop attached to the paint over the door. She quickly passed it over, then watched with admiring eyes as Dorn applied this to the top of the back rest, pushing down gently, dropping the seat back into place.

Dorn wiggled out and was now standing, a strange light dancing in his eyes. 'You have a friend in Pennsylvania,' he said.

'I know, Sweetheart.'

She watched as he covered each Maryland licence plate with dark blue replacements from the Keystone State, the backs holding flexible magnetic strips and allowing the signs to just slap into place.

'Are you sure their car will stop?' she asked quietly.

Dorn ignored her, strolling past the rear bumper, closing the trunk with a thud. 'Get in,' he said.

She did.

*   *   *

Jessica and Elmer Janson had been finishing double scoops of ice cream, sitting in a window booth at Svensk's Parlour on the other side of the mall.

'You certainly went quiet all of a sudden,' she said, watching the ice cream disappear.

'Sorry, Mom, how's your fudge?'

'Great, and your butterscotch?'

'Fine.'

'Elmer, you don't have to talk if you don't want to.'

'I'm okay.'

'I'll give you a penny?'

Elmer sat back in his seat, digging into the last scoop in his bowl, watching other families waiting in line to be seated. Jessica saw this and leaned back over.

'So what do you think?'

'Mom,' he asked quietly, 'did you and Dad ever go looking for buried treasure?'

'Why do you ask?'

'Well, his metal detector and all. It had been used, there was dirt all over it when I found it in the basement. When I was little, Dad said he was going to take me exploring . . .' and his voice seemed to trail off with sadness.

'Oh Red,' she sighed, 'is that why you went to play at the bowling alley?'

The boy hung his head.

'Elmer, your daddy wasn't looking for anything in particular, he was just interested in the past, he was a history buff.' She leaned forward across the table and touched him lightly on the arm. 'Most writers are, that was just a hobby of his.' Jessica forced a smile as she stroked his hair. 'Let's talk about something else, something happy, I don't want you playing with that thing any more.'

He nodded, staring down into his bowl.

'Elmer, would you like it if Gram stayed with us for your birthday? She could come for a week.'

'Sure,' the boy shrugged, 'but I'm not taking music lessons.'

She smiled, growing a bit annoyed. 'Oh you're not, huh,

and what makes you think Gram's planning something like that?'

Elmer's eyes danced lightly over her and returned to his bowl.

'You mean we're that transparent?'

He shook his head. 'You two talk about it all the time.'

'Oh, but you have no interest in music?'

'I want to be like Dad.'

'Elmer, your daddy played the guitar, wouldn't you like to learn something like that? A well-rounded person should be able to appreciate music and play an instrument.'

He shrugged.

'You're not crazy about it, be honest?'

'When I'm not at school I'd rather just be roaching around with Tripod.'

Jessica cringed and leaned forward. 'Stop using that term, it's very unpleasant.'

'Sorry.' He stirred the last bit at the bottom of the bowl into a cold soup. 'Mom, did Dad leave me anything, I mean adult things that I can have?'

'Yes,' she said confidently, 'yes he did, I'll give you something when we get home.'

'I mean grown-up things,' he said in a frustrated tone. 'Chet Morgan's father has a gun!'

Jessica closed her eyes with a frown, and thought it over. 'Finish your ice cream, guns are *not* toys, and you aren't going to play with them.'

'Did he?'

She nodded, holding up her right hand. 'Truth?' she said.

Elmer's eyes grew wide. 'Truth!' he agreed.

'Your daddy had several guns, including a pistol your Grandfather got in Germany, and these are yours,' and she swallowed hard, not knowing why she had said it, why this was important; truly unable to understand the male fascination with instruments of destruction. To Jessica Janson the world, though not without its troubles, did not need any more weapons or wars or killing, and she felt like shouting with frustration as Elmer's voice surely flowed with a new found joy.

'Can I see them?'

'Someday, they're locked away at the bank, but Elmer,' the boy had forgotten about ice cream and she quickly reached across the table pinching his arm, 'you don't get one until you're eighteen, that's the way he would have wanted it.' She quickly made a mental note to call Chet Morgan's father as the pent up breath spilled from Elmer's lungs.

'Thanks, Mom,' he sighed, and the wind drove a current of hard rain to hammer down against the window. They could clearly see the street outside, it was a glassy ribbon of flooded blacktop, cars were creeping through the downpour, although the lightning had stopped.

'It doesn't seem to be letting up,' she said, checking the bill, pulling her wallet from her purse. She counted out the exact change, right to the dime, laying this beneath the napkin holder.

'Drink some water,' she suggested, 'and for Pete's sake, Elmer, wipe your mouth.'

Elmer smiled broadly. 'Who was Pete? First Pete that comes to mind,' he cautioned.

The two instantly entered a trivia contest of free association they had played since the boy could remember. Anyone dropping an unexplained name or place had but one chance to explain, then face a new challenge.

Jessica frowned, straightening her shirt as she stood, then extending her hand. 'Pan,' she nodded proudly. 'I meant good old Peter Pan.'

'Then what did he use to stick his shadow back on?'

The young mother feigned deep thought, leading him slowly from the booth, then out into the mall.

'Just a moment,' she begged, 'I'm still working on it!' And she gave him a quick little tickle in the ribs.

Kiernan smiled. It was an answer she liked very much. The blonde's car would stop on command in the pouring rain, and she imagined her drenched like a sorry beggar, asking kindness of any passing stranger.

Dorn's eyes rolled as he talked. 'They really have no choice, it will be over in fifteen minutes, and when their car heats up, the antifreeze will blow like Mount St Helens. It will be spraying directly into the fan, so it should be quite a show.'

Jessica Janson drove a 1986 white Oldsmobile Cutlass powered by a six cylinder 3.8 litre engine with a two-gallon cooling system, and Dorn had made a precision hole in her lower radiator hose, boring through the top so that fluid would not leak out, staining the pavement, attracting attention. Having practised on, and followed other cars during the daytime, he knew with some certainty how long it would take, the maximum distance her car would be able to travel. To Kiernan it was mysteriously complicated and wonderful, a quick jab with what looked like a sharpened icepick.

'And they'll be where?'

'Stuck near that salt lick on Little Falls Parkway.'

'You mean that storage area where the mounds of sand are?'

He was staring out his rear mirror watching people leaving the mall for their cars. 'It's for snow emergency, absolutely the darkest spot along the Parkway, and the County reduces patrols to the hour on weekends.'

Irma smiled, 'And she thinks *she's* so smart . . .'

Dorn watched pedestrians passing by.

'. . . she just doesn't know us!'

He swung his head, seeing Irma's heavily made up lids. The humid air had produced blue cracks under each eye, and the rouge looked like dollops of meat.

'She'll know both of us soon enough,' he said flatly, 'just get it right.'

Irma was about to speak, cheer building in her voice, when he grabbed her by the arm, shutting down her response.

Son in tow, Jessica Janson was strolling towards them, walking with an athletic grace, speaking to Elmer as she passed through the stairwell's open door.

'Gram means well,' her voice echoed.

'I know, Mom, if it's that important to her, you know I'll do it.'

THIRTY-FIVE

It was nearing 11:00 when the pounding sheets of rain choked back customers, and the bar was beginning to empty. The brothers Dix were locking up early, turning off lights, closing the Zephyr's blinds.

Snake' and Younger spoke as they came down the hallway, towards the kitchen, passing the bathroom where the dogs had located Debra Patterson's scent. 'I still think we should stay open,' Snake complained, 'having only one long night a week is starting to cost us.'

'Most of our regulars are family types, home by ten, look at the weather. Besides, we're rich.'

'Well, extend the hours, we can get richer.'

They passed into the kitchen, pushing the spring-loaded door open, not looking back as they talked, too absorbed with each other to notice the figure sitting in the corner. He held the door to the wall and was now blocking any retreat.

'Damn,' said Younger, 'did you get the front light?'

'Is the Pope Catholic?'

'Pour me a drink, I'll count up.'

Snake nodded. 'I should have busted his nuts.'

Younger was half attentive, counting money, removing a grey metal box from beneath a chopping block on a floating island. 'If you mean that retarded cop, it would have kept us in court for a week, that's down time, and no one to pay for our trouble.'

'What's wrong with America?' Snake agreed.

'People don't know their place, harassing a family-run business. If we sued him we'd end up with some shitty little house on the tracks, and a used car. The score looks very good tonight.'

The pornography business was translating into thick stacks as Snake looked on, not bothering to count, for twins have an understanding of trust that's tied in the womb. 'Seven thousand so far, and I'm still going.' Younger smiled, taking a shot of bourbon, then marking onto a sheet of paper as Snake placed another pile of dirty bills onto the table.

Younger was lifting his glass in salute. 'To the new supply,' he said. 'Quality is our middle name.'

Snake beamed and was about to toast when a soft crying blew through the room, sounding like an alley cat complaining into a gust of wind. They looked at each other, then leaped into action, Snake grabbing a meat cleaver as Younger leaned over, lifting a large automatic pistol that lay under the island.

He immediately steadied his aim at the hallway, ducking behind the wooden block; as the door moved slowly shut, revealing a human figure in the darkness of the furthest corner. The two men were shielding their bodies, staring slack-jawed at the figure who was holding white-gloved hands into the air in a sign of absolute surrender.

'I'm going to cut you good!' Snake cried, turning to his brother.

'Shoot him!' he ordered Younger into action. 'Shoot the sonofabitch!'

But Younger seemed distressed, or at least confused, by what he saw.

It was a scarecrow. A human scarecrow. His head was a square burlap sack with a triangle cut where a nose protruded, the bulbous flesh sticking out, a bright and seamy lipstick red.

And the eyes were long horizontal slits that resembled black slashes.

The sack itself had once been splattered with house paints, green, red, blue, and was peeling badly, gathered at the throat with a silk tie, an ugly orange burst with a pattern of gold metallic swirls. In spite of the knot around his throat, the scarecrow had no chin, but a neck that looked like a rotting tree stump.

Snake noticed a small rectangle at the mouth, and behind this opening were inky black lips. The image was slow to register.

'Hey,' he screamed suddenly, pointing his blade. 'That's my best tie!'

Gun in hand, Younger was finding his nerve. 'He must be a goddamned psycho!'

The scarecrow smiled, the seams of his burlap sack suddenly pulling tight around his grinning head, when it occurred to the twins that he had yet to speak.

'Hey!' Snake took a small step forward, slamming the heavy blade into hard wood with a deadly thump. 'We're talking to you, asshole!'

The scarecrow scratched the back of his head, then peeled a piece of paint off a burlap cheek and dropped it onto the floor.

'He's wearing gloves,' Younger said quietly. 'Is he surrendering? What's he up to?'

Snake tapped his temple. 'The asshole thought he was gonna rob us!' he laughed, as Younger smiled sarcastically.

'Is this a stickup, do you have a gun?' He aimed his weapon casually into the corner. 'Bang! Bang!' he cried, then turned to his brother with a grin of achievement.

Gently, hands in the air, Rivers pulled his chair to the floor, his eyes darting between the two men, little blue flashes, the gaiety quickly dying. Younger wondered if his single-action .45 had a bullet in the chamber, revealing this thought by looking down, yet aiming the gun with deadly precision.

No one moved.

The scarecrow was standing.

Younger was watching in disbelief just as Rivers came forward, placing himself close enough to smell their sweat, biting off each word distinctly so there would be no room for further doubt in their filthy little minds.

'Fuck you,' he said.

Snake started forward as in one clean movement Younger cocked his gun and went to pull the trigger.

* * *

364

Time stopped.

Time stopped and the room blurred with an incredible swiftness, form becoming fluid as Rivers' entire body flew through air, a jagged flash roaring from the gun in his right hand, his left hand breaking his fall – all of this as the room just filled with the deafening crack of a single blast.

Snake caught only a glimpse as his brother's head seemed to explode in a thick red mist; his forehead bursting like a bad sprinkler, releasing a bloody spray, turning his face into a horrid red mask as the gun flew from his hand.

His lips parted and moved as his legs buckled, his body dropping backward through space, and before it had hit, Snake caught a flash of movement; coming down through the air with lightning speed, a solid white streak slicing through spaces above, delivering a deadly thump against wood that felt hot against his hand, painful as the blue lick of a cutting torch.

Younger was just hitting the floor as Snake screamed with agony.

Frozen with fear, Snake was; frozen with pain.

And as the room went still he was staring down in disbelief as a human thumb twitched hideously from the block, kicking like a frog's severed leg; and Snake stared at this, eyes wide, as if this slug of human flesh were someone else's thumb, and not his; and that his hand was not the screaming bundle of severed nerves that burned murderous fury as it pumped slick juices onto the floor.

The man screamed again.

The human Snake bellowed like a wild boar, cursing through a face that seethed and foamed with hurt and venom. 'You killed my brother!' he cried, staring in disbelief at a kitchen that resembled a dirty slaughterhouse.

'You killed my brother . . .' and his voice trailed into witless agony as he slumped to his knees, only to find himself staring up into the portrait of Debra Patterson.

His body shook like a wet dog.

'It will go numb,' the voice said flatly. 'Show some dignity, for Christ's sake.'

*   *   *

365

Snake was no longer a twin.

This realisation forced him to vomit until he could no longer respond physically. And according to his account, Debra Patterson had been at the bar. She had left the Zephyr alive. Her car was still parked when the brothers locked up and left for home.

The reason Snake remembered all this was because the top was down and the night was warm, so they had checked to see if sexual acts were being performed in the back seat, but it was empty.

Rivers wanted to be sure, he lifted the meat cleaver from the block and cleaned the edge on the man's shirt.

'God, no!' he moaned. 'I didn't do anything to her, I swear, I was just serving her drinks!'

'And you're sure she walked out of here of her own free will?'

'I swear it!' he cried. 'She left with those two other girls!'

Rivers nodded thoughtfully. 'And where does the kiddy porn come from?'

'We're only distributors, we don't make it, I swear we don't do the work!'

'Names, give me names and addresses.'

And Rivers observed that Snake was nothing like his reputation, once befriended he was an agreeable sort; eager to please was the best way to describe him.

Just as Snake had exhausted his knowledge, moving into a conversational circle for the second time, a horrible moaning filled the kitchen.

'Ooo . . .' the sound echoed. 'Ooo . . .'

Rivers strode across the room just as the groan was registering on Snake's mind, his marble eyes bulging from their sockets.

'Maa . . .'

Snake stared up at his attacker, then stared at the body, scurrying over, his stump releasing a trickle of fluid which he smeared with his knees.

'Rigor's setting in,' Rivers explained, 'the body grows stiff, driving air from the lungs.'

'Ooo . . .' came the sound, as Younger's lungs filled and emptied.

'Ooo . . .'

'Damn me for a mutt.' Rivers smiled, scratching his face, the burlap was starting to itch.

'He's breathing!' Snake rattled excitedly. 'Do something! Quick, do something!'

'Me?' Rivers chuckled, pointing a finger to his own chest. 'No, I don't think I will.'

'But he's not dead . . .'

Rivers bent at the waist, reaching down to Younger's forehead, down to where the darkest splotch of blood revealed a wound channel, about three inches wide, splitting flesh, showing a splinter of bone.

The gloved fingers were working, digging, scratching, as he peeled away a bloody slug and stood, dropping a crimson wad at Snake, who caught it with his good hand.

'What is it?' he asked with confused horror.

'Paraffin.'

Snake was trembling again, 'But you shot . . .'

Rivers shook his head slowly. 'You said you wanted to play trick or treat, that's best I could do on short notice. Next time I'll do some planning.'

'A game?' Snake hissed. 'This is a game to you?'

'No, I've seen people die from a wax bullet, looks like this one snipped an artery, maybe even busted his skull, must really hurt.'

Snake quickly drove through the comment, his voice betraying a brotherly love. 'But he could have shot you?'

'I looked down the muzzle, nothing but air in an empty pipe.' He leaned over, picking up the .45, then confidently pulled back the slide; but a menacing lead cartridge flipped out, spinning to the floor, coming to rest against the body. Both men felt the shock.

Rivers shrugged at the loaded gun. 'I would have dropped him anyway.'

'Moo . . . Maa . . .' The moaning returned, and Snake's face went to paste as he watched the scarecrow stroll back to the block and pick up a slug of flesh. Rivers twirled the severed thumb, tossing it into the air, catching it, tossing some more.

'Call 911, they'll save your brother.'

'But a surgeon could also save my thumb!' Snake cried after him, as Rivers walked through the door, the moaning twin's mouth popping open like a landed fish.

'Ooo . . . thar . . . Maa . . .' Like a braying lamb.

Rivers left with that pitiful sound on his mind. 'Maa . . . ma?' he parted his lips to repeat, shaking his head in disbelief, wondering if he could believe his own ears. He was quite sure the human sleaze was calling for his mother.

And as he stepped into his cruiser, he tossed the human thumb into the brush, dropping his stained gloves where they were easily seen by customers. He settled into his seat, turning the radio to the established frequency, wondering if he should call Jon Patterson about his daughter. The news was promising. Rivers now suspected that they were dealing with a runaway, for according to Snake, there were three girls together that evening, and they had been discussing pregnancy.

As he held the portrait in hand, he wanted to believe, his mind leaping forward to balance other responsibilities, organising tomorrow's MAIT team, yet finding time to work with this family. He was starting to pull through the alley as Mule Murphy's voice tore from the radio car, cracking against his soul like an icy whip.

'Base, this is Huskies,' he said flatly. 'The situation here is Red. Repeat. Code Red.'

The words hit Rivers like a bullet in the chest, his thoughts leaping for his radio as his body followed, throwing the fireball on the dash.

There was a scale of colours tearing through his mind, he had been the officer to establish the calls and codes.

Red was the colour of an abduction in progress.

Even with siren he was forty minutes away.

THIRTY-SIX

Afraid of being seen, Scott stepped up from the curb and stood in shadow, motionless, unaffected by the downpour that had come. He blinked once, water rolled down his cheeks as he studied the house, pulling his collar against the wind.

A car approached, speeding down the glassy street, high beams glancing off his worn raincoat, then vanishing into a bland suburban maze. He walked on, pulling a felt fedora low, shielding his eyes.

He came with the street light glowing at his back, moving quietly over a flagstone walk until darkness absorbed him. Rain streamed from his chin, and he stopped to listen, closing his eyes, but there was only the night coming to greet him, rain gutters beating like hollow, rolling drums; the wind rattling against wooden shutters; and the chirping of crickets from a window well at his toes. Abruptly, his shoulders fell slack, rounding into age and tiredness.

Scott was hesitant, feeling as if his arrival was unexpected and yet at the same time delayed, like something he had been putting off in his youth. It had now been nine days since they were killed, and he thought about that, watching tall oaks ascend with their branches, green leaves licking towards the windows on the second floor, and he studied the exterior.

The house was red brick. On the front lawn leaves that were once raked into neat piles were being pushed by stroking swirls of wind, blowing across the lawn, catching in hedges once squared with perfection. And he strolled, standing on the front stoop, peering down into the driveway to where branches were felled among soggy newspapers.

These were rolled and banded, their headlines just crumbling pronouncements important to none, and his eyes fell further, picking up an approaching car on the street below. There was a thunderous hiss as the treads pushed through rain, the headlights sweeping into the neighbourhood as if nothing but the present mattered. He started forward in the doorway as a cold wind rapped his teeth.

He stopped.

He stooped low onto one knee, inspecting an empty terracotta bowl filled with rich black soil, and alongside, in the shadow, he found a small trowel and glove.

Carefully, he picked this up, admiring the slender green and white fingers. Although he knew better, in his heart he felt like a stranger violating Diana Clayton's world, disturbing the recumbent solitudes of her former life, peering down into private corners that only held room for her.

Locked tight.

Scott was testing the door when a dried crust of mud shone with a glitter against the stoop's concrete seam. He picked this up. It was just a sliver of earth, round like a toe, curved with tiny indentations. It was small like the shoe of a girl he remembered with some clarity, though he had never known her; the impish grin, the wide eyes, standing in the doorway with her mother.

'Kimberly,' Scott said aloud, rubbing the dirt into dust between his fingers.

And he released a long and troubled sigh, then peering down, he took up this glove like a child's hand and applied the key.

He removed a penlight from his pocket and flicked it on, the tiny beam surveying the hallway and living room. He took one step forward and the foundations groaned as the walls closed around the house like an old blanket, still soaked with the smells of the living, casting out messages from every corner.

Scott paused, lowering his head.

That was the truth about a dead house, he thought.

The living, breathing truth that you did not find in books

or carry away from darkened theatres that popularise homes of atrocity. Such places live with a silent language that begins at the moment of death, and the horror kisses your heart with its hooks, and once it does, it never lets you go.

'I am the killer,' he closed his eyes to say. 'His skin is my body.' And he stopped in front of a mirror that hung just above a black babygrand, stroking white ivory, then peering in, pulling the beam back to his coat. It was not the face of Scott that he saw reflected there, the cunning eyes, a flash of teeth, a look, and nothing more. The mirror shattered in the centre.

Old enemy. Old friend.

12.21.

Returning to darkness. Seconds. Ticking.

He glanced up at the ceiling imagining faces relaxed into sleep, chasing childish dreams. A smile. A half-closed fist. A sigh as the room again filled with light, dancing across walls, spinning, orbiting, as a car went by passing into shadow; dust of shadows, all falling away through time.

As he neared the kitchen, the sharp odour of cedar chips found him, then defined him.

'What do you know?' Scott asked. 'Killing time? Am I waiting, or have I planned all of this?' And he stopped. Breathing deeply. Wetting his lips with his tongue. 'Tofu,' he said quietly, 'thousands of warm wet kisses.'

He was now peering down at the kitchen table, sweeping with his beam, not looking for death, but looking for life, looking with a question in his mind.

Something else, what was it?

Across the kitchen table a round water stain glinted where wax had been applied. He stroked this with a gloved hand. Toasted breadcrumbs mounted like a thin line of ash, small chips of bacon clung like grains of sand.

He removed a chair.

The beam working into corners; a bead of jewellery, a penny, a small clip of blue satin ribbon, these all obvious to the eye, all shining. And Jack Scott sat down on linoleum, looking up and under the table. Tofu's blood had puddled, smearing a wooden leg, and he moved on hands and knees towards the floor moulding; the coin blinking like a copper eye; the ribbon cut sharply, once knotted; the bead perforated, once strung or still waiting to be.

He left them undisturbed. Standing. Moving on towards the sink as an image stabbed in his mind; trusting eyes and a brooding *drip, drip, drip* as his flashlight searched with memory – as he focused sight and his mind went reeling, screaming to the sounds of life as a telephone was ringing, clanging, crying, the chambers of Scott's heart nearly bursting.

Images were colliding as he staggered forward, bracing himself on the counter where a red light suddenly snapped on beneath a white telephone with its message pad and pen at the ready.

'Hi ... this is Diana ... I'm Kimberly ... this is Leslie.'

He held his breath as the adult voice returned.

'. . . the girls and I are unable to answer at this time, but we thank you for calling, please leave a message.' It ended with an electronic beep, followed by a blasting dial tone.

Sharp. Biting. Endless.

Scott's lids fell shut, tightly. Shut. And he wished that he had not heard the voices, though his eyes popped open all the same as he turned towards the bedrooms.

He swallowed hard as his bladder tightened.

A shot of urine spat free.

Seeking in shadow.

With catlike feet he was climbing steps, toe to heel, one at a time, the blood roaring in his left temple. As he walked he imagined Diana, the chills had driven her to soak as her children tossed in their sleep.

He stopped, turning on the top landing.

It was a narrow hallway. At one end there was a small table on an oriental runner leading into the master bedroom. At the other, open doors and uncertain darkness.

He moved forward, first inspecting the table, a small lamp,

an arrangement of dried flowers, and above this a family portrait. There was a timer against the wall controlling the light, and he checked carefully, fingering the tiny buttons, the switch was set for dusk to dawn, yet the darkness remained?

'Afraid of shadows, perhaps, little Kimberly,' he said.

Scott moved on passing the table, creeping through the door to confront Diana.

Sitting down on her bed.

The turned down sheets released the smells of a fresh machine wash as the swollen mattress gave under his weight. Still waiting. The accent pillows all in place, all in a row, then Scott rose to the mirror above her desk.

'You would have liked this.' He grimaced, a flash of teeth, and then the bathroom door swung wide.

I am the killer.

She is waking into a nightmare bursting through her head. 'Who's there?'

Only now she sees my full form slowly coming forward, blackness covering my face, my hands, my head; a drum banging through her mind, thrashing her heart as she realises terror and her eyes explode from a sleepy state, her body still cloaked in a cloud of steam.

Do I know about the children? Thought number one. Has he seen the children but they could not scream?

She is trying to stand, the water ripples against naked legs, shaking into a trembling form that reaches forward but grabs only air.

'I came for you.' A comforting lie. The process. He is after the process.

She agrees, nodding her head. She dare not scream for waking the children, thinking . . . All the time, thinking . . . What can I do?

As the gun appears, coming out from behind my back, more like a plastic bag than a gun, and she stares with questioning horror, feeling a piercing blow smash in an instant through her teeth.

Her body jerks, I must break her fall . . .
. . . so quietly.
She cannot think, she cannot see.
Stiff and contorting beneath my hold, her instincts take over but it is too late.
The children are sleeping as five minutes pass.
She dies there.

Scott swallowed hard.
He stood at the door of the children's room, asking why. 'What did you feel?' he said aloud. 'What did you see?' The room was sparse for the crime, the lifelessness reaching up from every corner. His eyes cast about, then he walked slowly, moving directly towards the bureau dresser, trying to avoid detailed death, standing still in front of the mirror.
It had been shattered with controlled skill, not a shred of glass missing, long cracks snaking through the centre, moving up, coming down, and he was about to force a smile for his reflection, to look at this thing, when suddenly he recoiled with horror.
Scott closed his eyes and swallowed. The sudden silences were buzzing like hornets, then screaming through his head.
Broken with perfection.
In the wash from street lights, puddles appear like magic in the mirror, stains not visible to the eye directly; glistening, shining beneath two wicker chairs. The girls are parked together at the window.
Their dead eyes are looking out.
They are carefully displayed for anyone on the street looking in.
Scott could see with a clarity that forced air from his lungs, the scale of the atrocity dwarfed by the little room; the images bursting in his mind as he quickly fled.
Standing outside the door, breathing hard, regaining his senses. He trembled. Scott was staring down at his side when he saw her, when he *saw* Kimberly, standing alone at the end of the hall in a blue nightshirt, a fuzzy cell of a being, then

gone in a flash, a blink, a tick, just a turn of the head, and nothing more.

He closed his eyes.

'My images address me,' Scott swallowed, 'my images know my name.'

The power of his own imagination was such that he could conjure life and death from the black pool that was his mind. He knew that. He fought to prevent losing control.

'Keep it clinical,' the voice inside slipped out to warn him.

Scott quickly fumbled in his coat for a cigarette, finding this, then striking a match. Hot gases filled his lungs, throwing off harsher sensations, and as he held the fire to his lips, about to blow, he saw with a painful clarity.

Through the tiny blue flame, Kimberly Clayton came walking, moving past him from her bedroom, slipping towards the end of the hall. And Scott knew this was in his mind, for the child was too perfect, her expression exactly as her picture. Every detail, but dressed in a light blue nightgown with white silk buttons, stopping at the table, then turning to extend her hand. Forgiving him for failing, as only a child could do.

She vanished as the flame licked his hand.

Scott felt his eyes tear as the sting registered against his mind, but he did not jump, extinguishing the flame like a birthday candle that had flared only once; for the horror had hooked him, kissing his heart.

He thought of Commander Dobbs, of what he saw at the end, the apparitions becoming real; are these the silent images of the agent's disease that come in the night, haunting you for your sins, refusing to let you go?

Pictures and flowers, ribbons and wax, water and crumbs and beads? And, suddenly, all of his children were surrounding him, coming forth slowly. Lost faces offering smiles, taking him by the hand.

And Scott knew.

Instinct or guesswork, the faces faded, and it did not matter. Scott knew with his gut the way he had always known, and

375

with his mind, and it was only that; he called upon Kimberly at will, with a loving and bonded interest.

'Oh Mommy, just one more night?'

He closed his eyes and they were standing in the kitchen, the words echoing through the recesses of his skull. The playful life-loving voice. *Just one more night . . .*

Scott could see Diana Clayton reacting with guilt, her shoulders falling forward, a sheepish smile spreading across her face as she stood over the garbage pail, her youngest daughter having walked through unexpectedly. Diana faced with a heart-rending protest over losing something new, the words unfettered by the restraints and logic of an adult world.

Diana had already applied a coating of wax to the kitchen table in an effort to remove the troubling water stains, but she had never returned to wipe it clean. Something had interrupted. That something was staring at her now like she was the proverbial Grinch stealing Christmas.

And all the while a predator had been stalking. For about eight days, Scott was guessing now, that's what he would find. He was sure of it, because he knew.

He lifted the oriental vase with both hands, holding it above his head, looking up at the bottom, seeing a yellow skin of wax along the pale outer edge.

'Kimberly,' he said aloud, his heart pounding as he fingered the dried arrangement, then turned it upside down onto the floor.

Water fell. It splashed into a puddle. He swallowed.

Not dried at all, but yellow petals going grey, splashes of red fading to pink, and their stems drooped towards a brittle death. And he imagined Diana Clayton coming forward, towards him, gliding up the stairs dressed for bed, moving past, carrying the wilted flowers.

Scott was with them now, removing the china coaster from her closet, and carefully placing this beneath to protect the table's fine surface, then adjusting the timer on the light. And as he imagined they had, he returned the vase to its rightful place, where they would be close, for one final time before they languished and had to be discarded.

His throat choked tight.

Scott returned to the kitchen as time returned to the living.

For perhaps a week, Kimberly's flowers had spread their colours on the kitchen table where she could tend to them in a carefree manner, a little spill, a little slop, a little love, and who's to care?

But on the night of March 31st, Diana had cleared and waxed the kitchen table, and was about to throw them away, when she was caught in the act; the flowers were then brought upstairs to be nearby.

Scott tripped the ash off his cigarette and into the sink, then bending, he opened a door beneath the counter, removing a plastic trash can, peeling away darkness with his light.

And it was there.

Stuck to a wad of pink chewing gum, along with the blue ribbon once used for tying them, and directly under an empty packet of florists' preservative.

Carefully, he collected all seven of them, dried and brittle stalks, imagining how Kimberly had cherished them all, and so doing this with a tender hand. Flowers once picked by children, then thinned from an ageing bouquet, night after night, saving only the best, the best for last.

Yellow Loosestrife, the Swamp Candle.

THIRTY-SEVEN

'Oh come on,' Jessica Janson fumed, 'we're just sitting!'

The white Oldsmobile Cutlass edged out into traffic, the windshield wipers slapping at high speed as the rains came pelting down. The pavement was littered with fallen branches and debris, and she avoided this, merging left from the parking structure, dropping into a line many cars deep at the intersection of Arlington and Old Georgetown Roads.

Her left hand turn signal had been pinging, pulsing from the dash as the traffic light went to green, but the line remained motionless.

'Tomorrow, if it's not raining, can we go to the river?' Elmer asked.

From far in back came a belting honk, the line sliding forward by a single car length.

'I'm sorry, dear, what was the question?' She wiped her side window with a thin tissue, only to see flashing red lights beating from a block away down Arlington Road.

'About Sunday, after church can we go to the park?'

'We'll see, Elmer. I think we better find another route, there's an accident down there.'

She shifted to a right turn signal, trying to ease back into traffic, alternating her brakes with the gas, the car bucking at the gridlock. Behind her, headlights flashed once, signalling as a space appeared. She returned a wave of thanks without looking back.

'I'm cutting down onto Glenmoor and taking the parkway,' she said, switching the windshield defogger up a notch. 'It's a no left turn, but we won't tell?'

She glanced over at her boy, he was smiling.

'Crack your window, hon, I can barely see.'

They edged forward by inches, waiting for their turn.

'I wouldn't have done that,' said Irma Kiernan, batting at the fogged windshield with a tissue while working her face into a pout.

'Her car's heating up, would you like it to die in the middle of Bethesda?' Dorn was switching the windshield wipers to a higher speed just as he caught movement from the right corner of his eye.

'Irma, no!' he cried.

And she stopped dead. She was holding the seatbelt's chrome tongue with her right hand, inches away from inserting it.

'Sorry,' she said, 'I forgot.'

'You're sorry?' he sneered. 'No, Irma, you're just plain lucky.'

The button release on the attachment Dorn had screwed into place had been welded shut from the inside. Although it looked perfectly normal, once the seatbelt was snapped, the entire system had to be unbolted from the floor to free a passenger. The harness was an active restraint system, not much kinder to its wearer than a straitjacket.

She felt vulnerable, pulling her knees away from the dash, locking her door and then staring into space. Through the clouded windshield she was considering a choice of colours and texture, a flowing white gown complete with a veil, having never been wed she was truly entitled. Though, at her age, peach or pink might show more class.

'Jeff,' she mewed, 'what's your favourite colour?'

'Leave me alone,' he muttered, watching the Oldsmobile pull away.

So she considered dates, thinking ahead to the fall, pondering over the ceremony, the brilliant leaves, the harvest moon, the weather still warm enough for an outdoor reception.

Blue! she decided suddenly, jumping in place, though

keeping this to herself. A glamorous colour, touching on sexy, which brought her to cuts of satin.

'Whew!'

Jessica breathed audibly as she found herself on the other side of Old Georgetown Road, having taken an illegal left onto Glenmoor Drive, passing stately homes through a darkly lit residential area. They had left the heavy traffic mostly behind, winding their way west, towards the Parkway and home to River Road.

It had taken fifteen long minutes, and as Elmer spoke, she did not notice the temperature gauge on her dash as a red warning flickered, and then vanished again.

'Mom, do you want to play a game?'

'No, Elmer, I'm too tired, haven't we done enough tonight?' She tousled his hair as he sidled up to her, and the car sped through darkness.

From Glenmoor to Little Falls Parkway it was short minutes, leading through the intersection at Bradley Lane and into a wooded stretch of highway named for the nearby Potomac River. It looked empty but for the occasional car, tall oaks by the side holding vigil, their limbs branching in a dark canopy as the Jansons cruised through time, towards a destination they could not have imagined.

She felt a chill.

'It's not that I don't love you, but you should have your seatbelt fastened,' she said. Elmer, having grown sleepy, dragged himself away as a familiar blinking yellow light at Arlington Road passed behind them. They went bumping over railroad tracks, nearly home, when suddenly the car seemed to buck and kick.

'What the hell?' Jessica cried, just as a clattering filled the hood, just as a strange odour was filling the cabin.

'Something's burning,' Elmer stated nervously.

'I smell it too!'

She glanced down at her dash, the lights were glowing a bright and steady red.

'We're overheating!' she shouted, the trees spinning past,

starting to slow just as a blinding cloud of grey exploded in front of them, covering the windshield like a blanket, enveloping the car.

The road vanished from view.

In that deadly instant she hit her brakes, spinning the wheel as they hurtled through blindness, aimed for a black ravine.

It was there that Dorn was waiting.

He and Irma were parked on a side street, two hundred yards away on a hill, just across from this gully and through some woodland.

'Right on ... schedule!' he said, and his voice sounded queer, almost emotional.

'I feel old,' Kiernan responded.

'What?'

'I just hate my hair like this,' she pouted, referring to the netted bun which now hung against the back of her head. And although he agreed, he demanded, 'Let's see your eye makeup,' and she turned towards the back seat, batting her lids like a sorry Madame Butterfly, the blue mascara now gone, as well as the black streaks and fake lashes. To Dorn she looked for all the world like a stout school marm in an ugly green tank. On all windows were membership stickers for the AAA Road Service, it seemed more like a religion than a motoring club.

'Can we go now?' she whined, taking a more direct posture behind the wheel.

Dorn carefully scanned the Parkway through high-powered lenses. A car was approaching from the east, the headlights hogging the road, then slowing as it moved towards the Oldsmobile, which was sitting in a cloud of steam, its right side in the ditch. The interior light was on, he could see the woman clutching her child with both arms.

'Let her wait,' he said tonelessly.

'But Jeff, someone might help them?'

Dorn shook his head. 'This is Bethesda, Irma.' And he said that with a confident knowledge.

*   *   *

'Oh, Elmer, you're sure you're not hurt?'

He looked up, more concerned over the way she was holding him, rocking him so hard like a baby.

'Mom, it's only a bump on the head, but you look white . . .'

'We were lucky, God, that was awful!' She pounded the wheel. 'And I just had this stupid thing serviced! I can't believe it! Maybe they did something to the car?'

'Did you tip them?'

'Yes, Elmer,' she sighed, letting him go. 'You're too young to be concerned about things like that.' She watched his eyes, they were filling with hurt.

'Oh, Red.' She quickly pulled him back, hugging the boy all over again as the steam continued rising, obscuring their vision. A car was approaching slowly, just coming alongside, and a horn sounded. Jessica quickly rolled her window down just as a young man stuck his head out from a faded grey Cadillac and into the pouring rain.

'Can you call . . .' she started to say, as she saw water rolling off a naked torso, a menacing drunken face was leering at her. A beer bottle clutched in his hand, he was leaning out the window to his waist.

'Hey, Baby!' he yelled as the car came to a stop. 'Are you a part-ty ani-mal?'

She quickly rolled the window back up. 'Lock your door,' she said coolly.

'Hey, Baby!' the voice came again. 'Fix me, I'll fix your wheels!' They could both hear the sounds of men laughing, their drunken hoots and broken words growing more brazen.

'Mom?'

'Ignore them,' Jessica cautioned, and she could see a wildness burning in Elmer's eyes.

'Don't do that to your face,' she corrected.

'Mom, I think . . .'

'Hey, Sugar, come on out, we're having a wet T-shirt contest!'

With this a lewd laughter all but exploded as a soaked shirt landed on the hood with a heavy whack, followed by smacking

382

noises and jeers, as Jessica Janson fired the only weapon at her disposal.

She leaned into the horn button, and a minute quickly passed.

The sound was deafening, but she would not let go.

Dorn was delighted, having heard snatches of their remarks, watching the Cadillac coast away, gaining speed again.

'You see, Irma, there is a God.'

'And I want . . .'

'Yes,' he cut her off, 'you *want* to hit the red light at the next intersection, so pace yourself accordingly, I need thirty seconds to climb in and close back up.'

She put a hair brush into her purse, arranging this on the floor behind her seat, then turning the ignition key. The green Maverick started on the third hit, the rough idle growing steady as she rolled away with her lights off. A tree loomed from shadow and she hit her brakes, Dorn losing his balance, almost spilling onto the floor.

'Damn you!' he cried. 'What the hell are you doing!'

'Moving my seat forward, you have it too far back!'

She did this with her left hand, her whole body bobbing like a hinged puppet looking for a spine as she placed the car back into the proper lane. The street was deserted. The houses that lined it were dark as a pagan ritual.

'What if she screams?'

'Hey, that's a new one, Irma,' Dorn said with disgust, rejecting the topic. He just wanted to rescue the Jansons before the punks started to reminisce over what they had left. He leaned over the seat, his breath closing hotly on her ear.

'Are you getting cold feet?' he mouthed.

'No, but something could go wrong.'

'You worthless sow,' he barked suddenly, 'I could have been home relaxing . . .'

'Oh, Sweetheart,' she smiled, patting him on the hand. 'I just get hesitant, you know I'll be fine once we get started.'

The car moved forward in silence, the old oaks passing on the right like a wall of ancient sentries, she could just see the traffic light in the distance as they started down a steep hill approaching Little Falls Parkway.

'You know what to say, then?'

Irma nodded. 'Before I get out I make sure the overhead light is left on so that they see an empty car. I walk slowly to her window, knock if it's not open, then stand back so that they get a good look at me.'

Dorn shook his head, 'That's obvious, one more time Irma, do you know what to say?'

'Yes,' she nodded, 'the only thing I'm unclear about . . .'

'From the top,' Dorn ordered, cutting her off. 'We'll go through it one last time.'

She slouched forward, adjusting her bun while steering, and Dorn quickly corrected this behaviour with a backhanded slap, stinging her head with his fingertips. 'I'm Mrs Janson, you're standing at my window. "My car's broken down," I say, or words to that effect,' Dorn recounted.

'Oh my,' Irma answered, 'it is a bad night for that, could I make a phone call for you?'

'Right, make sure you don't blow it and just offer a ride, she'd get suspicious. "Oh that would be very kind!" Now what?'

'Well, I'm from Allenstown, PA, I'm just visiting family, so I don't know the area. What service stations are open this time of night?'

'The Shell Station, it's on River Road.' He was prompting in his own voice.

'Oh, is that far?'

'Make sure you sound concerned, Irma, that was a joke,' Dorn said in a biting tone. 'She has to feel you slipping away from her, use some subtle pressure or it won't work.'

She nodded. 'Oh my,' she exclaimed, 'I don't know that street, is it far?'

'Good, and then?'

'She tells me it's close, but I let her come to a conclusion on her own. I act confused, fumble with my hands, very uncertain about the whole business.'

'That part will come easy.'

384

'Jeff!' she pursed her lips. 'I'm not stupid, I have feelings too.'

The car inched forward, the headlights still dark, the intersection pulling closer. Dorn couldn't believe what he was hearing, but he continued all the same.

'Now at this point she'll be reaching a decision over what to do, should I ask for a ride or give this woman directions and hope? That will be going through her head, so give her time to think. Timing, Irma, everything comes down to timing.'

'Then I cut her off, when she pauses to think, go straight for the kid?'

'Exactly, let's hear it.'

'Well, he's adorable and I'm a third grade teacher.'

'Yes, but say it like you mean that, just between us girls, he's a nice one.'

Irma smiled, 'Sweetheart, you make him sound like a piece of fruit, he's a beautiful little boy, so it won't be hard. Besides, we're doing this for him . . .' Her voice trailed off, Dorn closing quickly on her comment.

'That's right Irma, now . . .'

'Jeff,' she barked, jumping back in. Dorn's teeth clenched. 'I bet you were too, I mean, a gorgeous little boy. Just think what would happen if we . . .'

'Later,' he corrected firmly, then put his hands against invisible bosoms and mustered up an effete voice. "Oh really!" he swooned. '"So you noticed how terrific my kid is! Well, he's a very good student, the brightest and most talented kid there ever was," or whatever dribble spills off her idiot tongue. She won't be able to stop talking, trust me.'

'So I act pleasantly surprised, like we're all one happy family, when I just happen to mention how silly it is to be standing here in the pouring rain, just talking away, especially with no man around, and it's a dangerous world . . .'

'No!' Dorn yelled. 'No, no, no! If you even say the word *man* that will give her mind something to bite down on. Just say I'm not comfortable here, and it's silly to be standing in the rain.'

'Sorry,' she puffed.

'She'll ask for a ride at this point, so make sure you're uncertain about that.'

'Is it too terribly far?' she cooed in response.

'And since the light in the car is still on, she'll think it's empty, nothing to fear unless you . . .'

'I won't,' Irma said, 'you're forgetting.'

Dorn nodded. 'Now you understand that all of this may not be necessary, she could just short-circuit the whole rap, come right out asking for a ride?'

'Of course, silly, the important thing is to make sure the boy gets in back.'

'That's critical, Irma, once I pop out from the cell and grab him, we control her easy. So what's the control?'

'I get in first, then as I unlock their door, I look right at the boy . . .'

'Yes, make sure he sees your eyes, he's very obedient.'

'. . . and I say, that seat's broken, it doesn't come forward. It's a bit of a tight fit, I'm afraid.'

'Right, and raise your eyebrows, challenge him, he'll jump right through the hoop. And if the blonde says anything?'

'Can you believe I've had it fixed twice, nothing gets done right any more.'

'Very good, Irma, real casual, little details like that can be important. Then what?'

'As I'm pulling away, I make sure she buckles up, and if she doesn't I ask her very quietly because of my car insurance policy. It won't cover anyone if we don't wear our belts.'

'Right,' his eyes rolled. 'When we hear that snap, she's ours, she belongs to us. I punch out from the back and hold a gun to the kid's temple, she'll be unable to breathe.'

'Well, Mr Perfect, don't you forget!'

Kiernan flicked on her headlights, slowing at the bottom of the hill, then stopping with precision for the light. She was preparing to take a right onto Little Falls Parkway when she glanced into her rearview mirror.

'Jeff?' she said.

The vacant back seat thrilled her in a way she did not understand.

A troubled sigh fell from Jessica's lips.

'No,' she said, 'we stay with the car.'

'But Mom, it's only a couple of miles, that's better than just sitting here.'

'Someone will come, Elmer, the police will be along, or a tow truck, you'll see.'

She noticed how dim the headlights were getting, the windows were thick with fog, it was like staring out from an eggshell, and she disguised her fears, feeling terribly cold and terribly lost. 'Are you warm enough, Red?'

'Sure, I guess so.'

And it was then that the car's interior bloomed with light, the gravel churning, crunching up slowly behind them.

'Mom, somebody's stopped,' Elmer said nervously, and she quickly started to wipe her side window, but the car was directly in back, the motor still running, and she could not see a thing.

'Dear God,' was her only thought. 'Those men have returned, they've been drinking for the last half-hour.'

Suddenly Elmer climbed into her arms to protect her as she shut her eyes, placing her hand against the horn.

Irma Kiernan felt a wicked delight.

Life was catching up with the Jessica Jansons of the world, that's what Irma thought, and she planned on discussing some beauty tips with the woman who had been flaunting her body on the merry-go-round, offending any sensible adult, showcasing herself at a time that should have been for the children.

'Cheap trick,' she said aloud under her breath.

And as she approached, she was Mrs Irma Dorn, a proud woman of regal stature, moving under the admiring watch of her man, a war hero and mythic champion.

'Mom, someone's coming,' Elmer cried nervously.

Jessica furiously tried wiping the window with the flat of

her hand, but as quickly as it cleared, it filled with fog.

She was hopelessly locked into blindness.

'Quick, Elmer, into the back seat, lie down on the floor.'

'No, Mom! No . . .' he exclaimed, and fear choked his voice as he struggled with her effort. He would not leave her, he would never leave her, and a sharp rapping came down against the window.

Three times.

Jessica closed her eyes tightly while leaning into the horn, the sound wavering from a weak charge, the cry failing to reach the road.

Words were running through Kiernan's mind.

'Little details are important, Irma, stand away from the car, let them see your body.'

Jessica Janson parted the window, rolling it down a fraction of an inch.

She was not sure how, but she was preparing to protect her child, wondering if Elmer would be able to sneak off into the woods, but more importantly, would he go if she ordered? She shook visibly at the thought, barely able to discern a form, a shadow looming over her, and it seemed small.

And a face.

It was coming down from above as Jessica pushed herself backward along the seat, the horn still weakly sounding, and her eyes transformed into slits as the dark features started taking form.

'What do you want?' she cried, and her voice filled with panic and fear, Elmer quickly coming to her side.

When suddenly. Without a word. She felt warm.

Her body and her breath relaxed in a sudden and unexplainable manner that she would take to her grave, never able to cast into words. Her heart backed off from a destructive tempo, her fists became hands again.

'Mom, who is he?' came Elmer's voice.

But there was only the sound of the rain beating against the shadowy brim of an old dark fedora. It was a man. An older man. While this face was kind, it was somehow punishing and worn, and in a painted bar of light cast from an oncoming car, the eyes radiated a concern that Jessica Janson had never seen before.

'Mrs Janson?' he asked quietly.

While she was thinking, *Do I know you? Should I know you?*, she suddenly unlocked and opened the door, her hands and legs shaking, stepping out into a horrid rain.

He was dressed in a battered grey raincoat, the hat shapeless and pulled low, the slacks worn and baggy. And he was holding a notebook in his hands, following a green car with his eyes as it passed closely by, slowing down, then gaining speed again.

A tear rolled from Jessica's cheek and she quickly brushed it away as Elmer took up her hand.

'Mrs Janson, my name is Scott,' he said carefully, extending a badge that gleamed in the harsh darkness.

And while a thousand questions went racing through her mind, they would not connect or form into words. And in the uncertain strangeness of that night, the three stood on the roadway, locked in time suspended; as if they were not really strangers, but rather old friends, and at last they had been reunited by fate.

'Our car has overheated.' She exhaled, and the words just seem to drift with the rain.

Scott nodded. 'I know,' he concluded softly.

Elmer tugged on her hand.

'It's all right,' she whispered, and she raised a troubled brow.

'Why do you know my name?' she pressed quietly, hesitant, almost backing away from the response. 'Please tell me . . .' her voice trembled. 'This was *no* accident, was it?'

Scott studied her eyes brimming with tears, a young mother fighting with enormous courage. 'It could have been, I would not take that chance. I am sorry. There's a small tracking device under your car, so I knew you needed my help.'

'Oh God!' she exclaimed instantly, biting down onto her fist. 'What have we done?'

Scott looked thoughtfully at her, his eyes warm and knowing. 'Well, that's a difficult question, Mrs Janson, although you've done nothing to deserve this directly, as I'm sure you've already guessed, an explanation might take some time.'

He took a step past them, removing the keys from her car and then turning off the lights. 'There's nothing to fear, let's have a cup of hot coffee, I'll do my best.'

And as his mother was about to respond, Elmer took a cautious step forward. Images and ideas had been popping off in his head like flash bulbs. 'Do you know Detective Rivers?' he asked quite suddenly.

Scott leaned over, water streaming down from the soaked brim of his hat. 'Elmer, I hear you have the spirit of a crusader and a lion's heart. You know that's very high praise coming from a man like Frank Rivers.'

At the sound of his own name, an explosion went off in the boy's head, so powerful that his heart went beating double, his eyes growing wide as Jessica's tears fell freely, the rain dropping her hair forward across her brow.

'It's that goddamned bowling alley!' she cried, looking up to Scott. 'That's the only trouble we've ever had!' She started to speak again but just shook her head with confusion, looking down at her child, wanting to anger, yet feeling only love.

'No trouble at all, Mrs Janson, I assure you. Let's just say that Elmer here opened a door on the past, we were the ones who happened to walk through.' And while this didn't make much sense to Jessica, the expression on Elmer's face said there was no misunderstanding. The stranger and her son seemed to grasp something, on a deeper and invisible level, that was totally lost on her.

'Are you him?' Elmer asked shyly. 'Did they give it to you?'

Scott nodded, fumbling in his pocket, his fist coming slowly out, then his fingers opening as if he had captured a moth and did not want it harmed. And it was there.

Elmer's coin.

A speck, a promise, a joy. Shining like a star through the red beginnings of time.

DAY THREE:

THE VILLAGE

The worth of mankind will be measured by only
those things that he was able to leave alone.

William Oscar Swensk

Evil is the nature of mankind.
Welcome, again, my children,
to the communion of your race.

Nathaniel Hawthorne,
Young Goodman Brown

THIRTY-EIGHT

She came like the grey promise of dawn, a shadow passing through the sleepy suburb, moving over the sidewalks with bandaged legs, her frail hands clutching a worn bible. The day was not yet warm to arthritic bones, so she wore a loose purple shawl across her shoulders, a cobweb clinging to another time.

Her name was Halford, from the English, a title meaning she was born among the privileged, that her family had been allowed into the great manor house of a Richmond dynasty. And she was Victoria. Born in 1892. The last of her clan.

She stood at an intersection while waiting to cross, shielding her face from a slight rain. With a turn of a traffic light she carried herself past waiting motorists, eyes would seem to stare upon her but fail to see; the snow white hair in thinning patches, the stooped back curved like some old walking cane, bent with the unseen weight of a mighty hand.

She did not look back, entering the parking lot, a shadow among shadows, barely moving, hardly there. And it took long moments for her to catch her breath, standing in her dress shoes among the foul weeds, beneath a huge section of pink aluminium, large as a billboard, that had once advertised Patriots Bowl in tall white letters.

Slowly she edged across the wet and broken pavement, coming to the wooden basket-weave fence at the rear of the lot. This was her destination. And with spindly hands she opened to a marked passage in the Good Book. With her head held high, thin lips went trembling over words that had carried her through a lifetime of toil. A threatening rain dampened pages as she lifted her face to the sky, remembering her singing voice, and this was something only she could hear, for the years had laid virtue to ruin. She hummed with a gentle dryness of breath under the secret gaze of a small boy who had come to share the final moments of her world.

Victoria Halford had stopped visiting when the lanes were operating, her time for remembrances host to drunken gamesmen. But at ninety-six years, Patriots Bowl's brief tenure over the land blew through her mind like candles on a cake, and she smiled, a dark line curving proud and contemptuous. Her position in the thick weeds offered a crooked line of sight to the Jansons' compact townhouse, and she heard voices, glancing in this direction while adjusting her shawl.

'Hi, Mom!'

'Oh Elmer!' a woman's voice scolded. 'Don't you Hi Mom me, your hands are like ice, this isn't summer.'

'But she's there,' he said shyly, and Victoria heard this; as somewhere deep inside the boy a shadow turned mournfully over.

The window closed with a sharp knock.

Victoria Halford lifted her head in hymn.

Jack Scott pulled a set of high-powered glasses away from his eyes, resting these on the Chrysler's dashboard, his face puzzled, yet filled with wonder.

'That's really incredible,' Rivers offered quietly.

'Yes, yes it is.'

'If we hadn't been looking for her, I'm not sure we would have seen this.'

'I saw,' Scott pondered. 'Where did she come from?'

From their position in the 7-11 parking lot on River Road, they had an unobstructed view of three long suburban blocks, which included the bowling alley some two hundred yards to the left; on the right, the intersection of Little Falls Parkway.

Almost directly across the street the small white church Jim Cooley had said was the last tangible remains of Tobytown was sandwiched between a twenty-six-storey highrise apartment and a modern office building. The latter had been designed by a Frank Lloyd Wright enthusiast who had failed lamentably in his basic understanding, and was rather typical of Bethesda.

Before she left the alley, Victoria Halford removed a small package from her purse, leaning it with care against the wooden fence, closing her hands in prayer.

'Pogo to base,' Rudy Marchette chirped through the radio, and while Scott heard only the words that came from inside the bowling alley, Rivers heard serious fatigue. The rookie was badly in need of sleep.

'Go ahead,' he responded, having grabbed the microphone.

'She's left something behind, a small package, do you want recovery?'

Rivers looked towards Scott for direction, he was dressed in his best charcoal grey suit, all three pieces, with a conservative silver and blue tie. He was continuing surveillance through a windshield that was heavy with mist that looked like a coating of wax. Around them, the pavement and buildings all but sparkled.

'Pogo, what's your rotation time?' Rivers asked.

'Uh, any moment, I hope.'

'Then make that a negative, the package can wait.'

'Roger, she should be on you about now.'

Victoria Halford came steady as time, pushing herself gently down the sidewalk towards the open doors of the Shiloh Baptist Church. The sun was just beginning to cast shadows as the street lights snapped off.

'That's affirmative,' Rivers spoke into the microphone, 'check back at your shift change.'

'Roger that.'

Scott put the glasses back on the dash. 'What did Jim Cooley find out?'

'If it's the same woman,' he reached for a notebook, 'she's from a family of masons and stonecutters, they used to work on the memorials, Lincoln, Jefferson, that kind of thing. Many of the foundations were laid with the rock and stone of Cabin John and other Maryland towns. Victoria Halford, that's what some deacon told him from the description, she's the daughter of slaves who were freed towards the end of the war.'

'She is truly astonishing,' Scott puzzled aloud.

Rivers shook his head. 'You want to talk amazing, Jack, how about a little ten-year-old boy and this ancient woman somehow hooking up and befriending each other, and no one even knew about it. That blows my mind. Elmer told me they share *his* secret place, but I'll bet Victoria Halford was visiting before I was even born.'

Scott chuckled. 'And Victoria leaves little gifts for him?'

'Well, one time she left him a hand-carved wooden boat, it's gotta be older than dirt. And then last year Elmer made her a bird feeder at school, then left it by the fence on Christmas Eve.'

Scott turned towards him. 'So where from here, Cooley suggested what kind of approach?'

'Neighbour to neighbour, he said showing a badge in church is like taking a shit in bed. It might help if you were black, you're gonna stand out like a sore thumb.' Rivers went silent as the lyric sounds of a choir came drifting from across the street, a hundred human voices like canting ghosts, marching distantly at first, then dancing closely with some clarity and rhythm.

'Gives me shivers,' said Frank.

'Gospel, moves the soul,' Scott returned, 'they must be practising, according to the sign services don't start for an hour.'

The sound was growing, swelling, beginning to echo gently against the highrise apartments. Glancing up, Rivers could see balcony doors sliding shut. 'So how do you assess our risk at this point?' he asked. 'You've got a make on Zak's car, an ugly duck like that's an easy target for an air search.'

'No,' Scott shook his head, 'that car will be well hidden, believe me, it's a waste of time.'

'But you're sure it was him?'

'It was him, the hole in the Jansons' radiator was way too precise, I'm sure he had a detailed abduction plan or he wouldn't have approached. At least we know he's working with a woman.'

'That part really turns my gut. How about with the Claytons, was she involved?'

'That's my best guess, so it's starting to make sense. At any rate I should formally thank you for placing a transmitter on the Jansons' car.' Scott was watching Victoria finish her climb up some steps and into the small church. 'The ones we ordered from Captain Drury just came in an hour ago.'

Rivers nodded.

'I checked on the Pennsylvania licence tags they were using last night, reported stolen six months ago and came from an identical car, an early model Ford Maverick. Zak Dorani is the only one who would care about those little details.'

'What shape is Elmer and his mother in?'

'Fine, considering what I told her, that Elmer's interest may have attracted a stalker, but she doesn't know what kind, just that we've been watching them and there's some danger. She's pretty well shook, but if you want to know the truth I think she's been sensing something all along, this is a very bright young lady.'

'I already know that,' Rivers stated with concern. 'I want them out of town, Jack, I won't allow you to use this woman as some sort of decoy.'

Scott turned, looking at Rivers. 'It wouldn't make any difference, Frank.' He rubbed a fist into eyes that had gone red from lack of sleep. 'Zak will just hunt other victims until she returns, then he'll take her and the boy when we're no longer around. He doesn't give up, in fact, this miss of his will be perceived as a challenge, very enticing, just adds to the thrill. No,' he paused, 'we've only got one chance at this.'

Rivers was draining the last from his first cup of morning coffee. 'Jack, I'm not doubting you, but about that car?'

Scott smiled. 'Am I sure it was a woman driver, it was pouring rain, and where was Zak?'

Rivers nodded.

'It was a female Pilot. And even if I hadn't seen her, the approach was way too tentative, just too cautious. In a hunter-prey situation like that a man's body dumps a chemical high-ball of adrenaline and testosterone, the system goes wild. So the closing attack would have been more dramatic and less controlled.'

'Then where was Zak, you said the car looked empty?'

'I've thought about that quite a bit, the floor would have been too obvious.' He removed his glasses from his top pocket. 'My guess would be in the trunk with some type of false access panel in the back. One of the things he craves is shock value, the pleasure of a quick and merciless attack.'

'Jesus, what evil . . .'

'Right,' he agreed, 'and just like all the other Pilots we've discussed, which are almost invariably men, he's outdone himself this time. He'll be manipulating her like a robot, Zak understands the psychology of this type of relationship better than we do.' Scott's voice sounded distant.

'What's upsetting you, Jack, the Clayton house? You saw something?'

'Yes,' he nodded. 'Zak and this woman are the perfect hunter-killer team.' Just then a car came roaring into the parking lot, heading directly for them and pulling alongside. A pleasant-looking man got out and strolled for the store.

'So what did I miss?' he asked apologetically.

'You missed nothing, Frank, and I have no tangible proof in terms of direct physical evidence for what I think.' With those words, Scott's voice changed, dropping a pitch while his face registered fatigue.

'Well, something's bugging you?'

Scott was rubbing fists into bloodshot eyes. 'This is hard for me to explain, but what I saw was a rather withdrawn and shy little girl, very passive and unsure, hardly able to speak above a whisper, which is nothing at all like I had expected.'

Rivers raised an eyebrow, uncomfortable with what he was hearing. 'You're a strange man, how the hell is it possible to tell any of that, no one I canvassed knew her that well, at least . . .'

Scott swallowed, holding up one hand.

'Hey, wait a minute!' Rivers caught up suddenly. 'That's what I didn't understand about you! I get it,' he said excitedly, 'you use your feelings to interpret a crime scene!'

'Very good, Frank,' Scott smiled, 'it's called emotional reading, the use of feelings, perception and imagination, the same type a writer or a painter uses. I've learned to refine mine into somewhat of an art, that's not an exaggeration.'

'No, I believe it.'

Scott nodded. 'Then you *do* understand the principles of the Devoid, like androids, robots of pure intellect?'

Rivers was smiling at himself.

'So my single most powerful weapon is precisely what they lack, the human substance, you could learn to do the same.'

'So you're telling me you felt them, the Claytons, I mean?'

'Last night I spent a good deal of time employing all the detail I'd memorised about their lives, envisioning each of them as individuals, and how they lived together as a family.'

'So what was different than you thought?'

'Everything,' he concluded. 'For instance, when I first saw Kimberly's photograph I was sure I was dealing with a mischievous little monkey who couldn't be controlled, she had this slight turn to her mouth,' he rubbed the corners of his lips with a finger, 'impish, almost teasing, a smirk, if you will. Yet inside,' Scott thumped his chest, 'she was grinning, even laughing, she was just too timid to produce or display that. Everyone else in the family smiled with a natural ease, but Kimberly was shy, even a bit withdrawn.'

'Go on, I'm following this.'

'So her mother was working to compensate. On Diana's nightstand I found *Small Wonder*, a classic text on childhood shyness. Based on this advice she had established little spaces throughout the child's territory like small comforting islands. A shy child engages in more quiet activities, so Diana was allowing Kimberly to plant flowers by the front door, I found only her shoeprints there. That space was Kim's because she was the first arrival home from school. She would play near

399

the front door because it gave her an open feeling, not quite as vulnerable, waiting for the rest of her family.'

'You're freaking me out, Jack,' Rivers sighed, 'I'm not sure I could get to know them that well.'

'We'll talk about it,' Scott concluded. 'How about a cup of coffee, I'm dragging like an old whore.'

'It's on me,' he quickly returned, and Scott leaned back into his seat checking his watch, closing his eyes as Rivers climbed out and an inky black Porsche pulled in, snout first, parking alongside the little blue Chrysler.

Scott turned his head away as a middle aged man popped out, swinging his legs onto the pavement, then straightening his light blue sports coat, tugging at the bottom seams. He spotted Scott's relaxed elbow poking in his direction and moved slowly alongside.

'Hi neighbour!' he smiled. 'Where are you from in Maine?'

Scott's face fell vacant as his thoughts went leaping into space, he had forgotten his car sprouted Maine licence plates, and this was of no significance to him. He had merely grabbed the first set from his trunk when he left New York two days ago, an entirely random selection from a dozen good choices.

'A small town, you wouldn't know it,' Scott returned absently. But the man shuffled closer, leaning down with some enthusiasm.

'Well, I might, I'm from a small town myself, Kennebunkport. Small's nothing to be ashamed of!'

Scott smiled weakly.

'So what town?' he beamed, and Scott blinked, still fighting to find himself after three hours' sleep, so he fired off the first name that came to mind.

'Moxie Pond,' he offered without tone.

'Hummm,' the man was surely humming with joy. 'That's not a seaport, all the same I should know it.'

'No,' he replied, still staring into space. 'It's an agricultural village in Western Maine, population 628.' And that's really about all he knew, except that a young woman by the name of Lacy Darleen Wilcott had come from there, that her life had been destroyed, and that her ravaged body had been dumped like so much garbage onto a trash pile off Florida's Coastal Highway. It had been discovered by a midnight hauler, and at 4:46 a.m., Scott had been notified by the ViCAT slot as Captain Duncan Powell of the Florida State Police was pressing for his personal and immediate inter-diction.

ViCAT was dispatching Agent Matthew Brennon as Lacy's parents were just being notified; and Scott's new neighbour had not stopped talking for one bleary second.

'. . . and so I think we will become well known as the family state, you'll see that I'm right.'

Scott looked up, his face tired and impatient. Rivers was coming up behind the man while sucking red currant jelly through a donut hole. He reached beyond the stranger, handing Scott a large cup of coffee.

'So I overheard,' Rivers questioned. 'You're a political speech writer?'

'Why yes.' The man looked puzzled. 'How did you know?'

'Your bumper-sticker.'

The man nodded. 'Are you also from Maine?'

'Nope.' Rivers lifted a lip, exposing front teeth, pointing to his face with a torpedo creampuff. 'What's this?' he hissed.

'I don't know.'

'That means I'm from the nut factory up the road, Dad here just paid to have my screws rethreaded so I don't hurt people any more.'

Scott spat black juice into his cup. 'Frank?' he frowned.

'Yes, Dad, can we go to the pet store? I'm still hungry.'

The man chuckled. 'You fellas are having some fun with me, good chatting with you.'

'And with you,' Scott returned.

As the man walked off, the Commander gave Sergeant Rivers a cold stare. 'Was that really necessary?' he asked.

But the resulting silences seemed to validate a mutual understanding that went deeper than speeches, far deeper than words. It was several moments before they spoke again.

'Hey, Jack, what was all that shit about, a kinder and gentler nation?'

Scott held up his hands in surrender. 'Hell if I know, but the American people will never buy it.'

THIRTY-NINE

Dudley Wren Hall had arrived alone.

He stood in the doorway of the command post clutching a paper bag that contained a blue enamel urn, a yellow cab waiting at his back while he was looking for a doorbell. If this was hidden, the Diggerman from Woodlawn had faith he could find it somewhere on the moulding of the funny tower of a house, not wanting to tarnish the shiny brass knocker with an uncaring and sweaty palm. He had been raised better than that.

He was dressed in his Sunday best, a light brown suit, faded blue shirt and red tie, this was extra wide at the bottom but since he kept his jacket buttoned it did not matter. He rested a large heavy travel case in the corner and had begun to look in earnest for the bell when the door swung wide. He was bent at the waist searching for wires along the baseboard as Frank Rivers spoke. 'Mr Hall?' he asked, raising his eyebrows.

'That I am,' he chirped through a missing front row, 'call me Duddy. Note said to ring the doorbell, ain't no doorbell.'

'Yes sir,' said Rivers, 'it's connected to the knocker, pull it back and the chime rings, pretty foolish, wouldn't you say?'

'That I would, son.' He straightened up. 'Cabbie wants a tip, they didn't give me no tip.' And he seemed either annoyed or disoriented, Rivers couldn't tell which.

'Come on in, I'll take care of it,' he said as a large man came forward across the blue carpeting to greet Dudley. He was wide with massive features and had the air of New England aristocracy.

'Hello, Charles McQuade,' he offered the Diggerman, 'I've heard a lot about you.'

'And I you,' Hall chirped, taking his hand firmly, then handing him the urn. 'Burnt man, they said it was important.'

McQuade examined the burial can, and its broken seal, and then turned to lay it on the coffee table in the kitchen. 'Thank you,' he said, 'can I . . .'

"You FBI?" Hall asked, cutting him off. 'Only lab that kin handle burnt man is the FBI.'

McQuade smiled. 'I'm from the Armed Forces Institute. Can I fix you a drink?'

'Flew in first class, filled me right up. Is that young fella in charge?' he asked, removing his jacket, then wandering for the living room. He slung his brown jacket over a sculpture that resembled a large paperclip melting. 'That get caught in a fire?'

'It does look like it,' McQuade agreed.

Hall had now unbuttoned and removed his shirt as Rivers was closing the door, approaching from the rear. From this angle the Diggerman looked like a human refrigerator, his large corded arms failing to hang limp, his shoulders and back massive for a little man, his neck like a block of wood. When he spoke, his voice sounded funny, high pitched, as if he had swallowed a bird whistle.

'Mr Hall, we've made up a room for you,' Rivers offered.

'That's very kind, young fella, I won't be staying long. Are there any archaeologists on your team?'

'No,' he shook his head. 'Dr McQuade does have some background.'

'I'm a forensic pathologist, I only dabble.'

'Whelp,' Hall chirped, 'we'll be working too fast to dabble, archaeologists bitch we're destroying things, ain't got no time for bitchin'.'

As Rivers and McQuade looked on inquisitively, Hall quickly pulled his work boots from a zipper bag, dropping his slacks, then slinging these over the artwork. 'Wonder what that was,' said the Diggerman, staring down at the sculpture. 'If it was bought by Department of State, could very well be their view of the world, you know, all twisted up and filled with shine like that.'

Rivers smiled incredulously. 'Scott told you about this place?'

'Known Jackie mostta my years, said this place would charge my battery, renew the old vinegar.'

'How's that?' asked McQuade.

Hall was stepping into his work clothes, a baggy suit of khaki overalls with a zipper from crotch to neck. 'This house was built by the federals, and I've been fighting a personal war with the IRS ever since Korea. Fools don't know the difference 'tween a knocker and a doorbell, but they're sure willing to spend my money to get it. I'll be writing my Congressman.'

There was no disagreement to be found as Dudley Hall reached inside his pants, adjusting his plaid boxer shorts. 'Where's dis place?' he asked.

'Across the street,' Rivers offered.

'And there's no warrant, Jackie said we're trespassing?'

'No paperwork at all.'

'Good,' Hall chirped, 'we're here to catch a baby killer, ain't that right?'

'That's right.'

Hall nodded as he lifted and then straightened his thin dress slacks across the polished metal, then found a bottle of talc, shaking this into his boots. As he was slipping these over bare feet his eyes wandered to the centre of the room, finding a leather couch with a chrome and glass coffee table. He was sitting to tie his laces when he saw it, his eyes caught by the human face that appeared with golden lenses glinting at him from a child's features. It was so lifelike he startled, raising back up, then pondering the clay and plaster bust, reaching to touch a cheek with a weathered palm.

Around the little girl's neck hung a shiny new silver chain, and Diggerman Hall held this in his palm, looking up at McQuade with an expression suddenly grown quite severe.

'You make this child?' he asked quietly.

McQuade nodded, looking down at the haunting face.

There was a special innocence that radiated from her smile and the high subtle cheekbones. Dudley Hall quickly glanced away, over to the empty corner of the room, and Rivers could see the man's jaw muscles ticking.

'What's her name?' Hall swallowed quietly, looking in the opposite direction.

'Don't know,' Rivers replied.

Hall nodded thoughtfully, returning to look at the child. 'Do you have any whisky?'

'Black Jack,' Rivers stated.

'One shot,' said the Diggerman, 'helps fight the dew.' And Rivers strolled for the kitchen as Hall returned to lacing his boots.

'When was she killed?' he asked McQuade without looking up.

'Thirty-one years ago, in April, we believe, cause of death . . .'

Hall had raised a massive, silencing hand. 'That little boy found her, yes, she was buried under the asphalt?'

'Correct,' said Rivers, handing him a shotglass of brown fluid. Dudley Hall made a fist around this, splashing the liquid back into his throat, handing back the glass.

'Does she have any kin?'

'No, not that we can find,' Rivers said sadly.

Diggerman Hall came abruptly to his feet, lightly stroking her head. The hair was fine and silken to the touch.

'She does now,' he chirped with conviction, 'that I'd truly have to say.'

'Aliens,' Elmer repeated under his breath, and he was embarrassed for the confession. That's what they had been to the imagination of a ten-year-old child, these weeds that didn't belong; weeds that were somehow different from all the rest.

The boy stood nervously in the bright morning light, his reddish hair freshly washed and shimmering, his mint green eyes looking up at Detective Rivers as his mother watched, growing increasingly uneasy.

'It will only take a moment,' he comforted, holding Elmer's

treasure guide in his hand. Jessica nodded agreement as Rivers began to read.

'Study plant growth, previous disturbances often result in a noticeable change in vegetation.'

'I was just playing,' Elmer said quietly, 'I didn't know I'd find a body.'

Rivers nodded, scanning the parking lot behind the old alley. To him, and to Charles McQuade and to Dudley Hall, it was very easy to understand what had attracted a curious little boy. If you made an effort to notice, and it did require an effort, then Patriots Bowl was a genuine eyesore. The building itself was low slung, set back from the street into shadow, and it sat on nearly an acre of littered ground. Around it, and directly across the street, expensive office buildings belied its existence with properties priced like ocean view lots.

There was a rusted fence that was overgrown with weeds, split and broken asphalt, a roof collapsing in sections, and paint peeling from holes and windows. More importantly, it was gloomy, dank, and forbidding. A very spooky place.

More importantly, it was boarded shut.

'And you had been watching where the plum-headed aliens were growing?' Rivers asked, looking down at the child.

Elmer nodded, as from inside the alley Team Pogo watched with interest as three men and a woman came marching through the lot, being led by a little boy.

In the rear of the alley, the blacktop was sinking in more than a dozen sections, and standing back, there were more than twenty fountains of weeds, plum-heads, standing tall against short croppings of green grasses and wild straw. Some sprouted just ten feet from where Elmer Janson had found the remains, and Dudley Hall hovered, holding a thin metal rod in his hand; a device which Scott had procured especially for him.

Hall tamped the asphalt with his toe, then grabbed a clump of wet weeds and tore them from the ground. Already, Jessica Janson was alarmed, checking her eyes against Rivers, who nodded, as Hall fell forward onto his knees, inserting the rod into a crack in the pavement.

He was now working this carefully, turning the rod between heavy padded work gloves, able to look directly eye to eye with Elmer. 'Sooo . . .' his mouth went round with the sound, and the boy backed up a few inches, standing before Frank Rivers.

To a child's eyes, Dudley Hall was a hard-looking old man, his face was worn, the leathery skin beaten into a patchwork of lines and crevices. He was now rubbing the rod back and forth between his palms, not looking where he was working, but Elmer could see the metal probe mysteriously sinking into the wet pavement.

'Young fella, hear you got a special friend, hellava good hound by the name of Dipper.'

Elmer looked up to his mother, and with a flitting breeze Jessica could smell whisky on the man's breath. She did not care for this, patting the boy's shoulder, bringing him to her side.

'His name's Tripod,' Elmer said shyly. 'He's part wolf.'

'Elmer,' she corrected softly, and Hall smiled.

'Every boy should have a dog,' he chirped. 'Your friend Jack Scott told me about him, missing a front leg, he said, he's missing a paw?'

Elmer was immediately defensive. 'He's still good as any dog,' he said under his breath as Hall worked the thin rod, nodding thoughtfully. The thing of steel was now some three feet down into the wet clay beneath the asphalt.

'Whelp,' said the Diggerman, 'there's something in that bag for him.' He tilted his head, nodding at a brown paper sack. 'I brought it special from New York City jest for him.'

The probe stopped moving and Hall pinched it between his forefingers, pulling it back like the string of a bow, giving it a snap. It sang for one strong second, just two feet of hard metal poking up from the ground and humming. Elmer Janson's eyes were bright and wide as he stared down at the bag and Dudley Hall came to his feet, lifting it, placing it at the boy's dress shoes.

'That's for him,' Dudley offered the mother.

She released her hold as Elmer's eyes danced. He was

leaning over the bag, peering in with curiousness, then reaching in with confusion, lifting an object he had never seen before. It was made of a heavy white nylon with bright chrome buttons, all connected to metal beams with three soft leather belts. The mask of freckles pulled tight across the boy's face as he examined it, confusion working on him.

'What is it?' Elmer asked excitedly.

Dr McQuade stepped forward, smiling broadly. 'You're very kind,' he said to the old Diggerman, then leaned over and took the thing from the boy, anxious to inspect the device. It was very professional, very precise.

'Elmer,' McQuade offered, 'this is a prosthesis, do you know what that is?'

The boy shook his head.

'It's a false leg, I've seen them on police dogs who were hurt, it's very rare.'

The grin that resulted looked to be breaking the boy's face, his green eyes wide and brimming with joy. 'A false leg!' he beamed. 'Mom, it's a leg for Tripod!'

Dudley Hall nodded, looking up to Frank Rivers. 'Young fella,' he said, 'you work with the K-9 Corps?'

'Sure do,' he nodded.

'Get one of them boys to help with this.' Then he turned to Elmer, placing his hands on his knees and bending down. 'Seen these work, son, that hound of yours will be running like he was born with it. A little patience, a little love, he'll never know he was hobbled.' And with that the Diggerman held three coarse fingers out, then added a fourth.

'What do you say, Elmer?' Jessica quickly nudged.

'Thanks, Mr Hall,' he said excitedly, 'thanks an awful lot!'

'You're very welcome. That was made for a famous police dog up north, an extra.' He straightened back up, his eyes levelled at Rivers. The detective gave a nod, turning to the young mother.

'Time to go?' he asked.

Jessica Janson stepped forward. 'Thank you so much, for Elmer and Tripod,' she said, smiling warmly at the old

Diggerman, then reaching up she kissed him lightly on the cheek. 'Bless you.'

'Sure nuff, sweet lady,' he answered through a broken row.

Rivers was tugging his tie, making sure it was straight, when he felt a soft hand against his forearm. With a slight smile Jessica moved to face him, gently pulling his tie, rearranging his collar, then pushing the knot into place. 'When's the last time you went to church?' she whispered.

'Mom,' Elmer said suddenly, slipping his hand up into hers, 'why do we have to go? We can make it up next Sunday.'

Jessica Janson had started to speak as Rivers turned quickly, grabbing the boy under his arms, lifting him through air and onto his shoulder.

'Time for church,' he said, his eyes locked on Jessica Janson.

'Pliers,' Hall demanded.

Charles McQuade pulled them from a toolbox and the Diggerman pinched the rod in a vice-grip, spinning the metal 360-degrees, twisting and twisting, like unscrewing a long thin bolt.

'It's dere,' he whistled, his face stern with concentration as he grabbed a wooden slab from his bag, threading this onto the rod through a hole. The block of wood dropped, slapping the ground, and he was finding a machine nut in a zipper pocket, then tightening this into place on top.

'Are you locked tight?' asked McQuade.

Hall stopped shaking the stiffness from his arms, then placed a boot on either side of the rod. 'Hold that ground,' he nodded at his toe, and McQuade stood closer, placing his shoes together directly over the spot.

Hall spread his legs, these like massive hams on his short frame, then leaning over he picked up the block, sliding it to the top of the rod where it formed a T-bar type handle. The device was an old fashioned retrieving iron known as a Dirt Cannon, the bane of professional archaeologists, for it always destroyed what scientists thought of as context, or the three-dimensional placement of an object in space.

410

There were other names for the weird tool, fouling gun, looter's spade, digger's sword; it had been used since the time of Dickens to discover and rob from the dead.

McQuade nodded, and the Diggerman lowered his torso at the knees like a sumo wrestler, grabbing the beam with leather work gloves, looking up to the gentle scientist. And with all the strength that was the Diggerman, he pulled and strained until his face looked like a ripe tomato, gas discharging in a flatulent tear as he moaned, the ground rising into a hill; McQuade's considerable mass rocking as if on the deck of a small boat.

Hall relaxed his grip and the wave of earth settled again as he spat, shaking the cramps from both arms.

'Is it?' asked McQuade.

'It is,' Hall said grimly.

Having applied his full mass beneath the fouling gun, Dudley Hall was pulling with all his might. The steel rod bent and tilted as through the hole between his boots the red dirt fizzed, spilling up onto his toes, the shaft seeming to grow by inches, the ground rising in a small swell which the scientist rode in anticipation.

Then, with a sudden tearing of asphalt, the rod snapped free, Dudley Hall stumbling backward with a wad of red dirt attached to the end of the tool. His barrel chest was heaving, his face a patchwork of blue veins as he held the instrument out to Dr Charles McQuade.

'Snagged cloth,' he winced.

McQuade carefully leaned the sword onto a sheet of clear plastic, scraping the tip clean as the Diggerman was already turning to insert it back into the fractured ground. 'Hold on a minute,' McQuade cautioned, 'we're directly over a skull.'

'How's that?' he wheezed.

'It's not cloth,' he said, 'it's hair.'

And he and Hall quickly dropped to their knees, working the wet wad with a small pick, McQuade's massive fingers separating the sections of dirt as a chunk of bone glistened in the light, holding the empty sockets of two teeth. Their eyes

411

met, Hall's face transformed into a mask of seething anger.

'How old, Doc?' he swallowed.

McQuade held a sliver of jaw and tooth fragment between his fingers. 'Second year molar, no surface wear, no tartar stains, late teens or early twenties. Female from the looks of the hair.'

'One thing's for sure,' the Diggerman said, 'that was not an embalmed body, the ground was turned fertile with flesh, I know the difference.'

McQuade agreed, rising to his full height, pointing at the next clump of aliens just beyond the *No Dumping* sign. 'Let's move on,' he suggested. 'This was a young Caucasian, her hair was blonde.'

Hall's shovel bit with dark precision, slicing through blacktop, lifting pieces away as if picking at a large pie crust, placing these into a neat stack while clearing ground.

The fouling gun had struck three times, McQuade was examining slivers of clothing, marking each find against a blueprint of the site. They were still outside of the building envelope, working their way towards the wall that was the alley's rear.

Dudley Hall took a long pull from a water jug, sprinkling his head, then edging a square into the ground, marking off a section. The spade struck dead centre, slowly slicing down at a tilted angle, and he was now working the handle, back and forth repeatedly, looking into the large brown eyes of Dr McQuade.

'We've got something 'ere, dirt's froze,' he whistled, wiggling the blade.

'Compacted?'

'Real tight.' Hall stopped, moving the blade a foot, then reinserting it with some precision and working it flat beneath the ground like a giant spoon. He lifted and discarded a slab of red clay, then grabbing a jug, he sprinkled water into the pit. He was kneeling over the hole, wiping with a gloved hand. 'Look here,' he said as McQuade stood over.

They were staring down at a naturally flat stone that had

412

been rather shallowly inscribed. With two massive arms, Dudley Hall heaved the object from its resting place, exposing a brass circular ring, picking this up and handing it to McQuade.

'What is it?'

'Casket handle, pre-Civil War, I'd guess.' He poured more water over the stone, the engraved letters showing in red where the clay had leached through the years. 'Cornelius T. Mott,' he read, 'died 1860. That's quite a marker for the time, well respected gent, would be my guess.'

'God, what is wrong with people?' McQuade sighed as Hall picked up his tools and moved on. 'This was a cemetery, they put a bowling alley right over it.'

'Yep, look around, dead been comin' to rest 'ere since long before we was born.'

'My guess is that they chose to build an alley because it was simple slab construction, it wouldn't require anything but a few inches of dirt beneath the building.'

'No cellar anyhow.'

'Duddy, from the lot size what would you guess the population would be?'

'Better than 600 souls resting 'ere, plus what the killer added over the years.'

They moved past the rusted engine block to a gold fountain of weeds that all but swirled with strange growth. 'Here's the way we think it happened,' McQuade offered, flipping through a bound report, the records of the River Road properties. 'They knew there was a cemetery, but the original building permit says it was a vacant lot as of 1957 when the property was seized from the Shiloh Baptist Church.'

'Back taxes?'

'Right, claimed by the county government, then sold to the highest bidder.'

'You can't legislate decency,' Hall spat, clearing his mouth, then dropping in a fresh chaw of tobacco. 'Who bought it?'

'January of 1958, two thousand dollars and change, the new owner,' he shuffled pages, 'was recorded as a Dr R. Jaffe.' Charles McQuade, reviewing the file, did not notice that the

413

ground next to him had broken free and that Dudley Hall was emptying his fifth shovelful of clay.

'Well, he should be ashamed,' Hall said, working the spade. 'And it also explains why this old building has never been torn down; if you dig this deep,' he pointed to the blade, 'you'll be swimming with caskets and headstones. Did our girl have a sister?' he asked in a sombre whistle.

McQuade quickly came to his feet, as with a gentleness that one would not expect from a gravedigger, Dudley Hall swung the shovel up with his right arm, cradling the blade with his left. At the end of an outstretched spade was a small human skull, stained red from years at rest in the clay, with long black hair carefully woven into braids that had endured.

There was a finger's worth of this fine hair neatly preserved between the jaws and teeth, a Latin style cross swinging before them, metering time, dangling from a rotted silver chain.

Dr Charles Rand McQuade did not require a close inspection; high brow, gentle and sculpted cheeks, large sockets to accommodate golden lenses.

This was family.

It had taken him twenty hours to build her sister, and he knew this child with his heart.

Dudley Wren Hall had nothing to say, here at the beginning; counting off, then marking other spots where outcroppings of lush weeds sprouted through spongy asphalt. The vegetation was growing thick from human nutrients in a sun that was hot and bright.

They removed their shirts.

They worked in silence.

FORTY

The Shiloh Baptist Church was a small hallway of brick and beam, built on a gentle rise of hill, and painted white inside and out. The roof was simple grey shingles with a plain wooden cross. The windows were thick leaded glass.

As Scott climbed whitewashed steps he could hear a deep bass voice reciting a passage from *Luke* and could see a gathering of bowed heads, all nodded forward in prayer. At the front of the assembly, the choir hummed quietly in bright blue robes, kneeling in a semicircle around the altar and orator.

There were twenty-five pews on either side of the aisle, and these were all filled with the faithful. As he stood in the doorway, a small black man came forward quietly, Scott guessing his age at seventy or better. He was a powerfully built little man in a starched white shirt and black suit, with arms and shoulders that seemed too large for his body. He wore a tie that matched his red braces, his hair a powdery white fringe, his voice and eyes like troubled pools. He extended his hand in greeting, and Scott noticed his knuckles were swollen with arthritis.

'Thank you for coming,' he said. 'I am the Deacon Atticus Cory.'

'John Scott,' he smiled, looking over him and through the doorway for Victoria Halford.

'Mr Cooley expressed your interest in speaking with Mrs Halford and I have mentioned this to her. He told you that her memory seems to come and go?'

'I understand,' Scott nodded, 'I wish there were some other way.'

The service continued as the gentle swell of organ music piped a prelude through the open doors. Scott watched with intensity as a large woman stood, leaving the rest of the choir behind, coming forward to the small white altar.

'We'll wait until vespers are completed, then we'll go in before the offering.'

'That would be fine, thank you. Does Mrs Halford live nearby? She walks to church, I am told.'

The deacon's eyes pinched ever so slightly at the corners. 'No,' he blinked, 'Victoria has her own pilgrimage every Sunday, and that worries us, her bones are very brittle. She lives in Tobytown, that's about twenty miles north.'

Scott nodded. 'And how does she get here?'

'Taxi to River Road, then she lets herself out at different spots along the way so that she can walk to church, that's very important to her.'

'Then she's alone,' he heard himself saying.

'No, Mr Scott, she is not alone,' the deacon corrected sharply, turning back towards the congregation as the organ music swelled and the soloist's alto voice bloomed, a sweet and graceful sound that was filling the little sanctuary and spilling blissfully through the open doors. The deacon took Scott by the arm, leading him over thick gold carpeting, moving slowly down the aisle. And he felt as if every eye were beating down on him with consternation as they came to the first pew and a young woman looked up, scooting down, making room. Just next to her sat Victoria Halford, her eyes closed in silent prayer, her white gloved hands clutched to her chest with ever a slight tremble.

Before he sat, Scott looked up towards the altar, seeing the blue robed choir at the ready, the candles burning in white fury before the saints, a carved crucifix suspended from above. He genuflected, crossing himself before taking the last seat on the row, and the Reverend, seeing this, lowered his head, though he did not smile.

As he positioned himself against the hard rosewood bench, Scott suddenly felt very relaxed, the firm support against sore muscles at his back easing a tired ache. He felt cool, and pleasantly so, an overhead fan pulsing gently from high ceiling beams, the downward draught producing a sedative effect on his body. He closed his eyes, feeling the fatigue of the last seventy-two hours dragging him down, and he found himself thinking back instead of forward, hearing Matthew Brennon's voice on the phone only two days earlier as he was just finishing lamb chops with jelly.

'Sweet Jesus, you've made a cross,' he had said, and Scott opened his eyes, fighting to remain alert with the congregation. Brennon had been studying the Clayton photographic crime scene on his office wall, and the choir was now humming a song that Scott did not know, though it touched him, just so, slowing the beat of his heart and making him feel light-headed. And he heard the questioning voice of Frank Rivers in his mind.

'What did you see in there, Jack, something's upsetting you?' Scott gave a relaxing sigh, rubbing fists into bloodshot eyes.

'My single most powerful weapon is precisely the substance which Recreational Killers lack, they are Devoid, they cannot feel. Without feelings, anything becomes possible . . .'

'Are you sure it was him?'

'I was in that house and I know it is so.' But did he really, Scott was asking himself, and it was back then, there in the grey dawn, that they saw the old woman appear, coming out from the shadows.

Scott watched as a tall young man came forward to the altar, thinking he looked like a law student, maybe a doctor. The man started a sermon, falling into a monotone as the rustle of voices and pages around him fell into total silence. Somewhere past the opening statement, Scott's chin fell gently against his chest.

He did not dream. He would not remember falling asleep.

The young woman was nudging him gently with her elbow.

The Commander started, hearing gentle laughter, the voices of children floating overhead like thought balloons, the sound of the organ pipes playing an interlude as he was opening eyes filled with embarrassment, staring down into a worn wooden bowl, a church heirloom used as a collection plate. It was filled with small white envelopes.

'Sorry,' he smiled weakly to her, then at the well dressed man on the aisle who was holding the tray at the ready. He fumbled into a coat pocket removing a twenty-dollar bill, which he laid on top, and it looked crude in its naked form, a vulgar green among the carefully sealed givings, and he felt eyes covering him again. Carefully, he took the plate into his left hand as it was passed, and he caught the soft brown lenses of Victoria Halford soaking over his form like drifting clouds. She was a kind but fragile-looking thing, her hands peaceful in her lap, her shoulders stooped and uncertain.

Scott gave a gentleman's nod, then quietly reached back into a deep pocket as she studied him, his fist coming slowly out, extending towards her in the tight space of the pew. Victoria saw his fist hovering over the plate just next to her, and so he gave *it* there, carefully placing it on the top of the collection.

Sealed in plastic and surrounded by white, the copper coin was burning in candlelight as Victoria's eyes grew wide with a certain recognition, and she blinked as the plate moved closer, then swallowed, her thin neck seeming to tremble as she nodded her head. Her frail hands, gloved in church white, were suddenly reaching past the plate and towards Scott as a hushed murmur began to fill the hall.

The young woman's smooth face went blank as she dropped her envelope into the dish, then passed the offering towards Victoria, helping her to support the bowl's weight as the old woman took the platter into her lap, closing her eyes; closing her arms around the thing as if cradling new born life. Alarmed, the Deacon Cory came to the aisle, studying her as gloved fingertips carefully lifted the John's Warning from its place, her thin lips parting as she inspected this, and then her mouth producing a pleasing, almost infantile sound as she rocked herself in her pew.

The deacon rushed forward, down the row behind them, his eyes locking onto her as Victoria Halford began to rise from her seat, the wooden bowl still clutched to her chest.

'What's wrong?' a child's voice could be heard, and Victoria smiled a thin, sad line, her head held high, her posture slowly unfolding with the weight of decades. She turned to face the full congregation as concerned whispers erupted and the deacon gently took the heavy bowl from her hands.

'Victoria,' he whispered, 'would you . . .'

But the *will* that was Victoria Halford, the invisible old woman from Tobytown, held up a silencing hand as she swallowed, fighting for strength, her eyes welling. She lifted her chin further still, turning directly towards Scott, and then to the amazement of all, she reached out with both of her hands.

'A pleasure,' he said in greeting as she cradled Scott's fingers, joining his hands as in prayer. And he moved towards her, his arms closing at the elbows as she held his hands to her breast. He could feel the rapid pulse of her heart, he felt his own trembling in desperate coils as he was peering deeply into her soft brown eyes. The congregation released a troubled gasp.

'Mrs Halford,' the deacon whispered, staring at Scott, eyes like hot pokers. 'Victoria . . .'

Her voice moved in a dry whisper, 'Many dangers, toils, snares . . .'

Scott leaned even closer, not sure he was understanding clearly, his police mind working its tight logic.

'. . . we have already, come.'

And the sound she made was primal, almost eternal, something he could not understand. 'I'm sorry,' he said, as a large black woman robed in a white satin gown appeared in the aisle, studying the confusion on Scott's face, then moving past him to Victoria's side.

She placed a comforting arm around her, this woman looking back towards Scott, and only because Victoria was looking at Scott. And it was hard not to see his tired anguish, so she too placed her hands over theirs. She then raised her head, adding her voice to Victoria's, and it was then that something moved deep inside of Scott; something moving that was lifting as Victoria tightened her grip, sure that the stranger would now understand, comforting him, as she gave comfort for herself.

> Through many dangers, toils and snares.
> I have, already, come.
> Tis Grace that brought me safe so far,
> And Grace will lead me Home.

And at that moment Scott felt quite certain that, upon seeing the medallion, Victoria had understood, and all of this on some deeper level that he could not cast into words, nor would he ever try. And the thought occurred to him that, somehow, though he could not be certain, it had been the old woman's interest that had captured that of Elmer Janson, and that she was the true reason he was here.

And at that moment in song, there seemed to be some sanity in the crush of madness, something decent left on earth, as the entire congregation was beginning to stand for her, coming to its feet in a spontaneous and joyful rising; Scott looking deep into wells of warmth that were her eyes.

> When we've been there ten thousand years,
> Bright shining as the sun,
> In Grace our souls will journey on.
> In Grace our work is done.

And with this hymn, with this spiritual giving he had forgotten, he found life reaching up from his own childhood with a song he somehow *knew* in his heart; yet he *did not* know it, he told himself, fighting for the words so that he would understand. And it spoke directly to him, just as he knew that for all the chorus, one hundred strong, and for all of the congregated voices surrounding him, the only sound was the whisper of Victoria Halford.

Amazing Grace, how sweet the sound
That saved a Wretch like me.
I once was lost, but now I'm found,
Was blind, but now can see.

FORTY-ONE

The beast was incredibly beautiful, graceful as any bird, soaring in endless circles through a void of blue. The large grey underbelly was gliding overhead, blocking the light, the scars of a lifetime like white needlepoint etched upon leathery flesh.

The eyes were cold black hollows. The mouth slid open with white flashes, closing again, the pectoral fins like two stiff wings.

Frank Rivers watched with fascination as it surfaced, the large triangular dorsal fin slicing with hardly a ripple, and he felt the tiny hairs on his neck go prickly as the woman beside him was bound with rapture.

'How can you love this thing?' he asked in disbelief.

'They're not like the creatures you hunt,' she said proudly, 'that's the most perfect predator of all.'

Her name was Tammy McCain, marine biologist, and the keeper of the shark. She was slim with fine blonde hair and dressed in a stylish grey jumpsuit. The tight-fitting velvet sheathed and revealed a figure that curved in all the right dimensions, and Rivers turned to her, instantly lost in glowing green eyes.

'So where's this little boy,' she smiled, 'his name's Elmer?'

Rivers nodded. 'You won't believe it, but I took him to church this morning, we're really two of a kind.'

'Can't sit still?'

He shrugged. 'It's an effort, I don't like being preached at, I don't think he does either, but it's what Jessica wants.'

'And you're in love.' She smiled, just as the fish made another pass. Rivers grimaced, conjuring human screams as it slid from some primitive depth to crush hapless victims into jelly, like sucking snails off a platter, he imagined. Tammy caught the seriousness of his intent, so took him by the arm, walking him even closer. As they moved, the softness of her breasts caressed his arm, and he felt his pulse quicken, as if someone were thumping him lightly on the head.

'You wanted to know, so let's start at the top,' she offered, but Rivers heard only the gentle lilt of her voice, and not her words, as the shark came directly for them; subconsciously he ticked the hammer of his automatic with a thumb, wanting to drive holes into its huge blank head, wanting to turn the Requiem display at the National Aquarium into a certain still life portrait of a fish.

'. . . and should they bite bone and loose teeth,' she nudged him, 'new ones just pop from the gums, sharp as razors, can cut an entire horse down to pabulum in a few seconds.'

'Swell,' he responded without tone, turning to stare at her. He knew Tammy liked swimming with sharks, even diving into caves where they slept, and that had always troubled him.

'How much does he weigh?'

'Nearly two tons, but it's a she.'

'That's a girl shark?' he repeated with amazement. 'It has to be twelve feet, I didn't know they got that big.'

But there was no time, as a huge fur-covered flank suddenly splashed into the water as the fin broke the surface, gaining speed, the mouth hanging open like a snare of knives. Rivers watched in wonder as half a torso, complete with hoof, spun towards the bottom and the large torpedo fish bolted into circular orbit, gaining speed, passing them as the eyes went to white, preparing to hit.

'What happened to its sockets?'

'Nictitating membrane, like a lizard or frog, it closes for protection just before striking. Like I said,' she shrugged, 'the most perfect predator.'

The fish was slicing through water like air as it hit with one enormous bite, the entire blank head taking it all at once, as its body gave one massive twist and the water exploded around them. From either side of its head, enormous gill plates released a foul white cloud as smaller fish began darting, pumping this micro-slime down into gullets, the shark leaving a trail as it slid back to the depths.

'My God,' Rivers breathed, 'that was awesome . . .'

Tammy smiled. 'Fifty pounds of buffalo leg, rounds out her diet. The National Zoo sends it over, death from disease or old age, so don't get humane on me.'

Rivers nodded, thankful he hadn't brought Elmer. 'And this flounder, you said you'd show me?'

'Patience, Franky, that's next.' She pressed the button. 'Okay, Mike, try the Red Hot, and tickle the water first, don't just drop it.'

From their position, looking up to a silver ceiling of water, they could see a live fish at the end of a blue net. As this was eased into the drink, its pale oval form was slapping, breaking the surface, and the shark felt the vibration.

Instantly it spun upward, coming towards Rivers, eyes white, the death-head like a blind torpedo.

'It's a flatfish from the Red Sea that has some rather miraculous properties, watch how it releases a milk when it senses danger, the fluid discharge comes from a spray behind the dorsal fin.'

The small flatfish peeled off, swimming for its life, aiming towards the bottom just as the shark's black maw swung wide; the little fish swimming madly as the shadow came over it, a white film being spewed into the water.

Instantly, the tank seemed to burst into a boil of anguish as the shark leaped violently, breaking the surface, its body twisting out of control; jaws locked open, unable to close, the huge fish twisting like a jet out of control.

'Watch the jaws,' Tammy whispered.

Rivers felt his heart pound as the giant killer went mad, flipping and twisting and spinning, haplessly, the head frozen into attack as the little Red Sea sole fluttered away and safely to the bottom.

The shark was raging now, gaining speed, circling and circling the tank, the teeth locked tight into an open position, fighting itself, confusion battering at the formidable killer. All at once, the great fish shot forward through the void, the jaw sprung, ramming into the thick plate with a tremendous thud that shook the heavy glass.

Rivers started, pulling back as the shark seemed to fall, drifting through the water, the eyes locked open, the face paralysed.

'What in hell?' he exclaimed.

'Wasn't that incredible? Watch what happens next.'

'Is it dying?'

The shark was veering over the sandy bottom, the entire torso trembling, shaking, convulsing, its compass broken as the belly turned up, then down again, drifting off into space.

'What the living hell is happening?'

'Just watch,' she whispered sharply, as the shark's face began to close, the teeth coming together, the jaws moving slowly as if they were old and brittle, the fish just coming out from a tremendous seizure. Then it was moving freely, though very slowly, twisting its head and body in confusion as it returned to cruising speed.

'It's clearing itself of the toxin, flushing water over the gill plates,' she explained. 'In a minute, everything will return to normal.'

'Tammy, that is really incredible, what is that juice?'

She smiled coyly. 'That juice is my research, we've collected thousands of those little fishies. They produce a nerve toxin, we believe it's a protein, but we're still working on it.'

'And it hits instantly?'

'One part per million in the water, it slams into the central nervous system like a Mack Truck producing an instant mini-stroke, paralysing the jaws in mid-strike. The Office of Naval Research is carrying all my costs.'

'To come up with a liquid shark repellant?'

'Exciting, yes?'

'Very.'

She reached up for the intercom, pressing the button. 'Thanks, Mike,' she said, then turned back to Rivers. 'So how's that for Show and Tell? Next time bring Elmer and Jessica.'

Rivers nodded, then shook his head in disbelief. For all their years, she never failed to amaze him with what she would find to challenge in life, or what she was capable of accepting. He had stood her up for their senior prom, yet even this she had taken in her stride.

'What?' Tammy questioned his stare, slipping her arm up through his.

'Wait until you meet them,' he smiled, 'Jessica looks so much like you, I couldn't believe it, and her kid,' he chuckled, 'this boy is bright and creative like you've never seen.' He quickly fumbled in his coat and then offered her a photograph, which she studied intently.

'She's prettier than I am,' she pouted, 'and her boy has beautiful eyes,' she added dreamily. 'He reminds me of you, Franky. Even as a kid you could melt snow with those baby blues.'

'Tammy,' he protested, 'Elmer has green eyes.'

She nodded, handing back the picture. 'You better go, Frank,' she said, pointing to her watch, 'I'll walk you to your car.'

FORTY-TWO

Jack Scott stood on the slate deck patio as the Deacon Atticus Cory helped Victoria Halford ease herself down into a straight-back chair which they had carried from inside the farmhouse. And he viewed Jim Cooley with a new perspective, the lean young man toting a small pillow for her, adjusting this behind her back. Jim had never met Victoria, nor did he know of her, that's what he had said. Her existence had been news to him as the events began to unravel.

Late last night, Elmer had told Scott of her visits to Patriots Bowl, and in turn Frank Rivers had prevailed upon his friend to make a few inquiries. Cooley had put his heart into the effort, and Scott had spent nearly an hour with him alone, waiting for Victoria to come from church, listening to Jim and learning, making notes, moving backward in time.

As recently as 1960, John's Cabin, Maryland, had been a relatively unmolested place, the people who lived there as enduring as the river along which the village had formed, changing course very little over the centuries. The Potomac itself started as a brook in West Virginia, then after hundreds of miles roared into the mighty cascades known as the Great and Little Falls, spilling nutrients onto farmers' fields, once promising a lifetime of rich harvests. It had been a plough-boy's paradise. And though there had been twists and turns throughout its history, life in John's Cabin never offered much to outsiders. It was too far from the city to support much of a life-style, even the state highway system had passed it by, though through the years men of ambition had tried to bring the outside world to its door.

During the early 1800s, engineers made a foolish effort to tame the river, building the Chesapeake and Ohio Canal. This ran parallel to the Potomac, but after a brief decade of construction, they called it quits, having carved an elaborate trench that stretched 296 kilometres through some of the most rugged terrain to be found east of the Mississippi. Almost two hundred years later tourists flocked to think about that, the dam-makers having left behind real and lasting beauty by engineering reflective lakes, huge aqueducts to lift the float barges. But as Jim had explained, the rapid transit of the train killed the canal even before it was done, and shortly after, the Civil War killed the train.

While slaves escaping from the South were using the waterway as a lifeline, the Union Army of the Potomac employed the steam engine as a supply route into Washington. So while Rebel raiding parties found it difficult to destroy the canal, they did the next best thing. By 1865 the remains of trellis and rails served witness to another doomed effort to connect John's Cabin with the world. The tracks were never rebuilt.

Jim Cooley was not a historian, he had corrected Jack Scott on that. He was simply the son of a John's Cabin farmer, born on the land, the youngest of two boys. So it was quite natural that they used to play among the historic ruins; cabins and lockhouses, man-made lakes and railroad structures. As with other families in small-town America, the Cooleys had been well known, and since Jim had been named for an uncle who was killed in the invasion of Normandy, his name had recognition beyond his own, recognition before he was even born.

James L. Cooley, he had explained, was a proud family name that had shone from a gold inscription on a monumental obelisk in the Village Commons, a tribute to the lost sons of John's Cabin, just one little slice of America's heart. And as far as Jim was concerned, that was true for almost a decade and the world seemed pretty all right; the world seemed pretty fair. Then in 1958 came a thing. A bad thing.

Without permission from the local residents, strangers

came to John's Cabin to change the name of the town. Just like that. Saying that it had been mismarked all along.

Road signs and maps were quickly amended, and soon after came another sour jolt. Protected by a court order, outsiders removed the John's Cabin war memorial from the town centre, just toted it off to some orphan field so that a shopping mall could be built on the spot. As Jim remembered, an old man by the name of Richard Duffy, a merchant who lived closest to the town centre, unloaded an entire box of twelve-gauge birdshot into the moving van, blowing out their radiator, windows and tyres. That seemed to be the high-point of the protest, as most farm families could not afford to risk violent confrontation. Going to jail could mean losing crops, even losing a farm, so the Cooleys broke the piggy to file a lawsuit against the County. By then, as Jim remembered, the fight was already over.

At the age of fourteen, he entered tenth grade a quiet, distrustful boy who took life seriously and had every right. He had worked tending crops since the age of seven, and his first adult memory was of attending Walt Whitman High and finding himself a second class citizen. The ill-fitting hand-me-down clothes, a bicycle instead of a sportscar, a thermos instead of milk money, the cruelties.

By 1964, Bethesda was starting to boom, and four years later his older brother was killed in the Tet Offensive as time began to lose meaning.

Old man Duffy, he remembered, had put Michael's picture in the window of his hardware store, since there was no longer a village green where his name could shine.

Since there was no longer a John's Cabin, Maryland, where it would have mattered in the first place.

Victoria Halford sat comfortably, sipping lemonade, her head held high as she looked out over rolling hills that were rimmed with giant pines. And it all seemed very strange to an outsider like Scott, the vast open spaces in subjective error against the landscape, the old farm tractor like some giant insect spat through a time warp and into a crowded suburb.

A bright sun was casting shadows from behind, creating a dark hollow where the slate patio met an endless wash of severe green. The sky had cleared. Now there was greyish blue overhead and everything sparkled with a wet shimmer.

Scott eased a lawn chair next to the old woman as she closed her eyes, hearing the soft patter of song birds nesting from the tree line. 'Victoria.' He spoke quietly, and the woman turned towards him, the eyes opening slowly, brown pools that came soaking over his form like drifting clouds, staying their flight, then finding Jim Cooley who was standing just before her and opening a drinking straw.

'Sorry,' Cooley interrupted, leaning past Scott, placing this into the old woman's glass. The icecubes tinkled, and she thanked him with a tight smile as she clutched the lemonade with both hands, raising this to lips that produced a pleasing, almost infantile sound as she suckled. Her eyes had wandered from Jim Cooley but for only a moment.

'Child,' she spoke to him, returning the glass to her lap.

'Yes, Mrs Halford.'

'Child, I know you,' she said, her eyes closing again, blinking away dryness, the corners of her mouth turning up. And James Lee Cooley, the gentleman farmer, started in his heart, though outwardly there was not a sign. He was wondering if this was true, when she spoke again, her voice like a harsh whisper.

'You are the image of Joseph.'

'Yes, Ma'am,' he said, thinking of his paternal grandfather, and there was genuine surprise in his voice as his thoughts were straining to remember if he had ever seen this woman before; he did not think so, maybe as a child. He was trying to peel back the years, trying to guess what she may have looked like.

'Your mother, bless her soul, was a good Christian woman, though I don't recall her name.'

Cooley swallowed. 'Marie Catherine.'

The old woman nodded. 'And should you still be wondering, Jim, my father used to crop and shed on one of your outbacks, tobaccos and strawberries . . .' She paused, taking a small sip as a cool breeze soaked the landscape, and her tone was weathered like her skin, which was a parched and wrinkled mocha brown.

Cooley smiled, his mind fighting for clear images in what seemed slow and thin as a dreamscape. 'That was before I was born.'

'Always treated us fairly, honest and proud Tillerman, and with you, here, working the land, why that's just fittin'.'

Jim Cooley glanced at Scott, thinking about the woman's age, considering this time and place, what she was truly capable of understanding. He shook his head. 'No, Ma'am,' he corrected, and there was a note of sadness in his voice. 'Times are much different now, but I do grow vegetables for the Farmer's Market, mostly for others in need.'

He turned sideways, pointing across the field to a rocky but distant outcropping, furrows were spaced neatly, squared into columns, ploughed from the soil. 'That's eight corn lines. If I grow too much the County will send inspectors, then I'll need a special licence. I'm a *residence* here, instead of a *farm*, technically, I mean, to the law I am.'

Scott was watching all of this with intense interest. The little woman's face and lips were pursed tight, she had understood. 'Come the judgement!' she leaned forward to say, her voice turning sour with the sound.

'Yes, Ma'am,' he offered in return, 'come the judgement.'

'Jim,' she said, and again she smiled, as if she liked to make that sound, but was not really addressing him.

'Yes, Ma'am,' he said, bringing his chair closer.

'Jim, do you remember the dogwood petals on your brother's picture?' she asked, and Cooley's eyes grew wide as he unintentionally gasped and his heart began to pound. When his older brother was killed, his photograph had been placed in the window at Duffy Hardware, and someone, though they never knew whom, kept leaving flowers there beneath the frame. By the time mourning was over, if it ever really was, a basketful of white petals had been accumulated. Jim had sprinkled them over his brother's grave.

'That was you?' he asked in disbelief, almost coming from his chair.

She gave a slight nod. 'That was I,' she whispered, the corners of her mouth turning up as Jim swallowed the ache in his throat. She returned to sipping lemonade, her lips producing a baby's suckle as she steadied the glass.

'Victoria,' Jim asked quietly, 'I'm sorry if I've missed something, but how do you know me, through my parents?'

She was rocking in her chair. 'Do you 'member that day when the signs came down?'

'Yes, very clearly,' he said, raising an eyebrow, 'I was eight years old.'

'Your father told us how that made his babies cry.'

Jim was looking at Scott in disbelief. 'That was 1958,' he reminded him, 'the year Tobytown burned and they changed our name to Cabin John.' Scott was writing this down, placing a small tape recorder on the table next to Victoria to preserve critical detail.

'We were upset,' Jim said, 'we were very, very young.'

'The time and soul of a place is as fragile as newborn life,' she said, 'take care and it will grow.' She looked away suddenly as tears welled in her eyes. 'They was jest killing time, Jim, your father was gonna fight, needed all us coloured to testify. But it didn't do no good, things was changing too fast.'

'He never told me that.'

Victoria smiled. 'You *are* the image,' she said proudly, then turning to Scott. 'Your friend has questions for me,' she blinked.

'No, no, please go ahead,' Scott urged, 'it can wait.'

Jim looked at Victoria, remembering the flowers that a stranger had left behind in his brother's memory. 'Why dogwoods?' he asked. 'I never could figure that one out, and my mother didn't know either.'

'Bless her soul,' she said, 'don't you like the flowering tree?'

'Yes, it is very pretty.'

Scott found himself leaning forward too rapidly, staring down at the *Kern's Wild Flower Guide* sticking out from his jacket, trying to appear casual as he picked this up and turned to the index. He searched for a page with a print, and then read aloud. 'The Eastern Dogwood produces flowers each spring, composed of four spreading white petals with red tips on each end.'

Victoria turned her stiff torso towards him. 'It is the Resurrection Flower,' she corrected, as Scott held the book in front of her. The four white petals leapt from the coloured page, resembling a Maltese cross, and Deacon Cory studied this carefully.

'The petals form the suffering of Christ,' she said, pointing with a frail finger to what looked like four bloodstained tips. 'From His image on the cross of Calvary, as His mortal life flowed a branch fell at His feet, and to this day we are blessed with the dogwood to remind us.' She turned back to Jim.

'That is why I left them for your brother,' she swallowed, 'that is why . . .'

As she spoke Scott noted an intensity in her voice that had not been there before. 'Victoria,' he offered quietly, 'can you tell me about the Yellow Loosestrife, the Swamp Candle?' He had quickly turned to a dog-eared page, holding this picture up, but her eyes failed to see, they did not need to.

'Sweet Primrose,' she whispered, 'the life eternal.'

'The Swamp Candle, it's a symbol of the life everlasting?'

'It is the Easter flower,' she stated without hesitating, 'we used to collect them for services Good Friday and Easter Sunday. In parts of the South it is the traditional offering of the children . . .' Her voice seemed to float beyond him as Scott was filled with a release of tensions, like a coiled spring unwinding for the first time. His body trembled as he emitted a heavy sigh that made both of them pause.

'I'm sorry,' Scott said, clearing his mind, for it was as he suspected, there was a tangible link connecting each victim backward in time. In 1989, Good Friday had come on March 24th, seven days before the Claytons were killed. He surmised that Jennifer Doe had been collecting Candles on or near March 28th, the last Friday of March 1958, thirty-one years before. And Victoria, again, closed her eyes. When she opened them, Scott was holding the copper coin in his palm.

'John's Warning,' she whispered, and her lips parted as she began rocking herself for comfort.

'Victoria, you were crying when . . .'

She held up a frail hand, silencing him, lifting her head. Her eyes blinked with heavy lids and she cleared her throat, this sounding more like a long dry cough as her pupils narrowed. 'Jim Cooley?' she asked, reaching out for him with a shaky hand. He quickly rose to her side.

'Yes, Ma'am,' he said, 'I'm right here.'

'Jim, didn't I hear you and your brother used to play at the Widewater?'

He felt his throat go tight. 'Yes, Ma'am, we did, we surely did.' He noticed there was a pinch of panic in her tone that was pulling down at the corners of her mouth.

'Did you see the remains of two old houses near the poplars, where the dogwood clearing begins?'

Cooley moved a chair, sitting next to her, never once dropping his hold. 'Yes,' he said, 'we imagined those ruins belonged to John-the-Free, that he would hide there from the Rebs and make his war plans.'

'That's where I grew up, Jim Cooley, where you and your brother were playing.' As she said this her eyes came forward, locking onto him. 'Our house was the one with the large stone chimney,' she said proudly, and again she went silent. Every spring since Jim could remember he had gone there to see the forest colours.

'The foundations are still there,' he forced a smile, 'and one fireplace of smooth cut quarry stone.'

'Are there sweet blueberries, are the bushes there?'

'Yes, Victoria, enough for the largest blueberry pie in the State, the entire overlook is just thick with them.' He was glancing up at Scott for direction, the policeman nodded, pushing him on.

'Daniel Stoner is the name you want. Daniel, myself, and my mother planted those,' she stated, and suddenly her face contorted as water welled over her eyes. 'We were gone many years before you were born, but I knew 'bout you, Jim. From time to time we'd see your parents in Bethesda, so I know about you . . .' And she started to weep.

'Yes, Ma'am,' he said, stroking the back of her hand. It trembled, but not from fear.

The deacon was on his feet, standing over them. 'Is this really necessary?' he asked sternly.

'Please,' Scott nodded, 'I know of no other way.' And suddenly Cooley stared down. Victoria Halford was patting the back of his hand in a comforting motion, her head high, first looking at Cooley, then to Scott.

'That Warning,' she said, 'that Warning belonged to Daniel Stoner,' and she closed her lids unbearably tight. 'I know because I helped him drill that coin when we were still children, we made a new word from John's Cabin . . .'

'*Join*,' Scott stated softly, 'the word is *Join*.'

Victoria nodded. 'The chain Danny wore it on was mine, from my mother. He lived next to us in John's Cabin, I had given him the chain for his tenth birthday, he could not afford to buy one.'

'And the Token was then passed down from Daniel to his daughter?' Scott asked.

'Samantha.'

He swallowed, leaning forward. 'And how old was she?' he asked quietly.

Victoria's eyes came over him. 'Twelve,' she remembered with certainty, 'she was twelve the year she vanished.'

'And that was about the time Tobytown burned?'

'Only months before, she was gone, her sister and mother too.'

Scott could see she was fighting her emotions, so he altered the subject as Cooley reached back over, thin fingers closing around his as Scott unrolled an ancient river chart borrowed from Dr Robert Perry's *Treasures of the Civil War South*. He was holding the map in front of her.

'Victoria,' he asked, 'can you show me where your family first lived, and where you were resettled to?'

The old woman was breathing deeply. 'We settled in John's Cabin,' she pointed, 'my father built our house in 1863,

435

before I was born. Nathan Stoner, Daniel's grandfather, already lived there, he was a Union Freeman during the States' War, Daniel was an only child. We lived there until 1954.'

'And you were farm families?'

'No, the Halfords, Motts, and Stoners were quarry men and brick millers, mostly shaving and cleaning lodestone for the government pit bosses fashioning L'Enfant's city. Our men laid cornerstones for Lincoln in 1914, then Jefferson . . .' her voice went dry and she sipped at her drink.

'And you owned that land,' he stated.

'Yes.' She pointed with a fragile finger that shook against the parchment. 'We were moved up to River Road where we built the church, named our new village Tobytown after the cemetery, the County said they wanted us to have that land instead.'

'The cemetery was Tobytown.' Scott shook his head. 'Can you show me where that was?'

She looked at him with a dark smile. 'I think you know,' she whispered. And Scott nodded.

'From Patriots Bowl to where?' he asked. 'As far as the gas station?'

'They came at night, moving the dead, hauling them away, a week or more.'

Scott breathed deeply, his anger growing. 'The boundary was Little Falls Road, wasn't it?'

'A country mile.'

'And that's why you visit the alley, your . . .'

'That part was never cleared, my parents and my husband, resting there . . .'

'Near the fence by Elmer Janson's house, you do know . . .'

She turned, staring at him, tapping her chest. 'A fine boy, he has a poet's heart. We share, that is his secret place.'

Scott was amazed. 'And why were you forced from John's Cabin to Tobytown?'

She smiled, a dark and contemptuous line. 'The river land had become more valuable, the County Welfare people came

436

with papers. We didn't have sewers, we was living under unsanitary conditions.'

'Most families still have septic,' said Jim.

'And did Daniel Stoner move his family there at that time?'

'Yes,' she was rocking, 'built a nice house where the TV station is.'

Jim leaned forward. 'That tower is the tallest broadcast antenna on the coast.'

'And by this time he had two children?'

'Victoria, born 1943. Samantha, born in the winter of 1946.'

Scott sighed. 'The oldest after you?'

She did not answer, but closed her eyes, forcing tears into streams. 'When he moved his family, Daniel was a brick cutter for the Smithsonian Castle.'

'He would have done most of his work on Brickyard Road in Cabin John,' Jim said.

'Did Daniel have any troubles that you know of, was anyone upset with him?'

'In 1956 we heard that private houses was to be built on our river land, Daniel was hiring an attorney from Baltimore to fight them, it was going to court, everyone said he stood for a good fight.'

'But then Tobytown burned and his family was reported missing?'

'She was set to blaze and went in a single night.' She turned, facing Scott directly. 'The smoke was so heavy you could taste it in the water weeks after, it wasn't fit for drinking.'

'So you were asked to move again?'

At this question her face became a cold mask. 'We were told. Somebody else needed our land, so the Welfare folks came again with their papers, gave us a new Tobytown halfway to Baltimore, with new houses donated as charity. Never,' she said through pursed lips, 'never did we need charity!'

'And where was Daniel in all of this, what happened to his wife and children?'

'No one knows,' she sighed. 'During the ruckus they

437

disappeared, some said his Emma ran away and took the little ones, but they were planning on having another child.'

Scott took a deep breath. 'Daniel looked for them?'

'Yes.' Her eyes were again filling with tears. 'He searched without sleep, even started doubting hisself. Some said they had gone to swim in the river and drowned, but Emma Dysan grew up on the bayou, so he went to Louisiana but they weren't there.'

'Victoria,' Scott guessed quietly, 'Daniel is dead?'

She nodded. 'His heart died.'

'When?'

'That same year, on a tree by the river.' She closed her eyes. 'Hung by his own hand.'

With that Jim Cooley's body shuddered as Scott rose from his seat, removing a colour photograph from his briefcase, then watching carefully as he moved the portrait of Jennifer Doe closer to Victoria; the image coming into a slow focus when she turned abruptly, pushing at the picture with outstretched hands. She uttered a small gasp, closing her eyes as a mournful, infantile sound flowed from her lips. Jim placed a protective arm around her as the deacon hovered over in angry confusion.

'I'm sorry,' Scott pressed, 'is this child Samantha Stoner?' But Victoria Halford had clutched deep into her shawl, wrapping her hands around the Holy Bible, remembering her singing voice, and she raised her head at them in a harsh whisper.

'Samantha,' she said, 'my heart . . .' And her voice erupted into harsh song. 'Oh way down South in Dixie, with my body hung in the air, I was asking the white Lord Jesus, what is the use of prayer . . .'

'She's been through enough!' the deacon cursed suddenly.

'. . . I was asking the white Lord Jesus, what road should we travel on? And he answered with a Freeman, and we came to the House of John.'

Jim closed his eyes, holding the frail woman's head to his chest.

'And we lived by the word of John,' she whispered, 'on the banks of the river Peace. And we sought God in Bethesda, for Christ had slain the beast.'

FORTY-THREE

To Matthew Brennon both the flight and the day seemed
nonstop. He had been up all night collecting materials concerning Aaron Seymor Blatt, having made a study of the company known as DIDS, Dental Instruments of Dallas.

The corporation was the parent of a national chain of
Freestanding Dental Clinics, small private practices that
were franchised, and in his mind Brennon saw these as
the fast food of medical dentistry, the Burger King of tooth
pickers.

According to the ViCAT data search one thing was certain.
From Maine to Florida to California, consumers routinely
had their teeth drilled, their gums sliced, their crowns
fashioned, and their dentures refitted by DIDS; yet the odds
of them having ever heard that name were extremely long.

He was sitting with his table folded down, the roar of a jet
engine at his left ear, his the only overhead light as he
skimmed a recruitment blurb in the *Journal of Medical Dentistry* aimed at students.

As a dentist starting out in the world, a graduate could
work long hours to make someone else rich, then hope for a
partnership, or there was DIDS. They calculated the start-up
costs for private practice at $650,000 to purchase basic equip-
ment; drills, sinks, X-ray machines, chairs and work stations,
funds that few graduates could hope to borrow, except from
DIDS. Once placed in this context, it seemed a viable option.

With an accredited degree in dentistry, a DIDS partnership provided everything required for a student to start grinding teeth into paste; every tool, every die, every bit of equipment, and then, just when you thought it could get no better, turn a profit in two years and DIDS paid for your full education. After that, they owned thirty-one per cent of your silly butt for life.

'Did you want sugar with that?' asked an attractive red-headed woman, standing at his side with a hot cup.

'Just one, thanks,' Brennon returned, and she placed a small envelope on his tray.

'Cream?'

He shook his head, 'No thanks.' He lifted a photograph taken from a medical journal that was critical of the concept, while wondering if his own dentist were not a franchise. The thought made his gums itch.

'Sir, did you want the scrambled eggs or the waffles?'

'I think I'll skip breakfast.' He frowned, holding a photograph of the first DIDS, sandwiched between a pet store and a dry cleaners, circa 1960. Beneath a sign which proclaimed *Dental Office* was the proprietor's name, Dr Aaron S. Blatt, then in large lettering, *Daytime, Nighttime, Holidays Too!*

'How very convenient,' Brennon murmured.

'Sorry?' responded the stewardess, having arrived to refill his cup.

He smiled, 'Talking to myself.'

She moved closer. 'Doctor, do you have a moment?' she whispered, and he looked up, seeing her for the first time, dropping deep through bright blue eyes that twinkled in the early glow that had begun to stream through half-closed windows. Most of the other passengers were in that half-sleep state of red-eyed jet travel, having eaten their heavy micro-wave meals.

'I have this tooth,' she whispered quietly, leaning against his chair, her long legs bumping his arm as a bit of turbulence stroked the plane.

'Sorry.' Brennon lifted the stack, and this next statement

took a great deal of courage. 'I'm not a dentist, but I sure wish I was.'

She smiled coyly at him.

'This is just research for an interview I'm conducting,' he continued. 'I'm a journalist, *Lifestyle* magazine, it comes out on Sunday.'

'Oh,' she said with disappointment, 'my fiancé reads that all the time.'

In Fort Worth, Texas, there are some stately homes, and if the length of a driveway is a measurement of substance, then the Blatts had more than most, complete with a *yield* sign after about a minute.

Just in case he was being watched, Matthew Brennon slowed carefully before pulling his rental car through the private intersection, creeping around a greenway circle with a sculpted bronze of galloping horses, then onto expensive looking brick, coming to a stop under a massive white-columned overhang.

Such was the stately manor of Myra Isadora Blatt. It looked like the White House, particularly when standing in the portico beneath a lofty chandelier, between rows of blooming roses. He was about to ring the doorbell when the huge wooden door swung wide on polished brass hinges, the latchwork surely gleamed, and he was looking into the face of a man servant, late middle-aged and dressed in starched black, an ageing uncle type with a neatly trimmed goatee and salt coloured hair slicked back against his head.

'Good morning, Sir,' he said.

'Hello,' Brennon offered.

'Are you Mr Brent Masters?' the man inquired, and his accent was thick with old, manor house English accompanied by a slight lisp that sounded phoney. Brennon responded by handing him a business card, the gold lettering had cost him twenty bucks extra.

'Please enter, Sir,' he said, his thin face like boiled chicken. 'I am Sydney Oliver, at your service.'

'Pleased to meet you,' Brennon responded, though the servant had not offered his hand.

'Miss Blatt is expecting you, follow me.' With that Brennon found himself inside, strolling over expensive Italian marble beneath vaulted ceilings that seemed high enough to trap thin air. It was a long, expensive walk, past a sitting area with velvet high-back chairs, a gaming room with felt-covered tables, a darkly lit den with African animals mounted on the wall. They came through another portico of domed and gilded ceilings, then rounded into a red carpeted hallway that resembled an art gallery. Oils and watercolours, some of these portraits, faces glowing from recessed lights.

Sydney turned back, finding him studying an oil of a man-child dressed in a tailored suit, a bright red flower popping from a lapel, a wry smile from lips that seemed too moist, and too thin. His face had an unnatural glow of rouge, his hair was jet black, a silk white *yarmulke* covered the back of his head.

'Master Aaron,' Sydney offered, 'his *bar mitzvah*.'

Brennon nodded. 'Very nice,' he responded. 'Where is Aaron these days, my secretary said he would not be available?'

'Miss Blatt is in the atrium.'

From the rear of the great manor house, the manicured lawn spread as far as sight, every angle correct to the eye, squared hedgerows, circular fountains, a covered tennis court, a kidney-shaped swimming pool with smaller mansion that, Brennon guessed, was the bathhouse. As they came to a break in a wall of ceiling-high glass, Sydney turned abruptly. 'Careful, Sir,' and he stepped down over glazed tiles with gold and purple edging, entering the atrium.

It was a hothouse of sorts, with rows of planters and flowers in every colour imaginable, the lofty ceiling a frosted glass, giving Brennon the feel of moving inside a lightbulb. At the far end of this humid room he immediately saw the figure of an older woman among the greenery, standing over what appeared to be yellow orchids. She was carefully snipping

443

with tiny pruning shears, removing one leaf at a time. She was dressed in a white blouse and slacks, with a gold braided chain on the outside of a high-necked collar. She looked to be eighty, Brennon guessed, her colour a subtle but powdery rouge, her grey hair pulled back into a bun.

Brennon noticed that her sleeves were rolled up, revealing a dark blue tattoo along the inside of her left forearm. He felt his stomach knot as she tugged self-consciously at her sleeve, covering the horrid markings. She did not look up, though she was aware of their presence as Sydney came alongside. Brennon heard a fluttering of birds somewhere, though he could not tell if they were inside the glass walls or out.

'Mr Brent Masters.' He bowed slightly, handing her the card, then she quickly surveyed the stranger, a smile appearing on a kindly face.

'A pleasure,' she said, offering her hand. 'I spoke with Mr Flores on the phone last night, a story on Aaron could not have been better timed.'

'Yes, Ma'am.' Brennon gave a courteous nod. 'Why is that?'

'The DIDS Centre for Research, you'll have the details before anyone else, I thought you knew?'

'No, Ma'am, but I'd like to. Depending upon what I learn, Aaron could very well lead our list of *Lifestyle* entrepreneurs.'

She smiled. 'Then we will get better acquainted and I shall tell you all about it,' she said proudly. 'It will put a positive spin on your story.'

Brennon smiled.

'Sydney,' she ordered, 'ice tea, and . . .' she turned.

'That sounds very good, thank you.'

'. . . and also bring some snacks, Mr Masters looks hungry to me.' She addressed him with a raised eyebrow. 'Are you eating well, young man? You should not skip meals.'

'Right away, Miss Blatt,' Sydney responded, and was gone.

'Well,' Brennon found himself confessing, 'it's a busy world out there.' She emitted a sigh and shook her head at him, her voice carrying a slight European accent that Brennon could not place.

'It hurts me you are so thin, a nice looking young man like yourself.'

'Yes, Ma'am,' Brennon said, and he stood alone with the unsuspecting mother of the man who had paid for Zachariah Dorani's burial urn back in 1966. And he could not help but feel lousy, as deceptive and cruel as the Devoid he was hunting. Typically they came stalking the innocent from behind the camouflage of their manipulative lies, that was a behavioural hallmark; men sleeping beside wives who never knew of their husbands' little whims, mothers embracing sons who belied their secret hobbies. And if this mother knew who he really was, or why he had come, her life would end in a tick. Matthew Brennon swallowed his own spit. He hated it when they were so nice, the mothers and fathers, why did they always have to be so nice?

Without hesitation the small woman gently pushed her arm up through his. 'We'll sit on the porch, it's more comfortable,' she said, gazing up into his eyes, leading him closely down an aisle towards the rear of the greenhouse. 'My Aaron gave all of this to me.' She smiled, moving closely at his side. 'I am very lucky.'

'Yes, Ma'am, I can see that.'

'Oh please,' she said, 'call me Myra. Your parents must be very proud, so tall and well cultured.'

'Cultured?' Brennon chuckled.

'A writer.' She blinked. 'But you're not married!' She reached, taking up his left hand, spotting where a ring should be.

'No,' Brennon shrugged. 'Not as of yet, almost, once that . . .'

'Don't tell me you don't have time,' she chastised.

'Well, I . . .'

'You'll find her when you least expect it, and you'll know, there's still time, you're very young.'

'Yes, Myra,' Brennon agreed as they walked onto a cool deck through an open door. The level of personal intimacy the woman had reached so quickly amazed him.

'I do *not* believe that my Aaron will ever settle down, he's in love with his business.'

'My staff told me he could not be reached, do you know where he is?'

A slight smile crossed her lips as they came to a small and intimate oasis overlooking a reflecting pool, an elaborate fountain of bronze dolphins cast in play, spouting streams of water under which a school of Koi swam merrily in circles. 'Neat,' Brennon said, 'these are really big guys.'

'Aaron had this built for my eightieth birthday, that was some time ago.'

Sydney came from between hedges sporting two silver trays, then laid these down carefully on a table, unrolling a cloth, carefully lifting the food onto the fine woven linen.

'Thank you, that will be all,' she instructed, and he bowed slightly, placing a silver bell near her plate, then pulling a chair out for her, helping her to settle in.

'I'm sorry,' she said, 'what were we saying?'

'That Aaron's not available.'

'Yes, he's in Florida on business, but he calls home every three days, we'll be speaking Tuesday night. Please try the lox, they're Danish and very high in protein.'

'Yes, Ma'am.' He started reaching for the tray, but instead of thinking of Florida, his thoughts wandered to a small agricultural village in Western Maine. Scott's theory had now placed Brennon into the position of deceiving some poor old woman over pink slices of seafood cut thin as wafers; and he found himself picking at these, careful not to tip the pile. She leaned over and grabbed his plate right out of his hand.

'You eat like a bird.' She fluttered with her fingers across the lox, ignoring the silver serving fork, pinching a healthy pile, then dropping this onto Brennon's open-faced roll. She continued in a methodical circle, stacking deli delights, then placed this back in front of him as she picked up the silver bell, ringing once.

'Thank you, you're very kind,' he responded.

'Eat, Brent Masters,' she demanded, 'it hurts me, the way you're so thin!'

446

The truth was, Matthew Brennon was hurting a whole lot more.

'Yes, Miss Blatt?'

Brennon dropped his eyes as he took another healthy bite.

'A large glass of cold milk.'

'Yes, Ma'am,' he nodded.

'I believe Aaron's been setting up two new DIDS offices in the Gulf area, but I don't meddle,' she offered, taking a sip of tea. 'Is something troubling you?'

'No,' Brennon breathed. 'This is wonderful food.'

'You are familiar with how DIDS works, funding other doctors who would not be able to open a practice on their own?'

'Yes,' he smiled, moving quickly to capture control of the conversation. 'Aaron is an only child?' he asked.

'No,' she said quietly, growing suddenly sombre, 'he had two older brothers killed during the war.'

'I'm sorry.'

Sydney was back, placing a large glass in front of Brennon.

'Aaron makes up for a lifetime.' She smiled at him, and Brennon glanced into light brown irises that shielded a painful reality that was almost palpable. He took a sip of cool milk.

'You are writing a personality piece?'

'Yes,' he lied, 'a profile.'

'Then you should begin at the beginning,' she said, 'it is a miracle that he's alive, he was a holocaust child, born in Poland in 1937, did you know?'

Brennon swallowed. 'No, I did not.' He removed a small tape recorder from his coat pocket, bumping the grip on his service automatic in the process, placing the electronic device on the table.

'Then you are from Poland?' he asked.

'No, our families originate from Hungary, our name was Himmelblatt, that was shortened in America. Aaron's father was a research doctor, and in 1932 he had taken a position at the Polish Medical Institute, so you see, medicine runs in our family. I was a nurse when we first met, Aaron was two when the Nazis came.'

Brennon swallowed hard, suddenly thinking of the chrome gutters of Rigby's creamer, he could only imagine the horrors of that dark period.

'Every day since the *Einsatzgruppen*, I see Aaron as a gift of life . . .'

'I'm sorry,' he interrupted, 'I don't know that term.'

'The SS,' she responded, 'very special units. On September 27th, 1939, they began roaming the village streets throughout Poland, going from house to house, dragging away men who might oppose the New Order. They were after intellectuals, lawyers, teachers, government officials, anyone who could speak out and become a leader. Aaron's father,' she sighed, 'he was well known by our non-Jewish neighbours so he was taken on the first day.'

'To the camps,' he concluded sadly.

'No, no, that came much later. They were murdering in the woods then, about two hundred a day. The rest of us were left alone until November, then Aaron's brothers were taken to Treblinka, but the SS left me with my baby, they did not take Aaron. Too much work,' she shrugged, 'or perhaps pity.'

Brennon had stopped eating.

'In June of 1942 Aaron and I were taken to Auschwitz. Since I was a nurse I was able to survive by working in the medical laboratories, I was able to keep my baby.'

'God, that's awful,' Brennon sighed.

She nodded thoughtfully. 'After the war I came to America with a nickel in my pocket and a hole,' she pointed to her chest, 'a hole through my heart. Put that in your story,' she sighed. 'Aaron survived and was able to achieve beyond measure!'

Brennon waited a moment, finishing his milk, staring down at the take-up spool through a plastic window. 'Mrs Blatt,' he lowered his head, 'Myra. That picture of Aaron in the hallway, if he was born in 1937 and he had his *bar mitzvah* at age twelve or so, then that painting was commissioned around 1950?'

'Yes,' she agreed, 'that's about right.'

'That type of artwork is very expensive for someone who came to America with a nickel?'

She smiled at this. 'A probing question, you have an insightful mind, Brent Masters. The early portraits were paid for by a friend of Aaron's father, a doctor who was with me in the camps. In fact, he helped Aaron to make his start in the world, so if you have time he'd be a good man to interview.'

'Yes,' he agreed.

'Dr Rubin Jaffe. He helped with the expense of Aaron's education, then later in starting the DIDS corporation. Aaron paid him back, right to the penny.'

'Is Dr Jaffe in Dallas?'

'No, he resides in the Maryland countryside. The important point for your article is that, although Dr Jaffe has been a great benefactor to many children who survived the camps, my Aaron would still be a self-made millionaire, it's a question of drive, Rubin will tell you it is so.'

'Yes, Ma'am, a point well taken. Do you recall another friend by the name of Zachariah Dorani?'

'No,' she shook her head, 'a friend of Aaron's?'

'I guess not.'

He watched as Myra Blatt rose from her chair. 'We'll take a peek at Aaron's bedroom,' she whispered, 'I'll show you something very special.'

In a manor large enough to be a grand European hotel, the bedroom of Aaron Seymor Blatt was amazingly small, on the fourth floor, and just below the attic stairwell.

It had taken real time to arrive here, two elevators and a long walk, but finally they stood in front of a crudely finished wooden door that had been painted green. Myra caught the questioning expression on Brennon's face. 'Brent,' she soothed, 'this is off the record?'

He agreed.

'Aaron had all of this, including the door, dismantled from the house where he grew up on Mission Lane in Dallas,

449

exactly as it was. He does have another bedroom, more adult, it overlooks the pool.'

Brennon nodded.

'He saved everything so that he would never forget where he came from, poor but proud.' She stopped to insert the key as behind them the wooden attic stairs creaked and the valet appeared, his face stern, his chin thrust forward.

'Yes?' she questioned.

'Only checking on Madam,' the servant whispered as she turned a worn lock that could have come from a scrapyard.

'We're fine, thank you.' She waved him away, then whispered to Brennon, 'This is supposed to be Aaron's secret, Sydney's too protective.'

Brennon had to lower his head to step beneath the ceiling beam.

The little room was a fresh sky blue, the walls completely naked. There was a single mattress lying on a circular rug in the centre, the white bedding made to perfection, not a wrinkle to be found. Across from the foot there was a highly polished wooden bureau with a dozen small dishes, neatly holding a man's dressing accessories beneath a spotless mirror.

Brennon's eyes moved quickly.

Beneath a small windowsill there was a workbench constructed of raw two-by-fours, though these had been sanded smooth, and he followed as Myra made her way there. The surface was neat as a pin, not a tool in sight, only an electric vacuum cleaner and brush lying next to an architect's model. This sat beneath an adjustable spring-loaded light, and she reached past him, turning on the beam. 'DIDS Clinical Centre,' she said proudly.

Brennon was looking at an expansive structure complete with tiny cars parked in front of the main entrance, which resembled a neo-modern recreational centre. Brennon thought it antiseptically strange, and was hovering over the white and silver-sided model when he spotted a perfume bottle in the corner of the bench.

He thought it was seashells, in an odd sort of way, dozens of tiny shells soaking in a blue solution, but something strange. And he kneeled, pretending to study the building's entrance.

'It's his dream come true,' she said, and Brennon cringed, fighting the swell of his breakfast.

The bottle was filled to the crystal lid with human ivory.

'The design was his idea, he went through several qualified architects.'

Brennon swallowed hard: teeth of every size and shape, molars, incisors, eye teeth, the gumlines showing as a darker shade of white, and he was straining to find a hint of gold or silver in the collection, but there were none. These were young teeth, hundreds of them, bright, shining, soaking in a sea of blue.

'Ever since I can remember he's been interested in premature decay and gum disease, the centre will address both, a place for serious research.'

'That's wonderful,' he answered tonelessly, coming to his feet, quickly scanning the room for a file or bookshelf, pleased that there were none. He turned to face the proud mother, the man who would have her son executed by the State.

'I've read that Aaron's not a serious researcher, which is why he has never published,' he said in an accusatory voice.

'Oh, but he has!' she snapped, a hurt expression on her face. 'I will show you!'

With that she turned, walking briskly through the door. 'It will only take a second.'

Brennon was working quickly now.

Removing a pair of white gloves from a jacket pocket, he pulled these on while studying the bottle of teeth, taking a black zipper kit from his jacket and lying it alongside. From within he removed a small aerosol can, spraying the entire glass, then quickly wrapping it in a solid sheet of sticky tape, rubbing it into place with his fingertips, then lifting, peeling away.

Yellow fingerprints and smudges came free, and he rubbed the jar with his gloves to remove the fine forensic pollen, setting it back on the table, adjusting the desk beam as he twisted the lid open.

Molars, incisors, wisdom, and eye teeth all glimmered at him, the room filling with a medicinal, chemical odour as the top came free.

He spread his fingers, he sought to steady his hands.

First he sucked juices up into a syringe, sealed the needle, then laid five small evidence pouches in a row on the bench, carefully working the zippered seams, reaching down to a gangly wisdom tooth with four long roots.

The fluid stirred to his touch, swelling into a blue stain on gloved fingertips as he removed the human ivory, holding it to the light, the roots curling inward like the tentacles of cancer, a bit of greying flesh still clinging between them.

He swallowed, his hand steadied by hate.

If Scott was correct, then Lacy Wilcott's teeth would come next, carried like so many pearls in the hands of a killer. Her only sin, having left the protection of Moxie Pond.

And he quickly returned the jar to where he had found it as Myra Blatt came through the door.

Brennon turned to face her, but could not.

He could no longer look into the eyes of this mother.

At 10:58 a.m., Brennon stood at a phone booth at the Rise and Shine, an open air bar at Dallas International Airport, waiting for his connection. Although he and Scott had been reviewing their mutual progress, they were both silently scanning notes and documents, double-checking against the record.

As Brennon turned to another page in his notebook, seeking out the date that Aaron Seymor Blatt enrolled at Georgetown Dental School, he was also being forced to share his personal breathing space with a man who was demanding five dollars.

'To help the children.' The stranger pushed again at his captive audience, a collection can coming forward as Brennon fumbled through his papers.

'I already gave,' he muttered, but the man stood firm,

bedecked in black, suggestive of a priest, which he was not.

'For the poor and the crippled,' he insisted, 'the aged and the ill,' and Brennon found himself quickly fumbling through his pockets, finding a crumpled dollar, handing this over, then looking the other way as a voice boomed into his ear.

'Matt,' Scott said quietly, 'I'm looking at the deed to County Plat 178, the River Road properties, which includes the bowling alley. Is the name of Blatt's mentor one Rubin Jaffe?' he asked with a nasty bite.

Brennon closed his eyes with a nod and then smiled. 'One and the same, Jack, I don't know what that means, but we've got a hit.'

'And what did Mrs Blatt say about this man, other than the fact he was a victim of the Nazis?'

'She couldn't stop talking about him, a self-made millionaire, very religious, generous to a fault, and the silent political muscle that makes Washington move. He's known the Blatts since Aaron was a baby, his mother worked with Rubin Jaffe until 1945 when the camps were liberated. I have a feeling Jaffe paid for most of Blatt's education, so it's safe to assume they are still very, very close.'

Scott nodded. 'When we checked on the land, we discovered that Jaffe owns most of the River Road properties, and damn near half of Washington and Bethesda. I'll start on him from here. What else do we have, did Mrs Blatt say how long her son lived in this area?'

Brennon checked his notebook. 'Five years total, starting in 1955, then he moved back to Texas in June of 1960 and founded DIDS. My understanding is that Jaffe also helped to bankroll his business, I'm having numbers run on their mutual financial status, maybe we'll get another hit, or at least something else we can hook into.'

'No,' Scott corrected course, 'that's not as important as linking Blatt directly into the Florida spree. His mother confirmed he has business there?'

'Blatt calls her like clockwork every week, so she would know.'

'And you're meeting with Duncan today?'

'That's affirmative, Jack, in about two hours. Any special instructions?'

'Are you carrying your tape recorder?'

Brennon smiled, 'Let's go,' he challenged, reaching into a pocket, removing a small black rubber suction cup, then wetting this with his tongue. He quickly stuck this into place on the back of the telephone receiver. 'How much tape do you want to roll?'

'Thirty seconds, three . . . two . . . one . . .'

Upon hearing Scott's command, Brennon checked his watch, hitting the button and letting the spool roll forward on record, counting, then snapping the machine off.

'What else do we have?' Scott returned.

'Teeth,' Brennon stated grimly.

'And Mrs Blatt knew they were there?'

'Hell, Jack, she's a very fine old lady, if we're right, this is going to kill her. And besides, what's a bottle of teeth when your only boy is a millionaire dentist?'

Scott nodded. 'And you got prints off this collection?'

'A good dirty dozen, if they're on record we'll be able to get a background sheet, provided you make the . . .'

'It's done,' he cut him off. 'I told FBI that if they scratch and deliver the wrong files like the last two cases, I'm holding a press conference on their front porch. We don't have time to kill on this one.'

Brennon laughed. 'Duncan Powell told me that their data base budget is being increased another five times this term, maybe they'll start hiring from McDonalds . . .'

'Matt,' Scott cut him off, 'please, let's stick to the issues. What about this servant, Sydney, let's run him down just to be on the safe side.'

'All right, Jack, but I'm betting he's not a player, he sticks too close to the old woman, but consider it done. But be careful with the alley, I've been thinking about that, and I really don't like it . . .'

Scott nodded. 'I understand, but imagine what would happen if we went for a search warrant. Considering Jaffe's budget and political weight, it would take many weeks even if we were successful, which I rather doubt.'

'If we get caught, it blows the case.'

'I've worked that out with Dudley Hall, he understands the problem, and I've known him since 1953. He's the fastest digger alive, get in quick, get out quick, and if anyone raises the issue, then he found the graves working as a freelance looter of Civil War sites.'

'You're kidding, you think that will wash?'

'Yes I do, Dudley's brother lives in Wheeling, West Virginia, and that's his line of work, Civil and pre-Civil War antiquities. Dudley will say he was on his way there, having just robbed from the dead. Anyway, he's prepared to take the fall.'

'Jesus, Jack, he'd lose his pension!'

There was no answer, as Scott was already moving for another destination in his mind, planning his approach, working through the details.

'We'll talk again from Duncan's radio car,' he said, and Brennon grabbed his bag and headed for the gate, suddenly fearful that the covert nature of this particular investigation had gone too far. And he had nothing but time to think about that.

The plane to St Petersburg boarded one half-hour late, at 11:18 a.m.

It then sat on the runway for nearly an hour.

FORTY-FOUR

Aaron Seymor Blatt diverted his eyes, holding a collection of
human ivory in a tin box, rattling these, looking out from a
dirt road into a thickly grown patch of woods.

The young woman in blue was struggling, suspended in
the air, kicking backward with naked heels and fighting for
her life against the hold of an angry fat man. Gregory Corless
had wanted her for intercourse, not sex, but for pure physical
domination. Seymor Blatt had wanted her as a toy, a human
living mouth which he could fondle and pick, study and probe;
the fascination no deeper than most other men's lust for a
woman's softer parts, breasts, buttocks, legs, hands, and
he was absorbed in what he required for excitation, while
thinking other men equally abnormal for not sharing his
concern.

He heard the last breath leaving her body.

Carol Barth was almost dead. He knew that sound with his
gut and so turned back to face the end of a macabre dance
as the fat man's belly jiggled and the young woman's battered
body slipped towards his boots. He removed a cord from her
throat. The warm torso leaned against his feet.

'Well, well,' Corless said tonelessly, his upper lip twitching
with sweat as the lifeless form slid limply off his boots and he
turned, walking towards his partner. They were standing at
the edge of a remote and wooded lot, thirty short miles from
the city of Fort Myers, an hour from the Florida Keys.

456

What had started as a game of Happy Puppy ended here, with a brief three-minutes' worth of actual killing, with their hearts pumping, filled with excitement. Corless seemed more relaxed, more pleased with himself than he had been all morning; while Blatt felt a tranquillity that could not be touched.

And they wanted to stand there forever, just like this, no sound, no sweeter moment, no interruptions.

The simple act of killing for them was better than fine and blissful dreaming, better than pools of money, better than owning the planet.

Killing made them feel alive, and yet, it made them feel boundless, like they were travellers through time. 1989 lost meaning until it held no significance, nor did the place where they were now; no Florida, no rules, no cities, no concerns of a modern age. Just the living, raging world of primitive man on ancient safari.

After twenty minutes, when they found themselves talking again, it was in whispers and they did not want to leave.

'Carol and Lacy were awfully good for us,' Blatt offered quietly.

'They had no choice,' Corless corrected.

'Bakker One-Seven, this is dispatch.'

The desk sergeant's voice boomed through the grey box mounted between the handlebars of a bright blue Electro Glide Harley Davidson. Glades County Highway Patrolman John Brougham was unit One-Seven, six-feet-five-inches' worth of motorcycle cop who lived in a small house just on the other side of the wooded swamp preserve known as Waltzing Waters.

At 10:30 he was dunking a donut in front of Marty's Coffee Shop on Route 78, enjoying the fine weather, preparing to finish his weekend shift at noon. He had been on duty since that evening, having faced a rather routine Saturday night. There were the usual DWI and traffic accidents, one drug bust for recreational use in a parking lot, and a domestic altercation in a seedy motel near the town of Alva on Highway 80. That had been the high point.

At 3:00 a.m. he had been the first officer to respond after a woman busted a gin bottle over her sleeping husband's skull, an unemployed trucker who had, earlier in the night, blackened both her eyes and broken her arm. So, in his mind, John Brougham was editing his incident report down to a 413, wounding in self-defence, even though she had been feigning sleep for hours before she got the chance to clobber him.

'Dispatch, this is One-Seven,' he said in clipped tones between bites of a redcurrant jelly donut.

'John, your wife just called, she says to plant more often, you'll know what that means?'

'Roger,' he gulped, and the radio cackled with laughter. It was a code that wasn't all that difficult to figure out, and he immediately regretted not helping to devise something just a bit more clandestine. Mr and Mrs John Brougham were having difficulty in conceiving their first child, and having ruled out infertility, his seed was the only possible culprit. They had been waiting a week for lab tests to be returned, the family doctor had obviously called at Sunday dawn, knowing how concerned the couple were. The thought occurred to Brougham that all available units had just been informed.

'John, that's good news,' the sergeant offered through the box, 'a below normal count isn't unusual, just keep trying.'

'Thanks,' he sputtered back, knowing the man was being genuine, a real paternal type, just a bit out of touch, enough to have forgotten the pitch and jive of uniformed units. Brougham knew he would be facing locker room harassment in the days to come.

'Bakker One-Twelve, what's your 211?' the sergeant was asking another unit.

The radio hissed, sparking with laughter. 'Speed trap mile marker five, we can cover for One-Seven . . .'

'Roger that, One-Twelve, take his position intersect I-17 and Gables, traffic monitoring.'

'Roger.'

'Bakker One-Seven, shave the clock, Johnny,' the sergeant offered, 'it's a slow shift.'

'Roger,' is all John Brougham said. And he dropped the silver blue visor down on his helmet and fired the powerful machine into thunder, picking the microphone back up as he sped into the wind, approaching third gear.

'One-Seven to dispatch,' he called.

'Go ahead.'

'Thanks,' he said, and he meant that. Inside he was a big enough man so that a good laugh, even at his expense, didn't trouble him.

'Are you going to leave her like that?' Blatt whispered.

Corless shrugged, using an obscene gesture, for he really didn't care and the physical high they had felt was now over, their existence transformed back into a bland world where everything seemed grey, everything seemed the same. No highs, no lows, no peaks, no valleys. They had been to the mountain, they had arrived in a desert wasteland.

'That's not what I meant, Greg, we're only a mile from the main road.' Blatt's head spun nervously on a long stalk of neck, straining to find an intrusion, but there was only the sound of twittering birds coming up from behind them.

Corless was turning back towards Carol's body, trying to regain his sense of thrill, but staring down at this and finding none. In life she had been graceful and slim, now her violet eyes stared aimlessly upward, her mouth was a dark red hollow that lacked the sparkle of teeth.

The powder-blue tanktop was torn open, although she had been allowed to dress, and Corless pushed with his right boot, lifting the light torso, heaving it with ease over the edge of the embankment. The body slid limply into a ravine, dark hair streaming behind, coming to rest against a rotting tree stump. The partners waited for a few moments in this peaceful solitude, feeling calm in the still quiet of early morning while grey squirrels scurried about the body expecting a treat.

'Where is Newport News?' asked Blatt.

'How the hell would I know?' Corless returned. 'In Virginia somewhere, who cares?'

'I liked her accent,' Blatt smiled.

'I'm glad, Seymor. If you bought that jet we could spend more time up there.' Corless turned back towards the van. 'Let's grab some food on the way.'

'Greg, we can be at Page Field in a half-hour, it's only 11:10.'

'Poor pitiful Seymor,' Corless hissed, 'this safari's still a day ahead of schedule and you're ready to leave? How about one more, we haven't used half our trick bag.'

'Greg,' he said quite honestly, 'I wish you'd stop saying we're on safari, that bothers me.'

'Sure, whatever makes you happy,' and he climbed into the cab, waiting for his partner while turning on the radio.

'What would make me happy is an early lunch in North Carolina, and we could still be in Washington in time for dinner.'

'If you let me pilot; I gotta fly, Seymor, you know I gotta fly.' His voice had dropped a pitch into seriousness. Blatt knew this was important to Corless.

Like so many middle-aged men who flew small private planes, his manhood was somehow inexorably tied into the cockpit and controls; tied directly into his personal sense of well being, defining who he thought he was, as if any of this took uncommon skill. To Blatt it was absurd, but Corless was pushing his ideas on him.

'I've been thinking . . .'

'No,' Blatt cut him off, 'I am *not* buying you a jet.' He knew that courteous voice of Greg's, so unlike him to begin with, and Corless was cursing mad at the response.

'Seymor,' he pushed, 'you're rich as a damn sultan, what's the harm, buy it as a tax write-off, it would cost nothing.'

'Hardly,' Blatt puffed.

'If we had a jet, just think of the ground we could cover, an air van, Seymor. A goddamn air van. Able to go anywhere, anytime, and supersonic too. West Coast for blondes. Northwest for pasty skin. Southwest for tanned girls. And the east for society types. We could even bang 'em down in Mexico. Real diversity!' His face wore a manic intensity.

460

'Twin props are good enough, we already have a Beechcraft, don't push,' he sniped, his thin body plugged firmly in his seat.

'Fuck you!' Corless spat suddenly. 'You greasy little Jew . . .' And he was about to continue just as Blatt froze, his eyes locked wide with fright like a rabbit too scared to run from a predator. There was a sound approaching from beyond the tree line, like an engine without a muffler, or an all-terrain vehicle, seeming to come directly at them, the sound growing louder.

'Oh my God, Greg, it could be the police!' Blatt cried, quivering, barely able to control himself.

'Well then, it's just time to pay for the party.' Corless shrugged, his voice dripping with blackmail. 'Every man for himself.'

'Greg, don't say that!' he whined with fear, as the sound was looming, flaring from a thicket on the dirt drive they had found off the interstate. It was so remote a location Corless was guessing it was maybe a teen on a go-cart of some type, and he was wondering how old the kid might be.

'We wait until they go by, then pull away,' said Corless.

'It's the death state!' Blatt cried, gulping air through his rubber neck.

'Cool it.' Corless shook his head, and he casually grabbed the binoculars from behind his seat, adjusting these and staring through the windshield.

Just beyond the treeline he could see a form coming down the soggy roadway, moving very slowly over the dirt, the bright blue metallic paint gleaming as he came. He said not a word to Blatt as his hand reached down, wrapping around the grip of the stovepipe revolver, lifting the heavy black Magnum into his lap.

Blatt's eyes grew wide, his face frozen in horror with the sound of an engine coming for them, ever steady, coming down on them from the roadway.

'Oh God, Greg, what is it?' he cried.

'A cop,' said Corless, and his face was calm and cruel.

*   *   *

461

Trooper John Brougham was off duty and on his way home through the backwoods, cutting twenty minutes off his clock by using the State land. He crept along the path in an effort to keep dirt from his bike, his visor pulled up, mostly watching for larger stones that could chip paint.

As he reached the clearing he saw a van, not taking much notice of this since the fishing season was now upon them and there was a male partnership, and quite typically so. But these men were studying a road map.

It was this stall, the use of a map, that caused him to stop.

If Greg Corless hadn't felt they needed to look busy, John Brougham would have just kept going; he would have never stopped to help with directions.

'Oh God, he's coming straight at us!' Blatt whined.

And Corless produced his best grin, lifting a lip and showing teeth because that's what a smile is.

Isn't it?

The bright blue machine pulled next to them.

'How you folks today?' Brougham offered to Corless, resting comfortably on his bike, the engine still running, waiting to be asked directions.

'Just fine,' Corless responded, 'how are you?'

'Good,' Brougham nodded, and he straightened up, looking beyond to the other middle-aged male, who seemed a bit fidgety, his eyes blinking too rapidly, his neck bobbing with a nervous tick.

'How's he?' Brougham asked, growing concerned.

Blatt tried not to squeak, fighting to control his bladder. 'Just fine offi-cer,' he gulped heavily.

'So where are you headed?' Brougham asked, 'here for the crappies?'

Corless responded thoughtfully. 'Heading north, St Pete, just taking a little rest.' Officer John Brougham removed his helmet, looking up at Corless with penetrating green eyes. The back roads of the Everglade lowlands called Waltzing Waters seemed a strange place for a rest stop, and though it could have been innocent enough, he remembered an APB from the State Police.

Two men, middle-aged, van or stationwagon, one thin and neat, the other portly. He turned off his engine, knocking the kick-stand forward into place, trying to remember the rest. Something about a decal, that was the best he could do, though he was certainly trying.

'Oh God,' Blatt shivered under his breath, 'he's staying.'

The policeman dismounted, maintaining eye contact with Corless, then stepping back to what he had been taught, in the academy, was a safe distance from the van. About six feet, close enough for observation, yet far enough to prevent physical contact. His black boots covered this area in one stride as he smoothly unsnapped his holster, instantly whipping his .9 mm to chest level with both hands on a steady regulation aim.

'Step out of the car!' Brougham shouted, studying Corless. 'Put both your hands on the wheel, and I want to see fingers . . .' As an explosion boomed into a deafening stillness; an explosion ripping into Brougham, the jagged flash from the stovepipe blowing through the van's thin door, shredding glass and metal like paper, hitting him squarely in the chest, knocking him backward; his body lifting into air as it tumbled onto the bike; as the cabin screamed with a thunderous roar.

The muzzle's flash was still brilliant in their eyes after the sound had passed from the van.

Corless had kept the .357 in his lap, bringing the gun to rest, muzzle first, two inches from the door, and they sat in the van listening to shattered window glass tinkling in its channel.

The heavy bullet had slammed through the trooper's chest, and he lay on his side, a lobe of his heart poking out through his back, still beating as Corless was on him, with Blatt scurrying out the driver's door in an effort to catch up.

'I'll be damned,' said Corless, staring down at this.

'Greg, I beg you, I'll buy the jet, let's go, please . . . I'm really scared . . .'

'Of course you are, little buddy,' he said, wrapping his arm around him, walking closer to the wounded officer until they were directly over what had been John Brougham.

And there's no way to tell, but the odds were that the officer could not see or feel anything, not even the presence of his attackers as they hovered above. His eyes were locked open, but these were dark pools, for shock must have taken over, his life just a biological fact and nothing more, no human element anyway.

And so he very likely did not feel or even know that two more violent charges came ripping into his side in one burning instant, though one arm seemed to come alive with the impact, flapping upward, twice; the road becoming visible through a body cavity as the blow-back dust and gunsmoke cleared.

Then silence.

Without hesitation Corless put on gloves before dragging the bike and the body off into the ditch, kicking these downward where they came to rest next to Carol Barth. And they listened for sirens, standing there together, but there were none.

'I want to go, I want to get out of here!' Blatt was screaming with hysteria.

'Yes,' agreed the man who would pilot the plane, 'we can be ready for takeoff in fifteen minutes.'

And as he walked, Corless found himself thinking about the protest signs he had seen on television the day they burned Ted Bundy. Now he wasn't sure, exactly, why he had thought of this; maybe because they were in Florida, or maybe he felt that he had beaten the Reaper that took Ted. But there was something deeper, something more.

'God, I love this country,' he breathed hard as he climbed into the van.

Blatt was his partner, what could he say?

464

FORTY-FIVE

NOON
POTOMAC, MARYLAND

The Blatt investigation, and the discovery of Samantha
Stoner's identity, brought Scott to a country estate called
Kilimanjaro, thrusting him into the middle of Washington's
powerful high society. Or at least that's what he had been
thinking when he arrived, but now he knew better.

If one was just willing to scratch at it, then there was really
nothing sophisticated about what he saw before him, which
was money talking in a loud and predictable manner. Kilimanjaro was a huge white mansion in a world of other huge white
mansions, row upon row, all gated, all with plaques on paved
driveways declaring pretentious sounding names. Tara had
become Scott's favourite, Southland was another, and Wild
Mountain still another.

To make matters worse, there were no mountains at all in
Potomac, Maryland, and certainly no Mount Kilimanjaro,
only a silly little green hill on the poor side of the road
where he sat in his Chrysler, watching the estate through
high-powered lenses. Scott was truly horrified by what he
saw.

Kilimanjaro was a modern fortress, and staring down from
a meadow onto a front yard of perfect green, Scott saw the
place was surrounded by heavy steel Cyclone fence topped
with razor teeth. A roadway lay between him and the private
drive that ran through the menacing wire, and he could see
a dark blue uniformed guard smoking a cigarette, cap tilted

back, his arm wrapped around a middle-aged blonde in a grey servant's dress. They were closest to the main house.

Immediately to the right was an equestrian centre, including a series of barns and what looked like a riding stable with eight stalls. To the left, in a picket fence exercise ring, a stately grey Arabian trotted over yellow straw as a handler held a restraint, turning in lazy circles.

There was a guest house and indoor swimming pool. A tennis court in one side yard. In the other, a detached garage large enough to enclose a half-dozen good sized cars.

The front gate was deceptive, for there were two, stacked together, back to back. The first was ornate iron, a white lattice work to match the house, and the second stood about ten feet from this, composed of chainlink and mounted on small rubber wheels to enable a guard to push it aside. There was a guard house, again painted white, where a uniformed sentry appeared to be watching television as another approached, walking a black Doberman pinscher on a short leather leash. They were moving together as a tight team, coming down a gentle rise in the bright sun, and Scott could not bring himself to believe that what he was viewing stood in the most affluent suburb of Washington DC.

Here, in Potomac, Maryland, just one short mile from the private residences of two Supreme Court Justices, the Secretary of State, and the Attorney General of the United States.

The dog snarled at the roadway, lurching against his lead as a car filled with church worshippers slowed near the fence to admire the wealthy landscape. The dog was instantly released, breaking into attack, the handler grinning as the dog viciously charged the fence. The car sped off. And Scott immediately found himself remembering back to a rumour he had heard one April, scuttlebutt between boys playing kickball on the streets of New York.

As quickly as it had come, this ugly rumour had been dismissed as just that, rumour. But by September of 1946 a series of pictures appeared in national magazines, and Scott's father had called him in early in order to take his entire family to Mass. On the way to church, his parents gave one big sorry effort to explain, but they never could, Scott remembered.

Could anyone?

The twisted bodies lying for miles in bright sun. Iron doors caked with ash, their hinges dark and grey. Piles of human hair, pigtails tied with ribbon. And the gallows, strung with wire and the death they made there, of every size and shape, of every sex and age. Private rooms of horror. Meat hooks. Stained floors.

Dachau. Buchenwald. Treblinka.

These were the first images to arrive in the world, and the names that Scott remembered best; names that begged for mercy when said aloud, but names that did not belong to the factory where human beings suffered in the corruptible name of science. News of that came later. Men of medicine inflicting wound channels for study; mothers forced to watch their daughters being sexually destroyed.

Auschwitz.

Backed by a figure of six million souls, and with John F. Scott having made a lifetime of study: *The Devoid, the Psycho-Pathology of Recreational Killers*.

If a former victim of Auschwitz was living here, behind the snarling dogs and black uniforms and razor wire; and if this compound did *not* speak directly to that man's memory, filling him with terror – then either he was *no* victim, or Scott was *no* psychologist.

Walking briskly, with a slick military precision, the sentry was coming towards Scott, who quickly started his engine as the team crossed the roadway.

Upon hearing the starter, the man immediately released the dog from its leash and the jaws quivered and snapped, as the K-9 awaited instructions.

Slowly, Scott pulled back onto gravel, coasting across the street, passing them, moving down the driveway and towards the gate. A tall young man stepped from the booth, holding up a palm, approaching in a uniform that was expensively complete with a black tie and matching cuffs. The car came to a stop as the man leaned towards Scott's open window.

From his rear-view he could see the K-9 patrolman trotting into position from the rear. Near the guest house on his left, a young woman was sitting on a large white stallion.

'May I help you?' the guard asked politely.

'Yes,' said Scott, and he held his badge to the light. The man read the identification card and gave a precise nod.

'Commander Scott,' he said with ease, 'you do not have the right address.'

Scott nodded. 'Dr Rubin Jaffe?'

The guard glanced over the car to the K-9 unit, then back to Scott, establishing eye contact. 'Sir, do you have an appointment?' he said in a clipped, hard voice.

Scott yawned. 'Didn't know one was required.'

The woman on horseback was coming forward, riding an English mount, her jacket a bright scarlet, her boots and hat an inky pitch black. She slowed her gait to a walk as she approached. A child, Scott thought, sixteen at best, with dark brown eyes and pale skin.

'We have strict orders,' the guard glanced at a clipboard for effect, 'no one is allowed on the estate without an appointment. I do not see your name, so I'm sorry, Commander, I will have to ask you to leave.'

Scott nodded thoughtfully. 'Son,' he said in a condescending voice, 'do you know what a warrant is?'

'Yes sir.' The man's face was stone.

'Then pick up the phone,' Scott nodded at the booth, 'and tell Dr Jaffe that I'm here for a friendly visit and that you are making that *unfriendly*. I do not take rejection well, I'm afraid, and I do have considerable grounds.'

'Yes sir, but . . .'

'And tell him that I can be a very unpleasant man, in fact, a real son of a bitch when I get cooking. With a search warrant, I'll bring in a backhoe and dig up his entire lawn, and I mean that.' Scott glanced at his watch. 'And the stables too, plus drain the swimming pool and drill for evidence.'

'Sir, I . . .'

'Do it!' Scott raised his voice in a nasty bite, something he rarely did.

The guard looked to the handler, then walked directly to the booth and followed instructions, picking up a red phone. Words were exchanged, Scott seeing only his back, then he quickly returned.

'Sir,' he said nervously, 'there are no firearms allowed in the residence.'

'Open the gate!' Scott ordered.

And he did.

His face was cold and gaunt, withered as if by desert winds, his eyes a colourless grey. These were watching Scott with grave intensity, set deeply in a freshly barbered face, his jowls sagging with the translucence of age.

His belly protruded, but this was all but concealed by an exquisitely tailored suit, a tasteful gun-metal blue with pleats to cut a figure where there was little. Dr Rubin Jaffe was standing impatiently in a marbled foyer against the sounds of water splashing down from a stone fountain.

They made eye contact as Scott came through the door, and he noticed that Jaffe was a tall man, and that he moved behind a walker, a cage with silver and black ebony struts, the curved handles like two polished baby elephant tusks. The doctor was watching him with contempt for the disturbance, receiving him without a word, observing Scott's every move as he strolled through a high vaulted room with a servant on either side. The Commander was sure they doubled as body guards for the ageing holocaust victim.

Upon request, with his eyes locked on Jaffe's, Scott removed his service automatic, snapping out the clip, then laying this on the tray held towards him. The old man started forward, and it was at once obvious that the cage was no prop, his torso turned awkwardly, his legs were working stiffly, the thing was gliding towards Scott on small soundless wheels.

'What is this about?' he demanded, and his face and tone were cruel.

Scott raised an eyebrow, coming straight to the point. 'Serial murder, a criminal investigation.' And in terse language, he explained how the remains of Samantha Stoner had been found beneath Patriots Bowl, a property which Jaffe had purchased directly from the County in 1958, the year she was killed. The doctor did not respond in any manner, no words, no expression, but simply turned his cage away, hobbling down the hallway, the thing gliding as a childish giggle sounded behind them.

Scott turned quickly, catching a glimpse of what looked like a girl, but in a strange sort of way. He was guessing eight or nine, with harlot red lips and thick mascara, and he was about to inquire when the doctor, never looking back, interrupted his thoughts.

'My nephew,' Jaffe said flatly.

Scott felt a twang of nausea as he followed the caged man down a draughty corridor. 'I bet you have a number of them,' he stated sarcastically.

The doctor did not answer.

There were towering double doors of inlaid oak on two sides of the study. It was dark, the walls were panelled in wormwood, with one picture window looking out onto a bright green yard and swimming pool. The tall wire fence was hidden from this view by a forest of trees, and as they entered the room, the doctor, with a slight gesture of one hand, motioned Scott towards a red leather couch while moving to sit at a huge mahogany desk.

Jaffe hopped quickly, adjusting himself in a high-back executive chair, and Scott was about to speak as a waiter appeared through a side door. He stood patiently awaiting his master's wish.

'Tea,' Jaffe said flatly without looking up.

'And you?' the servant asked without tone.

'Coffee,' Scott ordered, 'black.' As the waiter vanished, Scott surveyed the walls.

There was an old collection of primitive artifacts, including an array of menacing spears with bright knifelike tips. He recognised these as a Morro warrior's from the Philippine Islands, and above, a series of hand-fashioned helmets made from reeds. There were six enormous swords mounted into a huge star, the thick blades reflecting afternoon light, and Scott felt the penetrating stare of Dr Jaffe, who was inspecting him with some curiosity, perhaps disdain, summing him up, but reserving his opinions.

'Morro Indian?' Scott asked.

Jaffe's brow lifted slightly, and he nodded. 'You know your weapons, Mr Scott, those were a gift from a tribesman. I visited the Morros in the late 1950s.'

Next, Scott's eyes came to rest on a large wild cat, mounted after death and now springing from the wall with half a torso. In the corner of the room was a leopard standing on its hind legs like a trained bear, holding an arrow in its teeth.

'Ituri Forest, the Congo,' Jaffe offered, 'six hundred pounds, took him with one shot.'

Across the great wall to his left there were hundreds of artifacts, made from reed and wood, cloth from hammered bark, bows and spears, small drums and musical instruments fashioned from monkey skins, and one sporting the head of a howling red monkey beneath what looked like a thick buggy-whip, a serious instrument of the lash.

'Do they beat their food before eating?' Scott suggested.

Jaffe turned his head but did not smile. 'That is a *Fita*, a whip used for sacred ceremonies by the forest people of BaLese.'

'Stanley's dark continent.'

'Yes, the very heart.'

'You travelled there extensively?'

Jaffe leaned forward in his chair. 'You are a cultured man, Mr Scott, what is it you want of me?' And he said this almost absently, a man who ruled his universe with an absolute power. The waiter appeared, serving his master first, then quietly placing a small silver coffee pot and cup before Scott on a three-legged table. The men waited for the servant to disappear.

'So, Jack Scott, tell me about yourself, an Irish cop, what will they think of next?'

The Commander smiled. 'Tell me about Tobytown,' he

said without tone, dropping a sugar cube into his cup before pouring.

'I'm afraid I don't know it.'

Scott's eyes locked Jaffe's into a head-on stare as he confidently poured the hot black liquid, then began stirring with his spoon. 'Make that the River Road properties, both sides of the street, you own the entire block as well as fourteen buildings, a gas station, a television station, and two banks. The only thing you don't own is the Shiloh Baptist Church.'

Now the old man smiled as if tasting sweets for the first time. 'Yes, that is very true, and years ago I also tried to buy that church. Offered quite a lot of money for the silly thing, but the fools turned me down. Even so,' he waved both his hands, 'I have no knowledge of this Tobytown, other than the housing development which I donated from the goodness of my heart to some displaced persons.'

Scott smiled at the sarcasm, Rubin Jaffe was toying with him. 'So, you are a charitable guy, a real fine fellow?'

Jaffe nodded without expression. 'Ask anyone, Earth First, B'nai B'rith, Centre for Creative Nonviolence, Save the Bay, Earth Watch, numerous fine arts, the list is endless.'

Scott sipped his coffee. 'The village of Tobytown existed until July of 1958, then burned to the ground. Arson would be my guess. The following September you bought the entire block, lock, stock and barrel of ash.'

Jaffe exhaled with pleasure. 'Yes, that was years ago, these properties are parts of cities now, we house and employ the masses, Mr Scott. Are you sure that's what they called it?'

'Tobytown, named for the cemetery that was destroyed to make way for development.'

'Well, it's a pity, good thing I was around to help.' He smiled, sipping his tea.

'And how much weight did you gain at Auschwitz?' Scott asked flatly, as Jaffe's eyes narrowed with never a flinch, his mouth turning upward with amusement as he steadily refilled his cup from a copper kettle.

'Well, you're a slick sonofabitch,' he mouthed, 'what do you really want?'

'Who struck the match?'

Jaffe huffed with a chuckle. 'Statutes, you should know better. The limitations are long expired if, as you are suggesting, there was some type of crime involved.'

Scott did not respond.

'You *do* know who I am, Mr John Scott, you do know who you are talking with?'

He shook his head. 'Why don't you tell me?'

Jaffe nodded, leaning into his high-back leather chair with a knowing smile. 'Read *Forbes*, you will find I'm wealthier than a king, the top ten billionaires. And I do have friends, powerful and worthy ones. While I won't bother you with my net worth,' he paused for effect, 'you should know where it all came from.'

Scott smiled. 'Well, we surely can't venture a wrong guess on anything this important.'

'Good,' he agreed, 'because I was thinking you might have to move at the end of the year when your lease expires.'

Scott did not take this bait.

'Tell me, Jack, you are a federal employee, so what building do you work in?'

'World Trade in New York or the Federal Headquarters Center in Washington.'

'Well, well,' Jaffe said, 'in both instances that means I am your landlord.' And Scott cocked his head.

'You see, Commander, I am landlord to most of the United States Government, since they are prohibited from owning too many buildings, I own for them, then lease back. I own nearly every building that houses federal employees by day, plus many they live in by night. Some of the most powerful men on this planet call me just to get a bit nicer office. So you see, I am an unheard of industry, and I've been able to corner that market by following political corruption. Greed, Mr Scott. When the government sells out, they sell out to Rubin Jaffe.'

Scott nodded, thinking this over. 'That's quite an angle, there's a code putting a cap on federal ownership of real estate?'

'Only buildings, I'm afraid.' Jaffe sipped noisily at him. 'That code has made me rich on your taxes, so I do hope you're current. You should know right now that your little theory about Toady Town, while it amuses me, I find no threat there, anywhere.'

Scott nodded. 'I'm glad,' he stated flatly, 'fear is a wasted emotion.'

Dr Rubin Jaffe smiled darkly, sipping his tea, watching with amusement. 'I find you to be very perceptive, that alone is of interest. So entertain me, Jack Scott.'

Scott considered this offer, he could not tell if it was genuine so he fashioned a question to test the waters. 'Tobytown, do you believe it was torched?'

'Yes,' he said without equivocation. 'Land is money, where should I have banked it, where do you put yours?'

'In your pocket,' Scott smiled, 'I thought we established all of that, though I do find great reward in what I've chosen to do for a living.'

'And you do what, exactly, I wasn't clear on that?'

Scott watched his eyes, they seemed to dance with a cunning intelligence. 'I'm a manhunter, Dr Jaffe, I remove killers from society.'

Jaffe nodded thoughtfully. 'But you seem so small and meek to me, Mr Scott, do you really have the stomach for it?'

'I do, and I find a great wealth in saving lives, and in the characters I am able to meet, the people I deal with. You'll find no luggage rack on my hearse, I'm afraid. Did you pay to destroy Tobytown?'

'Well, I like that!' Jaffe chuckled suddenly as his eyes danced. 'A man with a philosophy, that *is* rare in this age, very entertaining. Rich with the lives of others, and yes, while I'll give no confessions, who else could it have been?'

Scott nodded gratefully. 'And the man who lit that fire . . .'

'Only one?' Jaffe cut him off with a sarcastic smile. 'That was over thirty years ago, is that the best you can offer?'

'Correct me.'

'I cannot, you know the law, Jack, skirting the edge of incrimination.'

'I've assumed the job was to drive people from Tobytown in any manner possible?'

Jaffe nodded. 'They were trying to pay their back taxes, if there was such a place, and they came close, that was my understanding.'

'Then does the name Samantha Stoner mean anything to you?'

'I'm sorry, it does not.'

Scott reached into his briefcase, producing a colour picture of the clay bust, then walking with this to the large mahogany desk, laying it in front of the older man who merely glanced at it and shook his head.

'Nothing,' Jaffe said, 'although I do remember a Negro accusing me of kidnapping his family, so maybe . . .'

Scott nodded gratefully. 'Do you remember anything about him?'

'A stone-cutter, I believe, we bought and sold his business, nothing more than that.'

Scott felt sick, the Auschwitz victim was talking about Samantha's father. 'This child was killed in April, three months before the fire was set.'

'Is that what you're after, some crime from our ancient and collective past? Oh come, Mr Scott, relevance, please. I demand relevance.' Rubin Jaffe's face grew huge with disbelief. 'You disappoint me, you seemed such a bright and cultured man.'

'Did you pay the fire-starter?'

Jaffe shook his head. 'That is very unprofessional, rather accusatory.'

'Then he wasn't a local man?'

'I hired no one, but the towns of Cabin John and Bethesda were rife with inbreeding, tight, and very, very small. We changed all of that, built the cities and people did the rest.'

'The rest?' Scott puzzled.

Jaffe tilted back in his chair, clasping his fingers together. 'They breed, Jack, *ergo* they did the rest. It is mankind's only true and predictable behaviour, if you put people together they *will* fuck. Any man that accepts that can make a fortune. Humans breed like space is not a finite thing, and it is this behaviour,' he paused to smile, 'that makes men like me wealthy beyond reason.'

Scott removed a photograph of Zak Dorani from his file, approaching the desk slowly. He held this in front of the doctor and watched his eyes carefully, there was no change, no expression at all.

'Then I thank you for your time,' Scott said, returning to close his briefcase, his posture curled into intentional defeat, sagging shoulders, chin turned down slightly as he was preparing to leave.

'You are a very cunning man,' Jaffe said darkly, 'your body language is a skilled performance, you are very good, really.'

'No,' Scott stated, 'I've taken enough of your time.'

'I think not.' His eyes smiled with amusement. 'Your mind is bursting with questions, yet this, for whatever reason, is the most important to you?'

'Perhaps,' Scott stated.

Jaffe leaned forward on his desk. 'I never saw his face, and I never knew his name. Tell me his name.'

'Zak Dorani.'

The doctor gave a knowing nod. 'Quite possible, from that old photo I can tell you that he *would* have been my choice, but I leave those things to others so that I have no immediate knowledge.'

'Fascinating, but why would he be a candidate? How would you know?'

Jaffe sighed with annoyance. 'Oh please, better than that, I grow weary.'

And Scott's mind flipped instantly back to the camps, to the pictures and films he remembered as a child. 'The eyes,' he concluded. If Jaffe had really been there he'd know, and he obviously did, for he was nodding thoughtfully.

Slowly, Dr Jaffe placed a finger under each lid, and then pointed directly at Scott's heart. 'No one home,' he spat, 'emotionless. And yes, I truly have seen it before.'

'Then would it trouble you to know that women and children were disappearing at his hand because he enjoyed his assignment so much?'

'That is unfortunate,' Jaffe stated coldly. 'I am not a killer, and that was not part of the request.'

'And your involvement ended there?'

'What involvement?' He held up his hands. 'The *darkies* have always been good for me, Jack, they rent my slums, they give me properties to develop.'

Scott stood slowly, holding his stomach together by sheer will, he wanted to vomit into the man's face. Instead he walked to the monkey head on the wall, then admired a row of sticks set into a design that resembled the spokes of a wheel. 'May I?'

Jaffe nodded, watching with a great curiosity as Scott stood on his toes to finger them. They were black, darkened from fire, sharp as needles to the touch.

These, in turn, were surrounded by shiny steel rods of half the length and thickness. Scott tried not to choke while fighting the sickening tide that was now pulsing, coursing through his body as he stared into the open maw of a red monkey, the thin white teeth glistening like angry needles.

'And these?' Scott asked.

'The metal ones are fléchettes, the wooden ones are *Njobo*, they are really one and the same. One modern, one ancient, death's most perfect instrument.'

'Very interesting,' Scott responded, and his voice sagged. 'These are hand-held instruments?'

'No, no, again you disappoint me, such limited knowledge. The wooden shafts are from the lost tribe of Ituri, proving that peoples of the Congo are not so primitive as the Western world would like to think.'

Scott shrugged, raising a questioning hand, and though this trembled slightly, he did not believe the ageing doctor saw it.

'They are used in various forms to kill and control *Nyama*, or the devil spirit of the forest. They had a saying for it, *evil controlling evil*, that's the rough translation. The shaft is actually the weapon, the delivery differs according to purpose.

The steel fléchette was developed by the U.S. Army's Armed Forces Special Weapons Project in 1956 and is based entirely on the primitive system.'

'I don't understand.'

Jaffe looked at him with puzzlement, rising from his desk, pushing the walker before him. He reached the display easily, removing a wooden shaft, then handing this to Scott.

'Feel how light it is, the balance and strength, the metal toughness, cuts through air like a deadly spirit. Certain tribes thought it was spirit, made from a living thing, every speck of the forest is thought to have a soul, even trees and fire, they were used in combination.'

Scott did not have to examine too closely, he had held this a thousand times before, and was fighting with those images now.

'During a hunt,' Jaffe continued, 'a *BaMbuti* warrior could place several of these into his prey from a great distance, depending upon the skill level. While it would slow a being down, it was not uncommon to see the head of an adversary filled like a pincushion.'

Scott swallowed. 'So death was not instantaneous?'

'Hardly, those are special bolts used for shooting the red monkey you see grinning at you, he took ten, the precise number to steal evil, transferring it to the warrior. This makes him stronger, increasing his powers.'

'And the method of delivery?'

'A blowgun, very accurate, very effective for stunning prey. They whistle through the air like deadly insects, impaling the victim's head, and it is impossible to know the direction of attack.'

'And the fléchette?'

'Potentially the deadliest small arms projectile ever designed, but it was dropped by the armed forces as inhumane. They were also used as small arrows, what we would call bolts or quarrels. My fascination was with the surgical precision of both the ancient and the modern version, it is because they are so thin that their velocity is so great.'

Scott blinked, he had seen footage of blowguns at work,

478

they were silent and capable of delivering a projectile with incredible violence.

'When it comes to the fléchette, nearly every country on earth has experimented with them. As for the ancient version, more than a hundred living tribes around the world still use them. But these,' he held the black wood in his hand, 'would only be known to the most serious of hunters, the study of them is an art by itself.'

Jaffe was pointing Scott towards the door, the wheels on his cage gliding across a Persian carpet.

'Then that technique you explained,' Scott said, 'ten nails or better, according to the ancient beliefs of the Congo that was considered killing deeper than life?'

Jaffe nodded. 'You are a well educated man, a pity we will not speak again.'

'And my question?'

Jaffe smiled darkly as his man servant moved before them, opening the giant wooden door to the world outside and offering Scott his gun.

'The ancient fléchette is used to extract power from death and suffering, it kills the body, but more importantly, it kills the soul.'

Scott stood on the front stoop looking deeply into the doctor's eyes. 'And did you explain all this to Aaron Seymor Blatt before or after he hired you an arsonist?'

The man's dark pupils instantly constricted into pinpoints, though his expression never changed. 'Good day,' Jaffe said as he turned away.

'Indeed it is,' Scott added as the door closed tight.

FORTY-SIX

Jack Scott strolled down from the gas station on River Road, having parked his car in the rear of the church. 'Entertaining,' he repeated aloud, his voice filled with disgust, that's how Dr Rubin Jaffe had explained the ancient blowgun and its fléchette, the use far more satisfying to a killer than a firearm or bow.

A swift, fatal and silent weapon that in turn offered the user myth, magic and perfect control for either slow or instant destruction of life. Since the shaft was shaped for balance, there had been no markings to tell of its origin, only the slight spittle from the attacker, lost to forensics after only a few days. As he walked he remembered the hands of a victim, batting at her face, having to be restrained as she fought off invisible hornets, batting at the air without being able to explain. And there had been others, the shafts removed after death even before Scott had arrived on the scene.

Why, he thought back, had they not known? Even if the police sciences were in their infancy, that was his job, that is what he did; looking into his mind and watching women and children batting away deadly insects, it was obvious. And suddenly Dr Chet Sanders was there to tell him otherwise, Scott remembering how sympathetic his manner always appeared.

'There is nothing you can do, save yourself,' Dr Sanders was saying now, and Scott could hear that old man's voice, soft but clear, tired but never despairing.

'There's still hope,' Scott remembered, that's how he had responded, and he couldn't believe that now, how hard he had tried to cling to hope, to his own failings, to not being able to fail. A part of the job, he told himself, and he carried his mental baggage down one short flight of crumbling concrete stairs to a damp hole in the ground that was a metal door. This had once been red, but the paint was badly faded into a tomato soup pink and covered with dirt.

Scott knocked softly with the flat of his palm, hearing Sanders' voice in his mind, he'd been a towering man with dark brown hair and warm brown eyes. 'She's too badly beaten, Jack, the meninges, the protective membranes enveloping the brain. I'm sorry . . .' Scott heard footsteps. Mercifully. Footsteps were coming.

'Hi Jack,' Rivers offered. 'Any luck?'

The door opened with a retarded moan and Scott looked up into the hard-looking face of a friend, though they had met only forty-eight hours ago. Instantly Scott felt an abiding sorrow for the young detective, and he felt like warning him of what his life could become if he stayed in the game, in the manhunt; a haunted old fool with festering memories, it was on the tip of his tongue.

'Jack?' Rivers pressed, and Scott forced his thoughts into paths of logic.

'Sorry, how are we making out?' His grey eyes appeared bloodshot and worn.

'That depends on your point of view. Come on in. Dudley Hall is really something, never seen anything like it.'

Scott nodded. 'Good,' he said, crossing the threshold. And they were standing inside an enormous ghost, the ruins of what had been a gaming theatre for fun and recreation, the festive atmosphere decayed beyond much recognition.

The once-polished wooden lanes had been torn apart, revealing strips of concrete with scatters of boards where the glue had resisted. The ball return gutters had been removed, leaving metal support rods poking up from the floor like strange sculpture. At the end of the lanes, where family and team members once cheered for strikes, there was a series of plastic lights dangling from rotted wire. And an entire third of the building, at the further corner, was a still and festering pond where insects and rodents traded places in the food chain.

It was a breathing darkness.

Only around splintered plywood by the main door did light come streaming through, and as his eyes adjusted, Scott glanced across the wide expansiveness of Patriots Bowl to where a snack bar must have stood, the counter still in place, the wall behind it destroyed in the removal of sinks, stoves and fountains.

Dudley Hall turned towards him, a smile spreading across a toothless jaw as he watched them approach, his arms swinging at his sides with excitement.

'Scotty Dog!' he whistled, coming for him in quick steps, embracing Scott like a small bear and unintentionally lifting his feet from the floor.

Scott chuckled loudly. 'Hey, great to see you, Duddy,' he gasped as the air was crushed from his lungs.

'Well, let me look!' Hall commanded in an excited chirp. 'A sight for sore eyes!' He held him back by the shoulders, shaking his head. 'Ah, Jackie,' he sighed, 'your hair's grey.'

Scott smiled. 'Put on some weight too, can't stop the years.'

'Old, you say?' he whistled sharply. 'Born at the step of the grave, why we jest getting younger!'

Scott nodded, looking over his shoulder. 'Hello, Charlie,' he said, and Dr McQuade came forward from shadow. 'So how do you like working with a real Diggerman?' Scott asked, patting Hall on one massive shoulder.

'I can't keep up,' McQuade smiled. 'A truly remarkable talent.'

Hall was leading Scott by the arm towards the battered counter. 'We've got eleven.' He paused. 'You do want to work, Jackie?'

'Yes,' Scott nodded.

'Then eleven it is,' Hall whistled. 'Thought we'd make twelve, but the yard's clean, jest one final check.'

Scott was staring down at a series of human skulls, all washed and lined up in a neat row with numbers scrawled on their foreheads in black marker. The shades ran pinkish to

482

burnt red, the product of years beneath Maryland clay, twenty-two dark sockets staring back at Scott, filling him with blame. He startled, releasing a heavy sigh, fumbling in his pocket for a cigarette.

Rivers reached over, giving him a light, the familiar gases drilled his lungs. 'God save us,' Scott mumbled aloud, reaching towards a skull with seven black fléchettes protruding in a sharp circle. The largest skull was an adult, the smallest the size of a large grapefruit.

'Do you know what these are?' Hall asked quietly, holding a stick.

Scott nodded. 'Yes,' he said grimly, and it was clear from the hard expression on his face that he would not be pushed further. The men watched as he walked, back and forth along the snack bar, moving like a military commander inspecting troops, nodding thoughtfully at each one. Scott turned. 'What about Samantha's family?'

McQuade moved closer, pointing with a heavy finger. 'Her sister Victoria,' he offered, then counting eight down, 'and Emma.' This skull was of an adult, and Scott swallowed, his eyes narrowing.

'And you're sure?'

'I can't be certain of the mother, but there's no mistake about this child.' McQuade lifted the skull of Victoria Stoner, cradling it in one massive hand like a small globe, the teeth grinning at them.

'Note the similar nasal bridge as Samantha, the high cheekbones, the splendid curving of the forehead,' he offered, turning to lift the mother. 'They were a pretty people, Jack, even in the bone structure there's a great deal of similarity.'

'Yes,' Scott swallowed, 'a pretty people. I see no darts, Charlie, how did they die?'

'Impossible to tell for sure, but I believe a sharp blow to the cranium on Victoria, notice the hole, the splintering . . .'

Scott saw and quickly turned his face away. 'And the lethal instrument?'

'My guess would be a small hammer, that kind of thing, not a bullet punch. Death was instantaneous.' Scott was thinking that the killer might have slipped, delivering a harder blow than was really necessary.

'And the mother?' he asked, holding up a hand. 'The short version, please.'

'Strangulation, a broken neck.'

Scott nodded. 'And you believe the property to be clean at this point? Was there a graveyard?'

McQuade raised the skull towards Dudley Hall. 'Yep,' he whistled, 'damn near buried out. Whoever discarded them,' he pointed at the red skulls, 'he sure knew what he was doing. Jackie, we think the reason this property hasn't been resold is that folks who own it know there's a graveyard.'

'Can't miss it?'

'Ain't no place a blade can hit that won't produce dead.'

'Duddy, how old is it, when did it start?'

'Can't tell for sure, most country yards jest start as a family plot, then develop over generations. First real busy period was around 1840, lots of stones from then, Civil War was mighty active, right up after World War I.'

'And they're mostly black?'

'The graves or the modern victims?' McQuade clarified.

'Sorry, graves first.'

'Whelp, there's some white folk, not many,' said Hall.

'As for the victims, six black, the rest white,' said McQuade.

Scott nodded. 'What now, Charlie?'

'We were just taking a break when you arrived, we have a few holes to cover, and a few spots to recheck.'

Scott smiled thoughtfully. 'Thanks,' he said quietly, 'I really appreciate it.' And he wandered away, making eye contact with Frank Rivers as they moved for the door.

FORTY-SEVEN

1:05 P.M.
ST PETERSBURG, FLORIDA

Matthew Brennon laid a tape recorder on a marble coffee table as Captain Duncan Powell looked on, motioning with a massive hand for his driver to leave the room. The young officer nodded, then quickly dismissed himself as the Captain turned to Brennon.

'I have a working relationship with the family,' he said calmly, his bass voice filling the small room. 'I will tell you when time is needed for composure, and I will ask the questions.'

'Yes, sir,' Brennon said with precision.

Captain Powell was a natural leader who was known for having never raised his voice in anger, yet when he controlled a situation it was with absolute authority; his demeanour was sobering, yet kind, a professional from the old school of police brass.

Brennon could see that quite clearly in the tall and polished stance, barrel chest thrust out, feet parted one length, hands placed behind his back, holding a gold braided officer's hat by the shiny black brim. This revealed a full head of silver hair as he nodded slightly downward. The truth was that the young federal agent felt relieved at the overwhelming presence of Captain Powell, for this large man in full dress, his face like chiselled granite, was preparing to shoulder the tremendous burden that would surely come, and then carry the responsibility on his wide and rigid back.

Brennon took a deep breath as he watched Philip Caymann stroll into the room, a minister at his side, though Powell did not look up until spoken to directly.

'We have told her what is required,' Caymann said softly, 'she is preparing herself.'

He was a small man, only made smaller by the Captain's presence, and Phillip Caymann's face was the colour of his suit, pale grey, and badly in need of warmth and colour. On March 29th, their eight-year-old daughter, Lisa, had been playing in their backyard, 1606 McDowell Drive, in the sub-division known as Silver Shores, a middle class neighbourhood. As Denise Caymann recalled, she had left her daughter for only a moment to answer the phone, and shortly thereafter the State Police were called in on suspected abduction. It was a clean and professional job. No witness. No evidence. Only a vague recollection of a telephone conversation with an insurance agent and some material evaluations from Lisa's body, which was found in a gravel pit covered by a blanket. The Caymanns had been mourning for only two days as ViCAT dispatched Brennon from Fort Worth.

Duncan's bass voice filled the small room. 'I apologise, but it is a necessary intrusion,' he said to Caymann, then extended his hand to the pastor. 'Hello, Father, I'd like you to meet Special Agent Matthew Brennon, who has been working with me.'

'A pleasure. Thomas O'Brian,' he said, shaking Brennon's hand.

As the men became better acquainted, Brennon felt a light-headedness from lack of sleep, certain that he was coming down with a flu from the plane flight. It wasn't a far enough trip for jet-lag, he thought, though something had caused his stomach to sour, and he was sipping a cup of hot tea, his tape player at the ready, waiting for Lisa's mother.

She had not been up from her bed since the news of her daughter's death, and Brennon thought back to his dog-leg where he had seen the remains of a girl from Moxie Pond, the pathologists hovering under hot surgical lamps, the chrome gutters, the sound of high-speed instruments.

*   *   *

'Well, someone will have to identify the body,' cautioned Dr Cyril Kline, the Jacksonville coroner. Brennon had turned his back as Captain Powell stood fast at the dead woman's feet.

'I've spoken to the father, but I will not allow him to see this,' the Captain countered. 'We've located a friend of the family who is willing to take the trip.' He handed a slip of paper to the rubber-gloved pathologist, who laid it off to one side without looking at it.

'You better be damn certain, Duncan, we have no dental forensics to work with on this one.'

'How's that?'

The white coated assistant was now mowing across Lacy Wilcott's blonde head with a barber's shaver, sweeping hair into a bag, as Kline reached, holding her jaw with one hand.

'If you don't use family, I'll need a signed affidavit of the relationship for my files.'

'I understand,' Powell said grimly.

Brennon stepped forward. 'Cause of death was strangulation from behind?'

'Yes and no,' Kline muttered, 'she would have died anyway.' He turned, lifting the sheet. 'Any of these wounds could have been fatal, but technically . . .'

In an instant Brennon's face went to white as he stumbled into a drip gutter, fighting a tremble in his stomach and a weakness at his knees, remembering the pink lox that Myra Blatt had served him for breakfast.

'Matthew?' Powell cried with concern, but that came too late.

Brennon shuddered in one wild hot instant as the pit in his gut became a fast rising ball and vertigo took him violently by the throat.

'Cover her back up,' Kline had quickly ordered, then snapped off the overhead lamps.

Brennon had remained silent for most of the day, his stomach was just beginning to settle.

A ghost of a woman was now entering the room, her black hair had been combed with nervous abandon, her face was drawn and pale. She was small, wearing a pink bathrobe that was tied at a thin waist.

A nurse moved slowly at her side, and there was no worse illness, Brennon reminded himself as she came to her husband's side, greeting Captain Powell, then the preacher, looking straight at Brennon. He could see the dilation of her pupils. Denise Caymann was heavily sedated, and though he knew her to be but forty-three, she looked much older.

They were all standing, and waiting, this scene reeling in slow motion as she took a chair by the table, her eyes rolling to the nurse, down to the tape recorder, then up to Captain Powell. He nodded at her, and then following his lead, everyone sat but Father O'Brian, who came to the woman's side, standing just behind her chair.

'Have you found them?' she asked flatly without looking up.

'Perhaps,' Powell said, and his bass voice filled the little room. 'As I explained earlier, it will take some time, and we require help.' He introduced Brennon, who stood to take her hand; it felt cold as death.

'Phillip said you wanted me to hear?'

'Yes,' Powell said grimly, 'tell us if it is the voice you heard, and please, take your time.' Without further delay he nodded at Brennon who pressed the button, and the tape spun onto its take-up spool as a stranger's voice popped from the small speaker.

'Hello, this is Jack Scott, I'm not available to answer your call, but if you leave a message I'll get back to you when I return.'

Brennon quickly stopped the machine and leaned slightly forward on the couch, looking carefully at the expression on the woman's face. Her eyes were dark and deep, lacking sparkle, her lips pulled tight. The silence was like a cold blanket as he pressed the button a second time.

'Hey now, this is Duddy Hall,' the voice chirped, 'I'm not available, but if you leave a name, I'll call back.'

The woman's eyes narrowed and she sighed, looking up to her husband and shaking her head. The Captain nodded.

'Hello . . .'

Denise Caymann responded as if to a gunshot, flying to her feet, her body shaking towards convulsions as Father O'Brian and the nurse quickly held her, keeping her in place as her torso grew menacingly stiff, her eyes burning with a murderous rage.

'Kill him!' She found her voice and screamed. 'Kill him for me . . .' and she released a horrid cry that sent a corkscrew of ice through Brennon's spine, that caused Captain Powell to bite into his cheek, that forced tears to roll from the face of a father.

They were all on their feet now and moving through the chaos, instinctively trying to help as Phillip Caymann quickly grabbed his wife, locking the struggling woman into his arms.

'Play it!' she shrieked, and Brennon looked at Powell, then the voice filled the room.

'. . . this is Aaron Blatt. I'm not available to answer your call in person, but if you leave a message I'll get back to you when I return.' The woman released a torturous screech that hit them all like deadly bolts.

'Kill him!' she screamed again through clenched teeth, fighting at anyone who was near, her fists pounding against her husband's frail chest.

Lisa Caymann was buried that week, one short mile from her home.

FORTY-EIGHT

On the way back to the command post, Frank Rivers came cruising down the George Washington Memorial Parkway, turning up onto MacArthur Boulevard, passing through the town of Glen Echo, then north towards Potomac and the home of Mr and Mrs Jonathan Patterson. As he drove he radioed for messages.

Rudy Marchette was having troubles at home and would be late for his return detail as Team Pogo, covering the alley; while Toy Saul and Mule Murphy had taken an early dinner break and were proceeding directly to the Jansons' home.

Rivers was considering breaking Team Huskies into two, perhaps putting Mule inside the condemned structure, but decided against that. Scott did not believe the next twenty-four hours would be that pressing, so Rivers' mind flowed back over MPR 780, Debra Ralson Patterson.

What Rivers had determined with the kind assistance of the twins, the Brothers Dix, was that Debra had been drinking with two other girls on the previous night. And while Debra had left with one, the third girl, described to him as a blonde in her twenties, had stayed a bit longer.

Now just a short week ago, that news, alone, that Debra frequented bars, would have horrified the Pattersons into a seizure, perhaps ruining their lives, but it was all joyful news to them now. Life-and-death pressures have strange effects on normal people, Rivers reflected, things turn upside down faster than a snake can spit.

There was a dark side to Jonathan Patterson's daughter that her parents never knew existed, and this, he thought, was one hell of a way to find out. Even if she turned out to be a runaway, the FBI stats claimed better than twenty per cent of all missing teens were abused or exploited before they were found, and no man felt the clock ticking more than Jonathan Patterson, who dashed out the door as Rivers was just pulling into the driveway, coming under the circular overhang.

The man was running forward to greet him, still carrying a telephone book in one hand and clutching a paper bag in the other. His thin face was pale, there were dark circles under brown eyes, and although he looked drained, this time there was some life and excitement to his voice.

'Frank!' he said excitedly. 'Thanks for coming, I have something to show you.'

'Good to see you, sir, you managed to get some sleep?'

'Yes, first time last night.' He was holding out a bag and pulling it open. 'Look,' he said, 'we found it in her room!'

'A pregnancy test,' Rivers concluded.

'Yes, and we've tracked it to the pharmacy up the street, we think she was going there for another kit when she left to get milk, the instructions say to test two times if the first one is positive!'

'Well, that would be good news,' Rivers sighed. 'Did anyone recognise her photo?'

'The druggist, though he couldn't remember which night she came in. A nice chap, he says these things are very popular with the high school kids.'

'I'm sure. How's Mrs Patterson holding up?'

'Better,' he sighed. 'Your information lifted her spirits like I cannot tell you, thanks so very much.'

'No sweat, Mr Patterson, I have a feeling that if we keep pushing something will break.' He forced a smile. 'Do we have any idea as to who the other two women are that Debra was with?'

'No,' he shook his head, 'not so far, but we're calling everyone back, that's our best hope right now, don't you agree?'

Rivers nodded, as Jonathan Patterson was a man obsessed. By five o'clock that night he had already distributed photographs of his daughter to damn near every abortion and

491

pregnancy clinic in the immediate area, while his wife continued to man the phones. For extra measure Patterson had distributed flyers to other teenagers, visiting haunts and hangouts that young adults Debra's age were known to frequent. Yet nothing had been forthcoming.

'Frank,' he said quietly, 'your sources, did they say she was . . .' he stammered. 'Dee, I mean, did they say she was in good shape when she left the bar?'

'Yes,' Rivers comforted, 'she wasn't sick or drunk, just plain unhappy about something. We'll find her, if we just keep trying.'

Patterson placed an appreciative hand on his shoulder. 'Would you thank them for me?' he asked, with a desperate sincerity in his voice.

'I'm sorry?'

'Your sources, whoever they are, will you thank them personally for us, Mrs Patterson included, I can't tell you what a difference they've made. They've given us hope . . .'

As his voice trailed off, Rivers thought about the brothers Dix, of their perspective on the world, and of their callous disregard for this man's pain and his daughter's life. 'I already mentioned that to them,' he smiled warmly, 'I'm sure they understand.'

At 5:49 p.m., Sunday, April 10th, the Montgomery County Police became officially involved in the missing persons case of Debra Patterson, opening their investigation now that their seventy-two hour rule had been fulfilled. Assigned was Sergeant Tyler Conroy, for he had taken the first essential information that previous Friday.

Officer Conroy arrived at the house at 6:00 p.m., very much relieved when he found that the mother had returned home. Simply put, he had not believed Patterson's mission of mercy story about a relative being sick in some other state, and he expected to find Mrs Patterson cowering from fear, covered with bruises and welts.

Sergeant Conroy took his watch in front of the Pattersons' television, pleasantly surprised but not distracted, as he studied quietly for the County's Detective Exam.

FORTY-NINE

In the kitchen of the command post Jack Scott hung up the phone just as Frank Rivers came through the front door, untying the laces on his running shoes, then kicking these from his feet and pulling off his socks.

He stood in the hallway, massaging sore feet, then draped the sweaty things over a gold sculpture that looked like a giant corkscrew. Scott came towards him over the blue carpeting. 'Any luck on the clinics?' he asked in relation to the Debra Patterson case.

'Negative, how about with Brennon, wasn't he finishing up with Lisa Caymann's family?'

Scott's eyes looked pinched. 'We've got a positive on Aaron S. Blatt,' he said tonelessly. 'His voice was the one that distracted Lisa's mother.'

Rivers shook his head in disgust, lifted off his shoulder harness, slung it across his back, then started towards the kitchen where he could hear Dudley Hall and Dr Charles McQuade talking. 'Do we know where Blatt is? You said he has an appointment to testify before the FDA, what's that about?'

'Blatt's mother told Brennon that he's coming to Washington to announce the opening of some sort of research centre, it sounds more like a PR push to get the health regulators off his back. At any rate, he's not due for another week, so unless they have some serious change of heart, they'll stay in the field, and that bothers me. We've ordered taps on all Blatt's phones, including his mother's, so maybe something will come in over the transom. They could be anywhere.'

'Did Brennon find out who his partner is?'

'No, a complete dead end, but Captain Drury is running data for me on Blatt's private plane. That gives them real mobility, a KingAir 300 Beechcraft with a cruising speed of better than 350 miles an hour at 18,000 feet. It cost better than a million bucks.'

'Good for him,' Rivers frowned.

'Pocket change for the right dentist. The important thing is that Blatt doesn't know we're looking for him, so if he should file with the FAA, and if he lands in a major airport, then we've got him.'

Rivers knew the procedure; for a private carrier to fly, an IFR, or Interstate Flight Rules plan had to be registered with an FAA official, containing such relevant information as the plane's identification number, the type and number of passengers, route of flight, time of departure, and true air speed. 'How much damage can they do in a week?'

Scott glared. 'A lot,' he said sadly, and they walked into the kitchen eating area where McQuade and Hall were staring down into the sockets of yet another skull recovered from River Bowl.

Rivers and Scott stopped in the doorway as McQuade was snipping at a thin lock of hair, the colour of red clay, and this scalp-lock was still attached to the brow. It was an adult skull, albeit young, with a neat hole just over the right eye socket. There were twelve of these, arranged in size from small to large, with packing boxes carefully laid out for each. Scott strolled towards the macabre collection, looking at Emma Stoner, Samantha's mother. Even reduced to bone there was a family resemblance.

'And you're sure this is all of it?' Scott asked rather callously.

'Yep,' Hall said, coming from his seat towards the counter. 'That alley couldn't swallow another victim if it had to, only thing left are cemetery bones,' he chirped, 'embalmed, except for the slaves.'

Rivers was studying a chart on the wall near the back door. This was now almost entirely filled in, yet it still took some puzzling to sort through. To the right there was the heading *Clayton Killings*, step by step, every room, every face. On the left was a photograph of Samantha's reconstruction, and the words *Stoner Family*. Directly beneath these:

1. *Zak & female partner;*
2. *Jaffe/Tobytown burning;*
3. *Blatt & male Devoid partner.*

To the right and left of the Claytons and Stoners was the cutout picture of Yellow Loosestrife, and above this a photograph of Great Falls Park, showing a dramatic scene of waves crashing through a rocky gorge.

'So you believe that the common link between the Claytons and Stoners was this flower?' Rivers asked, pointing at the red and yellow trumpets. It seemed incredible to make that connection so far back in time.

Scott came closer, handing him a can of cold Coke from the box, opening one himself, then standing beside Dudley Hall, though addressing Dr McQuade. 'What about it, Charlie, am I chasing smoke?'

McQuade rubbed his eyes. A set of magnifying lenses were strapped to the top of his broad head and they jiggled as he yawned. 'Well, let's take a look,' he offered, coming across the room. He counted out skulls, then picked one up. It was medium in size and smooth as thought, and behind this was a patch of aged cloth that looked like a pad of bad cheese.

'Notice the pale and colourless nature of this weave,' he said, poking at it with long thin tweezers. 'My guess is that this is a blouse, or perhaps a dress, but if you look very closely you will see little red dots, and just a smattering of gold or yellow.'

The three men all leaned into a semicircle and studied this closely, the Diggerman turning the splotch over to review both sides. 'It does have red specks dere, Jackie.'

'And that,' McQuade's voice was deep with resolve, 'is precisely the bias of colour that we found on Samantha, though in her case it was more pronounced. The stain comes

495

from the Swamp Candle, and these,' he reached for the counter and into a large evidence bag, 'are what Jack found in the Claytons' garbage.'

He was now holding a collection of stems, the petals had become brittle, leaving a network of burnt orange and mustard gold on starlike veins.

'So both families were attacked while pickin'?' Hall questioned.

'Perhaps,' Scott confirmed, 'I believe it is so.'

'And Jimmy showed you where these grow?' Rivers questioned.

'Yes, and not surprisingly, it's very close to where Victoria Halford was raised. In 1958, when the Stoners were abducted,' he pointed to a circle on the chart, 'that property would have still belonged to them, although they had moved to Tobytown up near the church. Zak was watching them pick flowers in the woods at their old home site, and when he grew bored with this, he challenged Samantha and her older sister, Vicky, along with Mrs Emma Stoner.'

'But because of the remains we know that he killed them elsewhere?' Rivers asked.

'They were abducted down by the river, but I do not believe they felt threatened at this time. Maybe he appeared as a cop, or a security agent of some type, then drove them away. He could have come up with a thousand stories about how they were not safe there, and needed to go with him. Each girl was still carrying flowers, that's the key, they were lured into a false state of security, otherwise they wouldn't have cared about the flowers and would have left them behind.'

'Which is why the stems were so routinely dumped with the bodies, he was just cleaning up after the kill,' Rivers concluded.

'Yes,' Scott agreed, 'Zak must have driven them to the Tobytown cemetery, because the alley hadn't been built then, it was just being planned. Perhaps he stopped so they could place flowers on a grave, their grandparents were buried there.'

'And this is the only spot where the flowers grow?' Rivers

asked, pointing at a circle on the wall chart. Scott inched closer, then tapped at it thoughtfully.

'It's hard to know for certain where they grew in 1958, but it's a safe guess it was along the canal somewhere.'

'Very likely,' McQuade offered quietly, 'that descendants from the original plantings are still nearby or within easy reach, the Loosestrife are a hardy lot, the only thing they cannot survive is drought.'

'But Jackie,' Hall asked with confusion, 'what would the Clayton girls be doing in the same area more than three decades later?'

'In 1971 the canal was named a National Park, and this is a big city, not many places to go if you're looking for nature, or wild flowers, anything like that. Your choices are limited. Also, these flowers, plus the dogwood, are religious offerings and well known to children, who use them at Easter time. That's when the killings took place. I will bet that when Charlie gets a time fix on the rest,' his hand swept over the skulls, 'he will discover most were slain in early spring.'

Hall nodded. 'So while children were pickin' flowers, a killer was pickin' dem. Sometimes the world's not worth livin' in.'

'I agree with you, Duddy, this wild garden that he's used for abduction over the years is what we call a site magnet, a natural attraction for women and children.'

'Flowers,' McQuade sighed, 'beauty attracts beauty.'

'Yes, and he may have worked other site magnets as well, there's just no way to tell.'

'Then what about Blatt?' Rivers pushed with his finger on the name. 'You're saying that he and Zak were partners?'

'I am, at one time, but that was long ago. Like myself, I think Blatt fell for Zak's funeral trick and thought he was dead. Blatt was duped, I was duped . . .'

'But how'd he do it?' Hall whistled. 'A body was cremated.'

'That's true, and according to prison records there was a death, another prisoner. We'll never know, but my guess is that Zak left prison in a pine box after disposing of the real corpse right on the prison grounds somehow, he was working in the infirmary. He had to have come up with another body for a contractor to burn, maybe it was a hitchhiker, whoever knows, Duddy.

'The important thing is that rather than attending services for a yardbird, Blatt bought an urn for Zak, and that was their only major blunder. Going back in time, it ties them together very neatly.'

'He was 'fraid of the funeral?' Hall chirped.

'Not the way you mean it,' Scott corrected softly. 'As a graduate of Georgetown with society types for friends, he wasn't in a position to expose his dirty relationships, or let his hobby spill over into his professional life.'

'Then how they hook up with dis old Jew?' he chirped, pointing at the name Jaffe on the display. 'He was their leader?'

Scott shook his head. 'Yes and no. Jaffe is not a killer, at least not in the strict legal sense. His passion is money, and I believe he recruited Zak to burn Tobytown for him, and Blatt was the middleman who negotiated the deal. At about that time Aaron Blatt was living at Jaffe's house while completing his dental degree. Blatt and Zak met under his roof, finding common interests. They started by employing terrorism in an effort to drive Tobytown residents off their land.'

'And the final act was to target the Stoner family, abducting their children,' McQuade concluded. 'It makes sense, didn't you say Samantha's father had hired a lawyer to fight them?'

Scott nodded. 'To fight the County,' Scott corrected. 'Jaffe always works with direct governmental pressure, and the County served a tax notice for him. So yes, he made this family a target, that's my best guess.'

'Yes,' McQuade said pensively, 'it makes sense. When the abductions didn't work, maybe it even united the people, then they simply torched it.'

Scott sighed. 'I'd guess Zak did most of the violence, while Blatt served as businessman and observer, at the same time protecting Jaffe from direct involvement.'

'Non-prosecutable?' McQuade questioned.

Scott shrugged. 'With Jaffe we'd never be able to prove a

thing, except that he's a heartless leech. If we said one unkind word about the man in public, then we'd also have to fight every Jewish defence group in the world. The man was in a concentration camp, and ever since he has used that as a shield from honest criticism or criminal investigation.'

'The holocaust *is* the ultimate sacred cow,' said McQuade. He was about to go further when Rivers pressed forward.

'Sorry, Jack,' he shook his head, 'I don't buy it. You're saying Jaffe has spent his life fucking people, even ordering abductions and executions?'

'I am.'

'No,' Rivers scoffed, 'if he was in a concentration camp the horror of his memories wouldn't allow him to act that way, I'm sure of it.'

Scott's face was a sorry statement. 'I didn't say he was a *victim*, Frank, I said he was there. Interestingly enough Aaron Blatt's mother was with him in Auschwitz, so believe me when I say Jaffe did not spend money spoiling her child from the kindness of his puny black heart.'

'Hush money?' Rivers asked incredulously.

'No, not as we think of it. But Myra Blatt does know something that Jaffe doesn't want public, that's a guess, but I think a very good guess. Ever heard that old Mafia saying, *Keep your friends close, but your enemies closer?*'

Rivers nodded as Dudley Hall filled a cheek with Redman chewing tobacco, offering this around as heads began shaking at him.

'Well, old Jaffe became such a good friend and benefactor to the Blatts that he has nothing to fear from their memories of him. Regardless of his crimes, here or elsewhere, Dr Jaffe will leave this world only when his money fails to buy him a new body, and even then he can afford plenty of spare parts.'

'I'll give him a transplant,' Rivers hissed.

Scott shrugged. 'If you want my humble opinion, I think Washington deserves Jaffe as much as Jaffe deserves the Washington he created. The material fact is that Blatt killed for the first time about thirty-five years ago when he lived under Jaffe's charge, and Blatt's partner was Zak Dorani.

Both of them are still alive, both are out there killing, and both are young enough to continue for another ten or fifteen years.'

McQuade stepped forward. 'So Samantha was murdered when Blatt lived with Jaffe, and they had hired Zak Dorani to burn the village,' he repeated. 'Jack, the urn ties them together, and the time and location is correct, but is there any other evidence?'

Scott nodded, pointing at a stick in one of the skulls. 'The fléchette,' he stated coldly. 'A perfectly balanced needle made of wood or steel that can be fired from a blowgun, crossbow, or rifle. During this same time period Jaffe was bringing back an odd assortment of these weapons from all over the world. While this little killing instrument fascinated him as a medical doctor, I'm betting Blatt and Zak were the ones who actually went to employ them in the field. They started making their own, a bit cruder than the ones in Jaffe's collection,' he shrugged. 'Then again, practice makes perfect.'

'Then where does Victoria Halford fit in?' McQuade asked, changing the subject. 'We found a headstone with her name on it, Shelby Halford, husband of.'

Scott winced. 'Well, I've got a good team,' he said as the Diggerman smiled through tobacco-pink teeth.

'Jackie, where's that bottle of sipping whisky?' he asked. Rivers immediately went for the bar in the living room, returning with two glasses and a bottle. He gave one to Hall and McQuade and then poured a shot for each. Hall kicked the fluid back against his throat.

'You was sayin' about Victoria?' he whistled.

'Yes, her only connection is that she happened to know the Stoners, and quite well. Plus she still comes to Patriots Bowl, although to her it's still a cemetery. She visits her relatives, and will until she joins them.'

'Jack,' McQuade offered, 'maybe you can get Jaffe to donate the land as a park, it's not being used.'

Scott shook his head. 'Don't count on it,' he sighed. 'Anyway, what's interesting to note is Victoria's age, think of the changes to that one small tract of land that she's seen, from

500

a dirt road cemetery, to an entire town, then to a huge city block on a superhighway. She saw Elmer's house being built,' a smile returned to his voice, 'she remembers the weekend that his parents brought him home from the hospital.'

'No kidding,' Rivers chuckled.

Scott nodded. 'When Elmer was about three, his father was worried as to why this old woman was loitering, singing near the window, that kind of thing. He approached her, and to that end Victoria has a picture of the boy.'

'Amazing grace,' McQuade observed.

'Jack,' Rivers asked, 'this guy Zak has been hitting houses with first-rate locks, yet he gets in with no sign of entry. How does he do that, he has to . . .'

And suddenly there was a sharp rap on the front door. Rivers braced himself as a man in an expensively tailored uniform entered, his face drawn, his shoulders beaten, his mouth covered with dried antacid paste.

Captain Maxwell Drury looked like stress alone would drop him any moment as he rushed into the kitchen. Alarmed, Scott came forward, the group breaking away from the counter, the skulls staring up at Drury in a blank horror.

'Captain,' Rivers gave a grim nod.

'Hello, Frank,' Drury acknowledged, then challenged Scott with trouble burning in his eyes.

'What is it, Max?'

'A new ball game.' His voice was gravel. 'Duncan Powell just called me at home, rather urgent news, so I came myself.'

'Lacy Wilcott's companion?'

Drury nodded a sorry head while removing his cap. 'Carol Barth, she was found at a place called Waltzing Waters in the Everglades, but there's something else, John . . .'

The four men in the room could feel the stress. 'What happened, is Duncan okay?'

'No, no he's not.' And his face and body stiffened with anger. 'They killed a cop,' he said flatly, 'a highway patrolman. Just blew his heart from his body, when one shot would have been enough.'

There was an ugly silence. Rivers' jaw started to tick as he paced past Dudley Hall, who handed Drury a shot of whisky. The Captain slapped this into his mouth, swallowing hard, then spoke again.

'In savage mockery they manipulated this policeman's body into a suggestive position with the dead girl, they're worse than animals . . .'

'Jesus,' Rivers swallowed, turning sharply where he stood.

'. . . and it gets worse. They're heading this way, John.' Drury sighed, his voice heavy and wooden as a vein in Scott's neck blistered out.

'I need Frank,' he concluded. 'The vile bastards just filed a flight plan from South Carolina.' He handed Scott a slip of paper.

'Columbia to Richmond to Washington,' Scott read.

'They're running straight at us.'

FIFTY

On two Sundays of every month, Great Falls National Park
opened its gates to volunteers who provided scenic educational tours to church groups, school classes, and senior
citizens. Guided Adventures through history, as they were
called, were given by invitation or appointment only.

At a lockhouse overlooking the C & O Canal, the docents
had assembled by 11:00 and were preparing to educate and
entertain the classes that were now arriving, elementary students from four nearby public schools. They were dressed in
turn of the century clothing, the waterway garb of old, with
heavy black work-boots, dark dresses and broad bonnets,
some with wire spectacles, others with leather work
gloves.

Off near the lock, two men were hitching five mules into a
train, preparing to harness them to a wooden barge anchored
in front of the visitors' centre. Jessica Janson was making her
way there, holding a tired little boy by the hand.

'Can't I just go on the ride?' Elmer asked, pointing towards
the mules.

'You have to take the tour first, the ride is last.'

'But Mom, they . . .'

'You wanted to come, Elmer, you accepted the invitation,'
she corrected him.

'But what are you going to do?'

'I'll talk to other parents and have a soda.' She sighed.
'Maybe I'll buy some crackers and feed the ducks.' Jessica
smiled at him, for once they had arrived she knew why the
boy didn't want to go. He was shy in front of classmates, and

as they approached, his mother saw a little brunette girl staring at him.

'She's cute.'

'Yuck.'

'Now you be a gentleman,' she countermanded as they came to a stop at a throng of parents and children, the crowd still forming. The mother of the little brunette smiled at them.

'Hi,' Jessica offered, holding Elmer in place.

'Hello,' the woman said warmly. 'I'm Janet Lynch, Mrs Martin's third grade class.'

'Pleased to meet you.' They shook hands. 'Jessica Janson, that's our class too.'

'Then they must know each other,' she replied, looking down at the little girl who was soaking up the boy with her pretty hazel eyes.

'Hi, Elmer,' she mewed, and Jessica was appalled that her son turned rudely away. She squeezed Elmer's hand tight enough to drain colour from his cheeks.

'Hi, Beverly,' he snipped, then returned to studying the mules. Jessica glanced down at Elmer with a daggers.

'He's being a brat,' she teased, 'today's brat day.' Elmer blushed visibly.

Janet Lynch smiled. 'So I wasn't sure why we were honoured with invitations for this event,' she questioned, watching the crowd milling about.

'Oh, they invite a different class every time, it's supposed to be very interesting, supported by the county education board. They take the older children camping.' They watched as a matron dressed in a colonial period dress with wire hoops at the hem came forward from the house, clutching a stack of papers and a clipboard.

'Attention!' she called out in a high-pitched voice. Children and adults stirred and went quiet as the woman came forward. 'Thank you for attending the C&O Canal Sunday Retreat, a four-hour Guided Adventure and field study for children. We would like to extend a special warm welcome to Mrs Martin's third grade class.' The woman paused as the crowd turned inward to survey itself.

'For the children, the trip will begin just on the other side of this bridge.' She waved across a liftlock and a dozen fair maids all waved back. 'These docents are volunteers who will be working with small groups so that more can be accomplished in a short time. Please have your invitations ready,' she demanded, and the crowd began to shuffle for papers, Jessica removing one from her purse, then handing this to Elmer.

'Can't we just leave?' He squirmed at her side.

Jessica stroked his hair. 'Give them a chance, it's only a few hours, you may like it.'

'Children,' the matron commanded, 'say goodbye to your parents now, and as you start across a docent will place you into a group. Girls, if you have a purse, you should leave it in the lockhouse, you will want both hands free.'

The children started forward, Elmer turning to face his mother. 'See ya,' he said quietly, and she rubbed his freckled nose with an index finger. As he strolled off little Beverly Lynch was tagging right alongside, watching him with admiring eyes as from across the waterway two old mule skinners with Dutch-boy hats struck up a banjo chorus of *Erie Canal*.

'Parents,' the woman continued, 'for those of you who wish to wait, we have refreshments inside the lockhouse. The classes will return at four o'clock, but we ask for your patience should any group be tardy.'

Jessica watched as the children formed on the other side of a chained area, handing over their invitations, and in return receiving identification markers. Beverly was having a blue ribbon tied into her hair by an older woman.

'I guess they'll be in the same group,' Janet Lynch offered quietly. Jessica smiled, for Elmer was rolling his eyes at her, barely able to stand still as an old mule skinner was pinning a green clover to his chest.

'Well, that's that,' Jessica said, watching the small crowd being factored off, according to colour, by characters in period clothes. 'I'll buy us a soda.'

* * *

505

'Let's all get better acquainted,' the docent smiled easily, moving her flock of six children closer to a huge shade tree by the river. The banjo pickers were singing now, and the canal was making a gurgling sound as water flowed through the gigantic liftlock.

The docent was an older woman with a bluish-grey bonnet fastened beneath her chin, this pinching at thin flesh that looked uncomfortable to Elmer. Her eyes bulged from behind old style horn-rimmed spectacles, her boots were tight black leather with rows of buttons. Around her waist there was a white apron, this covering a light grey dress with a metal hoop for fullness, and Elmer thought it strange that grown-ups would go to such lengths to capture the past, when the woman's bright pink nail polish gave it all away.

'Today I am dressed as a lock-keeper's wife.' She smiled. 'Does anyone know what year that would be, when the Chesapeake and Ohio Canal was in full operation?'

The children looked at each other but would not venture a guess. The docent leaned forward, placing her hands on her knees, the giant hoop reaching out into the semicircle as she studied Elmer Janson's mint green eyes.

'I'll bet you know,' she said softly, 'there's no need to be shy.'

Elmer swallowed his spit, fidgeting in a pocket, Beverly Lynch admiring his every move. '1860?' he asked shyly.

'That's very close,' she mewed, 'the correct time period is thirty years earlier, 1828, just before the Civil War. Now let's all pretend that's the age we are living in, and introduce ourselves.' She leaned over, smiling at the boy, extending her right hand.

'My name is Irma Kiernan,' she said.

They had been strolling for nearly an hour, stopping to sip drinks and learn about the park, when they came to the end of a harsh gravel path, their images reflected by the still water of the C & O Canal. Overhead there was a wooden bridge. Just to their left, a liftlock and small white house. Although this was boarded shut, it was well kept, and there was a lawn composed entirely of wildflowers in every shape and colour of the rainbow. Irma slowed her pace, stopping here, looking out over a splendid view of the raging Potomac river, huge granite cliffs, and horizons as far as the eye could see. She was holding Beverly Lynch by the hand.

'Children,' she said, gaining their attention, and they all gathered around. 'Does anyone know where we are?'

'A liftlock,' Elmer offered, 'near Little Falls.' By now he had become comfortable with the group.

'Very good,' she smiled, 'this house is where the lock-keeper by the name of Horace Marsden lived, and we will be showing you pictures of his family when we take the boat ride. Now the lock-keeper's job was more than waiting for a boat to come. If you look overhead,' she turned and the children studied the wooden bridge, 'you will see a series of rope elevators. These were used for lifting cargo down onto the boats. What do you imagine that cargo was?'

'Food,' Beverly said.

'Yes,' Irma agreed quickly, 'grain and livestock. They'd lower pigs and cattle from these ropes onto the decks, then the boat would proceed into Washington. What else would Mr Marsden be in charge of?'

'Building supplies,' Elmer said quickly.

'Very good,' Irma winked at him, 'bricks and stone, as well as coal for heating the cities. Other cargoes would include tobacco, furs, iron ore, whisky and timber. Now, while Mr Marsden looked after the cargoes from Cabin John, what duties did his wife have?'

'Cooking,' said Beverly, 'she would bake all the bread and clean the house.'

'Yes, plus she had to be a teacher, for there were no schools, and she had to be a veterinarian as well, taking care of the mules and other livestock. A boat would only come about once a month, so that's how often they had visitors, and Mr Marsden would hook up his mule team and continue down towards Washington. Then, when he arrived in Georgetown, what did he do with his boat?'

'Bring it back,' said a tall black girl by the name of Audry Morris.

'No, they could not go back, so they would dismantle the boat and then sell it for lumber. Many of the early houses built along the river had boat in them!' she smiled, and several children giggled.

'Now, Mr Marsden and his family lived here from 1836 to 1884, but they were not the only family on the waterway. Who else would have moved here?'

'Slaves,' Elmer said in a quiet voice.

Irma Kiernan heard this and was impressed by his knowledge, the child was bright for age ten. 'Elmer knows,' she said almost proudly, 'and that's the correct answer. In 1860, Negroes began escaping up the river from the South, now why would they choose to live here?'

There was not a sound. From the back of the group a thin black child with a bright red cap offered his opinion. 'Maryland was the Free State so they came to find freedom.'

'Yes,' Irma confirmed, 'Derrick is correct. But once they arrived, why did they stay? Once they crossed into Maryland they could go anywhere, so why not take the boat into the city of Washington?'

It was a hard question, and the children were both restless and quiet. 'The answer,' she said slowly, 'is religion. From out of the cruelty of slavery, the American Negro managed to build a way of life by worshipping what you see around you right here, symbols of the freedom God could give. Can anyone pick out such a symbol?'

'The river,' Elmer said quickly.

'Flowers,' said Beverly. Irma Kiernan was smiling, for the children had grasped the concept.

'The trees and the forest,' said Derrick.

Kiernan nodded. 'That's fine, these are all powerful images of freedom, a piece of heaven right here on earth. Now who can find where the slaves lived, who can find the chimney in the woods?'

The children turned excitedly, scanning the horizon, and

faint as a scar an object was jutting up from the treeline. Irma saw the boy's eyes grow wide, locking onto this.

'Let's follow Elmer,' she offered, 'I think he's found it.'

They came to a small clearing in the centre of a wooded grove, standing high overlooking the Great Falls. To their right was an expanse of canal, an aqueduct known as Wide Water. There was a stone foundation, a fireplace, and a rock chimney, and Elmer's heart quickened, thinking of what could be buried beneath this. The ruinous hint of past lives filled him with the spirit of adventure.

Surrounding the house were millions of bright blueberries and scads of wild flowers, and Beverly quickly wandered off to explore the bright colours, the children all stirring with excitement, bounding through the glade like noisy ants and into the old foundation.

'What do you think this was?' Irma asked of them all. 'What type of house?' There was no answer. 'This was all made by hand from the natural things you see all around you, rocks from the river, limbs from oaks and redwoods, bricks from red clay, slate from the falls.' She pointed to a rocky gorge that frothed and churned with a raging, powerful current.

'Runaways settled and made this house,' she continued, 'in the beginning of the Civil War. As they were escaping, they followed the river and the canal. Notice all of the lush plants and bushes, these were started by them and then used as food and decorations.'

'How many were there?' Derrick asked with a sense of awe, moving from room to room, looking at where the walls had been.

'No one kept track, but this was a big house, so as many as ten families all slept under this one roof. Notice that there are two fireplaces, slaves were poor, there must have been crowds of them in here.'

Elmer was crawling into an enormous stone fireplace, the huge granite rocks still held together by a fine grey mortar, and little Beverly was moving beside him, her index finger following a line of concrete. 'Look,' she said excitedly, 'some-one wrote something with a stick.'

Elmer edged forward, blowing dust away from the fireplace as Derrick came alongside on his hands and knees. 'Can you see what it says?' he asked with a smiling voice.

'I dunno,' Elmer puzzled, 'I think it says *picky*, it's real fancy writing.' Both boys were working the scrawl with their spit. Beverly forced herself between them, then the three started digging on hands and knees.

'It's a *V*,' she announced with a giggle. 'That not a *P*, silly,' and she pouted her face at Elmer who was working at what looked like a date.

'*Vicky*,' Derrick stated, 'it's a *name*! And there's a date too!'

'Children.' Irma came from the yard and was hovering over them. 'Please back out of there, spiders and bugs, we can't have that.'

'But there's a date!' Elmer repeated with excitement. 'I think it says 1918?' and his voice was bewildered. 'Hey, Miss Kiernan, there weren't any slaves in 1918.'

'That must have been when the house was rebuilt by pres-ervationists, now I want you to back out of there now,' she said firmly, 'it's dangerous.' And the children complied, although begrudgingly.

'We have ten more minutes to explore the slaves' quarters, so let's split up and have a quick look around. Now be careful not to touch any plants that have three bright green leaves or funny berries. There are some very special flowers that you should look for, they have bright red and yellow petals and were once used by the slaves to celebrate Easter. Who can find such a flower for me?' She then took two sly steps to be closer to Elmer.

'Do any of you boys have a pocket knife?' she asked, though she was careful not to make it appear as if she was addressing anyone in particular. Derrick was still fumbling in his pocket as Elmer held his knife towards the teacher.

'I do,' he said proudly, handing her a scouting blade on a key ring. This had belonged to Elmer's father and was some-what of an antique, and Irma was fighting a smile as she stared at the single key which was swinging from a brass metal loop. She took it in her hand and glanced at the knife.

'Thank you,' she said, then turning away. 'We are going to pick Easter flowers to take home, so everyone look around and select that group of plants that looks the prettiest to you.'

With that the children scurried off, running noisily through the damp glade, pouring over the native colours. Beverly and Derrick and Elmer were now somewhat of a team, and together they raced to a bluff that suddenly dropped, and quite steeply so, down into the raging river. Below, the currents went howling, roaring into white waves, and at this spot, in the moist and swampy ground, there were thousands of flowers of every shape and colour.

Some had huge white petals, like the Dutchman's Breeches, and stood as high as Elmer Janson. Some were blue with what looked like purple fruit, the Jack-in-the-Pulpit, though the children did not know these names. Others had bright orange blooms, like the Sweet Clover, and there were tall and furry Cattails that resembled large corndogs on a stick. Just at the bank of the river the colours came like explosions, red and yellow, as far as the eye could follow.

'Look at that!' Beverly cried with delight, as the children all seemed drawn by these fragrant and gentle blooms, marching along a small creek that ran in a furrow down a hill. And they gathered here, pinching and touching, stroking and collecting the vibrant trumpets of the Swamp Candle. They bloomed in a shower of glory across the wet ground; the brilliant spires rising into star-like petals, the deep green stalks, the smell like a magic summer rain.

Irma Kiernan had not counted heads as she briefly watched the children packing flowers into small tight bouquets. Her heart was fluttering, driving into a rapid beat as she brought herself to the task at hand, sweat popping onto her brow as she carefully reached into her dress, removing a small black tin that said *Hide-A-Key* across the top. She steadied the box in her left hand, then quickly slid the lid open, placing her back to her brood.

Within lay a grey mixture of plastic clay that resembled a huge flat eraser, and she took Elmer's key from the knife, holding this between her index finger and thumb, laying it flat, then pressing, kneading with both hands. With expert care, she worked the key's toothy edge with her thumb before lifting it out, leaving an impression that was clear and precise. Next, she turned the key over, and had just begun the process again as Beverly Lynch came bumping into her hoop, rolling it slightly, tugging on her dress from behind.

Kiernan jumped, but did not turn around.

'Miss Kiernan?' she said shyly. 'Miss Kiernan . . .'

'Just a minute,' Irma muttered, pressing with both hands, her heart now beating into her throat.

'Miss Kiernan?' the small voice was distressed, asking again, as the woman worked the key down into the mix and back up again, making certain that the centre groove showed clearly and without any slop. Jeff hated that, she remembered, when making an impression of a key, shoddy work could mean extra metal that had to be filed away by hand.

'I have something in my eye!' Beverly suddenly cried from behind.

'Yes, Honey,' Irma said quietly without looking, 'we'll wash it out when we get back.'

'But it hurts . . .' she was crying now.

A one-second mistake, Irma knew, could cost Jeff an hour of extra filing, and as the child sobbed behind her, Kiernan completed an impression that was clean and nearly exact, then rubbed any fouling away with her apron. She carefully sealed the box, dropping this back into her pocket. When she turned around, Elmer was inspecting Beverly's eye, trying to remove a fleck of dirt from her lower lid, his finger covered with a shirttail.

Derrick came up alongside, placing his flowers on the ground, then peering into her pretty hazel eyes.

'Stop that!' Irma barked at them. 'You could make it worse!'

Elmer startled, his mouth falling open, his arms coming limp to his sides. Kiernan quickly took Beverly's chin in her hand, staring down into her face.

'Well, you weren't doing anything . . .' Elmer said under his breath.

'I heard that!' Kiernan fired back, her heart thumping madly.

'Well, it's the truth,' he said quietly, 'she hurt herself and . . .'

Kiernan was on him. 'Don't you backtalk me,' she warned, aiming a finger, 'I know what is needed here and you are *not* it!'

The boy backed off quickly as Irma bent at the waist to assess the problem. Beverly's left eye was red, tearing badly, while Kiernan suddenly found herself wondering just why in hell her man wanted to save the Janson kid, who at the age of ten was pushy beyond redemption.

'*Men*,' she muttered to herself.

'But it's all very simple,' Dorn had instructed, 'why do women have to make things so complicated?'

Irma Kiernan could almost hear his voice as she looked down at Beverly Lynch. The tears were drying, but the eye was starting to go puffy, swelling from the bottom, covering up the speck that was buried in the soft tissue of her lid.

'You have the mould, Irma, it's new plastic, and you know how to work it. Now stop complaining and start practising.' They had been driving from their house in Wooded Acres, down River Road and towards the canal.

'But he'll be watching me,' she had said, 'we've never done it this way, all of the others . . .'

'Damn, just forget them. Janson's only a little kid, why is this such a problem?'

'Well, last night, I thought . . .'

Dorn cut her off. 'An old bum in a trench coat, they got lucky and you just waited too long. If you had made it ten seconds earlier he would have seen us and just driven away.'

'But it's too much of a coincidence that he stopped . . .'

Dorn shook his head, applying the brakes while slowing for the light at River and Falls Road, a half-mile from Great Falls

Park. 'No, for the love of God, he was from out of town. You said Maine?'

'Yes,' she mewed.

'So he probably came here to feed off the public tit, the Vice-president's campaign manager comes from there.' The light changed and he pulled the black BMW ahead, slapping in a tape of Chopin's Nocturnes.

'Oh, honey,' she had questioned, 'he'll be suspicious, can't we wait for a girl? There's no one around when they put their purses in the lockhouse. I have all the time I need to get their keys, no one's watching, it's worked every time. You liked it when . . .'

'No!' he snapped. 'If you can't handle it I'll do it myself!' His voice was dripping with venom. 'You and Jessica Janson are like beauty and the beast!'

'Oh Jeff,' she sighed, 'that's a terrible thing to say to me, you don't mean that . . .' her voiced trailed off weakly as Dorn shook his head apologetically, it had just slipped out.

'So you ask if anyone has a pocketknife, the kid's real proud of it. Jessica talked to his grandmother for hours over the stupid thing, deciding if she should let him have it. The first thing Elmer did was to attach his house key, so it's perfect.'

'You're sure this is the right thing to do?'

Dorn's stare was ice. 'How long did it take for that bitch to mail in the RSVP for an event as worthy as the Adventure?'

'The Jansons were the very last ones.'

'Well you see, Irma, that's how involved she is with his life, she doesn't give a shit about his education. So just make sure you're standing closest to Elmer when you ask for a knife, all little boys have one, regardless of what Mrs Janson thinks.' And he pressed the stopwatch he was holding with his right hand.

'Two minutes and thirty seconds, you have to do better than that, now try it again.'

'Miss Kiernan,' Elmer said, looking at Beverly's hurt eye as they walked. It was nearly swollen shut, so he was holding her hand, unintentionally slowing down the flock. They had been walking for nearly ten minutes, Derrick on the other side, telling Beverly when there were larger stones in the towpath.

'Yes?' she crooned absently as his voice just registered, for she was dreaming in the golden light that was filtering through the thick wood. It was late afternoon, soon the sun would set, and she was pondering a wedding in such an ethereal glow. For the correct light, timing was important, and she had almost decided on an early evening service as the boy, again, was interrupting her thoughts.

'Miss Kiernan, you still have my knife!' Elmer stated loudly, and the woman blushed. She had been holding it tightly in her right fist, and she quickly turned it over to him.

'Elmer?' Beverly cried suddenly in a shy and unhappy voice, and the boy swallowed, picking up his pace, coming back alongside.

And only because she came right out and asked, and for no other reason; and because little Beverly had really hurt herself, Elmer politely took up her hand again as they walked. Derrick was taking notice of this and gave him the old rolling eyeballs, but he was a pretty decent sort and said nothing.

'What's a guy gonna do?' Elmer shrugged.

'Tell me about it, I got two sisters.'

From his fishing spot at Wide Water, Jeff Dorn was watching through powerful field glasses, and he was pleased by what he saw. Whenever Irma had failed at something, her shoulders and face fell like a mud slide.

He saw her now, prancing dreamily down the path, holding flowers beneath her chin.

By the time the Jansons arrived back home, shadows clung, the night had begun to settle.

DAY FOUR:

THE CITIES

I shall tell you a great secret, my friend. Do not wait
for the last judgement, it takes place every day.

Albert Camus

FIFTY-ONE

It was all one and the same, and Seymor Blatt, who had spent a great deal of time there as a young man, recognised this to be true. Bethesda, Cabin John, Potomac, Silver Spring, Falls Church, and countless other once smail villages in adjoining strips of real estate known as Maryland and Virginia, had been reduced to being just parts of the same huge, singular and sprawling city.

That city was Washington DC, land of monuments and commuters, and from the cockpit of a luxurious KingAir 300, they followed an ugly stretch of highway dubbed the Inner Beltway, which appeared as a crooked river of red lights. It was the first sight that caught their attention as they sliced through the heavy cloud cover that had dogged them from the moment they had reached the coast earlier in the day.

Gregory Corless, who did not understand this urban ring, believed that to stay at a hotel in Bethesda was to be away from Washington, and not smack in the middle of its affluent upper core. While Blatt had tried to explain, Corless thought being near the seat of federal government would somehow place them where the action was.

'Greg, there *isn't* any action,' Blatt corrected, 'the Bethesda Hyatt is absolutely *it*, we couldn't do better. In Washington everyone leaves after five o'clock for the suburbs, it's all the same, the city is the suburbs.'

'But it's got a view, the room has a view?'

'Yes, I had to use a favour to get the executive suite, and in Washington favours are like toothpaste, when you use them up they're gone.'

'I appreciate that,' he said sincerely, 'I've never spent any real time here.'

'Sure,' Blatt nodded.

'Roger, Nancy-five-one-eight, you're clear for approach, runway six, wind northeast at seven knots, time 8:04:10.' The radio was clear as crystal, and Seymor Blatt placed his highball glass back into its holder, grabbing the microphone with his right hand, then pressing the button. They were tired and hungry and anxious to land.

'Tower, Nancy-five-one-eight prepared for landing.'

'Come ahead five-one-eight.'

Greg Corless drained the last from his martini glass, licking the lip with his tongue before handing this to his partner, dimming the already soft cabin light.

'I didn't want that interrupt feature,' Blatt said, turning up the stereo. When the tower kicked in, it interrupted the music, and the Beach Boys were playing in concert. He loved the Beach Boys, once he had wanted to be a carefree surfer, but he had decided it just wasn't a very secure lifestyle.

'*There's a place where I can go and tell my troubles to . . .*' Blatt was rocking and singing as the tiny blue strobes of National Airport were pulsing in near perfect time, and the Washington Monument came into full view, the powerful white lights streaming upward along the bright marble, then filtering off into low cloud cover.

'Buckle up,' the captain ordered smartly, and although Blatt shook his head at the fat man, he did just that. As an experienced pilot, he knew how tricky the wind coming off the Potomac could be, even though the overhead gauges were showing a calm night.

With effortless skill, Corless straightened and adjusted his wing tips as the plane soared in, the blue and red lights streaming from blacktop, the wheels hovering scant feet above the ground. There was a gentle swell as they touched down, the engines quickly spinning twin props in reverse, Corless applying a gentle braking motion that could hardly be felt.

'*In my room, in my room . . .*'

'Hey, Seymor, let's settle in quickly and get some supper, we haven't eaten since morning.'

'We had ham on rye, that was pretty good . . . *and leave the world behind . . .*'

'Welcome to Washington National, five-one-eight, hangar deck C-4, take tarmac Alpha-Seven.' Corless turned the plane according to alphabet, rolling towards the white temporary housing that was Washington's idea of an airport.

'I don't think they'll ever finish this,' Blatt complained, fingering a button. 'Roger, tower, five-one-eight proceeding to hangar C-4.' He had waited to respond for 'In My Room' was playing, and he loved that song almost as much as 'Surfer Girl'. He opened a small blue box and slipped a pair of perfect ivory choppers over his grey dental posts, these looking more like flat grey nails than teeth.

'Thank God,' Corless spat as he parked at a loading bay. They both felt relaxed, the giant KingAir provided a cockpit with all of the comforts of home.

'I'm going to leave the trick bag and the collection here,' Corless stated, unbuckling, then stretching to the ceiling.

'Do you think that's a good idea, Greg? This is a public place even if we do pay for the slip.'

He shrugged. 'It's always been good enough before, besides, that alarm system of yours is class, real class.'

They performed a ten-minute drill, transforming themselves into expensively tailored but conservative executives. Blatt had learned well from Dr Rubin Jaffe, the Washington power broker he once described as combination rabbi and coach. 'Remember,' Blatt said as they prepared to disembark, 'this is a town where attitude and appearances are everything, so please call me Aaron until we leave, it's more formal.'

'Who cares,' Corless huffed, he was moving Happy's cage down into the storage bay, it was filled with pictures that had helped to break the monotony of air travel.

'We do,' Blatt corrected. 'We are representing DIDS, so for the sake of appearance you and I are business associates.

Try to remember, in Washington no one has permanent friends, only permanent interests.'

Corless grunted.

Through the American terminal, they were entering a city that judges character by the cut of clothes, by what you drive, by how you talk. And for these reasons alone, they were immediately men not to be tampered with, not to be taken lightly. Their clothes were expensive, their manner elite, and they stood patiently waiting for a limousine to take them to a better hotel, not a house for the masses.

Unfortunately, their car was one of many stacked into a solid wall of identical limos, while employee-grade travellers scurried around them for cabs and buses.

A man holding a placard to his chest hurried by, an older man with baggy slacks, and although Blatt scanned the crowd quickly, he did not see him. The man's open collar spelled *no count being*. His battered old fedora cast a line of shadow across his face, though beneath this his eyes were edged like flame and his mind cut quickly into them.

Five-six, balding, wide eyes, cupid lips, long neck, frail face, expensive dentures. Commander Jack Scott knew Aaron Seymor Blatt on sight; thin, neat, precise. From his dress and demeanour it was clear that Blatt was the type of man who would analyse everything, every little detail down into infinity; how a person dresses, how much he drinks, how often, how he carries himself, where he lives, what he drives, how he speaks. His suit was dark European, his shirt a frosted white, his tie an arty but smart Armani in shades of purple. This, Scott reasoned, was his little fashion statement.

Six-two, 245, clean shaven, eyes close-set, pudgy hands and fingers, wide of chest, thick neck and lips, double-chin, his hair but a memory. Corless, though Scott did not know his name, had a face so full it resembled a hog's backside with human features.

'So this is Blatt's partner,' he whispered to himself, standing off to the right, holding a sign that protested fare-hikes. The fat man was clad in the classic uniform of Washington, a blue blazer with tan slacks and Italian tasselled loafers, these were extra wide to support the heavy load.

The two men were talking, chatting with each other without a care in the world, while Rivers sat directly across from them in a small ten-minute parking lot.

He was watching through high-powered glasses.

'Panther, this is Eagle One,' the voice of Steve Adare, the designated MAIT team pilot, boomed in the tan Crown Victoria as Rivers held the microphone with an easy hand.

The Loach jet helicopter was panning, swinging high in the air, for the blades sounded thin over the radio, like playing cards on the spokes of a bicycle wheel.

'Go ahead, Eagle . . .'

'They crossed over to the American terminal on foot, they should be passing to you about now, coming onto the sidewalk. Their hangar is still being sealed off.'

'Roger that, we've got them.'

'I'm maintaining, do you want me to hold?'

'Affirmative, Steve, they'll be taking a limo, we'll flag it for you, then everyone follows.'

'Roger.'

Scott had returned and was opening the door, swinging in as Rivers pulled the fireball off the dash and onto the seat. 'All set?' he asked, as Rivers was double-checking a .45mm Combat Elite, locking this into place under his left arm, the tension spring adjusted to mush. In a highride holster at his back he inserted a .45 Commander, the hammer locked into the stage-three position.

'Let's do it,' Rivers said quietly, and there was an unsettling calmness to his voice while fires burned in his blue eyes. Scott watched as the man popped an aspirin, grinding this into paste, his jaw ticking as he stared into another world.

'Frank?'

'Yeah, Jack, just thinking about Waltzing Waters. You know, I have no idea where that is. I sit here looking at those two bastards, the way they just stand there, and without a care in the world, and only this morning they killed some poor kid and then, just for fun, blew away a cop. It's insane, I don't care what you say, it's crazy.'

Scott shook his head at Rivers. 'We take them as planned, Frank, in their room at the Hyatt. Wouldn't you like a vacation to Florida so you could watch them burn in the chair?'

Rivers nodded, his eyes dancing, jaw ticking, holding his hands in front of him and spreading fingers, closing, opening, exercising; moving his shoulders in round limbering waves, slow sweeps, preparing himself. 'They put that officer's tool into her mouth, I can't cope with that. As far as I'm concerned this is show time, Jack, the rag is off the bush and this is what I do best.'

Scott was watching Blatt and his partner in a new light as they calmly bought a newspaper from a vendor, then eagerly divided this into sections. His stomach tied into a sorry knot as he turned back to Rivers, their eyes locking tight in one sudden and deadly instant, like two bolts of fire striking in mid-flight.

They held this position for a long, merciless moment, then Scott was looking down calmly at his watch. 'They're going to be armed,' he cautioned. 'If they smell a cop they will not hesitate . . .'

Rivers nodded. 'I'll deal with it, I just don't like being away from the Jansons, this is not good timing.'

Scott nodded.

'I'll need the air cover,' Rivers said flatly, and with that he opened his door and stepped out into his own shadow, his long strides carrying him with almost a lazy certainty.

On his back he carried a plastic dry cleaning bag, slung without purpose, working into darkness, his mind cooking his own private terror.

By April 11th, Scott had come to understand him, not the details, but he knew. It had something to do with a Cambodian village he once thought of as family. Qua, he had called it. As a young man Rivers had been responsible for them, protecting them, using that village to monitor enemy troop movements. In July of 1969, he was returning from long range patrol, coming across a mountain ridge, hoofing it solo when he saw them.

The zombies, he had said, like walking dead. Their eyes filled with shock, women and children savagely tortured, but seeming to work the rice fields. As he entered the village, they greeted him in the silence of atrocity, laying baskets at his feet in offering, for this had been ordered by the VC who had spent the night.

'There was nothing I could do,' Rivers had explained, 'they were like family, so I helped them fish out the limbs, then matched them with bodies. They butchered every male in the village, including children.' Scott could still hear his voice.

'Something called a Spider Patrol, it took me months to track them all, but I did, every last one.'

Scott watched him blending with shadows, fearless and brave to a fault. As a young man he had given horror a face, and he wore it well, Frank Rivers did.

His armour was a village called Qua.

FIFTY-TWO

For Aaron Seymor Blatt it was a hightech world of modern convenience, though at times that world seemed to go very wrong. He looked at his watch. It was 8:34 p.m. They had been waiting forty minutes even though he had called ahead from his KingAir reserving a limousine. He had specified white, but now he knew that was truly a fool's folly.

'Well, that's it,' he said suddenly, 'I'm not paying!'

'Let's take a cab.'

'That's image busting, I've got an image.'

'Suit yourself,' said Corless, as he turned back to eyeing the crowd. As a rental cop strolled at their backs he leaned into Blatt's left ear. 'Bang, bang,' he whispered, and the dentist cringed.

'Don't do that,' he sniffed.

Corless shrugged. 'But it brings luck.' He pointed to a white sedan that was cruising their way, coming around a traffic circle, pulling quickly across the lanes and threading traffic. The large wheels crunched an empty can, and they watched with disdain as a driver climbed hurriedly out, holding up a sign that read DIDS.

Blatt was on him in seconds.

'You've killed our schedule!' he spat, grabbing the card from his hand and throwing it on the street.

The driver was dressed in a black coat with white shirt. 'Sorry sir,' he said slowly, 'there was a bad accident, are you with DIDS?'

'Obviously!' Blatt fumed, as the driver quickly came around, opening the rear door for the two men. Corless was studying a young woman in a tight skirt, Blatt emitted a heavy and troubled sigh.

'The Hyatt Regency, sir,' the driver checked, 'we should be there in twenty minutes.'

Blatt huffed as the driver waited for a response. 'Well,' he barked, suddenly staring him in the eyes. 'Are *you* going to get the damn bags?'

Instantly the beleaguered driver hopped into action, popping the trunk, then grabbing two suitcases as Corless leaned into Blatt's space. 'What's the problem?' he asked.

Blatt shook his entire body. 'I hope he's careful with his ancestors,' he said as the bags disappeared into the trunk. 'My luggage is genuine pig skin.'

'Then we have to?' she asked.

'No,' the man shrugged, 'but we really should.'

'But why can't it wait until morning?'

'Because,' he sighed, 'I want them to see the lights.'

'They're very tired, Thomas,' she said with reserve, and she used his full name only when extremely frustrated. On his lap a young boy had fallen asleep.

'Oh Lindsey,' he sighed wistfully, 'it's something special, something they'll never forget.'

And Thomas Alvin Wheeler watched his wife carefully, looking for signs of surrender. Her name was Linda, and in her arms she cradled their daughter Katie, nearly five years' worth of muff who was worn to the bone. She was wearing her good pink dress with white frills on the bottom and shoes to match, and she yawned, looking up at her father with bright blue eyes, her blonde hair shining like America's best hope.

Linda and Tom had been married for twelve years. They had been up since dawn, starting their day with the Capitol Rotunda, then touring the Smithsonian Institute, the Air and Space Museum, and finally, the U.S. Mint. They just finished supper at Bob's Big Boy in the upper northwest part of the city. By 8:15, they were done.

They sat in a shiny new Toyota mini van, in the parking lot on Wisconsin Avenue. The licence plates were Iowa green, and they were from Osceola, just south of Des Moines. Katie started to yawn.

'Come here, Cupcake,' he smiled, scooping her up, then holding her alongside her brother. She grabbed his earlobe and gave a curious pinch.

'They're just too tired, Tom, Michael's sound asleep.'

'Oh, Lindsey,' he said again, 'I can still remember when my father took me, I was even younger than Mikey.'

The boy stirred, opening his eyes. 'Kennedy?' he asked with a sleepy voice. Michael was seven, and about to start first grade.

'No, something better,' he whispered, patting his head, and face to face with his father the resemblance was striking; blue eyes, fair skin, bright teeth, brown hair. This shone like it was wet, but was not. They were both looking at the young mother.

'Okay,' she sighed, 'I guess it's important.'

They headed south, into the city of monuments.

By the time the passengers in the limo had passed the 14th Street Bridge, they had gone silent, sipping drinks from the bar. For a while Corless had fiddled with the small television, but there was nothing of interest. And again, Blatt moved forward, his hand resting on the front seat.

'Take a left,' he ordered, as they slowed to a stop at the intersection of Constitution Avenue and 23rd Street.

The driver laid a lazy arm across the seat. 'It's out of our way,' he said pleasantly, and Blatt's eyes narrowed.

'You!' he cursed. 'You just damn well do what I say!'

'Take it easy,' said Corless.

'And,' Blatt huffed, 'you can start by putting on your cap!'

The driver complied without response, shaking his head as he pulled away with a jolt, moving towards the Lincoln Circle. Within minutes they were cruising slowly behind the enormous white monument.

It was lit with huge powdery lights that caused the structure to gleam with almost an ethereal brilliance, as if it were the stone, itself, that were glowing.

By the southwest corner two men in their mid-twenties

were huddled together on the lawn, watching the flicker of the Eternal Flame from John Kennedy's grave across the river and into Arlington. These were the only tourists, unfriendly-looking men who were passing an orange flame between them, this light ballooning with a match.

It was unmistakable that they were smoking a Dipper in a liquid narcotic known as PCP, a cigarette that had been soaked, the ether creating a small fireball on ignition. They were standing now, dancing, skipping in boxer-like steps as a tan Crown Victoria slowly rolled in, circling the building, the riders in the limo oblivious to this presence.

'Stop the car!' Blatt ordered sharply as the driver slowed in front of the massive structure, the steps rising under the scornful watch of a stone president.

'Well, I'm not going anywhere,' the fat man puffed.

'Greg, there's an elevator, it will only take a moment,' Blatt spoke as he opened his door.

'I'll go with you, sir,' the driver offered kindly, stepping out of the car.

'Oh no you won't,' Blatt corrected.

As the two men walked out into the night, the chauffeur closed their doors for them, shaking his head in dismay. And he found himself thinking about a raise in salary, he just didn't get paid enough to put up with this kind of personal abuse, though he understood the harsh restraints that Captain Drury faced daily.

For the past nine years, the State Police budget had been tighter than teeth, and Frank Rivers knew that was true for all of law enforcement but the FBI and US Department of Justice.

Scott pushed the fedora back on his head as he approached the white car on foot. He was watching the partnership tackle the monument.

Since there were fifty-six marble steps to be faced, they immediately headed for the handicapped elevator off to the left, moving down a neatly trimmed path lined with greenery.

'We're all set,' Scott said, coming into a line of trees next to the limo. 'We'll take them in their hotel room when we get to Bethesda. Can you tell me what we're doing here?'

Rivers grimaced, removing his cap. 'Blatt saw a movie once and has to talk with Abe. I feel like I'm driving a garbage truck.'

Scott nodded. 'Did you get the name?'

'On his luggage, Gregory R. Corless. It looks like he has a .357 in his belt, but I can't be certain. What's the deal on the limo?'

'We smash it, we own it.'

Rivers watched intently as headlights approached and a car pulled in slowly, a silver Toyota mini-van with Iowa plates, father, mother, two children, and a dog; their faces all pressed to the glass as they admired the marble man.

'Oh just great!' Rivers hissed, his lungs emptying completely. 'That stupid son of a bitch thinks he's a goddamned Norman Rockwell canvas!'

Scott turned, and as the van eased in, stopping in the empty parking lot, Rivers could just see the two men on the lawn extinguishing their Dipper. In quick time they were strutting towards the darkness of the south wall facing the street, their features vanishing in the shade.

Scott shielded his brow; the sharp glare of floodlights covered the entrance to the monument, sidewalk, and elevator path. The man and his wife were stepping out of the van, opening the side door, each taking a child by the hand, then hurrying forward.

'I better stop them, we could have a problem here,' Scott said with concern.

'Tell me about it,' Rivers said flatly.

'Cupcake,' Tom Wheeler spoke sweetly, swooping his girl up into his arms while moving towards the bright building, 'do you know who that man is way up there, do you see that man?'

'Bob?' she squeaked, her eyes were bright and wide.

'No, no,' he hushed, whooshing her quickly forward down the path, his wife hurrying alongside and holding Michael by the hand. The boy was pulling her forward with excitement.

Once on the dimly-lit path, Tom Wheeler eased his gait.

'Children,' he said proudly, 'that's Abraham Lincoln, our finest President.' As he said this, a form suddenly appeared from shadow and onto the concrete sidewalk directly in front of them. Wheeler saw this and stopped.

He was tall, black, and dressed in a dark T-shirt with the sleeves ripped out, coming at them with a purposeful strut, swinging his arms in time to an inner beat. Instinctively Linda edged closer to her husband, taking Katie from him, then rocking her gently. 'Tom,' she trembled, 'he has something in his hand.'

Wheeler felt his pulse climb, the man closing, locking into eye contact with him as his wife spoke again, quickly grabbing Michael's hand. 'There's another one behind us,' she said with panic.

'Mommy,' a small voice cried, and as Wheeler turned his back to assess the threat, both men suddenly rushed the family, not a run, but a strutting sweep, a knife appearing from behind, a gun appearing in front.

'Hey mudderfucker!' yelled the gunman, not ten feet away, coming directly at them, and the family instantly closed around each other, scared witless.

'My God, Tom!'

'It's going to be all right,' he whispered.

'What will we do?'

'I'll reason with them.'

'Don't hurt us!' Wheeler yelled with sudden fright, his hands in the air, staring down into the black hollow of a gun muzzle. In panic, Linda was turning away.

'Don't ja go anywhere, Ho!' the man with the knife yelled, as the children began crying, grabbing her by the legs.

'What do you want of us?' Wheeler cried.

'I want your life, you white mudderfucker,' the gunman quickly laughed into his face, jamming the gun under his chin, twisting this, pushing his head into the air.

'Take my wallet!' he screamed. 'Please don't hurt us, please take my wallet . . .' he was reasoning with them.

'Yeah, I'll take your wallet and I'll take your Ho!'

'Mommy . . .' Katie cried.

The man with the knife started for Linda and her children, grabbing her forcefully by the hair when something happened. Something strange.

Though Wheeler could not hope to see, for this took place at·his back, a man quickly appeared on the sidewalk in front of the memorial, moving forward, intentionally walking directly for them.

And this man did so totally without fright while whistling a tune, which everyone heard echo from the vault where Lincoln sat.

'Whattda fuck?' said the knifeman.

They heard a low and mournful series of whistled notes, which sounded like an old Negro spiritual; every head now followed the sound, including Katie's and Michael's and Linda's, focusing on this strange figure. As he stepped into the bright white lights, he smiled an easy smile, slowing his pace but ten feet away, then casually putting a cigarette into his mouth.

'Who datt? Who datt?' the knifeman asked nervously, jumping behind the young mother, forcing her to face the stranger.

The intruder lit a match, a tiny blue flame glowing under the brim of a battered fedora as he puffed, hiding eyes that never once failed to see them clearly.

'Whattja want?' the gunman said suddenly, his eyes glazed, his thick lips moist and parted. 'He's jest an owld bum, Louis, dat's all he is.'

'What's he want, Roy?'

Just as he said this, Blatt and Corless came strolling from the elevator tunnel, coming down the neatly manicured path and towards the Wheeler family, oblivious to the threatening situation.

'Hey you!' the gunman yelled at Jack Scott, 'whattja want, you owld mudder, you want some snatch, why you owld dawg!'

With a careful ease, Scott removed his hat and tossed it away, for he had heard their comments quite clearly. 'No, Roy,' he said in pure unaccented English, 'I want you and

Louis to lay down your weapons very slowly while you still can.'

'Say what?' the gunman charged, ramming the pistol hard under Wheeler's throat, enough so that blood trickled from a laceration just as Corless and Blatt stepped out into the light, stopping quickly, the fat man instantly fighting the curve of his belly to draw his gun. The sight snagged his ample midsection, then came free at last. He was now pointing aimlessly towards the Wheelers, uncertain as to who was the threat.

'Please put that away,' Scott said quietly to Corless, as Blatt stood shaking just behind his partner.

'Greg, let's go, I don't like this.'

'Who datt?' the gunman barked, for Roy was holding Tom Wheeler and was unable to turn around.

'Mudderfuck!' Louis growled, grabbing Linda around the waist.

'Oh my God,' she sobbed, closing her eyes, and her captor reached up, smacking her hard on the chest as her children clung to her side. Katie was crying now, almost screaming.

'Mommy?' Michael whimpered. 'Mommy . . .'

'I'll do him, I'll do him right now!' Roy suddenly snarled, his face seething with the drug.

Corless had not moved, watching the show with interest, then studying Scott with intense curiosity, sizing him up as if the others simply did not exist. This little grey-headed man in baggy pants was unarmed, yet calm as a duck in water. Something, he knew, was terribly wrong.

'You *can* walk out of here slowly,' Scott offered Corless, pointing towards the street and careful to misdirect, as Frank Rivers was easing closer from the green hedgerow by the path. He was wearing his grey jacket and holding a .45 in each hand.

His left was aimed carefully at Corless, the other at Linda Wheeler's attacker. Unfortunately this was a bad shot, the angle, Rivers knew, would drive a slug through the knifeman and into the woman's back.

'Please,' Scott said quietly, 'you don't need that, you can put that away and return to your car.'

'What?' Corless hesitated, his eyes growing large.

'Whattda fuck?' Roy echoed.

'Oh please . . .' Linda began to beg as her daughter shook violently. Rivers was moving forward in careful strides, walking on his toes. He stopped on Blatt's left, his gun aimed at the fat man's head.

Suddenly Blatt spun and recoiled in shock, seeing his chauffeur with two guns and a gold star swinging from a chain around his neck. Rivers' eyes narrowed and locked, as Blatt's went wide with horror.

'Greg!' he screamed suddenly, and Corless turned, swinging his large frame with panic.

'Go ahead!' Rivers spat, snapping both barrels on Corless from scant feet away. The fat man swallowed hard, his face a cold mask.

'We're backing up!' Corless immediately shouted, turning his gun on Rivers. In that instant Scott drew his gun, locking Corless into the sights of his .9mm, slowly kneeling to reduce body mass.

'Say what?' Roy barked nervously, twisting his gun into Wheeler's throat as Rivers was now easing, one step at a time, towards the street, going for an angle that would allow a margin of safety for the young mother.

'Dear God!' Linda wept as her attacker tightened his grip.

'Don't mess with me!' Louis screamed at Rivers, who stopped instantly, his right aimed at the black man's head, his left still levelled at Corless. Blatt's hand dug nervously into a pocket, producing a small pistol, his body trembling.

'Whattda fuck?' said Roy.

Louis cursed, staring at Scott. 'He ain't no goddamned owld bum!'

'Jack,' Rivers stated calmly, 'I'm going to take my left off the *fat* man, if he shoots, drop him.'

'Like a brick,' he answered without tone, kneeling with both hands gripped to his gun.

'But we were backing up!' Blatt complained, as if this wasn't fair.

'On three, Jack.'

'Right.'

With a swiftness that was nearly invisible, Rivers snapped his left into position on the knifeman's head. Startled, Louis lifted Linda's feet off the ground.

'Mommy!' Katie cried. 'Mommy!'

Rivers emptied his lungs. '*Three*,' he breathed.

'Whattda goddamn!' Roy yelled, jamming the barrel harder into Wheeler's throat.

'Greg!' Blatt implored.

'Don't you get it?' Corless snapped, staring over his sight, his puffy cheeks now raised into quivering jowls. 'They know who we are Seymor, why do you think that punk was driving?'

Blatt was mute.

'Isn't that true,' Corless stated flatly, aiming his barrel at Scott's chest.

He returned a slight nod. 'Lisa Caymann,' he said quietly.

Blatt froze, stunned but quivering.

'Her mother sent us.' Rivers' voice was ice, but Corless had no real expression for any of this.

'Lacy Wilcott,' said Scott, 'and Carol Barth.'

'Jenna Simpson and Janet Moore,' added Rivers.

'Bobby Vought and Darlynne Cooper.'

'Officer John Brougham.'

'Whattda fuck?'

And suddenly, without warning, with the bursting howl of a halogen beam, daylight came blasting down from above even before the sound of a jet engine had reached their ears; night becoming day in that instant, only brighter, as the terrible roar came thundering down, Eagle One dropping like a stone.

The blades were now a violent blast as little Katie opened her mouth to scream as in that one terrifying, chaotic moment, time stopped.

The world exploded.

Rivers pulled his triggers, Corless did, Scott did, Blatt did; the monument grounds bursting in a terrible blaze as the deafening blasts roared into the night, echoing against marble like godless cannon fire.

Instantly, Linda Wheeler toppled onto both children, a dark jell splattering over them as Rivers' guns kicked. Louis fell backward, his head exploding off his neck like a split melon.

Scott was rolling onto one hip as a slug slammed pavement, driving concrete across his face, drilling his torso.

Corless fell backward, crying out as a sledgehammer blow tore through his gut. He fought for control, his face a seething mask. He raised his gun at Rivers who was spinning, both hands releasing red flames, sending precise bolts into the fat man's shoulders, then once to the midsection, then turning away.

Corless screamed in agony, thrown back with such force that his head cracked pavement. Blatt, ten feet away, stumbled backwards while aiming with both hands, jerking at the trigger. Rivers flinched as a bullet caught the bone of his left shoulder. Ignoring it, he leaped into air, slamming Blatt in the middle of the chest, punching the human weasel onto the concrete.

Rivers was all over him.

He reached out, grabbing Blatt around the back, laying a forearm against his throat, then lifting him skyward, staring into his face, folding his torso slowly backwards.

Blatt screamed with horror as he felt his spine begin to splinter like a hollow stick.

'Lisa,' Rivers hissed as Blatt's torso dangled. Then he threw his full weight into him, crushing the killer's ribcage and snapping his spine in half.

Blatt shrieked in high-pitched agony as he came apart with the sound of ice being crushed. Rivers' face was twisted in vengeance as he folded him backward until Blatt's head thumped against his rear pockets. 'John Brougham,' he cursed, dropping him, delivering a swift kick, aiming for his right temple but missing this, connecting with his mouth. Blatt's teeth came flying out, spinning and clattering over pavement, landing by Corless in a puddle of human fluids.

'I'm gonna do him!' Roy screamed through narcotic rage, pulling Wheeler from behind as he backed away from Scott,

536

who was now on his feet and moving towards them, his face peppered with stones and blood. His left eye was closing, his pants torn, his belly a dark brown pool.

'God, please . . .' Linda cried, clutching both children, watching her husband being dragged into darkness as Officer Steven Adare appeared behind them in the grass, quickly assessing, laying his assault rifle down.

'Quickly!' he said to Linda, reaching down, grabbing the woman by the arm. 'Get them out of here!' The woman covered both children in a huddle, walking crablike, scurrying through terror.

Once they were safely away, Adare dropped into a prone position, the laser-scope on his .308 HK-91 laying a bright red dot on Wheeler's face, flitting from side to side, drawing a line as he tried to sight on the black gunman, but it was no good.

Roy's body and head were shielded from Adare, for Wheeler was much taller. And suddenly, without provocation, Roy tore into Wheeler's throat with the front sight, creating a red tear in his skin. 'I'm gonna do him! I'm gonna do him now!' he screamed.

'No,' Scott said calmly, 'you don't want this, Roy, you haven't killed anyone yet, there's still time to save your life . . .'

'Fuck you!' Roy shrieked, his eyes glazed and rolling with PCP, his teeth bared with instinctual terror.

Scott was peering over his gun sight, seeing Adare's red beam flicking from Wheeler to Roy to Wheeler.

'We will take your habit into consideration,' Scott said, appeasing him, 'the drugs are *not* your fault.'

Roy responded by grabbing Wheeler by the hair, jerking his chin up, exposing smooth skin as he jammed the muzzle under his victim's jaw.

'Please don't kill me,' Wheeler was begging. From his perspective he knew he was going to die at the hands of this rabid animal. And all of this in sight of the Lincoln Memorial, so clean, so ageless, so American. As if staring through the wrong end of a telescope he watched Abraham Lincoln growing smaller and smaller as Roy dragged him into darkness. Then, strangely detached, he looked down the barrel of Scott's gun, finding a curious peace.

He made this peace with himself, very quickly, for he had seen his family moved safely away and they seemed unhurt. Unhurt physically. And though he wasn't sure why, his mind started calculating assets; life insurance, stocks, savings, money market, and he had started to work on how far that would go as the world burst around him in a bright jagged flash.

Orange and red daylight, that's all Wheeler saw, then his eyes went blind into white as he felt his body falling through space, his ears roaring, a warm stickiness slapping his face, then pelting down on him in a slippery rain.

Roy was gone.

Roy had backed up into Frank Rivers who had placed his .45 one foot from his skull, behind his left ear, and fired.

'Oh Lord,' muttered Scott, shaking his head.

'Shit, are you okay, Jack?' Rivers asked. 'You look like death . . .'

'No.' Scott was checking himself for the first time. 'No, I'm not all right, I hurt all over.'

Wheeler lay there on his back, digging jell from both eyes. And as his vision cleared he was staring up into a man's face, his eyes blue as bottled glass cleaner.

'Your family's doing just fine. You okay, buddy?' Rivers asked.

Wheeler was speechless as sirens screamed through the capital city.

Gregory Corless was sitting upright like a fat Buddha, staring vacantly. As Scott and Rivers approached he was trying to move, moaning against the stained concrete, just as he heard a quiet splat from flesh ripping open.

And he *heard*, rather than felt this.

It was only then that he caught the smell of what was happening to him. Corless had been trying to turn for his gun, twisting his torso slightly right, his mass moving downward,

538

forcing his bowels to split open, releasing a foul and sickening odour that even he could not believe.

He squirmed, trying to ease the painful pressure. His liver seemed to moan as it ruptured, starting to slip downward.

'Oh God!' he cried, and with that, he froze.

The pain was growing, expanding in his gut. It had started as a sharp fire just under his ribs where bullets had slammed into him, but now that fierce agony was blinding, his belly felt like someone had driven a jagged spear clean through and turned the blade inside him like a corkscrew. And he sensed things inside him just sliding around, slithering, as if his organs were coming alive and were starting to crawl.

In his mind he was moving his hands over and across the tear in his belly, holding his hands in place so that his liver would not slip free. But bullets had severed the nerves in both shoulders, and his arms would not obey. In an animal urge, he twisted his torso towards Blatt for help, trying to cry out when there was the sudden sound of a bedsheet being ripped.

There was no bedsheet.

For all the world Corless looked like a beached whale, leaning forward, sitting on two giant hams. There was a brown slipper between his legs, and another large piece of him was poking through.

'Help me . . .' he groaned, his eyes fixed, his body slung forward but unable to move as the two policemen stood over him.

'No,' said Rivers, 'I don't think I will.'

'So, Gregory,' Scott was leaning over, down into his face. 'If you're so smart why are you so dead?'

'Help . . .' his lips moved as his gut discharged a cough of brown fluids.

Scott squatted directly in front, lifting Corless' head from his chest with one hand, looking him directly in the eye. The pupils were dilating, the lids had stopped blinking. 'You know, your life wasn't a total waste,' he offered.

'How so?' Rivers asked.

'Think about it, that poor family of civilians. If there had

539

never been a Corless and Blatt, we would not have been here tonight.'

'That's true,' Rivers nodded.

'And I think Roy and Louis would have killed them, at the very least they would have done real damage.'

Rivers was nodding thoughtfully as Scott edged even closer to Corless, his nose almost touching the fat man's face. 'Thank you, Gregory, for saving the lives of a nice family. You didn't know *you* did that, but *you* did!'

'Help me . . .'

'You're dead, Gregory!' He bit these words off sharply. 'You died in order to save a little girl and boy, and *you died* so that a family can live. Just think about that on your way to Hell, all because of you and Aaron Blatt, they're going to live happily ever after.'

The fat man couldn't move, or Scott was sure he would have. Corless was trying to speak, the heavy layers of skin on his throat quivering as Scott threw a disgusted hand to the sky, flipping Corless onto his back as they heard a strange sound.

A sound like a knife ripping through a canvas sail.

The inner mass that was Corless was moving swiftly downward, his belly emptying into his shirt.

He moaned with agony.

He did that several times before he really died.

FIFTY-THREE

Sitting at his kitchen table in Wooded Acres, Jeffery Dorn slipped a needle into red meat, driving fluid from a syringe with his thumb.

Irma Kiernan was watching, flipping through a catalogue of summer fashions while listening to a live performance of classical music broadcast over WETA public radio. Dorn returned the needle to the vial, filling it again, jabbing it violently into a flank steak.

'Oh, Sweetheart, please be careful with that.'

Dorn shot her a wild look, his dark eyes glinting in soft light as the music swelled and Irma lifted the small bottle, inspecting the clear fluid. *DANGER*, a label warned, *DMNA dimethyl nitrosamine.*

'What is it?' she asked.

'As far as I'm concerned it's heart medication,' he said tonelessly, lifting the steak and flopping it over onto a serving dish. 'It's actually a corrosion inhibitor for rocket fuels, but it's also used in cancer treatments. When ingested, it causes the heart to explode.'

Kiernan cringed as he took the bottle from her hand, jamming the needle back in, sucking fluid with the plunger.

'Is this for her?' she asked, and her face carried a dizzy expression.

He shook his head.

'Then who's it for?' she pressed, and Dorn reached over and touched her hand.

'Tell me about this Beverly Lynch,' he demanded. 'You said her father has filed for divorce and left town?'

'Oh Jeff, she seems happy to me, she doesn't need us.'

'Irma, you described her as *sullen*, that's a symptom of abuse, all those years of specialisation and you don't know that? We should rescue her as well.'

'Oh Jeff.' She rose from her chair and sidled up to him. 'Let's stay home tonight, just the two of us.' She was rubbing his ear with her fingertips as he continued to work.

'Last night you said it was too early to make another try at the Jansons, you said you needed time to plan . . .'

'I've planned,' he cut her off.

'*MASH* comes on in ten minutes, it's your favourite.'

'I have another show in mind. Go polish the key, a little extra steel wool wouldn't hurt.'

'Oh, Honey, I've worked it to death. Would you like to talk about the wedding?' She flipped to a page in her magazine, there was an advertisement for a bridal boutique. Dorn was injecting the meat until it glistened, small pools of liquid popping up from the flesh.

'Hand me a paper towel,' he demanded. And soon he had covered the platter, patting it down, soaking away surplus. He waited as more fluid leached through, patting it again, flipping it over.

'I don't think this is right,' Irma said quietly. Dorn lifted his head, his eyes dark and punishing.

'Don't start with me,' he warned.

'But what will you do with Elmer, Honey, how will you save him?'

'It doesn't matter.'

'Yes,' she pouted, 'yes it does.' She looked as if she was about to cry.

'You nitwit,' he said absently, 'you're a big part of this.'

And Irma Kiernan began to weep, as Dorn stopped work with a heavy sigh.

'Irma, what the hell is the matter now? You know the plan, why do you do this to me?' She looked over at him, her eyes pinched and troubled.

'Jeff, you're not being honest with me,' she said softly, and sobbed once more.

'What? Irma, why are you doing this?'

'You've been sick,' she cried, 'and you didn't even tell me . . .' And with that Jeffery Dorn rose abruptly from his seat, smacking his forehead and staring up at the ceiling.

'Goddamn you, Irma, you've been reading my mail!'

'Oh, Honey,' she whined, 'are you going to sue Dr Landry?'

Dorn's face drew a perfect blank. 'What are you rattling about? Why would I sue him, Irma, dead men can't sue anyone!'

And with that she pulled a plain white envelope free of her dress. It had been torn open by a nervous hand when the stress of so much mysterious correspondence finally broke the woman down. Dorn looked upon this as if it were a vile and alien thing, then quickly snatched it from her hand and started to read.

When he had finished his face was contorting without control, his knees were shaking his entire frame, and he felt bile rushing up from his stomach.

'My Lord,' Irma cried nervously, 'what's wrong? That's good news, Sweetheart, you should be happy.'

'I can't believe this . . .' Dorn muttered, swallowing hard, and he seemed to be out of breath and fighting for air.

'Sweetheart, if you're mad at him, then I think you should sue! Mistakes like that don't happen without a price, they either screwed up in his office or at the testing facility. Either way, you should be happy. You're so brave, Jeff, living with something like this all by yourself . . .'

'Shut up!' he cut her off, and then read the letter again.

As stated in our previous correspondence, the mix-up between your blood sample and that of a terminal cancer patient was made at the Wyro Technical Center. Frankly, we are concerned since we have not heard from you as to your course of action in this matter . . .

'I can't believe it, the goddamn insufferable incompetence! Bastards! God, Irma, we have to get busy!' And while Dorn's

543

personal message to Scott flashed through his mind, Irma Kiernan was on her feet, twirling in place.

'What, Jeff?' she said perkily. 'I think we should celebrate, a dark cloud has been lifted from this house!'

'Stop it! Irma, you don't understand the trouble we're in!'

'It will pass, Jeff, you were never sick. I know how hard this . . .'

'No!' he cried, and he held up a silencing hand. 'What happened to the Claytons could have drawn attention to us, and that kid was found . . .'

'Jeff, that family wasn't your fault, you were trying to help them.'

'If that kid keeps digging, it's over for me, Irma, and over for you. Goddamn, I can not believe this has happened to me . . .'

'I don't understand, Jeff, what are you saying?'

Dorn released a heavy mechanical sigh. 'It doesn't matter,' he said quickly in a confused and confidential voice. 'People are out to get me, you'll just have to accept that. From now on you help without questions, Irma, I don't want to waste any more time answering your . . .'

She stood suddenly at this, crying with alarm. 'Hold me, Jeff, hold me.'

FIFTY-FOUR

Jessica Janson was in her bedroom, listening to the rippling of flutes and the lazy depths of cellos as the Fourth Movement of *Fantasia* played over the radio. As she folded clothes, she was wishing she could have afforded tickets to take Elmer, for the London Philharmonic was something that he would remember, especially at the Kennedy Center.

And then and there she resolved not to give up on her efforts to instil an appreciation of music in him, though the strings, piped into her bedroom speakers, were sounding a pinch shallow. She frowned noticeably.

'What's wrong?' Elmer asked.

'Be a doll and go downstairs and adjust the bass to the right setting,' she whispered. He had been sitting on the end of her bed, digging through her jewellery box and toying with treasures.

'Mom, what's this?' he asked, holding up what looked like a dozen very thin rings all interlocked with each other into a four-inch chain. She smiled, sitting alongside him on the bed.

'That's a puzzle ring from Egypt, your daddy gave that to me in 1979 when he was covering Secretary Vance's trip to the Middle East.'

'Why is it apart?'

'Because,' she poked him in the tummy, 'the tape that held it together fell off, and I don't have time to go to Egypt to find a puzzle master to fix it.'

'Can I have it?'

'It's very expensive, Red, you can play with it if you like.' And he shoved it into a pocket.

'What's this?' he asked, opening a long velvet box, which she quickly took away from him.

'That's for another night, you have school tomorrow.'

Elmer pushed off the bed as Tripod stood, tail wagging, preceding him out the door. 'Mom,' he asked shyly, 'do you like Mr Hall?'

'I think he's a very nice man, very special.'

'Can we invite him over for dinner?'

'Yes, Elmer, if he hasn't returned to New York we can ask.'

'Mom, are you in love with Detective Rivers?'

At this Jessica shook her head, then reached over to pinch him gently on the ear. 'Elmer, why do you ask questions like that?'

'I saw you hugging.'

She emitted a heartfelt sigh. 'Red,' she said softly, 'that was just a thank you hug for helping us. I think it's getting late. While you're fixing my speaker will you get me a soda?'

'Orange?'

'Gingerale, and no ice cream scoops for you, either.'

It was an expensive intercom, manufactured by JBL and installed by Elmer's father just to the left of the refrigerator facing the hallway. Elmer flipped on the light as he came through, quickly adjusting a speaker, then opening the door to the freezer.

Inside he saw a box of chocolate covered bonbons, and he squinted, flipping the switch to his mother's bedroom.

'Just one,' she responded before he had asked, and Elmer smiled.

'Mom, do you want a cookie?'

'No,' her detached voice said firmly, 'no cookies. You can have a bonbon, or you can have a cookie, not both, and you have to brush your teeth again.'

'Okay, Mom.'

He peered back in at the ice cream as Tripod raised himself on hind legs, pressing against the boy's back, pushing him forward. 'Oh, hold your horses,' he giggled, pulling at the box, then removing two balls of ice cream with his fingers.

'Sit!' he ordered, and as the dog obeyed he held an ice cream ball at his nose. Tripod gulped without chewing as Elmer popped his, letting it melt in his mouth. He then grabbed a vase from beneath the sink and began filling this with tap water as the dog suddenly rammed him from the rear.

'Tripod!' he laughed, poking him gently in the nose, and the dog sat on his hind legs wagging his broom-like tail. Over the sink and just to the left, Elmer opened a cupboard and removed a box, this with a smiling cartoon puppy on it. He was just reaching inside the flap, grabbing a handful of cookies which he held to the dog's muzzle, when suddenly, Tripod dropped forward, his jowls quivering.

The skin on his nose was raised into a snarl, exposing teeth, looking eye to eye with the boy. 'What's wrong?' Elmer started, sniffing the biscuits as the dog suddenly hopped away and towards the back door.

As Elmer came alongside, the dog released a low, menacing growl.

'Come on, boy,' he comforted, stroking the ridge of fur on Tripod's neck. But the Shepherd would *not* come, instead, he reared up and rapped at the door with his front foot.

'Mom?' Elmer quickly threw the intercom lever and spoke excitely into the wall-mounted speaker.

'What is it, Red?'

'Tripod hears something.'

'Yes dear, he always does. Now only one bonbon apiece, and I've counted them.'

'Not like this, Mom, Tripod is really upset.'

'Give him a cookie and come upstairs, Elmer. It's almost ten o'clock, way past your bedtime.'

Elmer looked at the dog's snarling head. 'What is it, boy?' he leaned over to ask, as the Shepherd was locked into a seething growl, his large brown eyes fixed into a menacing stare out the window as saliva dripped to the floor.

'Come on,' the boy urged, tugging at his collar, but the dog would not budge.

Elmer flicked a wall switch and as the outside yellow light

came on, Tripod reared onto his hind legs, his body stiffening, his massive head tilted slightly down as his fangs glistened.

But there was only the wind.

And a shadow fading into darkness.

Jessica Janson was sipping a gingerale while putting up her hair, combing this straight up, then gathering it directly on the top of her head. With practised ease she took an elastic tie from between moist lips and secured a tight bundle. Rivers had been right in his earlier description, the result was a funny little ponytail that resembled a straw fountain. From her scalp it bloomed in every direction, and she batted this down into place.

Sitting in bed, she kicked her feet into the air while pulling slacks from her hips, standing to shake the wrinkles out, then hanging these with care. *Fantasia* was still playing, so she glided with the strings towards the closet and back, retrieving her choice of dress shoes for the morning, parking these beneath her side window by a night-stand.

It had been a long day, she reflected, alone for the first time that weekend. Elmer, who had seemed sad on Friday, had certainly perked up when Rivers was around. How the boy had tried to mimic the way that Detective Rivers walked, quiet and confident; it was almost comic, though she had been careful not to snicker. She wondered what it was like for a boy Elmer's age to be missing a male role model.

'Should have had a brother,' she said aloud. The truth was that at times she did feel that need in her struggle to raise someone who would be worth knowing. And that was really her only criterion, that her son grow into a man that made a contribution to the world, and not just take from it. Frank Rivers was just such a man, she thought, strong and caring and dedicated, and yet somewhat of an enigma, a mystery she wanted to decipher. 'That will take some time,' she said aloud, removing a package of stockings, breaking open the plastic seal. Then she proceeded to lay out a pale grey executive suit.

Verdone Apparel, she remembered, and her gears were shifting quickly. Since 1983 she had been the commercial account executive, and through no fault of her own, they were going to run over budget on a television campaign, and she wondered how the agency would absorb that.

Check with accounting, she dashed quickly onto a notepad, staring down at her briefcase, and while she started to pick this up, she stopped abruptly, settling for the warm and subtle chords which went swirling through the room. She stretched, catlike, pushing her arms above her head and releasing a relaxed yawn.

This behaviour was contagious.

Irma Kiernan was yawning with her.

Not more than forty feet away, the two women were facing each other through the window, though Jessica was oblivious to this presence. The older woman could barely tolerate the way her man had been staring up at Jessica, breathing heavily as the blonde tart really went into an act, slowly unbuttoning a blue silk blouse. As she did this, Kiernan wanted to throw stones through the glass, and *not* to alert her.

Irma wanted to resurrect the witch trials of Salem and burn, stone, crush her into nothingness with large rocks. Even without binoculars it was easy to tell how smooth and taut the woman's skin was, and that made Irma feel old beyond years; her back rounding, her sagging chin and face falling forward in defeat. She quickly looked away.

From the rear, the light in Elmer's bedroom was casting out shadows, these landing against the fence near the alley, while Jessica's room was in the front northeast corner. Her side window faced the lot between houses, and Dorn stood here, looking up from a neighbour's wall through binoculars.

Once the wall had been painted white, but Jeff had explained how old the owners were, and the red brick was showing through in ugly strips, there was no one to maintain the property line. As she steadied herself, flecks of paint stuck to Kiernan's palms in the humidity, so she came forward again, brushing herself off, growing quite angry as the woman in the window was slipping off her shirt, exposing herself in a peach-coloured bra. And just when Kiernan thought it could get no worse, Janson suddenly unsnapped this in one sweeping motion, letting her breasts bounce free.

The woman did have a substantial figure, and seemed to be tracing red lines with her fingers. Kiernan could stand this no more, and she looked at Dorn, quickly interpreting this display for him.

'Nothing special there!' she laughed, having quickly come over a patch of lawn to his side. Dorn did not respond, he knew better on two counts.

First, it was a rare night when the Janson house wasn't shut like a tomb with the wooden shutters drawn tight, so he reasoned that the boy must have toyed with these. Second, Jessica had curves that could fog a camera lens, while Irma thought her too slim, her breasts too large, her hair too blonde.

More than this, she thought Janson's style too assertive, her manner too suggestive and showy. The window was partially open to the cool night air, the classical music was swirling through the yard, reaching them. To distract herself, Irma tried looking up to a scattering of clouds. The stars came stabbing down like angry needles, and she was thinking of other ways to distract Jeff when they heard voices.

'Mom?'

Jessica quickly threw on a silk bathrobe, then turned for the hallway.

Dorn's face was a perfect blank.

'In for a penny, in for a pound.' Irma was pressing an argument.

'No,' Dorn corrected, 'I'm going in alone. We go back home, I assemble my gear, then you'll drop me off again.'

'But Jeff, I think . . .'

Dorn held up a hand. 'Irma,' he huffed, waving the tainted meat at her, 'it will take time for this to work anyhow.'

'But isn't the dog in the house? He'd be barking at us.'

'Very good, Irma, they always unlock his doggy door just before they go to sleep. He'll come out and have a nice snack, and then,' he rapped his chest, '*blam-boom*, he'll blow like a cheap party balloon.'

With that Dorn strolled the short distance of green to the rear fence and, standing on his toes, peered over, studying the backyard. He selected a spot near a small elm tree, then removing the meat from a plastic bag, hurled it with some precision. There was a muted thud.

'But how will I know when you're done?' Irma was standing behind him, and Dorn shook his head with frustration.

'I told you,' he whispered wearily, 'it will be about four or five hours, so I'll call, just wait by the phone.' He turned towards the street and began to walk.

'But why so long, Jeff, I still don't understand why you will take so . . .'

'Irma!'

'Oh, Honey, that's dangerous, you shouldn't use the phone.'

Dorn was almost to the street, turning for their car which was parked down the road. 'Reach out and touch someone, that's why we have phones.'

'And you're sure she's guilty, she uses the boy for . . .'

'Irma, you saw her public striptease, you read that article about her? She's a kinky slut and that kid needs us, he's in for some real trouble.'

As they headed down the street towards the car, Irma considered this, though not so carefully, as the next question was more pressing, overpowering, nagging. 'Jeff,' she squeaked, pressing herself into him.

Dorn turned, walking backwards. 'The answer is no, Irma! I do *not* want to touch her, you are my only bed partner.' He paused for effect. 'I'm happy the way things are.'

She smiled coyly as Dorn laid a hand to her cheek. Her skin felt cool and lifeless as vinyl.

He opened the door.

Kiernan believed because she wanted to.

FIFTY-FIVE

Scott and Rivers had left their cars, including the limo, taking Eagle One to Suburban Hospital, more than ten minutes away by air. There were many closer choices, including the Washington Hospital's MedStar Unit, but they wanted to be near the command post.

Scott had been in surgery for nearly an hour, not for the severity of wounds, but for the sheer number of them. Corless had shot the concrete just at Scott's feet, driving debris into his legs, crotch, stomach, chest.

As of 9:52, the Commander had taken thirty-nine stitches, and as the count continued, Rivers sat on a table in the gun wound operating theatre.

'Then it's not that bad?' he questioned, peering into the warm brown eyes of Dr Anh-Bich Pham, a Vietnamese American with skin like smooth cream on the face of an angel. She was still in her operating blues and was taking his pulse.

'Mr Rivers . . .'

'Frank, please, you've inspected my entire body.'

She dropped his arm. 'You better use that sling, the muscle is badly bruised, and torn in two places. I'd suggest lying on your right side when you sleep, and don't plan on working for at least a week.'

'I appreciate that, Doc, how long until it closes up?'

'That depends on how you treat yourself, but there's a piece of cartilage that may have to come out, we'll see in a few months. In the meantime I would recommend bed rest, no exercise on this side until you're mended, and I'm also putting you on antibiotics.'

'Is that really necessary? They fry your guts to hell.'

'Yes,' she smiled, 'they do. Now stand up and bend over.'

'I beg your pardon?'

'Bend over, Sergeant, I have a little present for you, that is unless you want lockjaw.'

Rivers shrugged and assumed the position, dropping his pants to his knees. 'Is this going to hurt?'

'Fiercely,' she winked, 'but you're a tough guy, so . . .' And she quickly hit home.

'Eeeeee yow!' he cried. 'Damn me for a mutt!'

'Told you, tetanus, it's not a nice shot.'

'Terrific,' he winced, rubbing one cheek, 'just terrific.'

'And I'm serious about my instructions, Frank. I can see you don't listen to doctors very well, but this time you'd better.'

'How's that?'

She pointed to a scar on his chest and another on his left forearm, this like the sealed flap of a small envelope. 'Who sutured these?' She gave a nasty stare as she examined his flesh.

'Oh, those are mine, safety pins, it's an old trick.'

She nodded. 'Very macho, Frank, you gave yourself stenosis in the tissue, come see me in another twenty years when those scars become cysts, or tumours.'

He smiled. 'You've got a deal, but the arm's going to mend okay. Just take it easy?'

'That's a nasty little wound channel there, you're lucky it was a .25 and not something bigger, the bullet was on the surface because it hit the bone and bounced back out. It really is more serious inside than you can tell, so take it easy, you've lost a pint of blood.'

'I'll eat some liver.'

'I'm sure,' she glanced at her watch, 'and your friend's going to be another thirty minutes, so you might as well get comfortable.'

'He is going to be okay?'

'Mr Scott has taken nearly forty *real* stitches so far, and they're still picking stones out of him. The bullet carried the full path of debris into his skin, the slug tore a hole right through his pants, you knew that?'

'It hit him?'

'No, the bullet sliced neatly through the baggy seam at his crotch, he was very, very lucky.'

Rivers swallowed hard. 'It mustta ricocheted.'

'Yes,' she smiled, turning for the door. 'I'll be giving you something for the pain, you are going to hurt when the IM wears off.'

'Sorry?'

'Intramuscular injection, pain killer. I did quite a bit of digging in there, as well as curettage against the bone, which you couldn't feel, but you will. This will start to hurt, believe me, so I'm going to get you started on something very hippie.'

'I'll take it later.'

She gave a nasty smile. 'We'll see. Your captain's waiting for you if you'd like to see him.'

Rivers nodded as he rubbed his wounded shoulder.

'If you need me, you call, that's my beeper,' she said, handing him a card. He slipped this into his pants without looking at it.

'Thanks, Doc, I really appreciate it.'

She smiled warmly. 'Try to duck next time, Frank, you have enough hard miles on that body of yours.'

'Tell me about it.'

She nodded thoughtfully and edged closer. 'Who shot you in the face?' she gave a concerned whisper. 'I didn't see a reference to that in your medical history.'

'Oh,' he sighed, 'it's that obvious?'

'No, no,' she pouted at him, 'I was a trauma surgeon at Da Nang Air Field, I know reconstruction when I see it, and you have a replacement cheek.' She stroked his right lightly. 'It's beautiful, no one would ever know.'

Rivers grimaced. 'Please don't put that in the file.'

She shook her head at him. 'Our secret, but it was Vietnam?'

'Cambodia.'

'That's a very special job they did,' she smiled, slowly opening the door as Captain Maxwell Drury suddenly rushed in.

'Sweet Jesus, Frank, I've been worried sick.'

'Hiya, Max, I just gotta thump is all.'

'Detective Rivers?' Dr Pham questioned, waiting until she had his full attention. 'Take those pills, you're going to need them, all of them.'

Rivers waved. 'Thanks.'

'My God, Frank,' Drury cried with dread, 'that lousy bastard almost shot off Jack's goody bag!'

'I know,' Rivers grimaced. 'What about Jessica, Max, if you're here, I take it you put an extra team on their house?'

'Are you all right, son?'

Rivers stood suddenly, 'I'm fine, Max, what about the Jansons? Did you pull Toy and Murphy out of the bowling alley? They can't see the house from their position!' His voice was flushed, his tone accusatory as Drury was breathing deeply, his eyes flinched with anger.

'Don't you start with me, Frank,' Drury cautioned suddenly, 'I've just been reviewing the contents of Blatt's plane, and I'm damn near fed up. They recovered enough teeth to make three mouths, plus a shitload of the cruellest videos your mind can imagine – those bastards were playing a weird sadistic sex game, trading their pleasure for a little relief from torture . . .'

'Max!' Rivers cut him off, raising a hand. 'I don't want to hear it. If Blatt's dead there's no one to prosecute. What about Jessica?'

Drury's eyes flared and then narrowed as Dr Pham held open the door to the recovery theatre. What appeared from shadow was a patient who bore the look of a man brought back from death. Scott's eyes were swollen and hollow, his face bruised and covered with tracks, and he looked old. Very old. He limped forward with a body that trembled.

Drury stared at the apparition.

'Captain,' Dr Pham said nervously, helping Scott to a chair. 'This patient has refused admission, and . . .'

'Oh, Jack,' Drury cried, 'you should stay and get some sleep.'

Scott slowly shook his head, watching as Rivers laced his jogging shoes. 'What about the fat man?' he swallowed, his breathing laboured.

'Gregory Richard Corless, superintendent of public schools for Mercer County, Alabama. We don't know his history with Blatt just yet, but he's married and has three children. Two of them are girls.'

Scott nodded.

'Blatt all but came apart into two pieces when they cut his clothes off, I was going to ask Frank about that.' And though Scott had started to respond, he knew with a glance that words were not necessary. Rivers was quickly holstering his guns, his shirt still open across his chest, his eyes like stones, his jaw muscles ticking with anger.

'The Jansons, Max,' Scott charged quickly. 'Who is covering for you?'

Before Drury could answer, Rivers pushed out the door.

556

FIFTY-SIX

In the Janson backyard there was an undisturbed silence, a departed stillness by the corner of the house, under a small elm, and it lay lifeless and undone.

Dorn looked skyward.

The ten o'clock shuttle to New York roared overhead, gaining altitude, and the Sunday traffic on River Road had slowed to a handful of parading cars. The air was cool. His black body sock cut the breeze, so he only felt this on his face. The Dacron hood was tucked back behind his ears, enabling him to discern the direction of any noise.

On his waist he carried a gear pouch, this was black nylon, and he removed a lipstick from here, applying this to thin lips that were quickly going dark blue, with three more strokes, nearly black.

He stood in the very rear of the side lot, looking over the gate and into the backyard, the light in Elmer's window casting a muted glow. Dorn could just see the form of Tripod lying near some bushes, still as a stone. And this delighted him.

All along Jeffery Dorn had known something about this particular dog that had gone unnoticed by most people. At one time he must have been a trained attack dog from some military or police K-9 Corps, though he didn't know which. His educated guess was armed forces, for the Shepherd rarely barked, even when there was a threat. The mutt had been trained in stealth, though the boy was starting to ruin the animal's instincts.

Tripod's type of attack, Dorn knew, would be silent and

merciless and without warning, the product of professional conditioning. And it almost seemed a waste to kill such an obedient instrument of destruction. After only one bite of tainted meat, the mutt had crawled into the darkness to die.

And die, he did. Dorn checked his watch. 10:42 p.m. It was quiet now.

Through the upstairs window he could hear the Kennedy Center's final prelude, and he could see Jessica's graceful shadow gliding by above him, a form cast against the half-drawn shades.

'Good night, Mom,' a voice flitted through.

'Night night, Sweetheart. Did you let Tripod out?'

'Yes.'

'Elmer, did you say your prayers?'

'Yes, Mom. Tomorrow can we take Tripod to the park?'

'Monday's a work day, Red, you know that. Next weekend, okay, and you have to do well on all your tests. School's almost over, then you'll have all summer to play.'

'Mom?' he asked shyly.

'I'm right here. Elmer, aren't you tired?'

'Thanks for everything, I mean the pizza and movies and all.'

'You're quite welcome, baby, give us a kiss.' There was a pause that caused Dorn's heart to flutter. 'Good night,' the woman sang, 'don't let the bed bugs bite.'

Dorn closed his eyes, breathing hard, as Jessica turned out the light in the boy's bedroom. The voices, the stillness of the yard, the key in his hand; all of this was almost more than he could take without screaming.

In Jessica's room, the lights stayed on, and he placed his ear to the outside wall, hearing the music fail as the sounds of running water filled in behind. From the street there was only the blinking traffic lights on River Road, and he waited, seeing headlights slow before moving on.

In his younger years, he thought, he would have simply used the dog's plastic door as an entrance, lying on his side, wriggling through with ease. Now, in his later years, the scoliosis of his spine and the age in his joints had taken their toll, and he was half the man, forced to live with memories. And in the torn light he remembered dropping right through a chimney on Christmas Eve and into a living room, savouring that, recalling the terrorised expressions that greeted him.

He was moving now, down along the front of the house, against the hedges, towards the front door. He had considered the rear, but the back light was left on, casting a glow that could reflect a tall shadow.

A car came veering from the intersection towards him, and instantly he pulled back, the headlights streaming through the sleepy suburb, passing the little house, dropping off into distant dark. He stood quickly, removing a pair of rubber gloves from his bag, these with a soft and subtle cotton lining which felt clean as death on his fingertips.

He held the key to his face. Irma's key. She had polished it until a shine glowed from smooth edges, the teeth like gold.

With the practice of a gameshow host, he inserted this gently, as with his left hand he covered the hardware, muffling the sound of a bolt lifting.

It turned freely, and his eyes fairly burned.

Like so many others who had entertained him over the years, the woman made use of a safety chain, rings of tarnished brass dangled against the jamb. In scant seconds he slid the metal tongue from its groove with rubber-coated forceps, the thing slipping with ease through its track. He startled, the chain swinging once as he skilfully steadied it, his heart now pumping with a mad and merciless pursuit.

And he *felt*. Something. Not sure what.

But it was wonderful, this feeling, causing his skin to go crawling, writhing, forcing sweat to the surface as his pulse continued to climb. He felt the blood tingle through his torso, battering at his brain, driving his senses wild. Looking out from the hood, his eyes were like moist coals, wild with delight, and he could now hear his own twisted life-tide roar in an angry ocean, rocking him, bursting in his ears as the door swung open.

It was dark, and he walked in.

It was the violated spaces that he craved.

'Jessica,' he said aloud, practising her name, closing the door behind him. 'There is nothing, Jessica, that you will not do to please me!'

Her voice came drifting down the stairs after him. It was a tired voice, yet filled with hope. 'I think he really would love an instrument, Mother, just not this year,' she was saying. 'Right now he needs boyish things.'

She was on the phone. And Dorn stood in the living room listening to this as his eyes adjusted to the darkness, very slowly. He felt his pupils grow as he smelled the domestic wonders around him.

Every house, he knew, was different. Odours came alive, having soaked into fabric and wood. Some pungent, some sweet, he had smelled them all. Yet for the aroma of wet dog food, the Janson house smelled *clean*, somehow, and as he strolled for the kitchen he decided he would change all of that. Change the smell. The dog would help some, so would Jessica, maybe her kid, he wasn't making a detailed plan, just kicking it around a little. And he stopped. A calendar in the breakfast nook caught his eye, then he saw the morning's breakfast which was placed neatly on the counter.

Cereal, bread, jams, and a pan for eggs.

'Mother,' Jessica sighed, 'that's not at all what I'm saying.'

Dorn glided for the sink. The smell of ripe dog chow hung in the air, and he didn't care for this. The refrigerator released a quiet, steady hum, and posted on the door he saw Elmer's report card. While the silly woman had penned a gold star on top, there was a B in math circled in red. He imagined that really chewed on Jessica, the kid wasn't perfect; Dorn guessed his love-making was also poor.

And standing there in the kitchen, moving towards the staircase, he felt like he had known them for years, though he hadn't really. And he was looking forward to meeting them for the first time, face to face, his heart pounding with sweet cruelty as he imagined hers.

He stopped.

In a photograph on the staircase wall, he saw his reflection in the glass. And even though this was an image of the entire Janson clan taken when Elmer was born, Dorn saw only himself. His features all but invisible as he lifted his upper lip, then tightened the masking over his head.

The stair creaked.

'Mom, I'd like to talk more, but I left the shower running.'

Dorn steadied himself with a gloved hand against the wall.

'Love you too,' she said, and there was silence. Formless and pure. Through the thin walls, pipes began to moan gently, down into a soft bass note as Jessica added hot water to the flow of her shower.

Moving quickly now, stopping midway up the steps, he listened intently. A door with a magnetic catch snapped open, the linen closet he guessed, as he heard the steady showerhead spray being interrupted by a human mass, the rapping echo less prevalent, then a glass door clicking shut.

He walked.

Toe to heel to toe, step by step, stopping at the top landing. Before him, on the burnt orange space rug, a large rubber bone. It had been chewed to death. Swooping this up, he strolled right for Elmer's bedroom.

The blue door was cracked a foot so that Tripod could nudge by, so Dorn batted at this, his fingertips making a scratching noise as he came peeking through.

Sound asleep, Elmer was, and curled around a stuffed panda. At his feet was a large beanbag doggie bed, the type sold from catalogues, but from the fur on Elmer's sheets, it was clear this wasn't used.

'Bedbugs,' Dorn mocked tonelessly under his breath, as he reached down into his pouch. And he gave the boy a chance to wake, holding a pair of brightly polished handcuffs by the chain, rattling them at him, then rolling the rubber bone across the carpet.

The boy would not wake.

Dorn turned, sliding the door shut, so silently. And even before he had entered the master bedroom, steam came pouring out to greet him, making his oval face tingle in the tight mask, as every nerve was now coming alive.

Jessica had let the hot water spray during the length of a phone call, steam filling the air, this seeping through the bathroom door. And he could clearly hear water thumping against a glass cell, echoing from her bathroom.

He entered with a nod, for the bed was readied, the sheets meant to receive him and turned down with hotel perfection. Interesting, he thought, a glass of water on her night-stand. Dorn quickly placed a gathering of rope on her pillow, the kind bought at the better sporting goods stores; and with gloved hands he picked up the glass, holding it to his lips, testing the temperature with his tongue.

It was cold.

He drank it down in a single shot, moving soundless as thought for the bathroom door. Dorn knew Jessica would be quickly out, not for the lateness of the hour but for the way she had tied her hair. She would cover this with a rubber cap, instead of washing it, and he knew how the steam would cause fluff if she stayed too long. Jessica had mentioned that to her mother once.

Vanity, he thought, *thy name is vanity*. And he was imagining how she would be willing to soak it, just to please him, or shave it off completely. With two fingers he pressed against the white wooden door.

It opened by inches.

Peering right, directly into a wall mirror, her blurry form was reflected from the shower stall. He decided to watch as she danced about a glass jar, cold and inky black eyes darting over her naked form. She was thin and tall, her hands held in back of her neck, rubbing with a washcloth while both elbows went poking out with her breasts saddled between. She turned, facing the far wall, her left foot rubbing the calf of her right, and he heard an audible sigh.

Suddenly, she tilted her head backward, opening her mouth, letting the water rush over her face.

With a soaring pulse, he eased onto the carpet, closing the door quickly, for he did not want a draught to warn her.

Not this time.

Dorn wanted Jessica to see him pressed against the glass, and so what if she screamed? That was fine. The possibility excited him further.

She turned, the water rolling down her back, one hand on each shoulder, bending slightly forward at the waist.

Dorn approached. He removed his gloves.

Again she turned, facing the wall as Dorn quickly propelled himself forward, standing just to the right, his heart like a sick animal beating at his ribs. She rubbed her eyes, tilting her head back.

She was closing her eyes, her beautiful eyes, caressing her face with light fingertips, letting the water stream in restful strokes.

Blindness. Dorn saw she was blind. If only for one second, and that's all it took.

With an instant step he came into position directly in front of the glass panel, a movement that brought incredible pleasure, a thousand times better than anything he knew. Standing directly on top of her with certain perfection, man against prey, the little gun steadied in his right hand.

Standing within inches.

Watching her play with ribbons of water, streaming off her chin, tunnelling through cleavage, flooding over belly where her hands were cupped. Collecting a pool of bath water, splashing her face. She repeated this several times, as Dorn rolled his eyes, the whites popping up.

Mouth opened, he thrust his jaw forward. He licked his lips, wetting these until they fairly dripped, pressing his face against smooth, warm glass; moving closer still with every tick, edging his entire body, laying his features flat.

Chest, pelvis, knees, and then, as one final touch, he thrust a broad tongue onto the pane, sealing his face with its glue.

The woman's hands gently crossed her chest as she yawned; as Dorn was contorting every muscle, twitching like a hellish mask of impossible cruelty.

Then, as if sensing something that should *not* be; that could *not* be, the woman's eyes suddenly snapped open and she

563

turned, facing him in one wild hot instant; their bodies flat against the glass, his face mocking at her with obscene malevolence.

She opened her mouth to scream.

No sound came forth.

Her jaws yawned with absolute terror, and she tried, forcing air from her lungs, reeling backward in terror while fighting for breath; feeling her stomach empty as this nightmare image drilled into her mind.

She shut her eyes with a violent shudder, stumbling backward into the farthest corner; a shaking, vulnerable mass that Dorn was now anxious to see in full view, though he was savouring this moment as something special.

He was making memories.

He was opening the shower door, working his face into a heinous knot as Jessica's voice tore loose, crying with such clear and savage hate that it instantly struck Dorn with confusion – for it was coming from the bedroom outside.

'Zak!' she was screaming for all her worth.

'Zak Dorani!'

FIFTY-SEVEN

Dorn froze with terror.

At that instant he lifted his gun towards the hall as the shower door slammed open and a forceful hand seized his arm, grabbing his wrist as other human figures came pounding towards him through a frantic darkness.

Dorn screamed with rage.

'Freeze!' Frank Rivers yelled, pushing himself out of the shower, and Dorn felt a warm gun under his right eye as men instantly filled the room.

Dorn's eyes stretched wide with horror as he struggled against Rivers' vice-like grip.

'Drop the gun!' Scott suddenly charged forward, ramming a shotgun into Dorn's throat, leaning over and ripping off the hood as Dorn was deciding and he felt a sharp rap to his head, dropping him like a stone as the lights came on and he gazed up from the carpet. The room was whirring in his mind, he saw the faces of hate surrounding him in a blur; male faces, hard, unforgiving, their voices like spokesmen from Hell.

'You are under arrest, the charge is fifteen counts of murder!' cried Rivers, though Dorn could not see a face as someone else was grabbing him, approaching with handcuffs, and he screamed again, fighting to stand, throwing both fists as he felt his body moving under a great human force.

Dorn was spinning through air, slamming down onto the sinks with such power that his skull shattered the mirror and he felt something in his spine giving way.

'Shut up!' Rivers cried, as Dorn screamed with agony;

screaming into the night as he felt his arms being pulled and gathered, caught in a powerful vice by a wall of men, his heart nearly bursting.

Dorn's body was going spastic, shaking, trembling, as suddenly the contents of his stomach flew into the air, emptying out onto the floor. As he felt the cold metal collars pinching shut around his wrists he began to sob at the painful pressure. The human wall suddenly parted as an older man stepped forward, pulling his face down low, the brim of his hat against Dorn's brow.

Scott waited a moment for his image to register as Dorn shook his entire body in disbelief. 'You have the right to remain silent,' he hissed at the killer, 'I strongly suggest that you use it!'

Dorn's eyes stretched with terror, his face first frozen, then bursting into a quivering slab of absolute agony. His feral cry sent chills through each man, terrifying the woman behind them who was left cowering in the corner of a running shower.

Frank Rivers, dripping in his soaked jockey shorts, reached over and smacked Dorn on the top of the head with his open fist.

'Search him,' he ordered, then draped a bath towel over the shower stall, standing on his toes to look inside.

'You okay?' Rivers asked.

The woman was crying quietly, sobbing in the corner.

'Hey, fellas,' Rivers was suddenly yelling above their voices, 'she wants to get dressed, get that maggot outside!'

When the bathroom had cleared, Rivers opened the door and climbed in, turning off the water, wrapping the woman in a towel.

'Oh God,' she sobbed, 'Franky, that was so awful . . . I didn't even *have* to act, I couldn't even think . . .' And, again, she broke into tears.

'I know, Tammy,' he sighed, holding her tight. 'I know, but you did just fine.'

Tammy McCain cried up at him, her large green eyes still apprehensive, and she was shaking, whimpering softly. After a career filled with oceanic predators, she had now faced a true terrestrial monster in Jessica's shower. Where a thousand pounds of Requiem shark didn't faze her, the cruel little man had scared her to the bone, and she was sobbing for the horrid reality of what this thing did for kicks.

'He would have killed them . . .' she cried, breaking back into a sob.

'Everything is going to be just fine,' he comforted. And Rivers believed this to be true.

FIFTY-EIGHT

In the bright wash of kitchen lights, there was nothing particularly special about Jeffery Dorn if one looked closely. If anything he was a plain looking little man, with a thin face and thinning hair, his eyes so deeply set that they sparkled through shadow. Of outstanding characteristics, he had none, and what four policemen saw was a cowardly worm of a being that filled them with loathing. They had carried him downstairs. They had plopped him on the floor like an old rug that was rolled and could not be cleaned. It was clear from his rigid posture and glassy stare that he was in shock.

Scott leaned over, pulling him further into a corner by the rear door, by Tripod's water bowl, as Rivers entered.

'Don't drink any of that,' he scoffed, 'it would turn puppy's stomach. Jack, he doesn't look like he knows you.'

Scott nodded. 'Oh he knows, but he won't do anything to please us, and that includes recognition. Isn't that right, Zak?'

Dorn's face was stone.

Rivers huffed in dismay, his eyes narrowing as he strolled over to the intercom by the door. 'Listen up,' he said at Dorn, pressing the rewind button on the cassette player, the little killer watching with abject disdain. Then Rivers pressed play, switching the speakers to the kitchen as it caught in midsentence and voices filled the room.

'Good night, Mom,' Elmer's voice piped.

'Night night, Sweetheart. Did you let Tripod out?'

Jeffery Dorn had no expression for any of this, as Scott looked on and Rivers ejected the tape, then dropped in another. The voice of a small boy filled the room.

'But I don't understand, why does he hate us so bad?' Elmer was asking.

'What about it, Zak?' Rivers said, taking a step forward, and his face looked a stone killer.

'Frank?' Scott cautioned.

Dorn's head turned smoothly on its stalk, his lips moist and parting. 'This is entrapment,' he said coldly. 'I want an attorney.'

As Scott turned to face Rivers, Mule Murphy came quietly forward, a huge and powerful man standing over the little killer while pointing down at the massive toes of his combat boots. The older man saw this and backed up a step.

'That's what he wants,' Scott offered. 'In a minute Zak will be begging for a few bruises or cuts, a brutality charge, anything to blow us out in court.'

Murphy nodded, backing up again.

'I'm entitled to a phone call,' Dorn suggested quietly, and there was slyness to his voice. 'You're violating my rights, Scott, I know the drill and you're depriving me of counsel.'

Scott raised an eyebrow at Rivers. 'He's a lawyer too.' And with that he produced a notepad and pen, leaning down into Zak's airspace.

'Okay,' he offered, 'give me the number and I'll dial for you. After that you can meet with your attorneys in the state lockup.'

There was no answer, no recognition.

'All right.' Scott turned to the men. 'Take him out of here while I call to arrange transport to Jessup, I think we'll go for federal maximum security, but I'll need a court order.'

'My call!' Dorn suddenly barked. And Scott nodded, holding up a hand to stop the men, then picking up the phone.

'I'll hold the phone to your ear, but the cuffs stay on,' Scott offered the man he knew was Zak Dorani. 'What's the number?'

Dorn's eyes glazed with a secret amusement. '555-0817.' Scott punched it in, holding the phone to Dorn's ear, it was answered on the first ring.

'Irma, red button!' he yelled as Scott jerked the phone away violently. 'You bastard!' Dorn cried. 'I'll ruin you in court, you old psycho!'

Scott nodded, touching a finger to his temple, listening intently.

'Oh Jeff! My God! Sweetheart?! Are you there . . .'

Instantly Scott hung up the phone. All he needed was a number, an address was seconds away. 'Drury is waiting at the command post,' he said to Murphy. 'Radio the number and tell him the charges are conspiracy to commit murder and attempted kidnapping. On second thoughts,' he paused, 'tell Max to throw in murder one, I don't want her making bail.'

'Jack,' Rivers suddenly protested, 'let me work with Drury, I accused him of dropping the entire setup, and . . .'

'Frank,' Scott corrected, taking a step forward. 'We both did. I even cursed him out for leaving them alone, when he had already moved the Jansons from the house. Let me talk to him later, I'm hoping this is nothing that can't be healed over.' He looked to Murphy, and with a nod of his head, the policeman lifted a radio off his belt and began to speak.

'Let's go, Zak,' Rivers snapped, coming forward. 'We're moving.'

'Go easy, Frank. Your shoulder,' Scott reminded him. Instantly Toy Saul and Murphy hovered over Jeff Dorn as well, Mule's massive, grinning head looking down at all the smaller detectives.

Rivers nodded.

'Don't touch me!' Dorn hissed, and Murphy reached down, jerking him hard into the air, bringing Dorn's face up into his.

'Be nice,' Mule demanded.

On the way out the door, just past the Commander's sight, Murphy shook him violently, using a third of his strength, Dorn's head slapping like a rag doll coming unstuck.

'Hey, Franko,' Toy Saul offered, 'shouldn't we let Zak see the dog?'

Rivers shrugged.

'Well, I haven't seen it,' Mule said, bouncing the killer under one arm. As they approached the elm tree, Rivers blinked with pleasure as the Mule held the little man by the waist, his legs and upper torso folding, dangling in air.

'It's really something,' Rivers explained, 'it took Doc McQuade less than four hours to build and assemble the entire thing, framework and all, a fairly complete dog. He's a serious genius, just look at the eyes.' Rivers leaned over, pulling the K-9 mannequin from the shadow. From a short distance it looked very much like the lifeless remains of a Belgian Shepherd, in reality it had been Mrs Drury's lynx coat.

'Hey, that really is remarkable.' Mule swung his head at Dorn, showing thick white teeth. 'But I wouldn't have fallen for it.'

'I want a lawyer!' Dorn demanded with disgust.

Rivers said nothing, but was staring down at the glistening slab of tainted meat as Murphy carried Dorn through the back gate, placing him on his rump, leaning him against the house. They were well in the shadows, the lights streaming through the windows creating a dull wash of white.

'Mule,' Rivers said as the man straightened to his full height and backed away. 'Can you imagine what those apes will do to a mouse like this in the big house?'

Toy Saul laughed a big easy laugh, Mule grinned, as Dorn seemed to be having some kind of fit, his head swivelling back and forth, his tongue wagging as his eyes rolled.

'Bring me Elmer and his crippled dog!' he shrieked suddenly, and then his voice broke into a wicked laugh as Rivers' eyes flashed with a menacing clarity.

Dorn laughed. Then smiled. Then suddenly he began to cry, his tears flowing in heavy streams down his face as he sobbed a fit; then snapping this display off, he laughed again, staring up at them and hissing over his teeth.

'God, that's creepy,' said Mule.

'Wonder if that's the last thing his victims saw?' Toy asked incredulously, and with that, Dorn's tongue thrust from his face as he rolled his eyes to white.

Toy Saul moved away, uncomfortable with this

performance, stepping over to Rivers. 'I can't take this,' he said softly, 'I'll be waiting out front.'

'Nigger babies!' Dorn suddenly shrieked after him. 'Kill the niggers!' Jack Scott appeared through the back gate, running from the house, coming alongside and placing a calming hand on Toy's shoulder. He was struggling to get at the little man, his eyes wide with rage.

'Detective Saul,' Scott said in a calm and commanding voice. 'He's not worth it, his life is finished.'

The prisoner released a savage cry and then started to laugh. 'Scott's a fucking loon,' he mocked, 'the man is crazy as a squirrel.' Then Dorn smiled, pursing his lips, cooing like a baby.

'Fuck you,' Murphy stepped forward and spat at his feet.

The Commander turned to Rivers. 'Frank, we've got her name and address, I'm leaving you here with him. It shouldn't take thirty minutes, and a uniformed unit will take Tammy home.'

'Is she doing okay?'

Scott nodded, looking at his watch. 'She's recovering, said to tell you Zipper can't compete with this, whatever that means, I think she's still shook.'

Rivers smiled.

'You old burnout case,' Dorn muttered at Scott's back.

Scott turned, his eyes seething, the left nearly swollen shut. 'I'm going to watch your brains smoke,' he said coldly, then turned to look at the troopers. 'The worst thing we can do to him is just walk away, without an audience he's nothing.'

With that Scott turned towards the street and started to stroll, and as the men vanished into shadow, Rivers pried a cigarette loose and lit up.

'Burn me?' Dorn asked pleasantly.

Rivers ignored him.

Then came a shrieking, hollow cry that touched Rivers right on the spine, and he turned, facing him. Dorn was grinning, eyes going white, flashing his teeth.

'That's not a smile,' Rivers spat, leaning over and into his

572

face. 'You don't know who you are dealing with, so I'd suggest you shut up.'

'Hit me!' he barked.

Rivers backed up, leaning against the wall, listening to the sounds of distant sirens. His left shoulder was growing stiff, giving him pain.

'I'll be out in five years, and Elmer will be fifteen . . .'

Rivers spun, the bolts of fire in his eyes startling the animal, who broke into a fit of girlish laughter. 'Elmer,' he whined, 'that's it . . .' as in a single stroke, Rivers cut Dorn off with the barrel of a gun levelled at his head, then poked the tube down into the soft tissue under his right eye.

Dorn winced, twisting uncomfortably.

'No,' Rivers glared, 'this time you're wrong.' And he watched Dorn blink uncomfortably. It was not a normal looking gun, but had a long, thick barrel.

'A sexual device?' Dorn suggested calmly.

'No,' Rivers shrugged, 'it's a prison, a prison cell with a life term.'

Dorn's face was a blank.

'Take a good look, Zak, smile at your chamber. The gun itself is not that big a deal. Hell,' he puffed, 'I could deliver my load with damn near anything, a blowgun, a slingshot, a crossbow. But I chose this . . .'

'An air gun?' Dorn sucked in.

Rivers gave the barrel a little twist. 'That's close enough, it's a CO_2-powered dart gun, I learned all about it on *Wild Kingdom*, and that's where I'll be sending you.'

Dorn's face was stone. 'A tranquilliser pistol, so you're going to put me to sleep . . .'

'No,' Rivers shook his head while baring teeth. 'I'm going to drill you with a fléchette,' he stated flatly and Dorn froze.

'Only it's much smaller than the type you use, the shaft in here carries a very special type of toxin, they think it's a protein, and I'm going to seal your brain inside a dead body.'

Dorn shook, then regained control. 'If there was such a thing I'd know about it.'

Rivers took in a puff of smoke, then exhaled slowly. 'It

stops a one-ton killer shark, one part per million in water.' And he said this so convincingly that Dorn's eyes went wide as he began to tremble.

'Wait a minute,' he was hyper ventilating, 'you can't get away with this . . .'

Rivers removed the gun and took a step back. 'Sure,' he offered, 'and I'm going to nail you with plenty of witnesses too. The only thing they'll see is a stroke victim,' he tapped Dorn on the head, 'just an ugly little frog doing his last dance.'

'But you're a cop!' he protested loudly, as if this wasn't fair.

Rivers nodded. 'To serve and protect, I take that very seriously even when the systems fail. No,' he paused, 'your mistake was mentioning Elmer, you see, the kid adopted me, I'm his Uncle Frank. And as for his mother,' Rivers sighed. 'I don't think I'll ever meet a finer, more sensitive woman, or a better mother for that matter. You know . . .'

'Kick me!' Dorn cried with a sudden panic, struggling to hit Rivers with his right toe.

And while Rivers really did think this over, he just walked away.

'No,' he said thoughtfully, 'I don't think I will.'

FIFTY-NINE

Irma Kiernan was horrified, her hand shaking as she hung up the phone. She had heard panic in Jeff's voice, and that, alone, filled her with a questioning fear.

'Jeff said the code was red,' she muttered, fighting to steady herself. 'Jeff said to implement the plan . . .' her voice trailed off as she hung her head, her eyes glazed with a certain shock, then she walked away from her perch at the kitchen table.

With small animated steps she moved towards the living room, one careful foot at a time, then pushed herself slowly down the stairs and towards the basement. The hallway was cool and dark. In the soundless passage she heard her own laboured breaths, her pounding heartbeats falling in small uncontrolled bursts as she rounded the steps and came to a door. Jeff's door. And she stopped for a moment considering this.

His den was his sanctuary, a private place, but more. Though Irma did not know why, this was the well from which he drew his strength, and although she did not want to intrude, she needed that strength now, she reasoned; they both needed it desperately. And yet her body would not obey as she reached, in her mind, for the latch. For greater than her wish to protect their lives from outsiders was her simple fear of the mirror that waited just inside, plus whatever secret it held behind its menacing wet silver.

Jeff had warned her many times.

She stood frozen like a jacklighted deer, conjuring images in her mind that might protect her, dreams of gallant knights and fairy tale endings, and while she prayed for this, she reached with a cautious hand and pulled as her body shuddered and the door swung wide with a sharp breath.

It was there to greet her.

And her face twitched as she laid eyes upon her own full size image, recoiling for an instant, then coming forward under her own gaze. Irma trembled at what she saw, for there was another woman staring back at her as she crossed the floor, and this other was nothing like Irma imagined; tall and stately, well curved and feminine, and the truth screamed at her, calling her by name.

She stood at the mirror. And it was a brutish sack of a being that moved as she moved, blinking together, studying eyes like dull grey marbles on either side of a bulbous nose. With her lips pursed tight, she suddenly reached to pinch a fold of loose skin that sagged below her chin, then shook her head, hearing her own heart, forcing her stubby frame into movement.

'Minutes,' she remembered, and the words seemed so unreal to her now, Jeff's voice reeling through her mind, coming back from a distant time. 'You will only have minutes . . .'

And as she considered this the face in the mirror fell from obsession, just a troubling witness to her movements as she pushed, toe to toe, confronting her image with an unwonted purpose; reaching and then grasping the silver frame with both hands, her arms shaking as she began to lift.

The mirror was coming free, rising from the wall, coming into her hands and she felt its weight pushing on her like a slab of lead, and she double-stepped, stumbling backwards under the enormous weight.

The mirror fell with a crash, the glass breaking, the frame landing on her knees. Irma Kiernan saw blood, and she fought to right herself, her pounding heart stealing her breath.

'Oh dear,' she sighed, looking at her cut and bleeding hands. 'Oh my!' As she lay wounded under shards of broken glass, she began to sob, but not for the sharp silvery needles that had sliced through her fingers. She was sobbing for Jeff. All his life he had worked with a hero's courage to help others, and against such great odds; and Irma knew how the world had treated him. Like old tissue, once used, ready to discard.

Lesser men hounded him, persecuted him, unable to face their own inadequacies when placed in his large shadow. She knew such men had come for him now, had taken him captive, and more than ever she was determined not to let that happen without a good fight.

Steeling herself, she pushed the shattered frame from her body with a great resolve, seeing the thick envelope taped on the back. With some reverence she removed this, opening the flap with care, her heart pounding in her throat as she spilled the contents onto the floor.

A child's hooded skating key fell loose. And a note. In Jeff's handwriting, so she smiled, for it was addressed to her. She breathed deeply, closing her eyes. The opening salutation was causing her heart to flutter like an enraptured schoolgirl.

Darling. Jeff was addressing her as *darling*.

'My darling Irma,' the note read, 'if you are reading this, then tragedy's dark shadow has come over our house . . .'

'Oh my,' she pursed her lips, 'this is not good.' Her hands trembled nervously, she was sipping each and every word like a sacred and aged wine.

'. . . only you can save us, it will take great courage!'

Irma closed her eyes, reaching into a pocket, feeling the warm tears rolling off each cheek.

She placed the Legion of Merit around her neck.

Jeff had called it the Atomic Cafe, and Irma followed his instructions to the letter, inserting a hooded key into a dark little smudge, then pressing with both hands against a panel.

Instantly the dank little chamber bloomed into life, beckoning her through a tiny hallway, a soft light coming on the moment the seal was broken.

And though it startled her, this strange entrance to a world she did not know, she thought the mysterious humming of magnetic fans a pleasant sound, filling the buried shelter with swirls of cooling air that came fluttering against the tiny hairs on her face and arms.

She hunched, scurrying forward.

She stood looking down into what she thought had been removed and filled in years before, not really angry with Jeff, for their problems ran much deeper than that. Irma Kiernan was more curious than mad as she watched her shadow grow tall in the recessed confine, blooming large and stately across the little room.

As she entered it spread like a giant black wing over the white domed ceiling. Her eyes immediately touched an antique lamp made from brass, the muted glow sending a sparkling golden aura spreading out in every direction, filling the little chamber with a soft romantic glow. She reached, gently stroking the shade, a lovely tan leather, and quite old, Irma thought, fingering a small pink butterfly that lay suspended in the centre of the buttery hide.

'This should be upstairs,' she mewed, turning the shade. It was shaped in a pentagon, and she rotated this as a small blue flower came into view. To Irma Kiernan, the image seemed a small distorted painting, the purple stalk and bluish petals looking somehow withered, and she did not care for this. She was turning the lamp again, rotating until a splendid bloom came before her, and this was a beautiful and symmetric thing that calmed her pounding heart.

The colourful image came glowing from the muted backlight, a blood red rose with black outlines, the full petals seeming to come alive. Just beneath a green and blue stalk, the word *Rose* was scrawled in dark blue letters, and Irma smiled for the first time.

'Oh, we all know that,' she said, thinking that Jeff had crudely drawn the word with a rounded hand. But when she turned to the fourth side, her heart began to pound, for she had seen this image before.

She swallowed hard.

Locked dead centre of the buttery hide was a bright red heart with a large blue arrow passing through, and underneath the name *DAVID*, in all capital letters.

Irma Kiernan quickly closed her eyes.

She closed her eyes as she felt something hot rising fast

into her throat, and she fought to swallow with all her strength, then gulped for air as her knees trembled.

She looked down onto the table as her hand went twitching, faltering at the wrist, fighting to grasp a large photograph that Jeff kept there; she breathed deeply, her entire body beginning to tremble as she pulled the picture closer to the light.

The image registered.

Vertigo slammed into Kiernan like a bullet in the chest as she fell, dropping to her knees, coughing once before spilling down onto her own vomit.

She had been staring at the naked figure of a rough looking teenager with long dark hair, and above the girl's right breast, just below her shoulder – was a tattoo. A piercing heart. The same heart she had been touching on Jeff's lampshade.

She screamed, fighting for her feet.

Disoriented, she grabbed for the display case, fighting to stand, staring up and into the blank sockets of a dark hanging form. And although it took all her remaining strength, she rose, pulling frantically on the doors while Jeff's letter came burning in her mind with impossibly cruel deception.

Irma Kiernan nearly tore the doors off their hinges, violently grabbing his albums, one by one, throwing them onto the floor.

'My Darling,' the note had instructed, 'please do not look at the albums, these scrapbooks are *not* mine. You must ignore these things and quickly press the red button over my display case.

'You must trust me . . .'

But Irma's trust had fully and fatefully expired as she looked down into the face of a mummified head suspended neatly with wire in front of a wanted poster listing a runaway teenager from 1979; and she had started to read the name when suddenly she began shaking with uncontrollable violence, her knees folding, then her body dropping like stone as she gave a wild and torturous cry.

'My God . . .' She wept freely, her eyes locked open with shock, the pupils dilating into dark little pools. 'No . . .' she moaned, moving her hands in the manner of the blind, her fingers crawling over the carpeted floor for the instrument she had seen there.

Her mind knew.

Kiernan's mind knew by the hot flame that licked into her palm, and though this was split open as she grabbed, the warm fluid running down her arm, she did not react. She was holding one of Jeff's many straight razors, and without closing her eyes, she placed this against her right wrist, sucking a deep breath, then drawing a sharp and violent bite across thin flesh.

Each wrist.

It was with a cold and deliberate malice that she used all of her strength to kill Jeff Dorn in the only manner she knew.

'If you don't destroy these things, they will destroy me,' the note had said. 'You must, Darling, you must . . .'

As her world began to vanish, expanding into a soft and blurry focus, Irma Kiernan recited a prayer while hearing voices gathering above her, hushed and kind, and she smiled, imagining that a fairy-tale knight had finally come to save her from the darkness.

Oceans of darkness, coming now.

The waves beating from some distant shore, closing over her as a last breath came seeping from her lungs.

'Jack!' Drury cried again, as Scott's anxious shoulder rammed a second time against the front door, thumping painfully.

'Break it down!' he ordered, as Murphy quickly came forward, looking at his captain, who gave a nod.

With one sharp step backward, Mule's right boot slammed against the lock face with such power that the entire jamb crumbled inward, breaking loose in fragments of splintering wood. Before Murphy had even cleared the space, Scott was pushing against the beam of Drury's flashlight, and a hallway appeared from shadow, lifeless and gloomy with the smell of boiled cabbage.

'Spread out!' Drury ordered, his gun drawn. 'Scott has point, if she so much as touches a weapon, do not hesitate!' With that cold caution the men rushed in, guns drawn, filling

580

the little house with sweeping lights. In minutes they had covered the first two floors, and stood joined in the living room near a buff recliner.

It was then that they heard, or thought that they heard, a small moan, like some animal's dying gasp, drifting up to them through a kitchen door. Scott sparked instantly into action, peering over his gun sight, moving with a clocklike precision.

He passed through the hallway and into the kitchen, spotting a syringe and bottle on a table, though he did not stop, pressing quickly for the basement door. And though his body was torn and bruised, he travelled the downward steps in seconds, the stairwell behind him teeming with men.

Scott rushed in.

The basement room was a crisp white, nearly barren, and his eyes strained to focus, following a glitter of glass and the spoor of his wounded quarry, which appeared as a drizzle of red across the green carpet.

When he saw it, his eyes stretched with hate. The panel removed, the maw of a hidden room screamed at him with murderous secrecy, electric motors filtering air, buzzing at him like angry wasps, buzzing in the recesses of his mind.

'Careful, Jack!' Drury cautioned, as Scott was gone in that instant, pushing down into the dark corridor as fast as his feet would carry him.

Then Drury heard Scott scream.

Drury heard him cry with anger and frustration as he followed through, dropping into the sunken confine where he found Scott banging with both fists at the chest of a fallen woman, pulling himself back upright, then grabbing beneath Irma's neck, pinching her nose, breathing his life into her lungs.

'Tie her wrists!' Scott yelled, gulping air, staring into the dilated eyes, then pressing his mouth over hers. As her lungs emptied, he crossed his hands over her chest and began to pump. Drury laid a stoic palm on the man's shoulder.

'It's over, Jack, she's gone.'

'One one-thousand, two one-thousand, three one-thousand . . .'

Scott breathed again, forcing air, filling her ribcage.

'Jack, it's a code blue . . .'

Scott shook his head, he hadn't noticed that he had been kneeling in a dark pool, the circumference spreading every time he pressed against her ribs. Without her wrists being tied, each thrust had pumped more blood into a hideous puddle, which Scott now felt being drawn into the coarse fibre of his slacks as he continued to work in the sticky sweetness.

The smells began to choke them both.

'Jack, let her rest,' Drury offered quietly, lifting Irma's right hand, placing this higher over the body to prevent further drainage. He draped the other arm across her chest as Scott pushed himself back, releasing a heavy and mechanical sigh, then fighting to right himself as Drury took him by the arm.

'Is this a torture chamber?' he asked, pulling Scott to his feet.

Scott shook his head. 'More like a trophy room,' and he leaned over, picking up a scrapbook, placing it beneath an arm as he watched anger register on Drury's face as he studied the mummified head in Dorn's case, the skin like leather stretched across an obscene grin.

'And official Washington says the threat of serial killers is overrated.' He breathed hard, voice sober, his face like stone. Scott gave a heartfelt sigh, they were communicating on a level of understanding beyond the politics of crime, and they knew what was next.

In an effort to close the standing case list of 17,435 people who had simply vanished without a trace, investigators and relatives of the missing would soon be flooding Drury's office with requests, calling from every state, then waiting in line for information that could help. Mostly it did not.

Drury pushed past Scott. 'It's the calls from parents that hurt the most,' he said grimly, moving through his own voice and up into darkness.

Scott nodded, he knew it was so.

SIXTY

'I'm entitled to my day in court,' Dorn stated coldly, his face etched with outrage. 'I have a right to face my accusers!'

Rivers glanced over his shoulder at him. 'You bet,' he answered without tone, thinking about Diana Clayton and her daughters, and the rights he had given to them; then the remains from the bowling alley, and his cruel designs on the Janson family. He had started to think about the rope he had placed on Jessica's pillow, when he suddenly removed the dart gun from his sweatshirt, jamming this back under Dorn's left eye.

'One more word,' he cautioned.

Dorn twisted his head. 'But I have something you want,' he said quietly. 'I have answers!' And his dark eyes seemed to gleam with spite.

Rivers dropped a cigarette into his mouth. 'Okay,' he breathed fire, 'did Rubin Jaffe hire you to torch Toby-town?'

Dorn grinned, lifting a lip. 'It *was* his money, but I was hired by another, a serial killer, I will give him to you if you hit me hard.'

Rivers shook his head. 'Tell me who Dr Jaffe is, tell me about him.'

At this Dorn's eyes closed and opened, his face twisting into a wicked knot. '*You* are Jaffe,' he said flatly, '*we* are Jaffe. He is *every* man!' And he started to laugh, as with an incredible swiftness, Rivers delivered a controlled kick to his thigh. Dorn hissed back into silence.

'Do you know anything about Debra Patterson?'

Dorn's lips pursed tight, his eyes laughing at the man. 'She begged me!'

Rivers nodded his head with a murderous fury in his eyes, his body pulling tight like corded steel as he unbuckled his belt, pulling it free, then wrapping it across the knuckles of his right hand. He was reaching over with his left, grabbing the man, when a voice broke through the yard.

'Frank!' Scott cried, running with a painful hobble.

'Quick, do it!' Dorn yelled, and his mouth appeared to become his entire face, as Mule Murphy grabbed Rivers around the waist and hauled him backward through the darkness.

'Frank.' Scott looked deep within him. 'That's what he wants, don't give in.' Captain Drury and Toy Saul and Rudy Marchette appeared, trotting with three uniformed officers; Toy carrying a canvas strait-jacket and video camera. The team was preparing to transport the prisoner according to the strictest provisions of the law, documenting every procedure to counterclaim the inevitable brutality charges.

'Who gave him his rights?' Drury barked as eight men gathered round, standing in a semicircle before the accused.

'I did,' Scott answered, 'it was clean, Max.'

Drury brought a questioning stare onto Rivers. 'Did you hit him?'

Rivers rubbed his wounded shoulder, 'No, Captain, I'm barely able to move, but what happened to you guys? You're covered with blood.'

Drury answered with a nasty stare, turning to Toy Saul. 'Give Frank the camera, I consider this my collar.' And the man complied, handing Rivers the equipment as Dorn was writhing, fighting for his feet.

'He's going to kill me!' Dorn howled suddenly, as Rivers took a cautious step backward. 'He's going to shoot me!'

Rivers shrugged.

'Stop him!' Dorn screamed. 'Stop him . . .'

'Take it easy, Zak.' Drury's voice was gravelly as the men moved in. The prisoner released a horrified cry, his eyes wide, glaring at Rivers who was backing up one foot at a time, bringing a video camera into position.

'He's going to kill me!' Dorn cried with panic. 'Don't you understand he's trying to shoot me?!'

Drury turned suddenly and glanced at Rivers. 'We know,' he winked, 'I told him to.'

While all eyes were on the prisoner, Dorn watched in horror as Rivers was working in shadows, expertly removing an air gun from his shirt, placing this under the camera for support. Murphy was bending over to take hold of Dorn's right arm.

'Killer!' Dorn screamed. 'Please . . .'

The outburst caused the policemen to pause, stepping back to examine their approach – just as Dorn suddenly came leaping straight at them, up into the air, propelled by a violent and unseen force, his legs and torso thrusting stiffly as if he had been hit by a massive electric charge; shaking, flipping, shuddering in rapid vibration as if he were holding a raw powerline between his teeth.

'God save us!' Drury yelled, backing up.

Dorn's body slapped the ground violently, then he raised up on his shoulders, bouncing again like a paratrooper slammed to earth without a chute; his entire torso going rigid in that instant. He spun onto his stomach with a powerful thrust, flipping again, shuddering with a tremendous quake.

'Do something!' Drury yelled at the stunned faces, while Dorn's mug was frozen, his body convulsing; head, legs, arms and torso shaking stiffly without control. The Captain quickly dropped to his knees, throwing away his cap.

'This man is having trouble breathing!' he yelled. 'Frank, you're a trained medic, for crying out loud!'

Rivers sauntered forward, shaking his head. He laid his camera on the lawn, then peered down. Dorn was stretched flat, his face skyward in frozen agony, his maw locked open. He was vibrating with a violent inner spasm, as suddenly, a foul odour discharged and his body went slack.

'Jesus Christ!' Drury exclaimed, standing quickly as the sickening smell hit him and Rivers nudged by.

Drury started to pace. 'I've never seen anything like it,' he concluded anxiously, 'that was a bizarre fit!'

'A stroke,' Scott agreed flatly.

'Sir, it looked to me like he'd been struck by lightning?' Saul questioned excitedly. 'Medical assistance will be here in one minute.'

Drury was face to face with Scott as the other men went silent, Toy working a handheld radio as Rivers leaned over, staring into Zak's stony eyes, then discreetly pinching his right thigh just above the knee.

'Told you no one would notice,' he whispered, 'I need my dart back.' He jerked a small black needle from his flesh.

'What's that, Frank, speak up!' Drury ordered.

'Sorry, Captain, I said it's not a heart attack.'

'Oh for crying out loud, Frank, we already know that!' Drury cried with frustration. 'Why do you have to say things like that?'

SIXTY-ONE

Alsop's House on the Virginia side of the Potomac in the suburb of Falls Church had been named for Isadora Gene Alsop, a grand old matron from the age of suffragettes, though Jonathan Patterson doubted very much that she had ever fought for equal rights, or rights of any human kind.

Standing in the tight little lobby, surrounded by young women, he could discern many things from the woman's stare, which was cold as a tomb. Her hair was worn in a tight bun. Her four-cornered nursing cap carried the cross of the ages. Her white uniform was crisp and precise, and there was a bible on her lap. In her right hand was a large ruby-studded crucifix; she held this outstretched, readied to ward off evil.

Alsop the Protector, the brass legend read beneath the oil painting. And there were joyous giggles from pregnant women, who were really just girls, as the 11:30 television broadcast of the *Dating Game* had started. There were about a dozen teenagers, and though their eyes fell over him in the stuffy wood-panelled receiving room, they did not see. And Patterson felt like the invisible man, standing there, waiting, wondering; his heart pounding into his throat as his armpits and palms were cold and wet.

His journey had started an hour earlier after an unsolicited phone call. Two of them in fact. And eventually they had brought him here in clandestine search of his daughter and before the punishing stare of Madam Alsop, where children Debra's age were preparing to have children. What troubled him was the thought of the childhood these girls were abandoning so easily, the lives they were giving away, instead of

587

bringing new life into the world. His mind wandered back to the way he had been staring bewildered into the phone, incredulous, fear and anger coursing over his face as his wife began to panic by his side.

'Who are you?' Patterson demanded, quickly summoning Sergeant Tyler Conroy of the County Police to his side, expecting a ransom demand. The telephone voice dripped with secrecy.

'First tell me if the reward is good, I have a poster from the drugstore that offers $5,000 for information.'

'Only if she is found, if the information leads to her. I need your name and . . .'

'Oh no, I've got to go, I'll call you back.' With that the conversation had terminated, leaving Patterson with a dial tone.

Minutes crawled by with agonising torment, every sweep of the clock's hand a painful exercise in waiting until the phone finally rang again, and Patterson answered before the first ring had ended.

'Is the reward still good? I mean, I have expenses and this is very dangerous for me.'

'In what way? Why is it dangerous?' he demanded with fright. 'Where is my daughter? Do you have information about . . .'

'I work in a halfway house and if anyone finds out that I've broken the rules of confidence, I'll be fired, I need my job.'

Patterson breathed deeply, mustering his reserve. 'How old are you, son?' he asked gently.

'Eighteen, this is the longest I've held a job, I'm the building engineer.'

'And how much do you make a year?'

'Eight thousand, plus my meals.'

'All right then,' Patterson said calmly, 'tell me about this, confidentially; if you get fired I will pay you a year's salary if we find Debra.'

'Well,' he paused, considering this. 'I think it's the same girl, but the flyer I got was wet and the image was blurry. Does she have curly hair?'

Patterson's heart crashed. 'No,' he said weakly. 'Does the face look the same as the photograph?'

'I think so, but I'm not sure, but I could sure use the money.'

'Where do you work son, what's your name?'

'Brian Daily, I work at Alsop's House.'

He, himself, was a child.

As Patterson stood beneath the canvas of the patron that founded the shoddy little house, a young man dressed in jeans and a Madonna T-shirt strolled to the television set in the corner and adjusted the picture contrast, which did not need adjusting.

As he did this, he winked at Patterson, the girls seeing this, then turning back around. He was lean like an alley cat and his face was scarred with acne. He sauntered across the room as if he often came forward just to study the portrait. He was now staring up at the *Protector*.

'Are you Brian?' Patterson asked quietly.

He nodded. 'Mrs Handry is in back with her and another girl, I only gotta minute.'

Patterson nodded and removed a photograph from his jacket, fighting his fears with enormous courage as Brian Daily positioned his body between the picture and audience. The man-child studied for a moment, his brows knotting, his lips making a weird clicking sound, and Patterson's heart all but crashed.

'Well?' he suddenly frowned, and the girls turned, looking up at them.

Daily waited patiently, rubbing a hand through a black head of hair that needed a shower. He nodded. 'She has curly hair now. I wonder when she did that, does she have a sister?'

'No,' Patterson shook his head. 'Is this the girl?'

'That's her, okay, she's in back with Mrs Handry.'

'And you're sure?'

'I dunno, yeah, sort of.'

'Why would she be here, is this for runaways?'

The expression that crossed Brian's face was blank with

confusion. 'You don't know what this is?' he asked, incredulous. 'This is a baby farm, a right-to-life house for expecting
mothers who can't afford to . . .'

Patterson held up a hand and gave a precise and sorry nod.

'You have no right to keep my daughter, she is not of legal
age,' Patterson was saying the moment the older woman came
forward, an official looking clipbook in her right hand and a
bible in the other.

Mrs Helena Handry, a wide load of a woman in a white
uniform and dripping with crosses, knotted her face at him.
'She came of her own accord because she had no one else to
turn to.'

'She could have come to me, and her mother!' Patterson
barked. 'She is only sixteen, so either you produce her now
or I'm calling the police and my attorneys, and then,' he took
a deep and satisfying breath, 'and then, I will close you down!'

'I will protect her rights to bear children with my last
breath!' the woman charged, raising her voice and her chin.

'Then you're going to need it,' Patterson hissed through
his teeth as he started at her, moving towards the dark hallway.
A figure emerged slowly from the shadow, coming into form,
a small suitcase in her right hand and tears streaming down
angelic cheeks.

'Debbie!' Patterson screamed her name, and instantly the
figure ran towards him.

'Oh Daddy, Daddy,' the girl cried. 'Daddy . . .'

In that painful instant, Mrs Helena Handry became their
mutual enemy, casting about the room for someone to give
instructions to.

'I'm going to have a baby,' Debra sobbed against her
father's chest while looking up into his eyes.

He sighed, holding her for all his worth. 'Why didn't you
tell us?' he wept, and as she started to answer, he stopped her
with a warm kiss. 'Never mind, we have time for all of that,
let me look at you!'

And he did. And they cried. And Jonathan Patterson held
onto his daughter, determined to never let her go.

'You said if I ever got pregnant you would disown me . . .' Debra sobbed suddenly at him, and the man's heart crashed to the abyss of parental anguish.

'Oh Dee, I never said that . . .'

'You did, Daddy, I heard both you and mother. She said she'd make me have an abortion and then lock me away for the rest of my life.'

Patterson winced, thinking back. He vaguely remembered that there had been a documentary on teenage pregnancy a few weeks ago, and he had been speaking with his wife – when it hit him. They had been drinking, they had just gotten the news about Debra's grandmother, they were upset.

'But we weren't talking about you!' he suddenly shrieked in anguish. 'We were talking about a girl on the television. You're our baby!'

'Oh, I love you, Daddy . . .'

'Dee, it's your decision, Honey, it's your life. Whatever you want to do we will always support you.'

'I don't know . . .' she was crying freely.

As they walked through the door of Alsop's House together, Brian Daily came rushing down the front path from the kerb. 'Psssst, Mr Patterson,' he whispered.

Jonathan Patterson nodded, holding his daughter with his right hand, removing a white envelope from his jacket with his left, then handing this to the young man just as a car came roaring to a stop. A frightened father quickly stepped out with a photograph in his hand.

He was haggard and his face showed a tired and aimless strain as he made eye contact with Patterson.

'Mr Coaler?' Brian Daily whispered quickly as Patterson ushered his daughter into their car.

Debra had been missing for just over three days, and on the way home they stopped for a cup of chocolate so that he could call and alert his wife; so she could leave a message of thanks for Detective Sergeant Rivers.

'Debbie, do you know where your car is?' Patterson asked quietly.

She nodded, 'I lent it to Jammie Wolfe.'

'Do you know where she is?'

Debra shook her head. 'She's run away from her boarding school, she'll bring it back. Oh, I missed you Daddy.' Debra suddenly burst into sobs, crying freely, unable to control her emotions any longer.

As she curled into his arms, Patterson closed his eyes tightly, the tears running off his chin, the nightmare finally over.

'Everything's going to be fine,' he comforted.

And for the Patterson family, this was true.

SIXTY-TWO

The Shiloh Baptist Church was gone with a blaze of head-lights as the tan Crown Victoria hurtled by, red and blue emergency globes pulsing off stained glass windows in a single beat, and nothing more, as Frank Rivers sped towards the city.

In short moments he was rounding a corner on Elm in the heart of a seemingly instant modern metropolis, with a glance catching a shimmer of lights coming off a patch of cobblestone that had once been a village street, laid from ship's ballast, then ripped from the ground. For a short moment he was speaking to Elmer Janson in his mind, of tall ships and sea-farers, of how they had plied a trade in a wrinkle before the Civil War; but the site was far behind as he was spinning left, speeding down onto Winsconsin Avenue.

The upscale diner came and went. A huge empty pit filled with light, and he remembered how the Deco Theatre had stood there forever; even in haste he could not help but notice these things, for they were the familiar, the pitiless remnants of another age found in a crush of high-rise glitter, glass and chrome; the personality of a temporary city born on the ruins of history and permanence.

'One-Echo-Twenty,' the radio cracked, and instinctively he reached forward, but it was too late.

Scott had grabbed the microphone and was opening the line, his mellow voice but a smear against images that carried Rivers through the night, and he was roaring by the stone Post Office, proud as an old matron, her mica-flecked quarry skin pulsing with red and blue, just an instant of light, and nothing more.

Gone in a blaze, 40-50-60, towards the main intersection at East West Highway, where he triggered the sirens, pushing by a nest of drivers forced to the side of the road as the sound came screaming through the concrete canyon. Rivers applied his foot to the floor.

'Slow it down, they're not going anywhere.'

But Rivers did not hear, only the sound of his heart as it beat a strange song, as the road was swallowed by his blaze of lights.

It was over, he was going to them.

Like the men who plied the waterways of old, his journey had been relentless.

Elmer Janson was sick of television.

There was nothing on, and it was a cheap little black and white image flickering against his dog's fur as they lay side by side on a soiled throw rug that Jessica guessed hadn't been cleaned since the late sixties.

'I wish you'd stay on the bed, Elmer, I don't have the strength to fight with you.'

'I'm okay, Mom, Tripod's on the rug.'

'I can see that. Can't you try to get some sleep?' She leaned over and tried brushing the bangs off his brow. 'Tripod's sleeping, let's both give it a try?'

'I'm not tired.' He had begun to renew his protest, when the dog suddenly raised his massive head, pushing himself forward with a healthy growl, then bumping into Elmer as he moved towards the door.

'Mom,' Elmer said cautiously, 'Tripod hears something . . .' And with that the dog released a growl from deep within, his head lowered, his brown eyes menacing and levelled.

'Elmer, come back here!' Jessica demanded, as the boy scampered, as the distant sounds of a siren became audible to the human ear, only weakly at first like a faraway cry, then screaming with demand like the piercing wail of life hanging in the balance.

'I'll bet it's Frank!' Elmer fidgeted nervously, reaching for the doorknob, his voice filled with excitement.

Jessica grabbed his arm forcefully. 'We don't know that,' she cautioned, then tested the chain on the door.

The wheels of the tan radio car burned with a fury as the sirens died and Rivers sped into a darkened alleyway, rumbling over a concrete drive that had warped and cracked years before. He was slowing as they approached, and it was at the very end of a series of driveways that he spun the wheel and turned through a chain-link fence.

They were moving towards a low slung building that resembled a series of stalls, an old fashioned apartment court, and as they pulled in, Scott spotted a sign, this over the only door with glass in its peeling face.

Furnished Rooms, Day/Week/Month.

The building's facade was a drab and uniform pea green, which reminded them both of the tasteless surplus store colour. 'So why here?' Scott asked as the car slowed, crunching over the broken gravel.

Rivers shrugged. 'Tripod and Elmer refused to be parted. Could you see them walking through the door at the Hyatt?'

Scott chuckled. 'Yes,' he smiled, 'I can picture that.'

'Anyway, who'd ever guess about this dive? Besides, this is the only lodging Drury could find that wasn't owned by Rubin Jaffe, either outright or indirectly. I wasn't about to trust anyone.'

'I'll wait in the car,' Scott offered, 'I've had enough excitement to last through the night.' Rivers didn't seem to hear as the red and blue fireball came bursting against the green shell like rain drops splattering a sponge.

The place swallowed light.

It was dark and seedy.

'Elmer, please stay away from that door.'

'But Mom, a car is pulling up, it has to be them! Look at Tripod, he's wagging his tail.'

She opened the door, but only to peek, as the dog bolted out with the boy fast behind.

'Frank!' Elmer cried, and his voice was surely bursting with joy as Rivers stepped out into shadow. He started forward, but before he reached his stride the team was on him, Tripod ramming his leg as Elmer was tugging at his jeans.

'Did you catch Zak?' he rattled a little breathlessly. 'Mom says I don't have to go to school tomorrow.' Rivers looked down at the child as a shadow of movement caught his eye.

Standing in a bar of painted light filtering through the doorway, Jessica Janson steadied herself as she watched. She looked tired and worn and beautiful, her hair shining in this half-light, her eyes wet, still fearful, still questioning.

'Come here, Elmer,' Rivers said quietly, and he reached down, swooping the boy up under both arms, then swinging him through the air until a spit of laughter fell free. He carried the child towards his mother as the dog nipped at the boy's running shoes.

'Mom, can we go in Frank's radio car?' he asked.

'We have our own car, Elmer, and we will follow Frank,' she responded, and her voice was firm. Disappointed, he turned his face away.

'She's upset,' he whispered. 'Are we still in trouble, Frank?'

'No trouble at all, Rooster,' he whispered back, his eyes steady on Jessica. 'Let me talk with your Mom a minute.'

He leaned over, and the boy's feet started to move the moment they touched earth, but Rivers held him back with a gentle hand.

'Can I sit in the radio car?'

'Sure, ask Jack if he'll let you have the wheel.'

It was a hard, biting and awkward silence.

Jessica's eyes were red, a film of water covered them, but never once did they fall from Rivers' blue stare. And he wanted to comfort her, to say something, anything, if he didn't come across sounding like a hard-bitten man with time on his hands; and he was thinking of how to do this when he noticed his heart was beating into his throat, that his spirit was falling inside him like a heavy rain.

'Are we safe?' Jessica suddenly swallowed, and he saw her lower lip tremble.

And for reasons he did not understand, this made him feel like he was coming apart inside, and he was suddenly fighting words in his head, trying to answer, just as he saw a tear tumble off one cheek.

And as if he was watching somebody else, his hand moved slowly forward with an alien gentleness and simply brushed it away, then stroked her cheek.

'You caught him,' she had started to say, when her emotions slipped to the surface and her knees buckled as she began to cry. Rivers caught her, and she laid her head against his chest where his heart beat like a watch wound to destruction.

'Frank?' Scott questioned quietly, appearing at his back. 'I'm going to take Elmer home, he wants to ride in a police car, you two can follow.'

'Thanks,' Rivers agreed, releasing the woman, who quickly brushed the tears from her face as her son came alongside, slipping a hand up into hers.

'Is it okay, Mom, can I go with Jack?'

'Yes, Elmer,' she said firmly, her eyes never once leaving Frank Rivers. And they listened together as the doors closed, the emergency lights pulsed back into life, then the headlights pulled away into darkness.

In a bar of painted light cast out from the little doorway, their eyes met in such a clear and certain way that words became a meaningless shadow. Rivers had started to speak as Jessica suddenly placed a finger across his lips, and he knew.

This feeling was like no other, far more than sexual, deeper and driving, begging him on; like the flame he found in the solace of her eyes, this feeling was like a great and lasting storm, a fear, a hurt, and a lifetime of need.

For the couple in the green motel, the room seemed to be drifting in time, not a shabby cubicle with a small single bed, but a place that held no meaning beyond themselves.

As he closed the flimsy wooden door, Jessica moved into him, her hands gently stroking his neck where a large white surgical dressing rose from his left shoulder. Frank studied her every curve and movement, the turn of wrist, the fingertip touch, the way her eyes seemed to lead or to follow, her lips pulling tight as they moved together, as she crossed the small room with a single stride.

Closer still Jessica came, as he leaned over to kiss her neck, the woman pulling her hair from place with a slender hand, then reaching up for him, accidentally touching his wound.

Rivers winced.

'Then it does hurt,' she stated in a whisper, but Frank only gave a slight smile, the woman's silken form had reduced pain to a meaningless concept as he studied the soft curves of her shoulders and arms, the splendid and silky skin that ran from her neck where her sweater had parted. With a feminine curiosity she watched his eyes drink, then took a last step backward as he tried to reach for her with both hands, an awkward movement, for his body had grown stiff and sore.

Jessica shook her head, her hair shimmering in the light, her breath falling into small bursts as she reached with her right hand to unbutton her sweater, wriggling free from its cling like a teenager, as Frank lightly stroked her throat, moving down over the swell of her breasts. His head was going light as he inched forward, enveloping her with both arms, locking her tight in an embrace as her mouth met his, her eyes closing as their bodies suddenly shuddered in unison.

They were closing upon themselves and closed to the world.

Exploring. Touching. Caressing.

They fell onto the bed as their clothes came undone, and Jessica quickly moved under him with a subtle grace, then even closer up into his arms, covering his mouth with hers to silence him, as Rivers had started to speak, had started to doubt, had started to think.

'Don't,' she whispered, reaching down for him.

With a soft female cry he felt a powerful union as she was pulling him from his elbows, burying her face into his neck.

And they fought with each other to get close. Closer still. Then impossibly close, moving like skaters in a tight and perfect dance, breathing each other's breath in mutual symphony, their eyes wild and undone with the merciless pursuit of each other's flesh.

They made a kind of mad and reckless love that Jessica thought could never be again.

A kind of healing and lasting love that Frank Rivers had never known existed.

'I think we're onto something here,' Jessica suddenly giggled as she lay spent in his arms.

'My entire life,' Frank stammered, then cleared his throat. 'My entire life I've spent looking for you,' he said, or thought he said, and in his mind his voice was sounding like it once had; like it must have once, he told himself, in a time so long ago that happiness was a distant memory.

And he heard this memory now like lost waves rolling on some faraway shore, and he steadied himself, his eyes locking onto hers to see if she had even heard; or if he had even spoken.

Jessica brushed his hair from his brow, pulling close to him, her lips gently kissing his eyes, these closing as Rivers' body trembled slightly.

'Then I only wish I had known,' she said quietly, and there was a sudden sadness in her voice that had not been there before. She pulled away in all of her splendid nakedness, then locked her eyes onto his, studying the deep blue pools, tracing the jagged scars that edged across his body with sorrowing fingertips.

'Frank,' she whispered, 'why don't you have a family?'

At this his body tensed and he started to speak, to explain, to reach out so that explanation was not necessary; and she quickly moved back onto him, pressing his lips with hers, delivering a wet kiss that saved them both from looking back.

SIXTY-THREE

The kid on the red Schwinn was coasting, aiming down the street in an easy glide, his red hair shining in late afternoon light, his mint green eyes sparkling and wide with anticipation. Down in front of his house, Sergeant Rivers held the boy's dog, as Tripod was whining, struggling for freedom, his large blond frame wobbling uncomfortably on all *fours*. His right front leg was a bright and shiny white.

'Okay, Elmer, call him,' Rivers said.

'Come on, boy!' Elmer shrieked, the mask of freckles pulling tight across the bridge of his nose as he increased his speed, leaning over the handlebars in a backward glance.

'Come on . . .' he urged, 'come on Tripod!'

With a tentative bobbing motion, the dog tried to hobble in his old and accustomed way, but could not. Tripod was landing stiffly on his right, where once there had been only air, and with sad brown eyes, he watched his playmate go whizzing by.

Tripod was edging forward, then suddenly stopping to sit, waving the alien leg in front of him. Upon seeing this, Elmer spun in place, kicking hard against the pedals in a power drive, then hopping the kerb near Dudley Hall.

'What's wrong?' the boy breathed hard as he dismounted.

'Elmer,' Hall chirped, 'go git him, jest show him what he needs to do and he'll follow.' As the boy approached, the dog instantly came leaping, Tripod punching him in the chest with two front limbs and driving him back.

'Woah,' Elmer laughed, and the dog snipped at his clothes with excitement. 'Tripod, sit!' he cried, as Hall came standing over them.

'He just don't know what it's for yet.' The Diggerman smiled. 'Git Tripper to walk for a while.'

Elmer did just that, rubbing Tripod's chest until a rear leg was thumping, then moving him forward. The dog was on all fours and walking cautiously.

'That's good, now jest put some weight on his shoulders so he knows it's gonna support him, he's gotta know he can trust it. Been a time since he felt dis part.'

Elmer complied, hugging his dog around the mane, applying some weight, then rocking him up and down. Tripod was enjoying this action, as his broom tail was swinging furiously in metered strokes.

Jessica approached, her face tired, eyes slightly puffy from lack of sleep. She carried a tray of drinks, walking gracefully towards Rivers.

'Where's Jackie?' Hall asked suddenly.

Rivers shrugged. 'Making memories, would be my guess.'

The braying of piston strokes echoed through the halls of Suburban Hospitals Emergency Critical Care Ward, sounding like Scuba divers snoring beneath the smells of antiseptics. Scott stood just outside room No. 7-B in a corridor of pastel blue with a swarm of medical personnel in green gowns running in every direction.

Medical teams went clattering by with crash carts and life saving equipment, and Scott stepped back, patiently waiting for someone to appear through the closed wooden door behind him. It had been fourteen hours, allowing the MAIT team a chance to shower and sleep, and he shifted his weight, standing in his grey suit, holding a notepad in his hand to jot down details.

The cuts from Greg Corless now burned with a fierce intensity, feeling like angry flames licking his legs and groin, and though he squirmed many times, he could not get comfortable.

He was reflecting back, wondering how Irma Kiernan had handled Kimberly and Leslie Clayton when they came to the park for their educational tour, demanding that they leave their purses inside the lockhouse so that she could make copies of their keys.

The door opened and Dr Anh-Bich Pham strolled from the room. As she saw him, she removed a blue mask from her face and she released a troubled sigh.

'How is he?' Scott asked quickly.

She raised a concerned eyebrow. 'You should be resting, Commander,' she said with a chilly voice. 'You'll be a very unhappy man if those stitches break open.'

Scott nodded thoughtfully.

'As for your patient, at this time we've exhausted our treatment, so we'll just have to wait. He has suffered a severe cerebral haemorrhage, a stroke, it seems as if three sections of the brain are involved.'

'Then he's paralysed?'

'Completely,' she sighed, 'except for the breathing mechanism. The stroke was about the most massive we've seen, the cerebellum and medulla have been destroyed, and with that,' she raised her hands, 'any chance of regaining motor function.'

'Will he live?'

'If you want to call it that. Like I said, he's regained his ability to breathe, but he will not recover, no one could. From the tests I can tell you that his brain looks like it's coated in black ink.'

'How long does he have?'

She shrugged. 'Six months, maybe more, it's impossible to say. If he could feed orally there would be more of a chance, but I'm afraid he has no movement capability at all. He can't even blink, so we are using drops to keep his eyes moist.'

'Can he see, does he have vision?'

'Well, yes, we have him hooked to an EEG, an electro-encephalogram, a monitor that reads brain function. According to machine response, he can think and see, so we won't be able to get a court order to justify termination of life support – at least not without a great deal of difficulty.' She rubbed her eyes. 'He'll be dead by the time a court came through, anyway.'

'But he is capable of understanding?'

'I don't really know, his brain waves respond to conversation, so his hearing is not seriously impaired. Now how long this will last I can't say, I can only imagine the terror of complete and total paralysis, being able to hear and see must only make it worse.'

Scott nodded. 'Can I visit with him, or is it too early?'

'Two minutes,' she said, turning to open the door for him. 'Just go easy, we can't predict how his heart will react to much more stress.'

It was a cubicle with pale white walls, and at the centre of the room was a hospital bed surrounded by machines. Spread-eagled on a flat slab with turned down sheets lay the animal who killed Diana Clayton and her family, and Samantha Stoner, her mother and sister, and Scott could only guess at the rest.

Even locked into a rigid body, his thin and frozen face looked cruel, the pinched cheeks, the lips like cut veal, the black eyes aimed up at the ceiling. His head was shaved and capped with white gauze.

To his left was emergency resuscitation equipment, to his right the scrolling blue EEG machine, monitoring his brain waves. From this pale but living corpse, tubes sprouted everywhere, through his nose, mouth, between his legs, down into each arm.

'This shows his brain activity,' Dr Pham explained, and as she spoke there was a bright little wave of light that bloomed and went rolling across a blue screen. 'He heard us coming in, watch this.'

As the line began to flatten she leaned over, placing a drop of fluid into each of his eyes. These were fixed and frozen in his skull. 'How are you feeling?' she asked softly, and Scott watched with interest as the monitor broke into a wavy blue line. She pulled off the oxygen mask and swabbed his lips and tongue with a moistened pad.

'See, he does hear us,' and just as she said this, the page beeper on her belt went off, emitting a piercing series of tones.

'Damn,' she sighed, 'two minutes, I'll be right back.'

Scott stood quietly, peering down at the little killer.

Slowly he moved to the right for a clear view of the brain wave monitor, and as he approached a flat blue line wavered a tiny bit and went still again. Scott remained just out of sight, waiting until the only sound was that dry sucking action of the patient's lungs, dark and empty like the bray of pistons produced by his victims.

Slowly, Scott edged his body nearer the bed.

'Hello, Zak!' he spat as the line boomed into a sharp curve and the black eyes rolled towards him with a vibrating fix. Scott removed Samantha's photo from his jacket, holding this just above his face, blocking his sight, as the monitor instantly took on the appearance of an angry ocean tide with jagged peaks and crests.

'I thought so,' Scott concluded softly, 'the Stoners send their regards.'

He quickly stepped back, waiting until the line approached horizontal again, pulsing down into softer waves, rippling quietly. Scott removed the portrait of Kimberly from his brief-case, the silver encased frame with the almost perfect looking little girl. The line was flat as he moved this into position, then suddenly the screen exploded into a mountainous range of wiggling swirls as Scott's jaw started to tick and bile filled his throat. He swallowed hard, dropping the photo onto the man's chest and leaned down so that his lips nearly touched him.

With a start, he reached behind Dorn's head and snatched away his pillow. 'Now you listen to me, you cruel and evil son of a bitch,' Scott heard himself hiss, 'at last you are receiving some justice, so let me explain what is happening to you . . .' And Scott quickly caught himself as the brain wave monitor beeped audibly, the lines hitting the edge of the screen as the black pupils spread like melting tar.

Scott waited, leaning back into him. 'I've spoken with the doctors and you are *not* going to get well, in fact, you are dying very, very slowly.'

Beep, beep, beep the monitor toned and went silent.

'Your body is drying up like a landed fish. Your feet, your hands, your legs, your arms, these will start to go one at a time, shrivelling like salted snails, rotting . . .'

Beeeeppppppp . . .

The monitor warned Scott off with a solid crest of waves, and he pulled only slightly back to a *beep, beep, beep*; lines and shadows of lines, pitching and falling, so he moved even closer until his lips blew moist against the killer's face.

'Your eyes will crack like drying grapes,' he hissed, 'and your lungs will tighten and rip like old paper bags. Eventually,' Scott paused, 'and no one knows how long, your liver and kidneys will begin to fail, but you will still be alive. You will *not* be dead just yet . . .'

The monitor beeped as the lines exploded and failed, Scott reaching over and lifting the killer's left hand, this feeling cool and limp. With a frightening malice, the tired policeman suddenly brought his right palm down hard over this in a tremendous stinging slap that cracked like a gunshot, sending the beeping little lines off screen.

Scott waited.

'And I'm going to be spending a great deal of time with you, *Zak*, because you no longer will be able to avoid my questions, your brain is hooked to a machine that will answer for you – and you have thirty-six years of killing and torture to discuss before you die. I will not allow you an easy death . . .'

Beeeppppp . . .

Scott backed away quickly, folding his arms across his chest, taking on a look of sad reserve as Dr Pham opened the door, rushing for Dorn, laying a hand on his wrist. She began counting.

'What happened?' she asked rather flatly.

Scott shrugged. 'I told him what happened to his friend Irma, how she failed in her mission to trigger an explosion in their toy room, and then how she slashed her wrists. But you know, Dr Pham, I didn't think he understood what I was saying . . .'

Again the monitor burst into a hot boil, solid, piercing, penetrating.

'Please,' the doctor cautioned, 'his heart . . .'

'We found her clutching the Legion of Merit, she had pumped her blood all over the damn thing . . .'

Beeeeepppp . . .

'Let him rest!' Pham ordered, and she then dropped fluid into his eyes. With a tender hand she closed his mouth, replacing the oxygen mask, then turning on the juice.

'Doc,' Scott interrupted, 'do you think he'll be seeing me in July? I'm coming back for a little boy's birthday party.'

'It's a good bet,' she said flatly, 'he just seems to be reacting to stress, the anguish of paralysis, we should let him sleep. And you as well, Commander.'

'Yes,' Scott smiled darkly. 'We sleep not, unless we have done mischief.'

Dr Pham cocked her head at him. 'That's sounds vaguely familiar,' she said, 'is that from the bible?'

'No, no, child, that's an old proverb,' Scott corrected, 'a favourite of a very old friend.'

'Please?' she smiled.

Scott nodded. 'And our sleep is taken away unless we cause some to fall. For we eat the bread of wickedness. And we drink the wine of violence.'

EPILOGUE

The late afternoon sunlight filtered through the trees in the Jansons' backyard, where a short night ago a killer had come stalking. Jessica was standing at her kitchen window with Jack Scott, preparing dinner, watching her child at play.

'Frank!' Elmer was calling with excitement, and his voice came bursting through the window with a sweet and innocent joy.

'Frank, Tripod's running!'

Rivers smiled broadly and waved them on, as Jessica suddenly pushed her arm up into Scott's. 'He's a very special man,' she said warmly, leading him to the kitchen table.

'Don't let him get away from you,' Scott advised quietly, and she winked as she pulled out a chair.

He sat awkwardly, the wounds licking at his torso with a day-old intensity, the woman seeing his discomfort.

'I don't think you should be out of bed,' she said with concern.

Scott nodded. 'I've felt better, but not in my heart.' And he watched intently as the young mother sat alongside him, sweeping bangs from her brow.

'Then would you please ask your heart something for me,' she said, her eyes puffy from lack of sleep, her voice concealing fear with a faint tremble.

Scott smiled warmly. 'I think I know what you're feeling,' he stated gently, reaching for her hand. And as he did this he could see tears welling from under her lids.

'You and Elmer are very safe, it's just the horrid reality of what has happened that you are dealing with, that's what troubles you now, the fact that men can be so cruel and for no reason.'

She pondered, looking down, testing this with her mind.

'It's not surprising this experience has left you feeling sad and alarmed. But I can tell you, while Elmer may become more cautious, he has *not* been harmed by this, in fact . . .'

'He loves the attention,' she finished his statement. 'But he's really just a little boy, Mr Scott, he never understood how grave the situation was, maybe he never will.'

Scott nodded agreement. And for long moments they sat in silence, watching Elmer and Detective Rivers and Tripod. From time to time the old Diggerman would offer the boy advice, then spit a stream of red juice onto the lawn and Jessica would quickly divert her gaze. Then suddenly, without saying why, she leaned forward, peering deeply into Scott's eyes. They were deep, sad wells.

'I know,' he stated grimly.

'Then you knew that I felt him? And I thought I was cracking up!' She placed a finger to her temple.

Scott nodded. 'That's not unusual, some mistake their feelings for the flu.'

'From the beginning,' she said slowly, 'I knew something wasn't right, but I couldn't put my finger on it, I had a very creepy feeling, a sensation,' she touched her heart, leaning closer across the table. 'Last night, even before Captain Drury came to get us, every hair on my body was just dancing, my heart fluttered.' She closed her eyes as a tear rolled down her cheek.

'Let me tell you a secret,' Scott offered quietly.

Jessica nodded, crossing her heart the way she had seen Elmer do a thousand times, and Scott leaned forward.

'What you have been feeling is instinct, pure and simple, your emotions and soul warning you of danger. You are safe now, but should you ever feel those sensations again, please trust them. They can save you, and rarely will they lie.'

Jessica nodded, her pretty green eyes blinking at the wetness.

'It is unfortunate, Mrs Janson, but in this country of ours, women and children are almost always the potential victims of exploitation and violence. I only wish that other mothers knew what you already do. Maternal instinct is a tremendous weapon, and with that you can feel what others cannot even see.'

She raised a questioning brow.

'Trust your instincts,' Scott said sharply, 'it's as simple as that. They will warn you better than anyone could, so listen to them, what do they tell you now?'

The woman closed her eyes, then thought for a moment. 'I feel depleted,' she said, 'very low and tired.'

Scott nodded. 'Then the threat is truly gone.' He worked his features into a smile as he stood, looking out the door. 'Your boy and his dog,' he said softly, 'for whatever reason they brought me here and I am truly grateful.'

They watched together as their two shadows came soaring across the lawn, side by side in perfect step, like a broken spirit that was suddenly made whole. Jessica pressed Scott's hand as he opened the door, and they strolled out onto the patio. To the right of the doorway there was a line of fragrant roses in bloom, a bright yellow climbing a green trellis.

'Elmer's father planted these.' She smiled, leaning over and snapping a perfect bud. She handed this to Scott as they toured the garden, standing over lilies which bloomed in a shower of colours, followed by tulips in sweeping rows of cultivated brilliance. Yet for all of the beauty of that spring afternoon, Scott felt drawn to a very simple cluster of weeds trapped in a plain vase near the door, where Elmer had left them.

He returned to these flowers as he knew he always would, the vibrant blooms glowing in the dying light, their ribbons of red like burning candles. Jessica sighed, touching Scott gently on the arm, seeing the red flame reflected in his eyes, a tired dove grey, his features hard and worn.

And though she did not know why, she suddenly knew that she would always remember him, and not like this, all battered and cut and worn; but standing in a cold and pouring rain on some lost roadway, there to comfort others that he did not know.

A windy gust suddenly flared through the yard.

Roses whipped in the wind. Tree tops sang, white petals fell from a dogwood tree. As these came flitting through the yard, circling at his feet, Scott instinctively placed his body into a protective posture around the little flowers.

He stood for a long and tender moment in the dying light, imagining Kimberly planting flowers by her door, waiting for her mother to come home. Then Victoria, and not the old woman, but the child once named for her. And then Samantha, hurrying by, chasing her sister through a flowered glade in a time so very long ago.

Her sculpted face and golden eyes were a haunting memory, never once failing to see Scott clearly. And for that fleeting second he saw all of his faces beginning to gather; lost faces, asking him why.

It was time to go, Scott told himself.

His promise was to the living.

MICHAEL SLADE

CUTTHROAT

In 1876 naturalist Francis Parker makes an extraordinary discovery before losing his life – and the evidence – in the horrific carnage of the Little Big Horn.

In 1987 Judge Hutton Murdoch is addressing the American Bar Association when his brain is blown apart by a high-velocity bullet. Two days later a second judge is pondering a complex point of law when a masked intruder slits his throat from ear to ear.

The hunt for an ingenious and brutal killer soon becomes a desperate search for the missing link between these apparently unconnected events. A search that will lead to a company engaged in bizarre genetic experiments, a sinister Chinese family with a centuries-old obsession – and ultimately to the horrifying secrets of man's earliest beginnings.

'There is no safety for the reader in a Michael Slade book'

Vancouver Magazine

'A master of horror'

Toronto Sunday Sun

Post·A·Book

A Royal Mail service in association with the Book Marketing Council & The Booksellers Association.
Post-A-Book is a Post Office trademark.

MICHAEL SLADE

HEADHUNTER

By the time the second mutilated body was found, the Press were talking about the Headhunter and the city of Vancouver was ready to explode with fear.

And then the photographs arrived. Carefully posed shots of the women's heads stuck on poles. Enough to convince Superintendent Robert DeClercq that they were dealing with a very special kind of killer. A killer who inhabited a bizarre world of cannibalism, torture and sexual perversion.

A killer who was only just beginning . . .

'Bizarre . . . full of tension and mystery with unforgettable scenes and weird happenings'
The Scotsman

'Well written, very well researched . . . a gripper'
Daily Mail

'Macabre . . . a very polished tale'
Sunday Telegraph

'A thinking man's Texas Chainsaw Massacre'
The Vancouver Sun

NEL BOOKS

MICHAEL SLADE

GHOUL

A violent spectre is haunting London.

Dressed in a grey cape and a top hat, with a bone-white face and a madman's eyes, the Ghoul crawls from the London sewers to kill – bloodily, perversely and inexplicably.

For Detective Chief Superintendent Hilary Rand, an ambitious woman in a man's world, the carnage must stop or her career will be finished. But hunting the Ghoul means stepping into her worst nightmare . . .

'As alarming a piece of Gothic as I've read in many a black moon . . . treads a perverted fantastic with droll skill'

The Times

'Slade runs a three-ring circus of suspense, salting the plot with red herrings and keeping the reader guessing until the truth is revealed in a grisly, sensational climax to which is appended yet another gut-wrenching revelation'

Booklist

'*Ghoul* almost finished me . . . Here's a book that gives you real shock value for the money'

Robert Bloch, author of PSYCHO

NEL BOOKS

WILLIAM BAYER

WALLFLOWER

Lt Frank Janek was flying home from Venice. A life-time dream, complete with a holiday romance, was suddenly destroyed.

A call to tell him of a murder. His goddaughter Jess, killed and mutilated while out jogging. A seemingly senseless, random crime. One of a countrywide series linked only by the grotesque method and detail.

But to investigate the murder is to investigate Jess's own life. And Frank Janek, driven but flinching, has to uncover layer upon layer that lead down to depths of complex madness and horror . . .

'. . . a graduate of the Hannibal Lecter school of fiction . . . well-constructed and chilling'

Sunday Telegraph

CORONET BOOKS

MORE TITLES AVAILABLE FROM
HODDER AND STOUGHTON PAPERBACKS

MICHAEL SLADE

☐	58428 3	Cutthroat	£4.99
☐	59112 3	Headhunter	£4.99
☐	59113 1	Ghoul	£4.99

WILLIAM BAYER

☐	58026 7	Wallflower	£4.99

All these books are available at your local bookshop or newsagent, or can be ordered direct from the publisher. Just tick the titles you want and fill in the form below.

Prices and availability subject to change without notice.

HODDER AND STOUGHTON PAPERBACKS, P.O. Box 11, Falmouth, Cornwall.

Please send cheque or postal order for the value of the book, and add the following for postage and packing:

UK including BFPO – £1.00 for one book, plus 50p for the second book, and 30p for each additional book ordered up to a £3.00 maximum.

OVERSEAS, INCLUDING EIRE – £2.00 for the first book, plus £1.00 for the second book, and 50p for each additional book ordered.

OR Please debit this amount from my Access/Visa Card (delete as appropriate).

CARD NUMBER ☐☐☐☐☐☐☐☐☐☐☐☐☐☐☐☐

AMOUNT £...........................

EXPIRY DATE ....

SIGNED ....

NAME ....

ADDRESS ....

....